Camellia

Jack looked at the sad, lovely face in front of him and felt a pang of fatherly affection. He could almost touch the mental scars caused by her scheming mother.

'Will you take a bit of advice from an *almost* uncle,' he said, his face flushing at the sudden tug of his emotions.

Camellia nodded.

'Put your mother, your childhood and all this away,' he said gently. 'Tomorrows are what count, love, not yesterdays. I love Bonny, so help me! But that's in the past now. Even dead Boony's twitching our cords, the way she did in life. Don't let her, Camellia. Be true to yourself.'

Lesley Pearse's first four novels, *Georgia, Tara, Charity* and *Ellie*, are all available in paperback. She lives in Bristol with her three daughters.

LESLEY PEARSE

Camellia

ARROW

Reprinted in Arrow Books, 1998

12

Copyright © Lesley Pearse, 1997

First published in the United Kingdom in 1997 by William Heinemann

This edition first published in 1997
by Mandarin Paperbacks and reprinted 5 times

Arrow Books Limited
The Random House Group Ltd
20 Vauxhall Bridge Road, London, SW1V 2SA

Random House Australia (Pty) Limited
20 Alfred Street, Milsons Point, Sydney
New South Wales 2061, Australia

Random House New Zealand Limited
18 Poland Road, Glenfield, Auckland 10, New Zealand

Random House (Pty) Limited
Endulini, 5a Jubilee Road, Parktown 2193, South Africa

The Random House Group Limited Reg. No. 954009

www.randomhouse.co.uk

A CIP catalogue record for this book
is available from the British Library

Papers used by The Random House Group Limited
are natural, recyclable products made from wood grown in
sustainable forests. The manufacturing processes conform to
the environmental regulations of the country of origin

Printed and bound in Germany by
Elsnerdruck, Berlin

ISBN 0 7493 1571 7

Chapter One

'Hey mister.' A small boy tugged at the police-man's sleeve. 'There's a woman in the river!'

Sergeant Simmonds put his cup of tea on the counter of the quayside snack bar, looked down at the carroty haired boy and grinned good-naturedly. 'Swimming, boating or doing her wash-ing?'

'She's dead, mister. Stuck in the mud!'

The boy was no older than seven, in torn shorts and a grubby tee shirt, his black gym plimsolls covered in mud, a handful of worms squirming in the bottom of a red toy bucket.

His expression was too earnest for a prank. He was out of breath and there were beads of perspira-tion on his little freckled nose.

'Where was this, sonny?'

'Way along there.' The boy pointed across the river, in the direction of where the rivers Tilling-ham and Breed meet and turned together towards the Rother and Rye harbour. 'I was digging up some worms to go fishing and I saw her arms.'

It was a glorious August morning, mist fast retreating with the promise of another hot, sunny day. Not yet seven, too early for holiday-makers to mar the tranquillity of the quayside, hours before day-trippers would arrive in their droves to admire the quaint old town.

1

Sgt Simmonds patted the boy's head. 'Go on home for your breakfast, sonny. Leave it with me. I'll check it out.'

'Maybe it's a stranded mermaid?' Alf, the snack bar's proprietor leaned forward over the counter, his swarthy, thin face breaking into a sardonic grin. 'That could be good for trade!'

'What imaginations some kids have!' Simmonds laughed, watching as the boy ran off down Wish Ward. 'Probably nothing more than a lump of driftwood. But I suppose I'd better amble round there and take a look.'

Bert Simmonds was thirty-six and easily the most popular policeman in Rye. Men admired his good humour and his prowess as a fast bowler in the local cricket team, children appreciated his friendly interest in them and the way he didn't always inform their parents about every act of naughtiness, not if he thought just a sharp telling off would do instead. As for the women, they just liked *him*, he was easy to talk to, just handsome enough with his blond hair and sea-blue eyes to set their pulses racing, but remarkably unaware of the effect he had on the opposite sex.

People were often fooled into thinking Simmonds was a soft touch because of his amiable disposition. In fact, there were few policemen in the rural areas of Kent or Sussex with as many arrests to their name, and very few with his tenacity or sharp wits.

Simmonds took his time going back along the quay and over the bridge, savouring the still cool air. Another hour or two and the High Street would be packed. He loved Rye, but it was too small a town to cope with the hordes of visitors it attracted in summer.

There was no real footpath on the other side of

the river bank, just a track behind the laundry, overgrown with struggling buddleia bushes and nettles. Several times Bert had to make a detour round old sheds and climb through fences, but if he'd taken the easier route along New Winchelsea Road he might just miss whatever it was that the boy had seen.

Bert looked across the river for a moment. It was easy to see why Rye attracted so many tourists and artists. Boats moored at the quay, the tall black warehouses, then the town, almost unchanged since mediaeval times, rising behind them. Tiny houses clung precariously to the walled hillside, a pretty hotchpotch of terracotta-coloured tiles and white weatherboarding, interspersed with patches of sugared almond blue, pink and green, and above them all the square grey tower of the church.

Bert walked on, smiling as he remembered other 'bodies' that had been reported to him in the past. One was an abandoned dressmaker's dummy, another merely a lump of wood to which some joker had attached old boots. Two very serious small boys had once informed him they'd seen a man burying a baby on the marsh. When they directed Bert to the spot it had turned out to be a dead cat. But all reports had to be checked out. There were a few boating accidents each summer and swimmers sometimes underestimated the strong current.

The tide was out now, thick glutinous mud gleaming in the early sun, the river just a thin trickle in the centre, making its way down to the sea. Ahead the marsh went on almost to infinity, broken only by the ruins of Chamber Castle and a couple of coastguards' cottages on the distant horizon. Black-faced sheep had the marsh all to themselves. The only sounds were the plaintive cries of the curlews and seagulls.

3

It was the seagulls which made Simmonds break into a run as he approached the sluicegates of the river Breed. Their shrieking and frenzied wheeling overhead suggested there was something in the mud, if only a drowned sheep.

But as he got closer, he saw a flash of turquoise. It lay on a high triangular mud bank, between the two rivers, brilliant against the brown mud. Four or five gulls were perched on it, pecking furiously and more were zooming down like fighter planes.

'Scram you blighters,' he yelled, hurling a stone at them. As they flew off squawking with frustration at having to leave their breakfast, Simmonds stopped short, staring in horror.

The boy was right. It was a woman. Instinctively he knew too who she was, even though she lay face down, half-submerged in mud. The curve of her hips, rounded buttocks and long slender legs gave her away immediately.

'Oh no, not you, Bonny,' he whispered, fighting against nausea. 'Not like this!'

He knew the correct procedure was to get help, before he even touched her, but he felt compelled to reach her and prevent the gulls pecking at her again. Throwing down his jacket on the bank, he lowered himself over the edge and inched forward.

In his fifteen years in the police force in Rye, this one woman had taken him through the whole spectrum of emotions. He'd admired her, desired her, and more recently despised and pitied her. As a young constable her sensual beauty had haunted his dreams.

There were cruel peck marks now on her thighs and arms, and as another gull swooped down to feast, he lunged at it.

'Clear off, you blasted scavengers! Leave her alone,' he bellowed, his feet sinking deeper into the mud.

The sound of a car stopping on the bridge by the sluicegate brought Simmonds back to his senses. As he turned his head and saw PC Higgins and Rowe clambering over the fence, he remembered that he could easily sink up to his waist in the mud without a rope.

'We had a telephone call at the station,' Higgins yelled. 'An old man out walking his dog saw something. We brought some waders just in case. Any idea who it is?'

'It's Bonny Norton,' Simmonds called back, struggling to regain his footing and his composure. 'We must get her out before a crowd gathers. Get the waders on and bring some rope and boards.'

It was obscene to haul out such a beautiful woman by her feet. The body which so many men had lusted after was revealed intimately as her dress was sucked back by the mud. Her lace panties were turned a filthy brown from the river, her golden skin smeared with muck. But as they turned her over on reaching firmer ground, one breast broke free from her bodice, pure white, pink tipped, small and perfect. All three men averted their eyes in embarrassment.

Higgins moved first, covering her with a blanket. 'What the hell was she doing by the river?' he said gruffly.

Rowe shrugged his shoulders. He was several years younger than his colleagues, a dour insensitive man who hadn't been in Rye long enough to have known Bonny in the old days. 'Drunk as usual, I expect.'

At twelve noon of the same day, Bert Simmonds came out of the police station and lit up a cigarette. He needed time alone to collect himself.

The police station was in Church Square, right opposite the parish church: a small Victorian red-

5

brick building set back from the rest of the terrace, almost as if it were apologising for having had the impertinence to sit amongst its fourteenth and fifteenth-century neighbours. A new police station was being built in Cinque Port Street, down near the railway station. Though Bert welcomed this move for practicality, he knew he would miss the peaceful churchyard, the splendid views of the marsh from the back of the station and its central position. But today he wasn't considering the beauty of his surroundings, as he usually did when he paused here. His mind was filled with Bonny.

Finding her body was one of the most traumatic events in his entire career. Now he was faced with breaking the news to her daughter.

It was so hot. His shirt was damp with sweat and his serge trousers sticking to his legs, still smelling of river mud.

'How do you tell a fifteen-year-old something like this?' he sighed.

From the first day in the summer of 1950 when Bonny, with her husband and baby, moved into the pretty house in Mermaid Street, she had made an impact on the town. It wasn't just that she was only twenty-one and stunningly beautiful, or that her serious-faced, much older husband was wealthy enough to call in craftsmen to renovate their home. She was outstanding in every way.

Bonny was an embodiment of the leap forward from the austere war-torn forties to the fifties. Her blonde hair was pure Hollywood glamour, she wore brightly coloured tight sweaters, mid-calf clinging skirts and high heels. The sight of her tight round buttocks wiggling provocatively as she wheeled her baby in a pushchair was enough to stop traffic, and the way she spoke airily of her time in West End theatres left her more retiring neighbours gasping in astonishment. There were those of course who didn't really believe she'd been a dancer, but she soon set the record straight when she joined in an amateur production and left the local girls looking like carthorses. The Desk Sergeant summed her up in a few well chosen words: 'I've seen pictures of girls they call "Sex Kittens", but until I saw Bonny Norton I thought it was just a photographic trick.'

Bonny was an enigma: a pin-up girl, but a loving wife and mother too – at least in those days. While men envied John Norton and secretly lusted after his wife, their women befriended her, tried to emulate her style.

Bert was guiltier than anyone of watching her too closely when she first arrived in town. He too was only twenty-one then, the youngest constable at the station, a shy, rather awkward young lad. It was a good couple of years before he so much as spoke to her.

One summer when Camellia was around three or so, Bert found her sitting on the doorstep in Mermaid Street playing with her dolls.

She was an odd little girl, very plain considering how beautiful her mother was, with poker-straight dark hair and almond-shaped dark brown eyes, old beyond her years. Bert guessed she was a bit lonely; he'd never seen her playing with other children. He paused to chat to her that day and before long their conversations became a regular feature of his beat. She would tell him where her daddy had gone on business, show him her dolls and books. Bert often brought her a few rationed sweets.

The first time Bert was invited into the Nortons' home was engraved deeply on his memory, perhaps because it was his first real close-up view of them as a family. It was a hot summer's evening, and as always he was lingering longer than necessary in Mermaid Street.

Camellia was sitting on the doorstep in a long pink nightdress, holding a small doll in her hands. As Bert approached her serious small face broke into a wide, welcoming smile. 'My daddy's come home,' she said.

'Has he now?' Bert crouched down on his hunkers beside her. John Norton was one of the top scientists for Shell Petroleum and was often away in the Middle East.

'Daddy brought me some new things for my doll's house. Would you like to see them?'

A gust of laughter from inside the house warned Bert the Nortons had visitors. He was just going to make an excuse when John came to the door. 'Bedtime, Melly,' he said, scooping the little girl up into his arms.

John Morton had the label of 'a real gent' in Rye. He was always impeccably dressed in hand-tailored suits, with sleek dark hair, a neat moustache and a deep yet soft voice. A great many women likened him to the actor Ronald Coleman. His face was too lean and his manner too serious to be considered really handsome, but yet he had a quiet endearing charm. He lifted his hat to women, always remembered people's names and asked about their families. Local tradesmen never had to chase him to pay his bills. He was courteous to everyone, however humble their status in life and he'd been accepted into the community in a way which was rare for a relative newcomer.

'This is Mr Simmonds, my friend,' Camellia said, playing with her father's moustache. 'Can he come and see my doll's house?'

'I've heard a great deal about you, Mr Simmonds,' he said and he smiled as if he liked what he'd heard. 'I'm pleased to meet you at last. The

8

house is packed as always, but do come in. I'm sure my wife would love to meet you too. Maybe Camellia might be persuaded to go to sleep once she's shared her new treasures with you.'

Bert had never seen the inside of the house before, but it was just as perfect as he'd imagined it to be.

There was only one large room downstairs, with polished oak floorboards, thick fringed rugs and antique furniture. Everything just perfect in that understated, classy way that rich people had of doing up their homes. The Nortons' friends were all plummy voiced strangers to him, six couples in all, elegantly dressed, standing around with drinks in their hands. They smiled as John introduced him, but Bert felt uncomfortable.

Bonny was at the far end of the room lighting long green candles on the dining table, which was laid for dinner with silver, starched napkins and flowers. Behind it open windows gave a view of a small walled garden. To Bert, who was only used to canteens and transport cafés, it looked like something from a film set.

Bonny turned to greet him, a little unsteady on her feet, as if she'd had a few drinks already. 'So we meet our baby's policeman friend at last! We didn't expect someone so young or handsome,' she said, making Bert blush with embarrassment. 'I hope she hasn't been pestering you, Mr Simmonds. She's a great deal like me, expecting everyone to adore her. Now can I get you a drink?'

It would have been hard for any man not to adore Bonny Norton, especially the way she looked that night. She wore a floaty blue dress with full skirt, her bare arms golden from the sun. Her hair was piled up on top of her head, loose tendrils escaping from the pins curled around her neck and ears, and her cheeks were flushed with the heat.

'I'm on duty,' he managed to get out, suddenly acutely aware of his rustic vowels. He'd heard rumours the Nortons entertained titled people. 'I'll just see Camellia's doll's house, then I'll get out of your way.'

Camellia's bedroom was the prettiest Bert had ever seen: a white bed with a kind of canopy affair above it, dolls, teddy bears and books arranged on shelves, a thick carpet and a padded seat at the window, with a view over the rooftops and the marsh across to Winchelsea.

Camellia bounded across the room towards the big Georgian-style doll's house. John smiled at Bert. 'I'm glad of this opportunity to thank you for taking an interest in Camellia,' he said, with genuine warmth and sincerity. 'I'm away from home so much and it's good to think she has a friend to share things with.'

'She's a lovely kid.' Bert felt an immediate affinity with the man. 'She counts the days till you come home you know!'

'Come on, Mr Simmonds,' Camellia said impatiently, beckoning him to join her at the house. 'These are the new things I got today – the piano, the lady sitting at it and the maid with the tea trolley.'

To a man of simple tastes like Bert, it wasn't a toy but a work of art. Everything was to scale like a real house. Little chintz-covered armchairs, table lamps, even plates of food on the dining table.

Camellia took out the piano and placed it in Bert's hands. It must have cost a small fortune, a tiny replica of a real grand piano.

'It even plays,' she said reverently, tinkling it with one small finger. 'Daddy finds me the best things in the whole world.'

It was soon after that evening at the Nortons' house

that Bert discovered Bonny was a tease. She sensed he had a crush on her and used it to her advantage.

She would invite him in for a cup of tea and it would always transpire that she wanted some furniture moved, or some other little job. Bert didn't mind this one bit, but she often asked him very personal questions, and sometimes he had the feeling she was waiting for him to make a pass at her. One sunny afternoon when they'd taken their tea out into the garden, Bonny had stripped off her sundress. Beneath it she wore a minuscule bikini, the first Bert had ever seen other than in pin-up pictures in the newspapers.

'Well?' she said with a provocative pout, lifting her hair and striking a model-like pose. 'Does it suit me?'

He was aroused instantly. Dressed she was sensational enough, almost naked she was ravishing: a tiny waist, long slender legs and the pertest of rounded buttocks. He gulped down his tea and left hurriedly, with the flimsiest of excuses, then spent the next few days wishing he'd had the courage at least to compliment her. He didn't dare confide his growing passion for her to any of his friends at the station. Superintendent Willis was very chummy with John Norton and Bert knew if it got to his ears he'd be out of a job.

When John joined the cricket team, Bert felt even more awkward. John was no longer a shadowy figure in the background, but a flesh and blood man who clearly wanted to be closely involved in the community. Bert liked the man's quiet humour, his intelligence and his total lack of snobbery, and if it hadn't been for his feelings for Bonny he knew they would have become very close friends. Sometimes over a couple of pints after a game, John would talk about both his wife and daughter, and it was clear they meant everything to him. He once confided that he had moved to Rye from Somerset because he had been afraid to leave his young wife alone in such an isolated place. He felt someone as vivacious as Bonny needed people around her, shops, cinemas and bustle. He was very anxious about being away on business so much, and Bert got the distinct impression John was asking him to keep an eye on his wife and daughter.

Bert tried very hard to see Bonny as just the wife of a friend, but he couldn't. He would wake from vivid erotic dreams of her feeling deeply ashamed. His heart leapt even if he saw her in the distance, and he knew he was guilty of inventing excuses to call at the house in Mermaid Street.

It was a bewildering and dangerous addiction, made worse by knowing she was totally aware of how he felt. She would fix him with her flirtatious turquoise eyes, her so-very-kissable lips pouting provocatively, and hold his hand just a little too long.

There were occasions too when she went a little further to tempt him, fastening her suspenders in front of him, leaning over so he could see right down her cleavage, on one occasion opening the front door to him wearing only a towel wrapped round her. What really baffled Bert though was *why* she played with him as she did. When she had everything any woman could ask for.

Bert knew the answer to that question now, some ten years later. Bonny Norton was a sensationalist who had to have a few admirers dangling on a string to satify her ego. Maybe if John hadn't died when he did, she might have grown out of it and come to realise how fortunate she really was. But John's death came unexpectedly. At twenty-seven Bonny was too young for widowhood and too giddy to cope with the pressures of bringing up a child alone.

'Poor Camellia,' Bert murmured. 'As if you haven't been through enough already!'

Chapter Two

Sgt Simmonds jumped as WPC Carter spoke at his elbow.

'A penny for them, Sarge,' Carter said. 'Wondering if you've posted your pools?'

Wendy Carter had been in the force a few years, but less than a year in Rye. She was an excellent policewoman, compassionate, sharp-witted, with a dry sense of humour. Bert thought she would go far. But she didn't know the Norton family history, or his involvement with it.

'Nothing so trivial,' he said. 'I was remembering Bonny as she once was. I wish it wasn't me who had to tell Melly.'

Carter looked puzzled.

'Melly! I thought her name was Camellia?'

'Her father called her Melly,' he sighed. 'He'll be turning in his grave at this moment. He once entrusted me to look after his wife and little girl. I didn't make a very good job of it.'

Carter studied the sergeant out of the corner of her eyes as they walked down East Street towards the High Street. Bert Simmonds was the kind of man she'd like to marry. Strong, dependable, good-natured and sensitive too. At thirty-six he was in his prime, with a firm muscular body and sun-streaked blond hair, just that little bit longer than the normal regulation cut. Not exactly handsome, but a good face, weathered by time and experience, his eyes grey-blue like the sea on a dull day. She thought Sandra Simmonds was very lucky. WPC Carter wouldn't mind being tucked up in bed with him.

Carter didn't get many offers from men herself. She was a plain stocky girl of twenty-nine with mousy hair and a snub nose, who had to rely on her intelligence and her cheerful nature to make friends, and those qualities didn't seem to get her very far with men.

Bonny Norton, on the other hand, had only to click her fingers and men came running. Carter had seen the woman many times, across a crowded bar, parading down the High Street, and like nearly everyone she had been fascinated by her. By all accounts Bonny was first with everything, the first woman to wear a bikini back in the fifties, the first adult to master the hula-hoop, and just recently the first woman of over thirty to dare wear the new short skirts. Carter admired such bravado.

Perhaps later tonight she'd discover if all the stories about Bonny Norton were true. Surely no woman of thirty-six could've done quite as much as she was credited with – turned down a Hollywood contract to marry John Norton, widowed six years later, then squandered half a million. Seduced half the male population, drank the pubs dry and finally ended it all by slinging herself in the river! Why stay in a sleepy little backwater like Rye if she was all she was cracked up to be?

As they arrived at Rowlands Bakery, Bert felt his stomach tighten. He could see Camellia behind the counter, chatting as she served a customer with cakes. Somehow the contrast between this plain, fat girl and her beautiful, slender blonde mother seemed even more poignant now Bonny was lying in the mortuary.

15

Camellia was tall, perhaps five foot seven, and at least twelve stone. A pale moon face, with dark almond eyes almost concealed by greasy flesh. Her lank dark brown hair was pinned back unflatteringly with a hair slide, advertising a big forehead. Her pink-and-white checked overall did her no favours either. It was too tight and there were bulges of flesh wherever it clung.

Camellia's face broke into a wide, warm smile as he came in the door. She was always pleased to see Bert. She'd continued to see him as a special friend throughout her childhood, but today her welcome cut him to the quick.

'Hullo, Mr Simmonds. What's it to be today? We've got some lovely chicken pies, just out of the oven.'

It was fair play to the girl that she tried to rise above her mother's reputation. She worked hard, she was always cheerful and according to Mrs Rowlands she was very honest too. That seemed to surprise the baker's wife more than anything.

'Nothing thanks.' Bert blushed. Until this moment he hadn't considered how he would get her away in private. 'Is Mrs Rowlands about?'

As he spoke, Enid Rowlands came through from the bakery wiping floury hands on her white apron. She fitted her job perfectly, as fat and round as one of her own doughnuts, a permanently flushed face surrounded by grey curly hair.

'Hullo, Bert,' she said, bright shoe-button eyes lighting up at the prospect of a gossip. 'What's been going on down at the river this morning? I've been hearing all kinds of rumours.'

Enid thrived on gossip. Nothing happened in Rye without her knowing the intimate details. Bert couldn't help suspecting she'd only taken Camellia on for the summer holidays in the hopes she might get some inside information about Bonny.

'Actually I want a word with Camellia,' he said, lowering his voice and praying that she would catch on it was something delicate. 'Could I take her out the back. WPC Carter will explain.'

Enid's eyes were instantly suspicious. She glanced across at her employee filling a box of cakes for a customer, then looked back at Bert. 'What's she done?' she mouthed.

Bert put his finger up to his lips, his eyes entreating Mrs Rowlands to use some tact.

Enid looked puzzled, but she stepped over towards the girl and took the cake box from her hands. 'I'll finish that off. Mr Simmonds wants a word with you, take your break now and go out in the yard.'

Camellia clearly didn't suspect anything, smiling at Bert for rescuing her from the stifling shop. She led the way, up a couple of steps, through the big, hot kitchen, and out through a side door into the yard.

'It's *so* good to get out of there,' she gasped, flopping down onto a small wooden bench in the shade and fanned herself with her hand. 'Do you know it's eighty-five already and I've been working since seven this morning.'

Looking at her now with a heart full of sympathy, Bert could see beyond the overweight body. She had a certain poise which even the humiliation her mother had dumped on her hadn't weakened. If someone could just get hold of her, make her lose that puppy fat, buy her some decent clothes she could do all right. She was bright, with a lovely smile, and she even spoke well. All she needed was taking in hand.

'No wonder Mrs Rowlands couldn't find anyone else to work in her shop this summer,' she laughed, showing small very white teeth. 'I was so pleased to get a job I never considered why no one else wanted it.'

Bert was used to people looking nervous when he wanted to speak to them. At any other time he would've found her open manner heartening. 'You're good in the shop,' he said, to reassure her she was there on merit alone. 'I'm sure Mrs Rowlands picked you because she knew you'd work hard.'

There was a moment's pause. Camellia continued to fan herself. Bert stared at a piled-up heap of bread trays and wished Carter would join him and help.

'What did you want me for, Mr Simmonds?' she asked suddenly.

Bert took a deep breath. All his experience of breaking news of death was to older people. He didn't know what to say. 'It's about your mum.'

Her face clouded over. Her expression was that of a mother with a troublesome child, expecting the worst as soon as its name was mentioned. 'What's she done now?'

Bert felt like screaming for Carter to come and help him out. She should be right here at his side to give the sort of comfort only a woman could give. But he knew she was staying in the shop purposely, believing him capable of breaking it more gently than they could together.

Bert got up from the bench, then crouched down on his haunches in front of her and took Camellia's hands in his.

'I'm sorry, Melly,' he said. 'There isn't an easy way to tell you, so I'll just have to come right out with it.' He paused, his mouth was dry, his stomach churning. 'Your Mum's dead, sweetheart. I'm so sorry.'

There was no reaction at first. Her fat pale face

18

was entirely expressionless, as bland as one of the iced buns in the shop window.

'She can't be. She's in London.' She put her head on one side, looking right into his eyes, then dropped them to look at his hands holding hers.

'She died here, in Rye,' Bert said, wanting to blurt out everything in one big breath. 'She drowned here in the river, early this morning.'

To Bert's astonishment she laughed, her double chin quivering. 'Don't be silly, Mr Simmonds,' she said, showing all her teeth. 'You've got the wrong person. She wouldn't go near any river. She's in London.'

Bert had heard of people going into denial when faced with something they didn't want to hear, but he hadn't expected it from Camellia. 'Melly, it was me who pulled her out. Don't you believe I know her well enough to identify her?'

Silence. Not a word or even a flicker of movement from her. Her eyes were focused on something above his head, blank and unblinking. He hoped she was remembering their close friendship when she was just a little girl, the cricket matches when she and Bonny came to watch, clapping him and John equally. But it was more likely she was remembering the times she saw her mother flirting drunkenly with him, or the times he called in an official capacity to get her to turn her music down. He wished she would say something, anything. He didn't know if it had sunk in.

Slowly her face began to crumple. Her wide mouth drooped first, her eyes closed, then tears crept out from under her lashes. As Bert watched, they formed into tiny diamond-bright droplets on her oily cheeks, rolling down one at a time.

'Who did it?' she croaked. 'Who did this to her?'

All Bert could do was take her in his arms, hold her against his chest and hope he could find the right words. 'We don't think anyone was involved,' he whispered into her hair. 'We believe she jumped in, sweetheart, because she was unhappy. No one had hurt her, she wasn't forced in there.'

'You're wrong.' She shook her head violently, pushing back against his chest. 'Mummy was happy when she went to London and she was afraid of water. She wouldn't jump in a river, not for any reason.'

Bonny had been very fond of speaking about the time she nearly drowned as a child. Bert had heard the story from her himself. He could visualise the wide, icy, swollen river in Sussex and the heroic rescue by her childhood sweetheart. Bert had put her fear of water to the police doctor as a reason why she wouldn't end her life that way. The doctor had disagreed, saying it was a further pointer to her depressed state of mind.

'People sometimes snap suddenly.' Bert tried to explain what the doctor had told him. He was aware that Carter had come out through the kitchen door, but he didn't turn to look at her. 'Sometimes lots of little worries build up together and make one huge problem that they can't solve.'

Camellia leaned against him sobbing into the front of his shirt and he just held her, signalling for Carter to tell her all those other details he couldn't manage.

Bert winced as Carter gently spelled out all they knew. The time of Bonny's death had been set at around two in the morning, at high tide. Her suitcase and shoes had been found under a bush. Camellia didn't react to hearing she would have to go to the mortuary to formally identify her mother, but when Carter mentioned a post mortem, she reared up, eyes wide with shock.

'You mean they cut her open? They can't do that!'

'There isn't any other way.' Carter came closer, putting one hand on the girl's shoulder soothingly. 'You see, they have to look for drugs, for drink, anything to build up a picture of what happened.'

As Bert held Camellia in his arms in that quiet little backyard, he shared her grief. Bonny to him was as much part of life in Rye as the old-world tearooms, the Napoleonic prison, and the quayside. Tomorrow he might feel anger that she didn't consider what her death might do to her child, but today he would just mourn an old, troubled friend.

Carter brought them tea a little later. Mrs Rowlands peered anxiously round the door, wanting to come out and offer some words of consolation, but like Bert she couldn't find the right words.

'Have you got a friend you'd like to have with you?' Carter asked. She looked very hot, sweat stains on her white shirt and her short fair hair sticking damply to her head. 'I could call them for you.'

Camellia drew herself up, wiped her damp eyes with the back of her hand and looked right into the well-intentioned policewoman's eyes. 'I don't have any friends,' she said, a new hard look in her dark eyes. 'Didn't you know? I'm like a leper. Mum saw to that.'

All Bert's good memories of Bonny faded at that moment.

'I'd like to be on my own for a few minutes, if you wouldn't mind,' Camellia said a little later. 'I mean before I have to identify Mum.'

Bert nodded. He had intended to say that tomorrow morning was soon enough for that, but he had a feeling Camellia would rather take all the shocks in one day. 'I'll come back for you in half an hour,' he said as he stood up. Then turning on his heels he ushered Carter away with him.

Once she was entirely alone, Camellia leaned

back against the wall and closed her eyes, remembering the day she was told her father was dead. It was 14 March 1956. She was just six then and it was also the day her snug, predictable world started to fall apart.

Aside from it being a particularly cold, windy morning, it started just like any other school day. She had porridge and a boiled egg for breakfast in the kitchen, and, while she ate, her mother plaited her hair and tied a neat ribbon bow on each end.

She had been so proud of her mother then. Many people likened Bonny to Marilyn Monroe because of her identical blonde wavy hair, and her glamorous pencil skirts and tight sweaters. Camellia thought she was even prettier. Even now, at eight in the morning, she was dressed in a pink wool two-piece and high heels, her hair just perfect.

'I hope this wind drops by tomorrow,' Bonny said as she adjusted the second ribbon. 'Daddy isn't a very good sailor.'

John Norton was in Brussels attending a meeting about the unrest in Egypt which it seemed could close the Suez Canal and prevent oil tankers getting through. He had taken the car ferry from Dover on Monday morning and was due back on Friday.

'I wish Daddy didn't have to go away all the time,' Camellia said wistfully. 'It would be nice if he came home every night.'

Bonny smiled and ran one hand over her daughter's hair affectionately. She was sure that this trouble in the Middle East was just a storm in a teacup. But John was afraid it might end in a war and he'd been very tense and preoccupied for some weeks. Bonny thought her daughter had picked up on his anxiety and this was what had prompted her remark.

'He'll be back for the weekend. If the weather's better, I expect he'll take you out on the marsh to see if there are any new-born lambs yet. I know Daddy would much rather be home with us too every night, but this is the way he earns his money, darling. He's a very important man.'

When Camillia reached the top of Mermaid Street she turned. Bonny was still in the doorway, ready to wave one last time. Camellia waved and plodded on. The shops were just beginning to open, Mr Bankworth in the greengrocers waved and shouted for her to hold her hat on, and Mr Simmonds her special policeman friend rode past on his bicycle and tinkled his bell at her.

All day the wind grew even stronger and it rattled the classroom windows. They learned the eight-times table and had a spelling test. Miss Grady gave them another ten words to learn by tomorrow morning, and said 'Woe betide anyone who couldn't spell them'.

It was something of a surprise for Camellia to find mother wasn't waiting for her at the gates at half past three. She met her most days, and sometimes they went down to Norah's tearooms by the Landgate for crumpets and tea. But Camellia didn't mind, it gave her a chance to look in Woolworths. Bonny didn't like Woolworths much, she said the wooden floor made it smell funny, but Camellia overlooked that as she loved to look at all the sweets and lemonade powder in their glass compartments and watch the assistants weighing them up in cellophane bags. It was her ambition to work there when she was grown up, though Daddy always laughed when she said that and said he thought she could aim a little higher.

As she walked down Mermaid Street, sometime after four, she sang Alma Cogan's 'Never do a Tango with an Eskimo'. It had been playing in Woolworths and she was determined to learn all the words so she could sing it to Daddy when he came home from Belgium.

The second surprise of the day came when the front door was opened by Superintendent Willis. He was a friend of her parents and sometimes came with his wife to dinner, but until today she'd never seen him in his police uniform before. He was a big man with a raw red face as if he'd been out in the wind for weeks, but today he seemed bigger than ever, filling the small lobby inside the front door.

'Hullo, Mr Willis,' she said, dumping her satchel on the floor. 'Where's Mummy?' Without giving him time to reply, she slipped in round him and into the living room.

She knew something bad had happened the moment she saw her mother. She was sitting in an armchair, her slim shoulders hunched, just staring into the fire, she didn't even turn her head as her daughter came into the room. There was a young policewoman with fair fluffy hair sitting there too, but she jumped up, her face flushing pink as if she was embarrassed.

'Mummy! What's wrong?' Camellia asked, rushing over to her mother, alarmed by her tear-stained face and puffy eyes. 'Has something happened? Why are the police here?'

There was a moment's heavy silence. Camellia could hear the grandfather clock ticking and the coal on the fire crackling and she instantly sensed that all three adults had been so immersed in whatever the problem was that they'd forgotten she was due home from school.

'Mummy?' She felt suddenly chilled to the bone. 'Tell me!'

'Oh, darling! It's Daddy,' her mother said in a strange, strangled voice, and all at once she was sobbing, grabbing Camellia onto her lap and holding her so tightly, she could scarcely breathe.

It was Mr Willis who explained what had happened. He crouched down in front of her and said Daddy had something he called a 'heart attack' while he was in Brussels.

'But when's he coming home?' she asked in bewilderment, looking from Mr Willis's red face to the policewoman's white one, then back to her sobbing mother. 'He *is* coming home isn't he?'

The man's big hand came down on her shoulder, it felt so very heavy and his usually jovial face seemed to sag. 'I'm afraid he won't ever come home again, sweetheart,' he said gruffly. 'You see, he died from the heart attack. Daddy's gone to live with Jesus.'

Much later that night Camellia lay beside her sleeping mother in her parents' bed, and tried to make sense of everything she'd heard and observed in the last six or seven hours. It seemed like a bad dream, but yet she knew it wasn't. Dr Negus really had called and given her mother the medicine which had finally stopped her crying and sent her to sleep. Mrs Tully, the cleaning lady, was now sleeping in Camellia's bed and Granny was coming tomorrow to look after them. Although it was warm and cosy in the big bed and her mother's body comforting, Camellia couldn't go to sleep.

There was enough light from from the street lamps out in Mermaid Street to see her parents' room clearly. Mirrored doors on the wardrobes reflected back more eerie light, Bonny's collection of perfume bottles on the dressing table glinted, and a white frothy negligee hanging behind the bedroom door looked ghostly. This room had always been a sanctuary to Camellia, both her parents' personalities were stamped firmly here, her Daddy's books and box of cufflinks beside his side of the bed, Mummy's hand cream and nail

25

varnish by hers. Even the bed smelled of them both, a whiff of Daddy's hair oil on his pillow, perfume on Mummy's. At weekends Camellia always got into bed between them in the mornings and over a cup of tea all three would discuss jobs to be done, places they wanted to go. But now as she lay there, her father's scent filling her nostrils, snippets of overheard adult remarks made during the afternoon and evening buzzing in her head, all at once she understood that everything which just this morning had seemed so permanent and secure, was shattered.

It was four weeks after her father's funeral when Camellia heard her mother and Granny arguing up in the big bedroom as she sat downstairs doing some crayoning. Camellia didn't want to listen, but she couldn't help it, their voices filled the small house.

'I won't have you speaking to me like this,' Granny said, her voice quivering as if she were crying. 'I came here to help, but I can't do that unless you co-operate.'

'Clear off back to London,' Bonny screamed at her. 'All you've done is criticise and fuss round me. I'm trying to get back to normal, but you won't let me.'

'You can't go out wearing a pink dress so soon after being widowed,' Granny retorted. 'What will people think?'

'I don't care what they think,' Bonny's voice rose even higher. 'I'm sick of looking like an old hag, sick of staying in with you while you clean, dust, wash and witter on like a frustrated mother hen. I'm sick of everything.'

Camellia began to cry. She was slowly accepting that without Daddy nothing would ever be quite the same, but she couldn't understand why her mother was so nasty to Granny. She alone had made everything seem just a bit better, she cooked and cleaned, she took Camellia down to the swings on The Salts, took her to school and taught her to knit and sew in the evenings. She was a bit of a fusspot, but she was kind and loving.

Until her father's death 'Granny' had just been the name of a faceless person who sent hand-knitted cardigans and beautifully dressed dolls for birthdays and Christmas. For some unexplained reason she hadn't visited before, at least not in Camellia's memory anyway, until her son-in-law's death. But now Camellia had got to know the old lady, she didn't want her to leave.

'I will go home if that's what you want,' Granny said, but now her voice rose too as if she were losing her temper. 'I've never understood you, Bonny. I've given you everything, I never thought of myself. You're nothing but a selfish, hard-hearted little baggage. Those tears aren't for John, just for yourself. You ought to get down on your knees and thank the Lord for the good years he gave you, for Camellia and your beautiful home. What did I have when Arnold died? A council house, a daughter who couldn't care less about me and a widow's pension. But I didn't mind about that, I just missed Arnold and I still do.'

The quarrelling finally stopped, but it was some ten minutes before Granny came downstairs. She had put some powder on her face, but her eyes were still puffy. She smiled at Camellia sitting on the settee, but her weak attempt at normality didn't fool the bright six-year-old.

'Don't go, Granny,' Camellia implored her. 'I like you being here.'

'I have to go, my lovely.' Granny flopped down on the settee and took her on her lap. 'Maybe Mummy will be better once I'm gone. She won't listen to me about anything, and I can't do any more.'

Camellia had no argument to come back with. She cuddled into the woman's arms, wishing she could think of something to say to both older women to make things right.

'How will we manage without you?' Camellia asked. It wasn't so long ago that her mother had stayed in bed all day, even now she left everything to Granny. 'Will Mummy make the meals and do the shopping again?'

'I'm sure she will.' The older woman sniffed. 'She'll have to, won't she?'

'I miss Daddy dreadfully,' Camellia blurted out, knowing somehow that saying such a thing to her mother would only irritate her still further. 'Will it always be like this?'

She meant would the big hole he'd left in her life ever be filled? Would there ever be a night when she wouldn't remember how he always read her a goodnight story? Or a weekend when she didn't think of their walks together out on the marsh. Mummy had never taken as much interest in what she did at school, about her friends, or even what she thought about as Daddy did. She had tried to stop thinking about these things, but she couldn't.

'It will get better,' Granny said firmly. 'I can't promise it will overnight and all those memories of your daddy will stay in your mind, because they're special ones and you'll want to hang onto them. But you will find they don't hurt so much soon.'

'Were you like Mummy when Grandpa died?' Camellia asked.

'No, I didn't make a big fuss when he died,' Doris said carefully. 'But then Grandpa was seventy and I knew he couldn't live forever. It's different for Mummy. She'll still only twenty-seven and she expected your Daddy to be with her for years and years.'

There were a great many more things Camellia wanted to ask, like why her mother didn't seem to care about her any longer. Why she wanted to put on a pink dress instead of the black one, and why if Granny was Bonny's mother did she seem to dislike her so much? But somehow she knew these and other questions niggling at the back of her head were best left unasked.

'Will you come to see me again?' she asked instead.

Again Doris hesitated. She knew she would catch the next train down if ever Bonny needed her, despite everything that had been said. But a sixth sense told her that her daughter was intending to cut off her entire past, because she was through with grieving.

'I'll come if you need me,' she said quietly. 'Maybe Mummy will let you come and stay with me during the holidays. Write to me, my lovely. Always remember I'm your Granny and I love you.'

Camellia's memory of her father's death had started the tears again. She wiped them away with the hem of her overall and stared up at the sky. But another vivid, and this time shameful memory slipped into her mind.

It was five years after her father's death, in February 1961 when Camellia woke one Friday night to the sound of Johnny Kidd's 'Shakin' All Over'. The music wasn't just loud, it was deafening. Switching on the light Camellia saw that it was ten past one, she wondered how long it would be before one of the neighbours called the police.

If it wasn't for the photograph beside her bed, she might have thought those cosy, quiet days of her early childhood were just a fantasy she'd dreamed up to comfort herself.

But there they were, in black and white, a family group. Camellia was five when it was taken, wearing a velvet party dress with a lace collar, her mother in a now rather dated waisted costume, and much shorter hair than she had at present, and her father standing behind their couch wearing a dark suit.

Camellia could see she was plump even then, but she looked kind of sweet, albeit too serious. Now she was fat, really fat, and her dark eyes seemed to have retreated into puffy flesh, like two slits. John Norton was dead. Sweet little Camellia was now a big lump. And Bonny wasn't a real mother any more.

Even the happy days at Collegiate School were over, snatched away back in December, two days before her eleventh birthday.

Bonny claimed she had been advised by the head teacher that as Camellia wouldn't pass her eleven-plus exam, she might as well go to the state junior school, in the new year, then on to the secondary modern next September. But that was a wicked lie, she was always near the top of the class and Miss Grady had often said she was clever enough to win a scholarship to one of the best girls' schools.

Camellia switched off the light and pulled her pillow over her head to shut out the noise. She didn't need to go downstairs to see what was going on. She could imagine the scene in the lounge because she'd seen much the same thing countless times in the past. Bonny would be centre stage as always. She probably was wearing her long hair up in a ponytail and one of her dresses with a full circular skirt, a wide belt nipping her waist into a hand's span, beneath it a cancan petticoat with a hundred yards of frothy pink and white net. She would be jiving with someone, possibly that awful man who dressed like a teddy boy in a long red drape jacket and shoestring tie, unless he'd had the heave-ho recently. All the other men would be watching Bonny's legs to get a glimpse of stocking tops as she twirled.

Who all the men were was a mystery to Camellia, they just appeared late at night, but she knew they always far outweighed the few women who came to these impromptu parties. Bonny had no women friends any longer. Auntie Pat, Babs, Freda and Janice had disappeared in the same way hot cooked meals, ironed school blouses, help with homework and nights by the television with her daughter had.

For a year or two after John's death, some of the old friends still dropped in occasionally for a cup of tea and a chat. Superintendent Willis, Mr Dexter the dentist, and Malcolm Frazer who owned the Mermaid Inn in particular, though they never seemed to be accompanied by their wives. But gradually they'd stopped coming too, and Camellia sometimes thought she'd actually dreamt that the dining table used to be laid with starched napkins, flowers and candles and that her mother had once spent all day in the kitchen preparing special dinners for groups of friends.

She must have fallen asleep again, for when she woke again the music was turned off and the house was quiet again, except for a thumping sound.

She listened for a little while, trying to place where the noise was coming from. It sounded like a branch banging on a window. It wasn't at her window, and as her mother's overlooked the street and there were no trees there, it couldn't be there. But as she listened the noise grew more insistent. Puzzled Camellia got out of bed and went out onto the landing.

31

Number twelve was over three hundred years old and all the rooms were on slightly different levels. At the top of the stairs was the bathroom, Camellia's room was next, up two steps there was a short passage and another step up to her mother's room which covered the entire front of the house. Next to the closed door was an even narrower staircase which led to two tiny attic rooms kept for guests. Camellia assumed the noise was coming from there. The house was prone to funny sounds, the pipes bubbled and the boards creaked. She thought perhaps one of the attic windows had been left open and the wind was banging it.

But as she crept forward in the darkness to go up the stairs, she stopped short at another sound. It was just like a pig grunting and it was in time with the thumping!

Her initial instinct was to run in to her mother, but as her hand closed round the door knob she suddenly realised not only that the noise was coming from within Bonny's room, but what it was. She froze, too shocked to move.

Her knowledge of sex was scanty. She knew there was some kind of special cuddling which made babies, and if you did it when you weren't married it was very bad. She'd heard too, boys saying nasty swear words in the playground and she instinctively knew what she was hearing now was that word 'fucking'.

As she stood there, unsure whether to burst in and stop the man from hurting her mother, she heard Bonny's voice above the grunting.

'Harder, do it harder. I love it!'

Camellia felt herself go hot all over, like someone had just opened a furnace door in front of her. She backed away, covering her mouth with her hands, afraid she was going to be sick.

Back in her room, huddled up in bed, suddenly

everything which had puzzled her for several years became crystal clear. Why all the old friends had stopped calling. Why the neighbours whispered behind their hands when she walked down the street, the odd looks she got from men, and why her old school friends from Collegiate stopped asking her round to play. But most of all the meaning of the word 'whore' which a horrible boy at school had called her mother.

From that night on things seemed to get worse and worse. Bonny bought herself an expensive new outfit each week, but Camellia was still wearing clothes she'd long outgrown. The parties became more frequent, noisier still, with coarse men rampaging drunkenly up the stairs and often bursting into her room mistaking it for the bathroom. Soon Bonny made no attempt to cover up that men stayed the night, the smell of their perspiration lingered in the bedroom, there were stains on the sheets which were seldom changed and the beautiful rugs in the living room had cigarette burns and beer stains on them. Bonny was often drunk during the day too, sometimes insensible on the settee when Camellia got in from school. Any attempts at housekeeping were abandoned, the only food in the house bread and jam. Camellia had a stodgy school dinner, bought a couple of stale buns from the baker's as she walked home, then Bonny sent her out for chips later.

Often she was left alone all weekend, a ten-shilling note left on the table to feed herself. But Bonny had only to sweep through the door on Sunday night, a silly soft toy in her arms for Camellia and say she was sorry and it would never happen again, and Camellia forgave her.

The neighbours were less forgiving, there were no longer polite requests to turn down the music but hysterical screaming at the door and hammering on the windows. Vicious, abusive unsigned notes were stuck through the door, endless warnings of legal action, sometimes threats against her person, but Bonny only laughed and tossed them airily on the fire. She said the neighbours were small-minded and jealous, and that soon she and Camellia would move away.

It was two weeks before Christmas in 1962, when she was almost twelve, that Camellia discovered her doll's house had been taken from her room while she was at school.

A sense of foreboding filled her as she looked at the space on the carpet where it been that morning. For some time she'd had a feeling that something very bad was going to happen. Bonny had been moody and withdrawn for several weeks – she hadn't mentioned anything about Christmas, not even about the decorations and there hadn't been any parties at the house for three weeks.

She plodded back down the stairs. She had grown even fatter during the summer and running was now beyond her. She didn't like anything much about herself, but she hated her size more than anything. Not quite twelve, she was forty-two inches round the hips and she weighed eleven stone.

'Where's my doll's house?' she asked.

Bonny was sitting in an armchair, smoking a cigarette and reading a typewritten letter. For once she wasn't made-up, in fact her hair didn't even look as if she'd brushed it and she had a stain down the front of her pink twinset.

'I've sold it,' she replied, without even looking up.

'You've sold it!' Camellia was incredulous. 'You couldn't have! You're joking aren't you?'

'I've got more on my mind than making jokes,'

34

Bonny snapped at her, putting down the letter and looking up at her daughter. 'Come on now, darling. You're too old for a doll's house and I needed the money.'

'But Daddy bought it.' Camellia's eyes filled with tears. 'It's all I've got left of him. How could you?'

'If you really understood how bad things are, you wouldn't ask that,' Bonny retorted defensively.

It was only now, perhaps because Camellia was angry with her mother that she noticed she didn't look as pretty as she used to. Her eyes had dark shadows round them, her skin looked grey and there were tiny lines around her eyes and mouth.

'Why didn't you take some money out the bank if you needed something?'

Bonny looked at the child's reproachful tear-filled brown eyes and sighed. She knew she shouldn't have sold it without asking, but she was desperate, she'd run out of alternatives now. Sometimes she forgot that Camellia was still just a child. She might be quick on the up-take about most things, but clearly she hadn't grasped their situation.

'There isn't any money in the bank, darling,' Bonny said more gently. 'I think it's time I explained a few things to you.'

Camellia slumped down onto the settee and listened in ever growing dismay as her mother reavealed she was not only broke, but in debt so deep that the house was going to be taken from them.

'That's why you had to leave Collegiate,' she finished. 'You see Daddy didn't leave me enough money. I tried to cut down the spending, but it's all gone now.'

'But what are we going to do?' Camellia sobbed. She wanted to remind her mother that only last week she'd bought yet another new dress and a couple of new records, but even in her own misery she could see Bonny was on the point of tears and she hated to see her cry.

'I've found a little house in Fishmarket Street.' Bonny wrinkled her little nose in distaste. 'I'm afraid it's not very nice, but it was all I could find. I'll get a job and we'll make it cosy together.'

Camellia sobbed again. She was fat and plain, she hadn't one friend, everyone at school laughed at her and said nasty things about her mother. Her doll's house and all those beautiful things her father had bought to furnish it were gone too, to another little girl who would never understand how precious it had been to the previous owner. Now, on top of it all, she was being forced to leave the home she loved.

'I'm sorry, darling.' Bonny drew her into her arms and enveloped her in the smell of Joy. 'I haven't been a very good mummy to you, have I? I'm selfish, lazy and a spendthrift. But I do love you!'

Camellia dried her eyes yet again and got up from her bench. Even after everything Bonny had put her through, the men, the drinking, squandering money and the neglect, she still loved her mother. Neighbours and town gossips might only remember the bad things, but she had a small store of precious golden memories, which all seemed so much more important now. Picnics in summer, trips to London Zoo. Laughing helplessly at each other in the hall of mirrors on Hastings pier, racing down the dunes at Camber Sands. Bonny had been a child herself at heart, always ready for fun and mischief. They might have been mother and daughter, but they were always best friends.

Chapter Three

'Bert's outside in the car waiting for you, lovey,' Enid Rowlands said as Camellia came out of the toilet wearing her navy-blue skirt and white blouse. She picked up a damp cloth and wiped the girl's face again for her. 'And I've told him he's to bring you back here afterwards. We've got a nice little spare room upstairs. You can't be alone at a time like this.'

Camellia thanked her. Until that moment she hadn't even considered where she might sleep tonight or in the future. Somehow it made Bonny's death even more real, it meant she didn't have a home of her own any longer either.

Mr Simmonds said very little on the ride to Hastings. Now and again his hand reached out for hers, squeezing it in silent sympathy, and she was glad he didn't feel he had to make any conversation. Camellia watched the people in other cars. They were nearly all families, driving home after a day at the seaside, tired and sunburnt, the children in the back seat dropping off to sleep. She recalled that when her father was still alive she'd always knelt up in the back of the car and waved at people. Perhaps children didn't do that any longer.

The mortuary was tucked away in a back street. An old red-brick building with painted-over windows. As Mr Simmonds took her arm and led her in, her stomach lurched and she suddenly felt faint with the smell of antiseptic.

'It's okay, some of us do feel a bit queasy in these places,' Mr Simmonds said very soothingly. 'But it's only the hospital smell, nothing more. You won't be seeing anything nasty. Bonny will just be in a room on her own, on a trolley, all covered up. We'll just take a look at her together and you confirm it is her. That's all there is to it.'

They were led into a small room by another man in a white gown. It was exactly as Mr Simmonds said. The man waited until Camellia was standing by the trolley and then lifted back the sheet covering her.

It was of course Bonny, despite the frantic prayers Camellia had offered up that it wouldn't be. She looked just the way she did in the mornings after a night of drinking. A bluey tinge to her skin, older and kind of hard. If it hadn't been for her hair stained darker by the mud, Camellia might have believed she was still asleep.

She confirmed it was her mother, but she couldn't kiss her. Her heart was telling her to. Her whole being wanted to stroke that golden hair, hold her tightly one more time. But she didn't. Instead she just looked, then turned away as if she didn't care.

Camellia lay back in the seat and closed her eyes as they drove back to Rye. Bert knew she wasn't asleep, it was just her way of dealing with what she'd just seen. But as he glanced at her pale, expressionless face so close to his shoulder, he was reminded of another time he had driven down this road with her, some eighteen months earlier. It had been about the same time of day, around four thirty or five in the afternoon. Not a hot sunny day though, but a bitterly cold afternoon in February and already dark.

He was driving back from Hastings towards Rye in his Morris Minor, a tricycle for his son's fourth birthday on the back seat. It was Saturday and so cold he was sure snow must be on the way. He couldn't wait to get indoors and warm himself by the fire. The heater in the car wasn't very good.

As he drove he was thinking about the past. It was incredible to find he'd been in Rye for fourteen years. It seemed such a short while ago that he was a young constable out on the beat. Now he was thirty-five, a sergeant, married with two small boys. To think, until he was twenty-eight, he believed he could never love any woman except for Bonny Norton!

Bert winced. What a fool he was over her! Always looking for her, hoping and wishing but never quite daring to do anything about it. Thank goodness Sandra came along when she did! Bonny was anyone's now for the price of a drink or two. If he'd got tangled up with her after John died, his career and happiness would have been finished.

Sandra was a total opposite to Bonny. Small and dark-haired, shy and loving, she didn't have a devious thought in her head. He had met her out at Peasmarsh, the year after John Norton died, she worked there as a nanny for Clive and Daphne Huntley. They were rich folks, the kind that couldn't be bothered with their kids. They'd had a burglary one night and he'd gone out to take a statement from them while the CID looked for fingerprints. Sandra made them all tea and before Bert left the big house he'd persuaded her to meet him on her night off. Eighteen months later they were married and living in a policehouse.

As he went over the brow of the hill at Guestling, his headlights picked up a figure some five or six hundred yards ahead. It looked like an old lady. He wondered if she'd missed the bus, as he couldn't imagine anyone choosing to walk along this dark, deserted stretch of road without good cause. He slowed down. She was hobbling, and just the way her shoulders were hunched up suggested she was in distress.

Bert went on past her to where there was a lay-by on the side of the road. A stream of cars coming through from Hastings obscured his vision for a moment. Leaving the engine running he got out of his car, pulled his sheepskin coat round him more tightly and called out.

'Would you like a lift, love? It's a bit cold and dark to be out walking on this road!'

He anticipated a rebuff. Old country women were a tough breed and she wouldn't know he was a policeman.

He could see her a little better now, not her face as that was partially obscured by a hood or scarf round her head, but enough to see she was fat and shabbily dressed.

'I'm a policeman,' he called out again. 'Sgt Simmonds from Rye.'

He thought he heard a sob, though it could've been only the wind. He walked towards her.

A car sped past in the opposite direction and for a second its headlights lit up her face clearly. To his astonishment it wasn't an old lady at all, but Camellia Norton.

'Camellia!' he gasped. 'What on earth are you doing out here?'

'Is it really you, Mr Simmonds,' she said, moving a little faster towards him.

The rear lights of his car weren't bright enough to see her face clearly, but he sensed she was crying and saw one hand move to wipe her eyes.

'Come on, love, get in the car,' he said. 'You must be frozen.'

Bert hadn't seen the girl for some time, even though he'd run into Bonny on many occasions in the George and the Mermaid. He knew all about their eviction from Mermaid Street and the move to Fishmarket Street, but Bonny just laughed it off and had implied that things were on the up and up for her. As Bonny always looked unfailingly glamorous, despite her drinking and chasing men, Bert hadn't actually believed all the rumours about how dreadful her daughter looked these days.

But now as he put on the car's interior light to get a better look at Camellia, he was shocked to find they weren't rumours but truth. He knew she must be fourteen now, but she looked much older because she was so fat. Her complexion, which as a young child had been clear and glowing, was now sallow, with a crop of vicious spots on her chin and forehead. She pushed back her hood to reveal hair which, aside from being dull with grease, also appeared to have been cut off abruptly with garden shears, and her thin gabardine school mackintosh was several sizes too small, pitifully inadequate against the wind and cold.

Bert took her icy hands between his own and rubbed them. They were red and chapped, nails bitten down to the quick.

'What's happened?' he asked gently. He could see she was trying not to cry, too cold to even shiver. 'Why are you out here all alone?'

'I lost my bus fare,' she said weakly, turning her face away from his, as if unable to meet his close scrutiny.

'Well, you're all right now,' he said comfortingly, shocked that she'd already walked some four or five miles from Hastings and appalled at how she might have ended up if she had walked the entire way home to Rye. 'A hot bath and a cup of tea will sort you out. I'd better get you home. Your mum will be worried about you.'

'She isn't there,' Camellia said in a small voice as

Bert started to drive. 'She's gone away for the weekend.'

'What! And left you on your own?' Bert's head jerked round to her in astonishment. 'Surely not?'

'She goes away a lot these days,' Camellia shrugged. 'I'm usually all right, but this time she forgot to leave any money for the meter.'

The story came out in fits and starts. It was clear Camellia didn't want to divulge anything, even to someone who knew her mother as well as Bert did. But once she got going it came out like a torrent.

On Friday evening she had arrived home from school to find her mother had gone away. She got herself some fish and chips, then settled down to watch television. She hadn't even finished eating when the meter ran out and she went round the house with a candle looking for a shilling.

When she failed to find any money she went to bed, but a further search this morning brought nothing more than sixpence and a few pennies.

'I couldn't ask any of the neighbours,' she whispered in shame. 'They talk about Mummy enough already. I had just enough to get almost into Hastings on the bus. I took one of Mummy's rings to the pawn shop in the Old Town.'

Bert thought this was very resourceful of her, such a solution would never have occurred to him. But then Bonny had probably acquainted her with such places.

'The man gave me two pounds for the ring,' she said wearily. 'It was so cold in Hastings I thought I'd go straight home again. But when I got to the bus stop I found the notes had gone from my pocket. I must have pulled them out with my hanky. I walked back to the pawn shop looking everywhere, but I didn't find them.'

By the time they stopped outside the house in

Fishmarket Street, Camellia was warmer and she'd dried her eyes.

'I'll come in with you,' he said, before she had time to make an excuse. 'We'll put some money in the meter and make sure everything's all right.'

He was furious with Bonny, determined to take her to task at neglecting her daughter and leaving her on her own for a whole weekend. But at the same time he didn't want to make too much of it to Camellia.

She made no protest, but he sensed her embarrassment as she opened the front door and a smell of old fried food and damp wafted out. Bert struck a match and put some money in the electric meter, but as the lights came on he had to repress a gasp of horror at the black mould on the hall walls, the paper hanging off in strips.

He'd seen plenty of grim places in his years in the force, but this beat most of them. It was so cold he shivered even in his thick sheepskin. Walking into the living room he could only stare in shock. The square of carpet was thin, sticky with spilt drinks, its pattern lost in a dirty film. Camellia turned on an imitation log fire with a couple of electric bars across the front. The logs were broken and dusty, the red light bulb beneath showing through. There were a couple of fireside chairs with greasy seats, a black plastic coffee table decorated with two swans and a pre-war settee with the stuffing coming out of the arms.

Maybe it wouldn't have been so shocking if he hadn't been in their old house. How could anyone adjust to living like this when once they were surrounded by antiques, Persian carpets and luxurious furnishings?

'It's awful isn't it.' Camellia hung her head and shifted from one foot to the other in nervousness. 'I didn't want you to see it, Mr Simmonds. Mummy

43

was going to get it done up, but she hasn't got enough money now.'

Bert gulped back a sarcastic reply. Just the price of one of Bonny's smart outfits would pay for this room to be redecorated, and she knew enough men who would willingly do it for her. He shifted back to being a policeman again, mentally noting all the evidence of Bonny's cruel indifference to her child's well-being, while she made sure she never went short of anything.

An expensive fur lying carelessly across a chair, a wooden clothes horse with dainty underwear left to dry. A bottle of Chanel perfume, a blue silk scarf and a pair of soft leather gloves shared the table with an almost empty gin bottle and a lipstick-smeared glass.

Bert went through to the kitchen and opened the drop-front cabinet. It was clean, he guessed kept so by Camellia, but so bare. Half a bottle of milk, one egg in a bowl and just a few slices of bread left in a bag. There were condiments, bottles of sauce and a pot of jam, but no evidence that Bonny ever went to the trouble to spoil her manicured nails with something as mundane as cooking.

'You can't stay here alone.' Bert turned as the girl came lumbering up behind him. It was painful to compare her appearance now with how she had looked when he first met her as a little girl. Her clothes had been so neat, hair shiny and well cut, plump even then, but now she was obese. What would possess Bonny to allow her to wear that dreadful pleated skirt or the shrunken grey jumper. Her shoes were scuffed and rundown at the heel and her grey socks were in concertinas round her ankles. 'I don't like it one bit, love. There's nothing for you to eat and besides a girl of your age shouldn't be alone at night.'

'I'll be all right.' Camellia's eyes dropped from

his. Her mournful brown eyes and her hair had been her best features as a child. Heaven only knows who had hacked off her hair, it looked terrible, and her eyes were now almost embedded in fat. 'Mummy will be cross if she comes home and I'm not here.'

'I shall be more than *cross* with her when she does come home,' Bert said tartly. 'She needs a good talking to. I'm taking you round to my mother's, I'll leave a note for Bonny.'

Camellia's face contorted into an expression of anguish.

'She can't help the way she is, Mr Simmonds.' She caught hold of his arm involuntarily. 'She's sad inside all the time, that's why she goes out a lot. Please don't get her into trouble?'

Bert thought about that plea from Camellia later that night when he was cuddled up beside Sandra. He had popped back to his mother's an hour ago and heard a great deal more that made him feel uneasy. Camellia was fast asleep upstairs, but his mother had described the girl's worn underwear, the untreated boils on her neck and chilblains on her inner thighs.

Camellia had opened up to his mother, as people usually did. But although she had confessed her diet consisted of fish and chips and sandwiches, she had staunchly insisted Bonny loved her. There were descriptions of picnics out by Camber Castle in the summer, days out to Hastings, and weekend trips to London. As Bert's mother pointed out, behind the visible part of Bonny, the drinking, the stream of men friends and wild spending sprees, there was a woman who cared enough to make some occasions memorable.

'I know it might seem kinder to get Camellia taken away from her mother,' his mother said as he left, catching hold of his hand, her eyes full of compassion. 'But don't do it, son. There is something between them that is fine and good, however it might seem otherwise to you. I can't explain this very well, but I know I'm right. Let's try and make things better for Camellia. Let me encourage her to come here for a bit of home cooking, and I'll teach her a few homemaking skills. Maybe I can help her with a diet too. Bonny's all she's got right now, and they need and love one another.'

Camellia sat up again as they drove up the High Street. It was quiet now, the shops soon to close and just a few people strolling along.

'Will you be all right with Mrs Rowlands?' Bert asked. He would have preferred to take her to his mother's again, but the baker's wife had been so insistent that Camellia was to stay with her.

'I'll be fine,' Camellia said, her tone implying it was all the same to her wherever she was sent. 'Don't worry about me, Mr Simmonds, you've got your own children to think about.'

That struck Bert as a remarkably adult retort. He felt she meant that his wife would take a dim view of him fussing over Bonny Norton's child.

'Well, I'll be popping in and out to see you. If things don't work out you can tell me then,' he said.

Some half an hour later, up in the Rowlands living room above the bakery, after Mr Simmonds had left, Camellia took the offered cup of tea in silence. Mrs Rowlands was talking ninety to the dozen, flitting from the amount of cakes and pies they'd sold that day, to what people had been saying about Bonny's death and then onto what they'd have for tea, without even drawing breath. The room was cluttered with ornaments, china or glass cats, dogs and other animals filled every surface, but it was bright, sweet smelling and welcoming, so very different from Fishmarket Street.

Camellia couldn't talk, or even cry. All she could think of was that she was finally released from a huge, impossibly heavy burden.

No more noisy parties, no 'uncle this' and 'uncle that' walking around the house in their underpants or waking her at night with the sound of bestial grunting and thumping. No more cleaning up vomit or finding the kitchen and lounge floor awash with beer and dog-ends blocking up the sink. Never again to face the humiliation of asking for credit at the corner shop.

She couldn't think of one thing she would miss her mother for. She was used to being alone, she'd been left for long weekends since she was eleven. The only difference now was that Bonny wouldn't dance back in with a bag of cream cakes or a soft toy and empty promises. This time her absence was forever.

Yet if she really was glad it was over, why did she feel as if she'd been torn apart?

Chapter Four

Camellia woke with a start, drenched in sweat. For a moment she was confused when she saw the sloping attic ceiling and the unfamiliar rose wallpaper. Then it all came back. Enid Rowlands had taken her in, a doctor had been called and given her a pill. It was real, not a nightmare.

The church clock struck seven. Pink curtains flapped at the tiny window, a picture of a little boy and a dog hung on the wall, a bedside lamp made out of a wine bottle and two china dogs with chipped ears were on the mantelpiece. The smell of baked bread was trapped up here, and under any other conditions she would have enjoyed being in such a clean, fresh room. But although Mr and Mrs Rowlands were kindly enough, she knew she was only here on sufferance, until someone else decided where she should go.

She got out of bed slowly. Her head was muzzy and she had an evil taste in her mouth. Looking down she saw she was wearing a pink nylon nightie that wasn't hers. On the chair was her navy skirt, white blouse and underwear. Mrs Rowlands had washed and ironed them, but even that made her embarrassed. Had she looked at that big cheap cotton bra and knickers, grey with age and careless washing, the elastic shedding bits of rubber and felt disgust?

Bonny had never worn such ugly things. She

threw clothes away when they got spoiled in the wash or went out of fashion.

The window overlooked the High Street, but she could see little besides the shops opposite and the church tower behind. It was so hot in here. Tomorrow morning when Mr Rowlands started baking it would get hotter still. She had to get out for some fresh air.

There was no plan in her head as she stood at Hilder's Cliff. It had always been her favourite spot and today was so clear and bright she could see right across the marsh to Lydd. Rye was at its most lovely early in the morning, before people broke the tranquillity. The ancient grey stone of the Landgate, brilliant splashes of colour from flowers in window boxes, latticed windows twinkling in the early morning sun, even the cobbles beneath her feet sparkled as if they'd been lightly sprinkled with glitter.

Behind her was Collegiate School, part of that dimly remembered happy past when her father took her for walks along the quay at this time of day, when visitors came down from London for dinner parties, when she was dressed up in a smocked dress to go out for lunch.

Fishmarket Street was down below. If she peered right over the rail she could just see their house to her right. Not that she wanted to look at it. She found it far more comforting to look at The Salts and remember being pushed on the swings by her father.

'I wonder what will happen to it?' she mused. Last summer she'd painted the living room herself in magnolia. Old Mrs Simmonds even gave her some better curtains to hang and showed her how to make covers for the two fireside chairs and it looked lovely for some time. But when winter came black mould crept up the walls and spoiled it.

Bonny consoled her by saying it would be the last winter they'd spend there. For once she had spoken the truth.

Camellia had no idea why she suddenly felt compelled to take the steep steps down to it. She knew, though she hadn't been told, that she wasn't supposed to until the police had finished their investigations. But she wanted to. Just for one last look.

All the other houses in the terrace still had their curtains closed and bottles of milk stood on each doorstep. Aside from a scruffy dog out on his early morning business, there was no one to see her. She slid her hand through the letter box and found the key dangling on its string inside.

The house smelled as musty as ever. In the narrow hall there was a theatre poster hanging over the worst of the peeling paper. Bonny had put it there herself. She said she used to know the actress Frances Delarhey who was billed as starring in the play. Camellia had no idea how Bonny came by the poster, but then her mother rarely explained anything.

Everything was just as she left it yesterday morning: the rinsed-out cereal bowl on the wooden draining board, one mug, a spoon and the milk turned sour in the bottle. She wandered aimlessly, picking things up, then putting them down, uncertain now why she was here. Unpaid bills on the ugly tiled mantelpiece, a mountain of ironing in a basket, even the almost empty gin bottle left on the table might indicate to an outsider that her mother was depressed, but Camellia knew that this was nothing compared with how things had been sometimes.

On the living room table was Bonny's make-up mirror, her bright pink nail varnish, emery board and an orange stick for her cuticles. It was almost as if she'd just popped out for cigarettes. If Camellia just closed her eyes for a moment, then opened them again, she might find Bonny back at that table, golden head bent over as she filed her nails to perfection.

The ironing board was still standing in the corner of the lounge, with the burn mark right through the cover. Camellia didn't want to remember now that only a fortnight ago Bonny had burned the skirt she'd saved up for weeks to buy.

Going on upstairs, she hesitated outside Bonny's room. This one room had always been out of bounds in her mother's absence and to poke around seemed like snooping.

'She can't say anything now!' Camellia said aloud. Her words echoed on the uncarpeted landing, and with the echo bitter memories came flooding back.

Bonny's room was the only one which had been redecorated. She got the horrible Stan who moved them in to do it and must have bribed him with the promise he'd get to stay here sometimes, because he worked like a slave at it. Not just painting and papering either, but building a whole wall of wardrobes for Bonny's clothes. Bonny insisted he'd start on Camellia's room when he'd finished hers. But maybe even Bonny balked at sleeping with the man just to get him to do jobs, because Stan disappeared suddenly without putting handles on the doors. Bonny had to do that herself and Stan never returned to do Camellia's room.

Pushing open the door, she walked in and stared round defiantly at Stan's handiwork.

Mirrors on the wardrobes reflected back the ornate walnut bed and dressing table brought from the old house. The deep pink curtains and carpet, white lacy bedspread and twin cherub lamps on little lace-covered tables gave an instant image of luxurious femininity.

Camellia could picture Bonny lying across the bed the day it was finished.

'It won't be long, darling, before the whole house looks as nice,' she said, drawing her onto the bed with her and giving her a cuddle. 'I'm through with all the silliness and parties. It's just you and me now. I'll get myself a job and we'll be happy here. Maybe I had to leave Mermaid Street to start again. There were too many ghosts in that house.'

It was all lies. The parties, the drunkenness and the men just went on and on. She didn't find a job and made no attempt to make the rest of the house nice. While Bonny had this comfortable pretty room, her daughter across the landing had bare boards under her feet, a piece of cardboard blocked a hole in the window and her bed had springs sticking out the mattress.

Camellia felt a surge of anger as she looked at the carefully made bed, the dusted dressing table with all those sparkling bottles of perfume arranged so neatly. Until now she hadn't really considered how odd it was that a woman who slept late, drank all night and who wouldn't even iron a school shirt for her daughter, somehow managed to keep this room immaculately clean and tidy.

The anger grew as she flung open the wardrobes to see row after row of dresses, suits and blouses. How many times had Camellia pleaded for a new school coat or skirt and always got the same reply. 'I'm a bit short now, darling. Next week maybe!'

So many excuses. She was going for an audition. This job interview was important. But mostly, 'He adores me, darling. I have to look right, just think how good it will be to have a new father.'

Who was the man she went to meet in London? Camellia had long since given up questioning

Bonny about her boyfriends, because all her relationships ended the same way. One moment she
was talking of flats in London, holidays in the sun
and her belief their luck was changing, then the
next it was all over. Bonny was like a fisherman,
idly dreaming away her life on a sunny river bank,
catching one, playing with him for awhile, then
throwing him back, always looking for the illusive
big catch.

Yet she had been unusually secretive about this
last man. She'd made long phone calls late at night,
her eyes glowing as if he really was important, and
kept hinting that something wonderful was around
the corner for both of them. Just a few days earlier
she had spoken of getting them both a passport.
Why hadn't she ever said his name or brought him
back here?

'I suppose he was married,' Camellia sighed.

As she flicked through dresses, tears welled up
in her eyes, splashing down her cheeks unheeded.
A memory of an evening some four weeks earlier
sprang into her mind, a good memory that softened
some of the anger.

Bonny was sitting at the dressing table brushing
her hair over her sun-kissed shoulders, wearing
just her bra and panties. Her stomach was as flat as
a board. She smiled as Camellia held out dresses
for her to choose from.

'That one's too dressy for drinks.' Bonny rejected
the emerald green one with beading on the shoulder. 'I don't feel like wearing black tonight. Get me
out the pink crepe!'

'I wish I had a dress like this one.' Camellia held
the pink one up to her and looked at herself in the
mirror. Her reflection made her cry. She was a fat
lump with piggy dark eyes, lank hair, sallow
greasy skin and she felt she would never look good
in anything.

53

She didn't hear her mother move, but suddenly she was there behind her, rubbing her soft perfumed cheek against Camellia's.

'You won't always be tubby, darling,' she said so very gently. 'One day you'll wake up and find it's all gone and you are beautiful.'

'How do you know?' Camellia sniffed back her tears. 'You've never been fat in your life.'

Bonny laughed, but this time there was no sarcasm in it.

'Because I had a good friend once who was every bit as plump as you. She turned out be one of the most gorgeous women anyone has ever seen. Besides you've got a lovely nature, darling, when the fat drops off, as it will, you'll be twice the woman I am.'

Camellia lifted out that pink dress and held it to her face and sobbed. She could smell her mother's perfume, feel that smooth cheek pressing against her own.

That night she'd gone to bed full of optimism. If she hadn't been so wrapped up in herself recently, perhaps she might have noticed something wasn't right with her mother.

All at once Camellia felt the full force of what Bonny's death really meant. She didn't care about the bad memories, the slights and humiliations. She just wanted her mother back, anyhow, anyway.

'Why Mummy? Why?' she whispered. 'If things were so bad why couldn't you have just come home and told me? You were always telling me to hold my head up and ignore spiteful people. I'm not a child any longer, I could have helped.'

It was a mixture of anger and grief that made her search through everything. Somewhere here she might find an explanation or at least a clue. She turned out everything: shoe boxes, old handbags, even coat pockets. She found almost a pound in change, but nothing else.

Next the dressing table, flicking aside the silky underwear with its waft of Chanel perfume, but still nothing.

A few photographs in an envelope of her father made her cry again. In the pictures he was just a tall, slim grave-faced man with dark hair and a moustache. She could barely recall his face to memory now. But she could remember how it was when he was alive, the feeling of utter safety, being loved and wanted. Hearing his deep voice wafting up the stairs at night, arms lifting her up above his head when he came home.

Maybe her mother had loved John more deeply than Camellia realised? Perhaps she was always searching for a replacement for him?

Not even the jewellery box held any surprises. The pearl necklace, diamond earrings and gold bracelet she'd been given by her husband were all there. Wouldn't she have pawned those again, if it was money troubles?

When Camellia had exhausted the possibilities of the room, she got down on her hands and knees to look under the bed, but even that revealed nothing but one laddered stocking. As she hauled herself back up though, holding onto the bed end, she noticed the bedspread was tucked in accidentally in one place, as if her mother had lifted the mattress to slide something beneath.

Holding the mattress up with one hand, she put her hand in, moving it along slowly. Her fingers met something hard and flat, and out came a large brown envelope.

It contained school reports, her parents' marriage licence and her father's death certificate. There were more photographs of her parents, many of them at their wedding, including one in a brass frame which had sat on the mantelpiece when they were in Mermaid Street. Her own birth certificate was there too, plus ten or twelve studio pictures of her up until she was about seven.

She put them all back carefully. The police would let her have them all later, she didn't have to take them now. But as she slid them back under the mattress, her hands swept further under. Again something smooth, flat and stiff. Hastily she pulled it out, sitting on the bed to examine it.

This wasn't an envelope but a wallet type file, made of stiff green card.

A sudden noise from the street startled her and she moved over to the window. The Colleys next door were packing their car with picnic things and she suddenly realised she had been in the house for quite some time. The police could turn up any minute or Mrs Rowlands would find her missing and worry. She must leave now.

Returning to the file she quickly flicked through it. It seemed to be letters from men, some of them so old they were discoloured. Bonny had tucked this away for safe keeping, along with the other envelope. It might only be old love letters, of no importance to anyone but Bonny, but the very fact it was hidden implied she didn't want just anyone to see them.

'I'll destroy them if that's all it is,' she whispered, feeling Bonny's presence so closely she could have been standing beside her. 'I won't let on to anyone. I love you, Mummy.'

It took only a minute to straighten the bedspread, close all doors and drawers. Another to get together a few of her own things in a bag, with the file tucked away beneath them and she was gone, closing the front door firmly behind her, leaving the key to swing on its string.

'Camellia! Where have you been?' Mrs Rowlands asked plaintively, turning from the bacon she was frying as Camellia came in the back way into the bakery kitchen. 'You can't imagine what I was thinking.'

It was the first time Camellia had ever seen Mrs Rowlands without an apron. She looked like an overstuffed bolster in her candy-striped blue cotton dress. The kitchen looked strange too – no heaps of baking trays waiting to be washed or uncooked pies and pasties stacked on racks waiting for space in the huge ovens. It was cool and very well scrubbed.

'I had to go out for a walk.' Camellia concealed the bag behind her back. 'I didn't want to wake you. I'm sorry if I made you worry.'

'Well, you're here now. Take this up to Mr Rowlands.' She handed Camellia a plate of bacon and eggs. 'I'll bring ours.'

Mr Rowlands was already sitting at the laid breakfast table in the living room, reading the *Sunday People*. He was as thin as his wife was fat, almost bald, except for a few wispy strands stretched over from one ear to the other, but his eyes were kind. He smiled as she put his breakfast in front of him.

Last night she'd been so very glad to be here. The small bright rooms held all the comfort and security her own home lacked. It was soothing to have a bath run, to be tucked into bed and be clucked over with sympathy, but now in the light of day it felt like a prison.

Mrs Rowlands was a gossip, and until yesterday she'd always been quite cool towards her. Wasn't it more likely that the woman offered her a home here, more from the value of sensationalism than real kindness.

'What's that?' As Mrs Rowlands came in with

Camellia's and her own breakfast, her sharp eyes noticed the bag immediately.

'Just a few things from home,' Camellia said, blushing with guilt. 'I was going past there so I thought I'd nip in and collect them.'

'You shouldn't have gone there alone.' Mrs Rowlands clucked round her like a mother hen, pushing her towards the breakfast table. 'The police didn't want you in there yet, until they've had time to look around. I could have taken you there later.'

Camellia felt tears pricking her eyelids. 'I only wanted my nightie and things. I didn't touch anything else.' She held her breath, terrified Mrs Rowlands might open the bag, but Mr Rowlands spoke out.

'Of course you wanted your things, my dear.' He reached out and patted her hand, his small, hangdog face full of sympathy. 'Enid can't help worrying, she's made that way. Now eat up your breakfast before it gets cold.'

At seven that evening a smell of yeast rose up through the house as Mr and Mrs Rowlands began mixing the dough for the next day down in the bakery.

Camellia crept out onto the landing to check one last time. She could hear their voices, muted by two flights of narrow stairs. Now was her chance.

The day had been interminable. Although she'd known the Rowlands for most of her life, she'd found it impossible to communicate with them.

It seemed rude to read a book, even ruder to ask if she could go to her room and be alone. Mr Rowlands had his nose in the newspaper and his wife kept up a stream of gossip. If she'd only talked about Bonny Camellia might have been able to cry, but instead she made a point of never bringing up her name.

During the afternoon Camellia had heard Mrs Rowlands talking about her on the telephone to one of her friends, commenting on how much roast beef and Yorkshire pudding Camellia had eaten. She'd claimed she didn't think the girl was upset at all.

It seemed as if Mrs Rowlands were intentionally embarrassing her. She'd remarked on the holes in her shoes, offered her a huge cotton dress of her own because Camellia's blouse gaped at the bust, and dabbed at her spots with TCP. Maybe she was trying to be motherly, but it felt remarkably similar to the cruel jibes Camellia experienced daily at school.

The clock hands went round so slowly Camellia felt she might break down and scream. Her whole being longed to be outside, walking in the sunshine alone. She was burning to read those letters, yet at the same time she felt guilty at taking them. When at last Mr Rowlands suggested she had an early night when they went down to the bakery, Camellia could have kissed him.

'You'll feel easier after the funeral,' he said in genuine sympathy, as if he'd guessed how it had been for her today. 'You're far too young for something like this, but we're here to help you.'

Camellia got into bed, arranging the covers so she could pull them up sharply if interrupted, and at last opened the file. There were two or three dozen letters in all and a few old photographs of people she didn't know. But if she'd hoped to find some kind of comfort in the letters, she was bitterly disappointed. All she found was betrayal.

It was hours after she'd finished reading them before she could cry. She lay in bed listening to the kneading machine down in the bakery whirring away and the rage inside her swelled up like rising dough until she felt it was choking her.

She heard the machines being turned off down-stairs, the clink of teacups and the whistle of the kettle as the Rowlands made themselves a last pot of tea. The church clock struck ten and she heard the stairs creaking as the Rowlands came up to bed.

Within minutes the house was silent. Outside in the street people were turning out of the George, high heels tip-tapping down the pavement to the occasional burst of laughter. It was only when the street was as quiet as the house that Camellia turned her face into the pillow and sobbed.

She could forgive Bonny for neglecting her, for drinking and sleeping around. She didn't care about the squandered family money. She had prepared herself for more humiliation, cruel jokes, gossip and sniggers behind her back in the weeks to come. But she hadn't reckoned on her mother robbing her of the one good thing she had left to hold onto.

John Norton, that kind, caring gentleman, was just another big fish Bonny had hooked by deceit. Not only had she tricked him into marrying her by saying she was carrying his child, but she'd told three other men the same thing and blackmailed each of them, starting even before John was dead.

'I hate you,' Camellia whispered fiercely into her pillow. 'Don't expect me to mourn for you, you lying whore. I'm glad you're dead.'

She had so many warm, wonderful memories of her father – sitting on his knee as he listened to her read, swimming with him down at Camber Sands, riding the carousel in Hastings with his arms holding her tightly in front of him. It was her father who took her to see new lambs and to find the first primroses in spring.

She had long since given up hope that she might become pretty like her mother, but she'd looked at his childhood photographs, seen that he was plump as a boy and hoped that like him at sixteen or seventeen the fat would vanish, that she'd become slender and elegant. Now she hadn't even that raft to cling to. She was the fat, ugly daughter of one of those other men.

For a couple of years now Camellia had believed her mother's selfishness, flightiness and lack of self-control were just minor character defects she couldn't help. But that belief was wiped out now. Bonny could help it. She was a calculating bitch who had lied and cheated her way through life. Even now she was probably laughing from beyond the grave, hoping each one of those three other men would be questioned, their families pilloried.

'I won't let it happen,' Camellia muttered as she tossed on her pillow. 'Even if one of them pushed you in the river, I don't blame him. You won't hurt Daddy again.'

Sleep wouldn't come. The file was hidden away under the wardrobe, but even in the dark she could still see those letters and guess at the torment her mother put those men through. She got out of bed and went over to the window, deeply breathing in the cool night air.

'You've got to get away from here,' she whispered, as she looked across at the church tower. The moon was hanging just over the spire, casting a silver swathe over the rooftops of the High Street shops. Any other night she might have been enchanted by the scene but all she could see now was ugliness. 'Forget about those other men. From now on you've got to look out for yourself.'

61

Chapter Five

Camellia put her suitcase down on the pavement, once again checking the address of the girls' hostel she had written on a scrap of paper. She was definitely in Hornsey Lane. It said Archway House plainly enough on the wooden plaque attached to the gatepost, yet she could hardly believe that such a welcoming-looking place was her destination.

It was mid-October, two and a half months since her mother died. That morning when Mrs Rowlands waved her off at Rye station it had been very cold, with sullen-looking black clouds threatening rain. But as she got closer to London the sky had brightened. Now in late afternoon the sun had emerged. It made the leaves of a large copper beech by the gate gleam, the windows sparkle. A few sparrows were sitting on the edge of a large ornamental bird bath in the middle of the lawn, watching one of their tougher brothers washing himself.

It had been a long uphill walk from Archway tube station and though Camellia had few clothes in her suitcase it had grown painfully heavy. She was a little dismayed too by the dilapidated houses and seedy shops on the route. The only part of London she'd been to before was the West End and somehow she'd imagined the whole of London being as smart. But, as she'd turned into Hornsey Lane and seen the big, rather splendid houses, her spirits had immediately lifted. Now she'd found the hostel she felt even better.

It must have been built around the middle of the last century: there were two Gothic fancy spires and an arched stone porch. The odd positioning of the front door on the right-hand side showed that it had once been two houses, but the conversion of the second door and porch into a large window was masked by a vigorous ivy scrambling right up to the attics. Turning it into a hostel hadn't changed its character: Camellia almost expected the door to be opened by a parlour maid or a carriage to roll into the semi-circular gravel drive.

She picked up her case and walked towards the stone steps which led to the front door. She was very nervous. It was all very well telling herself back in Rye that she was setting out on a big adventure working in a London store and that all the sadness was in the past, but deep down she knew she had a long way to go before she could wipe her memory clean.

Yet as she reached the steps she smiled. Someone had put a thin red scarf round the neck of a weather-worn stone eagle perched on the stone balustrade. She felt she was going to like it here.

'You must be Camellia Norton.' A thin woman with short iron-grey hair and thick spectacles smiled welcomingly as she opened the door. 'Do come in, my dear. Did you have a good journey? I'm Miss Peet, the warden, though I do hate that as a title. It makes me sound like a gaoler.'

Across the hall Camellia caught a fleeting glimpse of a room with half a dozen tables set for an evening meal. To her right was a wide staircase and to her left what looked like a lounge. Although it was as quiet as a church, it didn't have any of the institutional austerity she'd expected. The walls were painted in gentle pastels and there were carpets on the floors.

'Leave your case here,' Miss Peet said. 'I'll show you your room a little later. All the other girls are at work still, so we'll take advantage of the peace and quiet to have a cup of tea and get acquainted.'

Camellia followed the older woman along a passage to the far end of the house.

'What a lovely room!' Camellia gasped as she was ushered into Miss Peet's sitting room. The decor was autumnal, with chintz-covered armchairs, old gold velvet curtains and a fat tabby cat sitting in front of a real fire.

'This is Sheba.' Miss Peet bent down to tickle the cat's ears. 'If you ever find her upstairs shoo her down, she has a penchant for sharing beds and some of the girls don't appreciate it.'

Camellia suddenly felt very close to tears. She had been so very glad to leave Rye, yet all at once she felt terribly alone. 'I didn't expect the hostel to be this nice,' she said, struggling to control herself.

'We do our best to make it homely,' Miss Peet said, as she switched on an electric kettle sitting on a tea trolley. A tray was already laid with dainty bone china cups and a plate of biscuits. 'Now sit down and make yourself comfortable.'

Gertrude Peet glanced over her shoulder as she waited for the kettle to boil. The girl was hunched awkwardly in a chair, looking pale and frightened.

A teacher from the Secondary Modern in Rye had contacted Miss Peet to book a place for this girl, and through this teacher she had learned some of her family history. She'd imagined someone called Camellia to be very pretty; she certainly hadn't been warned that the girl would be so buxom and dowdy.

'What a glorious name you have,' she said as she

64

poured the hot water into the teapot. 'I've worked here since the hostel opened in 1948, but I've never met a Camellia before.'

'I prefer it shortened to Mel,' the girl said in a small voice.

It sounded as if she was used to having people make fun of her and her name, and Gertrude's heart went out to the girl. She had been plain herself: her nose sharp, her hair mousy and her body as thin and flat as a board. During the war she'd been in the WAAF and though she saw each and every one of her colleagues have love affairs, get married and have children, the closest she ever got to a man was at a dance in the NAAFI. She soon resigned herself to being a spinster. Now at fifty-eight with seventeen years' experience of looking after young women away from home for the first time, she could immediately identify with someone who felt she would never be accepted.

Gertrude Peet knew that many of the girls here at Archway House considered her an impediment to their fun, a dragon who watched their every move and swooped down at the slightest hint of rule breaking. In fact she understood young girls very well and cared deeply about the well-being of each and every one of her twenty-four charges. More often than not, the girls who came here were running away from their families. In her time she'd encountered everything from victims of incest, wanton cruelty and neglect, to those who had almost been suffocated by parental love. Oddly enough it was the last kind who were the most difficult: they were the ones who flouted all the rules. By all accounts Camellia Norton was quiet, hardworking and sensible, despite her mother's flighty reputation and her somewhat sordid end. But Miss Peet never took others' opinions on trust.

She believed in finding out for herself, as directly as possible.

'Well then, Mel.' The older woman put the tray of tea down on a coffee table and took a chair opposite the girl. 'Now I know about your mother's death and I feel very deeply for you, but I can assure you I am the only person here who knows. If you ever feel you need to talk about that or any other personal matter, that's what I'm here for and I can assure you it will always be in the strictest confidence.'

'Thank you,' Camellia whispered. She had been wondering all the way from Rye if the story had gone ahead.

'I know it is all very recent and grief can play some very odd tricks,' Miss Peet continued as she poured the tea. 'We all assume it's over once the tears have dried. But that's often the time we feel most confused. We get mixed-up feelings – love, resentment, guilt, sometimes anger. That's when we need to share it with someone.'

Camellia sat looking down at her lap. Miss Peet reminded her of the games mistress at school: skinny, a bit masculine, her grey hair cut unflatteringly short as if she had no time for any attempt at femininity. Even her Fair Isle cardigan and tweed skirt were old and worn. But her voice was soft, not the kind of bark one would expect from such an appearance. Camellia liked her.

'Do you feel any of those things about your mother?' Miss Peet asked gently.

'Yes,' Camellia whispered. It was the first time anyone had asked such a question. Perhaps most people thought they were being tactful, but to Camellia their silence had felt far more like indifference.

'Why don't you tell me about her?'

Camellia shrugged her shoulders, unable to meet the older woman's eyes. She wanted to say that a tight ball of hate was festering inside her, but she didn't dare. 'She was a dancer.'

'Was she pretty?'

Camellia opened her handbag and pulled out a photograph. It had been taken at a fancy-dress party a couple of years ago. She had no real desire to have it close to her or to show it to anyone. But this picture at least showed Bonny the way she really was, a glamorous show-off, and she hoped the plain older woman would understand.

'She hardly looks old enough to be your mother.' Miss Peet smiled in commiseration. It was difficult to imagine how such a beautiful woman could produce such a plain, big girl. 'A hard act to follow eh?'

'I don't want to be like her.' The words came out before Camellia could stop herself. 'She was cruel and selfish.'

She hadn't been able to admit this to Mrs Rowlands or even to Bert Simmonds, but now she found herself pouring everything out to this elderly and intuitive stranger.

Camellia had no choice but to leave Rye for good. Once the funeral was over, people treated her like a stray dog. They pitied her, offered her titbits, but no one really wanted her, or understood her feelings. Even weeks after Bonny was laid to rest they were all still gossiping about the expensive, anonymous bouquets of flowers which had arrived for the funeral. Not one of these mysterious admirers had the courage or the compassion to send a few comforting words to Camellia, or even a few pounds in an envelope to help her rebuild her life. The only letters which arrived were more unpaid bills.

Mr and Mrs Rowlands were kind, but in the

weeks Camellia was with them the debt of gratitude was mounting up so high she felt smothered
by it. She had been working like a slave in the
bakery to try to repay them. Getting a job in Peter
Robinson's in Oxford Street and living in a hostel
wasn't that much better than what she had in Rye,
but at least she could start with a clean slate.

Miss Peet did not seem at all surprised by
Camellia's outburst. 'Shall I tell you something?'
she said as she reached out across the narrow coffee
table and took Camellia's hand. 'I adored my
mother. She too was widowed when I was young.
We were so close I didn't want or need any friends.
But it wasn't until she grew old and frail that I
realised just how unhealthy that is too. I could have
travelled, made something of my life, but she held
me too tightly. I'm not sure which is worse, the
mother who loves too much or the one that doesn't
love enough.'

Camellia was a little thrown by this admission,
yet it reminded her of the things her mother had
said when Granny died. Camellia was only ten
then and she'd gone to London with her mother for
the funeral. Afterwards they'd gone to Granny's
house in Dagenham to sort things out. Bonny broke
down and cried when she saw the pictures of
herself as a child, almost filling the tiny living
room. Upstairs her old bedroom was just as it had
been when she was little – her dolls on shelves, her
nightdresses, socks and knickers still tucked away
in the drawers, almost as if Granny thought her
small child was just away visiting friends.

On the way home Bonny had tried to explain her
feelings. She said as a child she'd felt smothered by
love and blind adoration, that it was too big a
burden knowing her mother's sole reason for living
was for her. She went on to explain how the war
and evacuation had liberated her, that while other

eleven-year-olds pined for their mothers, she had hoped she would never have to return home again.

'So what did you feel when your mother died?' Camellia asked. Her own feelings fluctuated between anger, disgust and loathing, but every now and then a wave of pure grief would hit her and that was worse than hating.

'Mostly relief.' Miss Peet sighed deeply, as if this admission was painful. 'I knew I'd never have to get up in the night to give her medicine again. I could travel and live my life without having her to worry about.'

Camellia just stared at the older woman. She wasn't used to adults being so open about their feelings.

'I'm only telling you this to illustrate my point,' Miss Peet said gently. 'Both of us have had our lives spoilt by our mothers, though in entirely different ways. You're luckier than me in some respects because you have your whole life ahead of you. I was in my mid-forties before I was free. Remember the good things about your mother, Mel. Don't let bitterness get the upper hand. Now let's finish this tea and I'll show you your room. The other girls will be home soon.'

If Miss Peet hadn't brought the matter to an end when she did Camellia just might have told her about the file of letters she'd found. But as it was she felt better inside. Maybe she could show them to her some other time, and ask her advice.

Camellia sooned learned she had been wrong in thinking that her life was about to change dramatically for the better. In Rye her biggest problem had been gossip. In London it was a wall of complete indifference. There were many times in her first four months of living in the hostel and working at Peter Robinson's when Camellia would almost have welcomed being at the centre of another scandal, just so that someone would notice her. She felt as if she had become invisible.

She liked her job on the handbag counter at Peter Robinson's. She found she had a flair for selling, and was complimented by the floor supervisor for her skill at display, her attentive attitude to customers and her reliability. The store had been so busy in the run-up to Christmas, and afterwards with the January sale, that Camellia hardly had time to consider that all she knew of the other salesgirls was through observation and overheard gossip. But back home at Archway House she was totally aware of her isolation from the other girls. She had not made one friend.

An ache grew inside her as she saw the other girls in tight little cliques, closing ranks against her. Her weight, clothes, even her Sussex accent set her apart. It was just the way it had been at school, almost as if she had 'Reject' stamped across her forehead. So she pretended she liked to be alone, avoided going in the lounge, went to bed early with a book and on Sundays took herself off for long walks, mentally listing all the things she had to be grateful for. She had her own cubicle in a dormitory which she shared with three other girls. It was on the first floor overlooking the back garden, bright, clean and warm, with a very comfortable bed and her own pictures and posters on the walls to make it homely. The meals were always good with lots of fresh vegetables and fruit. She could have a bath daily if she wanted to, there were washing machines and irons in the basement and the only cleaning she was required to do was to dust her cubicle.

But at night she lay awake listening to the other three girls chatting and giggling. They borrowed each other's clothes and make-up, did each other's hair, but ignored Camellia.

Her sixteenth birthday went by without any cards. Christmas, a few days later, passed with only Miss Peet and a new girl called Janice, who kept bursting into tears. Everyone else had gone home to their families. Camellia had a card and a woolly hat from Mrs Rowlands, a gift voucher from Bert Simmonds and bath salts from Miss Peet. They ate roast chicken, pulled crackers and sat watching the television, but although Miss Peet tried to be jolly, even she seemed to be dwelling on happier times.

One morning in February, four months after she'd arrived in London, Camellia was travelling to work as normal on the tube when she felt slightly giddy. She guessed it might be that she was hungry: she had skipped the evening meal the night before and had rushed out that morning without any breakfast. But around ten, just before the mid-morning break when she intended to get a sandwich from the canteen, she suddenly felt strange again. There was a buzzing sound in her head, and her eyes wouldn't seem to focus properly. Before she could get to a chair to sit down, everything went black.

She came to, finding herself lying on the floor, surrounded by a crowd of customers and shop assistants. Suzanne, the small blonde girl from hosiery, was kneeling beside her smoothing back her hair.

Suzanne was the most popular girl in the entire store. She was the one everyone went out of their way to share their breaks with. Until now she hadn't so much as smiled at Camellia, much less showed any interest in her.

'I'll take care of her, Miss Puckridge,' the blonde insisted, helping the supervisor to get Camellia on her feet. 'I'll take her to the rest room and make her a cup of tea.'

As Camellia was led away supported by Suzanne, she was still too dazed from fainting to feel embarrassment or indeed to offer any explanation. It was only once the other girl had sat her down in an armchair, put the kettle on and then crouched down in front of her, her small elfin face full of concern, that Camellia realised she'd accidentally broken through the wall of indifference.

'You aren't pregnant, are you?' Suzanne asked.

Camellia shook her head. It was such a preposterous suggestion, but even in her shaky disorientated state she knew she must somehow turn her predicament to her advantage.

Everything about Suzanne made Camellia feel inadequate. She was a mod, and she looked good in her mid-calf tight skirts and Granny shoes: small and slim, with silky blonde hair which hung over one eye like a silk curtain. All day other girls risked Miss Puckridge's displeasure by nipping off from their counters to chat to her. She was only a year or so older than Camellia, but she had all the confidence and poise of a twenty-year-old.

'I'm certainly not pregnant.' Camellia managed a watery smile. 'Not unless you believe in immaculate conceptions.'

Suzanne laughed, her pale blue eyes crinkling up in merriment. 'Well, that's a relief,' she said, turning back to the kettle to make the tea. 'That leaves the other theory, that you've been starving yourself. Any truth in that?'

Camellia looked at Suzanne through her eyelashes as she poured the boiling water into the teapot. Not one bulge of flesh spoiled the line of her tight skirt. She even dared to put a belt round her jumper. Could she possibly understand what it felt like to be fat? 'Not trying to starve, but I have been dieting,' she said lightly.

'What on earth for?' Suzanne turned round sharply, her false eyelashes fluttering in surprise.

'Come on!' Camellia smiled. 'You don't have to be polite. I know I'm huge, but I've been trying to do something about it.'

Suzanne looked puzzled. She took a step or two back, one finger on her little pointed chin, and studied Camellia. 'I thought you were a bit podgy when you first came here,' she said thoughtfully. 'But honestly you aren't now. You can't possibly weigh more than nine stone.'

Camellia felt a moment of elation. Her clothes had got a bit baggy, but until now she just thought they'd stretched. She wasn't brave enough to weigh herself in a chemist's. 'A doctor weighed me for my medical, back in September,' she insisted. 'I was eleven and a half stone then and he gave me a diet sheet.'

Suzanne looked triumphant. 'Well the diet obviously worked. Have you weighed yourself recently?'

'I didn't stick to it.' Camellia dropped her eyes. 'I couldn't. I was working in a bakery you see. I was supposed to go back to him before I left Sussex, but I didn't. I guess I'd had enough of questions after my mum died.'

Suzanne looked startled. She covered her mouth with her hand, clearly embarrassed. 'I'm so sorry,' she said hastily. 'I didn't know. Was this recently? Is that why you came to London?'

Camellia had told herself after her initial talk to Miss Peet that she was going to put her mother's death behind her and never speak of it again. Seeing Suzanne's sympathetic reaction, though, she realised that this might have been a mistake. 'It's okay. It was back in August,' she said, hoping she could keep the girl's interest. 'She drowned you see. I'll tell you about it if you like. But maybe I ought to get a sandwich first. I don't want to keel over again.'

Suzanne put a mug of sweet tea in Camellia's hand, then went to get a sandwich from the canteen. Judging by the speed at which she came back, she had run all the way to the fourth floor.

The rest room was a small messy place with an adjoining toilet, used only for tea and cigarette breaks. The fug of cigarette smoke, the dilapidated chairs, piles of well-worn magazines and unwashed cups was at odds with the spotless and ordered department store just beyond its door. From time to time Miss Puckridge insisted the window was left open to air it, but the noise of the traffic from Oxford Street below meant her orders were disobeyed.

Camellia explained everything between mouthfuls of cheese sandwich and gulps of tea.

Suzanne's eyes filled with tears, and she even left her cigarette burning away in the ashtray.

'Oh, Mel,' she sighed at last. 'That's so awful. I can't imagine how I'd manage if anything happened to my mum.'

Camellia reached out a tentative hand and touched the girl's arm. 'I feel much better now. Thank you.'

They had a second cup of tea, even though Suzanne should've gone back to work by now, and Camellia admitted how lonely she'd felt, both at work and at the hostel.

'We all thought you were stuck up when you started here. I wish I'd known what had happened – I wouldn't have been so mean to you.' Suzanne's crisp London voice was subdued now, frown lines furrowing her forehead.

'You weren't mean.' Camellia smiled – all Suzanne had done was to ignore her. 'Besides the last thing I wanted was pity. I'd had a basin full of that. And I know fat plain girls don't set the world alight.'

There was a moment's silence, then to her surprise Suzanne started to giggle.

'You silly cow!' She caught hold of Camellia's hand and pulled her up onto her feet and over to a mirror on the wall. 'I've already told you, you aren't fat! You certainly aren't plain either. Take a real look at yourself!'

They stood side by side. Camellia saw what she expected: a big girl almost dwarfing the smaller blonde, hair scraped back into a ponytail, sallow skin, dark slanty eyes. But Suzanne caught hold of her skirt and cardigan behind her back, pulling the fabric tight to show the lines of her body.

'See what I mean? You aren't much wider than me. It's just those dowdy clothes of yours. And your face is great! You've got really good bone structure and skin, you just haven't learned how to make the best of yourself. Look at your hair dragged back like that! It should be cut nicely and left loose. If it's quiet this afternoon I'll get Carol on make-up to give you a few tips.'

They had to go back to work then, but Camellia's head was reeling with what Suzanne had said. She didn't believe for one minute that she'd got better looking, even though her spots had cleared up. Yet shielded by the counter, she ran her hands down over her hips. To her utter astonishment she found she could no longer grasp much flesh.

There was no mirror in the bathrooms at Archway House; the only full-length one in the dormitory was by Wendy's cubicle and she certainly wouldn't dream of studying herself in that in case someone saw her. Could just giving up sweets, cakes and pies really have worked a miracle without her noticing?

Camellia waited in Boots, the chemists, until a group of girls had moved right away from the scales, then slunk towards them, keeping her head down. It had been a very long morning, waiting for her dinner break so she could come here.

She stood on the scales, opening her coat before she put the penny in the slot to stop anyone else seeing the result. As the penny dropped she put her hand over the eleven as a precaution, but to her absolute amazement the indicator only went to nine stone eight pounds.

For a moment she could only stare in shock. Surely it was wrong. Could she really have lost over two stone?

'Are the scales accurate?' she asked an assistant at the counter.

'Of course they are,' the woman pursed up her mouth as if resenting such a question. 'They get tested each Monday without fail.'

If Camellia hadn't gone over to Suzanne and whispered the result of her weighing session as soon as she got back to the store, maybe the pretty blonde would've forgotten her earlier promise about make-up. But she looked around the shop, saw how few customers there were and escorted Camellia over to Carol on the beauty corner.

Carol, with her flame-red Cilla Black hair and talons to match, seemed even more formidable than Suzanne. Everything about her was perfection, from her creamy skin to her knowledge about cosmetics. She and Suzanne were the golden girls – pretty, popular and sought after. But all it took was one word from Suzanne and Carol whisked Camellia into a chair, dragged the rubber band out of her hair and brushed it through.

'You, my girl, have got all the classic features of a real beauty, not like me and Suzanne with our fair skins and dyed hair,' she said with enthusiasm. 'Your hair is naturally shiny and bouncy. It just needs a decent cut. I've been dying to have a go at you for ages,' she admitted.

Carol began by giving her a facial, tidying up her eyebrows, before starting on the make-up. 'You don't need a great deal,' she said as she smoothed on some foundation. 'You've just got to define the best bits, your cheek bones, eyes and those lovely luscious lips. Most women would kill for those!'

Even Miss Puckridge, the strawberry blonde, haughty supervisor, came forward with advice. She didn't seem to mind one bit that Camellia wasn't at her counter. 'Listen to what Carol tells you,' she smiled down at Camellia in the chair. 'Anyone who's ever seen her or myself without make-up would testify to its amazing powers.'

It was a shock to Camellia to discover her face was not round as she'd always thought but oval. There were interesting hollows beneath her cheek bones and, now enhanced with mascara and eye-liner, her almond-shaped dark eyes stood out in a way she'd never noticed before. When the girls went on to insist she tried a mod knitted two-piece with a long tight skirt, she was even more astounded. Her hips were only marginally wider than Suzanne's, her stomach was almost flat, and she had a waist.

'I don't wanna be horrible,' Suzanne said, picking up Camellia's navy-blue shapeless skirt and jumper with a disparaging look, 'but the best place for these is the dustbin.'

Camellia laughed. She would gladly throw them

away now. To think when Mrs Rowlands had helped pick them out in Rye she'd thought they were wonderful!

For the rest of that afternoon, Camellia stood behind her counter mentally adding up how much she had saved and what she could buy with it. Was she brave enough to wear tight sweaters or a clingy skirt? What if someone laughed at her?

But before she went back to the hostel, she had to thank Suzanne. She waited until Miss Puckridge had disappeared up to the first floor, then slipped over to the hosiery stand.

Suzanne was tidying up the stockings. Seen from the back, her small bottom in her tight skirt looked like two grapefruits.

'Suzanne,' she said hesitantly.

'Yes, glamour puss.' The small blonde spun round grinning.

'I just wanted to thank you,' Camellia said, blushing scarlet. She hoped she didn't sound pathetic. 'You've helped me so much today, talking and everything.' She stopped short, unable to get out what was in her heart.

'That's what mates are for,' Suzanne grinned. 'Me and Carol will help you sort out some new clothes. Just don't you go back slimming or skipping meals!'

For most of the tube ride home Camellia was lost in a wonderful daydream of how becoming slim and pretty would change her life. She could sunbathe in the parks this summer, and choose pink or red clothes instead of navy blue. She could go to dances and parties. She might even find a boyfriend.

But when the tube halted between Kentish Town and Tufnell Park, her thoughts suddenly moved on to that file of letters. Now for the first time she found herself thinking of those three men with interest rather than rage.

Which of them was her father? Was it Magnus in Bath, Jack in Arundel or Miles in Kensington? She had read their letters so many times now, that she'd formed images of all of them. She felt Jack was the childhood sweetheart who had rescued Bonny from drowning. He was clearly a rough, uneducated man, his address a garage in the same village in Sussex where she had been evacuated to during the war.

Magnus in contrast seemed older and very well educated, a married man who had been tormented by his illicit affair with Bonny.

The third man, Miles, had only written once, a coldly dismissive letter as if Bonny was beneath his contempt. Camellia felt she ought to know who this man was. She wondered if he and his wife were one of the couples who used to come to dinner when her father was still alive.

Then amongst these letters was just one from a woman. She signed herself 'H' and it sounded as if she were a dancer too. It was an odd letter, written in a very cryptic manner, but yet there was such warmth, such affection for both her friend and Camellia she had to be important.

Camellia was just about to get off the tube at Archway when in a flash of clarity she saw a new dimension to those letters. Back in Rye they had seemed final proof that her mother was just a cold-hearted, calculating tramp. She had been afraid to hand them over to Bert Simmonds, not just because of further scandal, or indeed because one of these men might have been the cause of her mother's death, but because *she* was scared of facing any more unpalatable truth.

But now with her confidence boosted a little by discovering she could make friends, that she wasn't quite as fat and as plain as she'd always thought, she wasn't so much scared, as curious.

She would need to work on herself and become *someone* before she had enough nerve to approach each of these three men. But she must do it one day. She wouldn't be a complete person until she knew the whole truth.

Camellia walked into Archway House soon after six thirty. She was so happy she felt she might burst. Fat, frumpy Camellia was about to be buried and a slim, potentially attractive new one was about to emerge.

Miss Peet was tidying up the notice board in the hall as Camellia came through the door. Even at a glance she could see something good had happened today. The girl looked quite different. 'You look happy,' she said. 'And it's not even pay day!'

'I feel wonderful,' Camellia beamed. 'One of the girls at work did my make-up and I weighed myself.' She stopped short, suddenly feeling foolish.

Miss Peet smiled knowingly. She had noticed Camellia was losing weight for some weeks now. She made sure all her girls had a carefully balanced evening meal without too much stodge and many of them grew slimmer and more confident because of it. She wished she could work such miracles where making friends was concerned, but perhaps now Camellia could manage that herself.

'A word of advice from the old dragon,' she said with a smile. 'No more skulking in your room, after tea, get down into the lounge with the other girls. You can do it if you put your mind to it.'

Camellia put her head tentatively round the door of the lounge. There were five girls there in all. Madeline, who was one of the girls in her dormitory, was sharing the big settee with two new girls who had arrived a week ago. Rose, a big redhead, and Karen, a small dark girl from up North somewhere, sat on the floor in front of them.

'Hullo.' Rose looked round and smiled. 'Coming in to join us? There's nothing on the telly, so we're all moaning about our lack of boyfriends.'

Miss Peet had endeavoured to make the lounge homely, warm and comfortable. The armchairs and settees didn't match, and some of them were old and shabby, but a big fire was lit every evening, the shelves were full of books, and there was a piano and a big television. Boyfriends were allowed in this room until ten, but they were a rare sight; for most young men it was hard enough to face Miss Peet at the door, let alone an evening with half a dozen giggling girls.

'Come on,' Karen smiled, with unexpected warmth. 'We don't bite.' Rose introduced the new girls and then paused for a moment. 'I can't tell you anything about Camellia,' she said to them with a tinkle of laughter. 'Until now she's been a hermit. Madeline believes she's about to take Holy Orders.'

All these months Camellia had been so immersed in herself it had never occurred to her that most of the girls in the hostel were as alone as she was. She found it hard to jump in and talk in the easy way Rose and Madeline did, but she listened to them attentively, biding her time before she told them about herself.

Rose had left home to escape her new step-mother. Brenda and Christine, the new girls, said they'd left Scotland because there were no good jobs there. Karen had come straight from a children's home, and Madeline had left her home in Birmingham after a row with her parents about her boyfriend. Yet the conversation wasn't centred on hard-luck stories, even though not one of them appeared to have the cosy comfortable backgrounds Camellia had assumed. They also spoke about clothes, pop stars and boys – and before long they wanted to know about Camellia.

The events earlier in the day had removed Camellia's intentions of hiding her past. Instinctively she knew if she wanted to be accepted by these girls she had to be open. She told the story simply, without any attempt to tug on their heartstrings.

As she looked at the girls' faces she saw not only interest, but complete acceptance. She knew then that her life was going to change. She was one of them at last.

The conversation moved on to discussing Miss Peet's insistence at an eleven o'clock curfew for the girls who were under eighteen. Rose said they would need to think up some plausible excuse if they wanted to accept the invitation from some boys further down the road to their party next weekend.

'They're all art students from Hornsey,' Madeline explained with a giggle that implied she knew the boys quite well. 'They are beats and they all smoke reefers.'

A ripple of unease passed across all the girls' faces. Camellia saw an opportunity to score a few points. 'Sounds like fun,' she said with alacrity, even though her knowledge of beats and reefers was limited to one magazine article. 'I'll ask Miss Peet if you like. She thinks I'm a goody-goody and if I say we're all going together she can't very well refuse.'

'What on earth will we wear?' Brenda, the Scottish girl, looked down at her tidy pleated skirt.

'Jeans,' Madeline said firmly. 'And sloppy sweaters. The place is a pigsty.'

A week later, the day after Miss Peet had finally agreed to lift the curfew so all the girls could go to the party, Camellia decided she must buy a pair of jeans.

On her day off earlier in the week she had thrown caution to the wind and had her hair cut at a salon in Oxford Street. She had gone armed with a picture from a magazine with a model with a silky bob, but when the hairdresser combed her hair down right over her eyes and began snipping off a fringe, she was terrified she'd made a mistake. The feeling of panic grew as the girl chopped off at least three inches all round, but once it was blow-dried she felt like crying with happiness.

A heavy fringe rested on her eyebrows, at once hiding her big forehead and accentuating her dark eyes. Her hair was now shoulder-length, thick, shiny and heavy, and even when she tossed her head it bounced straight back into shape.

The successful haircut stimulated her into breaking into her savings. She had already bought a tight skirt, a pair of Granny shoes and a skinny-rib sweater to wear to work, along with new smaller underwear. Now it was time for the jeans.

'Those are much too big.' Suzanne looked into the changing room, while Camellia was trying some on in her lunch hour, and held out a smaller pair. 'You've got to have them skintight.'

Camellia thought the size fourteen pair were just about right, but she didn't dare say so. Obediently she took them off and accepted the size twelve from her friend's hands.

She got them on over her bottom but she couldn't pull up the zip.

'They're miles too small,' she gasped as she struggled with it.

Suzanne was standing there grinning at her. 'No they aren't. Lie down on your back, you'll get them done up then.'

Camellia giggled at this ridiculous suggestion,

but she complied. She hoped no one would come in the changing rooms and see her lying there wrestling with a zip. 'I can't do this every time I go to the loo!' she squealed.

'They'll stretch, silly.' Suzanne was losing patience. 'You've got them done up now. Stand up!'

Camellia got up cautiously. She felt as if she were in a steel corset – she could hardly walk, let alone run or sit down.

'They look fabulous,' Suzanne insisted. 'Come out here and look at yourself.'

Camellia allowed herself to be led out to the mirror, blushing as a couple of customers stared at her.

But when she saw her reflection she gasped in astonishment. 'I look so skinny!' she exclaimed.

Jeans were a symbolic badge: they proclaimed 'I'm part of it all'. Camellia couldn't count the times she'd wished she could wear them. But now, seeing her bottom looking even sexier than Suzanne's, her stomach flat with no flab hanging over the waist, it felt like a miracle.

'How many times do I have to remind you of that?' Suzanne grinned good-naturedly. 'The only thing fat about you is your head. Now what are you going to wear with them?'

'Madeline said a sloppy jumper.' Camellia put her head on one side enquiringly. 'What do you think?'

'Only beatniks wear sloppy jumpers,' Suzanne snorted with disgust. 'You want something which shows your nice boobs. There's some really nice stripy Banlon tops over there. You'd look great in a red and black one.'

'They're too expensive,' Camellia frowned. 'I can only afford about three quid.'

Suzanne looked out the cubicle to check no one

was listening. 'Nick one,' she whispered. 'Stick it in your pants when you go home.'

Camellia stared open-mouthed. She couldn't believe she'd heard that. 'I can't do that!'

'Most of the girls do it,' Suzanne smirked, 'including me, but don't you go splitting on us mind.'

Camellia bought the jeans and got her staff discount and they were sent down to the staff entrance for her to pick up as she went home. But Suzanne's suggestion kept niggling at her once she was back at work behind her counter. The top didn't matter that much to her; heaven knows she had enough sloppy jumpers which would do. Yet the desire to be in step with Suzanne clouded the moral issue. It would be so easy: the top would fold up to no bigger than a scarf. Suzanne claimed she had once even worn a jacket under her coat. The security man on the staff entrance always checked their bags, but he'd never been known to frisk anyone. If she chickened out wouldn't Suzanne think she was feeble?

As the afternoon wore on Camellia kept nipping over to the fashion department to look at the top. The one she fancied cost £6.19.11p red and black with long sleeves and a scoop neck. The more she looked at it, the more she wanted it.

A rush of late afternoon shoppers made her forget about it. She sold a very expensive Italian bag and a purse to one difficult customer, then sold five cheaper bags one after the other. She wished Peter Robinson's gave their assistants commission: it was hardly surprising most of the girls didn't take much trouble with the customers.

At around five, Suzanne slipped over to her again.

'Someone's just left one in the changing room,' she whispered. 'Go on in there and get it.'

Camellia had no excuse now, not even a customer to prevent her. To refuse might push her back amongst the other wallflowers who spent their lunchtimes alone. She took her time walking to the changing rooms, hoping someone would have hung it back on the rails.

But it was still there, a small crumple of red and black on a stool. When she picked it up she found it was the right size.

Taking a deep breath she folded it up small, pulled up her skirt, tucked it into her suspender belt and looked in the mirror. There was no telltale bulge, but for safety's sake once she was back behind her counter she slipped on her old cardigan and did it up.

Suzanne appeared again, raising her eyebrow questioningly.

Camellia nodded and patted her stomach.

'I've got one of those,' Suzanne whispered, pointing out a white botany wool sweater displayed on a dummy. 'We'll go out together.'

The bell rang to clear the customers from the store, the security men came forward to lock the doors and the assistants put the white linen dustsheets over their counters. Then at last the second bell rang which meant they could take their till drawers up to accounts and leave.

By the time she reached the cloakroom Camellia was sweating and shaking. Suzanne was chatting to another girl as she put on a navy beret. She didn't seem the least bit nervous.

'Are you staying here all night?' Carol from the beauty counter touched Camellia's elbow. 'Come on, let's go and get a cup of coffee in the Wimpy before we go home. I'm dying for a sit down and a fag.'

Miss Puckridge was standing next to Wilf, the security officer, by the staff entrance. As always she

86

had that superior look. One by one the girls trooped by Wilf, holding out their opened handbags. Suzanne was in front of Camellia, Carol behind her.

'Goodnight, sweetie,' Suzanne clucked Wilf under the chin, when it was her turn. 'No kiss tonight?'

'Get on home, you hussy,' he growled, his dark eyes twinkling.

Camellia was next. She felt sick now, sure he would see 'Thief' written on her face. Wilf wasn't forbidding – he was sixty if he was a day and very jolly – but that would make it worse somehow if he suspected her. But he casually glanced in her bag, then moved onto Carol's behind her.

'Miss Norton!'

Camellia felt the blood drain from her face at the shrill call from Miss Puckridge.

'I think you've forgotten something, Miss Norton,' she added and Camellia's legs turned to rubber.

Miss Puckridge was nobody's fool, even though they all made jokes about her. She heard and saw everything that went on in the store and had been known to sack girls instantly for just being late. The thought crossed Camellia's mind that she'd been set up by Suzanne to discover if she was honest.

'Forgotten something?' Camellia repeated weakly. Her heart was thumping and every sweat gland in her body seemed to open to ooze out moisture.

'Your jeans.' The older woman smiled and held out a Peter Robinson's bag. 'Some of you girls would forget your head if it wasn't screwed on tight.'

All Camellia could manage was a faint smirk as she took the bag and made a dash for the door.

'So did you get anything today?' Suzanne asked

Carol once they were seated in the Wimpy Bar. To Camellia's surprise Carol fumbled under the table and pulled out a soft leather handbag.

Camellia wasn't only shocked that the glamorous Carol was capable of stealing too, but that she'd had the cheek to nick something from her counter, presumably right under her nose. 'But that's new stock,' she said. 'I only priced them today.'

'And it's not an easy thing to stick in your knickers,' Carol giggled. 'It prickled like hell. I would've told you earlier, but Suzanne hadn't told me then that you'd joined our merry band.'

Now it was Suzanne's turn to fumble under her coat. She pulled out her sweater and folded it neatly before slipping it into her handbag.

Camellia shamefacedly pulled out her top. 'I nearly wet myself when Miss Puckridge called me,' she admitted, smoothing over the top and tucking it into the bag with her jeans. 'I've never nicked anything before.'

'I reckon it's our due.' Carol lit up a cigarette and sat back in her seat. 'They pay us shit-all, expect us to be smartly dressed yet the discount we get on clothes is hardly worth having. I feel I'm just taking a rise.'

Camellia privately thought that thirty per cent off the jeans was pretty good, but she wasn't going to argue with her new friends.

'You'll soon have a whole wardrobe full of clothes,' Suzanne giggled. 'But don't ever be tempted to dip in the till, Mel. They've got millions of ways of catching us at that.'

The party in Hornsey Lane was something of a disappointment to all the girls from the hostel, aside from Madeline who fancied one of the boys in the flat. There was only beer or cider to drink, no food and the lights consisted of a few red bulbs.

The flat was disgustingly dirty as Madeline had warned them and the boys had only a couple of Rolling Stones LPs, no good dance music. Camellia thought the boys were all very arrogant considering they were grubby looking with straggly unwashed hair. The main entertainment was a beatnik playing guitar and singing protest songs. There was no sign of the promised reefers either; all the boys did was cadge the girls' cigarettes.

But even though this party didn't transform anyone's life, the shared scheming to persuade Miss Peet to allow them out until one in the morning, the help they gave each other with hair and make-up, and the giggling about the evening afterwards cemented new friendships.

A few weeks ago, weekdays had crept by for Camellia, while days off and Sundays had seemed even longer. Now, with friends at work and at home, they sped by. The party was just a taste of life outside the hostel, a glimpse of wild people who stayed up all night listening to music, went on protest marches and refused to conform. Suzanne said her mod friends took something called Purple Hearts so they could stay out all night dancing. When it was summer they'd all be going down to Brighton on their scooters.

As winter turned to spring, the fashions in magazines began to change, mainly due to the designer Mary Quant. Her clothes were made exclusively for the young, with vivid geometric designs and skirts way above the knee. Young girls responded eagerly, abandoning old calf-length mod skirts overnight, substituting boots for the old Granny shoes to counter-balance all that exposed leg. Someone in the media hit on the description 'miniskirt' and all at once a whole new look was born.

There was no stopping Camellia. She studied

fashion magazines, watched what other girls wore, and asked advice from anyone she thought knew better than her. And the items she stole almost daily from the shop were designed to set herself up as a fashion plate.

Her weight continued to drop off and by Easter she was under nine stone. She no longer slunk by shop windows afraid of catching a glimpse of her reflection, but looked at herself and smiled. She was the embodiment of a dolly bird with her swinging hair, eyes accentuated with black liner, pale pouty lips and long slender legs. Who would have thought that plain fat girl who'd once been nicknamed Camel would be the first at Archway House daring enough to buy a miniskirt?

Now and then Camellia found herself wishing Bonny could see how she'd changed. She would have liked her approval. Sometimes too she thought of going down to Rye. It would be sweet revenge to see the girls who'd teased her in the past reel back in amazement and envy. She didn't want to see Mrs Rowlands, but it would be so good to see Bert Simmonds again. He had been a true friend.

But 1966 was too exciting a year to waste precious time visiting a place that had nothing but sad memories. Freddie Laker introduced cut price air fares to New York. The space race between the United States and Russia was neck and neck. In April the Russians orbited the moon, and in June the Americans retaliated by landing the first unmanned spacecraft right on it. Labour won a landslide victory in March. The Moors murderers Myra Hindley and Ian Brady were jailed for life in May. In the summer England won the World Cup at Wembley, beating Germany 4–2 in a thrilling final. Bobby Moore, the Charlton brothers, Geoff Hurst and Nobby Stiles were public heroes and thousands of fans invaded the pitch. But the excitement of the year was overshadowed in October by the tragic Aberfan disaster when two million tons of rock, mud and earth ploughed into a small Welsh junior school, killing 147 small children.

Camellia wept as she read the shocking news of townsfolk, miners and firemen attempting to dig out the children with their bare hands until help arrived. All year she had been bursting with happiness, finding her feet with boys, going dancing and to parties. She'd even begun to make long-term plans to find a flat to share with Madeline and Rose in the new year. Suddenly she was reminded that joy and sadness were the two sides of the same coin.

Celebrations began with Camellia's seventeenth birthday on 21 December and continued right through Christmas until New Year, even though she had to fit in working flat out by day. Miss Peet laid on a birthday cake and Camellia had cards and small presents from almost all the other girls. The eleven o'clock curfew was raised till one so they could all go to a dance at the Empire in Leicester Square that night. Camellia wore a red crepe minidress with a white feather boa slung round her neck. One of her friends must have told the MC that it was her birthday, for the next thing she knew she was being pushed up onto the stage to be kissed by the entire band as they played Roy Orbison's song 'Pretty Woman', dedicating it to her.

Suzanne's parents, Mr and Mrs Connor, invited Camellia to spend Christmas with them in Hammersmith. Camellia had never met such a huge jolly family before. Suzanne was the youngest of four, and her two older brothers and sisters all had two or three children apiece. The house was in a three-storey terrace just off King Street and although Suzanne had told Camellia that her parents had been very poor while she was growing up, Mr Connor's building firm was now doing very well. The house reflected this sudden turn in the Connor family fortunes. They had an opulent orange three-piece suite, big enough for an airport, a twenty-four inch television and a tank full of tropical fish in their lounge, not to mention a seven-foot Christmas tree with flashing lights. Camellia loved all the flashy touches: a black and gilt bar in one corner, a mini-chandelier, carpets so deep they came over her shoes.

Their dining room table was already vast, but they added another at one end, and with ten adults including Suzanne and Camellia, along with eight children, sitting down to eat a turkey as big as an ostrich, it was something of a squash.

They played games in the afternoon, charades, Bingo and later when it grew dark, Murder. The children became more and more hysterical as the day wore on. The adults grew tiddly and told ruder and ruder jokes. The floor was littered with wrapping paper, toys, nut shells and selection boxes. Camellia felt as if she could live with this family for ever.

As soon as she and Suzanne were back at work on 27 December, there was New Year's Eve to plan, and Miss Puckridge had to remind them on several occasions that they both had counters they belonged behind and preparations to make for the January sales, not to mention keeping an eye open for shoplifters, as it seemed a great deal of stock had gone missing in the past few months. The girls waited until Miss Puckridge had stalked away, her nose in the air, then looked at each other.

'They should pay us to stay on a permanent

holiday.' Suzanne spluttered with laughter. 'That would solve the problem overnight.'

'Shouldn't we give up nicking things for the New Year?' Camellia said. She'd had an attack of guilt over Christmas. She had so many clothes now and she had real friends. Sometimes she had a feeling it could all be snatched away, that she'd be right back where she started. 'I mean, they might catch on to us.'

'They won't,' Suzanne said firmly. 'But remind me to wear something baggy to work tomorrow. I want to get one of those new Mary Quants for New Year's Eve.'

1967 came in with Camellia locked in the arms of a boy wearing a collarless Beatle jacket and matching hairstyle. He told her his name was Tony Blackburn and that he was a DJ on Radio Caroline, the pirate radio station. He did sound like him, but she couldn't quite believe a man as famous as that would spend New Year's Eve at the Hammersmith Palais and smooch all night with an ordinary girl like her. He said he would phone her in a day or two and take her out to dinner in the restaurant on the top of the Post Office Tower.

He never did, but that hardly mattered as she had plenty of other dates, both alone and with Madeline and Rose from the hostel. Each time they went to the pub up in Highgate they seemed to meet someone. January, February and March slipped by in a flash and still they discussed getting a flat together where they could have wild parties and stay out all night if they wanted to. But somehow they never got around to looking for anywhere.

It was in April that Camellia first became interested in the underground scene in London. There had been a rally of 10,000 flower children in New York's Central Park in March, and their bizarre clothing, their protests about the American involvement in Vietnam and their ideology of peace and love struck a note with her. The vast media coverage on the subject and the reports that London was 'The Swinging City' all convinced her there was something important happening right under her nose.

Around the same time Miss Puckridge issued an ultimatum that anyone arriving for work with a skirt less than twenty inches long would be forced to wear a nylon overall. As the majority of Camellia's skirts had, inch by inch, been shortened to less than sixteen, she knew she was a target and resented it. On top of this was a vague feeling of boredom with the girls at the hostel. She seemed to have outgrown them. Their only ambitions seemed centred on marriage, while Camellia wanted to experience life. Even Madeline who was the nearest thing to 'a raver' in Archway House, showed no enthusiasm for more adventurous nights out, like coffee bars and clubs in Soho. In fact when Camellia suggested they went to the Middle Earth, a new club which had opened in a cellar beneath Covent Garden market, she looked horrified.

'It's full of drug addicts,' she said, pursing her lips in disapproval. 'I heard someone comes up and sticks a needle in your arm the moment you get there.'

This seemed extremely unlikely, but Camellia decided to try Carol and Suzanne at work the next day.

'It's only those loony flower children who go there,' Carol said dismissively. She was a little surprised to find Camellia had come so far out of herself. 'I like places with a bit of style, not cellars full of weirdos.'

In the absence of anyone to go to the club with, Camellia had to resign herself to pubs and dance halls with the other girls, but it didn't stop her looking longingly at girls who wafted into the shop with bells and brightly coloured beads round their necks. She sensed their freedom, it wafted to her like the smell of their patchouli oil scent. These girls didn't wear bras beneath their flimsy cheesecloth blouses, their hair was long and tousled. She knew they didn't have to be home by eleven and she was sure no one would ever dare measure the length of their skirts.

But as summer arrived, at last Suzanne began to wake up to the idea that there was more to life and London than being bribed with a gin and orange by lads who wanted nothing more than to get their knickers off in the back seat of their Consul.

'Do you still fancy going to the Middle Earth,' she asked one evening as they hurried towards the tube to go home.

'Yes of course, more than ever,' Camellia said, feeling a surge of excitement. 'What makes you ask?'

'I met a real tasty Australian the other night who goes there,' Suzanne grinned. 'He said it was "mind blowing". We could try it out once, just to see. I think Carol will come. She's fed up with the Palais too.'

'Let's go there on Saturday,' Camellia suggested. 'But I'd have to tell Miss Peet I was staying at your house. Would your mum write me a note?'

As Saturday came closer Camellia was dizzy with excitement. In return for helping a friend of Suzanne's fill a shopping bag with clothes in the changing room, Camellia had an outfit so wild she could hardly believe she had the nerve to wear it: a red crushed-velvet tunic, with little shorts underneath and a huge studded belt to put round her hips. She spent almost a week's wages on some white, tight, long boots to wear with it. It was all packed in an overnight bag down with Wilf the security man. She was going home with Suzanne for tea and to change, and the Connors didn't have any kind of curfew in their house – in fact Suzanne had casually said they probably wouldn't be back until the tubes started running on Sunday morning.

The Middle Earth didn't open until after half past ten and when the girls arrived soon after eleven The Cream's 'Strange Brew' was blasting out with such force it almost singed their ears. As they'd been told, it was just a huge cavern like a cellar stretching right under Covent Garden market, the only seating planks on scaffolding in tiers, but to Camellia it was everything she'd expected and more. The walls were whitewashed, but transformed with coloured light shows. Strange shapes oozed and blobbed in time to the beat, each wall a slightly different image.

'To think I was worried I looked weird!' Suzanne giggled.

She was dressed like a Red Indian squaw, in a chamois-leather minidress with fringing and beads, more beads round her forehead and long brown boots.

'I've never felt more normal,' Carol sniggered. She had taken some persuading to abandon her normal dolly-bird image for a Victorian cream lace dress of her grandmother's she looked stunning in. 'I think I'll have to raid Gran's wardrobe more often.'

It was like walking in on a film set or a fancy-dress party. Hundreds of people, reflecting almost every period and style: girls in twenties and thirties evening dresses, still more in flowing diaphanous cheesecloth smocks, jeans, miniskirts and wild patterned loons; saris, gypsy skirts, even one girl like a belly dancer with a glittering girdle of gold chains. The men were every bit as remarkable: not a dark suit in the entire club and hair almost as long as the girls. Velvet trousers, brocade jackets, beaded Red Indian leather shirts and jeans. One man wore nothing but a pair of bright yellow hipster trousers, his bare feet and chest tanned a deep golden brown and his curly hair like a halo round his face.

'He must be a ballet dancer,' Suzanne said as he pirouetted and leapt into the air. A black girl joined him on roller skates, her buttocks undulating beneath a long red tube dress, flowers painted on her cheeks. Joss sticks burned everywhere, little bells around necks tinkled; it was somewhere between a fun fair and a carnival, a pleasure house for the young.

To Camellia's disappointment Carol and Suzanne seemed bored. 'There's no booze,' they kept saying. 'All the blokes are a bit weird. The music's too loud, maybe we should have gone down the Palais.'

The music wasn't loud, it was deafening. To Camellia it was like finally being dropped into the centre of all those happenings she'd read about. 'Don't be spoil-sports,' she implored them. 'Look, everyone else is enjoying themselves.'

'They're all on drugs,' Suzanne pouted. 'Now if we could get some Purple Hearts we'd be able to get into it.'

Camellia didn't need anything to make her high. But if some pills would keep Suzanne and Carol happy enough to stay, she intended to go along with it.

She perched on one of the platforms, with Carol just below her, and watched Suzanne walk towards a tall dark man in a long brocade jacket. He was very slender, with black curly hair as long as her own. He turned as Suzanne spoke to him and Camellia felt the hair on the back of her neck rise. A pirate out of a kids' book, was her first impression: a long olive face with thick eyebrows and a wide, flashing smile.

She was at least twenty yards from him, but when Suzanne pointed towards them he smiled and Camellia felt a quickening of her pulse.

He was at least six foot, judging from the way he bent down to listen to what Suzanne was saying to him. He wore a ruffled shirt under his jacket and velvet trousers tucked into long snakeskin boots.

Camellia put her hand down and touched Carol's shoulder, indicating the man. 'He's beautiful,' she whispered.

'He looks dangerous to me,' Carol sniffed. 'But then so does everyone. I don't know why we agreed to come here with you.'

Camellia took no notice of Carol's terse remark. Suzanne was walking back towards them, the dark man at her side.

'What are you after girls?' he said as he came closer. He looked up at Camellia and winked, almost as if he knew she'd been studying him.

'Purple Hearts or Blues?' Suzanne asked.

He dug in his pocket and pulled out a small envelope. 'All I've got is a few Bennies, want a couple each?'

'How much are they?' Suzanne had that cool, snooty expression she used when she wasn't entirely sure about something.

'Would I charge three tasty chicks?' he smiled. 'Have them on me.'

He hesitated before moving on. His gaze flickered up to Camellia and all she could do was stare back. His eyes were the darkest she'd ever seen, slanty with heavy lids and long black lashes, his skin tight and shiny smooth over protruding cheekbones. Maleness seeped out of every pore, drawing attention to his tight trousers and the suggestion of an iron body under the dainty shirt. Even his hair, which at a distance had looked like wild curls, was in fact made of tightly coiled spring-like ringlets.

'Wake up,' Carol nudged Camellia. 'He's gone now.'

'Was he really that beautiful?' Camellia smiled.

'Yeah,' Carol handed her a coke to wash the pills down with. 'But you can bet all the other girls think so too. So forget him.'

There were strange things going on all around her. A whey-faced, dirty-looking girl sat in the corner tightening a leather belt round her upper arm and to Camellia's horror she injected herself with something. In another dark corner a couple were making love just as if they were alone. Others mumbled to themselves, stumbling about with glazed eyes. On the dance floor couples jumped, swayed and writhed to the loud music, making her feel as if she had landed on a bizarre, alien planet. But despite all this decadence Camellia's eyes were drawn back constantly to the man who'd given them the pills.

Everyone knew him and tried to stop him as he passed by, but he didn't pause for more than a moment or two with anyone. Camellia wondered if in fact he owned the club. It was nice of him to share his pills with them.

She barely noticed first Carol, then Suzanne go off to dance, content just to sit and watch from her position up on the scaffolding, legs dangling in space, arms resting on another bar. Her friends had claimed to be so stoned they could barely sit still, but Camellia felt nothing more than a slight flush of excitement.

'Left you all alone have they?'

It was the man again, his voice deep and husky as if he smoked a hundred cigarettes a day.

'It's okay,' she smiled. 'I like watching.'

He jumped up the six feet to her as effortlessly and gracefully as a cat and sat down beside her. 'I haven't seen you and your mates before,' he said. 'Where are you from?'

'They live in Hammersmith,' Camellia replied. 'I come from Highgate.'

'I'm Dougie,' he said. 'And you?'

'Camellia.'

It was the first time she could remember giving her real name willingly. For some odd reason she felt like a Camellia tonight.

'A pretty name,' he smiled. 'It suits you. I think you've got the best legs I ever saw.'

Camellia blushed and giggled, instinctively pulling the little shorts down further.

'Don't do that.' He took her hand in his and smacked it. 'If you've got the nerve to buy something outrageous, wear it with pride and don't go getting embarrassed.'

Camellia had a surprisingly easy manner with men, compared with most of the girls she knew. She still didn't expect them to fancy her, somehow, so she didn't try too hard. As a result they tended to single her out to talk to. Working in a busy store had helped her still more, since she'd learned to respond with interest to anything customers might say. She'd also discovered that making an outrageous remark right at the beginning of a conversation, took people by surprise and kept their interest.

'I didn't buy it,' she grinned. 'I nicked it. I nick all my clothes.'

For a moment he just looked at her. It was difficult to gauge whether he was shocked or thought she was crazy. But his mouth curved into a wide grin and his eyes sparkled. 'Well!' he said. 'A girl after my own heart.'

It was only as she began to chat to Dougie that she became aware the pills were affecting her. As Suzanne had claimed, they made you chat a lot, made you feel powerful. She found she was projecting an image of herself that was entirely new, steering him to believe she was far more worldly and zany than she really was.

He asked her down to dance and though Camellia had a moment's trepidation that she would make a complete fool of herself, she found to her delight that she was swept away by the music.

'Are you a professional dancer?' Dougie asked. He hadn't been doing much moving about himself, more just a shuffle of his feet and a few waves of his hands.

'No,' she laughed. 'But my mother was. I suppose it's in the blood.'

Once or twice Camellia caught a glimpse of Suzanne and Carol, dancing on the other side of the club, but as they were obviously happy she forgot all about them. The more she looked at Dougie, the more she liked him. He wasn't like any other man she'd ever met.

The heat eventually stopped them dancing and they went over to one of the booths at the side of the club to get a soft drink.

Even here it was too noisy to have a real conversation, though Dougie pointed out a few of the more outrageously dressed people and told her who they were.

'See that guy in the orange robe?' he said, indicating a tall dark-haired man with a beard. 'Well he's an American lawyer, he gets his kicks coming down here when he's in London on business. Straight as a die he is, wouldn't know a drug if you shoved one up his nose, yet he gets all dressed up and dances all night.'

'What about him,' Camellia pointed out the man they'd thought earlier was a ballet dancer.

'He's an acid head,' Dougie grinned. 'He used to be with the Royal Ballet. The owner here lets him in for free because he makes a good floor show. That's what this place is all about really, a show. We get them all in here, the queers, the exhibitionists, and then a whole load of people who come to watch. It wouldn't be any fun if everyone was like that.' He pointed to a scruffy looking couple sitting against a wall, their eyes almost closed.

'They are on heroin,' he said. 'Losers both of them. They'll probably dip in a few pockets or handbags before the night's over to get their next fix. They started doing heroin for fun, now they don't know the meaning of the word any more.'

Camellia wanted to know a great deal more about Dougie, but without shouting to make herself heard, she couldn't ask him any more questions. He confused her a little. He knew everyone here, he seemed to belong here, yet he was cynical about the whole thing. Where did he fit in?

They had been back on the dance floor for only a few minutes when suddenly Suzanne was at her side twitching the sleeve of her tunic.

'Where've you been?' she said crossly. 'We looked everywhere for you.'

'I only went with Dougie for a drink.' Camellia stopped dancing for a moment. 'What's the matter?'

'It's nearly three. We want to go home,' Suzanne replied. 'Are you coming with us?'

Camellia looked across the floor. The crowd had

thinned out a little without her noticing. Carol was standing between two earnest-looking boys in denim jackets with Beatle-style haircuts. It was obvious even from a distance that the four of them intended to go together.

'It's early yet,' Camellia pleaded. 'Can't you wait a bit longer?'

'We won't get a taxi if we stay any later.' Suzanne's pupils were dilated so far Camellia could see no iris. 'Besides the boys want us to go back to their place for coffee.'

Dougie moved forward and slung his arm round Camellia's shoulder. 'You don't have to leave with them. I'll get you home,' he said.

Camellia looked from Suzanne to Dougie. She knew she ought to go with Suzanne – after all she was supposed to be staying the weekend at her parents' house in Hammersmith. But if she left now she might never see Dougie again.

'You don't want me as a gooseberry if you're with them,' Camellia nodded towards the boys. 'And I'd rather stay here.'

Suzanne frowned. She was torn. She wanted to go back with the boys, but she didn't like to leave Camellia here. Then there was her father. If they weren't in by eight in the morning he'd go crackers.

'Meet us at Hammersmith tube at eight,' she suggested. 'Don't be late. Dad will go ape if we don't get back together with the same story.'

'Okay,' Camellia thought this sounded a good idea.

'I'll see she gets there,' Dougie chipped in.

'Well, we'll be off then.' Suzanne still looked anxious. 'Are you sure you'll be all right?'

'Of course I will,' Camellia smiled, it was a new experience being fussed over.

Suzanne took a step back, then hesitated again.

'Go on! Don't worry about me,' Camellia urged her. 'And have a good time with those blokes.'

The music seemed to tug at Camellia's emotions once her friends had left. Lyrics she'd never noticed before now all seemed to hold a special message.

'All the boys in the neighbourhood, would love her if they could,' Dougie sang the words softly in her ear, holding her tightly against him, stroking her hair and back.

When he kissed her Camellia felt the club revolve around her. She had plenty of practice at kissing, and of fending boys off who wanted to go any further. But Dougie was a man, not a boy. He didn't lunge at her or try to squeeze the breath out of her. It was magical, tender and so very erotic.

It was almost light as they came up the steps from the club, ears ringing from the loud music. The market looked oddly skeletal closed up, yet there was still a faint whiff of flowers and fruit in the air.

Camellia shivered and hugged her arms around her body.

'It's far too early to go to Hammersmith yet,' Dougie said taking his jacket and draping it round her shoulders. 'Come home with me!'

Reason told her it wasn't wise to go home with a man she'd only known a few hours. But Dougie was right: it was too early to go to Hammersmith.

'Don't look so worried.' He lifted her face to his, kissing her lightly on the lips. 'It's only around the corner, you can leave just after seven and you'll be there in plenty of time.'

He held her hand and led her down a small alley, across another narrow street and into a tiny dark courtyard. He stopped by a printer's shop. 'Before we go in, I want you to promise you won't ever tell anyone where I live.'

A ray of early morning light cut down through a gap in the high buildings and drifted across his high cheek bones. Suddenly he looked sinister, and she drew back instinctively, afraid.

'You're safe with me.' His voice was low and compelling. 'I don't bring people here because I'm not a trusting person. But you're different, Camellia, and I feel something special for you.'

A couple of years ago no one in the world had cared about her. If being daring was the way to find love and adventure she wasn't going to duck the chance.

'I won't tell anyone,' she insisted. She would tell Suzanne she'd gone straight from the club to the tube.

But her fear returned as Dougie led her into the dark shop that smelled of machinery and printers' ink and through another door into total darkness.

'There's no light till we get to the top,' he said, locking the door behind him. 'Hold on to my hand, I'll lead the way.'

A stink of mildew made her recoil. She could feel bare wooden boards under her feet, and a sensation that mice or rats could be lurking made her shudder, but it was too late now to back off. Up and up they went, till at last Dougie switched on a light to reveal a square landing with smoke blackened walls.

'There was a fire here once,' he said calmly. 'The printer's old and I do a lot of deals for him, so he lets me live here. I'm going to get it all done up soon.'

There was one big dark room, with a primitive kitchen and bathroom leading off, filled with shabby furniture that reminded her of Fishmarket Street, with a big wooden bedstead the centre-piece.

Fear turned to horror when he picked up a big

steel bar and placed it in brackets across the door. 'Don't be scared,' he smiled, looking round at her over his shoulder. 'This is to keep people out, not you in.'

He lit the gas fire to take the chill off the room and put Sgt Pepper's Lonely Hearts Club Band on a Dansette record player. Camellia stood awkwardly, shivering, clutching his jacket more tightly round her. She wished she'd insisted on getting a cup of coffee somewhere.

'Come here,' he said, holding out one hand.

She came to him hesitantly, but he drew her into his arms and held her, his face against her hair.

'Isn't that something?' he whispered, pointing to the view.

Camellia looked out over the rooftops, but it was the sky itself Dougie was drawing her attention to: every shade from palest grey, up through blues interspersed with strands of pink and finally red, surrounding the giant melon sun.

He kissed her then, his warm lips coming down on Camellia's so softly she melted against him, losing her fear. His fingers entwined in her hair, drawing her closer and closer until they were as one.

'I knew you were special as soon as I saw you,' he whispered, kissing her neck, her ears and eyes. 'It's like that sky out there, Camellia, all new and shiny. I just want to hold on to you and make it last forever.'

Camellia was quite used to boys trying to seduce her. But this was different. He'd removed her belt and unzipped her tunic almost without her realising it and when he kissed her and slid his hands over the bare skin of her back, she trembled. Carol and Suzanne were always talking about sex at work, yet she knew they'd both think she was a slut to allow a man she'd only just met take such liberties with her.

Yet she was afraid to stop him, so terribly scared he wouldn't like her anymore. His arms held a warmth and tenderness she had not felt since she was a child. His kisses wiped out all the feelings she'd ever had of not belonging. Besides, she had pretended to be so sophisticated all evening. How could she revert to being a babyish little virgin now?

As he laid her back on the bed somehow he managed to remove her tunic all in the same move. 'Don't be scared,' he whispered. 'I only want to love you. Let me take your bra off and see your breasts.'

It was the wonder on his face when he touched her naked breasts for the first time which moved her. She had thought for so many years that she was ugly and unlovable, hiding her body from anyone's gaze. He sat back on his haunches beside her, took one breast in each hand and stroked them as reverently as if they were a work of art.

'You are so beautiful, Camellia,' he murmured, bending to kiss her nipples. 'The most beautiful girl I ever saw.'

Time had no meaning as she lay in his arms being kissed and cuddled. Each time he kissed her breasts she felt as if something was wringing her insides, tweaking an invisible cord which made her move closer and closer to him. Several times his hands moved down to remove her shorts, but somehow she managed to stop him.

'No further,' she insisted, although she might have weakened had it been dark. Her whole being wanted to be touched and explored, to find the seat of that burning inside her. If she could somehow have removed her boots, shorts, tights and knickers without him seeing, and got in under the sheets –

but sunshine was pouring through the window and she wasn't confident enough about her naked body yet, not to expose it to his eyes.

Eventually she stood up. 'I have to go,' she said. She didn't want to leave him but it was gone seven. Although Dougie's eyes kept drooping, Camellia was wide awake. It must have been the pills she'd taken: she felt faintly sick too and wanted a cup of tea.

'Meet me tomorrow. Covent Garden tube at eight,' he said sleepily. 'I think I'm falling in love with you.'

Dougie had fallen asleep in the time it took her to put on her tunic and belt and go to the toilet. Camellia noticed now the grime on the walls, the balls of fluff on the floor, the grey, stained sheets. But as she bent over to kiss him goodbye, her heart contracted painfully. His face in sleep had lost its hardness, his lips were slack and so very soft. She lifted a black curl, letting it coil around her finger like a spring. He said he was falling in love with her. She could change the way he lived.

Dougie was waiting as she came out of the tube station on Monday evening, he was leaning against a wall smoking a cigarette, but as he saw her he dropped it and almost leapt to her side.

'I didn't think you'd come,' he said, pulling her to him for a kiss regardless of people passing by either side of them. 'I thought you'd think better of it now you've seen where I live.'

Camellia just smiled and shook her head. She had thought of nothing else but him since she let herself out of that horrible dark printing shop, counting the hours till she could see him. She'd been excited about dates before, but never like this.

She had taken a big risk too, in stealing the dress she was wearing, before it was even priced. It was a Mary Quant mini, white with a black diagonal stripe from one shoulder to the hip, and only three had been delivered. She just hoped she didn't bump into any of the staff from Peter Robinson's.

'You look gorgeous,' Dougie said, taking her hand. 'Now where would you like to go?'

Camellia couldn't suggest anywhere, she knew so little about the West End's pubs, so Dougie took her to Old King Cole's down in the Strand which appeared to have been taken over by flower children and played loud rock music. As in the Middle Earth, Dougie seemed to know everyone.

The time went far too quickly. It seemed as if they'd only been there less than an hour when Camellia noticed it was half past ten.

'I must go,' she gasped. She would be hard pushed to make it back to Archway House by eleven.

They had talked about all kinds of things, yet she still didn't know much about Dougie. Why did he live in such an awful place when he seemed to have so much money? And why was he so evasive about his background, when she'd told him so much about hers?

'Stay with me tonight?' Dougie took her hand and lifted it to his lips. 'Please?'

'I can't. I'll get into trouble,' she said sadly.

'What's the worst that warden can do?' Dougie asked with a shrug of his shoulders. 'Throw you out?'

Camellia nodded.

'Well does that matter? You could always come and stay with me, we could do my place up together,' he said with a persuasive grin. 'You can't live being in at eleven. That's ridiculous, especially now you're my girl. I'm just waking up at that time of day.'

'I can't stay with you,' Camellia blushed. 'I might end up having a baby.'

'If that's all you're worried about I'll soon get that sorted,' Dougie grinned.

An hour or two later Camellia was in Dougie's bed, any earlier anxiety about Miss Peet or the rights and wrongs of staying the night with Dougie were gone in the joy of being held and loved.

It was too dark to see the ugliness of his flat. A soft, cool breeze was coming through the big open window and he had lit a couple of candles by the bed.

She felt as if she was lying on satin sheets, a fairytale prince making love to her. Maybe it was that pot she'd smoked with him that made her feel so secure and so happy, or just the way he kept singing snatches of the Beatles record 'Something' to her.

His chest looked golden in the candlelight, and it felt so silky. She had been a little alarmed at the size of his penis, rising up almost to his navel, the first adult one she'd ever seen. But he had been stroking and playing with her for so long, she knew the time had come when she must let him put it inside her.

'Let me put this under your bum,' he whispered, lifting her slightly to push a pillow beneath her buttocks. 'It makes it easier.'

A pang of jealousy stabbed at her. Somehow it showed how many other girls he'd been with.

It hurt. She wished she could push him off and say it was all a mistake. All the pleasure she'd felt earlier had faded. He wasn't gentle and loving now, he was saying swear words that made her cringe and they felt like a betrayal of trust, but still she held onto him, winding her legs around his back and arching herself closer.

It seemed to go on and on, making her sorer with

each stroke, but by now he was oblivious to her, grunting and groaning, biting at her neck.

Faster and faster he moved, until she thought she would have to scream, but suddenly he made a low roaring sound and it was over.

She lay there, squashed by his body, feeling damp and decidedly disappointed as his tremors gradually died down. Part of her was thinking 'So that's it, is it? Why do people make so much fuss about it?'

He was still for some moments, his harsh breathing slowly returning to normal. For a moment she thought he had fallen asleep.

But then he moved onto his side and drew her onto his shoulder.

Only one candle was still alight, flickering under a poster of Jimi Hendrix. She looked at the poster and wondered if Rose had given Miss Peet the message that she was staying with Suzanne.

'That wasn't any good for you, was it?' he asked in a curiously croaky voice.

'It was,' she lied bravely. She didn't want to hurt his feelings.

'Don't tell me fibs,' he said, wriggling away from her and leaning up on his elbow to look down at her.

He looked even more like a pirate or a gypsy now. His lips were very red and slightly swollen, his hair wild and curly.

'Let me make you come now,' he said. 'I want this first night to be beautiful for both of us.'

Camellia couldn't reply. She didn't know what he had in mind and she was a little afraid he would start all over again. But he took her silence as agreement and moved down the bed to kiss her breasts, parting her vagina with his fingers.

'Is it sore?' he whispered. 'I didn't mean to hurt you.'

She forgave him everything then, as he caressed her. Dipping his fingers right into her, then running them back. She held her breath, terrified he would stop, but still he kept on and on, driving her wilder and wilder.

How he got this experience no longer mattered. The ugly room disappeared as she was transported into a world of ecstasy. Suddenly she understood why her mother had kept going with men.

Sensation was the only thing that mattered now: breath hot and heavy, urging him upwards to kiss her, opening her legs wider and pushing his hands harder against her. Something was happening inside her, this great welling up feeling she couldn't control. A million stars twinkling behind closed eyelids, a rocket shooting her upwards to meet them.

'I love you,' she heard herself shout out.

'I think we were meant for one another,' he whispered later in the darkness, as he held her safe in the circle of his arms. The last candle had spluttered out, only a lingering waxy smell remaining. 'Be my chick forever?'

Chapter Six

'What are you doing that for?' Dougie came up behind Camellia as she was cleaning the windows, pressed himself against her back and cupped her breasts in his hands.

'They're filthy,' she said reprovingly. 'You can hardly see out of them.'

'I rarely got up in daylight before you came here, let alone looked out the windows.' Dougie tweaked at her nipples, burying his face in her hair. 'Let's fuck?'

'Don't you ever think of anything else?' Camellia dropped the cloth into the bucket. Dougie turned her on by merely being close to her, but her mind had been on making his flat more homely, especially now that it was getting colder. It was ten weeks since she'd first met Dougie, and the summer was nearly gone. 'We should paint the room, make it pretty. It's horrible in here during the day.'

She had cleaned it thoroughly, using copious amounts of Vim, bleach and other cleaning fluids, but though the kitchen looked much better, she could see little improvement in the main room. She dreamed of it all painted glossy white, with an orange carpet, Op Art large floor cushions and big bright framed prints on the walls. She had made little changes: a red tablecloth now covered the scarred sideboard, a red and gold Chinese lantern softened the overhead light, and two giant Zodiac-

113

sign posters covered the worst stains on the walls. But it wasn't enough.

Dougie opened the zip on her jeans and slid his hand inside, fingers reaching down towards her pubic hair. 'Sod painting the room when I could be fingering you,' he whispered. 'I'd rather look at your fanny than the walls!'

Since Camellia spent her first night with Dougie her life had turned upside-down. Maybe if she'd spoken to Miss Peet herself that night instead of leaving a message to say she was staying with Suzanne, she might still be living at Archway House and working at Peter Robinson's. But Miss Peet had been suspicious when she saw Rose's note and had rung Mrs Connor, Suzanne's mother, only to find Camellia wasn't there.

When Camellia got home the following evening, Miss Peet had called her into her sitting room to cross-examine her.

'Don't make things worse by telling more lies,' she snapped angrily as Camellia tried to pretend Rose had given the wrong message. 'I have a great deal of experience with teenage girls and I know you weren't with any girlfriends but spending the night with a man. What's more you haven't been at work today.'

If Miss Peet had been satisfied with giving a lecture on the dangers of pregnancy, venereal diseases, and the folly of rushing headlong into a relationship with a man she had only just met, Camellia might've stopped to consider that this older woman was only concerned with her well-being. But Miss Peet said that unless this 'boy-friend' was prepared to come to Archway House so she could meet him, Camellia would be grounded for a month.

'If he's a nice lad and cares about you, he won't object,' she said firmly, making it quite clear she would settle for nothing less. 'You are only seventeen and I am responsible for your safety while you live here.'

Camellia couldn't meet Miss Peet's eyes. She stared sullenly at the ceiling and refused to even apologise, much less agree to the woman's request. She could no more imagine Dougie with his long hair, tight trousers and cowboy boots waiting politely in the hall to meet this tyrant, than working on a building site, or going to church.

The next day Dougie was waiting for her as she came out of work. He looked like a rock star in a black sleeveless singlet, tight jeans and a huge studded belt.

'What's going on?' he asked angrily. 'I rang the hostel last night and asked to speak to you and some woman said I'd have to come out there so she could meet me. Who the hell does she think she is?'

Camellia explained what had happened. She was feeling very low: Miss Puckridge had given her a dressing down for not turning up for work the previous day and she had no good excuse to offer.

'Just leave the hostel,' Dougie said dismissively. 'That old bag has no right to tell you who you can see. And I'm bloody well not going cap in hand to her.'

Camellia couldn't think straight. On the one hand she was absolutely certain she was in love with Dougie. On the other hand a little voice was whispering that she should exercise some caution before jumping in feet first. She knew so little about Dougie, and his lifestyle seemed so strange.

'Couldn't you put on something smart and come out there just once?' she asked. 'It would make it so much better for me.'

'I can't see how,' he sneered. 'She'll take one look at me and decide I'm not suitable. She's a frustrated cow, I know that without even meeting her. It's up to you. Either you come and live in my pad and be my chick, or we leave it right here.'

He began to walk away, through the crowds of people rushing to Oxford Circus tube station. Camellia looked at his narrow hips and black curls gleaming in the late afternoon sunshine and she felt faint with the fear of losing him.

'Dougie!' she called out, running after him, elbowing her way through the crowds. 'Don't go like that.'

She caught up with him about twenty yards down Regent Street. 'Please don't be cross with me?' she pleaded, catching hold of his arm. 'I do want to be your girl. I'm just a bit scared.'

'Scared of what? I only want to have fun with you.'

Camellia wanted to admit that she hated knowing that Miss Peet and Miss Puckridge were disappointed in her, but she knew he would sneer at that. 'I don't know,' she said weakly. 'I suppose it's because everything's gone a bit haywire since I met you.'

He caught hold of her two arms and pulled her close to him. He smelled of sweat, he was hot and his almost black eyes burned into hers. 'I'll look after you. You belong with me.'

He kissed her then, hard and long, ignoring the curious glances from passers-by. When he eventually released her he cupped her face in his two hands.

'You've got this Saturday off haven't you?' he said. 'Pack your bags and catch a taxi to my place. You said you love me. Prove it.'

Camellia had agonised all week. Suzanne and Carol both advised her not to be hasty. Yet back at Archway House, Madeline encouraged her.

'You go with him if that's what you want,' she said forcefully, hands on hips. 'Miss Peet's as bad

116

as my parents, she doesn't want anyone to have any fun. So maybe it won't work out, but you'll regret it if you don't try. I gave up my boyfriend, Colin, in Birmingham because my parents didn't approve of him, and I've never met anyone I like as much since.'

In the end Camellia wasn't brave enough to give notice, or even say goodbye to Miss Peet. When she saw the older woman leaving on Saturday morning to go shopping, she hastily stuffed the last of her belongings into a couple of pillowcases and called a taxi. Rose, Wendy and Madeline all hugged her and urged her to stay in touch, but their eyes showed they knew they were seeing her for the last time.

Camellia hadn't really thought about what living with Dougie would mean, other than wondering how she would wash her clothes and where she would hang them. She was soon to discover his lifestyle was completely alien to everything she knew.

He had no set routine and time meant nothing to him. He slept when he was tired, got up when he chose, ate on the move and hated any kind of conformity.

Yet he was surprisingly organised in some ways. He erected a rail across an alcove for her to hang up her clothes. Within four days of her moving in he had found a doctor willing to prescribe birth control pills for her. She only had to mention wanting something, whether shampoo, steak or a jar of coffee, and he stole it.

Less than a fortnight after moving in with him, Camellia was given the sack from Peter Robinson's. She had been late on four consecutive days, arriving with dark-ringed eyes. When she couldn't offer a sick note to back up her claim she'd been ill, she was handed her cards.

Dougie was delighted. 'I'll teach you ways to make three times what they paid you,' he said, laughing at her protests that she needed money of her own. 'Don't worry babe, there's more to life than work.'

Camellia soon found that his last statement was entirely true. Once she'd got over the initial anxiety, she felt as if she were on one glorious long holiday. Idle summer days spent smoking dope, listening to rock music and making love, lounging in parks with Dougie's friends or cruising the boutiques in Carnaby Street, then moving on to bars and clubs for the night.

Dougie's friends were the sort she wanted to be like: fascinating people who laughed a great deal, who talked knowledgeably about exotic places, about music, art and poetry. Any form of authority was a joke to them. Love and sensation was all. Camellia was touched by the way they included her in their deep conversations, their wild clothes and their mystic ideology.

Although Camellia was a little disturbed at first to discover that all the money Dougie splashed around came from selling drugs, this was soon to become a source of pride.

By day they were just another couple of flower children, indistinguishable from thousands of others who thronged the West End, but as darkness fell and Dougie dressed up in velvet trousers, frilly shirts and snakeskin boots, he was 'The Man', sought after, admired and respected. Camellia's role was primarily a decoration on his arm, but also a distraction and lookout until every last packet of drugs concealed in his boots, crotch and pockets were gone, the money belt strapped under his shirt bulging.

As Camellia went with him from one club and bar to another, she learned for herself the difference between 'Tourists' and 'Heads'. The former could be made to pay twice the price; the latter were dangerous if the goods weren't up to scratch. Uppers, Downers, African Black, Lebanese Gold, Moroccan, Durban Poison, Acid and Grass, Camellia tried them all and learned to identify their peculiarities. She could spot a plain-clothes policeman a hundred yards off and became as practised as Dougie at giving them the slip.

They moved around: to the Hundred Club in Oxford Street, Tiles and The Scene, but mostly to UFO or the Middle Earth, fitting in the Whiskey-a-Go-Go or The Discotheque en route. London was buzzing, young people pouring in daily from all corners of England and further afield, and as that summer of 67 slowly turned to autumn, Camellia felt she'd removed the last traces of the fat, plain girl from Rye. Once or twice she'd tried to tell Dougie about how it was for her then, but he said it was only the present and future that counted, the past was as dead as her mother. Camellia had been a little hurt by that, she wanted to share everything with him. But she had come round to his way of thinking, and in private moments alone she thought of Bonny, understanding her a little better now that her own life wasn't squeaky clean.

Miss Peet, the girls at Archway House, and even her old job at Peter Robinson's were all so distant, a period in her life to be looked back on sometimes with nostalgia but mostly with relief that she no longer had to conform to their rules. Only the memory of Bert Simmonds occasionally prickled at her conscience. He would most definitely not approve of how she was living now. But she couldn't speak of that to Dougie, he wouldn't understand why anyone should consider a policeman's opinion important.

Camellia Norton was beautiful, so everyone told

her. She was in love, she had money in her purse. She was 'someone' at last; she had achieved her goal.

Dougie encouraged her to dress in tiny suede miniskirts, embroidered blouses that revealed her bare jutting breasts, Red Indian headbands and wild jangly silver jewellery. He wanted other men to lust after her as it all added to his prestige and Camellia was pleased to find herself the centre of attention.

But however exciting it was being Dougie's 'chick', seeing envy on other girls' faces and basking in his reflected glory, it was the time alone with him at home she loved most. For the first time in her life she felt truly wanted and needed. When Dougie barricaded the door and took her in his arms, all her little niggling doubts and insecurities seemed to vanish.

As Dougie's fingers delved deeper and deeper into her jeans, Camellia felt her enthusiasm for cleaning the windows evaporate. When he turned her round to kiss her, she dropped her cloth and responded eagerly.

Dougie was usually sparing with his kisses. Now she held him tightly, insinuating her tongue between his lips, pressing herself against him. She could feel him pushing her jeans down over her bottom and he nudged her backwards until she was resting against the windowsill.

Camellia found it hard to understand his preference for making love to her in strange positions and places. It seemed unnatural to her to be pinned-up against walls, on the floor or astride a chair when they had a perfectly good bed to lie on. But then he was unconventional in every way, and she had quickly learned that if she wanted to keep him interested she had to go along with him.

But when he dropped to his knees in front of her and pulled her jeans and knickers right off it seemed his only intention this time was to please her. He grasped the tops of her thighs, parting the lips of her vagina with his thumbs, looked up at her with a wicked expression, then thrust his tongue into her.

This was an unexpected treat, and all resistance vanished. Camellia bent forward towards him, winding her fingers into his dark curls, watching his long red tongue darting in and out, and moaned in bliss.

'Do you want to come?' He halted for a moment, grinning up at her, and then pushed two fingers deep inside her.

Camellia could only nod and pull him closer to her.

He looked up at her, his mouth wet and slack, his eyes black unfathomable pools of wickedness. 'Then promise me you'll go and nick some groceries afterwards?' he said. 'No bottling out like you've done before?'

She knew immediately she'd been conned. It wasn't passion which made him start playing with her, he was just asserting his power over her. Yet although she felt a moment's shame, she was helpless.

'I promise,' she murmured, throwing back her head till it banged against the glass behind her. 'Whatever you say!'

Over the last two years Camellia had altered immeasurably in her outlook and personality, but in the last few weeks Dougie had worked on her character too, already influencing her to think like him. She scorned the middle classes for their ordered lives, and regarded the teachings of the church and the law as just another trap to keep people in line. She was learning to believe too that drugs brought enlightenment, that only fools worked and that sexual experimentation was all important if you were to find your real self.

Yet Camellia wasn't entirely happy with the fantasies which came into her head while Dougie was making love to her. Deep down she felt shamed that instead of being filled with love for him exclusively, she sometimes imagined three or four men doing things to her in turn, being tied up and screwed senseless while vicars, doctors and even dentists took her in wild erotic situations. Sometimes Dougie played out these stories, pretending she was a school girl and he a teacher, doing things that made her blush with shame later when she was on her own.

This time she imagined someone watching from a window overlooking their room. A clerk in a pinstriped suit, masturbating while she writhed under Dougie's tongue.

She loved the way Dougie's eyes went all dreamy as he licked at her. Every now and then he looked up to see her reaction, stuffing his fingers inside her, smiling at her wild moans. She was afraid that he would suddenly stop, as he had in the past, taking her almost to the point of delirium, then getting up and walking away, making her beg for more. Other times he would throw her down on the floor and force himself into her, coming in two or three strokes, then getting up and going out without even a kiss. But then there were the other times when he only thought of her pleasure, hours and hours of playing and stroking until she had multiple orgasms, then sleeping, holding her in his arms.

Today Dougie was neither teasing nor cruel. He spread her legs wider, using both fingers and tongue with tantalising sensuality. She could see the tip of his cock rising out of his opened jeans and the imagined man outside the window disappeared as she looked down at his flushed, tender face.

She was coming, digging her nails into his shoulders, screaming out in ecstasy. While she was still shaking from the orgasm, Dougie turned her round, bent her over and pushed himself into her from behind. Now she had to hold onto the windowsill to prevent herself from falling as he gripped her hips and hammered away at her.

'You love my big cock, don't you?' he shouted.

'Yes,' she replied weakly, wishing he didn't have to be so crude.

'Can you feel it right inside your cunt? Eight inches of meat stuck up you.'

He came with a roar, reaching up and squeezing her breasts so hard she screamed out in pain. Then he was still, his sweat turning cold on her bare back as he withdrew and fell panting onto the bed. Camellia followed him, curling herself round his long body. She adored him most after sex, when his dark eyes turned to pools of melted chocolate and his lips lost their sneer. Even his body grew softer. For a short while he was all hers.

'I love you, Dougie,' she said with a catch in her voice, leaning up on one elbow to kiss his lips.

'Don't settle down and get comfy,' he said, turning his head away from her. 'The shop will be closed soon and you've got a promise to keep.'

Camellia crept down the dark stairs. She could hear Mr Tharrup's small press whirring away at the back of the building and she didn't want him coming out to speak to her. Mr Tharrup gave her the creeps, as did his dark, dirty building. He was well over sixty, obese, with a sweaty, red face and he leered at her whenever he saw her. Camellia still hadn't worked out the relationship between him and Dougie. Although she had seen printed flyers for clubs in the shop and Dougie claimed this was business he'd brought to Mr Tharrup, she had a strong suspicion there was something more to their relationship, something dark and unpleasant, just like the building. It seemed strange that a business-man would allow Dougie to live above his shop rent free.

Once out into Nottingham Court, Camellia pulled her black velvet antique cloak more securely round her. She had bought it in Kensington Market just for its beautiful jet beading; she certainly hadn't intended to use it as a cover-up for shoplift-ing. But it was ideal. Hidden beneath it she was wearing a Greek tapestry bag, slung over her shoulder. With two hands on show, hopefully no one would notice her popping the odd item or two beneath her cloak.

She crossed Endell Street and paused outside the Greek delicatessen on the corner of Betterton Street, trying to summon up her courage. It was quarter past six now and the street busy with traffic. But there were few pedestrians: this was an area of small businesses and most of the work force had already gone home.

Andreous, the flirtatious and portly Greek who owned the shop, was just inside, perched on a stool by the cash register, smoking a cigarette. Another half an hour and he would be closed.

' 'Ow are you today, pretty one?' he said, as usual. His accent was Greek but with a Cockney influence. Camellia liked him – his doleful dark eyes, his jollity and warmth. She knew she shouldn't be intending to rob him.

'Fine thank you,' she said cheerfully and picked up a wire basket from the pile by the counter. There were three or four other customers further back in the shop. With luck someone would want cheese or ham cut from the deli counter and Andreous would be distracted. 'And you?'

'Not so bad,' he grinned. 'Business 'as been better, but then it's been worse too. As Momma used to say "Andreous, not all the bottles of wine you open will be good ones." '

Walking down the shop Camellia put a bag of sugar in the basket. A tin of salmon went straight under the cloak, quickly followed by a large piece of rump steak from the cold cabinet. Biscuits in the basket, a packet of bacon and half a pound of butter into the bag. Dougie often got a bottle of gin or whisky but she didn't dare risk that. Instead she briskly walked round the gondola in the centre of the shop and selected a small loaf in full view of Andreous, who was just replacing a salami sausage on its hook.

'Have you got any mushrooms?' she asked. 'I can't see any.'

'Maybe I 'ave some out the back.' His dark eyes looked weary, he'd had a long day. ' 'Ow many you want?'

'Just a quarter. I'm sorry to put you to so much trouble.'

She managed to get a good bottle of red wine and forty Rothman's from behind the cash desk while he was gone.

Camellia was very scared while she was paying Andreous. The hidden bag was heavy and he had only to come round the counter and give her a playful hug for her to be caught out. Fortunately the telephone rang just as he gave her the change and he turned away to answer it. Camellia took her carrier bag in one hand, waved goodbye with the other and left hurriedly.

'Groovy,' Dougie enthused when she got back. 'I always knew you could do it. You'll be an even better tea leaf than me with a bit more training. I never had the nerve to take fags.'

Suzanne had once said that her only reason for stealing from Peter Robinson's was greed. In sixteen months of helping herself to clothes, Camellia had so many she was hard pushed to wear them all. But she had also discovered another reason, one she had never considered until she'd mastered shoplifting. The excitement.

Big stores like Selfridges were the best. With all that wonderful array of items just lying there on counters and rails. The more difficult and dangerous it was, the more the excitement grew. Leaving the shop was terrifying. Sometimes she would pause at the doors, expecting any moment to feel the hand on her shoulder and hear 'Excuse me, madam, will you come with me to the manager's office for a moment?'

Yet the moment she was well out on the street, scurrying away through the crowds of honest shoppers, Camellia felt absolute elation. It was better than drugs or sex, better than listening to Jimi Hendrix at full volume.

All through the autumn she felt like an actress, playing a dual role. She learned to win the assistants' trust in her, breaking up their otherwise boring day with a friendly chat. Her knowledge of store procedure helped: she knew how to spot detectives and recognise assistants who were easily distracted. All the time she was helping herself to anything she wanted.

Dougie was impressed at her skill and daring. He openly admitted she was far more adept at it than he was.

Sometimes Dougie worked with her. He would create a diversion while she stole something big to sell on to a fence, or she would stuff a bag to capacity with stolen items, then at a given signal she would swop her bag for his identical one, often filled with old paperback books and perhaps a couple of worn sweaters. Only once was she stopped by a store detective and although Camellia was sure the man guessed she'd been working with an accomplice, he had no alternative but to apologise for stopping her.

She and Dougie laughed helplessly for hours when they got home. Camellia acted out the whole scene for him, imitating the poor embarrassed security man, who had actually begun to stutter as he opened her bag. She felt all powerful, not just for beating the system, but because she'd found a way of becoming Dougie's equal.

Stealing clothes and household items began to lose its attraction once there was nothing more they needed. Camellia had got table lamps, crockery, kitchen utensils, bed-linen and towels, and the miserable cold flat began to look a great deal more welcoming once she'd stolen gay bedspreads to put over the old settee and a few colourful Indian durries to hang on the walls. She had all the pretty underwear she needed, dozens of sweaters, dresses, handbags, jackets and coats. But the thought of stealing just to sell the items on to someone else for a fraction of their value, somehow dampened the excitement.

One cold blustery afternoon in December, Camellia turned to pickpocketing. She was choosing a magazine from the newspaper stand at Piccadilly Circus when an American got out of a cab just beside her.

She probably wouldn't even have looked at him if he hadn't been arguing with the driver.

'Look, mate,' the driver was saying impatiently. 'If you think there's a quicker bleedin' way from

Notting Hill to Piccadilly Circus than the way I brought you down Bayswater Road and Oxford Street, then I suggest you catch an 'effing bus next time.'

The American was short and fat, wearing a loud checked overcoat that looked several sizes too big and a bright yellow wool scarf. As Camellia watched him dump his suitcases on the pavement and get out his wallet, she could see it was stuffed with notes. Instead of putting the wallet back into the inside pocket of his coat where he'd got it from, the American stuffed it angrily in his coat pocket, then picked up his bags and began walking back towards the Café Royal.

Camellia forgot all about the magazines she was going to buy. All she could see was the end of that black leather wallet sticking out of his right-hand pocket. She followed him, picking up speed among the crowds until she was just behind him.

The man's case and briefcase were so bulky that his arms weren't touching his sides. It was the easiest thing in the world to reach out from under her cloak, grasp the wallet firmly, pull it gently out, then withdraw her hand back into her cloak.

Perversely she still followed him, allowing other shoppers to come between them. She felt absolutely no guilt, only pleasure. He was obviously a rich man and a mean one at that.

Dougie was astounded when she showed it to him.

'You dipped his pocket?' His lean, olive face was a picture of disbelief, shock and awe. He touched the expensive wallet reverently and smelled the soft leather. 'Camellia, that's seriously bad. What if a pig had seen you?'

'The hand is quicker than the eye,' she laughed and snatching the wallet back from him, opened it and spilled the contents onto their bed.

They counted it together: two hundred and twenty pounds in twenty-pound notes, a hundred dollars and a few German marks.

They threw away the snapshots of his family and the return air ticket to Chicago. When they went out that night to eat at the Bistingo in Queensway, they didn't give the owner of the wallet a thought.

Camellia wore a white rabbit coat she'd helped herself to from C&A, over a new black Ossie Clark minidress; Dougie wore his new cashmere pea-jacket and a floral shirt she'd got him from John Stevens in Carnaby Street, and they took a taxi both ways.

It was a wonderful night. Over French onion soup, pigeon in red wine and a bottle of sparkling wine, Dougie held her hand across the table and spoke of his plans for their future.

'We'll start saving properly,' he said. 'I've got a couple of deals coming up just after Christmas, then in March we'll pack up and go to Morocco. We can live like this all the time there, Camellia. I'll get some contact sorted out there to buy dope. We'll find a real house by the sea. When we need more bread we just buy a weight of dope, smuggle it back here and flog it.'

He painted word pictures as picturesque and vivid as a postcard. Camellia saw them both in a little Arabic house, perched on a hill looking out to a turquoise sea, eating juicy peaches, drinking iced lemon tea. Their friends would drop by to visit them on their way through to Marrakech, they would swim and sunbathe all day and never be cold again.

That night, when they made love, it was tender and sweet. It didn't matter that the gas fire didn't heat the room or that the shutters rattled in the wind. They had one another and soon they'd be looking back on this awful flat with laughter.

Middle-aged American men around Piccadilly became Camellia's main target during December. She learned to track them down in banks and busy stores before robbing them in a crowded street. She dressed for this very carefully, never wearing anything which would make people suspicious, her fur coat left open to reveal a low-necked tight minidress, her hair and make-up as carefully done as if she was on her way to a wedding.

To her, the way these men displayed their wealth was obscene. They deserved to be relieved of it.

'Excuse me, sir.' She would smile right into their eyes, leaning forward a little so they could see down into her cleavage. 'I'm afraid a bird's done his business on your hair.'

They always reacted the same way, a hand moving to their heads, their fat faces flushed with embarrassment, never for one moment suspecting the pretty girl with shining long hair and a tiny miniskirt was going to rob them.

'I'll clean it off for you,' she'd say, smiling understandingly. 'It's supposed to be lucky but it isn't very nice, is it?'

With a tissue in one hand she'd mop away at them, distracting them with her cleavage, long legs and friendly banter. It only took a second to get her hand inside the appropriate pocket, another to slip it into hers.

Sometimes they tried to date her, almost begging her to come for a drink. 'You are a real sweety,' was her stock answer. 'But I've got to meet my boy-friend. Another time perhaps.'

She was off into the crowd before they could draw breath, down into the underground toilets to count the notes and dispose of the evidence, then home to Dougie to while away the rest of the day smoking dope, listening to music, making love and basking in his admiration.

Early in 1968 Dougie came home one afternoon grinning from ear to ear.

Camellia was huddled over the gas fire, with a blanket round her. It was a little after four, but dark outside. She had closed the shutters hours ago to try and make the room warmer, but it did no good.

Dougie had been gone since ten that morning. His Afghan coat was covered with snow and it gleamed on his dark curls like a sprinkling of sequins.

'It's still snowing then?' she said, just for conversation. Dougie didn't like to be asked where he'd been.

'Yup, it's six inches in places,' he said cheerfully, putting his coat over the back of a chair and coming closer to the fire to warm his hands. 'You should see Hyde Park, it looks like a Christmas card.'

Camellia didn't really want any reminders of Christmas. Dougie hadn't been able to get any dope, either for himself to smoke or to sell, and he'd been like a bear with a sore head. Camellia had cooked a chicken and all the trimmings, but he'd found fault with everything.

'How would you like a night in a posh hotel?' he asked. 'Long hot baths, loads of food and booze?'

'I'd die for it,' she said. In fact she would settle just for getting into bed.

'Well, princess, your wish is granted.' He made a low bow and kissed her feet. 'This Saturday, and get some kinky undies to please me.'

He said he wanted to take her for a long weekend to Brighton, but he was afraid the trains would be cancelled because of the snow. But as Camellia had never stayed in any hotel, not since she was a kid and came to London with her mother, she was just thrilled to be going somewhere smart.

*

'It's going to be like a fantasy,' he grinned as they chose underwear from a shop in Shaftesbury Avenue. 'I want you to make out you're a tart I've just picked up on the streets and I'll give you the time of your life.'

It was just after eight when they got out of the taxi in Upper Berkeley Street. It had stopped snowing two days before and the roads had been cleared, but there was still a great deal on roofs, trees and walls. The George Hotel looked wonderfully inviting, golden light spilling out of the half-glazed doors down white marble steps.

Camellia was wearing her white fur coat, and beneath it a tight red dress, black stockings and high heels.

She was glad Dougie seemed so confident. Just walking into the plush foyer with a uniformed doorman and a smart blonde receptionist behind the desk made her blush. But Dougie announced himself as Mr Green and signed the register as if he'd spent his life in such places.

'From now on you've got to play the game,' he said as they got in the lift.

Dougie had given her some speed just an hour before but it wasn't until they got into the room that she noticed how stoned she was.

The warmth and luxury wrapped round her like a blanket. The big bed was turned down in readiness for them, and the heavy brocade curtains, soft cream carpet and beautiful bathroom beyond made her feel like a film star. There was champagne in an ice bucket and a basket of fruit, and when Dougie switched on some soft music, Camellia felt herself being carried into the fantasy.

'Let me take your coat,' Dougie said, just like a gentleman. As he slipped it off her shoulders he bent to kiss her neck. 'Now some champagne.'

Camellia tried out the bed as Dougie opened the

bottle. She felt like bouncing on it, but that wasn't in character for the fantasy. The black basque bought in Shaftesbury Avenue was tight and restrictive, but it made her feel deliciously naughty. She lay back on the bed seductively, propping herself up on one elbow, and pulled her skirt up so Dougie would just get a glimpse of stocking-tops. A long low mirror on the dressing table and another behind her above the bed gave her a perfect, all-round view of herself, something she never got at home.

She felt she'd never looked so sexy. Her red dress was dramatic, the basque pushing up her breasts so they almost spilled over the low neckline. With her long dark hair loose on her shoulders and false eyelashes enhancing her almond eyes, she could be a beauty queen, or at least a high-class call girl.

Dougie had never looked quite so cool before either. In a new red velvet jacket, a frilly shirt and black tight trousers, his hair freshly washed and tied back in a ponytail, he made her think of cardsharps on Mississippi river boats.

'Come and sit on my lap,' he suggested, passing her a glass of champagne. 'Let's get to know one another a little better.' Camellia was only too pleased to do so. She kicked off her shoes, took a sip of her drink, giggled as the bubbles went up her nose, then wiggled her way over to where he sat in an armchair.

'You're very beautiful.' He stroked her hair, then ran one finger lightly round her lips as if it was their first date. 'Can I kiss you?'

This was the kind of fantasy that really got her going. Dougie smelled beautiful, he had shaved carefully and the drink was going straight to her head.

He kissed her the way he had on their first night together, so tenderly she was reassured he really loved her. If she wanted him to do this more often she would have to make the night memorable for him too.

Standing up, she turned the music up just a little louder and started to dance. Dougie smiled up at her, his eyes said he adored her. She was good at dancing and the soft lights, the deep pile beneath her feet made her feel wanton and abandoned.

Swaying her hips she teased him, slowly reaching behind her to unzip her dress and let it slide down her body to reveal the basque, stockings and those wicked flame-red, crutchless panties.

A glimpse of herself in the mirror brought a rush of excitement. The exposed breasts, the white of her thighs between the black basque and the stockings, and the mound of dark hair peeping through the panties made her think of photographs she'd seen in Soho bookshop windows. She was the favourite girl in a harem, brought on for her master's delight. Tonight she would do everything he'd ever dreamed of.

She opened her legs wider, lowered her hand to her vagina and parted her lips, gasping more at her own audacity than with passion.

'More,' Dougie urged her. 'More!'

He was always trying to make her masturbate in front of him, but until now she had always been too embarrassed. But it was as if she was someone else tonight. It was watching him that got her really excited. His eyes were glowing, lips red and moist, every now and then his tongue flickering across them. She put her fingers right into herself, groaning with pleasure and when Dougie moved from his seat to lift her up in his arms, she slid one into his mouth.

'Delicious,' he whispered as he laid her down on the bed. He didn't seem to notice they were facing the wrong way, but then it hardly mattered to her either.

The speed slowed things down, yet heightened the sensations. Each kiss was longer and deeper, as he stroked her thighs, her arms and back so lingeringly every nerve-ending responded. He moved one of the spotlights on the bed so it played right onto her open legs and pointed out her reflection in the mirror above the bed.

'Watch yourself come,' he whispered, thrusting his fingers into her already wet and ripe fanny. She had no need to fantasise about anything now to heighten the sensation. Just the sight of Dougie's pointed red tongue moving down to lick her, her nipples like two big raspberries sticking out above the black satin, the suspenders, stocking-tops and the opulence of the room was enough. Dougie was licking at her like a man possessed, still fully dressed.

'I want to suck you,' she commanded him, fumbling for the zip on his trousers. 'Now.'

Dougie peeled off his clothes slowly, pausing every now and then to touch her again or to bend and kiss her. He was wearing new tiny black underpants and his bulge looked enormous.

Camellia knelt beside him on the bed, stroking the bulge through his pants, holding his balls with the other hand. He was groaning, resting back on his elbows, watching her as his penis rose out of the pants, purple tipped and shiny. Wriggling down she lay beside him, taking one of his hands to her, while she closed her mouth round him and sucked.

She had never liked doing this before, but now his pleasure came before hers. Again and again she ran her tongue the length of him, then back to take it in her mouth. She liked his quietness – no crude words, just soft moans, his fingers burrowing into her like she was the most special thing in the whole world.

Camellia was on fire. Time and time again Dougie brought her to the edge of a climax, only to stop and change position; from behind like a dog, his fingers massaging her clitoris, then turning her over and bending her legs up above her shoulders and leaning over to bite and suck at her breasts.

'Make me come,' she kept calling out. 'Please, please.'

'Not until I do,' he grinned lasciviously, ramming fingers into her, turning round to make her suck him again and reciprocating with his tongue on her.

They moved from bed to chair, sideways, front ways and from the back. She felt as if she were in the middle of a whirlpool, being sucked in deeper and deeper. Her hair was damp with sweat. Rivulets ran down between her breasts and thighs making the basque stick to her. Still Dougie showed no sign of weakening.

When he turned over on his back for a moment, Camellia leapt astride him, impaling herself on his penis, dragging her nails down his chest.

'Fuck me,' she screamed at him. 'Harder!'

She came just moments before he did, riding up and down on him till she finally exploded inside. He rolled her over and with a few more long, hard strokes he was finally done.

Camellia was too exhausted to move. Her eyes wandered weakly to the clock and she saw it was after twelve. They had been making love for four hours.

'How was that?' Dougie whispered, pulling the sheets up over her.

'Wonderful, amazing,' she whispered back, reaching out to hold him.

'I'll just go and get us a drink,' he said. 'Won't be long, then we can cuddle all night.'

She was too drowsy to protest. She saw him pull on his trousers, heard the click of the door opening and her eyes drooped.

A faint knock opened them again, just seconds later. She lifted her head thinking someone had tapped on their door. Instead she saw Dougie had left it open.

From out in the corridor she heard him speak.

Suddenly she was wide awake. Earlier today he had said something about calling room service if they wanted a drink or food. Why hadn't he used the telephone? Wrapping a sheet round her she stumbled towards the door. She could hear another man's voice.

As she reached the door she strained her ears. What she heard Dougie say made her gasp in horror.

'Good performance, eh? Was she good or what?'

For a moment Camellia was frozen to the spot. A sick feeling washed over her. She looked back to the bed. Dougie had dimmed the lights over it as he left the room and she could barely see her reflection in the mirror above the headboard now.

A two-way mirror!

She didn't want to believe it, but it was the only explanation. He hadn't intended this to be a wonderful night of love, a taster of the kind of glamorous life he wanted to lead with her. It was a set-up!

Standing there by the open door she shook with rage. She wanted to burst into that room next door and cause a scene, but even in her anger she knew that could be dangerous. Turning away, she went into the bathroom, shutting the door behind her and locking it. There was only one mirror in here, above the basin, but as a precaution she hung a towel over it, stinging with humiliation.

Tears wouldn't come, she was beyond that. This was betrayal of the worst kind, treating her like a peep-show for a couple of perverts. She recalled every movement, every word she'd called out and the more she remembered, the more shame she felt. What would he do next? Hire her out to a friend for money? Stand by and watch another man make love to her?

She was in the bath when Dougie returned, the hot water right up to her neck.

'What you doing, babe?' he called out. 'I thought you'd be asleep!'

It was all Camellia could do not to roar out her anger at him. He had been gone almost half an hour. She imagined him drinking with these men, laughing and bragging at how much he turned women on. He was despicable, but she'd fix him this time.

Camellia got out of the bath and put on one of the thick towelling dressing gowns left behind the door. Her hair was wet, hanging like seaweed on her shoulders, her scrubbed face showing how young she really was.

Dougie was sitting on the bed. On the bedside table was a plate of ham sandwiches and two glasses of coke.

'Put something over that mirror,' Camellia said quietly. 'They've had their money's worth.'

The shock on his face was almost laughable. His mouth fell open, his eyes bulged right out of his head. 'You knew?' he gasped.

'Of course I did.' She made herself sit down and calmly pick up a sandwich. 'You don't think I'd bother to put on a performance like that for nothing do you?'

138

'But, how?' he started, his voice quivering and tailing off.

Inside she was quivering too. The pain was almost unbearable, but she knew the only way to get her revenge was to hit him where it hurt, right in his manhood.

'How much did we get?' she asked.

He had turned pale now, and a tick in his cheek was twitching. That always happened when he was scared.

'Fifty quid and expenses,' he said weakly.

'Well, you'd better give me half now,' she said curtly, holding out her hand.

She waited just long enough for him to count out her twenty-five pounds, then she reached out and took another ten from his hands.

'The underwear was part of the expenses,' she said crisply. 'I paid for those.' She turned away. 'Now ring room service and order a couple of Bacardi's to go with the coke. I'm just going to dry my hair.'

She came back into the room ten minutes later, feeling steadier. 'I was going to keep the money for Morocco,' he said. He didn't look like Errol Flynn now, but like any other unwashed hippie, with tangled hair, a faint hint of bristle on his chin and his pupils dilated by the speed he'd taken. She could see weakness in those full lips and sense the black hole where his heart should be.

'I'd rather spend mine on a new pair of boots,' she yawned and climbed into bed, flicking out the light. 'The bathroom's lovely, all pink and cream tiles with smelly things to put in it. I wonder what we get for breakfast?'

There was silence for a few moments, Camellia could feel his discomfort. He was brooding about his prowess now, perhaps wondering if she always put on an act in bed.

'I wish you'd told me you knew,' Dougie's whisper came through the darkness. 'You were so wonderful I forgot all about them, now I feel kind of empty.'

'It's about time you woke up to the fact I'm pretty smart,' she said. 'Don't ever take me for a prat again, Dougie, or I'll walk out on you. I went through this tonight to teach you a lesson. Just remember it.'

'I do love you,' he said fiercely, pulling her into his arms. 'When I said we were meant for one another it was true. I couldn't live without you.'

Camellia lay awake long after Dougie had fallen asleep. She had thought until now that all her old wounds were healed, but she could feel them breaking open again.

She felt just the way she did that day in the changing rooms at school, a hateful memory that she'd believed had been permanently erased from her mind. She was in her PE skirt and blouse, covered in mud from the hockey field and the games mistress had set one of the prefects on the door to make sure no one avoided taking a shower.

All the other girls were stripping off, shouting to each other, laughing and joking as they revealed pretty bras and pants, then all at once Margaret Davenport, a girl with a figure like a beauty queen but the nature of a wasp, spotted Camellia lurking in the corner trying very hard to become invisible.

'Get your clothes off, Camel,' she shouted. 'I can smell you from here.'

Twenty girls all stopped what they were doing at Margaret's shout, and the atmosphere in the changing room seemed to drop ten degrees instantly.

'Yeah, get them off!' someone else shouted and suddenly Camellia was surrounded. Mean faces leered at her, they began to chant 'get them off' viciously and hands reached out to pull her PE kit off her.

She slapped out at the hands, but there were too many of them. Someone tore away her skirt and the sight of her big flabby thighs prompted hysterical laughter.

Camellia had never known such terror. They weren't just girls any longer, but a braying mob. She was trapped in the middle of them, some trying to pull her shirt over the head, others dragging on the elastic of her pants.

'Fat Camel, fat Camel,' they chanted as they pulled her to the floor and wrenched off her shirt and underwear. As she lay there, desperately trying to cover her nakedness with her hands, sobbing with shame, her underwear was first examined, laughed at, then held aloft like flags of victory.

That ordeal had ended with the intervention of a teacher, but the degradation of it remained. She felt tonight's events would join it.

The next morning, as more snow fell outside, Camellia found the hurt was soothed by loving attention from Dougie and by the splendour of the room. He had breakfast sent up and fed her pieces of toast dipped in egg yolk, then rolled another joint and they made sweet, gentle love with the mirror firmly covered. It was a taste of all the good things in life, a bath together, the luxury of soft, hot towels and knowing they had more than enough money to go out later and eat somewhere smart.

Dougie opened up enough to admit the night had been set up by the head porter.

'The mirror wasn't put there for kinky purposes,' he explained as if it made a difference. 'Apparently this room was once part of a suite used for business. He found it one day during spring cleaning and since then it's been a good little earner for him.'

'Have you ever brought another girl here?' she asked.

'I haven't performed myself,' he grinned. 'But I have been a go-between before.'

Now the air was clearer Camellia felt a little easier. She would never forgive him entirely, but she'd learned something from the experience. She must assert herself more, stand up to him and even learn from him. She wasn't going to be a victim.

'This is what I want forever,' she said, stretching luxuriously, unashamedly naked in front of the window. 'If you won't get it for me, I'll find someone who will.'

'I never put you down as a gold-digger,' he laughed, sitting cross-legged and naked on the bed, his hair damply curling round his face like a King Charles spaniel.

'I come from a long line of them,' she grinned. 'You should have seen my mother in action.'

Suddenly she found herself talking about Bonny, laughing at remembered incidents. Dougie was interested now, laughing with her, and she felt it might prove to be a turning point in their relationship.

'Once she had a bloke who took her to a posh place in Brighton for the weekend,' Camellia said, a little surprised to find herself identifying with her mother, when once the tale had shocked her. 'They had a fight about something, probably because he wouldn't leave his wife, and he stormed off, leaving her alone in the room. Guess what she did to teach him a lesson?'

'Laid in wait to cut off his prick?' Dougie winced.

'No, nothing so barbaric. She nicked the towels, the bathrobes, even the bedspread and she put a pair of her knickers into his suit pocket and cleared off home. Not because she wanted the stuff, just to embarrass him. I bet he never left another woman alone in a hotel again.'

'So that's why you managed to act so cool last night?' Dougie looked at Camellia thoughtfully. Until last night he hadn't realised how much she had changed – she had grown harder, kind of ruthless. He wasn't sure that he liked it.

'I had good training,' she said defiantly. 'I'm growing more like Mum each day.'

Chapter Seven

'Fucking hell!' Dougie leapt out of bed, waking Camellia with a start.

'What is it?' she said sleepily. Even as she spoke, she heard heavy feet tramping up the bare wooden stairs towards them.

It was November, eleven months since the night at the George Hotel. Despite all Dougie's promises they were still living in the flat in Nottingham Court. Mr Tharrup still ogled Camellia and tried to grope her when the opportunity arose. Camellia still dipped pockets and shoplifted.

Dougie pulled back the heavy wooden shutters from the window before she could even lift her head off the pillow.

'Who is it?' she whispered. 'Why are you opening the shutters?'

'It's the pigs, stupid,' he hissed back. The light through the window was enough for her to see him pulling on his clothes at breakneck speed. 'I'm off. Don't open the door. Let them ram it in to give me time to get away. Tell them I went out some time after ten. They can't have been watching the house otherwise they'd have busted me earlier.'

Camellia's mind was reeling with questions, but Dougie put a finger to her lips and motioned for her to be silent. The heavy feet had now reached the landing outside their door.

'I'll be in touch as soon as it's safe,' he whispered, shoving his arms into his embroidered Afghan coat. 'Shut the window and lock the shutters behind me. Do it quietly so they don't twig. For fuck's sake give me time to get clear.'

At the first heavy knock on the door, Dougie snatched a duffel bag from under the bed, slung it round his shoulder and lifted open the window. He was onto the sill with the silent agility of a cat.

'See you soon,' he whispered as he dropped down onto the roof below. 'Lock it up and keep cool.'

Camellia saw him briefly silhouetted on the frost-covered rooftop, long slender legs straddling the apex, dark hair flowing out over his coat, hand raised in farewell. Then he was gone.

The banging grew louder at the door. 'Police, open up!'

In a flash Camellia had the window closed and the shutters locked and was back in bed, pulling the covers over her head. But her heart was pounding like a steam-hammer and she quivered with fear.

'Remember what he said,' she whispered as the banging grew louder still. 'Keep cool.'

A crash of a heavy boot against the door and the wood splintered. Another crash and the door just caved in, the steel bar clonking to the floor. As she peeped from beneath the covers, two bright beams of light shone into the room.

When they switched on the overhead light, Camellia made herself scream and sit up, clutching the blankets over her naked breasts. The light made her blink. It was easy to act shocked: she was.

Four uniformed policemen, truncheons in their hands, poured into the flat.

'Where is he?' One of them advanced on her.

Camellia backed up against the headboard, whimpering with terror. 'Who?' She curled her arm round her head, for one moment imagining they would actually beat her.

'Douglas Green, who else,' he snapped back, his big teeth yellow in the dim light from the Chinese lantern.

'He hasn't come home yet,' she stammered. 'Why? What's he done?'

The police were everywhere, all at once, rummaging around, turning out drawers, while the more senior one who barked out that he was Inspector Spencer tackled Camellia.

'Don't play the little innocent with me, girl,' he roared at her. 'We know he came back here, we saw him come in at half nine.'

'But he went out again later,' she said, guessing it had taken all this time to get a search warrant. She made a great play of reaching over for her clock. 'Goodness me! Is it really three o'clock? I was asleep till you came crashing in.'

She was terrified now. The expression 'losing your bottle' that Dougie used so often suddenly had real meaning. She wanted to go to the toilet so badly she was afraid she might just do it in the bed.

One policeman was pulling books off the shelves, scattering ornaments, packets of joss sticks and a collection of shells to the floor.

'What's your name?' Spencer barked at her again, daring her to lie to him.

'Camellia Norton,' she whimpered, tears welling up in her eyes. 'What's Dougie done?'

A sixth sense told her this was more than an ordinary drugs bust. Something had been up with Dougie yesterday.

He'd been pacing around the room, chain smoking and refusing to eat. He'd said a deal had gone wrong, but that could have meant anything.

'Three kids in hospital. That's what.' Spencer pulled her forward by the shoulder, ripping the pillows out behind her. 'By now they may all be dead and if you've got any sense you'll tell us where Green is.'

Camellia felt as if her blood had suddenly frozen. 'But what's that got to do with Dougie?' She forced herself to look stupid. 'He can't help three kids being in hospital!'

'Get up.' The policeman rolled his eyes with impatience.

'But I've got nothing on.'

'I've seen plenty of tarts with nothing on in my time,' he sneered. He snatched up a handful of clothes on a chair and threw them to her. 'Get those on, before I drag you out.'

The other policeman came back into the room as she buttoned up a shirt.

'He didn't go that way,' one of the younger men gestured towards the kitchen and bathroom. 'There's bars on the window. I found a substance in the fridge though.'

If things hadn't been so serious Camellia would have laughed. The window was the most obvious escape route, yet not one of them had thought to open the shutters. They'd be well brought down when they analysed the stuff in the bottle and discovered it was cough mixture!

Finally the youngest man, with pale gingery hair and eyelashes to match, made his way over to the shutters, barely glancing at her as she tried to wriggle into her knickers under the covers. He was so ham-fisted he couldn't even unlock the catch.

'I doubt he went out that way,' one of the others said. 'We'd have heard him.'

The young one got the window open eventually and peered out, shining a torch. 'It's a long drop,' he said. 'Should I check it out?'

'I told you he left through the door,' Camellia managed a token of defiance. She swung her legs over the side of the bed and stood up, reaching for her jeans. 'If you listened to what I said instead of hassling me, you might learn something.'

'Don't get lippy with me, girl,' the inspector snarled at her. 'And cover yourself up!'

Dougie had dropped the fifteen or so feet to the roof below without a sound, but the young constable was like an elephant. He lowered himself awkwardly over the windowsill, then dropped down like a ton of bricks, smashing something en route.

'Christ Almighty,' Camellia heard him say, his voice muffled. 'I've torn my strides.'

Over two hours later they finally took her down to West Central Police Station in Bow Street. She sat shivering on a stool while they turned out every drawer and cupboard, groped down the side of chairs, turned the mattress upside down, and tipped out packets of sugar and cornflakes to check there was nothing inside.

The most incriminating things they found were a few packets of red Rizla and the cardboard roach of an old joint in a wastepaper bin.

Inspector Spencer kept on asking her where Dougie kept his stuff.

'What stuff?' She kept up the display of complete ignorance. 'What are you looking for?'

She had to hand it to Dougie, he knew how to keep his drugs in order. All those times she'd laughed at him for being so careful to place everything in one box right by the bed. Now she understood why. He must have snatched it up the moment he heard the heavy feet.

When the policeman moved the rug by the window and found the loose floorboard, she had felt sick. Nausea quickly turned to anger when she discovered this hiding place was empty too. Their bank book, Dougie's passport and the wad of notes he'd put in there only days before were gone. Dougie must have expected a raid, yet he hadn't taken her into his confidence.

Back in the flat it had been comparatively easy to portray herself as a naïve yet somewhat rebellious teenager, but once in the station with the grim-faced Inspector Spencer questioning her, she found it far harder.

'Let me spell it out to you,' he said. The hanging flesh under his eyes and the slack, wet mouth reminded her of a bloodhound she'd seen once. 'Your boyfriend is not only a drug dealer, he's little better than a murderer. Not content with making money bending kids' minds, he had to make more by cutting this LSD with a poison. Suppose it was your friend lying there in agony on a hospital bed, vomiting up blood! How would you feel?'

It horrified Camellia to think of anyone in such a state, whether they were related to her or not. But as Spencer continued, he told her about other things Dougie had been involved in: burglaries in Essex where dogs had been thrown poisoned meat to silence them permanently; two old age pensioners in Islington who'd been robbed at knife point, then tied up while he ransacked their house.

'I didn't know,' she cried. This time she was speaking the truth. 'He never told me anything. I can't believe he was that wicked.'

The saddest thing was that in her heart of hearts she knew he was capable of all of it. He had no conscience and no respect for anyone. For most of the year he'd been out alone a great deal, and he'd become very secretive. It all added up.

'How old are you, Camellia?' The inspector put his hand on her shoulder, in an almost fatherly gesture.

'Eighteen. Nineteen in a few weeks,' she whispered.

'And your parents, where do they live?'

'They're both dead,' she replied.

She saw a momentary flash of sympathy in his eyes. But his next remark made her blush with shame.

'If I was to discover my daughter was living with a man like Douglas Green, I think it would break my heart,' he said. 'You couldn't have picked a worse man, Camellia, he's lower than a maggot.'

'But he wasn't bad to me,' she said, so scared now she could almost hear prison gates shutting on her too. 'He looked after me when I hadn't got anyone else.'

They left her alone for some time and she guessed they were checking up on her background. She hated to think they might speak to Sergeant Bert Simmonds in Rye. He would be so disappointed that she'd got herself into trouble.

But apart from the shame she felt, there was also the fear that they would discover she was a thief.

Supposing the security men at Fenwicks identified her as the girl who fainted in their store at approximately the same time four valuable furs were swiped from under their noses? Were there reports on file of a girl dipping into tourists' pockets around Piccadilly? So many people could tell the police that she was always with Dougie when he was out selling drugs in clubs and bars.

As the hours ticked by in the interview room, fright was replaced by despair. She wanted to cry. She'd spent eighteen months loving Dougie blindly, following his lead as if she had no mind of her own.

How often had she heard him justify selling drugs by saying 'If they don't get them from me it will be someone else'. He'd made her believe drugs were as essential to people's happiness as sunshine and love. And somehow she'd come to think shoplifting and pickpocketing weren't crimes, but a bit of a lark, a redistribution of wealth.

But it *was* wrong. She saw that now. By aiding and abetting Dougie she'd made him even worse. She should have got out after that night in the Mayfair hotel, when his real nature was revealed. Why hadn't she?

It wasn't even as if she'd been having fun with Dougie. All the drugs dried up for a time in February, and he'd begun to get morose and violent back then, yet she still foolishly thought she could handle him. No cannabis was coming through and the police found one acid laboratory after another. The Middle Earth was busted on three successive weekends and under threat of permanent closure.

Dougie got scared when plain-clothes policemen began mingling with the hippies around Soho, picking off the dealers one by one. Shoplifting had been almost a game until then, a 'V' sign to the capitalists. Now it became a livelihood and Dougie made her take bigger and bigger risks. 'Just till we've got enough money to split,' he would say. 'We'll take off to Morocco and live like spaced-out kings.'

But where was he when the store detective chased her up Kensington High Street? Would he have cared if she was caught dipping tourists' pockets? Where was he now with all that money she'd helped him make?

'Did Dougie give you that bruise on your arm?' the woman police officer left sitting with her in the interview room asked. They had already checked her for needle marks and found nothing, but clearly this fresh-faced blonde hoped sympathy would encourage Camellia to tell them everything she knew.

'No,' Camellia lied. 'I fell on the stairs a couple of days ago.'

'It looks like fingermarks to me.' The policewoman got up from her seat and came closer, cupping Camellia's chin and lifting her face so she could look right into her eyes. 'How did an intelligent pretty girl like you get mixed up with someone like him?'

Camellia wanted to blurt it all out. Being Dougie's girl was like being Queen of Soho. She was pointed out, looked-up to. Could someone who'd never experienced being a reject, possibly understand how that felt? She wanted to sob out that he needed her. Deep down, she knew that she endured being hit and sworn at because she felt that was what she deserved.

Even his old friends had urged her to leave him in the past few months. But how could she leave a man who shook so badly that sometimes he couldn't hold a cup or shave himself? His paranoia, his nightmares, all convinced her it was her duty to stand by him.

'I was just a kid up from Sussex with no family. He was so handsome and he knew everyone,' Camellia said at last, hoping this woman would understand. 'He looked after me. He made me feel I was somebody.'

The policewoman shook her head, an expression of bewilderment on her plump youthful face. 'But surely you must have guessed he was involved in something shady once you were living with him?' She ran her fingers through short blonde hair. 'Didn't you wonder where his money came from?'

'He told me he was a partner in the printers under his flat.' Camellia whispered the lie she had invented in readiness for this occasion. 'I thought he made deals for them. Mr Tharrup didn't charge us rent, so it seemed plausible.'

In all the time Camellia had known Dougie, the belief that he needed her and in his own way loved her was like a guiding star. She had been convinced that once they were away together, seeing the world, he would change for the better.

But now as she sat in this bare, brightly lit interview room, without anything to distract her from the truth, she saw things as they really were.

Dougie had never ached to see the Taj Mahal, or Niagara Falls. He didn't want the comfort and security of a nice home. All he wanted was to be stoned constantly, to live in a twilight world of idleness. The only reason he suggested India or Morocco was because drugs were readily available there and his money would last longer. Now faced with the organised way he had made his departure, making sure he had his drugs and money, but leaving her behind to take the flak, she couldn't even hang on to the idea that he needed her.

Inspector Spencer came back into the interview room a couple of hours later and patted her on the shoulder waking her from an exhausted sleep. 'I'm going to let you go,' he said.

'Go?' She stared at him stupidly.

'We'll get Green, I have no doubt about that.' His voice was low and stern. 'But I'm just as convinced that he won't come back for you.'

Camellia knew it too. Dougie was probably halfway to Amsterdam by now.

'But the kids in hospital?' she asked. 'How are they?'

'Fortunately for them, recovering,' he said icily.

Camellia felt a surge of relief and stood up.

'There's just a few things I want to point out,' he

said, his eyes like flint. 'I know perfectly well that you aren't as innocent as you would like me to believe. But unless I'm very badly mistaken, the events of tonight have shaken you up enough for you to take stock of your life.'

Camellia nodded. She couldn't trust herself to speak.

'I'll be watching.' He waved a warning finger at her. 'If I get so much of a whisper that you're up to your old tricks again, I'll come down on you so hard you'll regret it for the rest of your life.'

He knew everything. Camellia could see it in his face. She hadn't fooled him for one minute.

'That slum of a flat will be boarded up by tonight,' he went on. 'A WPC will go with you now to get your things. Take a word of advice from me, Camellia. Find yourself a decent job, make something of yourself. Don't ever make me regret my lenience with you.'

There was more shame as the policewoman watched her pack her clothes. No one would have believed that Camellia had once kept the flat clean and tidy. Now after the raid it looked like a derelict building a few tramps had slept in. The big settee stripped of its bright Indian bedspread had stuffing oozing out of it. The mattress had huge brown stains, the shower Dougie took such pride in building was just an old cracked sink embedded in cement. In a few weeks' time even the daisies she'd stencilled on the walls in the kitchen would be crumbling away with damp.

'Where will you go, Camellia?'

Camellia looked up from her packing at the question. The day before she would have been insolent, but she was beyond that now. The policewoman's plump face held real concern.

'I'm not quite sure right now,' she said honestly.

'I think I might move right out of London. But I need time to get my head together.'

As Camellia fastened the first suitcase she felt the bump in the lid-pocket made by her mother's file of old letters. Her entire life had been shaped by lies.

'Have you got any money?'

This time the question was almost maternal. Camellia saw the woman's hand move towards her pocket in a humanitarian gesture. Not all police were bastards, as Dougie had taught her, there was Bert Simmonds and now this one.

'Enough till I get a job.' Pride was all she had left, she couldn't take a handout. 'I'll manage.'

'Good luck then.' The policewoman held out her hand when Camellia was finished, her grey-blue eyes gentle now. 'Don't be too hard on yourself Camellia.'

It was only later in a café in Charing Cross Road that the full implications hit her. She was homeless, jobless and apart from about two pounds in her purse, broke and alone.

It was ten in the morning, a cold, dark, grey day. She needed to wash and clean her teeth, even her hair was tangled. She looked like a tramp. If only she hadn't left Archway House so hastily she might have been able to fall back on Miss Peet. But that was out of the question, so were Suzanne and Carol as she hadn't once tried to contact them before. What on earth was she going to do?

She cupped her cold hands round the cup of coffee to warm them, wondering if she dared spend a little of her money on a bacon sandwich. The only two other customers left, a blast of more cold air coming in as they opened the door.

'What's up?' A voice made her look up. It was the fat blonde waitress Dougie called 'Cream Puff', but her bright blue eyes were kindly.

'A touch of the blues.' Camellia tried to smile but her lips quivered.

The girl cleared the table where the two men had been and stacked the plates on the counter. She was wearing a tight blue nylon overall and where her black slip ended beneath it a bulge of fat quivered. She turned back to Camellia and asked if she could join her.

Camellia nodded.

'Dougie done a bunk?' The girl slid into the seat opposite and pulled a pack of cigarettes out of her overall pocket, taking one herself and offering one to Camellia.

For a moment Camellia was so surprised she could only stare at the plump pink and white face in front of her, framed by a mop of blonde frizzy hair. 'You know Dougie?'

The girl sniggered. 'Everyone knows Dougie Green.'

'Has he been in this morning?' Camellia's heart leapt for a moment.

The girl shook her head and lit both their cigarettes.

'Camellia, isn't it?' she said. 'I've often heard him call you it. It's a lovely name.'

Camellia didn't feel there was anything lovely about herself right now. 'I prefer Mel, especially when I look as rough as I do now,' she said. 'What's yours?'

'I've got a posh one too,' the girl laughed. 'It's Beatrice, would you believe. But I'd rather be called Bee. Now what's up? And what's with the suitcases?'

Camellia wanted to invent something, but she guessed by lunchtime the whole of Soho would know the truth anyway.

'We got busted,' she blurted out. 'Dougie got away. I've been at the nick all night.'

156

Bee didn't turn a hair. 'I can't say I'm surprised. I've been hearing whispers about Dougie for weeks, and all of them nasty ones. He's a louse to let you carry the can. Did they charge you with anything?'

Camellia was wary. Most of the girls she knew in the West End thrived on others' misfortunes. She couldn't think of anyone who wouldn't be gloating once this got out. She so wanted to pour it all out to this friendly waitress in the absence of anyone she knew better. But somehow it brought home to her just how friendless she was and she began to cry.

'Come on, love, it can't be that bad.' Bee put her hand over Camellia's. 'It's only a fine for possession. Is that what they charged you with or are you upset because Doug did a runner?'

Camellia had to talk, even at the risk of it all being repeated and embellished later. She told everything, encouraged by the kindly hand on hers.

Bee was a good listener, only stopping Camellia now and again to clarify a point. The nickname, Cream Puff, Dougie had given her was apt. The blonde curls, the sweet, pretty face and her plumpness were reminiscent of cream oozing out of a sweet, sticky bun. But there was something more to her than being a sympathetic ear, something Camellia identified with, yet couldn't put her finger on.

'I suppose you think I'm an idiot for trusting him?' Camellia said as she finished.

Bee shrugged her shoulders and dragged on her cigarette. 'I expect I would have too,' she said. 'But good-looking blokes like Dougie don't bother with girls like me, that's about the only advantage there is to being fat.'

The honesty in the remark jarred Camellia. She had once made such disparaging remarks about herself. 'But you've got a beautiful face,' she said. It

157

was true: Bee's face was lovely, kind of angelic with baby-soft lips that curved sweetly into a warm smile and dimples in both cheeks. 'You can lose weight, but I don't think you ever lose the label of being a mug.'

'Does it matter if wasters call you a mug?' Bee looked round towards the door, checking there were no customers about to come in, then sank back into the seat. 'I wouldn't lose any sleep about the opinions of Dougie's cronies. If I was you, I'd be thinking about making a new start.'

'Easier said than done,' Camellia tried to smile. 'How do you get a job when you can't explain what you've done for a year and a half?'

'There's one going here.' Bee drew deeply on her cigarette. 'The owners don't look too closely. I could say you'd been working abroad or something.'

A few weeks earlier Camellia would have laughed at the idea of making sandwiches and cooking egg and chips, but she was desperate now. 'Really? They'd take me on?'

The Black and White was close to being the seediest of the West End's cafés. Its black and white decor was a product of the late fifties contemporary style with spindly-legged tables and chairs. All the white was now yellow and much of the plastic padding along the counter and on the seats was cracked open. But it had a reputation for good cheap food and it was usually busy.

'Don't look so thrilled,' Bee chuckled, her double chin quivering. 'It's bloody hard work in the lunch hour, but the money's not bad and you get your food thrown in. I'll have to ask the boss when he phones later, but I could say you were just helping out as a casual until he gets a chance to see how you shape up.'

It was like being thrown a lifeline. 'Okay,'

Camellia smiled weakly. 'You're a life-saver. All I need now is somewhere to crash, I don't suppose you've got any bright ideas about that?'

For a moment Bee didn't reply. Camellia could almost see the girl wondering if she'd landed herself with a liability.

'You can kip down with me upstairs for a day or two,' she sighed as if she felt compelled to make the offer. 'But only a day or two, that's all.'

'I don't want to lumber you.' Camellia was embarrassed that the girl might think she was being railroaded. 'I appreciate your kindness. I'm not like Dougie. I won't take advantage.'

'You won't think I'm kind when you see the room,' Bee laughed, but her cheeks turned bright pink as if embarrassed. 'It's a slum. I only offered 'cos I can see you're breaking up inside. Besides, I get a bit lonely.'

At seven that same evening, once the café closed, Bee helped Camellia carry her suitcases up to her room on the first floor. Even though Camellia had been warned about it and was grateful for a bed anywhere, she was still shocked.

Clothes lay everywhere, and there were dirty dishes on the floor, some with half-eaten food congealed to them. Every drawer hung open; even the single bed was unmade. There were attempts at making it home: a few pop star posters, a green plant in the window and fluffy rug by the bed. But it looked what it was, a place a lonely teenage girl crawled into at night, a place that saw no visitors. It was almost as sad as the flat Camellia had vacated earlier in the day.

Below in Charing Cross Road the traffic roared incessantly. The smell of fried food trapped in the small grubby room made her feel slightly nauseous and she was swaying on her feet with exhaustion.

Her feet were sore, her hands reddened with washing dishes. She had never worked so hard, not even in the sales at Peter Robinson's.

'I'm a slob, aren't I?' Bee said cheerfully. 'I did intend to nip up here and clear it up before you saw it but there wasn't time. Still you'd soon find out about my slutty ways. Better to face it immediately.'

Camellia liked the fact that Bee didn't put on a false front. Neither, Camellia realised, did she sit in judgement on anyone. Bee probably knew and understood the West End better than she did. She'd worked in the café for four years, and although she was only a few months older than Camellia, she knew all the thieves, prostitutes, pimps, and drug dealers, along with club owners and businessmen. She talked to them, heard all their gossip, yet remained aloof.

'I don't care what it looks like,' Camellia said. 'While I'm here I'll help both downstairs and up here. I'm just grateful for a roof over my head and a job.'

'You're an odd bird,' Bee said reflectively. 'I got the idea when you used to come in with Dougie that you were a spoiled rich kid, know what I mean?'

Camellia sniggered. 'I could tell you some stories about me and my mother that would soon scotch that idea,' she said. 'But we've talked about me and my problems all day nearly. Tell me about your dreams and hopes?'

'The past is pretty shitty,' Bee admitted, but then laughed as if she intended to turn it into pantomime anyway. 'As for the hopes and dreams, well they're all about getting out of this hell-hole.' She found a tray, scooped the pile of dirty crockery from Camellia's hands and dumped them on it, then whisked it out the door.

She returned in just a few minutes and began to pick up clothes. 'All I really want is a nice flat and a job where I don't eat all day and stink of chips. I don't think much about knights on white chargers, or men festooning my fat neck with diamonds. Know what my favourite fantasy is?'

'A librarian who'll woo you with poetry?' Camellia joked.

'It isn't even a man. It's a room that's all white, with sun pouring in the windows and a single vase of daffodils on a polished wood table.'

Camellia didn't say anything for a moment. She was stunned not only by the simplicity of the fantasy, but her affinity with it.

Later as they curled up together on the bed with a cup of coffee each, Bee told Camellia her story, and as she listened Camellia felt she'd found more than a new friend, but a soul mate.

Bee was an only child. Her father had been a colour-sergeant in the army and her childhood had been spent in many different countries, including several years in Singapore. Until she was twelve and her father left the service she'd thought all children lived the way she did.

Her father was engrossed in his job, her mother in the army social life. There was a maid who saw to Bee's meals and cleaned the house.

'It was great,' she smiled. 'Mum was always off playing tennis or at whist-drives, there were loads of other kids to play with. The army organised everything, schools, housing, the lot. Dad was always strict, but then I hardly saw him or Mum really. It was only when they bought the house in Eltham and Dad went to work for the post office that I discovered what the real world was like.'

From twelve onwards Bee's life took a dramatic downward turn. She found it hard to adjust to a big

London comprehensive school, and she was bullied both there and at home. 'I didn't understand why my Mum suddenly became a ratbag when Dad left the army. She'd always been so elegant and cool, and suddenly she was in a tizz about everything. She never stopped moaning from morning till night. She couldn't cope with the simplest things like doing the washing or cooking. Then Dad came home from work and had a go at both of us.'

Camellia's heart went out to Bee as she heard more. A father, who after a lifetime of bullying men, started taking out his frustrations on his wife and daughter. A spoiled weak mother who resented having her life of ease snatched from her. A couple so wrapped up in their own selfishness and disappointment that they rounded on their only child and used her as a scapegoat for their own inadequacies.

'It was hell,' Bee said, tears springing to her eyes as she remembered. 'Mum expected me to do just about everything, as well as go to school and cope with homework. I'd never learned to cook, or wash clothes and of course I made a mess of it. Mum would scream at me, then tell Dad what I'd done when he got home. He thrashed me so often I could barely sit down. I was jeered at at school, I was tubby even then and I spoke differently. I got behind with my work and they stuck me in a dumbo's class. That made Dad even madder. I felt so alone, Camellia, can you understand that?'

'Oh yes,' Camellia sighed. 'I used to hope I'd get seriously ill just so someone would look after me.'

'I found out how to get attention when I was fourteen,' Bee admitted. She smiled, but there was a bleak look in her eyes. 'I started going with men. Not boys, they didn't fancy me because I was fat, but I used to let the man in the sweet shop near our house grope me in his stock-room.'

She made the story funny, describing him as a weasel. But Camellia couldn't laugh: the man sounded like the worst kind of pervert. Bee would go into his shop after school, still wearing her uniform and the Weasel would make her open her blouse and take off her knickers and get her to pose for him while he masturbated.

'He gave me ten shillings each time,' she said. 'He used to call me "his princess". But even though it was seedy and I knew I should be ashamed of myself, at least he really liked me, he used to talk to me afterwards and give me a cuddle.'

She went on to playing truant from school to spend the day with a travelling salesman she'd met in a café, or for sex in the afternoons with a milkman whose wife was out at work.

'I wasn't allowed out at night, not even to a youth club. I had no friends. So I turned to sex,' she said candidly, turning bright blue eyes on Camellia with such honesty it made her giggle. 'I used to seriously think about becoming a call girl when I left school. It was the only thing I was good at.'

'Did you run away from home then?'

'I didn't run. I limped away after Dad gave me a pasting. The milkman's wife found out about me, and confronted my parents with it. All hell broke loose then. Dad cracked two of my ribs, then flung me out.'

'How old were you?'

'Fifteen,' Bee shrugged. 'How could anyone throw a girl of that age out the house knowing she had no money or anywhere to go? I got the train up West and I ended up here in the café. I was in a terrible state, black eyes, the lot. I ended up telling Cyril the café owner all about it, just like you did to me. He offered me a job and a room on a trial basis until I got on my feet, and I never left.'

'Have you seen your parents since?'

'No,' Bee's eyes fell. 'I did write to Mum once. I tried to explain how I felt, but she never answered it. She sends me a Christmas card each year, but there's never a letter. I'm over them now anyway. I just don't care any more.'

Camellia suspected this was the first lie she'd heard all day. Someone as warm as Bee couldn't possibly not care about her parents, even if they were awful to her.

'Do you – well you know, with Cyril?'

Bee burst into laughter. 'Hell no,' she said quivering like a blancmange. 'He's a good man, and a straight one, happily married with five kids. If I'd let him into my drawers his wife would've had me in the bacon slicer without a second thought. I was just so grateful for being given a chance and treated like a human being, I've worked like a slave for him ever since. But gratitude runs its course in three years. I want something better now.'

When they undressed later for bed, Camellia saw why men would be drawn to Bee. Naked she was voluptuous rather than fat, her flesh silky and firm like the women in Rubens' paintings. The combination of her angelic face, fluffy blonde hair and such bountiful curves was womanly and very sexy.

Even though Camellia was exhausted, she lay awake in the sleeping bag long after Bee had fallen asleep in her bed. Anger at Dougie had replaced the smarting pain she felt earlier in the day and with it came the need for revenge.

'I'll show him,' she told herself. 'One day he'll come back to London and I'll have it all. I'll cut him dead and walk away and he'll regret everything.'

On 6 January, the girls paid off a taxi at 14 Oakley Street in Chelsea and, in fits of high-spirited giggles, proceeded to carry their belongings down the steps to the basement flat.

It was a raw, grey day, the wind coming right off the Thames with an icy force that lifted their coats and blew their hair every which way.

'This is the moment.' Bee put down the last of the boxes and cases outside, blew a trumpet like fanfare on her fist, then took out the key, waving it in front of Camellia. 'Now which of us is going to carry the other over the threshold.'

'Well, I'm not carrying you,' Camellia retorted. 'Let's just go in together!'

They had left the café for good. Just seven long weeks since the day they had met, they had the flat of their dreams.

It had come about from Bee overhearing a conversation between two men in the café. One was the tenant of this flat, tied by a long lease, and he wanted to get out of it quickly because he'd been offered a job abroad by the other man.

They were discussing putting an advertisement in the evening paper. As Bee listened she heard the tenant say he wouldn't ask for much key money as that would make it quicker.

Camellia had known Bee for less than a fortnight at that point and she'd already been surprised at how quick on the uptake the other girl was. But the speed she acted on that overheard conversation was phenomenal. Somehow Bee managed to approach the man, admit she'd been listening and ask him if she could have the flat. Within half an hour the man had agreed to let her have it for two hundred pounds, providing she could supply the right references to his landlords.

When Bee announced what she had done and admitted she had only ten pounds in the bank, Camellia thought she was crazy. She could see the attraction of it: the rent of the place was only ten pounds a week, and it had two bedrooms and central heating.

'But how on earth are we going to get two hundred pounds by the beginning of January?' she had asked, feeling almost faint at the thought.

But Bee had that worked out too. 'We'll get jobs as hostesses in a club,' she said. 'I know it will be hard, but we can make it. I know the right man to ask for a job. He fancies me and you'll blow his mind.'

Camellia had always assumed nightclub hostesses were really prostitutes, and said so.

'They aren't,' Bee said emphatically. 'They are just there to get men to drink more and they get ten pounds a night. It will be a doddle. It's coming up for Christmas. Every bloke stuck in London will be happy to hand over a few quid to drink with us. All we have to do is look pretty and make them feel important.'

There were setbacks: they didn't have the right kind of flashy dresses and it was a shock to discover they actually had to ask the customers for their ten-pound hostess fee. But they found a compromise. Camellia stole the dresses from a shop in Regent Street and Bee, who didn't find it so embarrassing to ask for money, asked Camellia's clients for her.

They were soon to discover it wasn't quite as much fun as they expected. The male customers were usually middle-aged and dull, and it was exhausting working all day in the café, then having to get dolled up to spend half the night, chatting brightly, dancing and encouraging businessmen to drink. They fell into bed at three or four in the morning, only to be up by eight and start all over again. But they stuck at it. They wanted the flat too badly to care about being tired.

Now they'd left the café they intended to continue as hostesses until something better turned up. As Bee had said at the outset, it was one of the easiest jobs going.

'How did you get the money for the legal fees,' Camellia asked as they swept into the flat arm-in-arm. They hadn't expected to have to pay a solicitor, and had been horrified when he asked for twenty-five pounds. Bee had said she'd see to it but until now Camellia hadn't got around to asking how.

'Don't ask,' Bee laughed, tossing back her hair and running around the empty lounge like a child.

Camellia looked at Bee sharply. She could guess how. Bee had gone out one Sunday night with a man she met in the club and she hadn't come back until Monday morning.

'Well don't ask how I got this then.' Camellia pulled a roll of notes from her pocket and tossed them to her friend. 'But it's just as well we were both naughty as there aren't any beds!'

Bee stopped in her tracks as she caught the money. She leafed through it and frowned. They had both confided all their past misdemeanours to one another. But Camellia had promised never to pick another pocket or steal clothes, and Bee had promised never to take money for sex.

'That drunk American when we left the club last night?' Her expression was a mixture of admiration and fear. 'You nicked his wallet while he was trying to chat you up?'

Camellia nodded. 'He was too far gone to remember what day of the week it was. Serves him right for letching after young girls.'

'But there's almost two hundred pounds!'

'I hit the jackpot,' Camellia giggled. 'All right I know what you're thinking. I promise I won't do it again! As long as you don't go swanning off to any hotel rooms either.'

Everything was forgotten as they explored the flat.

'Isn't it just perfect?' Bee ran from room to room, opening gleaming white doors and touching windows. 'A bedroom each, a proper lounge where we can entertain.' She raised one eyebrow at Camellia.

'It's heaven.' Camellia sat down on the carpeted floor and pulled out her cigarettes. 'He's even left the curtains and cooker, bless him.'

Despite the grey January day outside, the white-washed wall in the small yard beneath the street reflected light into the big windows of the lounge. A smart grey carpet covered all the floors, all the walls were painted white, and there were fitted wardrobes. All it needed to make it homely was a bit of furniture and some pictures on the plain walls.

'Ten measly quid a week!' Bee flung herself down on the floor by Camellia. 'Can you imagine saying to a taxi driver, "Oakley Street, Chelsea, by the river". They'll think we're bleedin' heiresses!'

'Shall we go and find some second-hand beds?' Camellia grinned. 'And a polished wood table to put your vase of daffodils on?'

Bee's eyes welled-up with happy tears. She'd forgotten she'd told Camellia that dream. She couldn't begin to say how much it meant to her to have a real friend, a home and a new start. But then she was sure Camellia felt exactly the same way. 'With two hundred quid in the kitty we can have the table, daffodils, beds, and some booze to celebrate.' She reached out impulsively to hug her friend. 'But first let's get my record player plugged in, then it really will be home.'

Chapter Eight

'We should get proper jobs.' Camellia's voice held little conviction. She lay back on the settee, dragging deeply on a large joint.

'Such as?' Bee asked from her position on the floor.

'I don't know,' Camellia let the inhaled smoke out slowly through her nose. 'Lavatory attendants?'

The girls had been living in Oakley Street, Chelsea for nearly eleven months. Bee had had her twentieth birthday that autumn, and Camellia's would be next month, just before Christmas.

Outside in the street it was cold and dark, even though it was only four in the afternoon. A strong wind was blowing leaves, bus tickets and sweet wrappers down into the basement area outside their front door, but inside it was snug. The central heating was on, Bobbie Gentry's hit single 'I'll Never Fall in Love Again' was on the record player and they were preparing for the night ahead.

Bee sat on a floor cushion, propped against the settee, wearing a fluffy pink dressing gown, rollers in her hair, flapping her nails as she waited for the shocking-pink varnish to dry. Camellia, still in jeans and a red jumper, was waiting for the water to heat again for her bath.

'I always fancied being a lavatory attendant when I was a kid.' Bee hugged her bare knees with her arms. 'I could see myself in one of those crossover pinnys, a little room of my own with a fire, a comfy chair and a couple of geraniums in pots, just nipping out now and then to check no one had laid a huge turd and forgotten to flush it.'

'But what if they'd laid it on the floor,' Camellia grimaced as she exhaled.

'I'd get a gadget made to scoop it up at arm's length!' Bee laughed, looking round at her friend lying behind her. 'Stop hogging that joint, I've hardly had any of it.'

Camellia passed it over, then lay back again, hands tucked behind her head, singing along with the record. They had only bought it yesterday and they'd played it incessantly.

Every month or so since they moved into the flat, they discussed the need to get real jobs, but they rarely got beyond opening an evening paper and ringing round a few vacancies. Aside from their lack of qualifications and the fact that they could only expect to earn around sixteen pounds a week in a regular job, compared with ten pounds a night at the Don Juan Club, they were trapped by the ease of their lives.

They were so happy in Oakley Street. Having a real home of their own had given them both the feeling of security they needed. Each piece of furniture had been chosen with care, haggled over in the second-hand shops in Portobello Road and transported home with pride. The green velvet Chesterfield Camellia lay on was the most expensive item, but they'd knocked the trader down to thirty-five pounds. The round Victorian supper table by the window had been a real bargain at ten pounds. It was badly scratched, but they'd found a man who did French polishing to restore it for the price of a couple of drinks.

There was little else of any real value. The wall

unit which housed the stereo was cheap wood and badly scarred but the damage was hidden by books and bric-à-brac. Camellia had re-covered the two odd easy chairs with remnants of jazzy materials. Studious studying of glossy magazines had been the inspiration behind a huge arrangement of beech leaves in a terracotta vase, a pile of yellow and green striped gourds in a basket and a collection of abstract posters in brilliant primary colours.

They rarely got up before noon. In hot weather they sunbathed in parks during the afternoon, went shopping or just lay around indoors when the weather was bad. Then off to the club in the evening. They had more than enough money to buy clothes, eat well and pay the bills. But now with Christmas just around the corner, Camellia's conscience was prickling yet again.

It wasn't so much the moral issue of whether it was ethical to earn a living by dolling themselves up and demanding a fee for keeping a man company while encouraging him to buy exorbitantly priced drinks. It was more that Camellia sensed the bubble had to burst one day. When it did, they might just be on the wrong side of the law. She never wanted to see Inspector Spencer or the inside of a police station again.

'What are you wearing tonight?' Bee's voice penetrated Camellia's train of thought.

'My red velvet.' Camellia was only too glad to be distracted. 'I always get someone tasty when I wear that.'

'Only because it hardly covers your bum,' Bee sniggered, wrapping her pink dressing gown more firmly round her. 'I think I'll wear my black one. With my tits and your legs on display, the other girls won't get a look in.'

They had been lured away from the Top Hat Club in Soho to the Don Juan in Mayfair back in

February. The Don Juan had a far more wealthy and prestigious clientele. In Soho, the men that used the club were invariably only in London for one night, and with no experience of club life they tended to think that the girls' hostess fee should include sex, particularly once they'd parted with twenty or thirty pounds for a few drinks.

The Don Juan was far more sophisticated. Its elegant black and chrome decor, young and attractive hostesses and less exorbitantly priced drinks meant wealthy businessmen returned again and again without ever expecting more.

A year of happiness and close friendship had brought changes to both girls, but the physical effects were far more noticeable in Bee. She had lost a stone in weight and tamed her frizzy hair into gleaming golden waves. Although still plumper than was fashionable she'd learned to buy well-cut clothes that distracted eyes away from her big bottom and thick legs towards her magnificent breasts and pretty face. The punters at the club fell over themselves to spend the evening with her. She was a heady mixture of child and sensual woman with her pink and white complexion, wide blue eyes, innocent mouth and her voluptuous curves. She liked men and they felt it. She made them laugh, flirted and teased, but she cared for them too. One regular customer called her 'His glass of champagne' and claimed he felt high just looking at her.

The changes in Camellia were more subtle. She was glossy now, as perfectly dressed as a mannequin, chic rather than outrageous. Her dark hair was longer, reaching her shoulder blades, washed daily and trimmed regularly. She had mastered make-up so men were fooled into thinking there was none.

She had true confidence now. Her body could

stand close inspection: her legs were long and slender and when she walked in a room full of men she sensed the rise in temperature and she liked it. Alone at home with Bee she was Mel, baring her soul, enjoying girlish giggling and silliness. But at the club she was Camellia, a little haughty, cool and controlled.

'Shall we go on to that party if we can get away from the club in time?' Camellia hauled herself up off the couch to run her bath. 'It might be a giggle.'

'Is it really our scene though?' Bee began to take her rollers out, dropping them on the floor beside her. 'I mean they're a bit heavy, aren't they?'

'We can handle them,' Camellia smiled. She liked men who were challenging, and Aiden Murphy was certainly that.

They had met Aiden and John in Finch's, their local, a fortnight earlier. Bee described them as 'heavy', merely because they had plenty of money to splash around, yet neither man would say what exactly he did for a living. Camellia didn't care much: she fancied Aiden, the irreverent, blue-eyed, black-haired Irishman, and just thinking about him made her stomach jolt.

They had been standing at the bar waiting to be served when they heard a man speak behind them. 'What'll you have, girls?' His musical Irish brogue made them both turn in surprise.

The man was well over six foot, with thick black hair and bright, inquisitive blue eyes, maybe thirty-two or three. The broad shoulders and healthy glow suggested he worked outdoors, yet his expensive hand-tailored grey suit could hardly belong to a navvy.

Camellia was thrown by his looks for a moment. A man as good-looking as this one was rare anywhere, but especially in Finch's where the men tended to be dropouts of one sort or another. She just stared at his laughing eyes and white teeth in surprise.

'So what's it to be?' he said, one bushy dark brow raised quizzically. 'You'll need an anaesthetic if I'm going to fuck you tonight.'

His approach was crude, yet it was original and very funny. In the circles she and Bee moved in, men rarely made them laugh.

Aiden's side-kick was John Everton. Next to Aiden he was ordinary, perhaps five-eight and slender, his fair hair unfashionably short. He was a wiry man whose bony, raw face somehow reflected his upbringing on a Fulham council estate. Later that night she and Bee nicknamed him the 'Day-time Cowboy' because of his studded Levi jacket and carefully pressed jeans. Yet even though he didn't share Aiden's quick repartee or his sharp mind, he had a courteous, gentlemanly quality.

The girls had intended to go to work that night, but the men bought them so many drinks they never made it. Later they all went to the Village Club in King's Road and stayed till it closed.

'I can't fuck you tonight,' Aiden said to Camellia as they got out onto the street at three in the morning. 'But would you like a glimpse of the purple death?'

Camellia was very drunk, holding onto lamp-posts for support. When he opened his fly and produced his huge, flaccid penis, she laughed so much she got a stitch.

'You won't be laughing, m'girl, when I use it on you,' he said, dark blue eyes full of merriment. 'When he grows to his full size he'll come up the back of your throat to be sure!'

It was the fun of that evening which stuck in both the girls' minds. These two men had danced, clowned, laughed and talked. They had alluded to sex countless times during the night, yet hadn't begun to try to get the girls into bed. They were aggressively masculine, and that came as a welcome change to the namby-pamby arty types in Chelsea and the fat cats with posh voices and soft hands at the club.

Since then the girls had been back to Finch's on several occasions, but neither man had been there. They had just about given them up for good when they got home a few days ago to find a note stuck through the door.

'Come to a party on Saturday night,' was all it said, with an address in South Kensington and a couple of pin-men drawings that could only be of Aiden and John.

Life in Oakley Street was never dull. Everything, from going to the Launderette to a drink before work was an opportunity for adventure. Chelsea was the epicentre of 'Swinging London': boutiques full of wild clothes, wine bars, clubs and pubs overflowing with young people. The tourists went to Carnaby Street, but the King's Road was for the more 'switched-on'. Pop stars bought flats and houses there; Sloaney debutantes, ex-public school boys, aristocracy and models rubbed shoulders with Cockney nouveaux riches. That year, 1969, saw Neil Armstrong become the first man to step on the moon, but to the young it would be remembered for the free pop concerts in Hyde Park and, across the Atlantic, the Woodstock Festival. The catch phrase 'free love' was on everyone's lips. The wide use of the contraceptive pill might have made sex safer, but it was the widespread intake of marijuana which led to real permissiveness.

At work in the club the girls portrayed themselves as a couple of sophisticates, with glitzy, slinky long dresses and diamanté or cocktail-style minis. They flirted, flattered, danced and fluttered false eyelashes, yet always went home alone.

But in Chelsea, on their home ground, they were out for fun and dressed outrageously, in everything from Chelsea market antique dresses, to revealing crocheted minis, flared loons and diaphanous voile shirts. Here they selected their partners not by the amount of money in their pockets, but by their play value. Men who got serious were soon abandoned. Time was too short for complicated, long-term relationships.

They rarely discussed their pasts now. Their friendship was based on knowing everything about each other and loving one another because of it. Each new experience tightened the bond between them. They shared everything: food, clothes, records, and sometimes even men. Camellia cleaned, and Bee cooked. They were all the family they wanted or needed.

'Join me for a late supper?' Duncan, a big Scot, covered Camellia's hand with his, his pale-brown eyes huge behind thick glasses.

It was sometime after twelve and Camellia had been keeping an eye on the time all evening as she entertained this businessman. Bee had already packed off her partner and was waiting at the bar. She kept looking across to Camellia. It was time she wound up the evening if they were to get to the party before it was over.

'I'd love to, but I can't.' Camellia returned the squeeze of Duncan's hand. 'I've got to drive down to Sussex now, my grandmother's ill.'

If it wasn't for the party she might have been tempted by Duncan's offer. He was nice – a real gentleman, even if he was close to forty.

'You've been such good company,' he smiled, his

full mouth very appealing. 'I hope I haven't bored you, going on about my family.'

'Not at all, Duncan.' Just this once she was entirely sincere; the time had flown talking to him. 'Your wife's a lucky lady.'

He got up with her, towering over her as he bent down to brush her cheek with his lips. 'Goodnight Camellia. Maybe next time I come to London?'

Camellia joined Bee at the bar for a quick, real drink before they left.

'What was old four-eyes going on about?' Bee asked.

The club was quieter than normal for a Saturday night. A quartet was playing gentle old standards while a few couples shuffled around on the minute dance floor. Four other hostesses were still working, encouraging their partners to drink, tucked away in the more intimate, black and cream plush booths.

'I want to marry someone like that one day,' Camellia said wistfully, looking back towards the door which was still swinging from his departure. 'And don't take the piss, he was lovely.'

'More than mine was then.' Bee looked gloomily into her glass. 'He was a fucking rep, chronic halitosis and terminally boring.'

'The night is still young.' Camellia brightened up as the large vodka slipped down her throat. She was ready now for a party. 'I hope you've got your best knickers on?'

'I'll probably take them off the minute I meet someone tasty,' Bee grinned, downing the last of her drink in one gulp. 'I've been so randy all night I expect I'd even have let that boring bastard grope me if his breath hadn't been so bad.'

Camellia smiled. Bee needed sex like Camellia needed fresh air and sunshine.

It was freezing and foggy outside in the street.

Camellia hugged her white rabbit maxicoat tightly round her as they ran down towards Oxford Street for a cab. She had bought it to replace the one Dougie had stolen for her, then sold when they were short of cash. This one was far nicer though, it had cost almost a hundred pounds, and she felt it was worth every penny. All men raved about a glimpse of long slender leg under a full-length fur and just putting it on made her feel sexy.

'Suppose they've got a couple of girls already?' Bee said as they got into a taxi. She took a mirror out of her handbag, put on a thick coat of fresh glossy lipstick, and ran a comb through her blonde waves. Then opening her coat she sprayed Je Revien down into her cleavage.

'Then we make sure they drop them,' Camellia replied confidently. She knew she looked good tonight. With her short red velvet dress, knee-length platform boots and the coat, how could Aiden resist her?

They heard the party even before they got out of the cab in Brompton Road. The Beatles' 'Why Don't We Do It in the Road' was blaring out at full volume.

Bee looked up at the house in approval as Camellia paid the driver.

Number 241 was smarter than most of the others in the long terrace. Its railings, doors and windows were freshly painted, the stone work recently cleaned. An uncurtained window on the first floor had fairy lights all round it and they could see silhouettes of dancers.

'It's looking good,' Bee remarked, sliding her hands under her coat and hitching up her black sheer tights.

The front door was open. As they walked up the

stairs to the first floor, a cacophony of music, laughter and revelry wafted down to them.

'Should we have brought a bottle?' Bee asked as they approached the polished wood door.

'Sounds like they've got plenty.' Camellia bounded ahead, reaching behind her to drag her less enthusiastic friend up a little quicker.

The smell of amylnitrate made them gasp as they walked in on the party. A man was in the process of inhaling it just inside the door. They paused in fascination, watching his face turn almost purple, veins leaping out of his forehead, then almost immediately he was normal again.

'A two-second hit,' he said, blue eyes bleary and unfocused, shaking the broken glass vial into a waste bin. 'But then you're supposed to snort it at the point of orgasm.'

The girls were no strangers to wild parties, but this one was beyond anything they'd seen before. They lingered in the small hallway looking into the softly lit, crowded main room, glancing a little apprehensively at each other.

The guests were two entirely different breeds: one group predominantly male Arabs, in sober dark suits, all over forty; the rest a mishmash of weird characters who looked as if they'd been picked up in one of London's sleazier pubs.

Two girls, no older than sixteen, were doing some sort of nymphet dance wearing nothing but skin-coloured body stockings, waving green chiffon scarves in their hands. Another girl was standing by a wall, topless, her partner chatting to her as if she were fully dressed. A pretty-looking young man wearing only pink paisley loons, was kissing another male in full view of everyone. Hard-faced brassy women danced with long-haired hippies half their age. A Jimi Hendrix lookalike played an 'air' guitar in the corner.

'I don't think this is our scene,' Camellia said, backing towards the door. She didn't mind the eccentricity. It was the Arabs she feared. They stood in small groups watching the proceedings with dark, brooding eyes, almost as if it was a cabaret.

'Hullo me darlings,' Aiden's voice made Camellia's pulse quicken, even before he pushed himself through the crowd to greet them. 'I'd given up on you. What kept you?'

'Work,' Camellia grinned at him. He looked like the Martini man in a dark suit, white shirt and a dickey bow. 'We're not sure this is really for us!'

'To be sure it is, or my name's not Aiden Murphy, party-giver to the stars,' he grinned. He put an arm round each girl, drawing them close to him so he could whisper in their ears. 'The flat belongs to the towel-head over there.' He nodded his head towards the only man in Arabic robes. 'Obas is a prince with pots of money.'

'Oh yeah?' Bee said sullenly, yet Camellia saw a sparkle of interest in her eyes as she noted this man's comparative youth, his aquiline nose and sensuous full lips.

' 'Tis true,' Aiden gave her bottom a playful smack. 'And didn't he just tell me he adores blondes with big tits!'

Closer inspection of the flat suggested it was a pied-à-terre, rather than anyone's home. Even in the dim light they could tell that the high-ceilinged lounge would be elegant when empty of all these strange people. Blue silky curtains with tasselled pelmets hung at the vast windows, though no one had bothered to draw them and the large semi-circular settees were just a shade darker. Camellia wondered if the central chandelier was real, or plastic – with the light switched off it was hard to tell. A professional-looking sound system, complete with strobe lights was operated by another wild-looking hippie, his bare chest festooned with beads.

'The prince must be pretty desperate for company to mix with people like this,' Camellia whispered to Aiden. 'They look like renta-crowd waiting for the pay-off!'

Even as she spoke she saw she had inadvertently stumbled on the truth. The sober-looking men were all Obas's friends, the strange people invited purely as a floorshow. Aiden had engineered the whole thing!

'Now will ye stop being a pair of Jonahs,' Aiden said, leading them towards the kitchen which was divided from the lounge by reeded glass doors, before they ran out on him. 'And get some grog into yous.'

On one side of the long narrow kitchen a bar was set up, complete with spirits, mixers and a huge silver punch-bowl. On the other side was food: houmous, pitta bread, and great salvers of savoury rice and kebabs. The girls hadn't expected much in the way of food and the sight of it weakened their resistance.

'Are you expecting us to perform in some way?' Camellia asked, helping herself to a large glass of punch and taking a kebab in the other hand.

Aiden didn't reply. He leaned back on a split-level cooker with his arms folded, a wide naughty grin showing brilliant white teeth.

'What would you like?' Camellia went on. Wicked men always made her feel more wanton. 'For us to seduce a couple of Arabs on the floor? To have sex with a donkey?'

'Seumus, the man with the donkey, let me down tonight,' Aiden retorted. 'But will ye take a look at the cucumber in the fridge and try it for size?'

Both girls began to laugh, and as the first glass of

the rum-laced punch went down, they relaxed enough to forget leaving.

'Take off your coats,' Aiden said, his hands lingering on Camellia's fur. He leaned close to her ear to whisper, 'I'll have you dressed in that alone later tonight. But for now let me put it where no one else can steal it.'

The girls went back into the lounge with their drinks to look at the other guests. It was all so bizarre. There weren't nearly enough women to go round, but the ones present were unforgettable. A statuesque brunette in a lace minidress that revealed more than it covered moved around kissing men indiscriminately. Another pint-sized redhead with flowered loons and a matching brief top wriggled her abdomen as she danced alone. There were some older hard-eyed women who she suspected were prostitutes, brought down by Aiden from Soho for a busman's holiday.

'Look what's going on in there,' Bee squeaked, pointing towards the open bedroom door.

Camellia's eyes nearly jumped out of her head and she looked away in embarrassment. Two couples were making love on a huge bed. There was no doubt in her mind that they were getting an even bigger thrill from it by knowing they had an audience.

'You have to hand it to Aiden,' Bee gasped. 'This party is like your wildest dreams. I bet those Arabs can't believe what they're seeing.'

Everyone was smoking dope. A hookah stood on a low table surrounded by several of the sloe-eyed Arabs. The two homosexuals paused in their dancing to snort coke, using rolled twenty-pound notes.

'Would you like some?' Aiden appeared at Camellia's elbow as Bee went off to investigate what was happening in the kitchen.

'Why not,' she smiled up at him. 'Everyone else seems to be doing it.'

She had tried it before, but not in the quantity Aiden used. He scooped out the white powder with a tiny silver spoon and laid it on a small mirror.

'Where's the twenty-pound note?' she asked.

'No need to be ostentatious,' he laughed. 'I never was one for overdoing things.'

The coke froze her nose and made her eyes water. Aiden took out a handkerchief from his pocket and gently wiped them dry.

'Let's dance?' he suggested. 'I've done my work for the night and been richly rewarded. Now I want a girl in me arms.'

The music was less frantic now, moving on from the Rolling Stones, Cream and Hendrix, to the Beatles and Bob Dylan. Bee was talking to Obas, sitting on one of the settees.

Dancing with Aiden's arms around her, Camellia was now more amused than alarmed by the decadent atmosphere. Some of the tarts had gone into the bedroom with the Arabs. She was glad she had Aiden for protection.

'Where's John?' Camellia asked a little later. She had spotted one of the hard-looking women looking balefully at Bee. She had a feeling it might be safer to get Bee away from Obas.

'Doing his knight on a white charger bit,' he said nonchalantly. 'Taking a bird home that was having a bad trip. He'll be there half the night looking after her, tomorrow she won't even want to know him.'

'Don't tell me you laced something with acid?'

He didn't have to answer: his expression said it all.

'That's really stupid,' she said angrily. She had never quite got over the thought of those kids who ended up in hospital because of Dougie. 'Suppose someone took it that couldn't handle it. What was it in anyway?'

'Turkish Delight,' he grinned, entirely untroubled by her horror. 'If she hadn't been such a pig she'd have been okay.'

'She might've overdosed!'

'It was too weak for that.' Aiden's eyes darkened. 'Look here, Camellia, every single person here tonight knows the score. They aren't doing anything they wouldn't do normally. The Arabs wanted to experience swinging London. I've got them stoned and supplied the cast. No one's being ripped off, everyone's enjoying themselves. I thought you and Bee were the kind of girls who'd enjoy watching it.'

Anger faded. Aiden was irresponsible and wicked, yet underneath it all Camellia had a feeling his intentions were almost honourable.

'You ought to be locked up,' she half-smiled.

'So I have been, frequently.' He kissed her nose tenderly. 'But I didn't invite you to be part of the shebang. I had other plans.'

'Such as?' She tilted her face up to his.

'A bit of lovin',' he said, running one finger down her cheek.

When Aiden disappeared later, Camellia felt absurdly sad. She'd really thought he intended to be with her tonight. She fortified herself with another large glass of punch and curled up in an armchair by the window.

Bee was sitting on a couch surrounded by Arabs, talking and flirting with them all. Obas kept touching her hair, her face, as if already deeply smitten by her.

The coke had made Camellia feel all-powerful, yet at the same time she had the sensation of being in a large glass bubble, detached, watching from a great distance.

To her left she could see right into the bedroom. A big, dark-haired girl was lying naked on the bed, her face concealed by a man's arse. She could see his testicles bobbing and the thrust of his buttocks. Another man was licking at the girl's fanny – a long red tongue darting in and out from a dark bushy beard – and he was masturbating himself as he licked. Above the sound of Joe Cocker singing 'Delta Lady', Camellia could hear the girl on the bed moaning.

She was neither shocked nor stimulated. She had the feeling that if she just blinked, the whole set would vanish.

A burst of laughter made her look round. To her surprise Bee was now devouring Obas. He lay back on the settee, Bee pressing him further back into the cushions, her mouth glued to his.

The ribald laughter came from one of Obas's henchman, and the object of his mirth was clearly Bee's bottom. Her black dress had ridden up, revealing minuscule black panties and tights. A big tear in the back seam showed a bubble of white flesh peeping through.

Camellia was suddenly jolted back into reality. She could sense a charge in the atmosphere. All the Arabs were looking intently at Bee; a couple of the older women were smirking malevolently. Even the two homosexuals looked round, their boyish faces hardening as they too sensed something.

Camellia thought for one moment. Bee would protest if she told her it was time they went. If she could just get her away from those men for a short while, maybe she could warn her that it was getting dangerous.

At least half the people had already gone. Perhaps twenty in all were left, at least ten of them in the bedroom. As Camellia got up, the front door opened and in came Aiden with John.

They paused, John frowning as he spotted Bee with Obas.

Camellia knew the men had come back for them, yet their arrogance irritated her slightly. She wanted Aiden, but she didn't intend to be walked over.

If the first opening chords of Wilson Pickett's 'Wait till the Midnight Hour' hadn't suddenly burst out, she might have allowed Aiden and John to rescue them. But she and Bee had invented a dance to the record one night when they were alone at home, and now the strong beat, the need to get Bee away from those men, and the desire to give everyone something to think about, made it irresistible.

She swayed to the beat as she made her way across the room, gave Aiden a flashing smile and pinched Bee's plump arm. 'They're playing our tune,' she said.

Whether Bee saw John in the doorway, or realised she was getting in deep water with Obas and the other men, Camellia couldn't tell, but she leapt to her feet, cottoning on immediately to what Camellia had in mind.

Pulling her dress down she patted Obas's head-dress and skipped away, leaving him looking startled.

'The whole bit?' Bee whispered, already gyrating her hips, running her fingers through her hair.

'Just like the rehearsal,' Camellia smiled wickedly.

They had devised and perfected this striptease dance at home with a great deal of giggling. But this time they gazed sombrely into each other's eyes as if they were in love, and danced so close together their breasts nearly touched, singing along with the record.

Like many plump girls Bee was a graceful dancer, light on her feet with the seductive charm of a belly-dancer, and Camellia had always put her ability to dance down to inherited talent from her mother. Slowly the men moved back; even the Arabs who'd gone into the bedroom came to the door to watch.

'Boots!' Camellia whispered. They had only done this in shoes and it was difficult to be seductive unzipping boots. But they managed it by perching on the arm of a couch each, lifting one leg at a time, then tossing the boots aside, towards the door that led to the bathroom.

Everyone was silent now as the pair moved together like one person, hands reaching out for each other, only to draw back. They lifted their dresses, enough to hook their fingers into their tights and slowly slide them down to their knees. It was a sticky moment as they balanced on one leg to remove the feet, but they managed to keep moving to the beat, and the tights landed by the boots.

A slow clapping began and now as they stood in bare feet they grew wilder, shaking their breasts, running fingers through their hair and revolving their hips. Camellia turned her back on Bee and let her unzip her dress, then turned back to let Bee do the same.

Now with dresses leaving their backs bare, the real show began, stroking each other, lowering one shoulder and kissing the flesh, then the other.

Camellia winked at Bee as they let the dresses fall to their waists, swaying their hips and gradually working the material down to drop on the floor, and kick them aside to their boots. They both wore black push-up bras and similar bikini briefs. Bee's blonde and Camellia's dark hair fused together as they embraced, aware every man in the room was watching.

The record was two thirds over, and they turned to each other, hips undulating, breast against breast as they reached up to unhook their bras, then turned back to back, holding their bras momentarily against them, strutting together towards the group of Arabs on the settee.

The clapping was getting stronger, the beat faster as they dropped their hands to expose their breasts. Obas's eyes nearly popped out of his head when he saw Bee's. A wild cheer broke out as each girl took her bra and waved it round her head.

Camellia could feel Aiden's eyes on her body and she performed just for him. Taking the bra between her legs she drew it back and forth, writhing on it, sighing with pleasure. Then dancing back to Bee they moved together, caressing one another's breasts, biting their lips so they wouldn't laugh.

The record was coming to an end. There was tension in the room as every man waited for them to remove their panties too, but they danced back towards the door which led to the bathroom and their clothes, turned and bent down to give one last view of their bottoms as the record ended.

'Let's go,' Camellia whispered as they faked a passionate kiss. 'They'll have us in the bedroom before long, shoving their dicks down our throats.'

Picking up their clothes they bolted through the door for the bathroom, as cheering, stamping feet and yelling broke out behind them.

As Camellia locked the door, Bee collapsed against the bath in laughter. 'We ought to ask if we could do it at the club,' she snorted, tears rolling down her face.

'We can't go back in there.' Camellia wanted to laugh herself but she was more than a little nervous now. 'Those guys you were with are too heavy. I hope Aiden and John will be standing by to rescue us. Hurry up and get your things on.'

As they zipped up their dresses a loud banging startled them.

'What's that?' Bee's eyes shot open.

Camellia listened carefully for just one second. She'd heard that kind of banging before and her stomach churned. They weren't in the flat yet, just at the outer door, but any minute they'd be in, rounding everyone up.

'It's the fucking fuzz,' she said, throwing Bee's boots to her. 'Get those on!'

'Oh shit,' Bee's face drained of colour. 'You mean a raid?'

Camellia was already moving to the window. Climbing up onto the washbasin she yanked the big sash window up, peering out into the darkness.

'There's a roof just below,' she whispered. 'It's about six feet down. Do you think you can make it?'

Bee's eyes were wide with fright, her mouth quivering. 'I don't know,' she whispered.

'You've got to. I'll go first,' Camellia was already up on the sill, pushing aside shaving tackle. 'I can catch you if you fall. Pull your skirt up higher!'

With one hand on a drainpipe the other on the windowsill Camellia slithered down, digging her boots into the brickwork, then dropped the last couple of feet, toppling as her feet hit uneven slates.

'Now you,' she called back, grabbing the drainpipe for support.

'Come out of there!' A voice roared the other side of the bathroom door. 'This is the police!'

'I'm just having a crap,' Bee called back sweetly, already astride the sill, her dress pulled up to her waist, plump thighs like sausages in the dim light.

'Hold onto the drainpipe like I did,' Camellia

whispered. 'That's right, now lower yourself to me.'

Camellia stopped her fall, clinging onto her. 'Now where?'

The light from the open window threw a brilliant shaft out onto the small roof, but left the gardens below in darkness. 'Over here.' Camellia took Bee's hand and they inched their way to one side to look down. A small patio lay beneath them. Adjoining the extension they stood on was an ornamental half-wall. Camellia scrambled down it, one ear cocked for the police coming through the bathroom door. She could hear muffled shouting immediately above them, and prayed silently that no one would catch them.

'Come on,' she whispered, as Bee climbed down. 'This way.'

Keeping in the shade of bushes, Camellia felt her way to the end of the garden. She hoped for a back gate onto an alley, but only the wall met her hands. It was around eight foot high, with no way out.

'Shit,' she hissed. 'We're bloody well trapped now.'

It was freezing, and all at once she remembered she'd left her coat in the lounge, with keys and money in the pockets.

Bee was shaking with fear, her teeth chattering. It was no time to tell her they would have to break into their flat.

'Another fine mess you got me into,' Camellia said, trying to make her laugh. 'Look I'll get up on the wall and take a recce.'

With the aid of an old lawn roller and a tree trunk, Camellia managed to climb up on top. There were perhaps ten gardens between them and the lights of Dovehouse Street to her left. As far as she could see the wall reached all the way along.

Sitting down on the wall she reached out for

Bee's hand. 'Feel with your hands,' she whispered. 'There's a brick sticking out you can get onto.'

Bee was hopeless at climbing, panting like an old woman with no co-ordination between hands and feet. Camellia practically hauled her up.

'I'm no good at this kind of thing,' Bee whimpered as at last she stood beside Camellia on the wall.

'It's okay.' Camellia took her hand to steady her. 'Turn sideways and just edge along. Don't try to rush it.'

It could only have taken minutes, but it felt like hours, creeping along with only the odd tree for support. Gusts of wind kept whipping their legs, threatening to blow them into the gardens below.

They were almost at the end of the row, streetlights beckoning them with friendly warmth, when they heard police crash through the bathroom door.

'Some've got out here,' a brusque voice shouted back and Camellia saw burly shoulders silhouetted against the bathroom light. There was no time now for hesitation. She peered down into the street, lay on her stomach and lowered herself, dropping the last three or four feet. 'Quick,' she hissed. 'They'll be round here any moment.'

Once on the pavement, they fled, running through the deserted streets blindly. Only when they burst out of a sidestreet into Fulham Road could they stop to draw breath.

'Look at your tights,' Bee panted.

Camellia looked down. She had torn both knees and blood was oozing out the hole in one. 'You don't look so hot yourself.' She stepped into a shop doorway, pulling up her skirt and wrenching the tights off to the point where they met her boots. 'The next problem is how we get in. My keys were in my coat pocket – and I suppose yours were in your bag?'

'Break a window?' Bee suggested.

They had run too hard to feel the cold now and they took the last lap of the way at a jog.

'Oh God, my coat!' Camellia stopped suddenly as they turned into Oakley Street.

'You can get another,' Bee said sympathetically. 'At least we're safe.'

'It's not the coat,' Camellia held her side, panting furiously. 'I've just remembered our address is in my wallet in the pocket. The police are bound to find it and come here.'

Bee's face blanched.

Camellia felt sick now. She had visions of them finding her name on record at Bow Street.

'Maybe we could say your coat and wallet were stolen a couple of days ago?' Bee said in desperation.

'But what about your bag?' Camellia's voice shook with fear. 'What are we going to say about that?'

Bee's face crumpled, tears welling up and dropping onto her cheeks. 'There's even a letter I wrote to my Mum!' she said. 'I changed my mind about posting it.'

'We'll just have to front it out.' Camellia put her arm round Bee and hugged her. 'Look we'll say we went earlier, but it was a bit kinky and we ran out leaving our stuff.'

'There's a bit of dope in my bag, too,' Bee whispered.

'Fucking hell,' Camellia exploded, grabbing her friend and frog marching her across the road. 'How many times have I told you not to take anything out with you. We'll have to get in now and check the whole flat. Put our nighties on and make as if we've been there for hours.'

They were shivering at their front door, trying to decide which pane of glass was the closest to the lock when they heard a car screech to a halt just above them in the road.

'Oh shit.' Camellia felt her insides turn to jelly. 'They're here already!'

Car doors slammed, followed by the sound of men's feet on the pavement. The two girls huddled together beneath the steps, hoping they wouldn't be spotted in the dark.

'Evening all!'

'Aiden.' Camellia breathed again. She couldn't see his face, but the voice was unmistakable.

John's white jeans appeared next to Aiden, his fair hair shining in the street lighting. 'I heard there was a party here,' he said.

It was then Camellia noticed John was holding something white over his arm. 'Is that my coat?' She wanted to laugh and cry all at once.

'Yours and Bee's,' John's gruff London voice had never sounded so wonderful. 'And Bee's bag. I checked it out and found two tampons, a lump of dope and some unidentified pills. What do we get for its safe return?'

'Anything,' the girls said in unison.

Once they were in, Camellia turned to Aiden. 'Coffee,' she asked. 'Then you can tell us how you escaped.'

'Coffee?' Aiden pulled a face. 'Show 'em what we drink, John!'

John pulled out a bottle of brandy from his coat. 'I nicked it.' He smiled shyly. 'While everyone was watching you two.'

Camellia took her coat and stroked it lovingly. 'Thanks Aiden, it would've broke my heart to lose this.'

'You can pay me back in kind,' he said, wide mouth curving into a delicious naughty smile. 'Me and John wouldn't say no to another show!'

'Bollocks,' Camellia grinned. 'We don't do en-
cores.'

'You two are full of surprises,' Aiden smiled,
sitting down and stretching out his legs while John
opened the bottle. 'Striptease, mountaineers, if
we'd come along any later I expect it would have
been breaking and entering too.'

'How did you get away?' Camellia giggled.
'Come on, tell us?'

'Well, we guessed you was planning to leg it,'
John grinned, his narrow face alight with pleasure.
'So we found your coats and Bee's bag over by the
window. I just happened to glance out and saw the
pigs arriving. We ducked out the front door and up
the stairs to the next flat.'

'Where I chatted up the young ladies to offer us
shelter,' Aiden smirked.

'He knew them already,' John looked sideways
at his friend with barely disguised pride.

'Anyway we heard the police rampaging down
the stairs and someone saying something about the
bathroom window. So we put two and two
together, got the girls to escort us down the stairs,
kissed them goodnight and here we are.'

'But what about all those other people?' Camellia
asked.

Aiden didn't look concerned. 'Down the nick by
now,' he said. 'And in court on Monday morning to
be sure. I dare say some of the towel-heads have
diplomatic immunity. They wanted a slice of
swinging London. I just gave them the whole cake.'

'That was without a doubt the best fuck ever!'

Camellia giggled at Aiden's deep brown Irish
voice and snuggled closer to him. 'I bet you say
that to everyone,' she said, biting his shoulder.

It was a week since the party. That night the four
of them had smoked dope, drunk brandy and

194

finally passed out. When Camellia woke later in the day she found herself on the couch tucked under a blanket, and Bee on cushions on the floor, equally well tucked-in. John and Aiden had gone.

All week Camellia had hoped Aiden would drop by, though Bee was less enthusiastic about seeing John. Then finally on Sunday afternoon just as she'd decided his interest in her was an illusion, he telephoned and asked if she would meet him for a drink that evening.

Bee had been quite relieved not to be included in a foursome and said she'd watch TV and go to bed early.

It was a wonderful evening. Aiden was a complete entertainment, mixing wild stories about his spell in the army and his time in prison, with gentle sweet ones about his large family in County Clare. He admitted having a wife, but avoided saying where home was. He was loyal enough to admit she was beautiful and long-suffering, laughingly calling her 'the shrew'. Whenever Camellia asked how he made a living his eyes twinkled and he invented something – anything from pimp to surgeon – but with enough conviction to make her believe he could in fact be anything he chose.

Camellia sensed that for all his charisma, he was a lonely man, disappointed by a cold, childless marriage which religion and upbringing prevented him from leaving.

He was even reluctant to make love, once they got back to the flat. He told her that he was forty, not the young man she'd supposed and asked if she was sure that was what she wanted.

But it was. Aiden fascinated her, bewitched her with his dark blue eyes, talk and ready laughter. From the first gentle kiss which expanded into wild passion the moment he crushed her into his arms, she knew there was no turning back.

Now he turned her face to his and kissed her on the nose. 'Sure I've said such things to other girls, but I don't remember meaning it before. Though why a girl like yourself, with all that beauty, intelligence and blarney, should waste herself on an old reprobate like me, that's really got me beaten.'

'Just practising till a big fish comes along.'

Aiden sat up in bed, pulling her with him and reached out for a cigarette.

The small table lamp on the bedside table cast a harsh light across his face. Dressed in a dark suit, he passed for thirty, but tired and naked his real age showed: a puckering of the skin around his mouth and eyes, a few grey hairs amongst the jet black, a stomach that was losing its tautness.

'Don't be a gold digger,' he said as he flicked his lighter. 'Settle for love, babies and suburban bliss. Money alone won't make you happy.'

'I was going to insist on a big cock too,' Camellia laughed, but something in his tone made her uneasy. 'Are you trying to tell me you are about to disappear?'

'If I could go back ten years I'd never leave you,' he said with surprising tenderness. 'But you aren't in love with me, Camellia.'

He was the wisest man she'd ever met, and when he wasn't telling huge, outrageous lies, the most honest. She sensed that deep down he was much like her, that even when surrounded by people, and the centre of attention, he too had the same lonely feeling as she did sometimes. Maybe that was why the lovemaking was so special. Somehow they had touched on this shared raw chord.

He was right of course: she wasn't in love with him. He was wonderful, probably the nearest thing to love she'd found in Chelsea, but it wasn't going to be forever.

'Don't go right out of my life, Aiden,' she whispered, playing with the long black hairs on his chest.

'I have to go away soon,' he said. 'And you've got to find another way of living before things catch up with you. I thought I felt that devil on horseback around here during the night.'

Camellia didn't answer. He had used that expression earlier in the pub, referring to something in the past. Now she felt the menace of it without knowing its meaning.

'Me Mam used to say that,' he smiled. 'Me Da was a devil for the drink and when I was little I thought she meant him. One night there was a terrible storm and she said it looking out the window. The next morning they brought me Da home on a cart. A tree had fallen on him on the way home and his back was broken.'

A shiver ran down Camellia's spine.

'What happened to him?'

'He died a day or two later. It was pneumonia, not the injuries. He'd been out there helpless in the rain all night, chilled to the bone.'

'Don't,' Camellia put one hand over his mouth.

'Just a word of warning,' Aiden grinned impishly and stubbed out his cigarette. 'I know how it is when you're young, you think good luck lasts forever. But everything in this life has to be paid for sweetheart. Like now this old man has to go to sleep or he'll drop dead later from exhaustion.'

Aiden had been in Chelsea for a month, but now, two days into the New Year of 1970, he was leaving the next morning as he claimed to have business in Sheffield. It had been a wild month. Camellia's twentieth birthday, Christmas and New Year had been an orgy of drinking and drugs, parties and clubbing and even John had deserted them tonight, too exhausted to face any more crazy scenes.

'So what do you want to do on your last night?' Camellia asked.

'Would you be prepared to do anything?' Aiden grinned wickedly at both girls.

Camellia laughed. Aiden was absolutely unique. A real man through and through yet with such a childlike sense of fun. He was irresistible and whatever he wanted to do she was prepared to do it.

'As long as I can do it sitting down,' Bee answered. She had spent most of the day lying on the settee nursing a hangover but now after half a bottle of vodka she was beginning to perk up.

'What about you, Camellia?' He put one arm round her and squeezed her tightly. 'My dearest wish?'

It was the way he looked at her that told her what he wanted, a little hangdog, but wicked lights in his blue eyes. He'd mentioned this fantasy on several occasions.

Camellia wanted him to leave happy, whatever it took, but she was also afraid of being jealous. Yet Bee liked Aiden almost as much as she did, and it would be sad for her if she was left alone on Aiden's last night in the flat.

'I guess so,' she said hesitantly. 'But only if Bee agrees.'

Bee looked from one to the other, clearly puzzled.

'Well Bee, are you going to join me and Camellia and make an old man happy on his last night in London?'

Bee's blue eyes shot open. 'You mean both of us?'

'Friendship's all about sharing,' he said nonchalantly, sitting down and taking a packet from his pocket. 'A little cocaine might loosen us all up.'

Camellia winked at Bee to reassure her she didn't really mind. The way she felt about Aiden it was probably a good idea. Alone with him she just might have started wanting more than he could give.

Only Aiden could have made it wonderful. They snorted two lines of coke apiece, then he led them into Camellia's bedroom holding them by the hand, lay down with an arm round each of them and kissed first Bee then Camellia until they were totally relaxed.

It was a delicious game. Camellia unbuttoned his shirt, Bee undid his trousers and together they slowly stripped him, kissing his neck, his chest, even his legs and feet.

His penis reared up like a barber's pole. Bee who had seen it many a time in a flaccid state stared in amazement at its size and ripped off her dress and underwear in record time.

When Bee bent over to take it in her mouth, Camellia slowly took off her clothes, watching Aiden's face. His blue eyes were on her, one big hand caressing Bee's neck. He held out his free hand to her and drew her down beside him, covering her mouth with his. Aiden's kisses were yet another thing that set him apart: all the enthusiasm and passion of a teenager, yet with a sensitivity and tenderness. He teased with his tongue, turning it into something astonishingly intimate. When Camellia opened her eyes to find that Bee had moved round and his fingers were gliding in and out of her, her arousal became stronger. It fascinated her to watch Bee writhing under his touch. Camellia slid down and joined Bee, licking at one side of him as she licked the other, their fingers touching as they caressed his balls. Aiden's fingers slipped into her too, groaning with delight at their joint effort.

The cocaine was having the desired effect, their inhibitions forgotten as they each took what they wanted. First Bee moved away, sitting astride his face and the sound of Aiden's lapping tongue and her friend's moans of delight increased the pleasure from the fingers inside her.

Camellia knelt between Aiden's legs, rubbing his penis against herself. Bee was crouched over him now, her plump white bottom moving up and down, revealing the tongue running against her.

The visual impact was too great. Camellia knelt over Aiden and with a groan of pleasure lowered herself onto him, masturbating frantically. Her own cries mingled with Bee's and she came almost instantly, screaming out with such ferocity Bee looked round in alarm.

'Oh shit, that was wonderful.' Camellia disengaged herself, crawling up the bed to Aiden, leaving Bee to take over. She smothered his face with kisses, undeterred by the musky smell that could only be from her friend.

Together they watched Bee come, her head thrown back, her mouth open as she moved up and down on Aiden. Her big breasts wiggled and swayed, her fingers rubbing herself. Aiden's mouth moved to take Camellia's breast, his fingers running over her nipples while he kissed her deeply.

'Let me kiss your pussy,' he whispered hoarsely as he began to buck fiercely. 'Don't stop Bee, I'm nearly there.'

Camellia came again seconds after she heard Bee shout out and then there was just wild grunting from Aiden as he finally came too.

Three damp, sticky bodies lay entwined, Camellia sighing deeply and Bee giggling.

'That's just about the rudest thing I've ever

done,' she said. 'What on earth would my mother say?'

'Brazen hussy, get to bed without any tea.' Aiden's voice seemed extra deep, his laughter directed only at himself. 'I suppose I shall have to confess this too. "Father I have sinned. I took two young ladies at the same time and it exceeded my wildest dreams."'

They had tea later, the three of them sitting up in bed laughing at everything and anything.

'I must go,' Aiden said eventually, turning to kiss both of them in turn. 'If I live to be ninety you two will always be my favourite dream. Look after one another.'

Camellia slipped on her dressing gown and went with him to the door.

'Come back soon, Aiden,' she said, reaching out to hold him one last time.

'Remember me fondly,' he said, stroking her hair back from her face. 'I wish,' he stopped short and just held her.

'What do you wish?'

'You know,' he said softly.

She knew. That he was younger, that he was different and that tonight didn't have to be the last.

'I love you, Aiden,' she whispered.

'Watch out for that devil on horseback,' he said, faltering for a moment, then turned away.

She watched as he bounded up the stairs to his car, biting back tears.

A sigh behind her made her turn. Bee stood in the doorway in her pink dressing gown, her hair rumpled, her face sweet and girlish.

'Now there was a man!' she said. 'He'll be a hard act to follow.'

Chapter Nine

May 1970

'Hi! I'm Camellia. Would you like some company?'

'Sure, honey!' The fat American's shoe-button eyes swept down her silky dark hair, lingered at her breasts bubbling out of her red chiffon cocktail dress and came to rest on her long slender legs. 'Sit down why don't ya. Let me buy you a drink.'

Camellia's professional fixed smile concealed dejection as she slid into the seat beside him. She'd drawn the short straw. It was only eight in the evening, the club wouldn't fill up for hours and this guy looked awful. It could be the longest night in history.

Camellia put her forearms on the table and turned towards the man as if he was the most important person in the whole world. 'Now what's your name and what part of America are you from?'

'Hank Beckwith, from Detroit.' He held out a podgy hand. 'Sure is swell of you to spend some time with a lonesome American.'

Camellia was repelled by the wet handshake, but fluttered her false eyelashes from force of habit. 'You do understand I work here as a hostess and I have to ask for a fee?'

He didn't reply and for a moment Camellia hoped he'd refuse. Instinct told her he wasn't a regular nightclub punter.

Then to her surprise he pulled out his wallet. 'How much?' he asked.

'Twenty pounds,' she said quickly, doubling the normal charge. It wasn't ethical of course, but Bee was at home in bed with the flu, and somehow Camellia felt justified in taking her share too.

The American frowned as he pulled out two new ten-pound notes and put them on the table.

'That's the worst part over.' Camellia folded the money and slipped it down the front of her dress. 'Now let's have some fun.'

Fun was the last thing she expected to have with this Hank Beckwith. He didn't look like he had it in him. Fat, red-faced and balding, his forehead was already glistening with perspiration. His big splayed-out nose, his wet, sloppy mouth and his loud checked suit appalled her. Without looking under the table she knew he was wearing her other pet hate: white socks.

'So tell me all about yourself,' she asked once the drinks he ordered arrived. Her first vodka and lemonade was real and she sipped it appreciatively, knowing the ones that came later would be just lemonade. 'Are you on holiday or on business?'

'Holiday? Do you mean vacation?' He stared stupidly at her. 'No honey, I'm here to work. My company makes packaging machines. I'm over here checking out your factories.'

In eighteen months of working in clubs, Camellia had met men in almost every line. But what could she say about packaging machines?

Unprompted, Hank began to reel off facts and figures: the targets he'd soared above and how much his company valued his expertise. Camellia fixed her eyes on him and pretended to listen avidly, letting her mind wander off.

She didn't want to work as a hostess anymore, it was becoming a drag. The thick carpeting, the chrome rails, plush booths and intimate lighting couldn't disguise the inherent sadness of nightclub life. How many more potted family histories would she have to listen to? If one more man told her his wife didn't understand him she felt she might just kick him in the balls and tell him he was lucky to have one at all!

It was all very well having nice clothes and plenty of money, but where was the romance, the thrills?

Aiden was partly responsible for this change in Camellia's outlook. His words about getting married and having babies seemed to have stuck in her head. Since the New Year everything had seemed a little phoney: the dressing up, the showing off, the so-called 'good friends' who came round to their flat for meals, but rarely bothered to ask her and Bee back to their place. Even the Beatles had disbanded back in April. Their songs had charted her life and emotions right through her teenage years and it seemed vaguely ominous that they should split up just when she was feeling it was time to move on.

Camellia was tired of one-night-stands, of hearing the same old glib chat-up lines. Aiden had made her want a real, meaningful relationship with a man, someone who just wanted to be around doing ordinary things.

There were no regrets about Aiden. He had given her what she wanted at the time, a light-weight romance with heavy duty sex, a caring friendship with no strings. He was a lovable rogue, the kind of charmer a girl only meets once in a lifetime, and he'd left her with something more than a few vivid memories.

But now Camellia felt she and Bee should plan for the future. They had become closer still since that night with Aiden, and they often talked of learning to drive, buying a car and travelling. Merely talking about it wasn't enough, though. Unless they made a concrete plan to save money, they would go on drifting.

'Tell me about your family,' she suggested when it seemed Hank had finally run out of steam about his damned machines. 'I'm sure a handsome man like you has one?'

He fished in his jacket pocket and pulled out the inevitable plastic concertina of photographs.

'This is Fern, my wife.' He pointed out a studio-posed picture of a moon-faced blonde in soft focus. 'She's put on a few pounds since then, but she's still a looker.'

Another snap of Fern gave Camellia a greater insight. Here she was wearing Bermuda shorts which looked as if they had a couple of cushions stuck down them, arms round two buck-teethed all-American brats.

'That's Marlene,' he pointed to the girl. 'She's eight now and as smart as her daddy. Buck's nine and he's gonna be a doctor.'

Every aspect of his life in Detroit was there: the white painted clapboard house, the Chevrolet, even the pet poodle called Misty.

'You're a lucky man,' Camellia said. 'You've just about got it all!'

'I'm luckier than most.' He snapped shut his pictures and stowed them away next to his heart. 'Fern ain't too strong on the intimate side, if you know what I mean, but she's a good wife.'

'Shall we have another drink?' Camellia knew from experience that such lines were usually an opener to an outpouring of a man's heart. She didn't want to know how Hank Beckwith supplemented his sex life. Getting him drunk and packing him off home early was a far better idea.

'One more maybe.' Hank put his wet fish hand

over hers. 'Why don't we go on somewhere, maybe grab a hamburger and go back to my hotel?'

It was the first time he had managed to surprise her.

'I think you've misunderstood what a hostess is,' she said in her best starched voice. 'I'm here to keep you company, nothing more.'

He gave her a sharp look. 'I paid for you, honey. I call the shots.'

She looked at his bloated face, and three chins, the quivering belly straining his shirt buttons and the wispy ginger hair and thought of having him thrown out by the bouncer. But the club was quiet. He might insist on having his money back and they'd discover that she'd asked for double the fee.

'You paid only for my company,' she said firmly. 'I don't know how it works in America, but here a hostess is a lady, not a prostitute. If that's what you want, please go and look elsewhere.'

'I didn't mean to insult you.' He looked confused now and a little embarrassed. 'Aw hell, honey, you're mad at me!'

'I shall forget what you said as long as you don't repeat it,' Camellia said crisply. 'Now let's have another drink.'

The club's income depended on making men drink heavily but it was clear to Camellia that this man resented paying the high prices. Begrudgingly he bought another round, but he sipped it painfully slowly.

He was such hard work. He answered questions briefly, never once bouncing spontaneously onto a new subject. Minutes seemed like hours and time and again she had to stifle a yawn.

'Would you like to dance?' she asked desperately. Two of the other girls were out there on the floor with a couple of businessmen. Sometimes the girls could engineer it so the groups joined together, that way making a lone male more affable.

'I don't dance,' he said firmly. 'Never saw no sense in it.'

There was no answer to this and Camellia racked her brain to think up some new ploy. 'When are you leaving London?' she asked. If he had an early flight booked, maybe she could nudge him into an early night.

'Maybe tomorrow,' he said. 'Got a few people to call up first.'

Camellia's desperation had almost reached screaming-point, when she heard his stomach rumbling. 'You're hungry,' she said solicitously. 'Haven't you eaten tonight?'

'No,' he admitted somewhat reluctantly.

'I could order you a snack here,' she said quickly. 'It's a bit expensive though.'

'I'm okay till later,' he said. His stomach rumbled again.

'The trouble is most of the restaurants near here close by midnight. There's nothing worse than going to bed on an empty stomach. Why don't you pop out now and get something?'

She saw suspicion on his shoe-button eyes. 'Trying to get rid of me?'

'Of course not.' She forced herself to pat his arm maternally. 'You can always come back afterwards. I don't like to think of anyone being hungry, it spoils the evening. Now there's a good, inexpensive steak house up by Marble Arch.'

She hoped he would gorge himself then think better of returning. At half past ten in the evening all restaurants would be packed and he'd have a long wait to be served.

He licked his lips, as if already smelling the steak. 'You won't run out on me?' he asked.

'Of course not.' She moved nearer to pat his

cheek, but recoiled quickly as his breath smelled so foul.

When he stood up she realised he was even more enormous than she'd thought. He had to weigh eighteen stone.

'See ya later then, honey,' he drawled and walked away to the door.

'Hard work, eh?' Denise, the bar manageress, smiled in sympathy as Camellia came over to her.

'The pits,' Camellia grimaced. 'Let me have a real drink, Den. I need it after him.'

Denise was thirty-five. Her bleached-blonde dizzy style, and low-cut dresses, concealed a knowing, hard-headed woman. Divorced, with a son at boarding school, a rich lover and a beautiful flat in Notting Hill it seemed to Camellia she had everything. She ran the club for Napier, had her spangly evening dresses made specially for her, and yet was caring enough to listen to all the hostesses telling her their troubles.

'He certainly wasn't prince charming,' Denise smiled. 'But you got rid of him early. How did you manage that?'

Camellia told her.

'Well, have that drink and shoot off home,' she laughed. 'By the time he's stuffed his face with steak and chips he'll be too tired for nightclubs, even with you as a lure.'

'But what if he does come back? He might complain about his fee,' Camellia said weakly. She didn't want Denise to know she'd overcharged him.

'I'll tell him your mother was ill or something,' Denise said helpfully. 'You can't really be expected to wait for hours for anyone. Give it half an hour, then go.'

Camellia agreed to this and sipped her drink.

'He was such a drag,' she burst out a few seconds later. 'Imagine being married to someone like that!'

'I was,' Denise said wryly. 'Promise me you won't ever be tempted by a loaded wallet alone. It's like being in purgatory.'

Denise often entertained the girls on quiet nights with tales of her ex-husband, his quivering belly, his belching and his insatiable appetite for kinky sex. Fortunately for her he met a nineteen-year-old model and left Denise to live in Florida.

Camellia smiled, but she still felt miserable.

'When's Bee coming back?' Denise asked. 'You seem lost without her!'

'I hope by the weekend. It's fun when we work together, even if the men are old farts. She's got this knack of bringing out the best in almost everyone.'

Denise nodded, but not exactly in agreement. 'You two should start to think about saving some money.' Her tone was almost maternal. 'I know you both think tomorrow won't ever come, but it does, sooner than you expect.'

Camellia smiled. Denise often used this line with them, but they usually laughed at her. Tonight however Camellia was beginning to come round to the older woman's way of thinking.

It was well after twelve when Camellia finally left the club. She had felt compelled to stay just in case Hank the Horrible did come back and she'd spent the time talking to Denise over another couple of drinks.

She paused for a second under the black and white club awning, looking out for a taxi. Davies Street was unusually deserted. For a second she thought of going back inside to phone for a cab, but Oxford Street was only a few minutes' walk and she could hail one there.

Two days ago warm sunshine had heralded

summer, but May was an unpredictable month and it had turned bitterly cold again. She was glad she'd decided to wear her white rabbit coat. Turning up her collar, she began to walk. To her delight a taxi was coming down from Oxford Street, pulling in some fifteen yards from her as if to let out a fare. Clutching her bag under one arm, she ran towards it.

But as the passenger door opened and a big leg in familiar checked trousers slid out, Camellia froze. It was too late to turn and run in the opposite direction. The rest of him was now out on the pavement and he'd spotted her.

It was only polite to make some sort of apology; besides she wanted his cab.

'I'm afraid I couldn't wait any longer for you to come back,' she said as he paid the driver. 'My flatmate is sick and I have to get home.'

'Could you take me to Chelsea please?' she said to the driver, insinuating herself between Hank and the cab.

'But I came back for you,' Hank said, his fat face slumping with disappointment. Camellia got into the car, but Hank held onto the open door, looking in at her. 'I didn't think you'd be this long,' she said weakly. 'Go on in the club, someone will look after you. I must go.'

The cab driver turned to look back at them, his expression irritated.

Camellia reached out for the door but Hank pulled it open further and began to get in.

'I'll see you home,' he said, his bulk filling the cab.

'That's not necessary,' she said, a little afraid now. 'Besides it's a long way.'

The driver cleared his throat. 'Look sir,' he said testily. 'I'm taking the young lady to Chelsea first.

If she doesn't mind I'll drop you off afterwards. All right with you, love?'

Short of making a scene, Camellia could only nod in agreement.

'The ABC in Fulham Road,' she said quickly so that Hank wouldn't discover where she lived. It was only a short walk from there to Oakley Street.

But the moment they drove off towards Piccadilly, Camellia regretted not having been tougher. He slung one big arm around her shoulders, and tried to force her face round to kiss him.

Just the mere thought of his slobbering lips on hers made her feel nauseous. 'How dare you?' She wriggled away as far as possible from him. 'Don't touch me again or I'll ask the driver to go straight to the police station.'

'You fobbed me off didn't you?' he sulked, slumping over against his window. 'Took my money and got rid of me.'

Camellia willed the driver to get a move on, wishing now she'd told him to drop her in Knightsbridge. 'It was you who decided to go for a meal,' she said snootily. 'I waited over an hour before I left. I could only assume you weren't coming back.'

It was so tempting to tell him what a fat, stinking bore he was. But she wasn't that brave.

The atmosphere grew heavier by the minute. Camellia stared out the window, and counted the landmarks. The Scotch House, Harrods, the turnoff to Fulham Road, the Michelin building – it wasn't much further now.

'I hope you enjoy the rest of your stay in England,' she said stiffly as she saw the ABC cinema up ahead. 'This will do nicely,' she called through the glass compartment to the driver.

He didn't say goodbye. Camellia was barely out

of the taxi before it pulled away and turned left up Beaufort Street towards King's Road.

She paused to light a cigarette, letting Hank get well away. She had always liked this bit of Chelsea: it wasn't as smart as some parts, but it was intriguing, almost like a cosmopolitan village. She was standing in front of Tully's brightly lit windows. Opposite was the Baghdad House, its Arabic-shaped windows alight with jewel-encrusted lamps. She could hear a faint hum of music and wondered if they had a belly-dancer performing inside. Beyond the cinema, now in darkness was Finch's, and the Hungry Horse café. She was shaking a little, unnerved by the big man. In all her time at the Don Juan, she'd never met anyone quite so unpleasant.

Shouting and a bright light spilling out onto the pavement opposite made her look up. A group of student types were coming out of a doorway next to an antique shop with bottles in their hands.

'Want to come to a party?' one of them called out, waving his bottle. 'It's only down in Finborough Road.'

Their cheeriness banished her shakes. Tucking her bag under her arm, she turned into Beaufort Street.

The road was deserted. Up ahead cars passed in King's Road but here all the residents were in bed.

This was the road she and Bee aspired to live in. Once at Christmas they had peered in at one of the elegant town houses through its wrought-iron gates. The front room was lit up, and the table laid for dinner, with silver candelabra, red napkins and flowers. A maid in a frilly apron was putting the finishing touches to it all. Enviously they soaked up the whole picture: a tree strewn with coloured lights in the garden, a holly wreath on the door, a silver Mercedes parked outside. Upstairs behind closed curtains the mistress of the house was probably zipping up a Bond Street evening dress.

There was nothing to see now. The windows were all in darkness. She could just make out the glint of glossy paint on front doors and a canopy of cherry blossom in the gardens.

A creaking noise startled her. She stopped, looking all around, but she could see nothing. Dropping her cigarette into the gutter, she walked on, assuming she'd imagined it.

She felt his presence split seconds before an arm locked round her neck. Before she could even scream a hand was slapped across her mouth.

It happened so swiftly. One moment she was walking, the next held captive. Her bag fell with a clatter to the pavement, scattering the contents. A whiff of foul breath told her it was Hank even before she saw the checked material on the arm holding her.

'You thought you were such a smart arse,' he hissed. 'I knew you didn't live back there, you said earlier you lived near the river. Took me for a sucker, didn't you.'

She struggled to free herself from his grip, but he held her too tightly.

'Do you know what I'm gonna do to you?' His voice was husky with menace. 'Would ya like me to spell it out?'

She couldn't reply. She tried to get her mouth free enough to bite him, kicking out backwards at his legs, flaying her arms around trying to get a grip on him.

But the more she struggled the more firmly he held her, pulling her head right back till it felt as if it would snap at the neck. He was using his knees to push her through an open gate, into the pitch darkness of a garden.

A flash of intuition told her that if he intended to

rape her he would have to turn her towards him. She stopped struggling, allowing him to move her forward, waiting for her chance.

As he took his arm way from her neck and momentarily let go of her mouth, she screamed at the top of her lungs, turning and bringing her knee up to his groin. But the scream didn't frighten him and he side-stepped the knee. In a flash he had her by the throat, squeezing her windpipe till she could feel her eyes popping out of her head.

'I was a marine,' he snarled at her. 'I know at least ten ways to kill you, but that ain't what I got in mind.'

Her chest felt as if it would explode as he squeezed her throat still harder. She was growing dizzy and could no longer see. All at once she felt rape would be better than death. He continued to hold her by the throat, yet kicked her legs from under her so she fell back to the ground. Still holding her, he followed, his knees either side of her.

'I had my bellyful of English girls during the war,' he croaked, one thumb right on her windpipe. 'Sucking up to us, asking for nylons and tins of food then laughing at us behind our backs. Nothing's changed, though we won the war for you. Still so goddamned arrogant.'

The oddest things sprang into her mind as he leaned forward onto her, using his entire weight to subdue her: Bee at home wondering where she was, the twenty pounds tucked in her bra, her lovely coat lying in mud. All so unimportant compared with rape or death.

He fumbled for something in his pocket. Holding her windpipe with just one hand, he thrust some material in her mouth, pushing it back till she retched.

Now she could only plead with her eyes. One of

his knees held her firmly to the ground; each time her arms moved to fight him off he squeezed her neck tighter.

'You understand at last?' he whispered as she became still. 'Now I'm gonna truss you up like a turkey at Thanksgiving.'

Something white and long appeared in his hand. He had a noose over her head in a second, pulling it tight round her neck. Then he grinned, and somehow that was even more terrifying than his scowls.

With one end of the cord he made another slip knot, putting her wrist inside it. But as he reached down behind him, yanked off her shoe and grabbed her ankle to add to the wrist, she saw what his intention was and knew that she was going to die, slowly and painfully.

Camellia put all her strength into struggling to get free.

Once he'd tied one wrist and ankle, then pulled the cord tight to fasten the other side, she would strangle herself if she moved.

She bucked her body under his violently, lashing out each time she felt him loosening his grip on her still free arm, but his weight was crushing her like a tank, and the rope merely tightened more round her neck.

As he pulled on the second leg to attach it to her wrist, it was agony. A sharp crack rang out like gunshot and she knew he had broken it.

Pain obscured everything now – the wet grass beneath her, his foul breath, even the expected rape. She was entirely helpless, any movement tightening the noose round her neck. She felt tears turn cold on her cheeks. Her attempted screams gurgled in her throat, inaudible to anyone but herself.

'I saw some guys do this to a nigger,' he said

almost casually, pulling her skirt up above her waist. 'If you lie still you just might live, struggle and you'll die.'

She was shivering and burning up at the same time. Her whole being centred on the pain in her leg and on stopping herself from trying to lower it. Even so she saw his hand move to open his fly as he kneeled between her splayed open thighs.

'Let's have a look at that pussy you wouldn't sell,' he said, reaching forward and snatching at her tights. The ripping of the nylon jarred her leg again, bringing a fresh wave of agony. Next came her panties, his fingers digging into soft flesh and yanking away the crutch. The cold breeze told her she was exposed, but that was nothing compared with the excruciating pain.

He knelt before her, his face in shadow. His jerking elbow was silhouetted in the faint light from a street lamp beyond the garden wall. Why didn't someone come along? How could the people in the house sleep while this was going on right under their windows?

He grunted, pausing for a moment, then the jerking movement started again.

'You bitch,' he spat at her suddenly, the sound of his zipper like a wasp in the darkness. 'You've even robbed me of that.'

She didn't see his leg move back as he jumped to his feet, just felt the blow as he kicked her with all his force right in the crutch.

'I think someone's trying to break in.' Diana Wooton nudged her sleeping husband into wakefulness. 'Gordon, wake up, someone's down in the garden, I heard the gate squeak.'

Gordon Wooton sat up, listened and scratched his head in the dark. He couldn't hear anything, but Diana would insist he checked.

'Okay,' he sighed, reaching for the switch on the bedside light.

'Don't put that on,' she whispered fearfully. 'If they see it they might hurt us. Just creep down in the dark and look. If there is someone there, call the police.'

Gordon fumbled in the dark for his dressing gown. By day in his office he gave the orders, and his staff jumped. But at home, and particularly at night, he obeyed Diana to the letter.

He crept into the sitting room first and opened the thick curtains just a crack. The arched wrought-iron gate was open, but there was no one in the garden. He went back into the kitchen and peered out of that window too.

Nothing but the glimmer of white blossom against the dark of the lawn.

'A drunk having a pee in the garden,' he muttered to himself, then groaned as he stubbed his bare toes against a box of wine he'd brought home the night before.

The squeak of the front gate in the wind halted him just as he was about to go back upstairs. Diana would lie awake for the rest of the night if he left it like that.

He walked cautiously down the brick path to the gate. Drunks had been known to do a great deal more than pee in their garden before now and his feet were still bare. He shut the gate securely, but as he turned he saw something white on the lawn, right up by the side of the house.

For just a moment he thought it was a swan, curled up with its head beneath its wings. He blinked, then looked again, then hurrying back to the house he switched on the porch light.

'Good God,' he gasped, hardly able to credit that what he was seeing was real. 'Diana,' he yelled at the top of his lungs. 'Call the police. And an ambulance.'

Camellia felt light rather than saw it: a pinkish glow which wouldn't clear. She tried to raise her hand to rub her eyes, but it was too heavy to move.

'Hullo,' a male voice spoke close to her. 'Can you hear me?'

She couldn't answer. She could hear questions shaping in her mind, but her mouth couldn't form them. She managed a croak, but nothing more and lapsed back into sleep.

The next thing she was aware of was a hand on her arm and the sound of pumping air.

Opening her eyes she saw a nurse in a blue and white striped dress.

'Welcome back,' she said. 'You've been out a long time. Are you feeling any pain?'

Camellia couldn't say: she was confused even by the question. The band round her arm was tightening, and she looked to the nurse for explanation.

'I'm just checking your blood pressure,' she said. 'Do you remember anything about last night?'

Memory came back as she tried to move and speak. There was a rope round her neck and as her hand came up a loosen it, Hank's leering face came clearly into focus.

As she tried to turn to one side to ease a throbbing in the lower part of her body, she felt a stab of pain in her legs. Her hands moved to soothe them and she found heavy plaster on one.

'Hank Beckwith,' she managed to croak out.

She was confused for some time. Fragments of memory floated by – lighting a cigarette in Fulham Road, Denise pouring her a drink, a canopy of cherry blossom above her head – but her throat hurt too badly to ask the questions which might fill in the blanks.

It was a policeman who helped the most.

'You are in St Stephen's hospital.' His deep voice was soothing and for a moment or two she thought it was Bert Simmonds. 'You were attacked in Beaufort Street at some time between midnight and three in the morning when you were found in someone's garden. It's nine at night now and you have had an emergency operation on your knee. But we don't know who you are or where you live. You must try to tell me so we can find the man who did this to you.'

Slowly Camellia managed to get the words out. Her fingers kept returning to her neck to try and ease the burning, constricting sensation. She was glad when a nurse came and injected her with something which made her sleepy again. She didn't want to be awake.

The next morning Camellia woke to find her mind clearer, though she ached everywhere and the lower part of her body felt as if it was on fire. She was in a small private room, and she was told she'd be moved back to the main ward once the police had finished questioning her. Her right knee was badly injured, and they still had to do more tests on her to discover whether there was internal damage from the kick in her crutch. It would be weeks until she could walk again. But she was lucky to be alive: if the people in the house in Beaufort Street hadn't found her that night, the police would be heading a murder investigation.

The American Embassy were searching their records for Hank Beckwith. All airlines had been alerted and a checking of London hotel registers was under way. An appeal had been put out for the cab driver who dropped Camellia off in Fulham Road. Late the previous night the police had called at the Don Juan to question Denise and the other girls.

Bee arrived to see Camellia at eleven in the morning, and was allowed in after the police had been through the entire story with her yet again.

Bee was distraught, her eyes pink-rimmed, her hair lank and bedraggled. 'Oh Mel,' she sobbed, even before the police were out of the room. 'This is like the worst nightmare. I can't believe anyone would do such a thing to you.'

A little later once she'd calmed down, she explained how she'd found out. 'I didn't wake up till ten yesterday morning. When I found you hadn't come home I just thought you'd met someone nice. I never thought anything bad had happened to you. I waited in all day, then I began to get cross because you hadn't phoned me. Eventually at nine in the evening I rang the club to ask Denise if she knew anything. Once she told me about that man I had a nasty feeling. Soon after the police called round. You'd only just come round enough to give your name and address. They told me what that man did.'

'It's over now,' Camellia said weakly. 'Try not to think about it, Bee, that's what I'm doing. I'll soon get better, you'll see.'

'But you don't understand,' Bee sobbed. 'They think we are just a couple of prostitutes and you got what you deserved for leading a man on.'

'Who thinks that?' Camellia asked.

'It's all over the papers today,' Bee raised her overflowing eyes to Camellia's. 'The journalists are camping on our doorstep.'

Camellia was in no fit state to even talk, much less think anything through.

'Find someone to stay with till it blows over,' she managed to croak out. 'Don't come and visit me again. Just stay out of sight.'

In the next few days, Camellia grew very glad that Bee didn't take her advice. She soon discovered she hadn't any other real friends. Apart from a warm letter and flowers from Denise at the club, no one else contacted her. She had always believed Bee and herself to be two of the most popular girls in Chelsea. Now she saw that was just so much worthless window-dressing.

The newspaper stories about her made her even more upset. Clearly someone from her past had been talking to them. Not only had they got an old photograph of her in an almost diaphanous blouse and no bra, but they'd dug up the story about her mother's death. It was pure sensationalism, the facts distorted, almost as if the editors had decided to use her as an example.

After a few days Camellia was moved down to the main women's ward. It hurt to see the hostile looks from the other patients, and to hear them whispering about her. When her leg was put into traction it seemed as if every time someone passed her bed they knocked it purposely.

But Bee's loyalty was unfailing. She was always the first visitor through the ward door, the last to leave. She made sure she sat in such a way that Camellia couldn't see herself being pointed out to the other women's visitors and did her best to soothe all Camellia's anxieties.

'I'm working every night now, so don't worry about the rent,' she said. 'I'm trying to save some money too so when you get out of here we can have a holiday somewhere.'

'You shouldn't be working there now,' Camellia said again and again. She worried about her friend every night, imagining that all the men there were like Hank. 'What if someone attacked you?'

'I'm quite safe,' Bee insisted. 'One of the bouncers sees all us girls into cabs now. Besides that Yank would never dare go in there again, would he?'

'They haven't caught him yet.' Camellia groaned as she tried to move into a more comfortable position. 'The police seem to think he gave me a false name. He's probably back in the States now.'

Bee saw Camellia wince as she moved. 'Does it hurt terribly?'

'The leg or knowing the world thinks I'm a tart who got her comeuppance?' Camellia tried to laugh but it was hollow.

'Your leg, silly.' Bee laid her head on Camellia's arm. She thought her friend was the bravest person she'd ever met.

'The leg isn't too bad,' Camellia said. 'As long as no one jogs the bed. It's the bruised fanny that's really doing me in, especially when they give me a bedpan. Why couldn't I find a nice straightforward rapist?'

Making jokes about her ordeal was the only way she could cope with it. The black looks from other patients, the journalists who kept asking to interview her, the anxiety and the question marks over her future were bad enough. But added to this was the constant physical pain and the mental torture, and combined they conspired to push her towards the deepest, darkest depression. Perhaps it was a little sick to joke about something so serious, but it was preferable to sobbing.

As Camellia's body slowly began to mend, it was Sergeant Rodgers, rather than Bee who showed her a way out of the dark morass her mind kept sinking back into.

He was the policeman who'd told her where she was when she first came round from the anaesthetic, the man whom she had mistaken for a moment for Bert Simmonds. Like Bert, he was a policeman of the old school, a man of integrity, committed to maintaining law and order, yet retaining compassion for those weaker than himself.

At first his visits were purely official. He took her statement and called in repeatedly for more information and to keep her abreast with the police inquiries. Gradually she found herself trusting this plain-speaking sergeant and opening up to him.

Camellia had been in hospital for almost a fortnight when he called late one evening to ask her to look at some photographs of men. Camellia had been crying nearly all day. She hated having to lie still in bed, forced to ask for everything from a bedpan to a glass of water. Outside the sun was shining. Hank Beckwith was out there somewhere, free as a bird, while she was still in pain. She'd become infamous overnight. Her past shamed her and she could see no future.

Sergeant Rodgers stood for a moment by her bed looking down at her, as if sensing exactly where her mind was.

'It will get better, Miss Norton,' he said gently. 'Your body will heal, the memory of that night will fade. You think now that this is the end of everything, but in fact it's a new beginning. Try to keep that in mind, you'll find it helps.'

He pulled up a chair beside her bed, and instead of launching into questions or insisting she looked at his photographs, he talked just as a friend would. He said he would arrange for someone from National Assistance to come and see her so she could pay her share of the rent at the flat. Camellia almost forgot he was a policeman.

Although later she found herself wondering if he was merely befriending her in the hopes she might be of some use later, that night she found solace by unburdening some of her fears.

Official reasons for calling on her had now all but dried up, but still Mike Rodgers kept coming. Sometimes he pulled a few sweets or an apple from his pocket, at other times he only had jokes to cheer her, but he always made her feel better.

'You are a very beautiful girl,' he said on perhaps his sixth unofficial visit. A nurse had managed to wash her hair for her today and it had lifted her spirits enough for her to put on a little lipstick too.

'Fat lot of use that is,' she joked, but she felt warmed by his flattery. 'I'll need more than a nice face to get a decent job when I get out of here.'

Mike looked at her thoughtfully. During his many visits and from his knowledge of her background, he'd gleaned more about her character than she realised. She was a good person at heart, a little easily led, but intelligent, brave and independent.

'You say you haven't skills, but you just aren't looking at them from far enough away,' he said.

'I'd have to get up close with a magnifying glass to see any,' she giggled, more from shame than amusement. 'I can't type or drive. I left school without any qualifications.'

'You've got a great understanding of people and a good personality,' he said dryly. 'Those are more valuable than exam results. I can think of many fields where those and your looks would be appreciated.'

'Such as?' Camellia raised one eyebrow.

'Personnel, welfare work, receptionist,' he came back with. 'You'd make a good probation officer too.'

As Mike's visits became more frequent, Camellia realised there was more than mere friendship between them. She found herself putting on lipstick and mascara, her ears constantly pricked for the sound of his firm step out in the corridor. She no longer spent time wondering what Bee was doing during the day, it was Mike she thought about. When he walked into the ward, his big face broke into the warmest of smiles, and she knew without him saying anything that she was as much on his mind, as he was on hers.

In her time at the Don Juan she'd become an expert at chatting up men and making them desire her. But she didn't dare try to use any of her old wiles to ensnare him. She just wasn't good enough for a man like Mike Rodgers.

When she asked whether he had a wife he laughingly replied that he was married only to his job. She knew he played rugby, that his favourite comedy show was *Monty Python's Flying Circus*, that he had a small flat in Acton. But it wasn't enough. She wanted to know everything about him: what he liked to eat, where he grew up, how old he was when he had his first kiss. Who the woman was who had let him down so badly, because somehow she knew he had been hurt.

But she didn't ask these questions. She merely soaked up little things about him to hold onto in the hours when she was alone. The way his lower lip curled petulantly when he disapproved of something, the dimple in his right cheek, the tiny chip in a front tooth and the light in his eyes which she knew was for her.

It was during the long, sleepless nights that Camellia did most of her thinking. She closed her eyes and tried to shut out the night-time sounds of the ward. The old lady in the end bed's wheezing breath, the faint scratching of a pen as the night nurse did her paperwork in the centre of the ward.

Influential people from her past paraded through her mind. Each and every character flitting by like a trailer for a film. Her mother in a backless blue dress, blonde hair waving over golden brown shoulders. Bert Simmonds in his uniform, Miss Peet in her shabby tweed skirt and handknitted jumpers, doling out the evening meal at Archway House. Dougie in his long snakeskin boots, tight velvet trousers and a frilly shirt. Other less important characters came too, Mrs Rowlands, Suzanne, Carol and Miss Puckridge.

Camellia knew now that no one in this cast was responsible for her failings, even if she had thought some of them were at times. Her mother hadn't been the best of examples, Suzanne and Carol had tempted her to steal, Dougie had introduced her to sex and drugs. But it was she, Camellia, who'd chosen to follow their leads and ignore her conscience. She alone conceived the idea of picking pockets and she'd never considered how her victims felt. Then there were all the men she'd slept with since Dougie. She couldn't even remember some of their names. What happened to the girl who once priced love above everything?

How could she even hope for romance with Mike? Setting aside her notoriety, which would harm his career and make him a joke in the force, there were all the dark shadows in the past of which he was unaware. She had breathed corrupt air for so long. She had no right to taint him with it.

Late in June, after six weeks at St Stephen's, the doctors told Camellia she could go home. Her knee had healed enough for her to have been taken out of traction the week before, and as she'd proved to be quite confident for short spells on crutches, there was no further need for her to be hospitalised.

Mike came in at seven that evening and found her practising hobbling along.

Camellia told him her news.

'I'm so excited,' she said breathlessly. 'I thought I was never going to get out of here. The summer's arrived and I hardly noticed.'

'Can I come and see you sometimes?' he asked. He looked faintly embarrassed.

'Let me try and get myself together first,' she said. 'There's more to mend than just my leg.'

Bee hovered in the doorway looking apprehensively at Camellia as she sat in an armchair, her plastered leg up on a stool. She had been home for two days and Bee had fussed round her constantly like a mother hen. She had arranged to do some modelling for a photographer this afternoon, but now she was nervous about it.

'Are you sure I look gorgeous?' she asked, fluffing out her blonde curls with one hand.

'Definitely,' Camellia reassured her for the third time, though in fact she thought the red minidress Bee was wearing made her look brassy. 'Go on, clear off.'

'Will you be all right?' Bee asked again. 'I'll go straight to the club I expect, so I won't be home till late,' she added with a blush.

'I'm not your keeper or your mum,' Camellia reminded her. 'Give the girls my love and get some gossip will you?'

'I'll do my best.' Bee picked up her handbag and made for the door. 'Mind you don't fall over!'

As Bee reached the top of the steps to the street, Camellia could see her bottom half as she waited for a taxi. Her eyes might be deceiving her, but it looked as if Bee had lost some weight.

Camellia sighed. Bee had seemed different the moment she got home: attentive, caring, but oddly secretive. There were stains on the carpet and scratches on the furniture as if Bee had held a party here in her absence, yet she hadn't mentioned one. She hadn't mentioned the girls at the club once either.

After eighteen months of sharing everything, Bee's secrecy was sad. Had she realised too that their relationship had come to a crossroads? To the left lay the clubs, easy money and excitement. To the right, real jobs, less money and hard work. Camellia knew which way she intended to go. Was Bee afraid to admit she couldn't join her?

Within an hour of Bee going out Camellia was bored. The days had passed slowly in the hospital too, but at least they were broken up by meals, visiting hours and doctors doing their rounds. Mike had telephoned her this morning to ask how she was coping and she sensed he was hoping she'd ask him to call round. She wanted to see him so badly, but not here, not amongst all the memories of her old life.

The flat felt like a prison. Camellia could see tantalising glimpses of people walking past the railings on street level, but it would be some time before she'd mastered the art of getting up the steps on crutches, and until then she had to stay put.

'Well, practise a bit,' she said aloud, reaching for the crutches and hoisting herself out of the chair. A few times up and down the passage to the bedrooms would make a good start.

As she got to the end of the passage and saw Bee's bedroom, she smiled. It was an absolute pigsty. Bee had cleaned everything else for Camellia's arrival home, but she must have run out of steam.

Pushing open the door Camellia went in. It wasn't just untidy, but very dirty. Clothes were strewn everywhere, drawers hanging open, the wardrobe almost empty. The dressing table had an inch of grey dust.

Sitting on the bed, Camellia started with the clothes, hooking them up with her crutch, then separating clean and dirty in two piles. She put the dirty ones in the pillowslip and added filthy stained sheets from the bed which clearly hadn't been changed for weeks.

It became a challenge to put everything right. She found a small shopping basket to carry unwashed china to the kitchen, then returned with it filled with cleaning materials. Camellia was surprised by just how much she could do. She pushed the dressing table stool with one of her crutches to where she wanted to tidy and clean, then sat on it.

The same method worked with the vacuum cleaner too, and bit by bit the room began to look nice again.

But as she pushed the machine under the bed a clonking noise alerted her something was there. Shuffling closer on the stool, she put one hand on the bed to steady herself, then lowered herself to the floor. She reached out for her crutch again, slid it under and nudged everything out. Two ashtrays, a gold earring Bee had lost months ago, a bracelet, some magazines and a handful of change came out with the first scoop. With the second came an old handbag and a large brown envelope. She put the china in her shopping basket and the rest on Bee's bedside cabinet, then hauled herself back onto the stool feeling very pleased with herself.

It was hard to make the bed again with clean

sheets while sitting on it. By the time she finally managed to replace the bedspread, she was tired and lay back for a breather.

Idle curiosity made her look in the brown envelope. She wasn't in the habit of opening Bee's things. To her surprise it was a batch of glossy, professional photographs.

The first one was of Bee in a black lace negligee. It was a good picture, capturing the essence of her character, the naughtiness and the sweetness all at once. She was pinning up a black stocking, showing cleavage and thigh.

Camellia smiled. Bee was clearly serious about modelling. She studied it for awhile, then turned to the next.

Her smile vanished as coy girlie pictures turned to pornography: one picture of Bee holding up her naked breasts, a lewd expression on her face, another of her astride a chair showing everything. By the time Camellia got to the last of the twelve, in which a man's hand was examining her intimately, she felt sick.

Closer inspection showed the photographs were taken here in the flat. The couch Bee lay on was theirs, draped with a leopard skin rug. The upright chair she sat astride was one from the kitchen. But worst of all were Bee's eyes. A stranger might assume the glassy vacant look, the dilated pupils were the throes of ecstasy, but Camellia knew better. Bee was drugged.

Camellia left the pictures on the bed and hobbled painfully back to the lounge. It was no good telling herself that she'd seen far worse than those pictures in magazines on sale at every newsagents. This was her dearest friend, her family.

Now she understood Bee's secrecy, the unexplained stains on the carpet, that tarty red dress. Someone was using her. While Camellia lay in hospital planning to start a new life, Bee had met someone whose influence was stronger, and she'd taken a couple of steps even further down the ladder.

When Bee finally came home it was after one in the morning. Camellia was wide awake, still with her bedside light on. She heard the click of the front door, the sound of shoes being kicked off in the lounge, then soft padding as Bee came down the corridor.

'Can't you sleep?' Bee asked, putting her head round Camellia's bedroom door. Her hair was tousled, and her make-up smeared. She looked as if she'd just got out of bed with someone.

'No,' Camellia replied. She had been crying for most of the evening and she turned her face away from Bee's so she wouldn't see her puffy eyes. 'My leg hurts.'

'I'll just get out of these clothes,' Bee said. 'Then I'll bring you some hot milk and a couple of aspirin.'

Camellia sighed. She had left the photographs out on Bee's bed. Would she be angry? Or would she try and convince Camellia that porno-modelling was an even better number than being a nightclub hostess?

She didn't have to wait long. Bee came back just a few moments later. She'd taken off her dress and replaced it with her pink dressing gown.

'You've been poking around,' she said accusingly.

'I didn't poke,' Camellia said stiffly. 'I just went in your room to clean it. I found them under the bed.'

'Is that what you've been crying about?' Bee asked. She folded her arms and looked defiant. 'I can't see why. There's no harm in it.'

'No harm in it?' Camellia hauled herself up to a sitting position. 'It's disgusting.'

'It's easy for you to say that, you didn't have to find a way to pay the telephone bill, the electric and gas.'

'But the club?' Camellia asked. 'You didn't need –' She faltered as she saw Bee's face crumple.

'I got the sack,' Bee said in a small voice. 'I didn't tell you because I didn't want you to worry. Don't be angry with me.'

'Who put you up to it, Bee?' Camellia said more gently, holding out her arms. Bee instantly flung herself into them and began to cry. 'Tell me everything.'

Bee was sacked because police and journalists kept coming into the club to ask questions after Camellia's attack. Denise felt that if Bee was no longer working there, they'd have no excuse for calling in. This seemed callous to Camellia but perhaps Denise was ordered to.

After a couple of weeks with no money coming in, Bee was getting desperate. She saw a small advertisement in a newspaper asking for models which said 'no experience necessary' and made an appointment to see a businessman called Jake.

As Camellia listened to Bee's explanation her heart went out to her friend. Jake had clearly flattered her, spun a story that she could earn a fortune and offered to take the initial pictures himself.

'I didn't really want to do it,' Bee sobbed. 'I knew you wouldn't like it. But Jake said I could tell you they were pictures for catalogues. He said the photographs of me would only be in magazines in Germany and Holland, not here.'

'But I don't understand how you could bear it,' Camellia said. 'He gave you drugs, didn't he?'

'Just a bit of coke,' Bee whispered against her shoulder. 'But it didn't seem so bad. By the time he took the pictures I'd slept with him a couple of times. I love him and he loves me.'

'But he can't love you if he makes you do things like that!' Camellia stroked her friend's hair. This man sounded frightening.

'He's an artist – he's different from the kind of men we usually meet.' Bee sat up, wiping her tears away with the sleeve of her dressing gown. 'He said my body is beautiful and I should be proud to show it off. It's not like I was letting a total stranger leer at me.'

Camellia sighed. 'You must stop it now,' she said gently. 'Look what happened to me through working at the club? You're in even worse danger doing something like this. I'm going to try and go straight, no more drugs, men or anything. If you can't go straight with me, then I'll have to go and live somewhere else.'

'Please don't leave me,' Bee began to cry again. 'I was so lonely while you were in hospital, I wouldn't have done it if you were here.'

Chapter Ten

Three days after Camellia found the photographs of Bee, she met Jake for the first time.

She was sitting in the lounge, reading, while Bee went shopping. It was hot and Bee had left the front door open to let in a breeze.

Camellia neither heard Jake come down the steps to the basement nor saw him walk in. He just appeared in front of her, making her almost jump out of her skin.

'Hi, I'm Jake,' he said, dropping into a chair as if it was his own flat. 'You must be Mel.'

He was every bit as handsome as Bee claimed: perhaps five feet eleven, with shoulder-length blond hair and a beaded Red Indian band round his forehead. A deep golden tan enhanced bright blue eyes and perfect white teeth. He looked around twenty-five, broad shouldered and slim hipped. His white voile shirt and washed-out pale jeans were spotlessly clean and neatly pressed. But despite his unexpectedly attractive appearance Camellia felt uneasy.

'How's the leg?' he asked. 'Tried having a screw yet?'

Camellia might've laughed if an old friend had asked her that. But given the circumstances of her injuries, and the fact that she'd never met this man before, she bristled. 'The break's healing,' she said curtly. 'Screwing, as you put it, is the last thing on my mind.'

She realised now he was older than she'd thought, possibly even in his thirties. As she looked close she saw too that the hippie image was contrived. His hair was too well cut, his jeans and shirt too expensive.

'Bee said you'd be snotty with me,' he said in pique. 'Could we be jealous she's doing some modelling?'

'I'd be snotty with any stranger who walked in uninvited and asked crude personal questions,' she snapped. 'But just for the record I'd hardly call the photographs I saw modelling.'

'So, you're a prude as well as stuck up,' he sneered, pulling a tobacco tin from his back pocket. 'Odd, considering you don't mind selling your fanny, that you don't approve of pictures of it?'

Her worst fears about this man were realised. 'I've never sold my body,' she retorted angrily. 'And I think men that get off on leering at dirty pictures are sick.'

Jake smirked and began to roll a joint. 'Well, you're more of a fool than I took you for. Porn's a growth industry. Bee can make enough to retire in a couple of years. Big knockers like hers are just what the punters want.'

'Bee thinks you love her,' Camellia flung at him. 'What sort of a louse exploits someone like that?'

'A businessman,' he shot back, rolling up the joint and licking the paper to stick it down. 'It's not so different to the way you led on those suckers in the club. Don't get snotty with me, you silly bitch. Bee gets a real kick out of it.'

Camellia smarted, not only at being called a silly bitch, but because she saw there was some truth in what he said. She couldn't retort that Bee was like an enthusiastic puppy, only too ready to lick the hand of anyone who appeared to love her. To admit that might give him even more ideas of ways to use her friend.

Her forebodings grew as she watched Jake lie back on the couch to smoke his joint. She had an awful feeling that he was going to become a permanent fixture around here unless she put her foot down firmly.

Bee arrived back from the shops minutes later, looking like a school girl in a pink gingham sundress. Her hair was tied up in two bunches and she was hot and sweaty.

'Jake!' she exclaimed, her face lighting up. 'What a lovely surprise.' She rushed over where he lay and went to kiss him.

But to Camellia's disgust, he pushed her away scornfully.

'What the fuck do you look like?' he said, his fleshy lips curling in scorn. 'You stink of BO too. Get in the bath and do yourself up. I wouldn't be seen dead with you looking like that!'

In the days that followed Camellia was to hear Jake insult Bee far more brutally. His vocabulary didn't seem to extend to words like beautiful, pretty or gorgeous, only ugly words that made Bee blush with unjustified shame. He found fault with her hair, her make-up, clothes and body, and only when she'd followed his instructions to the letter and turned herself into a sort of vacuous-looking Barbie doll, would he finally say she looked okay or passable.

At first Camellia did her best to find something to like about him, to understand why Bee was so besotted by him. But there was nothing to like, not a shred of decency or even humour. He had no conversation; it was all bravado, swagger and taking the rise out of others.

He quickly became a wedge between her and

Bee. Bee was so mesmerised by him that everything she did or said was for his benefit. Stuck indoors, Camellia had little else to occupy her mind but the changes in her friend's personality, and within a few days she realised many of them were caused by the speed Jake was feeding her.

Bee was restless, overly talkative and had lost her once hearty appetite. Camellia woke at dawn one morning to hear her opening and closing drawers in her room. Thinking that perhaps she was packing up to leave, Camellia got up and hobbled out on her crutches.

To her amazement Bee was wearing nothing but the briefest pair of lacy panties and her bed was piled high with clothes.

'What on earth are you doing?' Camellia asked from the doorway. Although she'd been aware Bee had lost some weight recently, it was only now, seeing her naked that she realised how much. She was almost skinny!

'All my clothes are too big now,' Bee explained. 'I thought I'd sort out the things I like enough to get altered.'

'At this time of the morning?' Camellia saw it was just after four. Bee had come home around twelve. But the time was hardly important. She saw immediately that her friend's pupils were very dilated, that her hands were trembling, and her breathing seemed laboured. 'What have you been taking?'

'Just a couple of Bennies,' Bee shrugged and pulled on the black minidress she'd worn the night of the Arabs' party. 'Look at this Mel! Remember how tight it was?'

Camellia remembered only too well how the dress had once looked. Bee's breasts used to almost tumble out of it, and it clung to her hips like a second skin. Now it was loose all over.

Having been fat herself Camellia could understand that Bee was excited to find herself losing
weight. But to lose so much, so quickly was risky,
especially when it was caused by dangerous,
addictive amphetamines.

'Bee, you've got to stop this,' Camellia implored
her. 'I'm worried sick about you. Jake's turning you
into a different person.'

Bee turned to Camellia and curled her lips in
scorn. 'Jake's right about you, Mel,' she said,
shaking her head. 'You're jealous, bitter and you're
becoming a real drag.'

'Jealous?' Camellia snorted. 'Of you having a
man who humiliates you, feeds you drugs and
walks all over you! Grow up, Bee, and look at him
for what he really is.'

'He only snaps at me because he's worried about
things at the moment,' Bee retorted. 'If he could
give up his studio and do his work here, he'd be
fine.'

Camellia's stomach turned over. 'Never!' she
said firmly. 'You let him in here, Bee, then I'm out
the door for good. That's a promise.'

There were two songs in the charts during this time
that seemed to capture Camellia's feelings. Mungo
Jerry's 'In the Summertime' was a reminder that
everyone else in London was out enjoying the hot
weather while she was incarcerated indoors. The
other was the Beatles' last and most poignant single
'The Long and Winding Road'.

She too had been on a long and winding road,
only to discover it was the wrong one. But on good
days, when Mike telephoned to ask how she was
feeling, she felt the road might yet eventually lead
to him and true happiness. Sometimes when Bee
went off somewhere with Jake, Camellia took a
blanket and a few cushions outside into the small

yard by the front door, to read books he'd recommended and dream daydreams of what might come later when her leg was better, when she'd found a job and Bee became disenchanted with Jake.

But there was no sign yet of him losing his hold over her. Instead his influence grew stronger daily. He took her shopping in King's Road and bought her diaphanous shirts, tight leather miniskirts with big studded belts and kinky long boots. Not even her hair escaped his attention. Jake got it permed in an Afro style, and now it stood out like a fuzzy blonde halo. She'd lost her wholesome pink and white prettiness, her warmth and her sense of humour. She looked like a blue-movie star, but acted like a robot, programmed only to please her master.

Two weeks after Camellia's discharge from St Stephen's Hospital she went back for a check-up on her leg. Jake used her absence as an opportunity to move in.

Camellia came home in a taxi, excited by the news that her plaster would be off within three or four weeks. But as she hobbled awkwardly down the steps to tell Bee, she caught a glimpse of Jake through the window, assembling his tripods in the lounge.

'You aren't going to move in here,' she shouted angrily, the moment she was in the door. 'Get it all out now!'

Bee wasn't there. Presumably she'd been sent out on an errand. Jake was wearing skintight white jeans, and a white singlet, a gold medallion round his neck and his hair in a ponytail.

'It isn't your flat,' he said grinning triumphantly at her. 'I looked at the lease. It's only in Bee's name.

And it's fine by her if I move in, so keep your mouth shut or I'll make her throw you out.'

Camellia shook with rage. He was right of course; legally Camellia was nothing more than a lodger. Alone with Bee later she tried to get her friend to back her up and throw Jake out, but Bee merely cried, insisted it would only be for a few weeks and begged her not to make any more scenes.

'Then I'll have to leave,' Camellia said, bitter that her friend thought more of Jake's feelings than hers after all they'd been to one another. 'I knew we couldn't stay together for ever, but I never thought someone as worthless as him would split us up.'

But however much Camellia wanted to leave, she couldn't. The only money she had was from the national assistance and that wasn't enough to pay advance rent elsewhere. Now that Jake was living with them, she couldn't even consider asking Mike round. A smell of cannabis hung in the air, there were pornographic magazines everywhere and she never knew which of Jake's dubious friends might drop in. Sometimes she was tempted to telephone Mike and confide in him, but he was first and foremost a policeman, and if he chose to get the flat raided, it was just possible that Bee might find herself up on serious charges.

As Jake dug himself into the flat, things grew far worse. The flat was no longer hers and Bee's, but Jake's. The lounge was littered with tripods, cameras and lights, making it impossible to clean up. He slept till lunchtime, then either spent the afternoons smoking dope in front of the television, or making endless phone calls to contacts. By six in the evening he was getting into his stride, objecting when Camellia wanted to cook a meal because it made 'his studio' smell. Total strangers came to be photographed. Scantily dressed women made free with the bathroom as a changing room, using her towels, dropping their cigarettes on the floor.

Music blared out constantly. Beer bottles, over-loaded ashtrays and piles of papers spoilt the home which had once meant so much to both girls. Jake had no respect for anyone's belongings or their privacy.

Often when Camellia was in the bath, sitting with her leg up on the side to keep it dry, he would march in to use the toilet, grinning broadly at her embarrassment. He ate the food she'd paid for and rifled through her room for cigarettes.

Each time she saw him brushing his hair, admiring himself in the mirror, she wanted to scream at him. She loathed him for his cutting remarks, his insolence and his violence to Bee. But she could escape to her room and lock the door. Bee had to live with his dominance.

Before Jake moved in, Bee went out a great deal with him, often not returning home until Camellia was asleep. But now she was in all day and night too, it was obvious how Jake had got her total subservience. He fed her drugs till she was in a permanent stupor: barbiturates to get to sleep at night, amphetamines to wake her up the next day. Her diet consisted mainly of yoghurt and oranges and as her weight continued to drop dramatically, she became gaunt and withdrawn. The bath was strewn with loose blonde hairs, her skin was dry and flaky and her eyes permanently dull and vacant.

In the early hours of the morning Camellia would sometimes awake to the sound of vicious sadistic sex – obscenities shouted out, the swish of a cane and screams followed by silence. Occasionally there was another female voice besides Bee's.

One morning she found Bee shivering on the settee wearing only a slip. One look at her tear-stained face was enough to know Jake had kicked her out in favour of another girl. For once she didn't appear to be drugged witless.

'Bee, you've got to pull yourself together,' Camellia implored her, making her tea and forcing her to eat an egg on toast. She ran her hand over a new bruise on her friend's now bony shoulder. 'He's evil, Bee, and you know it. Say the word and I'll round up a couple of Aiden's old mates to get him out.'

'You don't understand.' Bee's big, now dull blue eyes filled up with new tears. 'This is a mind game. A kind of test. He does love me.'

'Mind game!' Camellia shook her friend angrily. 'This is no game! He's all but destroyed your mind. Where's your pride, Bee? He's in there screwing another girl in your bed, on your sheets. He doesn't love anyone but himself, you poor fool.'

Four weeks to the day since she'd left hospital, Camellia went to stay the night with Denise in Notting Hill Gate, just for a brief respite from Jake. When she came home the next day it was raining hard, but Camellia was feeling more cheerful and optimistic. Denise had told her that a friend of hers who owned a pub out in Chiswick wanted a live-in barmaid. As soon as her plaster came off she could go and see the landlord.

The curtains were closed in the lounge, and at first Camellia assumed Bee and Jake were still in bed. She let herself in, but then stopped short at the brilliant light flooding from the lounge into the small hall.

She could hear nothing. Thinking Jake had left his photographic lights on by mistake, she went on into the kitchen, glancing through the half-open lounge door as she went.

To her horror, the room wasn't empty. Bee was

lying on the settee in only a black suspender belt and stockings, and by her head a naked, very hairy man was holding his penis to her mouth.

Camellia was so shocked she stood rooted to the spot.

'For Christ's sake, Bee,' Jake's voice boomed out suddenly, so close to Camellia that he had to be just the other side of the door. 'Don't just look at it. Suck it!'

The naked man turned slightly at Jake's command, but she barely looked at his face, for even semi-flaccid the man's penis was enormous.

Bee's open mouth was less than an inch from it, her eyes screwed up in disgust.

'Suck the fucking thing!' Jake shouted again and moved forward. All at once his back view was in Camellia's line of vision.

He was wearing nothing but a pair of white shorts, his muscular back bronzed from the sun. Holding the heavy cine camera on one shoulder, he shot his spare hand forward to probe at Bee's vagina.

'Come on,' he said huskily. 'You're keen enough to suck mine. Do it good and I'll reward you later.'

Camellia was trapped. If she went on out again now Jake would hear her. Stuck, she waited for an opportune moment to make her escape.

The dark man had rammed the end of his cock into Bee's mouth. Jake was practically on top of them with the camera.

'Come on, Bee,' he ordered. 'Play with yourself at the same time, stick your fingers in it. Hussein, start wanking.'

The man obliged willingly, his head thrown back, ramming the tip of his helmet into the wide mouth in front of him.

'It's good,' he shouted in a strange guttural accent. 'Hold my balls you bitch. Lick me!'

'Pull back,' Jake yelled. 'Let's see the spunk on her lips!'

As the Arab came, shooting it all over Bee's face, Camellia retched, lunging for the sink and dropping one of her crutches.

'Spying eh?' Jake was suddenly behind her. 'If you want to watch you only have to ask!'

She stood up again, holding the sink for support, her nausea replaced by fury. 'How could you?' she shouted. 'You bloody pervert.'

He caught hold of her arm and dragged her forward. She clung desperately to the one crutch and tried to prevent him, but he was too strong for her.

'Come and meet Hussein,' he said, smirking and putting his arm right round her, grabbing one of her breasts. 'I'm sure he's got another lot in there for you.'

Bee was hastily trying to cover herself, still with all that muck on her face. Hussein clearly thought he had been brought a new partner, and his low brow furrowed with frown lines as he studied the plaster cast on her leg. 'Who is theese?' he asked, rubbing his cock half-heartedly, sitting down on a chair, great balls hanging over the edge like a bull.

But overriding her fear and disgust was anxiety for Bee. She was completely out of her head, her pupils dilated so much her irises had all but disappeared. She couldn't even sit up.

'Leave her alone,' she kept mumbling, absent-mindedly wiping her face with the back of her hand. 'Let her go, Jake.'

On 1 August, nearly three months since Hank Beckwith attacked her, Camellia finally had the plaster taken off her leg. It felt strange without it. Her leg was oddly light, and the warm sun and breeze seemed to tickle the pallid flesh.

Taking the back streets, she crossed over King's Road, then went on to Cheyne Walk by the river. It was a hot, sunny day, and she was reluctant to go straight home, even though she'd been warned that it would take some time to adjust to walking normally again.

By the time Camellia reached the embankment, her knee was aching. She sat down on a bench and looked at the view appreciatively. The Thames looked almost clean today, silver and sparkly, the houseboats adding a gay, Mediterranean quality to the scene. A girl, little older than herself, was watering some flowers in tubs on a house boat. A fat brown baby sat by her in a pushchair, naked apart from a nappy, gurgling happily. Apart from the heavy traffic roaring away behind her, it was an idyllic place to waste a couple of hours.

Flicking back her Indian cotton wraparound skirt, Camellia stretched out her legs in front of her and compared them. One was lightly tanned, the other corpse white and a little thinner, the scar on the inside of her knee still bright red. She had joked when the nurse took off the plaster, about hanging one leg out of the window until it turned the same colour as the other. But her light-heartedness was gone now, replaced by dread of what was to come.

She had stayed with Denise for the past two nights, but today she had to return home and do what she should have done long ago. Bee would thank her for it one day. Perhaps as Denise suggested, she was hoping deep down that someone would rescue her.

A week ago Camellia had done some snooping while Jake was out. She discovered that he was setting up some sort of deal in Amsterdam, and found a bank book in which he had over three thousand pounds. This suggested he might be leaving soon, but she wasn't going to wait and hope for that now. Today she intended to hasten his departure.

Bee was in a very bad way. Aiden's predictions about devils on horseback seemed less absurd now, but Camellia was sure they could rebuild their lives once Jake was finally gone.

Mike Rodgers was the ace card she intended to use. She had met him for lunch a few days ago and she knew now that what she'd thought she'd felt for him in hospital was real and worth striving for. Her plan was to tell Jake quite casually that a policeman could be dropping in at any time to see her, and that he'd better remove all his filthy books and pictures from the flat if he didn't want to end up being busted. If she had his number correctly he would panic and make a run for it immediately.

It was only a short walk back to Oakley Street, but by the time Camellia reached the house her knee was throbbing and she was very hot. The curtains were still closed in the lounge, but the front door was wide open.

For a moment or two Camellia thought they'd been burgled. All Jake's equipment, cameras, tripods and lighting were gone from the lounge. But as she opened the curtains to take a look in daylight, panic turned to relief. It was no burglar; Jake had packed up and gone. His strewn clothes and his files of pictures had all been removed.

Camellia let out a whoop of absolute joy. The mucky, untidy room had never looked so attractive. 'Thank you God,' she whispered. Bee would be distraught for a day or two, but she'd get over it.

Camellia went along the passage, and peeped into Bee's room. The curtains were closed so it was too dark to see her clearly, but she was face down, entirely naked and fast asleep. For a moment Camellia was tempted to wake her, but she resisted the impulse. Better to let her sleep on, at least until she got the place straight, maybe they could go out to one of the parks later in the afternoon and lie in the sun together, the way they used to.

After changing into an old pair of shorts and a tee shirt, Camellia opened the lounge windows wide to let out the fetid smell of cigarettes and stale beer. Even though her leg was aching she could move easily, and as she vacuumed, dusted and polished away all traces of Jake, she was making long-term plans. Tomorrow she would go to an agency and get some temporary clerical work, maybe an evening waitressing job too. They'd repaint the lounge. Perhaps once Bee was feeling better again they could have a cheap holiday somewhere.

The kitchen was grisly. Dishes were piled in the sink, and there were beer cans, glasses and dirty cups everywhere. Flies hovered around the remains of a chicken curry, unrinsed milk bottles turning green.

While Camellia waited for the kettle to boil she got rid of the rubbish and washed the dishes. The whole kitchen needed spring cleaning, but that could wait until later. For now she would take some tea to Bee and have a real chat at last.

'Wake up, Bee! I've brought you some tea,' she said, pushing the door open wider with one foot.

There was no response, Bee hadn't moved since she last looked in.

'It stinks in here,' Camellia held her nose and stepped over the usual piles of clothes to get to the window, drew back the heavy curtains to let the light in. 'How you can sleep in it, beats me.'

But as Camellia turned to put the mug of tea down, she gasped in horror.

Bee was lying face down in a pool of stinking vomit, an angry red weal right across her bare buttocks.

'Oh shit, Bee.' Camellia put the tea down, and touched her friend's shoulder. 'Come on wake up and help me get you out of this.'

Bee didn't move. Camellia caught hold of her friend more firmly to roll her away from the vomit. As Bee's head lolled over and her hair fell back to expose her face, Camellia screamed.

Her eyes were wide open, cold and glassy, like a fish on a marble slab. The flesh beneath Camellia's fingers was icy cold.

'No, Bee!' she screamed. 'You can't be!'

While she waited for the police to arrive Camellia stood in Bee's bedroom doorway, too shattered even to cry.

'If only I'd come home last night,' she kept repeating aloud.

Flies buzzed round the room, hovering, then swooping down to gorge on the sickly mess on the sheets.

Bee's body had lost all its curves. Her hip bones, once padded with pink soft flesh, now stood out gaunt and sharp. Even her magnificent breasts had withered and shrunk, like two old chamois-leather bags.

'Death caused by inhalation of vomit.' The police doctor's deep clear voice wafted up the passage to where Camellia sat hunched in a chair crying.

'I can't say for certain until we've examined the contents of her stomach and run some blood tests, but I'd guess she'd taken a cocktail of barbiturates and alcohol. That cane mark on her buttocks is recent, as are the bruises on her upper arms, but much earlier than the ingestion of the pills. I'd put her time of death at somewhere around two or three this morning.'

Camellia felt as if she was paralysed in both

body and mind. She was aware of the police marching in and out, searching everything, but she heard their voices as if from a great distance. All she could see were Bee's glassy blue sightless eyes.

'Miss Norton.' A commanding voice, coupled with a hand shaking her shoulder brought her back to reality. 'Are you all right? Can I get you a glass of water?'

Camellia shook her head.

'You say you came in about twelve. Why did you wait until one thirty before you rang us?'

'I was cleaning up. I looked in at Bee when I first got home, but I thought she was just asleep.'

'But last night, what was she like? Did you hear anything unusual?'

Camellia lifted her eyes to the policeman. His face was just a blur, yet beyond his shoulder she could see people up in the street, peering down over the railings. 'I wasn't here. I've been at a friend's for two days.' She covered her face with her hands, rocking to and fro in grief. 'If only I'd come back she'd be alive now.'

A middle-aged plain-clothes policeman with a face like raw liver took over the questioning. 'What did Beatrice do for a living? Did she have someone else with her last night?'

'Yes, Jake. It was Jake,' she sobbed. 'You've got to find him.'

When one of the men came out of the bedroom with a pile of pornographic photographs in his hands, she became hysterical.

'Jake forced Bee to pose for them,' she yelled out. 'He drugged her and made her do it. Bee was a sweet loving girl, but he was evil and he controlled her.'

An hour or so later Camellia knew she might very well be arrested, but she wasn't concerned with that. They could poke into every corner, take samples of anything they liked, charge her with possession of the drugs they'd found, even blame her for killing Bee. She felt responsible. She should have been there.

Bee's body was taken out in a bag, yet still the police carried on searching. In and out they tramped, turning out drawers, cupboards, digging down the sides of chairs. It was like reliving that morning in Nottingham Court, only this time her dearest friend was on the way to the morgue.

A younger, fresh-faced officer took pity on her later. He made her a cup of tea and questioned her more gently about both Jake's and Bee's background.

Camellia told him everything she knew, including all she remembered about Jake's friends, contacts and his letters from Amsterdam. She felt she'd kill him with her own bare hands if he was to walk back in here now.

'Is there someone I could call to be with you?' the policeman asked. 'Your mother perhaps?'

'My mother's dead too,' she sobbed. 'I haven't got anyone.'

'You can't stay here,' he pointed out. 'We won't be finished with our investigations for some time. Now there must be someone who could help you?'

'I've got a friend in the police force,' she said weakly. 'Could you possibly ask him to call round? His name is Sergeant Mike Rodgers.'

The moment she said Mike's name she knew it was a mistake.

'Is he your boyfriend?' The policeman's eyes widened.

'Oh no.' Camellia shook her head. 'I just got to know him earlier this year when I was attacked in Chelsea.'

The plain-clothes man with the liver face had

been engrossed in searching through books and papers until then, and hadn't appeared to be listening. But at her last words his head jerked up, as if he'd suddenly made a connection.

As the two men went to one side of the room for a whispered confab, Camellia began to cry again. This morning she had actually believed she could put the past behind her. But the past was always on the heels of the present, and now everything would be raked up again, even though it had nothing to do with Bee and her death.

It was four in the afternoon when Mike eventually arrived. Camellia saw him speaking briefly to another officer outside the front door.

For a moment she was reminded again of Bert Simmonds, just as she had been when she came round from the anaesthetic in hospital and saw Mike at her bedside. His short fair hair was bleached by sun, his rugged face glowing with health. But like Bert, Mike was far more than a burly, competent policeman, with muscular tanned forearms. It was the inner strength which showed through, of someone who had witnessed every kind of foul crime, yet still retained his compassion and tolerance. He knew the law, but he knew people still better, and he'd never allowed himself to become disillusioned.

But as Mike came into the flat, signalling for the other man to leave while he talked to her, she could see he too was deeply shocked by Bee's death.

'I'm not here as a policeman,' he said, sitting down opposite her. 'Just as a friend. Tell me everything, Mel. I want to help.'

It was easy enough to speak of Jake, to pour out the despicable things he did, and her ideas about his whole sordid network of pornography. It was even relatively simple to explain why and how Bee was ensnared by the man. But the hardest part was to justify why she had done nothing while something so awful was going on under her own roof.

'I thought of phoning you dozens of times, long before we met for lunch the other day,' she admitted. Even now Mike wasn't judging her, just listening attentively, his eyes sorrowful. 'But I suppose I was afraid if the police raided our flat it would all backfire on me. I just kept waiting and hoping Jake would leave. That makes me a pretty low sort of person, doesn't it?'

'We are all self-protective,' he sighed. 'Given the circumstances you were in, with a broken leg, Jake on one side and Bee on the other, it was an impossible situation for you.'

'But that doesn't excuse cowardice does it?' Camellia began to cry. She could sense that Mike was withdrawing into his policeman self, closing down the shutters on the part of him that wanted her. 'Now, because of me, Bee is dead.'

'Mel, you weren't to blame for Bee's death. Yes, you should've informed us about what Jake was doing. But I doubt Bee would've thanked you for it.'

'It would have been better than her dying.' Camellia blew her nose and tried to compose herself. 'Maybe that way we could both have been straightened out.'

'I believe you straightened out the day that American assaulted you,' Mike said gently, wiping her tears away with his handkerchief. 'You mustn't try to carry the guilt yourself. Put the blame where it belongs, on Jake and on Bee too. She knew the difference between right and wrong – she wasn't an innocent child. You must carry on and put this behind you.'

'Like all the other things I've put behind me?' Camellia looked at his honest, open face and fresh tears sprang to her eyes. 'I've got a whole roomful of bad memories I've tucked away,' she said bitterly. 'But this time I don't think the door is going to close on them.'

'Of course it will.' His voice was crisper and more distant. 'Right now you're stunned by Bee's death, and you can't imagine ever coming out of this. But if you take one day at a time, you will eventually.'

Camellia was tempted to throw herself into his arms. She sensed that if he just held her, maybe kissed her, the man in him would override the policeman.

'You've been so very kind, Mike.' She got up and wiped her eyes, putting enough space between them to prevent temptation. She liked Mike too much to see him suffer by getting involved with her. 'I'll phone Denise and ask if I can stay with her for a few days. Thank you for coming here. It's been a great help to get everything off my chest.'

She saw his lower lip quiver at her politely formal words. 'I . . .' he hesitated. 'I mean.'

'Don't try to say anything.' Camellia went up to him and put a warning finger on his lips. 'I know how you feel, I feel the same way. But it was never to be, Mike, we both know that.'

He caught her finger and kissed the tip, closing his eyes. A single tear glistened on his lashes like a tiny diamond. She had never seen such honest emotion in a man's face.

She longed to tell him how he had kept her going in hospital and through the dark, last weeks with Bee. How she had woven dreams of a life with him – love, passion, even marriage. But it was kinder to let him go.

'Leave now, Mike,' she said firmly. 'I'll just pack a few things, then I'll be off to Denise's.'

Chapter Eleven

The moment Denise opened the door at her flat in Ladbroke Square, Camellia knew she'd had second thoughts about putting her up.

It wasn't just her guarded expression. She looked entirely different, almost as if she'd attempted to wipe out her blonde cocktail barmaid image. Instead of the customary flicked-up bouffant hair style, she had combed it flat and tied it back with a velvet bow at the nape of her neck and she wore a softly draped cream silk dress.

'I shouldn't have asked you,' Camellia blurted out, trying hard not to burst into tears again. 'But there wasn't anyone else.'

'Come on in.' Denise reached out and took Camellia's small suitcase from her. 'We can't discuss anything at the door. I'm still in a state of shock at the news, so you must bear with me.'

Denise went on ahead up to the first floor. As she looked back at Camellia hauling herself up with difficulty with her walking stick, her face softened. 'I bet that knee is giving you gyp,' she said. 'You've had a day of it and no mistake.'

Once they were inside the flat, Denise helped Camellia over to a settee and pulled a padded stool closer.

'Put your leg up,' she said, lifting it for Camellia and removing her shoe. 'I'll make a cup of tea, then we'll talk.'

Denise went out into her kitchen and Camellia

sat looking around at the coffee and cream elegant decor. She had always thought that this flat with its thick pile carpets, soft lighting and reproduction antique furniture was the height of luxury. But now faced with Denise's cool manner and her changed appearance, she realised her friend was scared.

Picking up a large framed picture of Philip, Denise's son, from the coffee table, Camellia studied it. Just a very ordinary thirteen-year-old, with sticking-out ears and slicked-down hair. Camellia slept in his room when she stayed here, but had never met him herself. He had always been away at school. Perhaps Denise was worried this might get back to him somehow?

She looked up as Denise came back into the room with two cups of tea.

'You aren't implicated in any way,' she said. 'It's been ages since Bee worked at the Don Juan, and the police will only ask you to verify I was staying here for the past two nights.'

'You can be terribly naïve sometimes,' Denise replied as she sat down opposite Camellia. She smoothed her skirt down over her knees rather nervously. Her green eyes looked very hard. 'When something like this happens they turn over every last stone, poke in every corner. If it isn't the police, it's the journalists. If I'd had time to collect my thoughts when you rang, I'd have suggested you went straight to a guest house or something. As it is, you can stay here tonight – I'll phone the club and say I can't come in. Tomorrow I'll find you somewhere else. Now, tell me exactly what happened?'

Denise didn't move closer to comfort Camellia as she recounted the entire story, nor did she show any emotion. But she listened carefully, as if weighing up all the evidence.

'I know I must appear hard,' she said eventually.

'I'm really sorry about Bee, heartsick, please don't think otherwise. I'm also very concerned about you, because I know what a terrible shock you've had. But I can't let you stay here after tonight.'

Camellia's lips quivered. Denise had been so sympathetic in the past.

Denise sighed deeply. She wanted to move over to Camellia and comfort her, but she knew if her instincts got the better of her she'd find herself up to her neck in the whole business.

When Camellia had confided in her on previous visits, Denise had known she ought to tip off the police herself about Jake, while Camellia was out of the flat.

But she'd done nothing about it. Camellia looked up to her, thinking she was astute and upright. But Camellia didn't know that she hadn't always been so. She might have changed her name and shut the door on her own past, but some things never quite got erased – not memories, not police records.

At the age of eighteen Frances Duckworth left Buxton for London, intending to become a secretary. Within a year she was calling herself Frankie and had been sucked into the Soho drinking clubs in search of easy money, in much the same way as Camellia and Bee were. But unlike Camellia, Frankie had to work on herself to get noticed. Her mousy hair was bleached blonde, her bra padded out with handkerchiefs, and she listened carefully to everything the older club girls told her.

Two years later she was turning tricks like a seasoned professional.

There was so much Denise was deeply ashamed of: all that sordid sex, the spell in Holloway prison, the decision to marry a man purely for his money. She had been down into a deep, dark sewer that few people ever crawl out of. There was only one thing in her life of which she was proud, and that was her son.

It was Philip she was concerned about now. When reporters came sniffing round the Don Juan after the assault on Camellia, she'd been terrified they would find out her past. But now a girl was dead, who'd worked at the same club. How long before an enthusiastic reporter with a nose for a story, discovered that one of the partners, Mrs Denise Traherne, was once Frankie Duckworth, call girl, blackmailer and thief?

'Camellia,' she said, bracing herself to tell the girl at least part of the truth. 'I'm not packing you off because I don't care what happens to you. But because I'm partly responsible for all this.'

Camellia frowned. 'You? What have you done?'

'I'm part of the set that corrupted you and Bee,' she said simply. 'Everything I have, this flat, clothes, furniture, jewellery has been acquired from men I've used. You must find good role models to look up to, not hard-faced bitches like me. Setting aside the fact that reporters will track you down, and I don't want any part of that, if you stayed around me, how long would it be before you got back into working clubs?'

'I wouldn't ever,' Camellia sniffed.

Denise shook her head, drop earrings jingling. 'You say that now and you mean it. But it would be a different story in a few weeks. I know, I've been there.'

Camellia was startled by the harshness in her voice. 'You haven't always lived like this then?'

Denise half smiled, but tears were glistening in her eyes. 'I've lived in places that would give you nightmares,' she said softly. 'I've met men who'd make Hank Beckwith look like a pussycat. All I've really got of value is my son, Mel. He means everything in the world to me. Please don't judge me too harshly. All I'm doing is trying to protect him.'

Denise found a room for Camellia the next morning and took her straight there in a taxi. It was in Nevern Place, Earls Court: a tiny, spartan room on the fourth floor of a student hostel.

'Just a place to lick your wounds,' Denise said, turning away to unpack a basket of a few essentials she brought for Camellia. She was riddled with guilt, afraid not only for herself now, but for Camellia's state of mind. She'd heard her crying in the night and this morning she looked close to a mental breakdown.

'Stay here till it all blows over. You can easily find a job, just about every restaurant needs a waitress. Phone me if you need to talk and I'll come round.'

Denise's carefully contrived coolness vanished as she said goodbye. She slipped a ten pound note into Camellia's hand, and then clasped her in her arms.

'I wish I could take away your grief,' she murmured into Camellia's neck, fighting to stop herself from crying too. 'Believe me, I do know how you feel.'

Later Camellia was to discover that Denise had paid a month's rent in advance for her and the unexpected and secretive kindness helped a little. But now, as she lay on the narrow single bed, she could hear laughter and chatter, the sound of girls rushing downstairs to the communal phone which rang almost constantly while she sobbed.

Losing her mother had been bad, but Camellia's bitterness and anger had balanced the grief. Bee left a scrapbook of glorious technicolor images nothing could fade: early morning bickering, afternoons of beautiful indolence, evenings filled with laughter. Sharing everything, from food, clothes and money, to dreams.

Now she felt like a Siamese twin, crudely separated from her sister. Alive, but unable to cope with the agony of being torn apart.

There were formalities to get through. The funeral, the inquest and cleaning out Oakley Street. But before any of these came the newspaper stories.

Camellia felt faint with shock as she read the lies and distortions. Beatrice Jarret was portrayed as England's queen of pornography, the flat in Oakley Street as a centre of vice and drugs. One tabloid had got hold of a picture of Bee and Camellia together and the headline read, 'Sleaze, sex and drugs'. The attack by Hank Beckwith was given a rerun.

But of all the painful things Camellia had to endure, meeting Bee's parents at the funeral was the most harrowing.

Bee had told her so many stories about them, that she'd turned them into caricatures. Camellia had imagined Mr Jarret as the old Raj type, with bristling moustache and riding breeches, his speech peppered with hearty 'jolly good's. As for Mrs Jarret, she had imagined her as languidly beautiful, the sort that had vapours.

In fact, they were so ordinarily middle-aged, they almost disappeared amongst the people waiting at the crematorium. Mr Jarret was thin faced, his hair fast receding, only his straight back and the knife-edge crease in his trousers indicating he was an ex-military man. His wife was short and dumpy, with skin as crumpled as a raisin.

Camellia approached them because Mrs Jarret looked so small and bewildered. She hoped to find that Bee had sensationalised their heartlessness and discover they had been waiting and hoping for Bee to contact them. But Bee hadn't exaggerated at all. Mr Jarret looked down his nose at her offered condolences, turning away as she tried to tell them how long she and Bee had lived together.

'She was always a difficult girl,' Mrs Jarret said spitefully, mopping at her eyes with a lace-edged hanky. 'She shamed us so many times, and now this.'

Camellia knew then Mrs Jarret's tears were all for herself, not for the daughter she'd cast out without a second thought.

There was nothing of Bee in these people. Was it possible that this starchy little woman with her mean mouth and crumpled face had brought such a warm loving person into the world?

Mr Jarret showed no emotion throughout the short service. He held his wife's arm, but never looked down at her. He proudly wore a military badge on the pocket of his blazer, but showed no love for his own flesh and blood. This was the man who had taken a stick to his daughter when she got bad marks at school, starved and locked her in her room because he saw a boy kissing her. A man who could not forgive his only daughter a couple of youthful indiscretions.

Camellia was jerked back mentally to her mother's funeral as she heard the soft whirr of the coffin slowly descending out of sight. She remembered it was at that point in the service that she became aware of the absolute finality of it all and the realisation from now on she had to be an adult. She had broken down then, crying for her mother, bitterness forgotten in her grief. Mrs Rowlands had cradled her in her plump arms to soothe her. Bert Simmonds had put an understanding hand on her shoulder.

Camellia's thoughts of both Bonny and Bee

merged as the coffin finally disappeared and suddenly she was seeing parallels between them which she hadn't seen before. They had both shared the same exuberant sense of fun, the love of men and sex, both led disorganised lives, living for the moment. For the first time ever Camellia found herself standing back and looking completely objectively at Bonny, understanding her just as she did Bee. Tears rolled down her cheeks. But now they were both dead.

Camellia tried to speak to the Jarrets again later outside as they filed past the few floral tributes. She wanted to give them the benefit of the doubt. Perhaps they were as stunned and shocked as she was.

'That one's from Mr and Mrs Cyril Potter,' she said pointing out the largest, a beautiful arrangement of red roses. 'They owned the café where Bee worked when I first met her. You ought to take the card, they've written some lovely words. And that bouquet of delphiniums and carnations is from an old dear friend, Aiden.'

Mr Jarret caught hold of Camellia's arm, his strong grip quite intimidating. 'There is nothing for us to be proud of here,' he hissed at her. 'How you've got the nerve to prattle on like this astounds me.'

'I'm so sorry,' she said starchily, looking into the man's cold eyes, 'but you see I loved her. For a moment or two, I thought you did too.'

Camellia took the little cards herself, then hurried away from the crematorium, through a barrage of ferreting journalists. When she looked back to check no one was following her, she saw Mr and Mrs Jarret having their pictures taken. She guessed in a day or two there would be more sob stories in the newspapers, this time centred on how Bee deliberately shamed her loving parents.

On her way home to Earls Court she went into a florists and bought a bunch of yellow chrysanthemums, in memory of Bee. It was the wrong season for daffodils. Back in her room she put them in an empty jam jar on the table by the window and reread the cards.

'Goodbye Bee,' Cyril from the café had written. 'We will always remember the sunshine you brought into the Black and White Café. Rest in peace, Cyril and Rose.'

Aiden's was short, written by someone else's hand. But the fact he'd wired flowers from wherever he was, was enough.

'Sweet memories never fade. Your old friend, Aiden.'

The simple posy of summer garden flowers that Camellia had given had gone on the coffin. She felt her heart had too.

Cleaning the flat and destroying anything that would bring further shame to Bee was all Camellia could do now. She separated seedy mementoes from more innocent ones. She buried her saucy underwear in the dustbin, sorted her clothes, the more outrageous items to go to a second-hand stall in Chelsea market, the quiet, ordinary ones folded neatly and put in the drawers.

She found an unfinished letter written by Bee in a maudlin moment's desire to be forgiven by her parents. Camellia tucked it into an address book so they would find it. She remembered Bee reading it to her, eyes filling with tears, then tossing it aside knowing she would never send it. It might soften their stony hearts – they wouldn't know it had been penned and forgotten months earlier.

While packing her own things Camellia came across the file from her mother, almost forgotten under a pile of old sweaters.

'Oh Mum,' she whispered, hugging the stiff card

to her chest, as if merely holding it would bring some comfort. 'I'm sorry I judged you so harshly once. You, me and Bee, we're all flawed, but none of us were entirely bad. Is that what you wanted to teach me?'

The inquest held no surprises. Just a cold verdict of death by misadventure. For Camellia it was like being transported back five years to her mother's inquest, a similar Coroner's Court full of sensation seekers and journalists hoping for a few last thrills. But this time Camellia took everything in, she was no longer protected by innocence.

Mr and Mrs Jarret sat close, but not touching, clearly not fully understanding the implications of the lethal cocktail their wayward daughter had taken on her last night. The words amphetamines, cocaine and barbiturates went over their heads, only the word alcohol made them exchange knowing glances.

A statement from a neighbour who had watched Jake carrying out equipment to his car and leaving just before midnight proved he wasn't responsible for, or witness to her death. But to Camellia he was a murderer, just as if he'd taken a knife and cut her throat.

Camellia didn't notice the summer ending, or even the transition to winter. She threw herself into work in an attempt to soothe the pain inside her.

Almost invisible in drab, plain clothes, her hair tied tightly back, she started her day at seven in the morning as a chambermaid, then moved on to a busy restaurant for the lunch-time, to a fish-and-chip shop for the evening. She ate at work, saved her money and avoided conversation with anyone.

Jake was apprehended in late September, stopped by customs men coming in at Dover with a quantity of cannabis. While he was awaiting trial, the police finally uncovered his pornography business: a small studio in Kentish Town and a far larger one in Amsterdam, with a network of mail order customers both in England and Holland.

Camellia was interviewed several more times, but whether it was because Mike had used some influence or just that the police had enough evidence without asking her to be a witness, the inspector in charge of the investigation made it quite clear she wouldn't be involved further.

Jimi Hendrix died of a drug overdose in September, and Janis Joplin followed him a few weeks later. In November a hurricane in Bangladesh killed 100,000 people, Camellia cried for all of them. Her twenty-first birthday in December came and went without celebration. Just one lone card from Denise. At Christmas she was compelled to put on a little make-up, smile and look joyous for the customers she served, but nothing broke through her reserve. She didn't contact anyone in all this time. Outside work she spent much of her time lying on her bed, sometimes reading, but mostly thinking.

Although she thought of Bee a great deal, and her own mistakes and misfortunes, it was Bonny who occupied her mind the most. She found herself dwelling less on her bad points. In the light of things she'd done herself she felt she couldn't be self-righteous anymore, and remembered instead the happier times with sweet nostalgia. Now and then she found that incidents which had once embarrassed or shocked her now made her smile. Bonny had always been such an extrovert.

As Camellia sifted through this store of old memories, considering how much of it was responsible for forging her character, it came to her that she knew very little about Bonny prior to her marriage. Bonny had never been one for reminiscing, she lived for the moment just the way Camellia had until now.

It was this which made her dig out the file of old letters again. She had read them many times when she first came to London, but in the past four years she hadn't touched them, except for once showing them to Bee.

To her surprise she found she viewed them now from an entirely different perspective. Maybe it was just that she had a better understanding of human nature that she no longer felt the same hurt or sense of betrayal. It was possible too that she had idealised her parents' marriage, they might never have been as happy together as she'd always supposed as a child.

She sorted out the letters from each of the three men. The ones from the man called Jack Easton were the most dog-eared, infuriatingly none of them were dated. She studied these first.

The most worn one, written on a piece of paper torn from a cheap notebook, had the address Tollgate Garage, Amberley, Sussex. Camellia knew this was the village Bonny had been evacuated to in the war to live with the dancing teacher she called Aunt Lydia. She had vague memories of being taken to visit there, both before and after her father died. It was a pretty village full of thatched cottages and Aunt Lydia had seemed almost like a grandmother, though tall and slender and not a bit like her real granny. She wondered now why Bonny had lost touch with her. Could it have had something to do with this man Jack?

'Dear Bonny, I can't say I'm sorry about what happened the other night. It was wrong but it was too beautiful to apologise for. I just wanted you to know that I'll be thinking about you next Saturday, I really hope it all works out for you and you end up happy. We had some good times, didn't we? You'll always have a special place in my heart. Love always, Jack.'

Camellia wondered what had happened on the Saturday referred to. Was it an audition for a show? Moving to a new town? The letter sounded as if it was intended to be a final goodbye. She wished Jack had dated it.

The one Camellia felt came next was on proper writing paper, from the same address in Amberley. This one was quite formal, merely congratulating Bonny on Camellia's birth, with a mention of his own daughter and a couple of references to Lydia who he said was dying to see the new baby. It was signed 'Yours affectionately, Jack'. She marked it 1950.

Camellia felt several years had passed before the next letter. It was on thick headed notepaper, this time from a garage in Littlehampton. Jack seemed to have become more successful. But his tone was cool and guarded.

'Dear Bonny, Of course it was good to hear from you, though I was very surprised. But no, I can't meet you. It wouldn't be right. We're both married, we've got kids and responsibilities. I'm sorry if you have some sort of crisis in your life. I'd like to be just a friend and listen, but we both know why that won't work. My fondest regards, Jack.'

Bonny must've written again pleading with him, as the next was virtually the same as the previous one, only this time it was a firm and emphatic 'No'.

But the second to last was the one which intrigued Camellia most.

'Dear Bonny, I thought I was through with being shocked by your lies, but this one is the biggest and most vicious yet. What you hope to gain from it I really don't know. I've seen pictures of your kid round at Lydia's, she's nothing like me and I've got the kind of colouring that gets passed on.

'You have everything a woman could want, a lovely home, a beautiful child and an old man who by all accounts adores you. Why screw it up, Bonny? What's going on in your scheming little head? You had your chance with me and you chucked it away. Even if we were both free, you wouldn't want a bloke with dirt under his finger-nails. I just laughed when you said you still loved me. Come off it!

'If blackmail's your game, it's a sick one. Just remember you've got even more to lose than me. Just one word from you to Ginny, and so help me, I'll swing for you.

'Jack.'

The last letter was one of condolence on John's death and made no mention of his previous ones. Like the first of the batch, it was warm and affectionate, offering sympathy and hopes that things would get better in the future. Jack was either a very forgiving man or he'd written this letter in the presence of his wife.

One of the old photographs was of a small group of children. Camellia recognised Bonny immediately: she was sitting right in the middle with hair ribbons sticking up on top of her head like rabbit's ears. She had a feeling the skinny, untidy looking older boy next to her might be Jack. He had a freckled face and a wide grin and his arm was round Bonny. Was he the boy she used to refer to as 'her childhood sweetheart'?

Next came the only letter from the man who signed himself 'Miles'. This one was dated September 1954, two years before her father died. The writing paper was top quality, cream heavy vellum with a hand-finished edge and an embossed address in London's Holland Park. The man's handwriting was a beautiful script, very different from Jack's scrawl.

'Dear Bonny,' she read. 'I am in receipt of your recent letter and astounded by the preposterous claims you make. My first reaction was to call on you and insist you retract this malevolent statement, but because of my high regard for your husband and Mary's affection for you, I have decided to ignore what you have said and put it down to a lapse of intelligence on your part, probably caused by jealousy and the consumption of alcohol.

'In your moment of spite, you have failed to appreciate that a blackmailer always comes off worse than his victim if he or she is exposed. You have a loving husband and a young daughter to consider, where as I am too old now to be concerned at a little mud slinging.

'Think on these things before you cast another stone into the pool.

'Yours sincerely, Miles.'

There were a great many letters from the last man Magnus Osbourne, written from several different addresses and over a long period. These told an almost complete story, about an older married man who'd fallen for a young dancer.

When Camellia first read back in Rye, she had known nothing of love, or passion. But now, as she read them again, she understood the undercurrents. The man was tormented, loving Bonny, yet his wife too. This was an honourable, highly intelligent man, she felt, caught up in a net he couldn't untangle himself from.

She gathered that Magnus had met Bonny while she was dancing at a theatre in Oxford – the first letter mentioned a show, a hotel, and a building project Magnus was about to embark on. He spoke of 'middle-aged madness', and in the same sentence he told her there could be no more between them, he asked her to write and tell him how she was getting on in her new show in Brighton.

In another letter he wrote nostalgically about a house on the Thames in Staines, Middlesex where he had taken her boating. He told Bonny she was a little witch who had enchanted him, and yet again said it must end before it was too late.

Presumably it was already too late. The letters kept coming, nine or ten of them in the period from 1946 to 1947. Camellia found these letters amusing, for by her more liberated standards they were very chaste.

She wished she knew where all these letters were sent. It seemed Bonny must have been touring and living in digs: he sometimes commiserated with her on the indignity of outside lavatories and no bathrooms. There were references to the pier at Brighton, and a charity event in London which might help her career. But after a mention of the Hippodrome in Catford, South London, where he hoped to find time to see her show, the letters stopped.

Camellia assumed that Bonny had met John Norton around this time and perhaps broken off her affair with Magnus.

He didn't write again until August 1954, from an address in Bath. This letter was puzzling. Camellia couldn't tell whether the Nortons and the Osbournes had been moving in the same social circle for some years, or whether Bonny had used a chance encounter to her advantage. The crucial element was the date. Just a month earlier she had received a remarkably similar letter from Miles.

'My dear Bonny, My first intention was to ignore what you said. You'd been drinking heavily and perhaps you just wanted to stir things up a little.

Maybe you got some sort of sadistic pleasure in giving me such a shock when both John and Ruth were within earshot, but whatever your reasons or excuses, I find myself dwelling on it constantly. You must tell me the truth. John clearly adores you and Camellia; from what I understand you have a happy life together. I would ask that you think of their happiness and security before making any further rash statements. Yours, Magnus.'

Again there was a long gap – the next letter was a note of condolence on John's death – but it was obvious that they had been in touch with one another during that interval. Bonny had clearly found a way of convincing Magnus that he was Camellia's father.

'My dear Bonny, I am so very sorry to hear of John's death. It seems unspeakably cruel that such a young man should die from a heart attack. It is always a difficult task to write letters of condolence, but in this case it is doubly difficult because of our past relationship. I liked and respected John, as you know, and it was my hope after our last talk that you would concentrate whole-heartedly on your marriage and be the kind of wife he deserved.

'But now on his death I find myself deeply troubled. I grieve to think of any child losing such a loving father. Knowing that Camellia is really mine puts me in an impossible position. I cannot acknowledge her: not only would it hurt my wife and other children, but it would hurt Camellia too. For all intents and purposes, John was her real father.

'I ask you now to consider only her. John has left you both well provided for. For her sake, let her take pride and comfort in his memory. Let old secrets lie buried, at least until she is of an age to understand them.

'I will of course give you financial assistance

should you ever need it. But I would ask that you address any correspondence not to Oaklands but to my solicitors, marking the envelope for my attention. I trust you will continue to behave with discretion in this matter, not for my sake, but for Camellia's.

'Yours, Magnus.'

Presumably Bonny did ask for help as the few letters in the years from 1956 to 1962 were short and businesslike. Camellia felt the only reason for them was that a cheque was enclosed. She felt Oaklands was a hotel as in one of the more recent letters there was a reference to guests. She wondered why there were no more letters after '62. Had Magnus refused to help out any longer? Or could it be that Bonny began to meet him again? Could he have been the man she went to see on her last trip to London?

Finally there was a single letter from a woman, written on saxe-blue paper, from an address in Bayswater Road, London. It was undated and signed 'H'.

'Dearest Bonny, How are things back there? I'm getting through, somehow. My hair feels like steel wool, my voice like a foghorn from lack of practice, and I'm so flabby I've joined up for a few classes. Saw "M" yesterday, I found it hard to look him in the eye, but it seems everything's going to plan. Meanwhile, I've got a job as a cocktail waitress to keep my mind off things.

'Yes, of course, my heart's down there with you and Camellia, but you know that don't you? Reassure me we did the right thing! Sometimes late at night I have panic attacks, but I suppose that's understandable. You know what I want, all the little details. Write soon and tell me. Kiss Camellia for me, and give my love to John. You are all in my thoughts, night and day. Love H.'

Camellia read and reread this letter. Clearly the woman was another dancer, and although there were no references to the past, the cryptic, almost code-like way she wrote suggested a long-term close friendship. Who was she? Was the 'M' she mentioned Miles or Magnus? And why couldn't she look him in the eye? 'Reassure me *we* did the right thing!' Had they hatched up something together? Was this 'H' woman in on the plot to blackmail all three men?

There was a well-worn black-and-white photograph of Bonny and another showgirl, wearing spangled costumes and feathered head-dresses. Between them was a man in a dinner jacket. Was the other girl 'H'?

But if she and Bonny had been such close friends, why had Bonny never spoken of her?

The man in the photograph was handsome, though probably over forty, strong rugged features, with thick fair hair and a wide endearing smile. Camellia felt sure this was Magnus. Miles didn't sound the sort of man who'd smile like that!

It was an intriguing puzzle, she decided, and an incomplete one at that. Her mother was always so disorganised. When they left the house in Mermaid Street she chucked out hundreds of old letters without even glancing at them. So *why* had she kept *these* and stored them away so methodically?

When Camellia first came upon them, she had assumed Bonny had intended the police to find them to create further trouble for the men. Looking at the letters now she found that unlikely, they were all so old. Bonny would have needed something far more recent to create any real mischief.

It could be that Bonny had put them under the mattress for safe-keeping, then forgot them. But a far more likely explanation was that Bonny was still in contact with one or all of these men prior to her death, perhaps even working on a new scheme to turn the screws on them.

Camellia didn't like that thought at all. She put the letters back in the file and put them away. She would have to deal with it one day. But not now, not yet.

It was not until February 1971, six months after Bee's death, that Camellia learned that Jake had been convicted and sent to prison. Overnight a blanket of snow had fallen and when she got to the restaurant for the lunch-shift she found it was closed. Her employer, a Greek called Costa, had been infuriated recently by power cuts, which had become a regular afternoon trial. And now decimalisation had just started. No one seemed to understand the new money at all, least of all Costa. Everyone was asking 'But what's that in old money?' Costa must have decided the snow was the final straw and stayed at home.

Camellia rarely bought newspapers or went into coffee bars, but she took a seat by the window of the Wimpy Bar on Earls Court Road and waited to see if Costa turned up.

If Camellia hadn't had time to kill, she might never have discovered about Jake's sentence. The front page of the *Daily Express* was devoted to a jokey story of decimalisation and the problems people were encountering, the second and third to a follow-up story about some of the victims of the Ibrox Park disaster back in January, which had killed 66 people when the crowd barriers collapsed. Jake's trial took up only one column on the fourth page and if it hadn't been for a small picture of him she might have missed it. His real name was Timothy Reading: it sounded like a middle-class bank clerk, not the perverted animal she knew him to be.

A year ago she might have thought six years' imprisonment a harsh penalty for smuggling cannabis and distributing dirty pictures. Had it been Aiden Murphy or John Everton she might have argued they didn't deserve anything more than a fine. But for Jake she felt six years wasn't nearly long enough. She knew he'd killed Bee.

When Costa didn't turn up to open the restaurant she went for a long walk, but it wasn't until she found herself in Kensington Gardens that she became aware of her surroundings. For months now she'd trudged through the days as if she was blinkered and her ears stuffed with cotton wool. Maybe it was just the beauty of the crisp snow underfoot, heavily laden trees glistening in the weak sunshine, but all at once she had an urge to run and even to smile at the rosy-faced children in their thick coats, bright woolly hats and mittens.

She stopped to watch a man and his children building a snow man, and dug into her pockets for two big black buttons to offer them as eyes. They'd come off weeks ago and she'd managed quite well without them all this time.

There was a holiday atmosphere everywhere in the park. Children were skipping school, businessmen disguised in sheepskin coats and wellingtons. Dogs gambolling in the heavy drifts, mothers dragging small children on sledges. A group of students pelted one another with snowballs and for once even the usual background roar of traffic had ceased.

The icy lump inside her was thawing. She felt it enough to scoop up a snowball and throw it for a dog. She laughed aloud as he ran to catch it, then turned in bewilderment when he couldn't find it.

Camellia knew then that it was time to move on. London held nothing for her but ugly memories.

She would travel, see the world and try to find something to like about herself. Maybe then she'd be strong enough to approach each of those three men and find out who she really was.

Chapter Twelve

Perspiration dripped down Camellia's sides and onto the grass mat. Lying face down her arms outstretched, wearing only the scrappiest of bikini bottoms, she was lost in the bliss of the sun's rays searing into her salt-flecked bronzed body and the sound of sea lapping just beyond her toes. The small beach was almost deserted and she was exquisitely happy.

'Inner peace.' Dozens of hippies arrived in Ibiza daily, chanting that phrase like a mantra. More often than not it eluded them, so they passed onto Morocco or even India. But Camellia had found it, without the aids of gurus or drugs, by looking deep into herself and recognising her failings and her abilities.

London, with all its bad memories seemed light years away. Even the scar on her knee had faded to just a thin pink line. But now she knew she must go back. Soon the bars and shops which relied on tourists would close for the winter. She was tempted to stay on, but she had plans and a career to find.

She sat up as she heard the sound of the ferryman's small motorboat coming in to the small rock-bound cove, slipped her bikini top back on and stood up. It was time to go.

A lump came up in her throat as she took a last

look at *her* beach. The sand was almost white, the sea turquoise, so clear you could see right down to the bottom even in deep water. There were no amenities here, no toilets or even a bar. Just a few scrubby-looking cactus-type plants separating the beach from the olive grove behind it, but it was the closest place she'd found to heaven.

The ferryman rang a bell to warn her and the other few sun-worshippers his was the last boat today. Camellia picked up her loose cheesecloth dress, slipped it over her head, rolled up her mat and stuffed it into a string bag with her towel.

She sat in the bows of the boat on the return trip to Ibiza town. She didn't wish to get into conversation with anyone for fear of missing all the last sights. She wanted to photograph them clearly in her mind, so that if anytime in the future she felt she was losing her grip again, she could instantly recall it and the inner strength she found here.

Camellia had heard about Ibiza from other hitchhikers as she travelled down through France and Spain. They spoke effusively about it being a Mecca for hippies, with the freedom to sleep on beaches without hassle and its low police profile. She had caught a ferry from mainland Spain and, even before the boat docked, she was enchanted. A mediaeval fortress high on a hill dominated her view; clustered precariously round it was the old town. No modern bars or ugly concrete hotels spoiled the sleepy harbour, just small restaurants and bodegas offering a warm welcome.

Everything she saw that day delighted her: the narrow winding streets, the old ladies in long black dresses, the ragged but smiling children who ran after her begging for pesetas. The smell of the fish in the market took her back to when she was four or five, holding her father's hand on the quayside in Rye and watching the fishermen turn out their baskets of gleaming herring. But here there were so many other fish, small pinky red ones, huge fearsome speckled ones, squid, sprats, crab and lobster.

On that first day she had climbed up and up the narrow steep streets, drinking in the colour and beauty: purple bougainvillaea, scarlet hibiscus, brilliant against white painted walls, faded green shutters on ancient houses, terracotta tiles on roofs. She was panting when she finally got to the fortress, but it was worth the climb. Sitting on a low wall, she surveyed the town beneath her, with its backdrop of brilliant blue sea and sky, loving the higgledy-piggledy way the houses were crammed in on different levels, no two identical. It seemed to be telling her that there was room for her here too.

Work was accountable for much of her new-found happiness and pride in herself. All summer she had worked as hard as any of the lean Spanish waiters. She was given a small room in a hotel down by the harbour in return for making the other guests' beds and cleaning their rooms. At lunch-time she waited at tables in a café by the market. Then in the evenings she was back by the harbour, serving drinks to the throngs of sun-baked thirsty people who sat at tables outside watching the sun go down over the sea and the world go by. Afternoons were the time she had to herself. Mostly she took this small ferry alone to *her* beach, and read and dozed in the sun, letting the peace and beauty of the place heal and cleanse her.

As the small boat chugged into the harbour, Camellia leaned on the bow and silently said goodbye to the fortress. Tonight she would climb up there one last time to look down on the town, but it was from this angle coming in from the sea that its true Moorish magnificence should be seen.

The ferryman tied up the boat and held out a

hand to help them step onto the quayside. The town was just waking up from its siesta now. Plump olive-skinned Spanish women hung flimsy garments up on hooks, wheeled out the postcard stands and the stacks of embroidered tablecloths.

Camellia could smell sardines cooking, and the acrid, smoky smell made her stomach rumble. She hadn't eaten anything all day except for a rather stale roll left from breakfast. Groups of hippies were gathering together, almost identical in their long hair, cut-off Levis and shapeless faded tee shirts. Some were arranging boards of handmade jewellery to sell, others unpacking tie-dyed tee shirts and sarongs, still more just smoking and chatting. Camellia had admired their fearless adventurous lives when she first arrived, but she'd turned a full circle now and decided they were merely aimless and lazy. She smiled as Pete Holt, a Nordic-looking six-footer from Birmingham gave her the peace sign, but although she liked him, she wasn't going to get embroiled with him, his chums or any large joints on her last night.

'*Buenas tardes, senorita,*' Pedro one of the snake-hipped waiters called out as she passed by Diego's bodega. Camellia smiled and waved. Pedro was sweet on her and very handsome, but tangling with a Spaniard wasn't her scene. In fact tangling with any man wasn't her scene anymore. She'd discovered back in July after a briefly promising affair with Christian from Cornwall, that although sunshine, sea and cheap Spanish wine might make you think a man was a god, there was also a price to pay. In Christian's case pay was the operative word: he had expected her to earn the money for them both, while he spent all day and night getting stoned.

It was nearly one in the morning when Camellia

crept into her tiny room on the top floor of El Tora after an evening of eating, drinking and saying goodbye to friends.

Although by day it was unbearably hot up here under the roof, a cool breeze was coming in off the sea now. Camellia had little to pack: she'd learned the wisdom of travelling light as soon as she discovered how heavy a rucksack could become after a couple of hours. She was down to mere essentials now – a pair of jeans, two pairs of shorts, underwear and a few tee shirts. She would donate her three cheesecloth sundresses to Michelle, the French girl who she'd worked alongside all summer. They wouldn't be much use back in London, but Michelle was going on to Morocco next week.

Sitting down on her narrow bed, she opened the window wide and lit a cigarette. She wasn't nervous about hitchhiking up through Spain and France alone, there was always someone to pal up with on the way and she'd learned the ropes coming here. Besides she had money from working all summer and living frugally. Once she got her pesetas changed up she reckoned on close to sixty pounds, enough to get a cheap bedsitter when she got back and tide her over till she found a job. All her belonging were at Denise's and she might offer her a bed for a few days anyway.

She turned to the small table by her bed and picked up a photograph of Bee and herself, taken in the Don Juan. Camellia was in white with a feather boa, Bee in black, her hair a golden storm of curls.

At one time she couldn't look at it without crying, but now she knew why she'd always kept it with her despite the pain it brought. Bee's sweet plump face was a reminder of all the dangers out there. It had kept her straight, even in moments of extreme temptation. So often this summer she'd been teased for refusing joints, for not giving friends free drinks in the bar, for not stealing so much as an orange in the little shops. But those people who travelled with their battered copies of Jack Kerouac's *On the Road* and the *Prophet*, who scorned materialism and lived on their wits, dope and other people's half chewed over philosophy, had never lost anyone dear to them. They had that to come.

Four days after leaving Ibiza, some hundred kilometres from Calais and the ferry home, Camellia discovered she'd been robbed of her money belt.

A businessman had picked her up early that morning just outside Montpellier in his Citroen and brought her all the way through France, dropping her at a crossroads.

She went through her rucksack three times, taking each item out painstakingly. But it wasn't there. She had worn it constantly back in Ibiza: she'd seen too many other people losing their money through being careless or too trusting. But today she had removed it because it was irritating her skin on the long drive.

Camellia wanted to scream with rage, but there was no one to scream at. It seemed like the middle of nowhere: flat open fields on either side of a road lined with the inevitable avenue of plane trees. From where she stood she couldn't see even one house. But even if anyone appeared, and she managed to explain in French, she didn't think she'd get much sympathy. Hippies were notorious for their hard luck stories.

She sat down on the roadside, thinking. The man in the Citroen had only stopped once, at a large services where they had coffee and croissants. Camellia knew she had it then as she'd offered to pay. The man had refused and she put it back in her rucksack. She had gone to the lavatories before getting back into the car. There were a couple of Dutch girls waiting in a queue and they'd discussed how disgusting the traditional French hole-in-the-ground variety was. It was the friendliness of these girls that had prompted her to leave her rucksack with them while she went in. They weren't hippie hitchhikers, but smartly dressed office girls, touring with their boyfriends.

'You bitches,' she spat out viciously, visualising the two fresh-faced blondes gleefully sharing out all that money she'd worked so hard for. But yet she didn't cry. At the back of her mind a small voice was reminding her of all those people she'd robbed back in Piccadilly. Now she knew how it felt.

It was half an hour before a truck slowed down at her raised thumb. Camellia picked up her rucksack and ran towards it. She wished she'd thought to change out of her brief shorts and replace her tight tee shirt with a baggier one, but it was too late now.

'Parlez-vous anglais?' she said haltingly, looking up at the man in the cab.

'I should think so, darlin',' he grinned broadly and tapped his arm on the outside of the truck door. 'What d'you think that is? Bloody Swahili?'

She was so relieved to hear an English voice, she could've hugged him.

'Are you going to the ferry at Calais?' she asked.

'Sure am, then on to London,' he said cheerfully. 'Hop in if you want a ride.'

He introduced himself as Reg, offered her one of his sandwiches and a can of beer, and listened to her story about the girls stealing her money belt.

'Well, you were a mug and no mistake,' he said. 'Me, I don't trust no one. But you're all right now with yer Uncle Reg. I'll get you home.'

As they drove on towards Calais, Camellia's

spirits began to rise again. It was a beautiful afternoon, fields of ripe golden corn, speckled with scarlet poppies stretched for as far as she could see, and Reg, though a bit grubby and uncouth, was kindly. She had to be philosophical about her stolen money: it would've been much worse if it had happened when she was still back in Spain. She had about twenty pounds in the Post Office. As long as she could get to Denise's she'd be fine.

The sun was beginning to set as they drove into Calais docks.

'Give us yer passport,' Reg said gruffly as he gathered together his papers ready to go into the offices. 'I'll pass you off as my girlfriend. There shouldn't be any problem.'

Camellia watched Reg with some amusement as he walked away from her and his truck. He made her think of a male pigeon, chest all puffed out with importance, as if he thought people were admiring him. Perhaps he'd once had a good body: his shoulders were wide and his biceps huge. But at over forty he was sagging. His beer-belly quivered under his tight dirty white tee shirt, and his sandy hair was very thin on top. She hoped he wouldn't get any ideas about her. She wasn't entirely comfortable with him passing her off as his girl-friend.

Reg spat noisily out the window several times as they waited in the truck for their turn to drive onto the ferry. It turned Camellia's stomach and she found herself noticing other unpleasant things about him. He smelled of stale sweat, his neck and hands were ingrained with dirt and he had tufts of hair coming out of his ears.

'Why aren't there any cars?' she asked, looking out the window as a uniformed man indicated the spot he was to drive into.

'Well, it's a freighter, love,' Reg replied. 'It's only

lorries come on it. You get good food too – none of the fancy prices they charge on the regular ferry. You look as if you could do with a bit of grub.'

The moment they set foot in the bar upstairs Reg was greeting the other drivers. 'Whatcha think of my new girl?' he bawled out across the bar to one of them, at the same time putting his hand on her bottom and squeezing it.

Camellia blushed scarlet with embarrassment. Her long brown legs in brief shorts hadn't raised an eyebrow all through Spain and France, but now she was painfully aware of every man's eyes on them. Foolishly she'd left her rucksack in the cab, but she wouldn't be allowed back down to the hold to get it and change. It was almost dusk and growing colder.

Reg insisted on buying her a meal. Camellia was a little dubious about putting herself further in his debt, but she was so hungry she lost her qualms at the sight of steak and kidney pie. Although his coarse banter with the other drivers and the way he sat protectively close to her was a little unnerving, he seemed genuinely concerned about her.

'You'd better get your head down in my bunk when we gets to Dover,' he said. 'I'll drop you off by Waterloo station, you'll be safer to hang around in there till the trains start running. Don't you go roaming around the streets till it gets light.'

It began to rain soon after the ferry left Calais. As the harbour lights of Dover came into view it turned into a full-blown storm. Camellia was freezing.

'You can get changed into something warmer in the bogs in the customs hall,' Reg said solicitously. 'Just hope they don't hold me up tonight. I wanna get home and into bed.'

An hour later Camellia was slipping off to sleep

in Reg's bunk. She had changed into jeans and a sweater in the toilets in Dover, and the sound of the radio playing softly, the swish of the windscreen wipers and the warmth of the blankets had lulled her into a sense of security.

She woke with a start as the truck stopped.

'We're here, sweetheart,' Reg said, turning in his seat to look at her.

Camellia sat up. It was still dark, and the road they were in was badly lit. 'Where are we?' she asked fearfully.

'It's okay,' he laughed at her expression. 'Waterloo Bridge is just up ahead. I ain't taken you to Timbuktu while you were sleeping. The station is just around the corner, but mind you stay there until it's light.'

Camellia climbed into the passenger seat, put her plimsolls on and fastened up her rucksack.

'Here,' Reg held out a couple of pound notes. 'Take this for your fare home.'

Camellia looked at his kindly weather-beaten face and felt ashamed she'd been wary of him earlier.

'That's very kind of you,' she said weakly. She wanted to kiss his cheek but the smell of his stale sweat deterred her. 'Give me your address and I'll send it back to you.'

To her surprise he laughed.

'What! The old woman'd throttle me if she knew I'd picked up a young girl,' he said. 'You just keep it and welcome. But be a bit more careful who you take lifts off in future. There's plenty of truckers who ain't got no respect for women.'

At eight in the morning Camellia was outside 34 Ladbroke Square. Mercifully it had stopped raining while she waited over a cup of tea at Waterloo for a more respectable hour. But she felt cold and very grubby.

She rang Denise's bell, bracing herself for a telling off for arriving so early in the morning. But she was excited too: she had so much to tell Denise.

By the time she'd rung three times and got no reply, Camellia felt vaguely sick. It hadn't even occurred to her that Denise might not be in. She rang the ground-floor flat.

'I'm so sorry to disturb you,' she said as a middle-aged woman in her dressing gown answered the door. 'I've been ringing Mrs Traherne's flat and there's no reply. Do you know where she is?'

'Off in Italy,' the older woman said curtly, clearly irritated at the intrusion. 'She left two days ago.'

The woman was already moving to shut the door, but Camellia moved forward. 'I'm in a tight spot,' she said, then quickly went on to explain about her clothes and money being stored by Denise.

'I can't help that,' the woman shrugged her shoulders, her face cold. 'I haven't got a key to her flat, and even if I had I wouldn't dream of letting a stranger in there. You'd better go to the police.'

By five in the afternoon Camellia was close to breaking down in tears. She had spent nearly the whole day at Charles House, the National Assistance Board in Kensington High Street, but all they'd given her was 75 pence, the daily subsistence allowance they doled out to vagrants. Until she had an address they couldn't give her more. But how could she get an address without advance rent?

She had begged tearfully, then got angry when they wouldn't listen. When she said she had twenty pounds in a Post Office, with which she could repay any loan once she got her book back from Denise, they merely pointed out she could try asking at a Post Office to see what they could do.

Everything was against her. In jeans and a sweater she looked travel worn and grubby, and her hair needed washing. Was it any wonder that she'd been turned away from her old student hostel in Earls Court with a flea in her ear? Was anyone going to trust a girl who had all her entire worldly possessions in a rucksack on her back?

Over another cup of tea in a café, she counted out her money. £1.48 was all she had left. She was sorely tempted to go to the West End and steal a wallet.

'No,' she whispered to herself, cupping her hands around the mug of tea and trying to ignore the growl of hunger in her stomach. 'There has to be another way.'

Thinking back to her days with Dougie she found it ironic that at that time any self-respecting hippie would offer a stranger shelter for the night, even if it was only on the floor. But the tide had turned, 'Love is all you need' had no meaning now in the 70s. People had become suspicious and self-protective.

By eight that evening Camellia was desperate and very cold. She'd walked from Charles House down to Hammersmith to see her old friend Suzanne, but found she and her family had moved to Watford two years earlier. Perhaps if she'd been a better friend and kept in touch she would have known that. Pride precluded even attempting to go out to Archway House, instinctively she knew she would get no sympathy from Miss Peet and any other addresses and telephone numbers of old acquaintances were all locked in Denise's flat with the rest of her belongings.

It was as she stood at Hammersmith Broadway

that Miles, one of her mother's old lovers, came to her mind. Holland Park wasn't that far away.

She had intended to have a good job, a decent home and be looking stunningly well dressed before she embarked on presenting herself to any of these men, but she was frantic enough to try anything.

It was a long shot. But this man had said he had great respect for her father and presumably he'd met her as a small child. She had nothing much to lose: the worst he could do was slam the door in her face. With luck he might offer her tea and a sandwich. If he was pleasant she might even be able to admit her predicament and get a bed for the night.

Camellia knew that Holland Park was an area inhabited by the rich. Miles's house was small in comparison to its neighbours. But as she peered through the arched wrought iron gate she felt her courage seeping away.

It was so very smart. A light over the front door illuminated the heavy brass knocker, glossy dark green paint and two bay trees in tubs. She almost turned tail and ran. A sixth sense told her she would get no welcome here, but perversely she opened the gate and walked up to the front door.

A bell echoed through the house. She saw a light come on in the hall and then heard the shuffling of old feet coming towards the door.

The door opened and a small, wizened man in a dark suit looked her up and down. 'Yes?'

'Miles?' she asked. 'I'm sorry, I don't know your surname.'

The man's lips curled scornfully. 'This is Sir Miles Hamilton's London residence.'

For a moment Camellia could only gape stupidly at the old man. Never in her wildest imaginings had she considered that the letters came from someone titled. This old man, looking at her so scornfully, must be a butler or manservant. She knew she had blown it. She should've done some homework before coming here.

'I didn't,' Camellia stopped short, racking her brain for a sensible way of introducing herself. 'I mean, I'm sorry to call without contacting Sir Hamilton first, but I've just got back from the continent and I wanted to have a word with him. Is it possible for me to see him?'

'Sir Miles is away at present,' the man replied sharply. 'If you would like to leave your visiting card, I will give it to him on his return.'

Camellia had a strong desire to turn and run. 'I don't have any cards,' she said weakly. 'My name is Camellia Norton and I believe he was an old friend of my father's. I came across a letter from him after my mother died. I just wanted to introduce myself to him.'

The man turned for a second, took a small pad from a table just inside the door and handed it to her. His heavily lined face was inscrutable. 'Write your name and address on here,' he said.

Camellia was stuck. 'I don't have a permanent address at the moment,' she said falteringly. 'I'm passing through London on my way to a new job. I'll just leave my name and perhaps I can write to him later.'

She wrote down her name and handed back the pad.

'I'm sorry to disturb you.' She tried to smile but she was dangerously close to tears. 'Goodnight.'

Camellia had slept rough in France and Spain, but it had been warm there and she'd had the company of a group of other people. In the absence of any alternative she wandered around until one in the morning, then made her way into Holland Park and curled up under a dense bush, her head on her rucksack.

She was too cold and hungry to sleep, and she smarted at her stupidity in calling cold on Sir Miles Hamilton. What was he going to think when he returned home and learned she called on him with a rucksack on her back? Well, she'd blown that one. She wouldn't dare contact him again.

It was a long night. From time to time she heard strange rustlings in the bushes which made her skin crawl and the cold penetrated through to her very bones as she lay there trying to make some sort of plan for the next day.

She thought of calling on a few hotels and restaurants in the West End, to see if they'd take her on as casual labour. But that still left her with nowhere to sleep. Then, just as she felt like sobbing in despair, she recalled Pete Holt back in Ibiza talking about Butlins holiday camp in Bognor Regis. He had done some spring cleaning there at the end of the summer season and it sounded grim. Yet he said he made enough money to get him onto Ibiza, and he got fed and had a chalet to sleep in.

As the first light of dawn appeared in the sky she got up and left, afraid someone with a dog might find her and call the police if she stayed any longer. As she walked back down the deserted Kensington High Street she was still thinking about Butlins.

It seemed a good idea to leave London, where people were so hard and suspicious. Even if it came to the worst and they wouldn't take her on at Butlins, the people in the national assistance offices down there would probably be more sympathetic. Bognor Regis had other advantages too. It was near to Littlehampton where Jack Easton had his garage, and Amberley, where Aunt Lydia lived.

Camellia had thought a great deal more about

her mother's childhood while she was in Ibiza. She knew she had been evacuated to Sussex during the war. Bonny had often said it was a lucky break for her, that Aunt Lydia had given her opportunities she would never have got back in London with her parents. Camellia wondered whether the bitterness she remembered between her grandmother and Bonny was due to this enforced estrangement. It would be good to meet Lydia, and find out more about her mother's childhood.

If she could just talk herself into a job, something to tide her over until Denise returned from Italy, she could investigate both Jack and Lydia in her spare time, then return to London.

Some sort of homing instinct made her walk through the back streets of Chelsea instead of taking a more direct route to the river and the South London main road. She knew no one in Chelsea now, but it drew her despite all the bad memories.

In Oakley Street she paused by the railings of number fourteen and looked down into the basement with a mixture of nostalgia for the good times she'd known there and deep sorrow. The people who lived there now had repainted the front door a glossy dark blue and a brass coach lamp was fixed to the wall.

Through the window she could see a large three-piece suite and a glass-topped coffee table. Camellia sighed, remembering Bee's poignant desire for a vase of daffodils in a white painted sunny room. There were no flowers now, just soulless expensive furniture.

Self-preservation was to the forefront of her mind as she hurried away towards Albert Bridge. She had to find somewhere to stay, today. If she spent one more night sleeping rough, it would show, and no one would take her on in any job, however humble.

Camellia did not arrive at the gates of Butlins holiday camp until nearly six that evening. She had been quite fortunate in lifts at first: one truck driver had picked her up in Battersea and taken her as far as Guildford, and the next had taken her to Milford and told her to get a lift down the A286 all the way to Chichester. But her luck had run out there and she'd walked miles along the Bognor Regis road feeling dizzy with hunger and so cold she actually contemplated asking for help in a police station.

But at last she was here. As she approached the security man in his booth she was determined to get a job even if she had to lie through her teeth and sleep with the devil to do it.

She had never seen a Butlins holiday camp before. As a child she'd heard people talking about them and got the idea they were paradise. She thought she ought to feel excited to be at one at last, but she was too tired, hungry and cold to appreciate it. There was a fun fair, over to her right, all lit up with coloured lights. As T. Rex's 'Get it On' which she'd heard constantly in Ibiza was blaring out, it seemed the best of omens.

'I've come for a job,' she said firmly, switching on a bright smile for the security man and concealing her rucksack between her legs. 'I believe you need people for the big clean-up.'

The man looked ex-military, a big chap in a green uniform with gold epaulettes and a moustache. Camellia had a theory about moustaches, based on her own experience, starting with her father. She firmly believed men who sported them were true gentle types, who grew them to appear more fierce.

'That's the first I've heard of it,' he said, looking

surprised, but his tone was genial. 'I'm sure we've got everyone we need.'

Camellia was dismayed and she let him see it. 'But I've come all the way from London,' she said, gripping the counter of his booth. 'I was told you always need people at this time of year.'

He gave Camellia the once-over. 'I'll ring personnel and ask for you,' he said.

Camellia sensed she had to present a stronger case for herself. The man's hand was only inches away on the counter, and she puts hers over it.

'Please use your influence,' she begged, looking right into his eyes. 'I really need a job badly. I'll work like three other girls.'

George Unwin wasn't usually a soft touch. Every day at Butlins, people tried to con their way in, to use the swimming pool, to steal purses or some other skulduggery. But he liked something in this girl's tanned face. She looked exhausted, and she had no coat even though it was growing chilly, but it was a good face, he thought an honest one.

'It would only be temporary,' he replied. 'You do know that, don't you?'

'I only need somewhere for two or three weeks.' She allowed her eyes to fill up with tears and quickly told him about losing her money. 'I'm really desperate,' she finished off.

'Okay, I'll see what I can do,' he said brusquely, but she knew he was now on her side.

She waited, politely out of earshot as he spoke to someone on the telephone.

He put the phone down after a couple of minutes and smiled at her. 'Looks like you're in luck,' he said. 'They could do with another pair of hands, but mind you keep your nose clean or I'll be for it.'

Camellia could've kissed him.

Two hours later Camellia was lying on a bed in a

staff chalet, hearing from Janice, the girl she was to share with, just how bad it was working at Butlins.

Janice was a pint-sized eighteen-year-old with thick glasses and wispy red hair. She was still wearing her uniform striped nylon overall, and she had a dirty tidemark round her wrists as if her hands had been in dirty water all day. As soon as she stubbed out one cigarette she lit another. Even her face had a yellow tinge as though stained with nicotine.

'Mrs Willows, the supervisor, is a dragon. We have to scrub every inch of the chalets, she never lets up on us. Next week they'll have us scrubbing out the kitchens and the dining rooms too. If it wasn't for my bonus I'd leave right now.'

Camellia didn't care how grim it was. After filling in an application form and being informed of her duties and the company rules, she had been taken to the cafeteria and given the biggest plate of fish and chips she'd ever seen, followed by spotted dick and custard and several cups of tea. She assumed this staff chalet with its bare wood walls and dim light wasn't quite the same standard the holiday-makers enjoyed, but it beat sleeping rough.

'Janice,' she laughed, stretching out on her narrow iron bed. 'I'm so happy to be here I'd gladly wipe people's bottoms for them if I were asked. All I want now to make my happiness complete is a hot bath and bed.'

'You won't be saying that in a day or two,' Janice said darkly. Then she smiled with some warmth and held out her cigarettes. 'Have a fag, Mel. It will be nice to have some company, it's been creepy being in here alone at nights.'

Janice was right, it was a terrible job. Mrs Willows, the Supervisory Housekeeper, was a female Attila the Hun. Nothing escaped her eagle eye, not a smear on a window or the tiniest piece of chewing-gum stuck to the bottom of a chair. The chalets Janice, Camellia and a team of other girls had to clean had been vacated the previous Saturday. The bedding and curtains went to the laundry, mattresses were carried away to a storeroom, the furniture had to be taken outside to be scrubbed with disinfectant, and then the floor and walls were scrubbed too before carting everything back. Camellia hadn't realised on her first night just how big the camp was. She soon lost any illusions that she was in paradise.

Wherever they were on the camp, they were always within earshot when Mrs Willows bawled some luckless chalet maid out for not completing the job to her satisfaction. On her very first morning Camellia saw the woman pull a girl by her ear into a chalet. She half expected to find that same girl in chains later.

By the second day Camellia's hands were red and sore, her back ached and she felt she had cleaning fluid in her veins instead of blood. The nylon overall she had to wear was shapeless, ugly and it made her smell sweaty. But the job had its lighter moments: the other chalet maids were a funny ill-assorted bunch of girls from all walks of life and they welcomed a new face in their midst.

The summer season was almost over. The few holiday-makers left in the camp were mainly elderly couples and families with under fives, all there at bargain prices. The staff were in a highly excitable state brought about by a combination of exhaustion and the promise of a good bonus when they left for good in two weeks. Janice claimed the entertainment had grown slack and the food dire, compared with the high season. But to Camellia both seemed pretty good. She could take a swim in the indoor pool at certain hours of the day, have a go at roller-skating and watch the cabaret show at night. In quieter moments, when Mrs Willows disappeared for a time, Janice and the other girls regaled Camellia with all the gossip about the various Red Coats.

It was on the following Tuesday, her day off, that Camellia decided to try and find Jack Easton and Aunt Lydia. She had been paid on Saturday afternoon and felt flush enough to buy a cheap day return to Littlehampton on the train.

The file of old letters was back at Denise's, so Camellia had only her memory to rely on. Although the name of the road Jack's garage was in escaped her, she was sure once she looked at a town map it would come back to her.

As she came out of Littlehampton station she had a flash of déjà vu. She could only suppose she'd been here before with her mother and father at some time. A large street map was right outside and as her eyes scanned down the index Terminus Road jumped up at her immediately. To her further delight she was actually standing in that road.

There was a garage right across the street from the station, but there was no name on the sign. It was a ramshackle wooden building with a corrugated iron roof, set back from the rank of small shops. Camellia spotted a man in a protective mask spraying a car just inside the door and went over to him.

'Excuse me,' she said in a loud voice to attract his attention.

The man looked round, halted his spraying and removed the mask from his face. He was around the same age as herself, with swarthy dark skin.

'Could you tell me who owns this garage?' she asked.

The man looked quizzically at her. 'Mr Stan Wells,' he said. 'Why d'you wanna know?'

'I thought a Jack Easton owned it,' she said. 'I was trying to find him.'

'In the market for a new car then?' His dark eyes ran up and down her, then paused on her breasts.

'Oh no,' she said quickly. 'I'm just looking for Mr Easton.'

'He did own this place once, donkey's years ago.'

Her heart sank. 'D'you know where he is now?' she asked. 'Does he have another garage?'

The man gave her the oddest look. 'Not a garage.' He grinned suddenly, showing surprisingly good teeth. 'But he's got a posh car showroom. It's up the Arundel Road a piece.'

Arundel Road started just around the corner, but after walking for fifteen minutes away from the town centre, Camellia wished she'd asked exactly how far 'a piece' meant.

As she came to a sign marked Wick, she saw the showrooms and all at once her confidence left her. No petrol pumps, greasy inspection pits and men in overalls, but a two-storey building with plate-glass windows, a showroom floor so shiny it looked like glass and gleaming new Mercedes on raised stands. Outside above a rank of equally gleaming second-hand cars a blue illuminated sign said 'Jack Easton Cars'.

She was scared, her palms sticky and her heart pounding. Although she knew she looked good with her tan and shiny hair, she wasn't sure jeans were appropriate for calling in such a place. The man might not want reminders of his past – and what if he remembered all that sordid stuff in the papers and slammed the door in her face?

She walked past the showrooms once, building up her courage to go in. There were two men inside, typical car salesmen types in sharp suits and highly polished shoes. But they were both in their early thirties, too young to be Jack. Stopping out of sight, she checked her face in a small mirror, ran a comb through her hair and put on some fresh lipstick. Then taking a deep breath she walked back to the doors and straight in.

'Good morning, madam.' One of the men almost bounded across the floor towards her. 'Can I help you?'

'I'd like to have a word with Mr Easton please,' she said, forcing a bright smile. 'Is he available?'

The man's face instantly became suspicious. 'Mr Easton doesn't see anyone without an appointment.' He looked down at Camellia's jeans and plimsolls. 'Are you selling something?'

Camellia did her best to disarm the man. 'Do I look like I'm selling something?' she laughed. 'No, I've just popped in on the off-chance of seeing him. I'm the daughter of an old friend of his.'

'Tell me your name and I'll see if he's free,' the man said, as his colleague came forward to find out what was going on.

'It will spoil the surprise,' she said quickly. 'Can't you just let me go up and catch him unawares.' She could see a staircase through glass doors behind the cars. She guessed his office was up there.

'Mr Easton doesn't like surprises,' the first man said flatly. 'Neither is he keen on interruptions.'

'Oh go on,' she urged them both. While they thought about it she wondered what she'd do if they refused. She didn't want to give her name: Jack Easton might refuse to speak to her out of hand. A false name was no good either. If he was hard to get to, he wouldn't be lured by a name which meant nothing. 'Look, suppose I tell him I nipped up the stairs while you were busy with a customer.'

The two men looked at each other reluctantly. As if fate had decided to give her a helping hand, the showroom door opened and in walked a couple who most definitely looked like potential Mercedes drivers.

'You didn't see me,' she said softly, and before they could stop her she was off through the glass doors and up the stairs.

Standing in the corridor outside a door with the plaque 'Jack Easton Director', Camellia was overcome by fright. Further along the corridor a door was open and she could hear two women talking and the sound of a typewriter. It would be so humiliating to be thrown out.

But taking courage in both hands she knocked on his door.

'Come in,' a deep voice replied.

Jack's appearance threw her. His hair was fiery red and spiky, his features almost thug-like. Had he been wearing overalls, and she'd had to speak to him while he serviced a car, she would have felt quite comfortable. But he was wearing a snowy white shirt and striped tie, sitting behind a vast black and chrome desk. She knew immediately that for an uneducated man, with such an unprepossessing appearance to have done so well for himself, he had to be as tough as he looked.

'I'm sorry to disturb you,' she said in a small voice. 'Please don't be angry that I came up here without asking first, but I had to see you.'

'Are you from the school?' he asked, getting to his feet. 'Has Amanda been up to something again?'

He was only marginally taller than herself, but his stocky build gave an impression of iron-hard muscle. His voice had a Sussex burr, yet with Cockney undertones.

'No, it's nothing like that,' she said coming right in and closing the door. 'You see, I'm Camellia Norton.'

For a moment there was absolute silence. He looked stunned, his mouth slightly agape.

'Bonny's daughter,' she said, taking another step towards him. 'I know you were friends years ago, I hoped you might be able to shed some light on something. You see Mum died a few years back.'

'She's dead?' His eyes opened very wide: they were light brown with flecks of amber, surprisingly expressive for such a tough-looking man. 'We were friends, as children,' he added, then paused as if wondering where to go from there. 'We were both evacuated here from London. But I haven't had any contact with her for years.'

Outwardly he appeared unruffled, but when he invited her to sit down and offered her a glass of whisky Camellia guessed it was more because he was shaken by the news than out of real hospitality.

She accepted the whisky gratefully to stop herself trembling, then launched into the story of Bonny's death.

Jack interrupted her as soon as she mentioned the river. 'Drowned! She hated water, never went near it.'

To another person that remark might have sounded aggressively dismissive. But to Camellia it proved just how close he had been to Bonny. She had reacted in exactly the same way when Bert Simmonds broke the news to her.

'The verdict at the inquest was death by misadventure,' Camellia explained. 'The police thought it was suicide. But I never quite believed that.'

Jack shook his head. 'She was terrified of water. She fell in the river at Amberley once and nearly drowned. We became friends because of it – it was me who rescued her.'

Camellia smiled.

'Why the smile?' Jack said brusquely.

'Because Mum told me that story so many times. She gave you a very heroic role. It's good to find it's true and put a name and face to you. She told me very little about her life before I was born you see, it's like having a blank page filled in at last.'

Again he stared at her. It was unnerving: she couldn't gauge what he was thinking. But he obviously hadn't read anything about her in the newspapers, or he would surely have said something about it by now. That was a relief. Perhaps her fears that people would remember her name were groundless.

'I'm sorry, I'm not thinking straight,' he said eventually. He ran his fingers through his hair and his tongue flickered over his lips. 'I should have said I'm sorry she died. You must think me very rude.'

'I didn't come here to gain sympathy and I don't think you are rude at all,' Camellia said evenly. 'My reason for coming is that I found a hidden batch of letters just after she died. I was only fifteen then and in shock, I kept them rather than giving them to the police, because everything I found in them disturbed me.'

His jaw clenched as she spoke, and his eyes grew harder.

'I assume you are about to tell me that some of the letters came from me?' His voice was suddenly icy. 'I just hope you aren't leading up to some sort of proposition?'

'Now you *are* being rude,' she said. 'My mother may have resorted to blackmail, but nothing is further from my mind. So kindly let me finish!'

He heard her out without interrupting.

'I was only a kid when I found those letters. It was bad enough losing my mother, but to suddenly find John wasn't my real father too, that was terrible. I adored him: he was the best father anyone could have, and the only thing I had to be proud of. It was the cruellest thing Mum ever did to me and for a long time I hated her because of it. But I've gone way beyond that now. I just want to get at the truth. Tell me, Mr Easton, just between ourselves. Could you be my father?'

Jack Easton gulped. He was not a man who was easily intimidated. His early childhood in a slum in South London had made him tough and self-reliant, and as a young man he'd had to work hard and fight every step of the way to achieve his ambitions. Bonny was the only person who had ever made him lose control and he often looked back at himself with loathing. She had manipulated him so often. This felt like one last try from the grave.

But there was nothing to remind him of Bonny in this young girl. She wasn't saucy, blonde or blue-eyed. He didn't think she'd inherited her mother's guile either.

He got up, walked round the desk, took both Camellia's hands in his and led her over to a mirror on the wall.

'Look,' he said, putting his face beside hers to make the comparison. 'Could I have produced an offspring as lovely as you?'

There was something comic about their two faces together. Hers was oval and olive-skinned with a perfect straight nose and almond-shaped eyes. Jack with his red hair, pale eyes and upturned nose bore no similarity to her at all. Camellia was forced to smile.

'I'm married to a woman with hair almost as dark as yours,' he added, as if to push his point home. 'But all my three kids have some red in their hair. They are all small and stocky and though Amanda has brown eyes, they are round, not like yours. Do you really believe Bonny and I, with our fair skins and hair, could possibly have made a child as dark as you?' He paused, taking a deep breath. 'Camellia, you are John Norton's daughter. Don't ever think otherwise.'

'But why did she say it then? You must have seen her around the time I was conceived?'

Jack faltered for a moment. He didn't want to admit anything which might incriminate him, but on the other hand he sensed nothing but the complete truth would satisfy this girl. 'There was *one* night only,' he admitted. 'But for my family's sake I'm trusting you to keep that under your hat. Bonny came back to Sussex in May to make her wedding plans with her Aunt Lydia. I drove her back to London because she'd missed the train. Things got a bit out of hand.'

'In May?' Camellia repeated.

'Yes, May. Ginny was away at her mother's,' Jack looked at her oddly.

Camellia made a fast mental calculation. Bonny had always claimed she was born prematurely. When she discovered after Bonny died that her parents had married in early June, she had assumed the claim of premature birth was a smoke screen so people wouldn't realise she'd been pregnant on her wedding day. A baby might have survived being one month early back in 1949, but somehow she doubted that back then a baby could be two months early and live. She guessed Bonny was pregnant before she had her last fling with Jack.

'I don't understand why a woman would do something like that when she was about to get married?' Camellia looked hard at Jack. 'Did she realise she still loved you?'

'I know why *I* allowed myself to be led,' he said quietly, blushing a little. 'But as to Bonny's motives, I can't say. With hindsight I suspect she knew she

303

was pregnant even then and that's why her wedding was so rushed. You've got to understand something about your mother, Camellia. She was devious and cunning, she liked to have power over men. She wrapped me up that night in her silken web, why I don't know. Maybe she had one last shot at all her old lovers around the same time.'

Camellia saw deep hurt in his eyes. She guessed that he'd paid for that one night of love with a great deal of guilt and sorrow.

'None of your letters were dated,' she said gently. 'Can you remember what year it was when she wrote and said she wanted to see you?'

Jack sat down again at his desk. He frowned as if thinking hard. 'It was the summer holidays. April, my eldest, was just about to start school so it must have been 1954, I think. I got in a panic when I got the first one because I thought Bonny might just turn up at the garage and April was often there with me.'

'1954 again,' Camellia said thoughtfully. 'I wish I knew what happened to her that summer. But you forgave her later when you wrote after John died? Was that because she apologised?'

Jack laughed, a rich warm sound. 'Bonny apologise! She never went in for apologies about anything. She just didn't write again, or visit, thank heavens. As for me writing when your dad died, well I had to, didn't I? We were old friends.'

Camellia sensed that Jack had had enough of personal questions. She decided to ask about the others before he got tired of the conversation and asked her to leave.

'Do you know anything about Sir Miles Hamilton?' she asked.

Jack grimaced and shrugged his shoulders. 'Not really. He was a guest at your parents' wedding, an old friend of John's, I think.'

'And Magnus Osbourne?' she asked. 'What do you know about him?'

Jack shrugged again. 'Never heard of him,' he said, and Camellia felt he was speaking the truth. 'But then she wouldn't tell me her lovers' names, would she?'

'Then there's a letter from a woman who just signed herself "H",' Camellia went on. 'What about her?'

Jack frowned. 'Can't think of anyone whose name began with "H". She had a girlfriend called Ellie, another dancer. I never met her though. She was Bonny's bridesmaid.'

Camellia paused for a moment before asking any more questions. She thought she had seen all her parents' wedding photographs, but there had been no bridesmaid in them.

They sat and talked for sometime. Jack gave her a few tantalising glimpses of Bonny as a young girl, the fun they had together, her early dancing shows. He spoke too of his heartbreak when she wrote and told him it was over, just before he came out the Army, and of how he continued to watch her career from a distance, until he married Ginny.

'I wish I could find out why she kept those old letters from all of you,' Camellia said in bewilderment. 'I can understand anyone keeping old love letters, birthday cards and stuff like that. But why throw those out and keep the nasty ones?'

'Nothing about your mum was straightforward,' Jack smiled ruefully. 'Logic wasn't exactly her strong suit. Or sticking to the truth.'

Camellia hadn't wanted to recount the depths her mother sank to in her last few years, but she felt obligated to tell the truth too. She told him how Bonny squandered the family money after her father's death, and about losing their home, the drinking and the men.

As Jack talked and listened to Camellia, he found himself impressed by her compassionate, yet sharp insight into people. It wasn't until he got around to asking what she did and where she lived that he sensed she'd been through some personal trauma quite recently. She was clearly reluctant to say how she'd lived since her mother died, passing off her present job in the holiday camp as a temporary measure. Then she swiftly moved on to inquire about Lydia.

Jack was shocked to discover that Camellia was unaware of the role Lydia Wynter had played in Bonny's life. Lydia had been far more than a wartime foster mother. She had loved and cared for Bonny as if she was her own child. Thanks to Lydia, Bonny spent the war years without hardship. Lydia gave Bonny everything: adoration, confidence, elocution lessons, poise. All the things she later used to entrap rich men.

'Lydia's dead, love.' Jack's voice crackled with emotion. He had as much affection for Lydia as for Bert and Beryl Baker, his own old foster parents. 'She died of cancer back in 1961.'

'Mum never said,' Camellia tried to think back. 'I don't remember her going to a funeral or anything.'

'That's because I made sure she didn't know about it.' Jack's face contorted as if the memory hurt. 'You might as well face it, Camellia, your mother was the most greedy, self-centred and cruel bitch in the world sometimes. She knew for two years that Lydia was ill, but she never came to see her, never telephoned or wrote. Finally Lydia drove over to Rye one day, just before she was too ill to do anything. They had a tremendous row and when Lydia got back home she called me round to tell me about it. She was heartbroken: she loved your mother like she was her own child, and she thought of you as a granddaughter. When she died just a few weeks later, I decided not to inform Bonny. I couldn't face her swanning back to Amberley, all glamorous in a black dress, playing the part of the grieving daughter and upsetting everyone.'

'I don't blame you,' Camellia said quietly. In view of what he'd told her about Lydia's relationship with Bonny, and his affection for the older woman, his bitterness was understandable. 'I just wish I could have met Lydia and talked to her.'

Jack looked at the sad, lovely face in front of him and felt a pang of fatherly affection. He could almost touch the mental scars caused by her scheming bitch of a mother.

'Will you take a bit of advice from an *almost* uncle,' he said, his face flushing at the sudden tug of his emotions.

Camellia nodded.

'Put your mother, your childhood and all this away,' he said gently. 'Tomorrows are what count, love, not yesterdays. I loved Bonny, so help me! There was a time when I'd have walked barefoot to the ends of the earth for her. But that's in the past now. Even dead Bonny's twitching our cords, the way she did in life. Don't let her, Camellia. Be true to yourself.'

'Can I come to see you again before I leave Sussex?' Camellia asked. There was still so much more she wanted to know.

'No, love,' Jack shook his head and his eyes were sad. 'Not because I'm not interested in you, but because of Ginny and our kids. My eldest, April is a little older than you, Amanda is fourteen and full of all the devilment I was at that age. Little Lydia is eight. I can't let them be harmed by gossip.'

'But surely we could meet somewhere away from Littlehampton?'

Jack smiled ruefully. Camellia was nothing like

her mother, either in looks or character, yet he could recall Bonny suggesting that very same thing back in 1949. Camellia's visit now was all tied up in that one night of weakness, and he'd lived with the guilt for years. He wasn't going to make a similar mistake again.

'People are so quick to gossip in these parts,' he said gently. 'Your mother is still mentioned in some circles. If they knew her daughter was around here and talking to me they'd soon be making a meal of it.'

Camellia got up. 'I have to go now.' She tried to smile, but her lips quivered. 'Thank you for your time, Jack.'

He had to hug her. Her face was registering all the sadness he felt inside, all the might-have-beens, the broken dreams.

'Look after yourself,' he said huskily as he held her tightly. As he released her he pulled a wad of notes from his pocket and handed her thirty pounds.

'Don't think that is a pay-off. I'm just trying to smooth your path a little, the same as I would with my daughters. Just promise me you'll drop me a line every now and again and let me know how you're doing and where you are.'

Jack watched Camellia going off to the station from his office window: a tall willowy girl with shining hair bouncing on her shoulders. If Lydia had still been alive she would have been thrilled to discover the funny little girl she liked so much had grown into a beautiful woman.

He felt saddened that he hadn't been able to tell Camellia anything which might have eased her sadness. But then he wished so many things. That Bonny had loved him as he loved her. That Lydia had never told him that on her last visit to Rye she'd found Bonny drunk, half naked and entertaining two men, while Camellia was at school. That he could have been honest and told Camellia that Lydia had left Briar Bank, her beautiful house in Amberley, to him and Ginny, because of that day.

Jack sighed deeply and poured himself another large whisky. The studio in the basement where Bonny used to practise her dancing was now a playroom. Ginny cared for the lovely garden, every bit as enthusiastically as Lydia did. Sometimes he looked at the big couch in the sitting room and remembered that was where he first made love to Bonny when she was only fifteen.

Lydia had wanted him and Ginny to be happy there, to give their children all the advantages she'd had, and to use it as collateral for Jack to set up the car showroom he'd always dreamed of. She had always been there for him, just as she was for Bonny. It was she who first taught him about cars when he arrived down from London, a skinny little waif, in 1939. She had stimulated his desire for better things all through the war years, comforted him when Bonny packed him in, supported and encouraged him right through those first lean years when he opened his first garage.

But above all Jack wished he'd been able to tell Camellia that Lydia had deposited several thousand pounds in a bank for her. But she had entrusted Jack and her solicitors with the task of passing it on to her when she reached twenty-five, providing she hadn't turned out like her mother. He wished he could have told her about it now, if only to prove to her that Lydia had thought of her as a granddaughter right till the end. But that would be breaking his promise to Lydia. He hoped she would keep in touch. It might be hard to find her otherwise.

Two weeks to the day that Camellia had been to see Jack, she left the holiday camp for good. It had been a rotten job, for even worse money and Denise still wasn't back at her flat. But Camellia had a plan now, one that excited her far more than going back to London to find a job. She was going to Bath, to see Magnus Osbourne and to settle the past once and for all.

Thanks to the money Jack had given her, she had a small nest egg. She intended to hitchhike rather than waste money on fares. She had a long grey raincoat, a couple of warm sweaters and a pair of stout walking shoes, all courtesy of unclaimed lost property. If it wasn't for feeling a bit off colour, everything would be rosy.

She'd had a sore throat for a couple of days. She'd gone to bed the night before shivering and aching all over. This morning she felt even worse.

A car stopped for her almost as soon as she was out of the holiday camp gates. By midday she was beyond Salisbury waiting for her fourth lift of the day and she reckoned she could be in Bath by three or four at the latest. But after she'd walked a mile or so in the rain, without anyone even glancing at her, let alone stopping, she had a feeling her luck had run out.

She was beginning to feel really ill now. Her throat was so sore she could barely swallow, and she was shivering as if in the depths of winter. Within an hour the rain had penetrated her raincoat and the stout shoes were giving her a blister. She stopped in a village shop, bought some more aspirin and a packet of plasters and asked if there was a bus to Bath.

'Not till five thirty, my lover,' the rosy cheeked woman behind the counter said cheerfully, in a rich Wiltshire accent. 'And I dunno rightly whether it runs this time of year anyways.'

There was no alternative but to trudge on, the rain growing steadily heavier, the wind stronger. Cars swished by her, spraying her with more water. A farmer with a lorry loaded with pigs picked her up eventually at around five thirty, but he was only going as far as Rode, the other side of Warminster, and over the noise of his old lorry, the rain outside and an untuned radio crackling away, Camellia couldn't even manage to tell him how ill she felt, or ask if he knew any bed and breakfast places nearby.

By the time they got to Rode it was pitch dark. She reckoned it was perhaps fifteen miles further to Bath. She plodded on, aware now that no one in their right mind would pick her up on such a dark, wild night. She just hoped she would come to a guest house before long.

It was scary walking in the dark. She veered between desperately attempting to flag down passing motorists and jumping into ditches to avoid being hit. She couldn't remember ever having felt quite so ill and cold.

She passed two pubs, and had a large whisky in both, but neither had rooms available. She was finding it increasingly hard to walk. The wind buffeted her from side to side, and several times passing cars blasted their horns at her. She was crying now, both her feet hurt and she was wet right through to her underwear, her soaked bell-bottom jeans slapping noisily against her shins.

As she came down a steep hill she saw a pub at the bottom all lit up with small lights. To her left she thought she could see a river, with what looked like a viaduct over it, but in the darkness and rain, in such a weakened state, it was hard to tell what anything was.

She summoned up the last of her strength and concentrated all her efforts on reaching that pub.

There had to be someone in there who would help her. She no longer cared if she ever got to Bath, she just wanted to lie down somewhere warm and dry.

Heat enveloped her as she pushed open the pub door. As she took a couple more steps towards the bar, it seemed to grab her and squeeze her so tight she could no longer focus her eyes. She saw a bright light, then a dozen more spinning before her and she felt her legs go from under her.

'She's soaking,' Camellia heard a man say. 'Freezing cold and soaked to the skin. Call an ambulance!'

Her fear of authority made her open her eyes. 'I'm okay,' she managed to croak. 'It's just the heat in here.'

She was lying on the floor surrounded by men, country types with tweed jackets and ruddy faces.

'Give her a bit of air,' someone said.

'Where were you making for?' another person asked.

Camellia felt someone put a hand beneath her back and she was lifted to a sitting position.

'I was going to Oaklands, a hotel in Bath,' she said.

She had had no intention of trying to find Magnus before she'd found somewhere to stay in Bath. But the words just sprang out.

'Oaklands, eh! Well you were nearly there.' The man who'd helped her up knelt beside her and put a hand on her forehead. 'You're burning up my girl. Best get you there right now.'

Camellia was too dazed to think straight. As the man helped her to her feet she was so glad that someone had taken over, that she didn't care what happened next.

She was helped outside again by two men. She was vaguely aware of them putting her rucksack in the boot and a rug over the passenger seat to protect it from her wet clothes, then she found herself bundled in.

The cold air brought her partially back to her senses. The car was climbing a very steep winding hill with thick bushes and trees on both sides.

'Have you come far?' the driver asked. He wore a checked flat cap and a gabardine jacket. His voice was brisk and well bred.

'From Sussex,' she replied with difficulty.

'Bad throat?' he asked solicitously. 'How long have you been out in the rain?'

She tried to reply, but it was just a wheezy croak. She held onto her throat and looked at the man hopelessly.

'Magnus will call a doctor for you,' he said. 'Were you going there for a job?'

Camellia nodded; it was easier than attempting anything else. But she was distracted as the man slowed down on a bend and a large wooden board with Oaklands came into the car headlights. It was fixed to an imposing old stone wall beside massive, open wrought-iron gates.

Her heart plummeted. In her imagination Oaklands was a largish house converted into a small tourist hotel. But this drive was through a dense woodland of huge great trees which met overhead in a thick canopy. Without even seeing the house she knew it wasn't going to be the sort of hotel the average tourist stayed in and they were hardly likely to welcome someone as bedraggled as her.

'Magnus is a man with great foresight,' the driver said. 'When he bought this place it was almost a ruin, we didn't expect him to make a go of it. Just looking after the grounds is a huge headache.'

As the car came out of the overshadowing trees, Camellia saw the imposing Georgian house floodlit before her and wished she was anywhere but here, anyone but herself.

In that second, before the car stopped by the front door, she knew she couldn't possibly reveal her identity tonight. She needed time to think.

A tall dark girl came forward as Camellia swayed on her feet.

'Quick, get her a chair,' she heard the man supporting her shout. 'Call Magnus.'

She must have blacked out again. The next thing she knew a strong male hand was holding her head down between her knees and asking questions.

'Did she say who she was, or why she was coming here? I wasn't expecting anyone.'

'She's come from Sussex,' the man with the car answered. 'About a job she said, but she was losing her voice.'

Camellia waited a moment before showing she was coming round. To the right of where she sat she could hear male voices and the clinking of glasses.

'I expect she's been walking all day,' he said in a growling voice. 'Soaked to the skin and probably hasn't eaten for a good while. She's got a fever, let's hope it doesn't turn to pneumonia. I'll give her a bed for the night Fred, and call the doctor, you get on back to your pint.'

Camellia moved then, fluttering her arms so he would release the pressure on her neck.

'Hullo, she's coming to,' the deep growly voice said. 'Well, girl, can you tell me who you are?'

As Camellia sat up he crouched down in front of her. It was like coming face-to-face with a lion. He had a mane of thick fair hair, a broad nose with two deep channels beside it, bushy eyebrows and penetrating speckly eyes of an indeterminate colour. She had expected to see the man in the photograph with Bonny and the other girl, but he seemed too young, hardly more than fifty-five at the most. The man in the picture had looked suave and debonair; this man was more rugged, as if he spent all his time outside. Instinct told her he'd be hard to fool.

'Mel,' she croaked. 'Amelia Corbett,' she said as an afterthought. It was the name of a girl she'd met in Ibiza and close enough to her own that she'd remember it. 'I heard you wanted a . . .' her voice gave way again and she merely mouthed the last two words 'kitchen maid'. It was a lame excuse but the best she could think of on the spur of the moment.

'Okay, Mel. Don't try to speak if it hurts you.' His voice was gentler now, and with that the driver of the car said his goodbyes and left. 'Just nod or shake your head,' he went on. 'Are you in pain?'

Camellia shook her head.

'You've walked a long way?'

A nod.

'Well, let's get you out of those wet clothes and into a hot bath.'

Magnus took her downstairs to the basement. He ushered her into a small bathroom, handed her a towelling dressing gown, and ordered her to take off her clothes.

'You must have a hot drink and some soup before the bath,' he said. 'I don't want you passing out in here alone.'

It was bliss to take off her sodden clothes, to hug the thick warm towelling around her and by the time she'd come out again, Magnus was coming down the passage with a bowl of soup and a mug of tea on a tray.

He sat her down at a small desk in the passage and she drank down the soup greedily despite her sore throat. Magnus disappeared again but she could hear him rustling things in a room further along the passage by the bathroom. There were other voices, coming from the direction of the kitchen, a male one with a French accent and a woman's, but neither of these people looked out at her.

'I've rung the doctor and run your bath,' Magnus said, when he came out again to find she'd finished the soup. 'Don't lock the door in there just in case you pass out. I'll be waiting out here if you need me.'

Gratitude that she'd been rescued was all she felt while she was in the bath. She felt too ill to contemplate the next day, when she would need to make explanations; for now it was enough to be warm. But as she climbed out of the bath, before she could even wrap herself in a towel, she was violently sick.

It was a horrible experience. It seemed to be coming out of her nose as well as her mouth and the stench of tomato soup mingled with the earlier whisky made it even worse. Magnus came rushing in, as she was leaning over the toilet bowl, giving her no time to cover herself. He picked up the dressing gown, put it round her shoulders, and pulled her wet hair back from her face.

'The soup was clearly a mistake,' he said in that now familiar growly voice. 'I suppose you've been starving for days while you slept rough.'

She couldn't speak to tell him this wasn't so. She managed to get her arms into the dressing gown and wrap it round her naked body, while he picked up her sodden clothes one by one from the floor, holding them distastefully between thumb and forefinger.

'I don't have any time for hippies,' he said, glaring balefully at the string of love beads around her neck. 'The doctrine of hitching rides, conning food, avoiding work and numbing your mind with opiates is anathema to me. However I wouldn't turn a dog out on a night like this, especially not a sick one. You can stay here until you are better, but I do not want to find you wandering upstairs for any reason. If you have any drugs in your possession, I suggest you flush them down the lavatory now.'

Camellia was soon safe in a warm bed, piled high with extra blankets, but although she was exhausted, she still couldn't sleep, for shame and embarrassment.

Camellia felt tears roll down her cheeks as she lay there. The room felt like a prison cell. There was just one small window high up in the wall and it had bars over it. The room was bare except for a plain small chest of drawers and a single upright chair.

She had blown it again. If she had let those people in the pub call for an ambulance she'd be safe in a hospital now. Well she wasn't going to tell Magnus who she really was. Let him think she was just a dirty hippie passing through on the lookout for a handout. She'd stay until she was better, take the pills the doctor had given her, then go. She didn't need a father who was as blinkered and bigoted as him.

Chapter Thirteen

Camellia came up the steps from the basement, skirted round the side of the house, then crossed the flagstone terrace to the wide stone steps which led to the lawn.

Once down there, partially concealed by bushes, she paused to look back at Oaklands. Soon Magnus Osbourne would be summoning her and this might be her only opportunity to look around before she was thrown out.

She had been in his hotel for six days. For the first two she'd been too ill to worry any more about what he or anyone else thought of her. She vaguely remembered Magnus coming into her room along with a doctor, but once her temperature returned to normal he made no further appearances. Mrs Downes, the housekeeper, and the French chef Antoine, who looked after her, said he asked how she was daily, but Camellia felt that only meant he wanted shot of her as quickly as possible.

Even down from the basement, Camellia had felt the house's magic and beauty. Now that she was at last outside, she saw it was even more magnificent than she'd imagined.

Looking at it from this position, across the lawn in weak autumn sunshine, was to see its best aspect. Like most Georgian country houses, it had been designed with its best side facing the view. And there couldn't be a finer one in all England.

The house sat proudly at the top of a lush green rolling valley. Below was the river Avon, the canal, the viaduct and the tiny village of Limpney Stoke, where Mrs Downes lived. Beyond that the hills rose up again. She could just make out the road she'd stumbled down before getting to the pub where she was rescued.

Camellia turned to look at the house again. Virginia creeper in its full autumn fiery beauty enhanced the golden-yellow stone, but she had a feeling that whatever the season there would be other climbing plants to take its place. She knew from Mrs Downes that behind the long elegant windows to her right was the dining room, that the ones on the far left belonged to the drawing room and that the room in the middle with doors leading onto the garden was the bar.

Mrs Downes had said that two of the ten luxurious guest rooms had four-poster beds, and she'd spoken of extensive renovation in the old servants' quarters, but although Camellia had hoped for more descriptive information, none had been offered. She could only guess that it was all as beautiful as the elegant entrance hall she'd seen briefly on the night of her arrival.

As she had surmised when she arrived, it wasn't ordinary people who stayed here, but the very rich, distinguished and famous. Magnus apparently took a pride in protecting those who might not wish the media prying on them, and she'd heard that staff had been sacked in the past for being indiscreet.

The hotel also served as a country club, where members could come and drink in the bar, have a gourmet meal, wander around the grounds, or just sit in the orangery over afternoon tea.

As she stood there gazing at Oaklands, a stiff wind blowing her hair into a tangle, Camellia felt a tug at her emotions. She knew what she was thinking was ridiculous, because within minutes Magnus was going to call her in and ask her to pack her bag and go. But all the same she wished she could stay here.

Part of this feeling was due to kindly Mrs Downes. Outwardly she was tough, uncompromising, briskly efficient and shrewd, yet her hard shell was mere protection for the softness inside her.

She lived down in the village with her husband, and came in daily. Camellia reckoned she was about fifty-five, a short, tubby figure with grey neatly permed hair and thick glasses. It was she who'd brought Camellia her medicine, and a constant supply of honey and lemon, she who'd found her magazines to read and comforted her in those first two days when Camellia had felt so ill.

Camellia had stuck to the name Amelia Corbett, but she'd kept to the truth as far as possible, saying that both her parents were dead and that she'd been brought up in London. To wipe out the need to discuss the last couple of years she said she'd been travelling and working all over the continent, ending in Ibiza.

In the last couple of days since she'd been well enough to get up, she had pitched in to help down in the basement, sorting laundry, ironing, polishing silver and folding napkins. Last night she'd got all the salads ready for the dining room under Antoine's eagle eye.

Antoine was excitable and temperamental: a tall, thin man with a hangdog expression which belied his exuberant personality. Mrs Downes had confided that he was forty and that he'd been in England for twenty years, yet he apparently still put on a thick Gallic accent when called into the dining room. Down in the kitchen his accent was an extraordinary mix of London slang and West Country phrasing, with an appealing Maurice Chevalier lilt. Camellia was intrigued by him. He was a brilliant chef, and the only member of staff who lived in. His room in the basement was extremely messy and cluttered and he didn't appear to have any sort of private life. She wondered why he'd never married: he was attractive with his glossy black hair and sparkling dark eyes. It had crossed her mind he could be gay, though nothing he said or did indicated this.

Aside from the housekeeper and chef, she'd only met one other member of staff – Sally, the girl who came in as a waitress in the evenings. But she knew there was a whole team of groundsmen, cleaners and casual staff.

'Mel!'

She looked up at the shout to see Mrs Downes beckoning to her from the bar doors.

She took one last gulp of the clean, sweet fresh air to brace herself and went on up the steps to join the housekeeper. Once she'd seen Magnus Osbourne face-to-face again she'd probably be only too anxious to leave. Mrs Downes and Antoine might think he was the wisest, fairest man in the West Country, but his hard words on her first night here were still ringing in her ears, and she wasn't anticipating any kind ones now.

'Are you feeling better?' Magnus Osbourne asked as she came into his office.

'Yes thank you, Mr Osbourne,' she said, keeping her eyes down. She didn't feel he was really interested in her health; it was more, 'I hope you're ready to push off now.' She looked up. 'You've been very kind letting me stay here. It was an awful imposition.'

The lion-like impression she'd had of this man on her first night hadn't left her. She had watched him from the basement windows in the last two days as he strode around the grounds purposefully, his fair hair blowing in the wind like a mane, his chin up, eyes scanning the distant horizon. He was a big man, perhaps six foot, with a healthy glow from working for long periods outside. She was amazed when Mrs Downes told her he was sixty-six; he had the vigour and strength of a fifty-year-old. Twenty years or so ago he must have been quite something.

'Sit down,' he said impatiently, indicating a chair by the window. His office was masculine, dark-red wallpaper, a cluttered mahogany desk, two brown leather armchairs and a filing cabinet. It overlooked the drive and the old stable block and it was rather dark. 'Now, let's have the truth about why you came here?'

His direct, straight-to-the-point approach unnerved her, as did his penetrating eyes. They were an extraordinary colour, blue predominantly, but speckled with green and brown. For a moment she thought perhaps he had somehow found out her real name.

'I didn't actually intend to come here that night,' she said truthfully. 'I was just on my way to Bath to look for a room. But I'd met someone in Ibiza who came from the West Country, who said she'd worked at a hotel called Oaklands, so I had it in mind to look for it once I was here. I went into that pub down the road and fainted. When I came round they asked me where I was going and I just said the name, I don't know why, I was dizzy and confused. Next thing they had me in the car and on the way here.'

He raised one bushy eyebrow. 'And the name of this girl you met?'

322

'Susie,' Camellia said defiantly. 'I never knew her surname.'

'You are an interesting phenomenon, Amelia,' he said, picking up a pen from his desk and playing with it. 'I feel you had some strong motive for coming here which you are hiding. Now could it be that your hippie chum mentioned also that this hotel is isolated and tends to be full of wealthy people?'

She was incensed by the insinuation of his question.

'You are insulting my intelligence,' she said coldly. 'If I wanted to burgle this place, I would hardly call to case it dripping wet with a dose of flu. I'd dress myself up, arrive in a taxi and flannel my way in as a welcome guest.'

'But you haven't any decent clothes have you?' he smirked. 'Everything you had in that rucksack stinks of that foul hippie perfume. Those jeans are so worn it's a wonder they don't split. You've spent all summer lying around on beaches getting out of your head on weed. You couldn't aspire to anything more than offering yourself as a kitchen maid.'

Camellia was suddenly furious. She stood up, her nostrils flaring. 'I was very grateful to you for giving me a bed and calling the doctor,' she snapped at him, her eyes blazing. 'But I did not spend the summer lying on beaches, smoking what you call weed, I worked. In fact I had three jobs. As for my clothes smelling of patchouli oil, well I'm sorry about that, I inherited the rucksack from a friend and it happens to be impregnated with it. I do have some very nice smart clothes, but they are in a suitcase at a friend's in London. Okay, you don't approve of people travelling and picking up work as they go along, well boring old you. I suppose you spent all your youth working out how

323

to become a millionaire? But I don't despise you for that. At least I know that not everyone marches to the same drumbeat.'

'Touché,' he said, and surprisingly his eyes twinkled. 'Well, it's nice to hear you've got your voice back, and heartening to know you aren't the little sniveller I took you for a week ago. Now shall we talk about a job?'

Camellia was so astonished that her mind went completely blank and she sat down again with a bump.

Magnus Osbourne was not a soft touch. As a young man he'd been full of altruism, but over the years he'd become aware that the vast majority of people abused generosity. He had learned to be suspicious, to hold back confidences and friendship until people proved themselves worthy of trust. Each summer he had scores of students coming here looking for work, and for every four he took on, at least one would attempt to fiddle him.

But Joan Downes really liked the girl and he believed her to be a good judge of character. She had praised Mel for her initiative, claiming the girl had done ironing and other tasks without anyone asking. Joan thought she might have faced some major disaster in her life not that long ago. It was partly this which made him goad the girl. He was intrigued by her. She didn't quite fit into any recognisable box.

She had pride, which he liked. In a nice frock, with make-up and her hair trimmed, she wouldn't look out of place. She spoke well, she was surprisingly dignified, and if she was capable of working hard he'd soon iron out the last of her wrinkles.

'Yes, a job,' he said, enjoying her look of utter surprise. 'As a live-in general assistant.'

'B ... b ... but,' she stammered. 'You don't like me or my clothes and you don't trust me.'

'I didn't say I didn't like you,' he smiled, raising one bushy eyebrow. 'We'd have to get to know one another better before I could make any judgement about that. As for your clothes you've already said you have smarter ones in London. You can go and collect them. And trust, well, I'm afraid we all have to earn that, my dear. Let's start with you collecting your clothes?'

'I haven't got any insurance cards,' she said weakly, so overcome she was almost hoping he'd change his mind. 'I've never had proper jobs.'

Magnus was pretty certain that once she disappeared off to London he would never see her again, but he hoped to be proved wrong.

'Well, I've offered you one now,' he said evenly. 'You can go and see the National Insurance people in the next day or two. They'll fix you up with a card. Off with you now, get rid of that red nose, and we'll discuss the finer points once you've got your belongings back.'

The girl who got onto the six thirty train to Bath at Paddington the following evening looked totally different to the one who had arrived at eleven that morning. She had put her jeans, sweater and plimsolls into Denise's dustbin and replaced them with a dark-red wool maxi skirt, matching fine-knit sweater, a wide brown leather belt, highly polished brown boots. With her long white rabbit coat, and her hair newly cut she looked like a fashion model.

It pleased her to be holding a suitcase at last instead of a rucksack. She was looking forward to wearing a frilly nightie again, to having slippers, petticoats and high-heeled shoes to put on. At Denise's suggestion they had swapped a few clothes: the slinky evening dresses Camellia had worn at the Don Juan were now hanging in her friend's wardrobe, and her own suitcase now held a navy-blue classic Jaegar suit, a cashmere twin-set and a pleated skirt. Conventional, middle-of-the-road clothes had never been Camellia's style, but they were needed in this job.

But best of all she would soon have an insurance card, with her new name on it. Denise had taken her to a solicitor, where she had changed her name to Amelia Corbett by deed poll. She only had to take this deed to the local National Insurance Office with her old number and she'd be issued with a new one. Camellia Norton was dead and buried now; Amelia Corbett, a girl without a shameful past was about to start a new career. Camellia intended to wipe out all the old memories along with the name. Plain, simple Mel would be what she'd call herself even in private thoughts.

Magnus had been waiting at Bath Spa Station for five minutes when an exceptionally attractive girl in a white fur coat came down through the barrier struggling with a heavy suitcase. He leapt forward instinctively to help her. It was a second or two before he realised it was Amelia.

'Well, I never,' he said, grinning broadly. 'You look the cat's whiskers.'

She was just as surprised to see him. 'You came to meet me?'

Magnus had left Oaklands thinking he was probably making a wasted trip. He was thrilled to have been proved wrong. 'Of course I came to meet you, Amelia,' he said, taking the heavy case. 'My staff are as important to me as my family.'

'Well, thank you,' she smiled. 'But please, call me Mel. Mrs Downes and Antoine do.'

There were more surprises in store for her when they got back to Oaklands. Magnus told her she had a new room on the third floor.

'It's the last one on the right, the only one

without a number on the door. Take your case up and unpack.' Magnus seemed amused by her wide-eyed delight. 'Give me an hour, then come on down again. There's your duties to discuss, your hours and wages.'

If it wasn't for the fact that this was the first time she'd been allowed upstairs, Mel probably would've flown, despite the weight of her case. But she took it slowly, marvelling at the wide, gracious staircase, the long arched window, the thick pastel-blue carpet beneath her feet. On the first floor landing there was a pale-green velvet chaise-longue and a walnut chest of drawers which looked as old as the house. Up she went to the top floor and here the ceiling sloped under the roof, the corridor side overlooking the stable block. She paused for a moment looking at the fresh flowers on a small table, the glossy white paint and the china knobs on the doors, then slowly, savouring each moment, she went towards her room.

As she opened the door, tears sprang to her eyes. There was nothing austere about this room: it was heaven.

There was a moss-green fitted carpet, flower-sprigged wallpaper, an old pine dressing table and a single divan with a green padded headboard. The last time she had stood in such a lovely room was at her childhood home, in Mermaid Street. The quilted counterpane matched the curtains. There was a small lamp by her bedside and another on a little desk. She even had a portable television. She opened one door and found a fitted wardrobe with shelves down one side and shoe rails at the bottom. In wild excitement she opened the second door, and there to her amazement was her own tiny bathroom, all pink and white perfection.

Tears of absolute joy were coursing down her

cheeks. She had *felt* reborn at Paddington station, but now she knew she *was*.

Crossing the room she drew back the curtains and looked out. It was too dark to see much, but tomorrow she'd wake to a view of the valley. She could see car headlights coming down that hill where she'd trudged. She looked up at the star-spangled sky and offered up a silent prayer of gratitude. She felt there was someone up there after all, someone looking after her and guiding her.

'You've been crying,' Magnus exclaimed when she joined him in his office later. She'd put away her clothes, arranged her few little ornaments and cosmetics. But mostly she'd just wandered around the room touching everything.

'It's nothing,' she laughed. She'd washed her face and tidied up her make-up, and had thought she'd concealed all trace of tears. 'I've just never had such a beautiful room before.'

'Mind you look after it then,' he said gruffly. In his opinion it was fairly ordinary. Sophie, his daughter, had never showed much delight in it when she slept there. Judging by her reaction, the rooms Mel had before must've been grim.

He got down to business immediately. Her hours would be from seven in the morning until twelve, then again from seven in the evening until eleven, with a full day off on Tuesdays.

'You won't always be busy during the weekday evenings,' he said. 'More often than not you'll be just pottering about, on call if necessary. But at the weekends it's often frantic, and though I have extra staff, I'll be relying on you to keep things running smoothly once you know the ropes.'

He wanted her to learn all aspects of hotel work – waitressing, housekeeping, reception, bar work – as well as giving a hand in the kitchen sometimes.

'Not all at once though,' he smiled. 'I'll break you in gently.'

When Mel learned she would get twenty-five pounds a week, on top of her keep, she nearly hit the ceiling in surprise. She would've been thrilled to get fifteen.

'You'll earn it,' he said with a wry smile. 'But now we come to the warnings and rules. Firstly you'll be on a trial for three months. I shall assess your performance week by week and if you don't shape up, then I'm afraid I'll have to ask you to leave. You must get a plain black dress for waitressing. I will supply the apron. When you are behind the bar or on reception I expect you to be as smartly dressed as you are now. You will always treat our guests and members with the utmost courtesy, even when they are obnoxious to you. You must never divulge any names of guests to anyone outside the hotel. If you are approached by any reporters, plead absolute ignorance and come straight to me. Likewise you will not discuss anything about the running of the place with anyone either. I do not want you making dates with any of the people who use the hotel. Finally, if I ever have reason to suspect you are involved with any drug taking, or consorting with people who do, you will be sacked immediately. Your room is for you alone and I will not tolerate any men going into it.'

Mel just looked into his odd-coloured eyes and promised to stick to his rules. She wanted to tell him there was no danger of drug taking or men in her room. She'd had enough of both of them to last a lifetime.

The sound of laughter made Magnus look up from the letter he was writing. It was Mel decorating the Christmas tree in the drawing room.

There had been a great deal more laughter here since Mel's arrival. After a mere ten weeks she was already indispensable. Aside from Joan, he'd never had an employee who was so intuitive or quick. She was unfailingly cheerful and the guests praised her to the skies for her little kindnesses to them. She was always asking questions – about wine, about the food, or the correct way to do any number of things. She sparkled behind the bar in the evenings, instinctively knowing the difference between interest and impertinence. She mixed friendly warmth with just the right amount of flirtation to keep the men coming in night after night, but she never over stepped the mark.

Yet it was the laughter she created that warmed Magnus the most. He couldn't help thinking how much Ruth would've liked her.

Magnus knew he ought to be over his wife's death by now, but he wasn't. Perhaps it was partly out of guilt that he hadn't always been the husband she deserved, but he grieved for her still.

Back in his twenties, when he first met and married the shy doctor's daughter, he'd believed he was the strong, dominant one in their partnership. While he forged ahead building houses, doing deals and making a name for himself, Ruth was at home in Yorkshire looking after the house, bringing up the children. She never complained about the amount of time he spent away from home; she encouraged, supported, nurtured and gave her love to both himself and the children unstintingly. He loved her then, and thought he knew her true value. But it wasn't until she was dying that he really understood all that she was.

A woman who put everyone else's happiness before her own, who understood people's strengths and weaknesses and never judged them. She could laugh away problems, kiss away hurt, cry for others, but never cried for herself. The bed still felt too big without her.

He could see those special touches she'd added to the hotel everywhere. Without Ruth he would never have understood that fine furniture, thick carpets and a good chef, wouldn't make a first-class hotel by themselves. It had to be built with love, the guests pampered as if they were valued friends or family. The staff too had to be trained and indoctrinated with this ideal.

Ruth would have picked Mel herself; he knew that. By now she would also have discovered the reason for that occasional sad, faraway look in the girl's eyes.

But Magnus didn't have that gentle talent. His way of finding things out was by goading people, and sometimes hammering them into compliance with his wishes. Somehow he'd managed to turn Sophie into a cold, calculating harpy, while Stephen was impossibly arrogant and lazy. As for Nicholas!

'You may have become a success financially and socially,' he murmured to himself. 'But as a father you are a complete failure.'

Another peal of laughter banished his introspection. He got up, opened his office door and looked across the hall towards the drawing room.

He could see Mel perched on the top of a stepladder. She was wearing jeans and a red sweater, her hair in two bunches like a school girl. In her hands was the fairy and she was trying, without success, to put it on the top of the eight-foot Christmas tree.

Joan was holding the steps. She too was laughing, her big chest quivering under her navy dress. Magnus turned to get his camera from his office.

He crept back across the hall without either of the women seeing him and stopped just to one side of the open door, lifting the camera to watch for a good moment through the lens.

'We haven't had the fairy on the tree for years,' Joan said. 'Margaret, who came after Mrs Osbourne died, thought a star was more stylish. It's much easier to fix too.'

'But a fairy's traditional,' Mel said, looking down at the older woman. 'And this one's so lovely. Look she's even got satin knickers.'

Magnus felt a tug at his heart as he watched. Ruth had dressed the fairy. He could remember her joking and saying, 'No fairy in my house goes knickerless!'

Mel had exactly the same expression on her face as Ruth had when she held dolls – maternal, yet like a little girl too, wanting to hold onto the magic of childhood. Mel was bracing herself on the top of the ladder while she tweaked out the fairy's skirt and wings. 'Now,' she said firmly, talking earnestly to the doll. 'You are going up there, you are going to stay there, and you won't come down until twelfth night.'

As she leaned forward Magnus waited, ready to click the camera. Mel's tongue was pointing out in concentration, her slender body arching towards the tree precariously. Joan was looking up, her plump face anxious, blinking furiously behind her thick glasses.

Magnus clicked and the camera flashed. The shock made Mel jerk and topple backwards.

'Ahhh,' she yelled, and fell off the steps.

The tree swayed as Mel crashed onto her back, bringing down with her several glass ornaments and a shower of pine needles.

Magnus couldn't resist taking another shot, this time of Mel with her legs in the air, still holding the fairy in her hands.

'You swine,' she yelled at him, but got up,

rubbed her bottom and burst into laughter. 'I bet you'd have taken that even if my back was broken. I've a good mind to sue you for industrial injuries.'

'I'm so sorry,' Magnus spluttered with laughter. 'I just couldn't help myself.'

'Well, you can go and help yourself to the hoover,' she retorted, 'and put this fairy up there yourself!'

An hour later, the tree dressed, complete with lights, glass balls and the fairy, Magnus lit the log fire in the grate. Mel was clearing away the last of the bits of tinsel and pine needles from the floor. Joan had gone to finish her duties upstairs.

'This room is so lovely,' Mel said in a soft voice. 'Do you ever come in here and just gaze at it?'

Magnus turned. Normally he would have retorted that he didn't have time to gaze at anything, but Mel's face stopped such cynicism short.

Her expression was rapt: her dark eyes full of wonder, yet sad too. Her full lips were quivering as if she was going to cry. She looked beautiful.

'Yes, I do,' he admitted, 'and I see Ruth's hand in everything. Do you know she hand-sewed the curtains? She said they would never look right if they were done by machine.'

The room was Georgian architecture at its best: a high ceiling, beautiful cornices and an Adams fireplace. Windows came down almost to the floor, looking out onto the terrace and the valley beyond. To the side were two more windows and a glazed door leading out into the courtyard. Everything was in soft greens and blues, the heavy sateen print curtains held back with thick silky cords, the pelmets tucked into soft pleats. Three feather-cushioned couches, two pale-blue, one green, a low Chippendale walnut console table behind one, holding a large Chinese lamp in the same colours.

'But there must be a hundred yards of fabric.' Mel touched the curtains reverently. 'She must've been such a patient lady.'

The more Mel had learned about Ruth Osbourne, the sadder she felt that Magnus hadn't been faithful to her. She sounded like a dream wife and mother, so very different to her own. But then she knew from experience that it was often the men with perfect wives who strayed. She could still recall all those men in the Don Juan who'd listed their wives' virtues, but still tried to grope her if she gave them as much as a kiss on the cheek.

'She was.' Magnus stood up, rubbing his knees as they were stiff. 'Patient, kind and very compassionate. I just hope our children inherited more from her than me. Patience certainly isn't my forte.'

'Children aren't always like either of their parents,' Mel said reflectively. In ten weeks she had come to admire and like Magnus more and more. But she still could find no similarity to herself, however hard she looked. 'I'm not like my mother.'

'How did she die?' Magnus asked.

'She committed suicide,' Mel said. Some weeks ago she had made up her mind to avoid telling lies as much as possible. She didn't volunteer information, but if asked a direct question she felt compelled to try to tell the truth.

Magnus was startled by such an abrupt statement. He moved closer to her. 'I'm so sorry Mel. That must've been terrible for you.'

'It was.' She flashed a weak smile at him, touched by his sad expression and his sincere words. 'But I'm over it now. She wasn't the best of mothers – she drank, told lies, and she was selfish. For a time I was full of anger. Nowadays I just try and remember the good things about her.'

'What was she like?' Magnus asked. 'I mean to look at. Do you have a photo?'

'No pictures, I destroyed them,' she replied. That was partially true; she had destroyed most, but not quite all of them. The remaining few were tucked away upstairs where no one but the most determined snoop would find them. She turned to the Christmas tree. 'She was a lot like that fairy up there, blonde, pretty, and just about as hard to pin down.'

Magnus looked up at the fairy. The blonde doll, with its glassy bright blue eyes reminded him of someone too. Someone he would rather forget.

'I'm glad to see her up on the tree again this year,' he said. 'Ruth dressed her too. She wouldn't approve of her languishing in a box in the attic.'

Mel felt a cold shiver run down her spine at his words. It was a reminder of what Jack Easton had said. Bonny was still tugging cords from the grave, even through a fairy doll.

Chapter Fourteen

Mel was sitting at the kitchen table reflecting that today was an anniversary. She'd been at Oaklands a whole year.

Mrs Downes came in through the door from the underground store outside. 'It's absolutely beastly out there,' she said. 'It's a good job Fred's coming to pick me up. I'd be blown away walking down Brass Knocker Hill.'

'It's just like last year.' Mel glanced at the kitchen window. Rain was battering against it, the wind making the frame rattle. She'd come down to see if Antoine needed any help, but nothing needed to be done. 'Did you know it's a year to the day that I arrived?'

'Well, I never,' Mrs Downes exclaimed, taking off her glasses to dry the rain off them. Without them she looked as kind and gentle as she really was, her face glowing pink from the wind outside. 'It doesn't seem as if you've been here five minutes.'

'Eet seems like five years, to moi,' Antoine said, putting his hands on his hips. 'As we French say, only wine improves with keeping. For me young Mel should never 'ave been allowed through la porte.'

Mel laughed. Antoine teased her all the time, usually in this silly cod-French. She waited until

Mrs Downes had gone out of the kitchen before answering.

'As we Engleesh say weeth such savoire faire, Bollocks!'

'Mon Dieu,' Antoine raised his eyebrows and backed away from her in mock horror. 'I must tell Mrs Downes what you say, she will not be amused.'

'Come on you escargot,' she laughed. 'Find me something worthwhile to do. Otherwise I'll just go up to my room and watch *Crossroads* and see what they do in real hotels.'

Mel's first year at Oaklands had been so very happy. She was proud to work in such a good hotel. She enjoyed meeting the guests, serving behind the bar, waiting at tables. And she got excellent wages along with generous tips. At night in her lovely room she wallowed in delight at its luxurious perfection and felt absolute security.

There were moments when she sometimes felt constricted by having to watch what she said and how she behaved. She was only twenty-two but had to act and dress in a mature manner. It would be good to have a close friend so she could go out, just occasionally, get roaring drunk and flirt with a few men, and she still found herself thinking about Bee. It was the girlie chats, the sharing of clothes, the helpless giggling she missed. She thought perhaps she always would.

Sometimes, hiding her past was a trial. Too often in the bar she'd overhear some old bore piously discussing something sensational in the newspapers and it was all she could do not to jump in with both feet and tell them not to believe everything they read. She had found that rich and successful people were often the most mean-spirited; their wealth didn't necessarily give them wisdom or tolerance. There were times she ached for more inspiring conversations, for someone as irreverent as Aiden Murphy to walk in and make her laugh. But when these thoughts came to her she squashed them and thought of all the good things at Oaklands.

Last December, Antoine had made her a cake for her twenty-second birthday, the first she'd had since she was seven or eight. On Christmas morning she found a small stuffed stocking hanging on the knob of her door and, when she thanked Magnus, he pretended to know nothing about it, laughingly upbraiding her for not believing in Santa Claus.

His real present down under the tree with the other staff presents, was a bottle of Estee Lauder Youth Dew. But as much as she liked that, the stocking pleased her more. It made her feel like one of his children.

She felt sad for him that none of them came for Christmas. Sophie arrived with her husband, Michael, for the New Year, but Stephen and Nicholas both cried off with other engagements.

There were times too, particularly during the winter, when she thought about love, and wondered if it would ever come her way again. Even if she had been allowed to date any of the men who came into the bar, none of them were her type.

Yet when she read in the papers about Bloody Sunday in Londonderry and the first cases of international terrorism which were to become a regular feature in the news during 1972, she was glad she was here, cut off from the real world.

In March she watched a green haze slowly creep into the valley as spring arrived. Each afternoon she'd put on a coat and explore the grounds, marvelling at the thousands of daffodils. She thought of Bee again as she picked a few, took them up to her room and placed them in the window.

Then spring turned to summer. Great clumps of purple wisteria quivered in the gentle breezes just outside the wide open windows, the roses bloomed and their smell wafted into the house. The cover was taken off the open-air swimming pool, and daily more people turned up for lunch out on the terrace, or to doze on sunbeds like lizards. But even on wet days Oaklands was beautiful. She could have the grounds to herself in the afternoons, wandering through the woods, listening to the peaceful sound of rain on leaves, smelling the good clean earth.

But now it was autumn again – the Virginia creeper on the house a fiery red, the trees on either side of the drive turning gold, brown, russet and yellow. She'd had a whole year of happiness here. But what had made it even more special was her growing certainty that Magnus was her real father.

On the day she fell off the stepladder when dressing the Christmas tree, she found they had a similar sense of humour. On Christmas Day when she discovered the stocking hanging on her door, she saw Magnus's tender side. All through the winter and spring her respect for him had grown as she watched how hard he worked, how fair he was with his staff, how caringly he looked after his guests. But it wasn't until one warm afternoon back in July that liking, respect, awe and admiration all came together and she realised that what she felt for this gruff, headstrong man, was love.

Mel had put on shorts and a tee shirt intending to walk down to the post office in the village, but she knew Magnus had been working out in the woods since ten in the morning without even a drink, so she decided to take him some of Antoine's homemade lemonade and a couple of chicken sandwiches first.

As she picked her way through the dense undergrowth, towards the sound of his chainsaw, she saw him up ahead in a clearing. He was bare-chested, wearing only a pair of faded khaki shorts and stout boots. Despite his age his body was as hard and muscular as a young man's, tanned the colour of old pine. He didn't hear her coming over the noise of the machine and Mel smiled at his youthful energy as he attacked the dense shrubbery, pausing every now and then to drag out the cut branches, tossing them onto a huge pile behind him.

'I thought you might like some refreshments,' she called out when she was close enough. 'That looks like thirsty work.'

He turned in surprise, his face dripping with sweat. 'Bless you, Mel,' he said, putting the saw down and taking a handkerchief from his pocket to mop at his face. 'I've been dying of thirst for well over an hour, but I was loath to go back to the house until I got this finished.'

He sat down on a fallen tree trunk and took the bottle of lemonade eagerly, drinking it so fast some of it trickled down his chin and onto his chest.

'You shouldn't work so hard,' she said reprovingly. 'Surely the groundsmen could do this?'

'Hard manual work has special rewards,' he said, smiling boyishly at her. 'It's far more satisfying than getting stuck into a pile of paperwork.'

His face, chest and arms were covered in small scratches, and his hair was sprinkled with burrs and bits of leaves. But his eyes were very bright. He looked supremely happy.

Mel sat with him as he ate the sandwiches. They talked about the people who'd been in for lunch and some guests who were expected later that evening. But when he'd finished eating she got up to go. 'I'd better leave you in peace.'

'Don't go yet,' he said unexpectedly. 'We never seem to have much time for talking. I've been meaning to ask you if you're happy here, and about your plans for the future.'

Mel sat down again. 'I've been happier here than I've ever been,' she said truthfully. 'I don't make plans for the future, but this is everything I ever wanted.'

'You are an odd girl, Mel.' He smiled and she saw affection in his eyes. 'I thought you'd soon get bored when you found out our guests were all old fuddy-duddies. Don't you sometimes yearn for a few people your own age?'

'Not often.' She laughed lightly, thinking of some of her old hippie friends back in Ibiza. She did miss that comradeship and the fun, but she knew that it was superficial. 'I feel complete here, at peace.'

'I wish my children had your tranquillity,' he sighed deeply. 'It's a strange thing Mel, and probably very disloyal of me, but sometimes I feel closer to you than to them.'

'My mother used to say it was a pity we couldn't choose our parents,' Mel said thoughtfully. 'She didn't think much of hers. I suppose it's the same with children. You might love them, but you don't necessarily like them.'

Magnus laughed softly, as if this struck a chord. 'Ruth used to say "We're stuck with our relations, thank God for friends." I suppose that amounts to the same thing. I never had anything in common with my older brothers. Stephen and Sophie seem very like them sometimes.' He stood up, raking the debris he'd cut back into a heap. Mel began to help him, pulling the bigger logs to one side and heaping them up so they could be taken back to the house for firewood. She didn't want to push him about his children, but if she stayed and worked he might confide in her further.

She had found nothing to like in either Sophie or Stephen on their infrequent visits. Since Nicholas hadn't bothered to visit Oaklands in her whole time there, she assumed she'd probably like him even less.

Sophie seemed seeped in resentment. At only thirty-eight she had embraced middle age eagerly, wearing the most unbecoming shapeless clothes, with her dark hair scraped back in a matronly bun. There was no joy in her: Mel had never heard her laugh, her smiles were tight and polite, and her overheard conversations always seemed to be laboured, as if she found it impossible to like anyone.

Michael, her banker husband, was almost as bad – a quiet, docile man who allowed his wife to dominate him completely. He sighed a great deal as if life had been a tremendous disappointment to him.

Stephen, the oldest son, wasn't a great improvement. He had taken over the running of the family estate back in Yorkshire and he was forever carping on to his father about the problems there. His wife, June, was like a grey mouse, with even less personality.

Magnus was silent for some ten minutes, dragging out more cut branches and old bushes onto his pile. But then just as Mel felt their chat was over, he stopped working for a moment and stood hands on hips watching her stacking the logs.

'When I bought Oaklands it was my intention that it would be a family run business,' he said. 'I never tried to brainwash them with the idea but when Stephen went in for estate management and Sophie chose catering, I assumed they too were working towards that end. Nicholas was only a small boy at that stage, so I didn't even think of a role for him. But when Ruth died, so did that dream.'

Mel squatted down on a log. 'It might not have worked out anyway,' she said cautiously.

Magnus chuckled and sat down beside her. 'You can say it. That a hotel run by frosty faced Sophie, with Stephen strutting about full of his own importance would be disastrous.'

'I wouldn't have the audacity to even think it, much less say it,' Mel said indignantly.

'Come on!' he teased. 'I've seen you looking at them both. Your face is an open book sometimes. Even Ruth, doting a mother though she was, used to claim they had less personality than a pencil.'

Mel laughed. 'Ruth sounds so funny and lovely. I wish I'd met her.'

'She would have liked you too,' Magnus smiled. 'She'd have winkled every last thing out of you by now too. When are you going to tell me properly about yourself?'

'There's nothing of interest to tell,' Mel said. She had agonised countless times over whether or not to tell Magnus who she really was. But the more she'd got to know him, the more she saw that it would put him in an impossible situation. He was still grieving for his wife, so she didn't relish reminding him of his past indiscretions. His children only seemed to come here when they wanted something, and she had no wish to be thought of as another fortune hunter. Besides she already had everything she ever wanted, the security of a good job, a home beyond her wildest dreams and the affection of this big man. She wouldn't gain anything more by revealing the truth and she might well lose what she already had.

'I disagree.' He slung one big arm along her shoulders companionably. 'I suspect your story is probably more action packed than my entire life. I'm not being nosey, Mel. I'm just an old man who thinks he's finally found a real friend, and real friends confide in one another.'

It was so still and quiet in the woods. Everything smelled so clean and pure. 'Magnus, if I withhold things from you it's not because I don't trust you, but because I'm ashamed,' she said softly. 'Nearly two years ago I paid very heavily for all my past mistakes when my dearest friend died from a drugs overdose. I turned my back on everything then. I turned over a new leaf and started out again. Please don't ask me to relive it.'

Magnus's grip tightened on her shoulder. 'Okay,' he said gruffly. 'I respect that. I've done things too which I'd rather lock away and forget. But I want you to know I've grown very fond of you, Mel.'

Since that day Mel had often gone out to work in the grounds with Magnus in the afternoons. It seemed as if each day brought new closeness. They discovered they both had a weakness for stodgy school dinner type puddings, escaping in lurid Harold Robbins books and old weepy films. Magnus told her stories of his days at Oxford University, his time in Canada as a young man and his exploits during the war in the RAF. He told her how he'd started his building business after the war, with the first plot of land in Staines. As he spoke of these things she was slowly putting more pieces into the jigsaw puzzle of her mother's past. She hoped that one day something might bring him round to mentioning Bonny, but although he admitted that back in those days he neglected Ruth, he never mentioned meeting anyone else.

Mel eventually got brave enough to confess one day that she'd once worked as a nightclub hostess. She even told him a few of the funnier stories about

Bee. She felt as if they were both circling round their own secrets, each day growing a tiny bit closer to the point where their last defences would drop.

But now it was autumn again. And Magnus was spending more time in his office. They might occasionally be able to work together outside, but realistically it would be spring before they had many more opportunities to talk.

Mel's reverie was cut off by Mrs Downes coming back into the kitchen buttoning up her mackintosh.

'Two more cancellations for dinner tonight,' she said to Antoine. 'Can't say I blame them. I wouldn't expect a dog to go out in weather like this. You'll have a quiet night, Mel. Magnus is off for his game of chess with the vicar and I doubt anyone will turn up for a drink. Make the most of it and get an early night.'

'Early night, what's that?' Mel giggled. She rarely went to bed before one and was up again at seven. Mrs Downes worried, but she didn't seem to need much sleep anymore.

'It will catch up with you one of these days.' Mrs Downes wiggled a warning finger at her. 'By the time you're my age you'll be as wrinkled as a prune.'

Mrs Downes had been right: it was extremely quiet. Two men came into the bar at half past seven, had a couple of drinks and left. There were only four people eating in the dining room and once they'd been served Sally, the evening waitress, went and sat at the reception desk.

Mel used the time to polish the glass shelves behind the bar and check the stock. The wind was howling outside, rain battering against the windows, evoking memories not only of that awful night when she'd arrived here, but of the year

345

before, when she'd been holed up in that little room in Earls Court, numbed and desolate from Bee's death.

It no longer seemed so important to piece together Bonny's life. As Jack had so wisely said, 'Yesterdays don't matter. It's the tomorrows that count.'

At around nine Mel heard a male voice out in reception. She assumed it was one of the guests talking to Sally, but a few minutes later a young man in a rain-splattered worn leather jacket came into the bar.

Mel knew most of the members now, but she hadn't seen this man before. If she had not heard him talking to Sally she might have asked for proof of membership: he wore jeans and a turtle neck sweater, when the rule for evenings was smart dress. Considering the weather outside, however, it seemed a little pedantic to do anything but smile warmly.

'It's an awful night out there,' she said cheerfully, glad of someone to talk to. 'What can I get you?'

'A whisky to warm me up, please.'

His voice was beautiful, detracting immediately from his shabby clothes: deep and resonant, the kind Bee used to describe as BBC. She saw now he was very handsome too, his streaky blond hair flopping over his forehead, his dark blue eyes framed by thick dark lashes.

'You must be the new girl, Mel?' he asked as she handed him his drink.

'Not so new now, I've been here a year today,' she said.

'Is that cause for celebration or commiseration?' he asked, his eyes glinting mischievously.

'Oh celebration,' she laughed lightly. 'In fact I'll treat you to that whisky to prove it.'

In a whole year at Oaklands, Mel had not met a

single man she was attracted to. Most of the younger members were flashy types, who sported gold watches and sovereign rings. Their hair was blow-dried, their suits were hand-tailored and their main reason for drinking here was to do some social climbing. But this man wasn't a bit like that.

She felt he took little interest in his appearance: his hair straggled over the collar of his jacket, and it had that neglected look that suggested when he did choose to have it cut, it was straight round to a conventional barber's for a short back and sides. He was around six foot tall, very slender, with beautifully defined cheek bones, probably in his mid-twenties. He had an aura of good breeding, much like some of the male students who worked the bar during the summer.

She joined him in a drink, taking pains to put the money in the till, even though Magnus didn't mind the staff having an occasional free drink with a customer.

'What do you think of Bath?' he asked. 'I always find it a bit stuffy.'

Mel had fallen in love with Bath at first sight, but she knew what he meant by the stuffiness. 'I love the city itself,' she admitted. 'But I must admit it's a snob's paradise. A bit la-di-dah, as my mother used to say.'

They spent some time exchanging anecdotes about some of the worst people they'd met in Bath. Mel told him how she'd gone into a jewellers to ask the price of a watch she'd seen in the window and nearly fallen through the floor in shock when she was told it was five hundred pounds.

'He said it was a Rolex,' she giggled. 'But that didn't mean a thing to me. When I asked if they had anything under ten pounds, he looked at me as if I had two heads, and said, "I think madam should try H. Samuel." I wanted to ask why anyone would spend that much on a watch, after all they all tell the same time, but I didn't dare. I just slunk out with a red face.'

The man told her he'd worked for a time as a waiter in Bath and described the meanness of some of the old ladies who came in for lunch.

'One old bat insisted on taking a table which I hadn't cleared. I thought it was just because it was by the window. Blow me down if she didn't help herself to the tip left behind, meant for me. Do you know, she filled up her crocodile bag with sugar lumps! She had her soup, then ordered the lamb chops, ate half of them and then said they were cold and she'd only pay for the soup. I found out afterwards she was Lady Something or Other with a stately pile in Bradford-upon-Avon. Apparently she was known for doing that in all the restaurants.'

Over a second drink Mel told him about her time in Ibiza and he described a summer he'd spent working in a bar in the south of France.

It was as if she'd known him for years. They flitted from subject to subject, laughing and commiserating at each other's hard luck stories. If Mel had met him anywhere but at Oaklands she would probably have told him some much more explicit tales. She felt they were on exactly the same wavelength. Somehow she knew he'd been to some of the dark places she had, not because of anything he said, more from his manner and a knowing look in his eyes.

When Antoine buzzed her on the internal phone to ask if she could come down to the kitchen, she saw it was nearly half past ten.

'I won't be long,' she said. 'If you want another drink ask Sally, she's only out on the reception.'

Antoine had cut his finger and was finding it hard to put a dressing on it. It was worse than she

348

expected, bleeding dramatically. She dressed it for him, then cleaned up the blood which he'd dripped everywhere, and put away food in the fridge for him.

She got back to the bar just before eleven. To her surprise the man was gone. Sally had turned off the bar lights, hung the towels over the pumps and locked up.

Mel felt very silly for having expected the man to wait for her. When she thought about it she realised she'd been flirting with him all evening.

The worst of it all was that she really liked him and she'd been absolutely convinced he was just as attracted to her as she was to him. Now she realised he must have been being polite. And yet try as she might she couldn't put his face, his voice or anything about him out of her mind.

Mel was clearing the breakfast tables the next morning when Magnus came striding into the dining room. He looked pleased with himself about something, his face had a rosy glow.

'What did you think of my Nick then?' he asked.

'Nick?' Mel stared stupidly at him.

'Well, by all accounts you spent half the evening chatting to him.' Magnus gave a rich belly laugh. 'He won't like it if I tell him what little impression he made on you.'

Her stomach lurched. 'That was your son?'

'Of course. You didn't realise?'

'No, he never introduced himself,' she said weakly, sitting down suddenly at the table she was clearing. 'I thought he was just a member.'

'I wouldn't give membership to anyone as scruffy as him,' Magnus chortled, but there was a certain pride in his voice. 'You shot off to bed a bit smartish didn't you? I came back to find Nick alone. He said you'd gone down to the kitchen. So I closed up the bar and took Nick upstairs. By the time I came down again to suggest you joined us for a nightcap, you'd already gone to bed.'

'I didn't know you were back. I thought Sally closed the bar,' she said, blushing furiously, remembering how she'd lain awake thinking about the young man.

'It doesn't matter that much. If he gets the part at the audition today he'll be around for two or three weeks at least. You'll have plenty of opportunity to get to know him better.'

Mel attempted to pull herself together. 'Well, fancy me not realising,' she said. 'I just didn't connect.'

'He connected with you, my girl,' Magnus growled, but smiled as if the thought pleased him. 'He wanted to know every last thing about you. First time I've seen him smitten with a girl in ages.'

When he left the dining room a few minutes later, Mel stayed, sitting at the table. She was shaken to the core.

This was one eventuality she had never imagined. She'd never for one moment anticipated liking Magnus's youngest son: everything she'd heard about him suggested he was even more unpleasant than Stephen, and he hadn't visited his father for over a year. Mrs Downes adored him, but then she'd been a second mother to him since his mother died. Yet even she'd said he was spoiled and over-pampered and that he ought to get a proper job instead of wasting his time as an actor and sponging off Magnus. His looks hadn't given him away at all, he was nothing like his father or his brother and sister.

She could no longer persuade herself that he hadn't been interested in her. Magnus's words had confirmed all her instincts. She wasn't naïve. She'd learned just about everything there was to know about men. Those tingles down her spine when she talked to him were due to dangerous mutual attraction.

'Mutual attraction with your half-brother,' she told herself, shuddering. 'You might've known something would put a spanner in the works. Now what are you going to do?'

Chapter Fifteen

'Mel!'

Mel ignored the shout from Nick and carried on walking up the drive as if she hadn't heard him above the wind in the trees.

'So you're deaf as well as impossibly snooty,' he joked breathlessly as he caught up with her. 'You've been lip-reading all this time and I didn't realise.'

'Did you call out?' she asked, hoping her cold tone would put him off. 'I was thinking, I didn't hear you.'

In the last few days Mel had become more than anxious about Nick. She was frightened.

He hadn't got the part at Bath Theatre Royal, and she knew only too well that his only reason for not returning to London was her. He'd been here now for four and a half days, and had gone out of his way to charm her at every possible opportunity.

It was working too. She wasn't just charmed, but bewitched. No other man had ever affected her quite so strongly as he did. In his company she felt light-headed and exhilarated, but once alone again, edgy and dejected. She kept telling herself she was overreacting and tried to put him out of her mind, but she couldn't. And he wouldn't stay away from her.

When she worked behind the bar, he was there

helping. He was by her side clearing the breakfast tables; if she went to the kitchen, he would turn up there too, chatting, making her laugh, teasing and flirting.

Everyone at Oaklands was talking about them, already convinced this was to be the romance of the century. Mrs Downes kept telling her stories about how sweet Nick had been as a little boy. Magnus just beamed and on Sunday he offered her an extra night off so Nick could take her to the pictures.

Mel had turned Magnus's offer down, she'd said quite simply that though she liked Nick, she had no interest in a date with him. But Magnus just laughed and said she was playing hard to get.

She thought she had atoned for all her past mistakes and wrong doing, that her new-found happiness and pride in herself was permanent. Now it seemed as if Nick had been brought into her life as further punishment. She didn't know what to do.

A small voice inside her urged her to go to Magnus and tell him everything. She had no proof he really was her father and he might know something which would put an end to her speculation once and for all. But how could she admit now that she'd been under his roof for a whole year under false pretences? She would appear so sly and deceitful. And if he really was her father, what then? He would either ask her to leave, or feel compelled to publicly acknowledge her. Knowing Magnus as she did, he was too upright to choose the more cowardly way out. And that would cause his entire family deep distress.

The heavy rain had gone on ceaselessly until the previous night, adding to her sense of oppression. When she woke that morning to find a blue sky and sunshine, albeit weak, she'd decided a long walk in the afternoon would give her time alone to think and maybe bring back her equilibrium. It was still very windy and a carpet of fallen leaves concealed deep puddles, but she was well protected by wellington boots, an oilskin coat and a warm scarf round her neck. She just didn't know how to protect herself from Nick.

She stopped short and turned to him. 'I'm just going for a walk. I don't want to hurt your feelings, but I'd rather be alone,' she said bluntly.

His mouth drooped petulantly, making him look very young. As usual he wore jeans and his leather jacket. His only precaution against the weather was a tartan scarf tied loosely round his neck, reminding her of Rupert Bear. His suede desert boots were hardly suitable for walking in mud and puddles.

In the last few days she had tried to avoid studying him too closely, but she had lost the battle. His slim hips and tight rounded buttocks aroused her, his ever watchful dark blue eyes brought her out in a flush. There was a tiny scar above his right eyebrow and on several occasions she'd itched to reach out and touch it. But it was his lips that really got to her, they were so soft and full, reminding her poignantly how long it was since she kissed a man.

'We've got to talk properly,' he said with a shrug of his shoulders. 'I know you're hung up that I'm the boss's son, but that's silly. Dad hasn't any objections.'

Mel sneered, even though her heart felt as if it were melting. She knew she'd got to find some way of wounding him.

'You are even more arrogant than your brother Stephen,' she said cuttingly. 'I am not some little Victorian kitchen-maid. I have a mind of my own. As I said, I like you, but that's all. I'm not interested in men full stop. I wouldn't care if you were Paul

Newman or Steve McQueen. I'd still say no. Can you get your head round that?'

She expected him to come back with an equally sharp retort. He was after all a man of the world and very eloquent, but instead he just looked at her, dark blue eyes full of reproach.

'I'm sorry, but I don't believe you,' he said in a quiet voice. 'Not because I'm an egotistical bastard who thinks all girls should fall at my feet, but because I can feel something between us. I know this might sound like the worst kind of cliché, but I felt it within moments of meeting you.'

Mel laughed at him. She'd heard from Mrs Downes that he was something of a playboy, a social butterfly who flitted through life with a different girl on his arm each week. 'I would have thought an actor could come up with something better,' she said.

'I'm good at clever chat-up lines when I don't mean it,' he said. 'But this isn't a joke, I'm telling you what's in my heart.'

His sincerity floored her.

'Look, Nick,' she said, finding it hard to meet his eyes. 'I don't know how much you know about me, but I've had a chequered past. I worked as a nightclub hostess, I'm a professional flirt. The way I was with you that night you came into the bar was just the way I am with everyone in there. If you read something more into it then I'm sorry. Now can I go on with my walk?'

'I'm coming with you,' he said taking her arm. 'I've got a great deal more to say to you.'

'I don't want to hear it,' she pleaded.

'I didn't mean I was going to harp on about us all afternoon,' he said. 'I just want to know more about you. I understand now why Dad thinks so much of you. Sophie and Stephen might think you've deliberately wormed your way into his affections, but for the record I know they're wrong.'

'Well I'm glad to hear it,' she said sarcastically, pushing his hand off her arm and stuffing her hands into the pockets of her coat. 'For the record, as you say, I've grown very fond of your dad too. He gave me a job and a new start. I owe him a great deal. I shouldn't think your brother and sister know him at all well if they think just anyone can "worm" their way into his affections. He's about the most astute man I've ever met.'

'You frighten them,' Nick said. 'You are everything Sophie isn't, beautiful, fun, vivacious and clever. As for Stephen, well he just thinks a woman's place is at the sink, he hasn't even got the imagination to think of them in bed.'

Mel had to laugh. 'I can't help your brother and sister's hang-ups,' she said. 'You can report back to them I'm not after their dad, or you. Tell them I'm a dyke if you like.'

'Neither of them would know what that was,' he said, catching hold of her arm again and twisting her slightly so she was forced to look at him. 'Okay enough of all that, let's just walk and talk. Maybe I'll grow on you?'

'Like moss?' Mel raised one eyebrow quizzically. 'I'd like to be friends, Nick, but let's get it straight right now, that's all. Okay?'

'Okay,' he smiled, showing perfect white teeth. 'Whatever you say.'

They walked down to the bottom of Brass Knocker Hill where the river had burst its banks, flooding the fields either side. But the canal towpath, though muddy in places and thick with leaves, was passable and sheltered from the cold wind by thick bushes.

'I'm sorry you didn't get the part the other day,' Mel said. She was feeling a little easier now. Maybe they *could* have a platonic friendship. 'Have you any idea why you didn't get it?'

'Just pipped at the post by a better actor,' he admitted.

'Well, that's honest,' she said.

He shrugged. 'I had to learn to be both honest and humble.'

Mel felt she'd hit a raw note. 'You weren't always?'

'No. I was King Brat,' he sighed, but then laughed as if he wasn't used to making such frank confessions. 'You see I didn't go to RADA or any other stage school. I thought I was so great in school productions that I didn't need it. I did a bit of extra work, then I fell into a couple of adverts through someone I knew. I never realised I was just lucky, I assumed I was naturally talented.'

'And you got your comeuppance?' Magnus had said one or two things in the past which suggested something had gone badly wrong in Nick's life at one time. She hoped he might tell her about it.

'That came later,' he said with a smirk. 'What really turned my head was getting the lead in a TV series. I was only twenty then. I got loads of advance publicity claiming I was a successor to James Dean, the lad likely to go to the top, and I believed every word of it. It was one of those gritty kitchen-sink type dramas, set on a South London housing estate. I played the Jack-the-Lad character, just back from a spell in Borstal.'

'Not *Hunnicroft Estate?*' she asked.

'Good God, someone remembers it!' he said dryly. 'Did you like it?'

Mel was too embarrassed to admit that she and Bee watched the first few minutes of the first episode, then turned it off. From what she remembered it was all swearing and young lads hitting each other with motorcycle chains. 'It wasn't quite my scene,' she said. 'But in those days I hardly ever watched TV.'

'It wasn't anyone's scene as it turned out,' he laughed again. 'The timing was all wrong, it was too hard hitting. People phoned up the television company and complained about the foul language and the violence. After the initial six weeks it was dropped like a stone.'

'And then?'

'Nothing more for me,' he said ruefully, kicking a stone along in front of him. 'I was type cast as a lout, all my dreams were down the pan and I didn't have the savvy to just lie low for awhile and wait for a second chance.'

Mel pondered on this for a moment. He must've been a pretty good actor to play a convincing lout. He certainly didn't look or sound like one in the flesh. 'So what did you do?'

'I acted the part of the big star. I went out clubbing it night after night, Annabel's, the Speak Easy, the Scotch of St James's. As long as there were a few dolly birds that recognised me, I'd stay till I was too drunk to walk. The money I'd earned was soon gone. All I had left after my five minutes of fame was a few glossy photographs and a couple of sharp suits.'

Mel was touched by his honesty. She'd been to all those clubs and met plenty of men just like that during her time in Chelsea. But then she'd been one of those dolly birds prepared to drink and dance the night away with them, bolstering their egos with flattery, just as long as they were paying. It was tempting to admit this, but some things were better left buried.

'You sound a bit ashamed,' she said instead. 'I know the feeling, there are bits of my life I'd rather forget.'

He gave her a sideways look, as if to gauge

whether he could take his confession further. 'I was a real prat,' he said with a faint humourless smirk. 'I used people until they dropped me, and I went down so far I thought I'd never climb up again. Fortunately I met someone who cared enough to offer a helping hand. She let me stay at her place while I got my head together again, insisted I got a job as a barman to support myself, and encouraged me to take some acting classes.'

'Is that the reason you haven't visited your father for so long?'

'Yes, I suppose so.' He looked a little ashamed. 'Dad's not a demanding type that expects me down every month or so. But I guess I couldn't face him until I knew I'd got myself together. But we've talked enough about me, tell me about yourself.'

Mel had a feeling he wasn't in the habit of talking like this, and that the whole story was probably as sleazy and painful to him as hers was. She felt such honesty deserved some reciprocal openness.

'I was just an empty-headed raver who thought she could burn the candle at both ends for ever,' she admitted with a sheepish grin. 'It was all pretty squalid. It's funny how you can delude yourself for so long that you're doing okay. Then one day you wake up and find it's all turned sour.'

She told him about Bee. But the same edited version she'd given Magnus, leaving out the pornography.

'I'm so sorry,' he said, and his blue eyes held the same compassion she often saw in his father's. 'I couldn't make out why you were so happy to be cloistered in Oaklands, I understand now.'

'It's the purity of life here that I like,' she said, turning to look back. Oaklands was hidden now by trees, but the rolling hills, the patchwork of fields, and the autumn colours in the valley were all so beautiful. 'I know that some of the guests aren't

359

everything they seem, that perhaps I'm cocooned away from real life, but when I look out my bedroom window I feel renewed and at peace. That's why I'm so grateful to your father, Nick. He's been like your friend that helped you. He took me in hand, threw out all the hippie claptrap I used to believe in. I like working hard now, and it's good to feel part of things here.'

Perhaps this wasn't entirely true, but she certainly believed Magnus had been the best and most formative influence in her life.

Nick sat by his father's bedroom window later that afternoon. It was already almost dark. This room was on the first floor, directly under Mel's with the same view of the valley, but larger windows. Next door was Magnus's private sitting room.

Here in the bedroom there were many reminders of his mother: needlepoint pictures, satin pleated cushions she'd made, fading now, their piping worn. Photographs of each of them as babies covered one wall and there were still more in silver frames on the dressing table. Nick always slept in the sitting room next door on the rare occasions he came home. He made the excuse that it wasn't worth messing up one of the guest rooms, but in fact it was because he liked to be close to his father.

When his mother was alive, they'd had private rooms on the other end of the house. Nick had bitterly resented Magnus moving out of those and into here on her death. But time and maturity had mellowed him and now he understood.

Ruth had loved pastels, dainty furniture and pretty watercolours, but once she was gone Magnus found it too painful to live with so many reminders of her. His new sitting room was as sternly masculine as a gentlemen's club with dark moss-green walls, leather armchairs and wall-to-wall books. Aside from one photograph of Ruth and Magnus on their wedding day, there were no jolts back to the past.

Nick stared out the window, watching as the sky turned dark. He knew he should have a shave, put on a suit and present himself downstairs for dinner with Magnus. But though he usually enjoyed meeting the guests and club members and playing the part of the prodigal son, tonight he was tempted to stay upstairs.

He could not get Mel out of his mind. He could picture the moment he first saw her as clearly as looking at a photograph.

One lone spotlight shone down on her dark glossy hair, tied back at the nape of her neck with a black velvet bow. She wore a slinky red dress which on many women would have looked tawdry, but she had the dramatic, almost Mediterranean-type colouring to carry it off.

When he saw Mel standing there behind the bar, he felt as if someone had winded him. Sophie had described Mel as some kind of raddled bar-fly, just waiting to get her teeth into their father. He knew Sophie exaggerated, and he'd wanted to see for himself what this harpy was really like. But he'd still expected a more buxom, obvious type; brassy, maybe even with an out-of-date bouffant hairstyle. This girl, and she was a girl, not a woman as Sophie had implied, was simply beautiful. For perhaps the first time in his life he enjoyed being anonymous.

A year or two earlier he would've been too puffed up with self-importance to really look or listen to her. But he found himself noting every last thing: the sensuality of that slightly fuller lower lip, the shape of her eyes, the jutting of her hip bone through her dress as she reached up to the optics to get him a drink.

All his girlfriends had been blonde, if he was

entirely honest with himself he'd admit he'd chosen them almost as accessories. At eighteen he liked them small with big breasts; later he'd progressed to the long-legged Sloaney kind with bony bodies. But Camellia would never settle for being anyone's fashion accessory. She had a mind of her own and a look that was entirely individual.

In some ways she was like Kate, the forty-year-old divorcee who had helped him get back on his feet two years earlier. Not in looks – Kate had been voluptuous with violet eyes – but in the warmth, the interest, and perhaps the passion. His relationship with Kate had been platonic, but he could see for himself that the passion was there, just as he could in Mel.

It was the passion he found himself dwelling on late that night as he tried to go to sleep on his father's settee. Mel would be hot stuff, he was certain of that. This was definitely a girl with vast experience of men. He found himself remembering all those humorous, incisive little remarks she made about her male friends in Ibiza. And the seductive way she'd looked at him.

Now after four days in Mel's company, Nick was puzzled. He had abandoned all Sophie's theories: Mel had nothing but pure admiration and affection for his father. From his conversations with Joan Downes, Antoine and other members of staff, he could tell she wasn't on the make in any way. If she were to leave Oaklands, they'd all be devastated: it seemed she practically ran the place.

They had so much in common: they laughed at the same things, they could talk so easily and naturally. He'd been honest with her about his past, though there was much more he could tell her, and she'd opened up to some extent about hers. So why didn't she want him?

Perhaps he was still a bit arrogant, but he *knew*

Mel was attracted to him. He could sense it, like being enveloped in a strong perfume. Why was she fighting it?

Later that night, Mel lay on her bed and sobbed her heart out. It had been one of the most painful evenings she'd ever endured. Despite her protestations Magnus had insisted that she joined him and Nick for dinner in the dining room. As she'd sat there toying with poached salmon, flanked by the two attentive men, she'd had the strongest desire to pack her bags and leave for good.

'I'm going back to London tomorrow,' Nick said, as he poured her a glass of wine. 'But I'll be back, continually, until I wear you down.'

Magnus just smiled beatifically, as if in his mind he was already arranging the wedding. 'That's right, son,' he said heartily. 'Faint heart never won fair lady. Mel's just out of practice. I've kept her under lock and key for too long.'

She could only blush and smile weakly. Nick looked so handsome in his dark suit and a pale blue shirt. How could she possibly feel such overwhelming *wanting* for him? Or betray the trust of Magnus, who gave her such fatherly affection without suspecting they were related?

Sitting there in candlelight, she was struck by similarities in all three of them that she'd failed to notice before. She had high finely drawn cheekbones, and so did Nick. The lines and softening flesh on Magnus's face had stopped her noticing them before, but she could see them now. Their hair and eye colour had prevented her from seeing other resemblances, yet Sophie had dark hair and eyes, and Magnus's own eyes were sometimes tawny, sometimes green, never a true blue like Nick's.

Their skin tone was another pointer: by day, one

only noticed that Magnus's was ruddy brown from working outside, and Nick's seemed pallid in comparison. But now she saw they all had the same underlying olive tone. And although Nick looked fairer-skinned, she remembered him saying that when he returned from Greece last year he was almost black. Even their lip shapes were a give-away. Each of them had a clearly defined Cupid's bow, a wider, more fleshy mouth than usual.

At one time she would've been delighted to find further evidence of her closeness to Magnus, but now she felt sickened by it. She longed to be an anonymous employee, with nothing more pressing on her mind than how to spend next week's wage packet.

The conversation had moved on to Magnus's future plans to install a gymnasium and an indoor pool in the stable block. He jokingly suggested to Nick that he could take a course as a fitness instructor so that he'd have something to fall back on if his acting career ever folded completely.

Nick had mentioned in passing before that he worked out in a gym in London, but hearing Magnus speak of it gave Mel a sudden vision of Nick naked. She drank more wine to cover up her confusion.

Then Magnus said he intended to see she had driving lessons. 'It's ridiculous you not being able to drive,' he said almost curtly. 'You could do the banking for me and get out more. I shall arrange the lessons tomorrow.'

It got worse as the meal went on. Every long-term plan Magnus mentioned included her in a major role. It was quite clear that he was looking ahead to his retirement, and intended her to be manager.

'I want to expand here,' he said, smiling at her, then glancing back at Nick as though they had already discussed this in detail. 'I'm looking into having an annexe built next to the stables, with another twenty rooms, I thought of incorporating a conference room too so we can offer businesses a complete package.'

A week ago Mel would've been wildly enthusiastic about these plans. She might even have suggested that they tried to attract more weddings. But now she just drank her wine and listened to the men, hoping against hope that some emergency would come up in the kitchen so she could rush off.

Nick was talking about his schooldays, describing how it had been when he was home for the holidays, back when Ruth was alive. It was painful to hear both men speaking so lovingly about her, knowing that during this time Magnus was writing to Bonny, about herself. Nick's childhood sounded so idyllic, a tree house up in the woods, school friends coming to stay for weeks on end, putting on plays in the stables with local children.

Yet Nick didn't once mention the time after Ruth's death and Mel sensed he had been as unhappy then in adolescence as she had been. Maybe that was when he learned to act, pretending to be tough and uncaring as his father withdrew into himself in grief: a lonely young boy forced to become a man too quickly.

'It's time you had a holiday, my girl,' Magnus said a little later, prompted perhaps by her unusual silence. 'Nick's always raving about the Greek islands. It's still lovely there at this time of year, how about the pair of you popping off there for a week?'

With hindsight Mel realised Magnus was just being kind, concerned because she wasn't sparkling and afraid that he'd been overworking her. But at the time she just saw it as manipulation. 'If I want a holiday I can arrange it myself,' she snapped without thinking.

She saw the two men exchange glances and realised she was a little drunk. Afraid she might make a bigger fool of herself she made a feeble excuse about having to have a word with Antoine. Before either of them could protest she got up and left the dining room.

Fortunately Antoine did need a little help, as the dishwasher had broken down. Mel took everything out and washed and dried it by hand while Antoine dished up desserts.

By the time she got back to the dining room, Magnus and Nick had retired to their sitting room with a bottle of brandy.

Sally smirked at Mel as she imparted this information. 'They asked for you to join them,' she reluctantly added.

Sally was the only member of staff Mel wasn't entirely comfortable with: a tall, thin rather Roedeanish sort of girl, by day a student at Bath university. Mel had wondered before whether Sally might be jealous of her; now she knew from her sharp tone that she fancied Nick.

'I'm not feeling too good,' Mel said lamely. 'I think I'll just go to bed. Will you tell them for me?'

She had just turned onto the last flight of stairs to the top floor, when the door to Magnus's sitting room opened and Nick appeared. When he asked her to come in, she offered the same excuse she'd given Sally and went on up the stairs. Nick followed her, taking them two at a time.

'What's really the matter?' he asked, catching up with her on the landing outside her room.

'I told you. I don't feel well,' she lied. Washing up had sobered her up a little.

'This evening's all been too much for you, hasn't

it?' he said. 'Dad's like a bulldozer when he gets going.'

The understanding in his voice brought tears to her eyes. The softness of it seemed to soothe the troubled place inside her. But as he saw her tears he drew her into his arms.

'There, there,' he said comfortingly. 'You mustn't mind Dad. He's just afraid of getting too old before he achieves all his dreams. He forgets that some things can't be rushed.'

It was so good to be held by him that for a moment she forgot her fears, even when his hands moved to cup her face.

'You're worth waiting for,' he whispered, kissing her nose. 'Sometimes I can be the most patient man in the world.'

His mouth came down on hers, and for a brief moment she yielded to him, losing herself in the sweetness of those hot, sensual lips.

But reality came back swiftly and with it absolute horror. She pushed him away forcefully. 'Don't ever do that again,' she said, wiping away his kiss with the back of her hand. 'I told you I wasn't interested. Can't you get that through your thick head?'

He took a few steps back from her, his face flushing a bright pink.

'I'd like to say I'm sorry, but I'm not,' he said turning to go back down the stairs. 'I don't know what it is with you, Mel, but I shall find out one way or another. You wanted to kiss me as badly as I wanted it. You don't fool me.'

As she lay in bed crying, Mel knew she was trapped. All evening she'd seen pointers to Nick's dogged determination, from the child who decided he would be an actor, despite opposition from his family, to the way he'd managed to climb back up that ladder after his initial arrogance had toppled him off. He might have been a playboy in the past, but he wasn't one now. He had decided she was his destiny, and she knew he would persevere.

'Why do this to me?' she whispered into the dark, to the same presence she'd once thanked for landing her in this beautiful room. 'What have I done to deserve it?'

Chapter Sixteen

Mel looked out of Magnus's sitting room window at the heavy, driving rain. It was not quite four in the afternoon, yet it was almost dark. The strong wind had stripped the trees of their beautiful autumn leaves, covering the lawn and terrace with a tawny patchwork. To her it was a poignant reminder of the day she arrived at Oaklands two years ago, and the day last year when she met Nick Osbourne for the first time.

'When are you going to tell me what's eating you?'

The growled question startled her. She pulled the heavy tapestry curtains to, then turned back to Magnus. He was recovering from pneumonia. It had started with a bad cold the previous month, turned into bronchitis after an afternoon spent working outside in the rain, and finally to pneumonia when he refused to take himself off to bed.

He was sitting in his high-backed leather chair, close to the log fire, wearing old grey flannels and a maroon smoking jacket. The tea tray she had just brought in sat on a small table beside him. He'd never been ill in his life before and he made a very bad patient, constantly getting out of bed, and delaying his recovery still further. But he was on the mend now, and next week Nick would be taking him off to the Canaries to convalesce in the sun.

'There's nothing eating me,' she lied. 'I was only thinking how depressing autumn can be.'

'I may be getting old but I'm not blind or senile yet,' Magnus retorted with a disbelieving snort. 'Come and sit down here.'

Magnus had been aware for some months that Mel wasn't quite herself, but he had put it down to overwork. The hotel had been busy all summer and they had been short staffed. During his period in bed however, he had sensed there was something more than the need for a holiday. She was deeply troubled.

Her smiles no longer seemed to reach her eyes, even though she still chatted and made jokes. Her brisk efficiency hadn't changed, and she was still every bit as pleasant to everyone, but the light inside her had dimmed. Now as she moved across the room to take the other armchair by the fire, he saw that the spring was missing from her step. Her whole body seemed tense.

Magnus poured tea into the cups, added milk and passed Mel's to her.

'Well?' He gave her a penetrating look, daring her to change the subject. 'What is it, Mel? And don't lie to me. I want the truth.'

Mel gulped. She had known for weeks now that she was going to have to leave Oaklands, but she had hoped she could keep it under her hat until Magnus was completely well again. She knew how much he depended on her, and they had become even closer during his illness. But she had too much respect for him to try fobbing him off now with a lame excuse.

For a whole year she had lived like a yo-yo: up, as long as Nick stayed away, down, the moment he returned. Wanting to see him, yet panicking the moment his battered red MG drew up in the drive. She'd prayed he would lose interest in her, find a job on the other side of the world and never return.

Last November he had joined a repertory theatre in Birmingham and for a few months she'd managed to fool herself he'd found someone else to focus his attention on. But at Easter he'd moved on to the Playhouse theatre in Weston-super-Mare for the summer season and he began to drive over to Bath at least once a week.

Magnus wanted to see each play Nick was in and he always asked her to accompany him. She had to go, to refuse would have hurt his feelings. But Magnus had no idea what agony it was for her.

Sometimes after a matinee the three of them would go down on the promenade for an ice cream and a walk, but just a brush of Nick's hand against hers, a kiss on the cheek would start her heart pounding. She was trapped in a hopeless, desperate situation, forced to display feigned irritation and exasperation whenever their conversations became personal.

Yet despite her pretended indifference, their mutual attraction flourished. His eyes followed her, just as hers followed him. On nights when he stayed at Oaklands she could almost hear his heartbeat through closed doors, feel his body against hers and imagine his kisses so vividly it shamed her.

She was safe surrounded by staff and guests; it was the chance encounters when they were alone she had to guard against. She was terrified of allowing herself just one moment of weakness. Nick was back in Birmingham now, but he would be coming home soon to take his father away, and after that she knew he meant to get work in Bath.

'Tell me, Mel?' Magnus's growl faded to a plea.

'You are far, far more to me than an employee and you know it. Don't have secrets from me now.'

Mel sipped at her tea, mentally dredging through all the explanations she'd invented and discarded, trying to find one which was plausible.

Everything she'd accomplished in her life had been learned here: bookkeeping, cooking, her knowledge about wine, how to drive – above all, self-respect. She could take her skills and use them elsewhere, but no other place would feel like home. She could hardly bear to think of life without Magnus.

'I don't know how to tell you,' she said, and she could feel her eyes filling with tears. 'You see I want to leave.'

'Why?' he asked, eyes widening with shock. 'Have Sophie and Stephen been getting at you again?'

It appalled him that his two older children continued to resent his affection for Mel; they couldn't seem to grasp that she had earned it. Mel did the work of three other people, and again and again guests returned because of her. She was the glue that kept everything together, just as Ruth had been.

Like Ruth, Mel too hid a great deal of herself. She rarely pushed forward her opinions, she didn't flaunt her many abilities, she preferred compromise to confrontation. She even concealed her beauty with subdued, often prim clothes. Yet behind her gentle manner and soft voice he knew there was a great deal more. No one could have such a deep well of understanding for others without having scraped the bottom of life.

Mel closed her eyes and clenched her fists willing herself to be strong enough to say what she had to and insist that he let her go.

'No, it's nothing to do with Sophie or Stephen,' she said quietly. 'I just feel I must move on.'

In the golden light from the log fire she could glimpse the younger Magnus as he appeared in that old photograph taken with her mother: a lean, craggy faced adventurer, who managed to look tough and powerful even dressed in a dinner jacket and black tie. Now that mane of unruly fair hair had turned to silver, his strong jawline was concealed by a white beard, grown just recently when he was too ill to shave. His once hard, muscular body was finally succumbing to old age, but his charisma, humour and keen mind were unchanged.

'I thought you were so happy here,' he said, alarmed by the tight sensation around his heart.

'I was, but not any longer.' She faltered, knowing this wasn't enough to convince him. 'It's Nick. I can't cope with him any longer. Please don't say you'll talk to him, or even stop him from coming here. That isn't the answer.'

She waited for the expected outburst, but surprisingly none came. He sat gripping the arms of his chair, his chin slightly uptilted, a proud, almost aloof look in his eyes.

'Do you understand?' she asked hesitantly. 'I can't ever be what he wants. It's better that I get out of both your lives.'

'It isn't better that you get out of my life,' he said, and to her dismay she saw a tear trickling down the deep groove in his cheek. 'It's better that you tell me the real reason you can't be what Nick wants. Because I *know* you are in love with him, however much you claim not to be interested.'

Mel felt faintly nauseous now. Although she hadn't managed to convince Nick they weren't meant for one another, she had thought his father had lost all his romantic illusions about them.

'That's ridiculous,' she said fiercely. 'I like him a great deal, but not in that way.'

Magnus looked at her steadily, his eyes calculating, unblinking. When he didn't respond immediately she felt even more uneasy.

Long seconds passed while he studied her.

'What is it you are hiding, Mel?' he said eventually. 'Are you married to someone else? Have you a child somewhere you haven't told us about? Or a disease you can't admit to?'

'No. Of course not,' she said indignantly.

He sighed, his eyes showing deep sorrow and some exasperation. 'I have to admit that when you first arrived here I had a strong feeling you'd come for a special purpose. As all the theories I had were proved wrong in the first few months, I put them aside. But while I was ill, with time to ponder why you were so troubled about Nick, one of those initial ideas came back to me. It seemed too far fetched at first, but the more I thought about it, the more likely it became.'

He paused, looking right into her eyes. 'Tell me now, are you Bonny Norton's daughter?'

Mel felt dizzy with shock at the question. For two years she had lived with the hope that one day he would mention Bonny's name. When he hadn't she had almost convinced herself it wasn't important to him.

The wind was howling round the house, like a vengeful wraith trying to get in. She couldn't deny it.

'Yes,' she whispered. 'Yes, I am Camellia Norton.'

His face blanched and he slumped back into his chair. 'Why didn't you tell me this two years ago?'

'At first because I was afraid to, later as I got to know you better, because I didn't want to hurt or embarrass you.'

'She sent you here?' There was horror and fear in his voice.

'No, of course not,' she said hastily. 'I told you that first Christmas I was here that she was dead. She never told me about you. I found some old letters from you.'

His expression was that of a man who'd just had a huge bandage ripped painfully from an old wound. His eyes were wide open, his lips trembled and he clutched his hands together as if to prevent them shaking.

'You'll have to start at the beginning, Mel. You see when you said your mother had committed suicide, I knew, or thought I knew you couldn't possibly be Bonny's daughter. She wasn't the type to take her own life. Aside from that I'd always imagined her child to be blonde.' He hesitated, a tick in his cheek making it twitch. 'You'd better tell me everything.'

Mel had long since wiped out any suspicion that Magnus could have played a part in her mother's death. But the shock in his eyes as she described that day eight years earlier would have proved it beyond all doubt.

'I found the letters the next morning,' she explained. 'I don't know now why I didn't let the police have them. I was just too devastated by them to think clearly.'

Magnus nodded. He moved his chair nearer to her and took her hand, listening as she spoke of the funeral, the shame, the gossip and slander.

'I was so young, a big fat lump of a girl whose mother was the town's tart. I just wanted to get away from Rye and start a new life. I shut the letters away in a suitcase, and it wasn't until I was much older that I began to want to find answers.'

She described how she came to Oaklands and her reasons for not telling him then who she was. 'I was happy just being close to you, Magnus. But when I met Nick last year, suddenly everything changed.'

Silence pressed in on them. The wind continued to howl and the rain battered the windows. Mel was trying to find the right way to reassure Magnus that what she'd told him would never leave these four walls. Magnus was staring off into space, forcing himself to look at a part of his life he'd buried.

'You see why I have to go, don't you?' she said eventually. 'I can't stay under the circumstances. But first will you just tell me something about you and Mum? I've pieced together part of the picture, but there's so much missing.'

'Yes, I understand how you feel,' he said slowly. 'It's impossible for me to justify myself. I won't even try. You are intelligent and worldly enough to understand that even adult, normally responsible men can behave recklessly sometimes.'

He cleared his throat and grimaced. 'I met Bonny at a time in my life when I was at a crossroads,' he said carefully. 'Behind me was my youth, and the war. I was forty-two, and there were several possible routes I could take. I could have gone back to Yorkshire, to Ruth and the children, but that would almost certainly have meant getting involved again with Craigmore, our family estate, and as I've often told you I had very little time for my elder brothers. Another possibility was teaching English and Geography, but there again the adventurer in me rebelled.

'Everything was so grey and grim in that post-war period. All the major cities were ravaged, and men who'd fought bravely for their country were coming back to find they hadn't even a home any longer. There were shortages of everything, from food and clothing to building materials. The government was dragging its feet, talking of rebuilding England, yet doing nothing at all about it.

'A golden dream was beckoning me, Mel. It might sound fanciful now, especially to children like you who never knew the deprivations of the thirties and forties. But I was incensed by the apathy all around me, and I felt compelled to use the little money and influence I had, and my knowledge of building, for the common good.

'I had just managed to get that first plot of land in Staines the day I met Bonny. I'd gone on to Oxford to meet an old RAF chum to celebrate. I certainly wasn't looking for a woman: I was happily married and I'd never been a womaniser anyway. But Basil and myself had rather a lot to drink, and we met these two dancers.'

He paused, looked at Mel and smiled wryly. 'If not for her I might've just organised the building work, then gone on home to Ruth, Sophie and Stephen. But she literally danced into my life and turned me upside down and inside out. She was just seventeen, and completely beautiful and I spent four wonderful days with her. In my naïveté, I actually believed I could have those four days, then forget her, but of course I was wrong. She whirled into my life bringing a kind of colour and passion I'd never known before and I just couldn't break away.'

Magnus lapsed into silence, remembering all those months of back-breaking work at the site in Staines. He chose the discomfort of hard physical work out of guilt. Yet if he had chosen the softer route and simply overseen the project he would never have accomplished all that he did.

'You really did love her then?' Mel could see he was struggling with painful memories.

'I always try to think that *true* love is what I had with Ruth: a peaceful warmth built on deep affection, sharing a life together,' he said gruffly. 'I never had that kind of peace with Bonny, it was more a kind of dangerous, destructive madness. She was travelling around, dancing in one town, then moving to another. Our affair was just snatched hours here and there. Yet it was love, for all that. She gave me something special, infected me with her spirit and daring. Giving her up was the hardest thing I ever did.'

'You broke it off then?'

'Yes,' he sighed deeply. 'When Ruth became pregnant with Nicholas I realised her feelings and the children's security were far more important than my own selfish needs.'

'But you didn't break it off entirely,' Mel said pointedly. 'Nick's two years older than me.'

'That's the hardest part to explain.' Magnus took her hand in his and squeezed it. His lips trembled and tears glistened in his eyes. 'I didn't see her again, not for over a year. I had built several small estates of houses in London by then and made a great deal of money too. I went back up to Yorkshire to build more houses there, and I found a new deep happiness with Ruth and the baby. I heard Bonny was seeing John Norton. I never expected to see her again.'

'Go on,' Mel prompted as he faltered.

'It was a fluke that I ran into her, a chance, meeting in a London shop. She was making plans for her wedding to Norton, and I was in London on business. We had lunch together for old times' sake. To this day I don't know how I allowed myself to be persuaded into taking her up to my hotel room.' He looked at Mel sadly. 'I've never ever felt quite so ashamed of myself as I was after that afternoon. I can blame it on drink, yet I still cannot justify my weakness, but that, Mel, was how you were conceived.'

Mel blushed. She hadn't expected him to admit it so readily.

Magnus saw her embarrassment and smiled. 'For the first time ever I don't feel quite so badly about that afternoon,' he said reaching out and touching her cheek with affection. 'I never expected to meet you, Mel. I certainly wish I could stop you hurting, yet a small selfish part of me is so very proud of you.'

Mel felt a surge of love for this honest, kindly man. Those last few words meant everything to her, it was all the acknowledgement she needed.

'Tell me what happened after that.' Mel thought of bringing up Jack Easton's similar claim of one night of lust with Bonny, but for now she wanted to know the rest of the story.

'John and Bonny married, some time later. I believe they went to live at John's family home in Somerset. I heard on the grapevine that they were very happy and they'd had a baby girl. I bought this place about that time and soon after Ruth and the children joined me here. It was a very happy, exciting period in our lives, like starting out all over again. I never for one moment ever considered that you might be my child, and I can honestly say I put Bonny out of my mind for good. But then fate stepped in, Ruth and I were invited to the opening of a friend's hotel in Sussex, to my horror John and Bonny were there too. Apparently they'd sold their house in Somerset and moved to Rye a few years earlier. It was that evening when Bonny told me you were my child.'

Mel could remember every word of the letter which followed the party.

'That was in 1954. You said in your letter she was

drunk, you didn't believe her. Why did you change your mind?'

Magnus grimaced.

'One thing I'd learned about Bonny was that though she was a practised liar, there was usually a grain of truth in her stories. Furthermore she had a very spiteful streak sometimes and ignoring her was like waving a red flag at a bull. So I agreed reluctantly to meet her.

'The irrefutable proof she had was blood tests of all three of you. John's blood group made it impossible for him to be your father, Mel, but the moment I saw them I knew I could be. The curious thing was that she made no demands or threats, she even apologised for blurting out the news to me at that party. Her only motive seemed to be that she wanted me to share her guilt. I got the impression it had been weighing very heavily on her shoulders.'

'But she didn't have any compunction in coming after you again once Dad was dead?' Mel said bitterly.

'It wasn't quite like that,' he said gently. 'I sent my condolences, remember I knew John quite well. He wasn't a friend exactly, but I respected him and I needed to know Bonny and you were well taken care of.'

'We were,' Mel said. 'Or we would've been if Bonny had looked after things, but she squandered the money and lost the house.'

Magnus sighed deeply, raising one bushy eyebrow.

'Is that what happened?'

Mel gave him a brief run-down of events. 'Didn't you know this?'

Magnus shook his head. 'I think you've been assuming we were in close touch during those years. We weren't, Mel. I didn't see her or telephone her. All contact from her was through my solicitor,' he said. 'She wrote and said John hadn't left enough money for your school fees. I agreed to pay them each term and I sent a little extra to cover other expenses. It was almost a business arrangement, she didn't volunteer any personal information and I didn't ask for it. I didn't even know your exact day of birth. To be honest I was so very relieved that Bonny made no further demands.'

'But she took me away from the private school,' Mel said, 'just before I was eleven. There weren't any letters from you after that time either. What happened then?'

Magnus looked thoughtful.

'I wasn't aware you'd already left the school. Early in 1962 she wrote to me via the solicitors and asked if she could see me to discuss your future. I had no wish to see her again in person, but I agreed to meet at my solicitor's offices in London. We made a deal that day which ended all contact with her.'

'What was the deal?' Mel asked.

'She told me that since you would be going on to the grammar school that September, there would be no further school fees, only the expense of uniform and equipment. She put forward the suggestion that I should give her a final lump sum, and sever all connections between us once and for all. My solicitor advised me that this was to my advantage, and after some discussion a sum was agreed between ourselves. Bonny signed a paper to that effect.'

'But I didn't go to the grammar school. I had to go to the secondary modern,' Mel exclaimed. 'I might have passed the eleven-plus if I'd stayed on at Collegiate, but the trauma of being moved into a state school made me fail.'

Magnus looked aghast. 'I wish I'd known that then. But there was no reason to doubt her word. My biggest surprise that day was that she didn't ask for you to be sent to an expensive boarding school.'

'She wanted cash,' Mel said darkly. She could make sense of some of the events in the past which had once puzzled her. The storm clouds had already been gathering back then. Bonny was already up to her ears in debt, and she'd cashed in a long-term policy for short-term gain. But she'd clearly squandered the money Magnus gave her as it was only a year later they had to leave Mermaid Street. It was a despicable act to rob a child of a good education, so she could carry on with the drinking and parties, but knowing Bonny as she did, she probably believed there was another crock of gold somewhere around the corner waiting for her.

'If I'd come to you when Mum died, what would your reaction have been?' she asked.

'I really don't know,' he said truthfully. 'Ruth hadn't long died, Nick was a troubled adolescent. Maybe if you'd written to me I might have worked something out for you. But just being someone's biological father doesn't necessarily make you behave with compassion, especially when it threatens the security of your other children.'

'Why did she leave those letters for me to find?' she asked bitterly. All the bad things she'd done swept through her mind like a whirlwind. 'I've been punished enough already for things I've done wrong. Now I'm paying for Mum's indiscretions too. Is that fair?'

'No, it's not,' he said wearily. 'I wish there was something I could say, something I could do that would put it all right. If it's any consolation at all, I'm paying the price for my past mistakes too. I

382

can't be absolutely certain you are my daughter. I feel you are, but that's not quite the same thing is it? But if you are, then I think I may lose my son along with you, when I explain this to him.'

His words brought her up sharply. Magnus looked very pale and frail suddenly. She hadn't expected that he might consider telling any of this to his family.

'Magnus, you must promise me you won't tell your children,' she clutched at his hands in her anxiety. 'I couldn't bear that. It must remain our secret.'

'Oh, Mel,' he sighed. 'Where did you get your big heart from?'

She looked at her watch and saw it was half past five. There was so much more she wanted to know, and she still wanted to discuss Jack Easton and Sir Miles's part in it all. But she could see Magnus was tired and she had work to do.

'I must go downstairs now.' She got up wearily, picking up the tea tray. 'Why don't you have a nap? I'll bring your supper up later and we'll talk again then?'

'Just tell me one more thing before you go. What was Bonny like as a mother? I mean when she wasn't drinking?'

A lump came up in Mel's throat at the tenderness in his eyes. 'It wasn't all bad. Sometimes she was just wonderful,' she said with a smile. 'She did actually like children you know. She had so much fun in her, so much gaiety. We used to go on picnics together, paddle in the sea. She was like a big sister not a mother.'

And when she wasn't wonderful?' His eyes grew darker, daring her to gloss it over.

'There were times when she neglected me,' she said, her eyes dropping to the floor. 'I hated her for spending money on nice clothes for herself when I had nothing, but I was fat and plain. Maybe she thought I didn't need them.'

He shuddered, guessing how much she was holding back. 'But you aren't fat or plain any more.' His voice was little more than a whisper.

She smiled down at him. 'I lost the weight myself, but I've got you to thank for everything else I am now. Sometimes I've hated Mum for things she put me through, but I can't be sorry that you might be my father, whatever happens.'

She looked back at Magnus as she opened the door. He was staring into the fire, hands on the arms of the chair. He had the lion look again, haughty, proud, arrogant maybe, but he would never be formidable again.

Mel paused at the top of the wide staircase and saw the dainty rosewood chair with the brocade upholstery where she'd sat on her first night before nearly passing out. Then she'd had only a glimpse of the splendour of Oaklands: the blue and green Chinese rug, the chandelier, the washed silk wallpaper. Now she knew every nook and cranny in the house. If burglars were to take every last item, she'd be able to describe them in detail to the police as if she'd lovingly bought every one of its treasures herself.

She went on down to the hall, crossing to the drawing room by force of habit to check everything was ready for the guests expected later. The curtains had been drawn, table lamps switched on. The fire was crackling merrily, a loaded log basket beside it, a large vase of white chrysanthemums on the Sheraton bowfronted mahogany sideboard. Outside it was bleak, wet and cold, inside an oasis of warm tranquillity.

'How is he, Mel?'

Mrs Downes came out of the bar, startling her.

The older woman was ready to leave, wellingtons on her feet, a long green mackintosh and her sou'-wester in her hand.

'Much better today, almost his old self,' Mel said. Mrs Downes worried about Magnus constantly. 'I'm taking his supper up to him again tonight, but I think by tomorrow he'll be well enough to come down.'

'I got Antoine to make him chicken and leek soup.' The housekeeper's face puckered into a slightly anxious smile as if she was discussing a favourite grandson, not her employer. 'That's always been his favourite.'

'You aren't planning to walk home?' Mel looked down at Mrs Downes's boots. 'It's wicked out there! Let me get rid of this tray and I'll drive you.'

'You'll do nothing of the sort,' the older woman snorted in disapproval. 'I'm not made of sugar and a breath of fresh air will liven me up. Tell Magnus I'll pop in tomorrow morning to see him. I think we ought to discuss redecorating the Blue Room. I thought the walls were getting a little shabby.'

Mel chuckled. 'One scuff by the door?' She raised an eyebrow. 'I doubt anyone but you would notice.'

'People pay for perfection here,' Mrs Downes smirked. 'My house is tumbling down from neglect, but then I don't charge a king's ransom for the privilege of sleeping there.'

She looked at Mel sharply. 'Talking of sleeping, you make sure you get to bed at a reasonable hour too. You've been looking peaky for some time.'

'It's only the time of year.' Mel forced herself to smile. There had been many times in the last year that she'd been tempted to confide in this kindly, wise woman, but she hadn't quite dared. 'I hate October, everything dying around me. Sometimes I wish I could hibernate.'

'You should be out dancing and having fun, my girl,' the housekeeper retorted sternly. 'When I was your age nothing kept me in.'

'I've done all the dancing I want to do.'

'That, Mel, is defeatist talk.' Mrs Downes put on her sou'wester, pulling a face at herself in the hall mirror. 'If I was twenty-five years younger and jitterbugging was still in fashion, I'd drag you out and show you a thing or two.'

Mel laughed. She couldn't possibly imagine Joan Downes doing anything more than a sedate foxtrot.

As she opened the door, an icy gust of wind swept in, sending the chandelier tinkling. 'See you tomorrow,' she called over her shoulder. 'And mind what I said, early to bed.'

At seven thirty Mel went upstairs again, this time carrying a tray loaded with Magnus's supper.

Laughter wafted up from the bar below: four businessmen and their wives down from London for a few days' holiday. A party of six were due for dinner, but they were regulars and if Magnus wanted to talk again she could easily leave the other staff to cope. She intended to get the file of letters and go over each one of them with him. She still hoped for a new piece of evidence to come to light that might miraculously change everything. If he could just remember in what month he'd had that last fling with Bonny, they might be able to discount the whole thing. Then they could check the records at the nursing home where she was born to discover if she really had been premature. Perhaps she should have done that two years ago.

When Magnus didn't answer her knock, she opened the door and walked in.

'It's only me,' she called out, assuming he was still having a nap in the bedroom. 'I've brought your supper, do you want it in there or in here?'

There was no answer so she put the tray down and went across to the adjoining bedroom. To her surprise he wasn't in bed: the bedspread was unruffled, although the lights either side of the bed were on, and a book was lying on the bed. It looked like he'd been intending to lie down and read. Perhaps he'd fallen asleep instead in his chair.

The bathroom door was open just a crack, golden light spilling onto the dark green carpet.

'Magnus!' She hesitated for one moment, afraid of catching him undressed.

There was no reply.

'Magnus!' She ran forward, pushing the door open, but it resisted.

'Answer me!' Her heart thumped painfully, beads of perspiration breaking out on her brow.

Wriggling round the small gap, she screamed before she could control herself.

He lay crumpled on the floor, mouth and eyes open, one hand still clutching a bottle of pills, the contents strewn on the floor around him. His maroon smoking jacket contrasted vividly with his white face and hair.

Mel pricked up her ears at the sound of footsteps in the hospital corridor. She jumped out of her seat in the waiting room and opened the door.

It was Sister Collins, one of the intensive care nurses.

'Is there any news?' Mel had asked this question countless times during the night.

By day hospitals were formidable enough, but at night there was a hushed empty eerieness. The faint sounds of bleeping machines, muffled voices and footsteps all had a hurried urgency, less noticeable by day.

'He's comfortable,' Sister Collins said wiping a handkerchief across her brow. In the dim light of the corridor her big, plain face had a greenish tinge as if she was exhausted and drained. 'It's quite normal for a stroke victim to stay in a coma for forty-eight hours, my dear. Now why don't you go on home and get some rest? Someone will telephone if there's any change.'

'I can't,' Mel said, tears starting up in her eyes again. 'Not until Mr Osbourne's son gets here.'

Mel's priorities in those crucial first minutes after finding Magnus unconscious on his bathroom floor had been to call the ambulance and accompany him to the Royal United hospital. She had left it to Sally and Antoine to contact Mrs Downes, Nick, Sophie and Stephen. In several telephone conversations with Sally since then she'd learned that Mrs Downes had come back to Oaklands to take over. A message had been left at Nick's digs in Birmingham and Stephen intended to drive down from Yorkshire in the morning, but so far there had been no answer at Sophie's home. Stephen had said he would get a message to her.

'If only I'd gone up to his room earlier,' Mel sobbed. She was distraught, terrified that Magnus might die, and that she was responsible for his stroke.

'Now listen to me, Miss Corbett,' Sister Collins said firmly, putting one arm round her shoulder. 'Men of Mr Osbourne's age are susceptible to strokes. If you'd been right by his side when it happened, it wouldn't have made much difference. But he's a strong man and I believe he will pull through. Now off you go and get some rest.'

The door at the far end of the passage opened and Nick appeared.

'Oh, Nick.' Mel ran to him. 'Thank goodness you've got here. I've been frantic.'

'How is he?' He caught her hands and pressed them, his blue eyes wide with anxiety, his face and brown leather jacket splattered with rain. 'I didn't get the message until I got back to my digs in the early hours. I came as fast as I could. What's happening?'

Sister Collins took over, explaining everything that had been done for his father. She repeated the reassurance she had just given Mel and said that Nick would be allowed into intensive care for a moment or two to see Magnus within the hour.

'Sister's right, you should go home, Mel.' Nick ran his fingers distractedly through his hair. He was very dishevelled – he needed a shave and he smelled strongly of cigarettes, as if he'd been chain smoking on the drive. 'I'm really grateful for all you've done, but I'm here now to take over. Take my car.' He handed her his keys.

'But!'

'Go,' he barked impatiently, then seeing the distress in her face, his expression softened. 'Look, Mel, you need some sleep and you're of far more use back at Oaklands than here. I'll phone if there's any change and I'll call a cab if I need to get back.'

When Mel got back to Oaklands she was too tense to sleep. Trees creaked in the strong wind, rain gurgled noisily in a gutter and from her bed she could hear a guest snoring further along the corridor. But these sounds didn't disturb her; they were reassurance she wasn't entirely alone. It was the terrible sense of guilt which prevented her from dropping off.

How could she face his children or the other staff if he died?

The thought tormented her for four hours.

At half past eight, unable to lie there any longer, she went down to the kitchen.

'You shouldn't have got up,' Mrs Downes said reprovingly. 'We can manage without you.'

'I couldn't sleep. Is there any news?' She poured herself some coffee and sat down at the kitchen table.

Antoine's face was as cleanly shaved and shiny as always. He stood calmly frying eggs and bacon as if it was any other day. Not even the possibility of Magnus dying prevented Mrs Downes from polishing each knife and fork as she laid trays for the guests who wanted breakfast in bed.

But Mel knew how it was for them. They were every bit as frightened and anxious as she was. Keeping their usual high standards was a matter of pride, and a way of dealing with the fear.

'Nick telephoned a short while ago,' Mrs Downes said, her lower lip quivering from suppressing tears. 'There's no change I'm afraid, but he's coming back in a minute for a shower and to have some breakfast.'

Magnus had been a dear friend to Joan Downes for some fifteen years. She knew that if he should die she'd feel the blow as keenly as if it was one of her own family. But when Mel walked into the kitchen her stricken face reminded Joan that at the end of the day she had her husband, children and grandchildren to go home to. Mel had no one else: she lived and breathed Oaklands. Magnus and the hotel were her life.

Mel looked like a waif again, just as she had when she first arrived at Oaklands. She'd gone through the motions of looking ready for work, put on a dark-blue dress with a lace collar, but her face was white and her eyes were full of pain.

'Nick must be feeling positive otherwise he wouldn't be coming back here.' Mrs Downes tried to smile as she put a couple of carnations in each of the vases on the trays. She wished she could wipe out that haunted look from the girl's eyes. 'And Magnus is a tough old nut, we all know that.'

The sound of tyres on the gravel drive prevented Mrs Downes from giving her a comforting hug. Mel had jumped up. 'It's Nick,' she said.

'Well, that's a relief.' Mrs Downes took two cooked breakfasts from Antoine, covered them with warming lids and lifted the heavy tray. 'I'll just nip up to the Blue Room with this lot. I'll be back to hear any news.'

Mrs Downes returned to the kitchen before Nick came down. On the face of it he seemed calm and collected, as if he'd just got up. He dropped a kiss on Mrs Downes's cheek, greeted Antoine with his usual impudent 'Bonjour Antoine.' Only the grey tinge to his skin and his red-rimmed eyes proved he wasn't as controlled as he pretended.

'Well, how is he?' Mrs Downes asked impatiently. 'Has he come round at all?'

'It doesn't look too good.' Nick's voice trembled. 'Even if he survives this stroke, it's pretty certain to leave him an invalid.'

Nick had told Mel how Mrs Downes became a mother figure to him when his own died. But as she saw the pair of them reach out instinctively for one another, she felt their love for one another. Mrs Downes was so short and tubby, Nick had to bend right over to lay his head on her shoulder, but that didn't prevent the older woman patting his back with her work-reddened hands as if he was just a small boy.

'There, there, Nick,' she murmured comfortingly. 'You know your dad's a fighter. I've seen lots of people survive strokes and I'm sure he will too. Now sit down and I'll get you some breakfast.'

Mel moved over to the sink to wash some dishes. She sensed Nick looking at her but she couldn't turn to meet his gaze.

'It must've been a terrible shock to find him like that, Mel?' His voice had a tender edge.

'The worst kind.' She turned slowly, dropping her eyes as she saw the concern for her in his. She had seen him in so many different roles: the aggressive male arguing at the bar, the charmer with the old lady guests, the debonair actor. But today there was something new in his face. He looked vulnerable, almost childlike, and it plucked at her heart strings painfully. 'I felt so impotent. I didn't know what to do.'

'I can imagine,' he nodded sympathetically. 'I thought Dad was indestructible. Seeing him lying in bed with all those tubes and wires stuck into him gave me the willies.'

Mrs Downes put another tray on the table and swiftly laid it for breakfast. 'I suggest you take this up to your Dad's office.' She looked at Nick sternly as if daring him to argue. 'And Mel can go with you.'

'I can't do that, there's too much to do,' Mel blurted out. The last thing she wanted was to be cloistered with Nick before she'd had time to sort things out in her head.

'There isn't. I've already rung my sister to get her in to help.' Mrs Downes gave her a motherly pat on the bottom. 'Aside from it not being nice to leave Nick to brood on his own, there's all the jobs that Magnus normally does waiting up there in his office. You two can do them together.'

Mel knew she was beaten. However much she would prefer the peace of changing beds and cleaning bathrooms, to being with Nick, she knew it would appear unnatural to say so.

'I keep seeing Magnus lying there in the bathroom,' she said weakly, as if that was a reasonable explanation. 'Supposing I hadn't gone up? He might have been there all night!'

'Well, he wasn't,' Nick said firmly. He took the plate of bacon and eggs from Antoine and put it on the tray. 'You heard Downie, you've got to help me. And later when I've gone back to the hospital, you'd better go back to bed. You look terrible.'

When they got upstairs, Mel found it was surprisingly comforting being with Nick. He took control in much the same way as his father always had and he didn't seem to wish to talk anymore than she did. He sat at Magnus's desk and went through the staff rota, telephoning some of the part-timers to arrange increased hours so Mel would be kept free to handle the jobs Magnus normally did, then moved on to place orders for wine and spirits.

Outside the rain had finally stopped. Weak sunshine was peeping through and the sounds of staff going about their business was soothingly normal. Mel sat at the other desk, opening the mail, separating bills from requests for hotel brochures and booking confirmations. She was just putting a sheet of headed notepaper into the typewriter to reply to some of the inquiries when Nick finally spoke.

'I think I'd rather see him die now, than end up gaga in a wheelchair.'

Mel's head jerked up in shock.

'Oh God, that sounded so callous,' he said, holding his head in his hands. 'I didn't mean it quite like it sounded.'

Mel looked at his stricken face and felt a tightening round her heart. 'I know what you mean,' she said softly. 'I just hope that if he is going to die I get a chance to speak to him one more time.'

Nick nodded in understanding. 'There's so much I need to say to him.' He shook his head sadly, his eyes glittering with tears. 'You know, stuff about

Mum. How he felt when I went off the rails and things. What do you want to talk to him about?'

Mel felt herself blushing. 'Oh, you know! About how grateful I am to him.'

'He knows that already.'

Nick was looking at her very intently. He could be just as perceptive as his father. The palms of her hands were suddenly clammy with sweat.

'You want to talk to him about me. Don't you?'

'Why should I want to talk about you?' Sarcasm seemed the appropriate way out, mingled with some truth. 'If you must know, yesterday afternoon I told him I wanted to leave Oaklands. I'd like him to know that I wouldn't leave until he was better.'

'You can't leave!' Nick's eyes flew wide open in astonishment. 'You belong here and with me.'

'Nick, it's you saying those sort of things to me that makes me want to leave,' she said quickly. 'I've told you dozens of times that I'm not interested in you in that way. I can't bear it.' It wasn't necessary to look at him, she knew those blue eyes would be dark with hurt, his mouth drooping, unable to understand the rebuff.

'Don't you know I love you?'

His words stabbed at her like a knife through the heart.

'I said I loved you,' he repeated.

She was thrown into confusion, staring at him in horror.

'I know you must've been badly hurt by someone,' he said, getting up from his desk and moving towards her. 'Maybe you are afraid of it happening again. But I know you feel the same as me, Mel. I can see it, feel it. It might not seem to be the right time to tell you, but I need you.'

He took another step towards her, arms outstretched. She shrank back into her chair, but his hands came down on her shoulders, holding her captive and his head bent to kiss her.

'No.' She pushed at his chest, but still his lips were coming towards hers.

Something snapped in her brain. The truth was the only way to stop this insanity. She couldn't find feeble excuses any longer.

'Don't Nick. I think I'm your sister!'

Her words stopped him dead. His lips were only inches from hers when he froze.

For a second their eyes locked, then slowly he straightened up, tossing back the lock of hair which had fallen across his eyes.

'What sort of sick joke is that?' he said in a whisper.

'Nick, it isn't a joke.' She got up from her chair and moved behind it for security. 'I would never have told you if you hadn't pushed me. But it was the only way I could stop you.'

The colour drained from his face so rapidly that for a moment she thought he was going to faint. He moved back fumbling for the edge of the desk to support himself.

'You can't be my sister!' His deep voice was strangled, his Adam's apple leaping up and down in his throat.

'I might be,' she whispered. 'Oh God, Nick! I didn't intend it to come out like this.'

'But how?' His lip twisted into a sneer. 'Are you suggesting my parents gave you away at birth?'

'Can we sit down and talk about this properly?' she pleaded with him. 'I can't explain when you look at me like that!'

This was how her whole life had been: pockets of brief, false happiness, paid for heavily with pain. Anger was replacing sorrow in his eyes; his broad shoulders were stiff with hostility.

'There's always been something odd about you,'

he spat at her. 'I don't want to sit down and talk. I want you to retract that malicious statement, then get out of here.'

'I will go if that's what you want.' She lifted her head in defiance. 'But not until I've told you the truth.'

He listened with his back to the window, arms crossed on his chest.

'If it wasn't for you coming on to me I would never have told you, or Magnus. I came to Oaklands two years ago to find out the truth, but I decided almost immediately that it would hurt too many people if I ever told him who I really was. Yesterday I told Magnus I wanted to leave and he wormed it out of me.'

'You bitch. You caused his stroke!' Nick lunged at her, as if to strike her.

Mel dodged away. 'Can't you understand that I love Magnus?' she shouted back at him. 'If it wasn't for you I would never have told him.'

'You flirted with me. You led me on!'

'Only that first night. I didn't know who you were then. Why do you think I've avoided you ever since, refused to go for a drink or even a walk? Have you any idea what torture it's been for me?'

'Why couldn't you have told me the truth?'

'How could I?' Tears of frustration rolled down her cheeks. 'I did everything I could to keep you at arm's length. I hoped and prayed you'd lose interest in me.'

'Why didn't you just slink out the way you came then? You bitch. You crept round the old man and then when you were tired of that you dropped your bombshell and gave him a stroke!'

'That's an evil thing to say.' She wanted to slap his face and make him listen. 'I tried to do the right thing by everyone. How can you even think I told him out of spite?'

'Was he disappointed his tart was dead? It must have made him feel ancient to find he'd outlived both his wife and mistress.'

'Stop it.' She rushed at him, pummelling him with her fists. 'You're turning it into something vicious.'

He caught her wrists, twisting them round till she cried out in pain, leaning forward and sneering at her. 'It is vicious. Did you convince him his legal children don't care about him? You've been so bloody clever. My sister was right about you all along. If Dad dies and I find you've got one penny I'll fight to make sure you never get it.'

She could see nothing but hate in his eyes now, as dark and venomous as the previous night's storm. The other side of his character, hinted at by himself, Mrs Downes and his father, was exposed: a man who had abused women, a selfish arrogant bully who pushed his way through life to get what he wanted.

She shook off his hands and backed away. 'Is money all you care about? I don't want anything of yours, Nick Osbourne. Since the day I met you I've had nothing but torture. If you loved your father half as much as I do you'd be praying for his recovery, not talking about his will.'

'Get out,' he screamed, taking a menacing step towards her. 'And if I ever hear you've said a word about this to anyone I'll drag you to hell and back.'

'You're quite safe,' she said as she brushed past him to the door. 'I wouldn't admit to anyone I had a brother like you.'

She flung the door open and ran upstairs, tears streaming down her face. She had to go now, for good.

There could be no tender farewells to all those people she had grown so fond of. Attempted explanations would only inflame the situation.

She stripped off her plain working dress, pulled on jeans and a sweater, then gathered together the barest essentials into one holdall. She didn't dare look round as she closed her door behind her for the last time. She'd had two years of happiness to which she wasn't entitled. Now she'd have to pay for them as an outcast.

Chapter Seventeen

The private room on the second floor of Bath General Hospital looked and smelled like a florist's shop. Baskets and vases of flowers filled the windowsill. The locker by Magnus's bed was almost hidden by a huge basket of fruit and a string along the wall held at least thirty get-well cards.

Magnus had stayed in a coma for almost thirty-six hours following his stroke. Although the doctor and nursing staff had continually reassured his children during that time, that this was quite normal, even they were surprised he'd suffered so little permanent damage when he finally came round. There was some paralysis down his left side, and his speech was slurred, but so far, five days since he regained consciousness, he seemed to be making an almost miraculous recovery.

Yet Magnus had aged dramatically in that short time. His skin had a yellow tinge, and it hung in loose folds under sunken eyes. The nurse had shaved off his beard and his rugged, square chin looked gaunt without the protective whiskers. Veins stood out like pieces of thick string on his hands.

Nick was sitting beside the bed looking through a newspaper. Gradually he became aware that his father was studying him and guessing what his next question would be, Nick attempted to forestall it.

'I'm getting really bored with all this Watergate business,' he said, closing the paper. 'How much longer are they going to harp on about it?'

'I couldn't care less if Richard Nixon is a mass-murderer, much less worry about scandals in the White House,' Magnus retorted with some difficulty. 'Stop treating me like an imbecile, Nick, and tell me why Mel hasn't been in to see me?'

Nick swallowed hard. Since he arrived back in Bath almost a week ago he felt as if he'd been through an emotional sandblaster: the fear that his father might die, the rage he felt towards him for having betrayed his mother, and his own sense of shame at the way he'd treated Mel. Worse still was trying to contain all this within him while he went about the business of hospital visiting and keeping things on an even keel back at Oaklands.

It had been reasonably easy while Magnus was still very sick to avoid any mention of Mel. He was only allowed one visitor at a time for just a few minutes and Stephen, Sophie and Nick had priority. All three of them had agreed for different reasons to say nothing about her departure until their father was stronger.

Part of Nick wanted to wound Magnus now, to call him all those names he'd muttered to himself during the long, sleepless nights of the past week. Yet the better part of him was overjoyed that his father had recovered enough to want to know what was going on back at the hotel.

'She's left, Dad.' He tried to sound casual. 'She went off the morning after you came in here.'

'Left!' Magnus's eyes seemed to come right out of his head as he struggled to sit up. 'She wouldn't have left while I was sick.'

Nick got up, put his hands on his father's

shoulders and eased him down again. 'Don't get upset, Dad. We can manage perfectly well without her.'

Sophie had arrived at Oaklands just an hour after Mel's rapid departure and Nick found some small degree of comfort in listening to his sister's malicious theories. She'd decided that Mel had run off because she feared they might investigate her closely now Magnus was in hospital: Sophie intended to go through the account books with Stephen when he arrived and was convinced they would find evidence that Mel had been systematically conning their father into giving her vast sums of money.

In Nick's aggrieved state he found it easier to go along with his sister's ideas than to reveal the truth to her or Stephen. In the days that followed, he even found himself believing them at times.

But it hadn't taken long before everyone, even Sophie, realised what a valuable employee Mel had really been. Oaklands simply didn't run so smoothly without her, however hard Joan Downes tried to cope with the extra workload. That quiet, unruffled way Mel had of working disguised how many different jobs she'd taken onto her shoulders. She was the one who silently filled in where necessary, darting from helping to prepare guests' rooms, to providing an extra pair of hands in the kitchen, making a few sandwiches and a pot of tea for a new arrival, or doing stock checks in the bar. No one had ever noticed that she saw to the flower arrangements, until they saw them wilting once she had gone. Nor had they observed before that the cutlery gleamed because she polished it. And now smears remained on mirrors and windows, with everyone insisting it wasn't their job.

Nick's anger hadn't eased the nagging sorrow inside him, or his fear about what his father would say when he found out. He could see that Sophie's waspish remarks about Mel had divided the staff into two groups: Antoine and Mrs Downes stoutly refused to believe she was guilty of any wrong doing; but Sally and the other part-time staff were delighting in scandalous tittle-tattle.

Magnus looked up at his son and saw anger burning in his eyes. 'She told you didn't she? And you threw her out?'

'Yes,' Nick admitted. He was very glad his father's mind was still so sharp, but his expression made Nick feel like a louse. 'And if you weren't so damned ill I might hit you. How could you have let something like this happen? Never mind about your children's feelings. It's an insult to Mum.'

Magnus turned his head away. It was the first time he could recall being afraid to meet another man's eyes. Only a few years earlier he had lectured Nick about treating women with sensitivity and respect; now he would have to admit his own failings in that department.

'I'm so sorry you're hurt,' Magnus whispered. 'It was all such a long time ago. If I hadn't had the stroke I would've sat down and explained it all to you.'

'So it's true then?' Nick's voice rose an octave. He'd hung onto the slim hope that Mel had been lying.

'I wish for your sake I could deny it,' Magnus said. It was an effort to talk but he knew he must. 'But I can't, Nick. I did have a child by another woman, and although I'm not proud of myself for being unfaithful to your mother, I can't say I'm ashamed to find Mel is that daughter. But you must believe one thing. She didn't come to Oaklands to make mischief. She just wanted to get to know me. If I hadn't forced her hand she would've left without saying a word. I know now why she wanted to leave: she'd fallen in love with you and it was tearing her apart.'

Nick's mouth fell open in shock. All this week he'd seen himself and his father as the victims, and Mel as a parasite who had preyed on them both. Now for the first time it dawned on him that she was as much hurt as himself.

Magnus closed his eyes again with weariness. He had to find the strength to tell his son how it was, even if by doing so he alienated Nick even further.

That afternoon after his talk with Mel, he had sat down at his desk intending to write down all his thoughts to try and clarify his feelings. He wasn't sure then if it was wiser to let Mel go and start a new life elsewhere, or to admit the truth to all three of his other children.

But that strange fuzzy sensation had come suddenly. He remembered going into the bathroom thinking he would take a mild sedative and lie down.

He was confused for some time after he came round. The events before he went to hospital were cloudy then, much like a half-remembered dream. But slowly as the days passed memories began to come back to him and with them the sense that things weren't quite right back at Oaklands. The card on the huge bouquet of flowers from the staff hadn't been signed by Mel, and it was odd that she hadn't come to see him, if only for a minute or two. Sophie and Stephen seemed unusually pleased with themselves and their insistence that every-thing was fine back at the hotel seemed too pat, when they were normally full of complaints. But Nick was the oddest of all: he was too damn hearty, as he'd always been when something was troubling him, and he hadn't referred to Mel once.

'Tell me exactly what happened?' he asked. He felt nauseous, knowing Mel would never have blurted out something so damaging until she was cornered. 'Were all of you involved?'

'No. Just me. It happened before Sophie and Stephen arrived and I haven't said anything to them.' Nick's lips quivered. 'Mel was gone before they came, they just think she ran out on us. But I don't want to tell you how it happened. Let's just say we had a row and in the heat of the moment it came out.'

Magnus winced. He could imagine the scenario. His fingers stole across the sheet to Nick's hand still clenched into a fist as he leant down over the bed. He wasn't a man given to tears, but even so he felt them welling up in his eyes. How cruel fate could be! One little seed carelessly sown years ago now threatened his son's happiness, and his own. 'Will you believe me when I say I'd have done anything to save you this pain?'

Nick looked at the big hand fondling his fist and felt his anger fading. His father was almost a legend in his own time. He'd bought a ruin of a house in acres of overgrown wilderness, and worked eighteen hours a day alongside his labourers restoring it. So many people had expected him to fail, but failure wasn't a word in Magnus Osbourne's vocabulary. Many of the young nurses here in this hospital had smilingly told him how their mothers had spoken of the big, handsome man who took Bath by storm all those years ago with his daring. Back at the hotel old friends spoke of his courage and his honour. But none of them had Magnus's full measure.

Magnus was the yardstick Nick measured all other men by, and found most of them wanting. His sensitivity, humour, passion, commitment and imagination were all still there, masked by white hair and wrinkled skin. Once he could have leapt over any obstacle, turned foes to friends by the sheer force of his personality. Now death was the only challenge awaiting him. How could Nick let him go to that without at least trying to understand?

'Tell me about Mel's mother?' Nick pulled up a chair and sat down, taking his father's hand in his. Nothing could take away the dejection he felt inside, but the truth might just make some sense of it. 'From the beginning.'

Magnus shut his eyes for a moment. He could see Bonny's face dancing in front of him, her golden hair, peachy skin and those vivid turquoise eyes. It was strange how even after so many years he could recall every last detail about her.

'It was in Oxford in 1947,' he said haltingly, hating the sound of his slurred speech. 'I was with my old RAF mate, Basil.'

He told Nick the story in much the same way he'd told Mel, but from a masculine viewpoint. Two old chums out on the town, hanging onto their evening together out of sentimentality because they both sensed it would be years before they saw each other again. The two dancers who'd captivated them, a few laughs and dances, a few more drinks. Taking the girls home to their digs.

'Bonny suggested meeting me for lunch the next day. I can't explain why I went, I knew it was folly.'

'I understand all that,' Nick said quietly. 'What I don't understand is why if you loved Mum you didn't break it off.'

'I think if you'd seen Bonny you would've understood that. I knew I was being a fool,' he whispered to Nick, tears trickling down his lined cheeks. 'I was over forty, she was just seventeen. I loved your mother and I never wanted to leave her, but Bonny was like a drug I couldn't resist.'

'Did she love you?' Nick asked. He didn't know why this was important to him – perhaps because he didn't want to believe his father had been a complete fool.

'That was part of it I suppose. I could never be entirely sure. She was devil and angel all rolled into one. She took me to heights I'd never reached before and depths of misery too. I worked like crazy at that time to try and get her out of my system, but that didn't work either. I finally made the break from her when your mother was expecting you. It was only then that I realised Bonny really did love me, in as far as she was capable of true love anyway.'

He moved on then to explain as he had to Mel about her conception and how over four years later Bonny had claimed that Magnus was her child's father. Finally he described the financial arrangement he'd made after John Norton died.

'But how can you say just by looking at blood tests that she was your child?' Nick said indignantly, tossing back a lock of hair from his flushed face. 'You must know as well as I do that one blood group might rule out John Norton being the father, but it's not proof that you were! There could've been other men she went with. Mel doesn't look a bit like you.'

'Since I've been lying here I've thought about that a great deal. There is a strong family resemblance,' Magnus said slowly. 'When Sophie lets her hair down it's just like Mel's. My mother had dark hair and almond eyes – if you go home and look in the old photograph album you'll see it for yourself. Your cheek bones too, Nick, they are just like Mel's.'

Nick was trying to find some argument against this. He still couldn't believe it but he could picture Sophie in her early twenties, her dark hair long, straight and gleaming. Before she took to wearing such matronly unflattering clothes her figure had been curvy too, just like Mel's.

Nick broke down then. He put his head on the pillow beside his father, holding the older man tightly, and cried.

In the past year he'd thought of little else but Mel. There had been many women in his life, but never one who had captivated him so completely. It wasn't just her looks, even though those dark eyes haunted his dreams. It was her character he loved most. She really cared about people, and she was always willing to help anyone. Yet she wasn't a goody-goody: there was a wicked glint in her eyes sometimes, she enjoyed a good argument and her sense of humour was earthy. She could put a man down with a brisk one-liner that cut right to the core, and just now and again her mimicry of people could be a little too incisive. More than anything he missed the friend she'd become. Oaklands felt empty without her.

'What do I do now?' he whispered. His father's honesty had killed his anger, but now he felt deeply ashamed. 'For a whole year I've wanted her. I never felt quite like this about any other woman. I feel so dirty now.'

'You haven't done anything wrong.' Magnus stroked his son's hair, tears rolling down his cheeks. 'I'd like to believe that now you know she might be your sister, the side of you that desired her will just cut out.'

'Maybe it will. But I've got to find her,' Nick whispered, his voice croaky with emotion. 'I can't bear to think of her out there somewhere alone, after the things I said to her.'

Magnus felt that Ruth's spirit had suddenly entered the room. Nick had been a difficult teenager, often seeming to care so little about others that Magnus felt he had none of his mother's genes.

But this burst of compassion proved Ruth was alive inside him.

'That could prove difficult,' Magnus said softly. 'In the two years she's worked for me she rarely talked about her past. I wouldn't have a clue where to start looking. She's proud too. I think she's probably hidden herself away somewhere we'll never find her.'

'Then you've got to tell me absolutely everything you do know about her. Any friends she mentioned, even in passing. There's bound to be someone or somewhere which was special to her. People go back when they are hurting.'

Magnus put one hand on Nick's cheek and smoothed it, the way he had when he was a small child. He could see Ruth in the boy's face, her quiet determination and surprising inner strength. 'Is that wise?' he said softly. 'Mel didn't talk about her past partly because it was too painful. Ask yourself whether it's going to hurt you still more before you dig into it.'

'I've got to.' Nick buried his face in his father's chest. 'Not only for me, but for you too. I know how much she means to you.'

Magnus lapsed into thought. He hated to think of Mel out there somewhere, with no one to turn to. But despite his concern and affection for her, his first priority had to be for his son's wellbeing. Nick had never discussed why his career had taken such a nose dive four years earlier, or what happened to the vast amount of money he'd earned then, or why sweet little Belinda walked out on him. Magnus had his suspicions, but he hadn't liked to look too closely.

It was possible that without some sort of rudder in his life Nick might drift back into his old ways again. The question was whether looking for Mel would be that rudder? Or whether Nick would dissipate the energy he should be putting into his work in a fruitless and perhaps heart-breaking search?

'Did she take the Morris Minor?' he asked.

Nick shook his head. 'She went off with only one small bag. The rest of her stuff is still up in her room. Perhaps she'll send word where we should send it on,' he added hopefully.

Magnus shook his head.

'I doubt that son,' he said sadly. 'She's not the materialistic type. My guess is that she's taken all the blame on her own shoulders and decided to close the door for good, hoping it will make things better for us. But when I get home we'll look in her room. Maybe we'll find something to give us a clue.'

'Sophie wants to clean it all out,' Nick sighed. 'What are we going to tell her and Stephen?'

Magnus was too tired to make any momentous decisions yet. 'Nothing for now,' he said wearily. 'Tell Sophie and Mrs Downes that Mel's room is to be left locked and untouched until I come home. We'll decide what should be done then.'

After Nick had left, Magnus found himself crying and thinking back to the day when Nick was born. He had taken that wizened little scrap into his arms and made a silent vow that he would be the perfect husband and father. Perhaps it was partly because when Sophie and Stephen had been small he'd always been tied up with work, and then the war had come along and prevented him from spending as much time with both them and Ruth as they needed. But mostly his vow was tied up with guilt about his affair with Bonny.

Yet only eighteen months later he forgot that vow when he had one more fling with Bonny.

Now over decades later he was being made to

pay dearly for that two hours of lust. Nick was badly hurt, Mel was out there somewhere all alone, and he was trapped in here, unable to help either of them.

Chapter Eighteen

Nick did not get an opportunity to search Mel's old room thoroughly until two months after Magnus's stroke. He couldn't do it in the first couple of weeks, not without arousing Sophie's suspicions, then just as Magnus improved enough for her to go back to her home in Yorkshire, Nick was offered a part in a play in Leeds, and had to leave Oaklands himself.

There had been no word from Mel, not even a request for the rest of her clothes to be sent on. Nick knew the staff joked amongst themselves about her room being 'Bluebeard's room' because it remained locked. But Mrs Downes who still retained her affection for Mel, despite all the rumours and speculation, had stoutly stuck by her employer's instructions. If she wondered why Magnus didn't want the room emptied and made ready for a new member of staff, she made no comment.

But now Magnus had been discharged from hospital and Nick had come home to help. Christmas was only two weeks away and both the hotel and restaurant were fully booked. With Magnus still very frail and unable to walk, and the staff already overstretched, Nick was needed here. Today however, he was determined to find some clues as to where Mel had gone.

Nick opened the wardrobe first, and a faint waft

of her familiar perfume took him by surprise. Instinctively he reached for the red crepe dress she had been wearing the first night they met in the bar. His fingers closed around the soft fabric and he drew it to his cheek, as a child would hold a comforter.

'I'm so sorry, Mel,' he murmured. 'I didn't mean those cruel things I said to you.'

Nick had been in here twice since she left. The first time he'd been alone, just checking to see what she'd done with her other things when he saw her rushing up the drive with only one bag. The second time had been when he caught Sophie snooping a day or two later. She had been taken aback by the neatness of the room. Of course his suspicious-minded sister had insisted this was because Mel was an accomplished confidence trickster, who knew how to cover her tracks. But then Sophie believed the worst of almost everyone.

Nick was an untidy person himself, whose clothes stayed where he dropped them, but he found Mel's orderliness appealing. Her dresses were hung on padded hangers, their zippers and buttons fastened, her shoes beneath in a row. There were surprisingly few clothes: five dresses in all, two suits, a few odd skirts, blouses and the plain black dress she wore for waiting at tables. He flicked through them all, checking pockets, but aside from a spare button in one, he found nothing. They were all recent 70s fashions: no old miniskirt, kaftan or fringed suede waistcoat from the 60s kept for sentimentality. Every woman he'd ever known had kept something from the past. But the day Mel became Amelia Corbett she seemed to have renounced everything that had gone before.

He moved on then to the chest of drawers and ran his hands over the contents. Everything was folded neatly: white pretty underwear from chain stores, not the kind of decadent frippery Sophie must have expected. Only the bottom drawer revealed a slightly different image: a white feather boa in a cotton bag, a minuscule spotted bikini, ragged denim shorts and a brilliant turquoise and pink sarong.

The drawer in the dressing table held nothing of interest: a few cosmetics, some odd pieces of cheap costume jewellery and coloured hair slides. He found a bundle of letters and sat down on the bed to read them, but was once again disappointed. They were all addressed to her here at Oaklands, from old members of staff, mostly students who'd helped out in the summer holidays. They were typical student letters, full of talk of parties, being behind with studies, the kind written in a nostalgic moment to someone they liked, but without the bond of lasting friendship. As each came from a hall of residence, and none had invited Mel there to see them, it was doubtful that she had made tracks to any of them.

When he found her post office book tucked under a drawer lining, he gasped in astonishment. She had a balance of over six hundred pounds. He looked at the entries: ten pounds paid in almost every week since she started work here. The only time she'd withdrawn any was the previous Christmas, presumably to buy presents. It made him feel more uneasy to think she was out there somewhere without even her savings to fall back on.

He checked all the books next, bemused by the variety of taste. Several Harold Robbins, George Eliot's *Mill on the Floss*, a biography on Florence Nightingale, another on the potato famine in Ireland, *Great Expectations*, *Jane Eyre* and several poetry and cookery books. There were no letters tucked into them, no interesting inscriptions.

Nick sat for a moment in the pink buttoned-back chair by the window. Just the way it was placed suggested this had been her favourite spot. The view over the valley wasn't at its best: it was a dismal, damp day, the kind that made everything seem as grey and dull as the sky. Nick was very disappointed by his search. It seemed inconceivable that anyone could have so few possessions and no sentimental clutter. If it hadn't been for finding her post office book he might've thought she'd purposely stripped the room of clues. But someone careful enough to leave no evidence behind would have remembered to take their money.

As he sat considering what his next move could be, a tiny raised tuft of carpet in the corner of the room by the skirting board caught his eye. In the days when Nick had been snorting cocaine and smoking grass he had often hidden his stash in such a place.

He was on his feet and over to it in a second. As he pulled at the tuft, the carpet peeled back effortlessly and he saw a green cardboard envelope file beneath it.

His heart raced as he opened it and found the old letters his father had spoken of. It was further evidence that she'd been too upset when she left to think clearly.

There was a photograph of a stunningly beautiful blonde on the top of the pile of letters. He didn't need to be told it was Bonny: she looked exactly how his father had described her. She was wearing a twenties-style short fringed flapper dress, but it had clearly been taken in the early sixties; not only was she doing the Twist, but her hair was set in an elaborate curled beehive and she had the Cleopatra black-lined eyes and very pale lipstick of that period.

'You were right, she was gorgeous,' he murmured studying it carefully.

Magnus's letters came next, fastened together with a paperclip. Just one glance at the bold, familiar handwriting confirmed they were genuine. Beneath these were some from another man, but just as he was about to start reading them, he heard Mrs Downes out on the landing. She was speaking to Betty who was cleaning the guest rooms. Afraid she might come in to see what he was doing, Nick closed the file, slipped it down the waist of his trousers, covered it with his sweater and left the room.

Mrs Downes was doling out fresh linen to Betty. She turned as Nick locked Mel's room and smiled hesitantly at him.

'Just checking to see everything's all right,' he said, blushing. It didn't seem right to be furtive. 'I suppose we'll have to pack all her stuff up soon, Downie, but Dad and I thought we'd wait till after Christmas. You never know, she might write then.'

Joan Downes had been hoping for an opportunity such as this. She was a little hurt that Nick hadn't taken her into his confidence about what happened with Mel. There was a time when he'd told her everything. She had dismissed Sophie's story that the girl had been fiddling Magnus out-of-hand. He was far too smart to allow anyone to fool him for long and Sophie had always had a wicked tongue.

Joan had arrived at the theory that Mel must have been pregnant, either by a guest or someone she'd met in Bath, and that she'd told Nick that morning after Magnus's stroke.

Joan felt equally sorry for both of them. It would be hard for any man to accept that the girl he loved was carrying another man's child, especially when he was frantic with worry about his sick father. It was understandable too that Mel rushed off without a word to anyone; Nick could be a real devil when he was angry.

'I reckon it was her who rang yesterday.' Joan went closer to Nick, lowering her voice so Betty wouldn't hear. 'Wendy on reception said a woman phoned to make inquiries about vacancies, then asked how Mr Osbourne was. Wendy said it was all a bit odd because the woman didn't sound the least put out about the hotel being full until after New Year; she didn't even want to leave her telephone number in case there was a cancellation.'

'What did Wendy tell her?' Nick asked. He wanted to believe it was Mel.

'She said he'd just come home and he was getting better, but it would be a while before he took an active part in running the hotel again. When Wendy asked for her name so she could pass on her good wishes to Magnus, she said it was Mrs Smithers. Magnus didn't recognise that name, and Wendy couldn't find any record of her staying here before.'

One of the nurses at the hospital had told Nick they had had several telephone inquiries from a woman who claimed to be an old friend but didn't give a name.

'I hope it was Mel,' Nick said. 'At least it would prove she still thinks about us.'

Joan put her hand on Nick's arm. 'I wish you'd tell me why she went like she did, lovey?' she wheedled. 'I know I've got no business to pry, but I miss her so much, and I worry about her too.'

'We had a bit of a squabble, Downie.' Nick made a sad face, wishing he could tell her the whole truth. He patted her shoulder affectionately. 'I said a few nasty, hasty things and then she went. I'm really sorry now, and both Dad and I hope she'll get over it and come back. If you can think of anyone she mentioned, friends or relations she might have gone to, let us know will you?'

Joan thought how typical it was of Nick to lash out at someone, and then assume a mere apology would put things right once he'd calmed down. She felt too that if he knew the real reason why Mel had left, he should have scotched Sophie's slanderous suggestions, not let wild rumours fly around the way he had. It was tempting to say these things – after all she'd known him since he was a little boy – but Nick was unpredictable, and she was, after all, only an employee.

'She didn't have anyone,' she shrugged, biting her lip. She hated to think of any pregnant woman alone and friendless. 'Leastways she never spoke of them. She used to want to hear every last thing about my family, but she never talked about anyone she knew in the past.'

'Christmas is when people remember good times,' Nick said soothingly, as much for his own benefit as for the housekeeper's. 'Even if she doesn't contact Dad or myself, she might drop you a line or a card. You'll tell me if she does, won't you?'

He went on down to his father's sitting room on the first floor. 'And how are we today, Mr Osbourne?'

Magnus was sitting in a wheelchair at his desk, jigsaw puzzle pieces spread out in front of him, glasses perched on the end of his nose. 'As well as can be expected,' he replied, with a hint of laughter in his voice. 'Or I will be when you lot all stop fussing.'

Nick had grown used to seeing his father dressed in pyjamas and dressing gown in hospital, but here in his masculine retreat they seemed to emphasise his age and frailty. The nurse they'd hired had sniffed at Nick's suggestion that he might feel more dignified in his normal clothes, and said it was more trouble than it was worth helping him change. Nick thought he'd wait a couple of days to see how this nurse shaped up, and if she didn't comply with his wishes he'd dress Magnus himself and find another nurse who wouldn't look on her patient as some old crock without any feelings.

'I haven't come to fuss,' Nick assured him, pulling the file from his trousers. 'And I've found a more stimulating puzzle than that one. Are you up to it?'

Magnus's face lit up, eyes twinkling. 'You found something in Mel's room?'

He had made a remarkable recovery. There was still a degree of paralysis in his left side, which prevented him from lifting with that arm and he couldn't walk again yet. But his speech was back to normal, he had no loss of memory and there was every reason to believe he would gradually regain the full use of his arm and leg with physiotherapy.

'It's letters, lots from you but others too and photographs,' Nick said jubilantly, pushing the jigsaw to one side and placing the file in front of his father. 'I haven't looked at them yet. Will you mind me seeing the ones from you?'

'Not really,' Magnus said, his faintly embarrassed grin showing he wasn't entirely sure. He took off his glasses, then supporting his weak arm on his knee polished them carefully on his dressing gown.

Nick had noticed how careful his father was to try and use his left hand as much as possible. Even when he was sitting watching television he would squeeze a rubber ball between his fingers for exercise. 'We'll leave yours till last,' he suggested. 'After all we know what's in those anyway.'

They didn't speak at all as they read the ones from Jack Easton, Nick looking at them first, then handing them to Magnus. To Nick's surprise his father didn't react when he saw that Bonny had accused Jack too of being Mel's father.

'So did you know about him?' he asked as Magnus struggled to put the letters back in order under the paperclip.

'Yes, she often spoke of a boy called Jack who was her childhood sweetheart,' he said gruffly. 'He was an evacuee from London like her, they were friends right from kids. She sent him a "Dear John" when he was in the Army, some time before I met her. Looks like she didn't give him up for good though.'

Nick picked up the attached photograph of a group of children. 'Did she ever show you this?' he asked.

Magnus smiled. 'Yes, she did. She always had it in her handbag. That's her of course.' He pointed out the small blonde with the sticking-up hair ribbons. 'The skinny boy with freckles and his arm round her is Jack. He was billeted with the station master. Bonny was with a dancing teacher she called Aunt Lydia. The other kids were "her gang".'

'He says "colouring like mine gets passed on",' Nick said. 'Did she ever say what sort of colouring he had?'

'Bright red hair,' Magnus chuckled. 'She said he was ugly too. But he was her best friend for all that. I liked the sound of him actually, she described him very vividly. A plucky sort of kid, plenty of derring-do.'

'Don't you feel angry that she was carrying on with him?' Nick asked heatedly. 'Why weren't you as tough as him when Bonny told you Mel belonged to you?'

Magnus shrugged. 'There's no point in having a post mortem now, Nick.'

'Well, what about this Aunt Lydia? Do you think Bonny kept in touch with her? Might she be someone Mel would go to?'

'Might be worth a try,' Magnus said, telling his son what he knew about this aunt. 'But you'll have to bear in mind, Nick, that Bonny told me countless lies. She claimed her parents were both dead, and I'm pretty certain that wasn't true. I was always led to believe this Aunt Lydia was rather grand and beautiful. We might discover she's impoverished and crabby.'

They read the letter from Miles together, Nick looking over Magnus's shoulder.

'Well, this is a turn-up,' Magnus said in surprise.

'Why, do you know him?'

'You know him too, if only by name,' Magnus said. 'It's Sir Miles Hamilton!'

Nick gasped and sat down with a bump. Sir Miles Hamilton was a well-known patron of the arts, with interests in theatre and a seat on the board of a couple of film companies. Nick had seen various articles about the man in *The Stage*, for although he was now in his eighties and had virtually retired, he still went to many premieres and award nights.

'Do you think he was her lover too?' Nick asked. Miles seemed old enough to be Bonny's grandfather.

'I can't imagine it,' Magnus frowned. 'He wasn't a friend, but I did move in the same circles as him at one time. I thought of him as a very upright sort of man and as far as I know he was devoted to his wife, Mary. Oddly enough I was instrumental in Bonny getting to know both Sir Miles and John Norton. I got the girls, Bonny and her friend Ellie, a little cabaret number at a charity bash in the Savoy, and they were both there too.'

'Were you there yourself?' Nick asked.

Magnus bit his lip and looked away from his son.

'Go on,' Nick urged. 'It's no good trying to hide things now.'

'It was a terrible night,' Magnus sighed. 'I regretted ever putting the girls' names forward to the committee. But I knew there would be quite a few show business people there and I hoped they might get offered a job.

'Bonny and Ellie were a terrific double act. Bonny was an outstanding dancer, and Ellie had the voice and the acting ability. My goodness you should've seen them together, they were dynamite.'

Nick was on the edge of his seat. This was the first time his father had ever given him an inkling that he knew anything about the entertainment world.

'Firstly, your mother was with me that night,' Magnus said gruffly. 'I'd warned the girls they were to ignore me, and they did, but I was still very uncomfortable. For the first part of the evening the girls behaved impeccably; they both looked gorgeous and when they did their act it nearly brought the house down. But after the cabaret was over, when supper was being served, Ruth, being the generous, good-natured soul she was, saw Bonny and Ellie looking for somewhere to have theirs and invited them over to our table.'

Nick chuckled. He had been in several tight spots with women himself and he could imagine his father's discomfort at wife and mistress meeting face to face.

'Well, Ellie saved my bacon,' Magnus sniffed. 'She whisked Bonny off sharpish in the direction of John Norton who'd spoken to them earlier. Fortunately Ruth didn't suspect anything. But then later on in the evening a man came in uninvited. To my further horror he made a drunken beeline for the girls and started a bit of a fracas.'

'Who was he? Another lover?'

'Hardly, he was a well-known pansy by the name of Ambrose Dingle. One time impresario, and ex-stage director of a show the girls had been in sometime before I met them. Anyway, Sir Miles got up and intervened. The next thing I know Dingle is about to swing a punch at Sir Miles, and everyone is rubber-necking to see what's going on. Ruth was horrified, she thought such loutish behaviour only happened in village halls in Yorkshire, and I was terrified Bonny might run over to me! But Sir Miles handled it very well and got Dingle thrown out, then took the two girls under his wing. Bonny, little show-off that she was, absolutely loved it all. She sat there with her head on Lady Hamilton's shoulder gaining her sympathy and batting her eyelashes at Sir Miles. She certainly knew how to put the little-girl-lost image across!'

Nick digested this. 'Could they have had a fling after that then?'

Magnus sighed. 'It is possible, I'm sure Bonny would overlook the man's age because of his money and title, but somehow I just can't see Sir Miles as a randy old goat. The girls did get taken on by his agency afterwards. In fact the show Bonny was in when I finally told her I couldn't see her any longer, was one of his projects. But a year or so later when Ellie got the lead in the stage version of *Oklahoma*, which was also one of his projects, Bonny wasn't even offered a part in the chorus, so I got the impression Sir Miles had only ever been interested in Ellie.'

'Is this her?' Nick picked up a photograph of Magnus in a dinner jacket, between Bonny and another dancer, both in sequinned costumes and feathered head-dresses.

'Yes, that's Ellie. It was taken back stage of a theatre in Wembley. I can't remember the name of it now. It would have been in 1947 anyway, not that long before Bonny and I parted. I liked Ellie. I was so pleased for her when she made it: she deserved it more than anyone.'

'What's her other name?' Nick asked, frowning as he looked at the picture. 'She looks vaguely familiar.'

To his surprise Magnus began to laugh. 'Looks "vaguely familiar",' he chortled. 'I should think she does. It's Helena Forester. You used to dote on her.'

Nick's mouth fell open in shock. 'Never!' he gasped. Helena Forester was a big Hollywood star. During the fifties and sixties she'd been a household name, and Nick had seen all her musicals as a boy. 'Why didn't you ever tell me you knew her?' he said petulantly. 'How could you keep that to yourself. I used to keep her pictures and read all about her.'

Magnus looked penitent. 'I was often tempted to. But how could I without admitting everything else?'

A few moments later Nick came upon a letter from a woman written on blue paper. 'Could this be from her?' he asked. 'She signed it "H".'

Magnus took the letter and read it through, Nick looking over his shoulder. 'I would say so,' he said thoughtfully. 'Of course I can't remember what her handwriting was like from all those years ago. I don't know that I ever saw it even. But it sounds like her.'

'Are you the "M" she refers to?' Nick asked.

'No,' Magnus shook his head. 'The last time I saw Ellie was back in 1947, the night I said goodbye

423

to Bonny. It could be Miles she means. Her first film *Soho* was made by one of his companies.'

'It's a very strange letter,' Nick said, reading it again. ' "Reassure me we did the right thing? Sometimes at night I have panic attacks." It's almost like it's in code. Have you got any ideas?'

Magnus shook his head and picked up a separate piece of paper on which Mel had written a few notes. 'Long-term close friendship' he read. 'Plotting together? Maybe joint blackmail. Is "M" Miles or Magnus? Why would her hair be like steel wool?' Magnus put down the notes and looked at his son. 'It seems that Mel was as puzzled as we are. She's right about the long-term close friendship: Bonny and Ellie were practically joined at the hip. But I don't think Mel knows who this letter's from. Now that's really odd. Back in the fifties there were huge queues outside every cinema to see Helena's films. Is it possible that Bonny didn't ever tell Mel that such a famous actress was her best friend? Bonny boasted about everything!'

'They must have fallen out,' Nick said. 'I wonder why?'

'Jealousy, I expect,' Magnus said thoughtfully. 'Maybe once Bonny saw Ellie's name up in lights it got too much for her.'

'Tell me about Ellie? What she was like?'

'She and Bonny were chalk and cheese,' Magnus smiled as he remembered. 'Ellie was a giver, Bonny a taker. It was an unlikely friendship really. Ellie's father died before she was born and she was brought up in the East End of London. Her mother was a dresser in a theatre, but she was killed in the Blitz. According to Bonny the poor girl had a terrible time during the war – she went to live with an aunt who was a drunk and virtually supported the woman until she too was hurt in an air raid. Oddly enough the aunt died later on the same night I first met the girls. Ellie was devastated: whatever her aunt had been, she adored her.'

'You really liked her, didn't you?' Nick could hear a warmth in his father's voice, different from the way he spoke about Bonny.

'Yes, I did,' Magnus sighed deeply. 'Sometimes I was tempted to tell her to split from Bonny, that she was wasting her talent. You see Bonny didn't share her friend's commitment to the stage and Ellie was a brilliant comic actress.'

'Did she ever get married? I don't think I ever read about her private life.'

Magnus shook his head. 'No, well, at least not unless that's the reason why she faded from the public view. Back when I knew her she had an actor friend called Edward, but she never seemed very interested in love and romance. Bonny claimed she still held a torch for a young fireman she'd met during the war. She had to choose between marrying him and her career on the stage apparently.'

'Do you know this chap Edward's surname?'

'No. I never met him, I only remember his name because Bonny was always moaning about him. He was in the first show they did together, and then the three of them went on tour. Bonny loathed him.'

'Why?'

Magnus smiled. 'Well you couldn't take anything Bonny said as fact! She claimed he was creepy, queer, a bit of an aristocrat, and that he was obsessed by Ellie. I saw a few photos – very good-looking, blond, Nordic type. Ellie spent a great deal of time with him.'

'Did he split up their double act?'

'Oh no,' Magnus said. 'I think it was really Ellie getting the part in *Oklahoma* and perhaps Bonny meeting John Norton which did it. And judging from that letter there where no hard feelings on either side about that. The following year, 1950, *Soho* was made, and Helena Forester took England by storm.'

Nick had seen this classic film several times and loved it: the story of a young girl who got caught up in the seamier side of war-time London. Many critics claimed that British film makers should have fought tooth and nail to keep such a fine actress working in England. The glossy musical comedies she made in Hollywood afterwards were trashy compared with *Soho*.

'Did Mel say anything about this letter?' Nick asked, waving the sheet of blue notepaper.

'No, but then she didn't have time to tell me about any of them. She was going to come back upstairs later that evening. But of course I had the stroke.'

'So you don't know if she's already checked out Sir Miles and Jack Easton?'

'No. That makes it doubly difficult doesn't it?'

Nick sat for a moment in silence, still with the letter from Helena Forester in his hands. He had hoped the file might also have had letters to Mel in it. It was disappointing to find it only contained things relating to Bonny.

'Dad,' he said eventually. 'There's something very weird about all of this. What would you say to me going to see this chap Jack Easton and Sir Miles Hamilton to see if they can throw any light on it?'

'I just wish I were fit enough to go myself,' Magnus said with a wry smile. 'But you'll have to be very tactful, particularly with Sir Miles. Lady Hamilton died some years ago, but men of his position and age are notoriously tetchy.'

Nick smiled. 'I can be the soul of discretion when I need to be. I think I should go down to Rye too, and find out exactly what happened when Bonny killed herself.'

'When do you want to go?' Magnus asked.

'I can't till after New Year,' Nick said. 'There's too much going on here until then and besides you need help until you can get about in that chair. But will you be able to manage without me then?'

Magnus cuffed his son's head playfully and smiled. 'Of course I will. One less wet nurse around me will be a relief. God I miss Mel, son, if she were here now she'd be making me laugh, not pandering to me as if I were senile.'

'I'll get her back,' Nick said softly. 'Just you wait.'

On 3 January Nick left Oaklands. Magnus waved goodbye from the side window in his sitting room until all that was left of the red MG was a puff of grey exhaust fumes amongst the trees on the drive. A tear trickled down his cheek as he turned his wheelchair away from the window and moved it back to the fire.

Christmas had been a very sad time for him: a glimpse of what old age and infirmity meant for many people. Alone in his room, the sounds of jollity wafted up to him from the bar and restaurant, cutting him off from all he'd worked for, reminding him relentlessly of happier times.

When Ruth was alive Christmas had been magical. She loved to give people surprises: she even filled little felt stockings for each of the guests, not to mention masterminding all the children's presents, dressing the tree, putting up the decorations and organising just about everything else. Anyone who stayed here at Christmas became part of the family for the day. Somehow she managed to balance being the perfect hostess with her role as mother and wife without ever looking harassed.

The lunch often went on for hours, the children slipping away, leaving the adults to lazily talk and drink in peace.

But since she died Christmas at Oaklands had become much like any other hotel: individual tables for each party of guests at lunch, the staff keeping an attentive and polite distance. Magnus and any of his family who came to stay ate their lunch down in the kitchen once the guests had retired to the drawing room. Magnus wished he could blame someone else for this change in the arrangements, but the truth of the matter was that he had neither the heart, nor the natural warmth that Ruth had, to bring ten or twelve strangers together with his family and make every single one of them feel special and wanted.

Nick had offered to help Magnus downstairs for lunch on Christmas Day, but he'd declined the offer. It was enough for him to share a special breakfast upstairs with Nick, and later to overhear him being the perfect host in his father's place.

Magnus had often felt guilty that he loved this child so much more than the other two. But during the long hours alone this Christmas he had come to understand why. Nick needed him more than his other two children.

On the face of it, Nick was blessed with far more than either Sophie or Stephen. He had boundless charm, he was handsome and amusing, and people took to him immediately. He had never needed to learn how to win friends. He had inherited the best features from each of his parents: Ruth's straight classic nose and generous mouth, Magnus's strong bone structure and height. Stephen had Ruth's short stockiness, but his father's craggy features, while Sophie was a throwback to her grandmother with the same tight mouth and pinched nose.

Magnus didn't feel responsible for either Stephen's or Sophie's failings: they'd had an idyllic childhood and they were grown up by the time Ruth died. She had once commented, 'Magnus, they are true Yorkshire Osbournes. They won't ever embarrass us or behave recklessly. Perhaps we should be grateful they are intelligent and steady instead of worrying about them being so dour.'

But Magnus did hold himself responsible for Nick's failings. When Ruth had died he'd been so immersed in his own grief he forgot his youngest son was still just a child.

'You should have got him home from school well before she died,' he murmured to himself. 'What sort of father leaves it to a headmaster to break that sort of news? He was only thirteen and you expected him to take it like a man!'

He sighed deeply, reaching over to pull out a scrapbook from his bookshelf. It was the only effort he'd made to replace the kind of special attention Ruth gave all her children: a collection of pictures, school reports, letters and later reviews.

He turned the pages slowly, sadly remembering other stories behind the snapshots. Nick in France, just a month after Ruth's death: a skinny tall boy, wearing only a pair of shorts, his hair bleached white by the sun. But Magnus had spent that holiday sitting in a bar drinking away his sorrows instead of swimming with his son. His first lead role in a school production of *Hamlet*; but Magnus hadn't been there to see it. Two years later a snap of him winning the cup at school for all-round sportsmanship: taller and more muscular now, his face showing every sign of the handsome adult he was to become, happy that day because Magnus was there to share his moment of glory. There were so many school pictures: cricket captain, rugby, swimming, athletics. Back then Magnus had been so proud of his son he overlooked the abysmal academic record and the master's strong hints that he was too arrogant for his own good.

'What happened to you?' he asked as he picked up a picture of Belinda, a girl with long blonde hair, a big bust and a sweet innocent face. He had only met her once, when Nick brought her here to Oaklands for the weekend. They had been engaged then, and though Magnus hadn't been delighted about that as they were so young, he had liked the girl very much. Nick never said why it ended; perhaps he just lost interest once he thought he was going to be a big star. Magnus wished he'd made a point of asking Nick what happened.

He turned to the glossy, moody studio pictures taken for the promotion of *Hunnicroft Estate*. Surly and aggressive in black leather, Nick sat astride a motorbike, stripped to the waist in torn dirty jeans. Then came the newspaper cuttings hailing him as the new James Dean.

There was a big gap in the book after the television series was axed. There had been letters from him during that time, but only requests for money. Magnus had kept the two lines about a court appearance and a fine for dangerous driving, but he'd never stuck it in.

'Why didn't you go up to London to see what was going on?' he asked himself. 'Or was it because you were afraid?'

Ruth would have known what to do, but Magnus for all his worldliness had looked the other way.

Yet he loved the boy. It was Nick's face he'd wanted to see, Nick's voice he'd wanted to hear. Nick was Magnus as a boy, Ruth as a young bride: the sunny, happy little boy whose presence ousted memories of Bonny and revived his love for Ruth, giving them both the happiest years of their marriage.

And now he was going off like a knight to the Crusades to discover the truth about his father's old mistress!

Magnus put the scrapbook back on the shelf, overwhelmed for a moment by shame.

'If he can do that for you, the least you can do is make yourself walk again,' he told himself fiercely. 'Stop feeling sorry for yourself and get out of this chair.'

He wheeled himself over to the window, put the brake on, then reaching out for the windowsill with his good hand, hauled himself up onto his feet. His left leg wobbled, but by taking most of his weight on the right foot he managed to swing his left foot forward, then support himself to move the right leg.

'You can do it,' he said, thrilled just to be upright. 'One step at a time and willpower, that's all it takes.

At eight thirty in the evening, with a gale force wind blowing straight off the sea, Littlehampton was deserted.

Nick smiled engagingly at the dark-haired woman behind the bar in the Kings Head. 'A pint of best please – and would you like something for yourself?'

Littlehampton was one of the dreariest towns Nick had ever seen. He had no wish to linger here any longer than was absolutely necessary. He had found a room in a small bed and breakfast, and eaten a greasy hamburger and chips. Now he hoped to get some help in finding Jack Easton.

'Well, thank you very much,' the barmaid smiled back at him. 'I'll have a half if that's okay.'

'It's a wild night out there,' Nick said. He glanced round the bar. There were only eight customers in all, three of them old men playing cards in the corner. 'First time I've been to Little-hampton – perhaps I should've waited for the summer.'

'I prefer the winter myself,' she said as she pulled his pint. 'It's packed out in summer. They steal the glasses, make a mess in the toilets and we're run off our feet. Where do you come from then?'

Nick could tell that she fancied him: she looked like the type who had a dull husband and a couple of kids at home and saw her work in the bar as a diversion. She was an attractive thirty-something, a bit overweight and overly made-up, but the kind a lonely commercial traveller away from home would make a beeline for.

'From Bath,' he replied, leaning towards her over the bar. 'It's a bit of a nightmare there too in the summer. We don't get many hooligans, but there's hordes of foreign tourists packing the streets, hogging all the seats in restaurants, and creating queues in all the shops.'

'Down here on business?' she asked, looking suspiciously at his worn leather jacket.

'Sort of,' he said. 'I'm actually trying to find a garage. I've got a bit of trouble with my car. Someone told me to go to a place called Easton's – do you know it?'

'You've got a Mercedes then?' she said, her eyes suddenly brighter.

Nick didn't know quite how to reply. 'That isn't all he repairs is it?'

She laughed. 'Easton's is a car showroom, not a garage. Jack Easton only sells Mercedes.'

The next morning Nick understood why the bar-maid had been so amused. It was clearly years since Jack Easton held a spanner in his hands. Five brand new Mercedes were displayed inside his sparkling showroom. Even the second-hand ones out on the forecourt were only two or three years old, and all in top condition.

'Lovely isn't she?' A middle-aged man in a sharp grey suit pounced on Nick as he paused to look at a silver-grey coupé. 'What are you driving at the moment, sir?'

Nick glanced sideways at the salesman. He couldn't be Jack, what little hair he had was fair. 'An ancient MG,' he said. 'To be honest I daren't even dream of a car like this. Actually I came to see Mr Easton.'

'Do you have an appointment with him.' The salesman lost his smile.

'Er, no,' Nick wished he'd thought before plunging in. 'Could you ask him if he would see me for a minute or two? I'm only in Littlehampton for today and it is urgent.'

'Your name, sir?' The man looked Nick up and down.

'Osbourne. That won't mean anything to him, just say I'm calling about a mutual friend.'

The salesman disappeared through a door at the back of the showrooms. He was gone some five minutes and came back in frowning.

'If you're selling something my life won't be worth living,' he said tersely. 'Go on up the stairs. The door at the end of the corridor.'

Nick knocked firmly on the door, then opened it.

Nick had expected Jack Easton to be something of a rough diamond, but he was taken aback all the same. His hair was not just red, but more like a flaming torch, and he was stockily built with a thick neck and a broken front tooth. His conservative grey suit and striped tie didn't seem to fit him at all.

Jack Easton leaned back in his chair, insolently

tucking his hands behind his head and looked Nick up and down. 'Mutual friends eh? If that means you know someone in the tyre or distributor business then you'd better push off.'

'I promise you I'm not selling anything. It's a private matter.' Nick held out his hand, even though the man hadn't got up from his chair. 'Nick Osbourne.'

Jack Easton ignored the hand.

'When I said we had mutual friends I don't even know if you were real friends exactly, but I'm hoping it may lead me to her daughter.'

The man burst into raucous laughter. 'That's about as clear as the oil in an engine,' he snorted. 'You'll have to do better than that.'

'Bonny Norton,' Nick said quickly before he lost his nerve.

His face tightened, his laughter cut short. He jerked up from a lounging position to sit bolt upright and folded his arms on his desk.

'Bonny's been dead for several years,' Nick quickly added, seeing he'd touched a raw nerve. 'Like I said it's her daughter I'm concerned with. Camellia.'

'Who are you?' Easton's eyes narrowed menacingly, as if he thought Nick was a private detective.

Nick was suddenly frightened. He had a feeling this man was quite capable of booting him through the window. 'I'm sorry. I haven't started out with this too well. You see I'm casting about in the dark. Two years ago a girl who said her name was Amelia Corbett came to work for my father. It has recently transpired that her name was really Camellia Norton and she had evidence that she was my half-sister. But before my father and I could talk to her further about this, she disappeared.'

'What's this got to do with me?' He relaxed marginally.

'Because the evidence she had was in letters written to her mother from three different men. My father Magnus was one of them. You were another.'

There was no movement in his expression or stance, yet he seemed to swell up in his chair.

'Look, Mr Easton. I haven't come here to make trouble or to dig up history. I've read your letters and I know how it was for you. My only interest is in finding Mel, and the only way I can do it is by backtracking.'

The man looked at Nick for a moment, his expression chillingly hostile.

'Why the hell do you want to find her?' he said eventually. 'If your father was involved with Bonny Norton he must know what a scheming little liar she was. Her kid belonged to John Norton.'

'I'd love that to be proved true,' Nick said. 'I don't want Mel for a sister.'

'Why? Afraid you might have to share out the family fortunes?'

'I wish it was as simple as that, Mr Easton. You see I'd fallen in love with her. It was only when I tried to tell her this that she admitted who she was. Then she ran away.'

To Nick's surprise Easton's insolent expression suddenly vanished. He slumped back into his chair. 'Oh God,' he said weakly. 'That damn woman. Even after she's dead she's still stirring up trouble.'

'That's exactly what my father said.' Nick moved tentatively towards him. He didn't quite dare sit down. 'But I have to find out the truth and I must find Mel. I thought you might know something that would help.'

Easton rubbed his face with his hands. 'I'm not her father,' he said at length. 'You can see that for yourself. A blonde and redhead don't make kids with hair as dark as hers.'

'You've seen her then?' Nick's heart leapt. 'When? Just recently?'

'Yup, I saw her,' Easton admitted. 'But it won't help you. It was well over two years ago. She came in here out of the blue, just like you have. I gave her thirty quid and told her to piss off.'

Nick was stunned.

'What, no anger?' Easton stood up. 'You public schoolboys are all the same. You never lose your stiff upper lip, not even when you should be sticking your fist in someone's face.'

'I doubt I could make much impression on yours,' Nick replied angrily. 'Besides I can imagine what Bonny put you through – it must have been a great shock, being confronted with her daughter.'

'How would you know?' Scorn twisted Jack's features.

'Because my father loved her and he's told me all about her. He was a married man too remember.'

'Then why is he such a damn fool to believe the kid is his?' Jack raised his voice. 'She married Norton. I saw the wedding photographs, Camellia looks just like him.'

Nick felt a surge of hope. 'Apparently Norton's blood group was wrong. But then that's no evidence that either my father or you were responsible. Once I find Mel maybe she and Dad can have further blood tests.'

'Do that.' Jack sat back down on his seat with a bump, as if he'd run out of steam. 'Look, I'm sorry, I'm not handling this very well, anymore than I did when the girl came to me. I was covering my back that day and I'm doing it again now. Sit down won't you.'

The man's sudden honesty was heartening, and Nick was glad finally to be offered a seat. 'I'm no threat to you,' he said. 'I came here to try and clear up a few mysteries. You don't know me from Adam and there's no reason why you should trust me.'

'I know a man I can trust from the set of his face,' Easton growled. 'It's guilt that's bothering me. I knew that girl had been through some sort of hell the day she came in here – but I just didn't want to get involved.'

Nick leaned forward in his seat. 'What did she say to make you think that?'

'Nothing. I just felt it. It was the tolerant way she spoke about things. People only get like that by going through the mill.'

Nick nodded. Easton was as perceptive as his father. It seemed Bonny went for a certain type. 'Didn't she tell you about her friends, where she'd come from, anything.'

'I just wanted her out of here,' Easton said quickly. 'All the time she was here I kept thinking Ginny would find out. I mean I don't get many young girls in here, people talk. But we talked a bit about Bonny and me when we were kids. She was desperate to know more about her mother.'

Over a glass of whisky Nick heard everything Easton could remember that he'd told Camellia – about Lydia Wynter dying and why he hadn't informed Bonny.

They discussed at around the same time the fact that Bonny had approached Jack and Magnus about Camellia.

'Why would she do that?' Nick asked. 'It doesn't make sense.'

'Attention I guess,' Easton sighed. 'She was always making things up so that people noticed her. I didn't get to the bottom of it though. She phoned me at the garage a couple of times, as well as writing, and she seemed very agitated. She said once that she was afraid her life was about to fall apart. I asked her all the usual things, like whether her old man was having an affair with someone, whether they were short of money? But it wasn't anything like that.'

'Strange!' Nick frowned.

'Tricky is the word I'd use to describe her,' Easton pulled a face. 'She must have known from Lydia that I was struggling to make ends meet in those days. If I'd had this place then it would have made more sense. But that's all long ago, over and done with. What's oddest to me is that she eventually drowned herself. I couldn't see her jumping in a river if the hounds of hell were after her. To be honest that's played on my mind a lot since Camellia told me. I even went down to Rye to look at all the old newspapers and check it out.'

'Did you find anything? I was intending to go there next.'

Easton shook his head. 'Maybe you'll have more luck than me though. I mean I couldn't go to the police and show any interest openly. You can if you're looking for Camellia.'

Nick got up. 'I'd better push off,' he said. 'Thanks for seeing me. Can I leave you my phone number just in case she contacts you again?' He took an Oaklands card from his pocket and left it on the desk.

'Of course.' Easton stood up. He paused for a second then grasped Nick's hand.

Their eyes locked in silent understanding, then Easton thumped Nick's shoulder.

'I hope it all works out for you,' he said gruffly. 'I liked Camellia, despite her mother. I like you too, Nick. Let me know the outcome?'

Chapter Nineteen

Sergeant Bert Simmonds approached the Mermaid Inn from the back entrance and paused to brush snowflakes from his sheepskin coat, glancing around to see if anyone fitted the description the library had given him that afternoon. He had been told the man was a typical journalist: young, well spoken, with untidy blond hair, and a brown leather jacket.

The Mermaid, standing near the top of Rye's most famous cobbled street, had once been Bert's favourite watering hole. It hadn't changed much since the fifteenth century: black beams hewn from old ships' timbers, ancient wooden settles and huge carved fireplaces big enough to roast an ox. Bert still had great affection for the place, but in recent years the old inn had become too much of a tourist attraction for his liking. Although Bert welcomed the prosperity visitors brought to the town, when he had a pint he liked his drinking companions to be unsophisticated, ordinary folk. These days the Mermaid seemed to be full of Americans with booming voices, or worse still Hooray Henrys down from London in their sports cars.

The snow storm which had started that afternoon had deterred any locals from coming out. It looked as if the few people in the bar were all guests at the inn. There was an elegant-looking couple sitting at the bar, and a lone male just inside the door – but he was at least forty and too well heeled to be the journalist. Two couples sat hugging the fire, but he could hear their American accents from across the room.

Bert was just about to move on when he spotted a young man tucked right up in the corner, half hidden by the side of the wooden settle, studying some notes in a shorthand pad. He wore a chunky navy-blue sweater, not a leather jacket, but Bert knew the chances of there being two such handsome strangers in town in January were very slim.

Bert walked straight up to him and smiled. 'Can I get you another pint?' he asked, picking up the empty glass.

The young man looked startled at such generosity from a total stranger.

'I'm Sergeant Simmonds from the local police,' Bert explained. 'I heard you were making some inquiries and I'd like to talk to you about them, if you don't mind.'

The other man leapt up, holding out his hand. 'Nick Osbourne,' he said. 'But let me get the drinks?'

Bert demurred and ordered two pints of bitter.

'Who told you I was making inquiries?' Nick asked once the sergeant had returned with the drinks. Nick thought he should have guessed this man was a policeman, even out of uniform. He was around forty-five, and heavily built, with a strong face, unwavering blue eyes and fair hair cut uncompromisingly short. His voice was pleasant; surprisingly soft for such a big man, with a rustic Sussex burr.

'Let's just say I have my sources,' Bert replied with a friendly smile. 'Now suppose you tell me why you're interested in this drowning?'

Nick was taken aback. He had arrived in Rye

soon after two and gone straight to the Library. He
had sensed a little hostility when he asked to look
at the local newspapers from July 1965 onwards,
but he had put that down to laziness on the part of
the women at the desk.

'Is it a crime in Rye to dig into the past?' he
asked, keeping his voice light. The two couples in
front of the fire got up and left, presumably to have
dinner in the dining room. Nick had eaten a couple
of sandwiches earlier, as the menu here was too
expensive for him. 'Or was there something
unusual about Bonny Norton's death that you
don't want people finding out?'

'Let's move closer to the fire,' Bert suggested.
They were almost alone in the bar now. Apart from
themselves, there was just the lone male and the
barman, and they were now deep in conversation.

'That's better,' he sighed once they'd taken more
comfortable seats in front of the blaze. He pulled
out his cigarettes, offering one to Nick. 'I'll be
honest with you. Here in Rye we are all sick of
sensationalistic journalists dredging up that old
story. Leave us be for goodness sake.'

Nick took a cigarette. He was confused now.
There had been nothing sensational in the accounts
he'd seen – in fact they had made very dull
reading. 'I think you've got me all wrong,' he said.
'I'm an actor, not a journalist.'

'Don't say someone's decided to make a film of
it,' the policeman groaned.

'I'm not writing a story or making a film,' Nick
said. 'I'm just trying to find Camellia Norton, the
dead woman's daughter. I hoped I might get a little
help here in her home town, but it seems I was
mistaken.'

'Camellia? Do you know her?'

'Of course,' Nick said. 'I wouldn't be looking for

441

her otherwise. She's been working for my father for the past two years.'

He took an Oaklands card from his wallet and handed it over. Then as an afterthought he pulled out a snapshot of himself and Mel taken by his father in Weston-super-Mare last summer.

'Does that satisfy you,' he asked with a touch of sarcasm. 'Now, I wonder if you could tell me whether you know if she's been here in the last three or four months?'

Bert Simmonds looked at the snapshot. The pretty dark-haired girl was willowy and sun-tanned, wearing a simple cotton dress. 'This is Camellia?' he asked.

Nick's irritation grew. 'I take it you've never met her.'

'That's just where you're wrong,' Bert said in a sharp tone. 'I knew Camellia right from when she was a baby. I just wouldn't have known her from this picture. As to whether she's been here or not, I doubt anyone in Rye would recognise this girl as Bonny Norton's daughter.'

Nick could see he had got off on the wrong footing. 'Look, Mr Simmonds,' he said more gently. 'Let me put you in the picture. This girl came to work for my father as Amelia Corbett. Both of us grew very fond of her, but it was only when she disappeared from Oaklands that I discovered her real name was Camellia Norton.'

'What did she do?'

Nick frowned. 'Do? What do you mean? Her position in our hotel?'

'No, I mean did she rob you? Or was it fraud or something?'

'Why should you think that?' Nick asked, scandalised. 'Mel isn't that sort of girl!'

For a moment the older man looked as confused as Nick felt. 'I'm sorry, it's just after all that last lot about her in the papers I guess I'm becoming as cynical as everyone else.'

Nick felt an unpleasant prickling down his spine. 'It seems to me, Mr Simmonds,' he said, 'that you and I are on different chapters of the same book. As you tracked me down here for some purpose and you've known Mel longer than I have, I think you should tell me all you know about her.'

Bert felt uneasy. He had come here tonight simply to try and make sure that there would be no repetition of the journalistic madness which had occurred three or four years before. There had been troupes of scavenging press men in town then, looking for a new angle to keep their squalid stories about Camellia's attack in Chelsea and the subsequent death of her friend going – and they found it when they discovered about Bonny Norton.

Town councillors, professional and tradespeople were appalled then to find their picturesque town suddenly linked with drugs, pornography and prostitution. They had panicked as they saw journalists photographing the Nortons' old home in Mermaid Street and the river where Bonny's body was found. Earlier today when Bert heard that questions were being asked again, he feared Camellia was involved in a new scandal.

His main aim had been to prevent any more adverse publicity for the town, but as a man who had once taken a paternal interest in Camellia he was deeply curious about her too. A sixth sense told him this young man was in love with her. Bert guessed that if he didn't tell Nick the truth, someone else would, and their version might not be as accurate or as unbiased as his own.

He told the story simply – the plain facts without any hearsay or embroidery – but just the same Nick turned pale.

'I'm sorry to be the one to break this to you.' Bert

put one hand on Nick's forearm in sympathy. He wished he'd stayed at home by the fire. 'You see I was very fond of Camellia when she was little. I was the one who found Bonny's body, and broke the news to Camellia. No one in Rye knows her family history better than me, and I have to say, after the example she was set by her mother, it wasn't really surprising that she fell by the wayside for a while.'

'I'm not upset by it.' Nick had a lump in his throat. 'Mel warned me she'd had a past – she said she worked in a nightclub, she even told me about her friend dying of an overdose. What's got me now is that I remember that case in the papers. I just never connected it with her.'

Bert went to the bar and Nick sank back into old memories. In 1970 he too had been living in Chelsea and used to drink in the Elm, a pub just around the corner from Beaufort Street. The case of the American and the nightclub hostess he brutalised had been the butt of many jokes: 'What do you call a tied-up tart?' The answer being 'Free and Easy'. Or 'What's a tied-up tart's favourite song?' 'Wriggle while you work.'

He felt absolute horror now that in those days he had found it funny. He hadn't had even a shred of sympathy for the girl. Even her unusual name hadn't registered; all he remembered clearly was thinking she probably deserved all she got.

As Bert came back with two whiskies he took one look at Nick's stricken face and felt a surge of sympathy. He'd been equally horrified when he discovered the girl was Camellia and felt so sad that life hadn't been kinder to her.

'Get this down you,' he said, passing over one of the whiskies. 'I can't take back what I've told you, and neither can I tell you where she is now, but I might be able to give you some useful background information. Suppose you tell me your side of the story first? And call me Bert, everyone else does.'

Nick hesitated for a moment or two. Aside from not wishing to admit Mel had withheld evidence at the time of her mother's death, he was also concerned for his father's reputation. But the policeman seemed to have integrity and a genuine affection for Mel. He had to trust him if he wanted to find out more.

He took a big gulp of whisky and launched into telling everything he knew. Bert listened carefully, his manner entirely sympathetic.

'Well, first off,' Bert said once Nick was through. 'I find it hard to believe Camellia wasn't John Norton's flesh and blood. She was dark like him, and she had his grave manner too. They were an ideal father and daughter, and he doted on her. Back in the fifties it was unusual for a man to be really involved with his children, but John was. Although he was away on business a great deal, when he was home he was always out walking with her, or down at the swings on The Salts. She was an old-fashioned little thing. She could tell you just where her dad was in the world, and he'd taught her to read long before she started school.'

Bert went on to tell Nick how the Nortons were always entertaining when he first came to Rye as a young constable, and how he used to stop to speak to Camellia when she was sitting on the steps outside their house. He blushed a little as he spoke of Bonny and Nick guessed he'd been sweet on her.

'Everyone was shocked when John died,' he went on. 'Presumably you've walked up Mermaid Street and seen how close the houses are to one another? Almost all of them are owned now by rich people, but back in the fifties there were ordinary folk living in many of them. Everyone knew one another, and the Nortons were liked – even if they

445

were newcomers and a great deal better off than their neighbours. Death is acceptable when someone is old or sick, but John was only just forty, and he left a beautiful young wife and a six-year-old daughter.'

'Did Bonny grieve for him?' Nick asked.

'Oh yes, for a month or so she was distraught. I believe Bonny never quite got over losing John. She certainly never found another man able to take his place.' He paused for a moment as if torn between his own opinion and those of others. 'But she didn't grieve openly long enough for some people. There are some who would tell you she appeared in a pink frock before John was hardly cold. As the years went by her behaviour made her a target for gossip. I'd have been hard pressed to find one person who didn't think she was glad to be a widow.'

'And Camellia, how did she take it?'

'On the surface, quite well. But even before her father's death she was a quiet solitary child, so it was difficult to know what was going on in her head. I was in a difficult position, being a young man then. I would have liked to have been able to pop in as I did when John was alive, but small towns being what they are, I had to keep my distance.'

Nick fell silent for a moment, digesting what he'd heard and adding it to information received from Magnus and Jack.

'I've got reason to believe Bonny had some sort of problem in the summer of 1954,' he said eventually. 'That was the time she met up with my father accidentally again, and contacted the other two men. Can you remember anything about that year?'

Bert frowned, trying to think back. 'Roger Bannister ran the four-minute mile and sweets came off the ration,' he smirked. 'I remember the first because I was a keen runner in those days, but he halved my speed record. As for the second I called round one day to the Nortons and Bonny was gloating over a huge bar of chocolate she'd just bought. She told me a story about a friend of hers who stole one like it in a village shop during the war and how she blackmailed him with it to let her join his all-boys gang. That brought her on to telling me about the time she nearly drowned.'

'I've heard that one, and met the chap who saved her,' Nick smiled. It was encouraging when stories he had heard were confirmed; it made the pictures more vivid. 'But can you remember anything more pertinent to the Nortons?'

Bert thought for a moment. 'Yes.' Suddenly he was very animated. 'Helena Forester, the Hollywood actress came to stay with them. Everyone was talking about it, she was red hot in those days, huge queues for her films everywhere and it was the first time a big star had come to Rye. I saw her and Bonny together in a big black Daimler, they were going off towards Hastings with Camellia standing up in the back waving like royalty.'

Nick leaned forward eagerly. 'Did Bonny tell you about this visit?'

'Did she!' he laughed. 'I don't think there was one person in Rye who didn't know Helena Forester was coming.'

'I meant afterwards,' Nick said.

'No, she didn't,' Bert shook his head. 'Now you come to mention it, she never said a word. Odd really, considering how she was always talking about the things they'd done together in the past and how she'd thrown up a part in a film herself to marry John.'

Nick smiled. Bonny had created quite a legend for herself with her tall stories, but this was the first he'd heard of a film part! 'Why do you suppose she didn't talk about it?'

Bert shrugged. 'Who knows! Maybe they fell out. I don't actually remember Bonny ever mentioning her again now I come to think about it. Helena certainly never came back to Rye. I'd remember if she had.'

'I've been told by an old boyfriend she contacted that summer that she claimed her life was about to fall apart. Have you got any ideas about that?'

Bert's clear blue eyes looked very knowing. 'She never said anything like that to me. Most women get a bit low sometimes for reasons us men can't fathom. Bonny liked to be centre stage, maybe Helena visiting made her feel a bit grey and dull.'

Nick felt there must have been a far bigger reason for Bonny suddenly wanting attention that summer than feeling 'a bit grey' – but as Bert didn't seem able to expand on it, he moved on to ask about the later years after John died.

'She just got wilder and wilder,' Bert said sadly. 'She spent money on clothes like she'd just won the Pools. She'd invite great parties of people in here to eat and footed the bills. Sometimes she took herself off to London and stayed in a posh hotel. Of course in those days we believed John had left her a fortune, but I found it strange that all the London friends she'd had while John was alive gradually dropped her. The rumours about her were rife – according to gossip no man was safe with her – and then the serious drinking began. I've seen her in here so drunk she couldn't stand. She used to joke that it was good she lived so close!'

'Poor Camellia had to watch this happening then?'

'That was the worst of it,' Bert sighed deeply. 'The poor kid grew fatter and fatter, more and more withdrawn. She had no friends – other mothers wouldn't allow their kids to play with her.'

As Bert went on Nick felt sickened. It was all so much worse than Mel had implied to his father. He heard about the bailiffs coming in to take the furniture from the house in Mermaid Street; the seedy drunken parties in the squalid house in Fishmarket Street; the men who came and went. When Bert graphically described the night he'd found Camellia walking home from Hastings, Nick felt tears prickling his eyes.

He felt ashamed too for the way he'd rebelled after his mother died. Magnus might have been distant for a time, and maybe he didn't attend every sportsday, but in comparison to what Mel had been through, his teenage years looked like one glorious picnic.

'My mother befriended her after that,' Bert went on. 'She taught her a bit of cooking, how to iron things properly, sewing and knitting, the sort of things her own mother should've seen to. Camellia never complained about Bonny though, she just accepted that was the way Bonny was. The moment she was old enough she got a Saturday and holiday job at the bakery and it was that summer that Bonny died. When I said no one in Rye could recognise Camellia from that picture, I meant as she was then. She was grossly fat, Nick. I'd say at fifteen she weighed perhaps thirteen stone.'

'Really?' Nick couldn't imagine Mel anyway but slim. Yet he remembered her encouraging one of the waitresses to diet, making a chart of her weight loss, and complimenting her at every lost pound. Now he understood why she took it so personally.

'What do I do now?' he asked. 'I don't have a clue where to look for her.'

'I wish I could offer some advice.' Bert looked

glum. 'But it's been my experience that people who run away, stay hidden until they feel ready to be found, whatever lengths we go to. If I were you son, I'd go home, get on with your career and just wait.'

Nick didn't think he could do that. 'Just tell me one thing more?' he asked. 'Was there ever any doubt in your mind that Bonny's death wasn't suicide?'

'A great deal of doubt,' Bert sighed deeply. His blue eyes were a little glazed now with the whisky, but there was something very resolute in them. 'If she was going to kill herself in my view she would have staged it like Marilyn Monroe's death, naked on silk sheets wearing nothing but Chanel No 5. She'd even have had her hair done that morning. But I dug and dug at the time. I went over that house in Fishmarket Street painstakingly. I read every last letter, studied every scrap of paper and I didn't find anything. I'm sure there was a man, somewhere. Camellia told me herself she'd heard Bonny talking on the phone to someone late at night and she said she had been excitable for several weeks, as if expecting something good to happen any day. Someone brought Bonny back to Rye that night and even falling down drunk, I don't believe she'd go walking by the river, much less jump in. It just wasn't her way. But I was a lone voice, saying things no one else wanted to hear. If I could've found one real clue it might've been different, but I didn't.'

Nick went out into the street with Bert at closing time. They were both a little unsteady on their feet but the long and intimate talk had created a bond between them.

Mermaid Street looked enchanting under its thick blanket of snow. Nick had to resist a childish urge to run down it making footprints.

'That was her house,' Bert said pointing out number twelve almost opposite. There was a light just inside the lattice window and Nick could see enough to get a picture of how it had been when John Norton was alive. 'Camellia used to sit on those steps on summer's evenings playing with her dolls.'

'Take it easy going home.' Nick grasped the older man's shoulder. 'Don't go falling in the snow.'

'I've got real policeman's feet,' Bert grinned. 'I might wobble but I won't fall down. Mind you I might get a rolling pin over the head when I get in, I said I wouldn't be more than an hour.'

A current passed between them, an unspoken message of mutual gratitude, understanding and even affection.

'Thanks,' Nick said gruffly.

Bert turned and moved away, but he stopped after a few yards to look back, big and burly in his sheepskin coat. 'Let me know how things turn out,' he called back. 'And if you find her, give her my love.'

It was two nights later in a guest house in Fulham that Nick finally gave way to dejection. There was nothing really wrong with the room he'd been given, aside from it being very cold. It was small and box-like, with an orange candlewick bedspread, an ugly central light with three imitation candles and a print on the wall of Looe in Cornwall. He wondered if Mel was in a similar room somewhere in London, sitting there reflecting bitterly on the past, as depressed and lonely as he felt himself.

Nick had so much background information about her now, thanks to Bert. By tramping around Rye in the snow the following day, with the help of the landmarks he'd been given, he'd recreated her childhood and adolescence. Perhaps if it had been warm and sunny, the images which came to him might have been less wretched, but walking from her pretty first home in Mermaid Street, down to the second in Fishmarket Street with icy slush under his feet and a chilling wind nipping at his ears, he could well imagine her desolation at being ejected from her beautiful childhood home and transplanted somewhere so grim.

Number twenty-two was as desolate-looking as Bert had described: its windows filthy, its paint peeling. Heavy traffic thundered past, splattering the narrow pavement, doorsteps and even windows with slush and grit. Nick walked on down to the secondary modern a little further on, imagining Mel as a fat, friendless teenager, going home to an empty house.

Later he climbed the steep steps up to the High Street and bought a sausage roll from the bakery. He wondered whether the plump rosy faced woman behind the counter with iron-grey hair was Mrs Rowlands. He didn't attempt to engage her in conversation, it was enough just to get a glimpse of the kitchens behind the shop and imagine Mel working there.

Finally before driving back to London, he went down to the quay and looked across the water towards where Bert said he found Bonny's body. It was high tide, the river brown and swollen. Seagulls were circling overhead, their squawking as plaintive as the grey sky. Nick was glad to get back in his car. Rye might be one of the prettiest towns on the south coast, but he'd immersed himself so deeply in Mel's sad and lonely childhood years that he never wanted to return. He was sure she wouldn't either.

When he got to London that evening he'd hoped

to make an appointment to see Sir Miles Hamilton for the next morning, then spend the afternoon in the newspaper archives before driving on home to Bath. Instead Sir Miles couldn't see him for a day, which meant staying in London for two nights. There was far too much time for him to sit and brood, not only on Mel's past, but on his own.

He had used to like reading sensational stories about famous personalities or even strangers in newspapers, but earlier today he'd discovered how painful it was to read such things about someone he loved. With the official details Bert had given Nick already, the story of Mel's ordeal with her American attacker took on a whole new sickening and harrowing perspective. But as he moved on to read about her friend Beatrice Jarret's death, his eyes had swum with tears of sympathy. To the journalists who'd bled the story dry, she was yet another casualty of the sixties, to be joined soon by Jimi Hendrix, Janis Joplin, Jim Morrison and Brian Jones. But whereas these famous people had been portrayed sympathetically as folk heroes, who'd just lived too hard and fast, Beatrice, and by association, Camellia, were portrayed as an affront to public morality, a symbol of a sick society.

Nick stripped down to a tee shirt and underpants and got into bed. He wished he had a stiff drink to warm him inside, because he knew sleep wasn't going to come easily. His mind was too full of vivid and painful images.

It was ironic to think that he and Mel could easily have met four or five years earlier. While she was living in Oakley Street, he had been less than ten minutes' walk away in Onslow Square. Had he met her and Bee then in 1969, no doubt he would have looked down at them as a pair of common dolly birds. In those days he felt he was very much part of the youthful Chelsea aristocracy, the beautiful jet set people who numbered rock stars, actors and high-bred rich kids in their decadent clan.

'Honky Tonk Woman' by the Rolling Stones was the song which seemed to epitomise those heady days. Nick had been at parties then with Mick Jagger, Marianne Faithfull, Brian Jones, Paul Getty and so many more famous people. All his clothes came from King's Road boutiques, ruffled silk shirts, velvet flares, tapestry jackets like a Regency dandy.

Chelsea and drugs were inseparable: they were as much part of being cool as handmade boots from the Chelsea Cobbler, antique lace dresses from Kensington Market, Harrod's trays of hors d'oeuvres and the sounds of Smokey Robinson, Otis Redding and The Cream at the many parties. Hand-mirrors left lying around held traces of snorted coke, the punch was as likely as not laced with acid and no number of lighted joss sticks hid the smell of cannabis.

Yet it wasn't the drugs Nick did in those days, or the pompous way he'd swaggered around Chelsea, which embarrassed and concerned him now, so much as the callous way he'd treated Belinda, the moment he thought he'd made it.

He had met her in 1966 when he was eighteen. She worked in the SKR, a café by South Kensington tube station, which was much loved by the bedsit dwellers in the area. Nick was then in a tiny room on the Fulham Road, living a hand-to-mouth existence with a bit of bar work while he auditioned for acting jobs. Belinda must have guessed he was hungry and broke that day when he came up to the counter for only tea and toast, because she passed over a free full breakfast with an understanding wink.

She was the prettiest girl he'd ever seen, small, blonde and blue-eyed with the added attraction of big breasts. The next time he went into the SKR he was feeling flush as he'd just finished some extra work and as the café was quiet, he invited her to join him for a cup of tea and a bacon sandwich.

Belinda was seventeen and lived at home with her working-class parents in Fulham, only streets away from the guest house he was in tonight. From that first cup of tea they were instantly attracted to each other. Nick couldn't claim he took her out, he rarely had the money, but Belinda would come to his bedsitter after work with a ready-cooked meal for them to share, or they'd have a drink in the Elm and then on to the ABC cinema.

Belinda was a virgin, with strong ideas about remaining so until she married, but she lost her inhibitions when they fell in love and Nick promised they'd get married as soon as he got a decent part in a play or film. He had meant it too: she was the centre of his world, and he would go to meet her at the café hardly able to contain his passion for her until they got back to his room. They were more than lovers, they were friends and soul-mates too. Nick could talk to her in a way he'd never managed with other girls and felt she alone truly understood him. Belinda would wash and iron his clothes for him, offering him loving encouragement when he went to auditions, commiserating when he didn't get parts, sharing his joy when he got the odd advertisement or walk-on part, and giving him money when he had none of his own. All he really gave her in return was a head full of dreams about the wonderful life they'd share once he became a big star.

Nick pulled the bedclothes round him tighter and tried his usual trick to make himself sleep, imagining waves pounding on the seashore. But tonight it wouldn't work. His mind slipped back to June 1969. He was in his new spacious flat at

Onslow Gardens. He could see himself sitting on the bare boards of the still unfurnished, undecorated lounge, talking on the telephone, when Belinda came bounding in from work.

It was just a few weeks before the first episode of *Hunnicroft Estate* was shown on television. Belinda had been his loyal, supportive girlfriend for almost three years and Nick had money at last. As Belinda's parents frowned on 'living in sin' she couldn't move in with him, but they planned to get engaged on the launch of the series and married within the year. Nick bought a double bed, a wardrobe and a cooker, but as he was off filming a great deal of the time, he hadn't got around to doing anything more to the flat.

Belinda dropped her shopping bag at the door, kicked off her white high-heeled shoes and ran across the room to him, smothering him in a hug that smelled of fried food, regardless that he was talking to someone. He sensed by her flushed face and her excitement that she intended to step up the pressure on him in some way.

Nick cut his call short and put the phone down.

'I've been into Peter Jones today,' she said in a rush. 'I've got lots of brochures to show you. I thought we'd have a cream carpet and a big coffee-coloured three-piece, then we could have one of those teak wall units all along that wall.'

Nick wasn't really listening to her, his mind was elsewhere. Everything had changed for him since he started filming. Other actors and actresses who'd barely acknowledged him before, suddenly wanted to befriend him, inviting him to dinners and parties. Suddenly he was aware there was a far racier, more glamorous world out there than the small cosy one he'd been sharing until now with Belinda. He began to have doubts about getting engaged, and even about Belinda's suitability as a girlfriend.

'I'll make some big cushions, and we'll have plants everywhere,' Belinda went on.

Nick had been out to lunch with his agent and aside from a couple of bottles of wine there, he'd also smoked three joints since getting home, another habit he'd picked up since starting filming. He resented Belinda steaming in with plans for *his* flat, and all the little things which had been irritating him about her for several weeks, suddenly erupted to the surface.

'Can't you just see it?' She danced round the room in her bare feet, oblivious to his surly silence. 'My brother and his mate will come and paint it for us at the weekend. I've got the paint samples in my bag, we'll choose them tonight and as it's my day off tomorrow we can get everything then and arrange for the furniture to be delivered on Monday.'

Nick could only stare at her. She looked common. Her pink minidress was too tight, emphasising her big breasts and showing the line of her knickers beneath it. Her long straight hair needed a wash, and she hadn't got the right kind of legs for short skirts. They were like milk bottles. He didn't like the way she drew starry eyelashes beneath her eyes either. It might look all right on Twiggy, but on her it looked cheap. But it was her voice that got him down the most: its high pitch and that awful London accent. He might be able to dress her up in something sensational to go to premieres and smart cocktail parties, but the moment she opened her mouth she gave the game away.

'Let's go to bed?' he said as a stalling tactic. He felt that in another moment she'd be pulling out brochures and paint charts from that huge plastic handbag, and he couldn't bear it.

'I was going to cook you some tea,' she said, her pale blue eyes clouding over. 'I got some sausages from work.'

If it had been steak and salad he just might not have lost his temper – he was hungry after all – but sausages left over from her crummy café were a further reminder of the ever widening divide between them.

'I don't want any fucking sausages,' he snapped. 'And it's dinner in the evening, not tea!'

Her face crumpled. 'Oh Nicky,' she said, holding out her arms like a small child. 'Don't be like this with me. I'm tired and hungry. I've been at work since six this morning.'

He held her from force of habit, smoothing her hair and making comforting noises, but inside the irritation was growing stronger. He didn't really want to hurt Belinda, but he couldn't help thinking of Lauren, the tall, slinky model he'd met a few days ago. She would be in the Village Gate club in King's Road tonight and he was hoping that Belinda would go home early enough for him to nip out later.

Belinda lifted her face up to his and kissed him, pressing her big tits against his chest. Despite everything Nick felt himself responding.

'Take me to bed.' she whispered. 'Never mind the food.'

Lovemaking with Belinda had always been wonderful; it had sustained him in the days when he thought he'd never get a break, and added extra joy to the good times. Before Nick met her there had been several other girls, but none of them had been as responsive, sensuous or giving as Belinda. Even tonight when his heart wasn't entirely in it, she still made him feel good.

She sat astride him, moaning deliriously, her hair tumbling over her big breasts. He reached forward for them, mechanically massaging them, letting his mind turn to Lauren and how she would look naked.

She was almost six feet tall and slim as a whip, her hip bones so sharp they'd grind against his, shiny dark hair flowing over her bronzed skin, brilliant-white even teeth and luscious full lips.

Lost in the fantasy of being with Lauren, he drew Belinda down to him to kiss her. As her hair floated over his face, the smell of chip fat brought him sharply back to reality and he lost his erection instantly.

'What's the matter?' she asked, moving back up to a sitting position.

'It's you,' he said, pushing her off and sitting up. 'You stink of chips.'

To his surprise she didn't burst into tears, but leapt off him and grabbed her clothes. 'I probably do smell of food,' she said, tossing back her hair from her face. Her eyes were blazing; something he'd never seen before. 'I've spent the last twelve hours in a kitchen. If you hadn't suggested we went straight to bed I'd have had a bath, then cooked you a nice "dinner". I even had a bottle of wine in the shopping bag.'

She was into her tiny black panties and bra so quickly, Nick was astounded. 'Where are you going?' he asked.

'Home,' she snapped. 'You've been getting pickier and pickier lately. Even if I didn't go to a posh school like you I'm bright enough to know why.'

'Don't be silly. I've just had my mind on other things,' he said weakly. He wasn't entirely sorry he'd provoked this. At least he could go out later to the Village Gate.

'You've had your mind on being a big star,' she said tersely, wriggling into her tight pink dress. 'And you don't think I'm good enough for you any

459

longer. Well, Nick Osbourne, I won't hang around and embarrass you. I just hope the next girl you meet wants you for yourself not your money.'

'You don't embarrass me,' he said quickly, all at once aware of how final this sounded. 'I'm just a bit uptight. Maybe I just need a bit of time alone to sort myself out.'

'Well, you'll get it now, won't you?' She tossed her hair back, opened the wardrobe and began to pull out the few clothes she'd left there.

'What are you taking those for?' he asked, sitting up as she began to stuff them into her shopping bag.

'Because I'm not coming back,' she snapped, without even turning to look at him. 'I know what you want, Nick, and it isn't me. Go ahead and do whatever it is you've got on your mind. Screw all those glamour girls who'll come crawling out of the woodwork as soon as you're on TV. Get some prune-faced debutante to iron your shirts. Just remember that I loved you when you were nobody.'

Nick was stunned. 'Don't be silly,' he said feebly.

'Silly am I?' She turned to him as she pushed her feet into her high heels. 'Do you know what you are? A conceited overgrown school boy. You think you're "it" now you're going to be on television. Well, let me tell you there's hundreds of actors out there who are more talented than you. You were just luckier than them, that's all.'

Anger made him leap off the bed and he'd punched her before he could stop himself. As she fell back against the wall the shock in her wide blue eyes cut him to the quick.

'I didn't mean to do that.' He reached forward to wipe away the trickle of blood from her lip. 'I'm sorry Belinda, I don't know what came over me.'

She backed away from him, but to his surprise

460

she didn't look frightened, only outraged. 'I know what came over you,' she snarled at him. 'It's the real Nicholas Too-Big-for-His-Boots Osbourne. Don't even try to get in touch with me again, you thankless bastard!'

She left then, sweeping out of the flat with a pride he hadn't known she possessed. His flat felt suddenly cold and empty.

Nick sat up, punched the pillow angrily and lay down again. He couldn't understand why his mind could recall shabby incidents in his life with such clarity, yet he had a job to remember phone numbers.

'Poor Belinda,' he whispered. 'You deserved so much better than that.'

But even though he tried to clear his mind of that period in his life, it seemed to be stuck there, forcing him to look at how he'd been.

He didn't give himself time to miss Belinda. That night and every other one he went out, playing the part of the rising star. Within the week he had been invited on a television game show, had two interviews on the radio and had been to a party in Cheyne Walk where he met Donovan and Steve Marriott from the Small Faces and he believed he had arrived.

The drug taking started as something all the stars did. Speed made everything more fun, acid opened his mind and a few joints helped him relax. He bought a Lotus Elan on hire purchase, filled his wardrobe with dandified clothes, and he slept with a different girl every night of the week. He never went home to visit his father.

His agent warned him to calm down, saying that one television series didn't mean his acting career was secure. But he didn't believe it, after all hardly a day passed without journalists begging for an interview. But his head was turned most of all by becoming part of the Chelsea jet set. New friends inviting him to fly off to Paris, or to a country house for a weekend. They were rich and famous themselves, knew he soon would be too.

But *Hunnicroft Estate* flopped. Nick could still see those terrible reviews as if they were printed permanently on the back of his hand. 'A shabby, desolate series.' 'Purile rubbish.' The reviews of Nick's personal performance were slightly kinder, particularly in the more subversive 'arty' magazines. But even so the telephone stopped ringing, and his agent looked embarrassed when Nick called at his office.

If at that point Nick had proved to producers that he was a seriously committed actor by going to every audition in town, he might have salvaged something. But he was too arrogant for that. Instead he went out nightly to Blaise's, Annabel's and the Speak Easy, believing that by acting the part of a big star, he would miraculously become one. He took 'sleepers' when he got home in the early hours, stayed in bed all day, then dosed himself up with 'leapers' to face the next night of posing.

Sometimes when he woke with his mouth feeling like the bottom of a birdcage and his hands so shaky he could barely hold a cup, he would think longingly of Belinda. But almost as soon as he'd popped another pill into his mouth he'd convince himself that he was about to be offered another leading role.

It was during this period that he heard about the girl being tied up and assaulted in Beaufort Street. He used to go in the Elm at lunch time to perk himself up with a few drinks before doing his daily swagger down King's Road chatting up girls in the boutiques, and calling in to see his agent.

But his agent was suddenly always out when he

called and his money was running out too. The Lotus Elan was the first casualty, reclaimed by the hire purchase company when he couldn't keep up the payments. The telephone was cut off next, and then an eviction notice arrived for non-payment of rent at Onslow Gardens.

For several weeks he used all his old friends by crashing in their flats, pretending he was looking for another flat, but he had no money by then even for another bedsitter and it wasn't long before he'd run out of friends willing to put him up.

The only jobs he was offered in that time were a dog food advert and a tiny part in a play that folded as soon as it opened, but still he refused to face what was happening. One by one his friends dropped him. Curtains twitched when he rang on doorbells, but no one opened the door. When he went into the Elm, his old drinking partners turned their backs as if they hadn't seen him. The only girls who welcomed him for the night were the dim sort who got their kicks from sleeping with anyone who'd had five minutes of fame and believed his stories that he was about to sign a film contract. They washed his clothes, fed him and lent him money, but the money went on scoring drugs and he never paid them back. When one got wise to him, there was always another. Acting parts might be thin on the ground, but there were gullible girls by the score.

It was desperation that made him attempt to gate-crash a party in Hammersmith in the spring of 1971. Nick had overheard a conversation about a party in St Peter's Square, where Vanessa Redgrave lived, and in his fuddled state he assumed the party was at her house, and that it would be teeming with actors, agents and film producers.

He didn't give himself time to consider the likelihood of being thrown out. Even through his

463

drug-induced haze, he knew he was in trouble: he had no fixed address and no money to get one, and he'd resorted to stealing food and drink from supermarkets just so the girls who put him up would believe he was sincere. If he could just get someone interested in him again as an actor, he could at least go home and ask his father to bail him out one last time.

He spent his last five pounds on a haircut, and promised a plain little girl in a dry cleaners a night on the town with him if she'd just press his velvet jacket and launder his best frilly shirt.

By the time he arrived glassy eyed on speed in St Peter's Square without even enough money for a tube, let alone a cab fare, he actually believed he'd been invited to the party. It was a warm night for spring and the sounds of Burt Bacharach wafted through large open windows at number five.

A burly man in evening dress opened the front door.

'Good evening,' he said. 'Nicholas Osbourne.'

To his surprise the man barred his way. 'Your invitation sir? I haven't anyone of that name on the guest list.'

Nick looked through his pockets, insisted that he must have lost his invitation, then tried again to walk on through the door.

A hand clamped down on the shoulders of his jacket, and before he could even protest he was manhandled down the steps to the pavement.

'No one gate-crashes Mr Soames' parties,' the man said shaking him like a rag doll.

'What on earth are you doing, Ronald?' A woman's voice rang out from behind them.

They both turned. The woman was standing at the top of the steps. She was perhaps forty, but as exotic as an orchid, with black lustrous hair and a deep violet low-cut evening dress.

'He's one of my guests, Ronald,' she said indignantly. 'What are you doing to him?'

Nick was so surprised by this magical intervention, he couldn't even speak.

'He isn't on the guest list, ma'am,' Ronald said.

'I forgot to add him,' she said, tripping down the steps towards Nick and taking his arm.

Nick allowed himself to be led back up the steps, before looking back to smirk at poor Ronald.

But as they stepped into the hall, the woman turned to him under the glittering chandelier, reached up to adjust the frills on his shirt and smiled knowingly. Her eyes were pure violet, just like her dress, and they danced with amusement. 'You naughty boy,' she whispered. 'This party is going to be an infernal bore, so I had to find out why on earth you wanted to gate-crash it.'

Nick had never fancied older women, but this woman's creamy skin, voluptuous curves and her low, melodic voice struck some chord inside him.

'I thought this was the Redgraves' house,' he whispered back.

She looked puzzled for a moment and drew back, appraising him. 'Well, it isn't, and they aren't likely to come either,' she smiled. 'But I'm Kate Hardy and I'm bored stiff, so if you still want to stay I'll be glad of your company.'

No stars turned up at the party. There were artists of the commercial variety, bankers and lawyers and their wives. Kate held his arm and introduced Nick as 'her actor friend'. If it hadn't been for her, he would have left: there was nothing and no one to interest him here.

The house had the same kind of dignified perfection as Oaklands: Chinese carpets, exquisite antique furniture and a collection of impressionist paintings in the drawing room.

'That's why Harry Soames is so careful whom he

465

lets into his house,' Kate said quietly. 'Do you know about art?'

'No,' he admitted. 'Nothing.'

'Thank God for that,' she laughed. It was the sexiest and most infectious sound Nick had ever heard. 'I've been surrounded by art bores for most of my life and I'm sick to death of the subject.'

Kate told him she sometimes acted as a hostess for Harry Soames, who was a bachelor. She pointed out a tall, thin man with hawk-like features talking earnestly to another middle-aged portly man in one corner. 'He's been my friend and lawyer for years,' she added. 'But these days my patience is growing thin. He will surround himself with the most tedious people.'

Nick felt the serious-faced, balding money men looking at him curiously, and several of their middle-aged wives sniffed in disapproval as if they suspected he was Kate's gigolo. He drank gin and tonic after gin and tonic and wondered how he could manipulate this strange twist of fate to his favour. The last thing he remembered was Tom Jones singing 'Love Me Tonight' as he danced with Kate in the almost empty drawing room. She smelled of lilac and her voluptuous curves seemed to mould themselves onto his body.

He woke the next morning to find himself in a pink and white bedroom. Kate was asleep beside him, as beautiful without make-up as she had been the night before, one big soft breast swelling out of a pale pink lace nightgown.

He crept out of bed and went to the window, drawing back the heavy silk curtains. The sun was shining on a lush green lawn. Beyond were trees, and between gaps he could see the Thames sparkling.

The garden and the bedroom suggested she was wealthy; the diamond ring and gold necklace dropped carelessly on the dressing table suggested she was also naïve. He felt he had fallen on his feet.

'What went wrong in your life?'

He spun round, surprised by such a penetrating question so early in the day. Kate was sitting up in bed hugging her knees, her black hair tousled, her violet eyes bleary.

'What makes you ask that?' he said, immediately on the defensive. He picked up his pants from a chair and hastily put them on.

'I know you were very drunk last night, but I felt your suppressed anger and disappointment,' she said, raising one eyebrow. 'Why don't you tell me about it?'

For the first time ever he couldn't think of a quick retort. Her questioning eyes reminded him of his mother. He wondered if he'd screwed her and whether it had been a disaster.

'We didn't make love.' She smiled as if she'd tuned into his thoughts. 'I showed you where the bathroom was and the next thing I knew you were in my bed fast asleep. Now, Nick, I'm not a rich woman looking for a young plaything, I brought you home with me because I guessed you had nowhere else to go. If you don't want to talk to me you can take your clothes and leave now, but if you would like to stay, as a friend, I expect honesty.'

At first he told her just enough so she'd let him stay. Her home reminded him of his mother's taste – the soft pastel colours, the dainty china and flowers – and it felt soothing. Despite his first impressions, Kate wasn't wealthy: it was an ordinary semi-detached house, decorated and furnished with care, and she earned her living doing accountancy from home. She later told him that her ex-husband had given her the house as a divorce settlement.

After that first night she put him in her spare

bedroom, a tiny yellow and white room that made him think of a nursery. She sent him back to Chelsea with only enough money for the return fare to pick up his belongings, and made him sign on at the Labour Exchange. He went along with it because he had no choice, but for the first day or two he spent a great deal of time considering stealing something from her and making off.

But Kate was wise to him: she gave him odd jobs to do around the house, leaving her office door open while she worked, and she had a knack of appearing with a cup of tea at crucial moments. As the days passed and his head cleared from the drugs which had been so much part of his life, he began to realise just how low he had sunk and how fortunate he was that he'd met Kate.

It was a long time since he'd had regular meals and Kate was a good cook. She made him help prepare the food and wash up, and in the evenings they watched the television together, listened to music or talked. She was restful company, interested in him, but not nosey, concerned about him, yet not overbearing. It was like a convalescence. Slowly he began to tell Kate about himself. The bitterness came out first: he put all the blame for his downfall onto other people and Kate listened and commiserated. Then he found himself moving back to tell her about his childhood, his older brother and sister, how his parents restored Oaklands, and the happy times until his mother died. Kate's gentle questions were like a key turning in a long-locked door.

He had never told anyone, not even Belinda how he hated his father for not bringing him home from school in time to see his mother before she died, but he told Kate. He told her how empty Oaklands had seemed in the long summer holidays, and described how he had made a conscious effort to do badly at school to get some sort of response from his father.

Finally he told her about Belinda, and what they'd had together. For the first time he was able to see that he alone was responsible for everything.

'Nick,' she said, fixing him with those lovely compassionate eyes, 'you haven't lost everything. You've just been flipped back to the start line. You are still young and handsome, you still have that talent which got you that television series. You have a father who loves you. You are healthy and strong. Now that's more than enough to start out again.'

'But my name is mud,' he said and to his shame he began to cry. 'I've hurt so many people. How can I start again?'

She put her arms around him and drew him to her big breasts as if he were a small boy. 'By looking deep into yourself and understanding why you did those things. It's my belief your mother's death is at the root of it all,' she said, gently caressing his neck. 'I suspect you locked your anger and sorrow inside you at the time. But these feelings can't stay shut away forever, and when they do finally rise to the surface we don't always recognise what they are.

'You felt powerful once you'd got your first good acting job. Maybe you were testing Belinda to make sure she loved you enough to stay forever, no matter how awful you were to her.'

'But I didn't want her then, I wanted to be free,' he sniffed.

'Did you?' She lifted his head between her two hands and looked right into his eyes. 'Then why did you blot out everything with drugs? Wasn't it because without them you felt exactly as you did after your mother died, alone and frightened? You

469

have to learn to be a man now, Nick, to take responsibility for your own life.'

Kate was right about so many things. She knew nothing about the drug scene – the wildness of the sixties had passed her by – but she knew all about people's frailties.

Nick got a job as a barman in a pub in Barnes and Kate introduced him to a retired drama teacher who coached him for a couple of hours each afternoon. Every week they studied *The Stage* together and decided which auditions Nick should go to.

Seven months later in November that year, Nick finally came home to tell Kate he had a part in a television play about the army.

'It's only very small,' he said, throwing his arms around her and bouncing her up and down in her kitchen. 'I'm just one of the squaddies, not the hero, and I'll have to get my hair cut short. But it's a start, isn't it?'

'A whole new beginning,' she smiled. 'I'm so very proud of you, Nick. Now get on the phone and tell your Dad and make him proud too.'

Nick gave up the struggle to sleep and sat up to light a cigarette. He wondered how Kate was, the last time he heard from her she was getting married again and moving to Suffolk. If she had still been living out at Chiswick he could have gone to visit her tomorrow before going home. He could bet she'd have had some suggestions about finding Mel.

There was only Sir Miles Hamilton left to see now. Would such an old man be able to remember anything about an event twenty years earlier?

An elderly man with stooped shoulders and wire-rimmed spectacles answered the door at Sir Miles's house in Holland Park.

'Do come in,' he said and ushered Nick across a wide hall with a polished wooden floor and into a library at the back of the house. 'Sir Miles will be with you in a few minutes, Mr Osbourne.'

The library was warm and impressive. A large coal fire crackled away in the hearth and the entire wall space right up to the ceiling was filled with books. Nick was too nervous to sit down in one of the winged armchairs by the fire so he stayed standing, quickly running his eyes over the books to try and get an insight into the taste of the man whose name was so often in *The Stage*.

There were the inevitable leather-bound classics, collections of poetry and legal books, but more interesting to Nick's mind was the enormous number of paperback thrillers. Somehow he had never imagined anyone with a title reading such books, let alone displaying them openly.

Nick braced himself at the sound of approaching feet, but as the door opened he was thrown. The black-and-white press photographs he had seen in the past hadn't prepared him for such a big or striking man.

Sir Miles wore a dark blue smoking jacket over grey flannel trousers, and a lighter blue cravat tucked into an open-necked shirt. He had several chins, a fat stomach and a somewhat bulbous red nose. Nick knew he was over eighty but he looked closer to sixty-five.

'Thank you for seeing me, sir,' Nick said holding out his hand.

Sir Miles gripped it firmly. 'I must confess to being a trifle intrigued by your phone call,' he said in a deep, almost growl. His eyes were almost hidden by folds of skin, showing only the dark pupils. 'You said it was a delicate matter.'

471

'Yes it is, sir. I'm still not quite sure how I should approach it.'

'It's quite private here.' Sir Miles motioned for Nick to sit down and took the other armchair himself. 'So fire away.'

If he knew Sir Miles better, Nick might have remarked how like W. C. Fields he looked. Instead he took out Sir Miles's letter to Bonny and handed it to him. 'This is the reason I wanted to talk to you, sir,' he said. 'This and some other letters from other men, including my father, were found by Camellia Norton on her mother's death.'

'Bonny's dead?' To Nick's surprise Sir Miles chuckled. 'What a relief for mankind.'

Nick had to smile. He liked irreverent people.

Sir Miles merely glanced at the letter, then tossed it back to Nick. 'Such a silly, empty-headed woman,' he said. 'Goodness only knows why Norton married her. She managed to charm my wife, but I never had any time for her.'

The old man's attitude was so indifferent that Nick felt his visit would prove to be a waste of time. But just in case he might get a little more background, he quickly launched into a brief explanation as to how he came by the letter.

'My father, Magnus, would have preferred to see you himself, but he isn't well enough,' he finished off.

'So you are Magnus Osbourne's son,' Sir Miles looked hard at him and frowned. 'I haven't seen him in years. We didn't know each other well, as I expect he's told you, but we ran into each other occasionally at social functions. A good man I believe.'

Nick wasn't sure that Miles had fully understood him; there was absolutely no reaction to hearing John Norton might not be Camellia's father. But

472

then it was a complicated story, and he was very old.

'I believe you were a guest at the Nortons' wedding,' he said. 'Did you have any reason to doubt John was Camellia's father?'

'None what so ever!' Miles exclaimed. 'I felt a great deal of sympathy for John that he was so besotted with that woman, but I saw him many times right up until a few months before his untimely death and everything he ever said about the child, pointed to her being his flesh and blood.'

'Would you mind telling me what Bonny said in her letter to you?' Nick said warily. 'You used the word "scandal" in your reply, and you sounded angry. I don't wish to pry into your affairs, I'm just trying to build up a picture of what happened back then.'

'It was clap-trap. She made up a ridiculous, vicious story which I have no intention of divulging. But you can take it from me that Magnus is not the girl's father.'

Sir Miles raised his voice as he spoke. It sounded as if Nick had annoyed him, and that those were his final words on the subject. But Nick wasn't about to give up that easily. 'Has Camellia ever called on you, sir?' He hoped he might be able to come back to the letter from a different angle.

'I'm told a girl did come here a couple of years ago. It may have been her. I was abroad at the time.'

'Then you've never met her?'

'I saw her, of course, when she was a small child. But not since.'

'Not since the letter from Bonny?' Nick prompted.

'Certainly not.' His face flushed an even darker red and his voice was full of indignation. 'And after

473

that dreadful business in Chelsea!' He stopped suddenly.

'So you knew about that then?' Nick couldn't help smiling. 'Then you must have known Bonny was dead too?'

'Now look here, young man,' Sir Miles blustered. 'How dare you come into my house and question me? I don't like your tone at all.'

'I'm sorry, sir, I didn't mean to be offensive,' Nick said ingratiatingly. 'But you see I'm just trying to piece together a puzzle. While doing so I have found out a great many things, and one thing is perfectly plain: Camellia is a victim of events which started before her birth. Even that business in Chelsea, as you called it, wasn't her fault – and neither was she guilty of any wrong-doing.'

'Rubbish, she was a prostitute.'

Nick smarted, but he was determined to charm something out of this old man at all costs. 'Sir Miles,' he said quietly. 'You are a man of great experience. I'm sure you know as well as I do that not everything in the papers is strictly true. Camellia was a nightclub hostess; she was never a prostitute. Please consider for a moment what Camellia had been through. She lost her father at six, her mother at fifteen and during the years in-between not only did all the old friends of her parents who might have given her life a little more balance jump ship, but she saw a parade of men pass through her home, and all her father's money squandered. She came to London without any friends, family or qualifications. Becoming a nightclub hostess may not have been the smartest thing to do, but then she had no one to guide her. She learned her lesson the hard way.'

'She was a prostitute,' the old man said belligerently.

'She wasn't. I spent an evening two days ago

474

with a policeman who knew everything about the case. She was just a hostess.'

'Same thing,' Sir Miles said stubbornly.

'You know it isn't. I'm sure you've been to clubs often and met hostesses. Are you saying every single one of those was a prostitute?'

'Yes, loose women the lot of them.'

Nick could see black humour in this situation. Sir Miles was sitting there dressed like a playboy, a lifetime of the theatre behind him, yet staunchly pretending he thought all nightclubs were dens of vice.

Sir Miles pulled a large handkerchief from his pocket and mopped his brow. 'Look at the rest of the evidence against her? She'd hardly recovered from her injuries and her girlfriend dies of a drug overdose. The police found endless pornographic pictures of the girl.'

'Not Camellia,' Nick said firmly. He wanted to comment on what a strange memory the man had, but he didn't dare. 'She wasn't even called as a witness when the photographer was on trial.'

Sir Miles snorted and lapsed into silence.

Nick waited for a moment or two before pressing him again. 'Let's put all that business aside now,' he suggested. 'You see it's not really relevant anyway. For two years now Camellia has worked hard for my father. He has become very fond of her and she practically ran the hotel. Look at this picture, sir?' Nick reached into his pocket and pulled out the photograph of himself and Camellia taken in Weston-super-Mare.

'That's what she's like now,' he urged him. 'Does she look like some cheap hooker? Isn't she entitled to have made a few mistakes along the way and be forgiven for them?'

The strangest expression passed over the old man's face as he looked at the picture. Nick couldn't read it at all. There was an element of surprise, but there was more to it than that. The length of time he took to study the photograph was odd too: most people would have glanced at it and then handed it straight back.

'No, she doesn't look like a hooker.' Sir Miles's voice had lost its growl. 'But I can't help you, Nicholas. I know Magnus isn't her father, surely that is enough for you.'

'How can you be so certain?' Nick was studying the man. He was ruffled; he did know more.

'The eyes,' Sir Miles snapped. 'Your father's are blue, as I remember, and so were Bonny's. I believe it's impossible for two blue-eyed people to produce a brown-eyed child.'

Nick felt a surge of wild elation. 'We never thought of that,' he managed to say. To his shame a tear rolled down his cheek.

'Come now,' Sir Miles said, leaning from his seat and patting Nick's arm. 'There's no need to get emotional about it.'

Nick wiped the back of his hand across his eyes and began to laugh. This whole interview was so strange.

'That's better,' Sir Miles chuckled. 'If I'd known that was all it would take to get rid of you I would've said it straight away.'

It was then that Nick saw the old man's eyes properly. In laughter they opened wider and despite the bags of flesh beneath them, he saw they were darkest brown and almond-shaped. Just like Mel's.

'What we both need is a brandy.' Sir Miles's tone was jocular now and his eyes retreated back into the flesh again. 'Now let's get off this subject. What production are you in at the moment.'

Nick told him his situation and mentioned things he'd done recently. Rather shame-facedly he also

476

added *Hunnicroft Estate*. He'd discovered this now interested agents and producers. Enough time had passed for it to have become almost a cult series.

'So you were the thug?' Sir Miles poured the brandy and passed it over to Nick. 'I remember it well. The script was appalling, but you played a good part.'

'You watched it?' Nick gulped at the brandy, amazed at this turn of events.

'I always make a point of watching new series, especially when they claim to be controversial. That one certainly was, such awful language! Had I known you were Magnus's son then, I might have been able to help you. As it is I'll drop your name in a few likely places, maybe something will come of it.'

Nick was suddenly on his guard. It felt as if he was being offered a carrot to go away and ask no more questions. He finished his drink. 'I think I'd better be off now,' he said, standing up. 'I've taken up enough of your time. There's only one more thing I'd like to ask, if you don't mind. As you were a guest at the Nortons' wedding, do you have a photograph? Call it nosiness if you like, but I've never seen a picture of John Norton.'

Nick saw relief flood across the man's face.

'Yes, there's one here somewhere,' he said with a smile. 'I'm sorry if I've been a little churlish with you, Nicholas. It was just that dreadful woman. I don't mean her child any harm and I hope you find her.'

He opened a drawer and pulled out three fat albums. Leafing through the first one quickly, he moved onto the second. 'Ah! Here we are.' He handed over a glossy picture of the bride and groom with other people around them. 'This was my wife's favourite one.'

Nick could see exactly why men fell for Bonny.

477

She was breathtakingly lovely in white satin. In this picture she was laughing, brushing confetti from John's jacket, her veil thrown back. John Norton was much as Nick had imagined, tall, slim with a rather aristocratic nose and a small moustache. Yet apart from his colouring there was no real resemblance to Mel.

'Who are the other people,' Nick asked. There were three women, one tall and slender, around forty or so and very attractive, the other two older, all three in fancy wide-brimmed hats. Beside Bonny was Sir Miles, still stout but without the sagging skin round his eyes. Nick saw Mel's eyes staring back at him. He felt faint and looked again, but he wasn't mistaken. They were identical to Mel's.

'That one was a charming lady, Linda, Lorna, something like that,' Sir Miles said, pointing out the younger of the three women in the picture. 'This one is my late wife, Mary. The other was John's godmother, Lady Penelope Beauchamp. She died a year or so after John from a brain tumour.'

'Would that be Lydia Wynter?' Nick asked going back to the attractive younger woman. Magnus would be pleased to know Bonny hadn't lied about her; she did look rather grand and extremely photogenic.

'Yes, that was her name, a dancing teacher. She was a second mother to Bonny, poor woman. Have you met her?'

'She died too,' Nick said quietly, suddenly aware that Sir Miles was the oldest in the group and the only survivor.

Sir Miles took back the photograph and slipped it into the album again. Nick knew this time he really must go. 'Thank you for seeing me,' he said. 'You've been a great help.'

'Chin up.' The older man smiled, with a hint of smugness. 'I don't doubt she'll turn up again. As

478

for your career maybe that'll brighten up too. Now go on home and stop worrying about things past. Get your father to have a blood test – that will give you both peace of mind.'

Nick paused for a moment at the door. 'One more question and I'll be off. Do you know why Bonny fell out with Helena Forester?'

Sir Miles was busy placing the albums back in the drawer, but his head jerked up sharply. 'Helena had nothing to do with any of this.' A red flush flooded his face. 'She is a serious actress. All there was between the two of them was a stage act.'

After leaving Sir Miles's house Nick went into Holland Park gardens and sat on a bench. He wasn't absolutely sure Miles was right about two blue-eyed people being unable to produce a brown-eyed child. In any case Magnus's eyes weren't a true blue – they were speckled with green and amber. But he'd check that out.

For some reason that last retort of Sir Miles's seemed the most important thing he'd said. Why should he say Helena had nothing to do with anything? She hadn't been mentioned in the entire conversation until then. Wouldn't any normal person say something like, 'I don't know, perhaps Bonny was jealous', or 'they grew out of one another'.

Suppose Sir Miles had been having an affair with Helena? Suppose Bonny lured him away for a while, perhaps thinking he would further her career too, and got pregnant by him?

That could have caused the girls to fall out and finished their friendship – especially if Helena had a close relationship with Miles. Perhaps Bonny had written to him out of pure spite, threatening to tell his wife about their child.

Although Nick couldn't imagine two such young

479

pretty women squabbling over an old man's affections, it was the most likely answer yet. It would also explain Miles's animosity towards Bonny, and why he'd read every last word about Mel in the papers. Why else would a man keep such close tabs on a child?

Chapter Twenty

Mel got off the bus in Wandsworth Bridge Road, Fulham and walked disconsolately towards Stevendale Road and her bedsitter. It was six months since she fled from Oaklands, and she'd just been turned down for a job with the Grand Metropolitan group of hotels, because she couldn't give references from her previous employment. The personnel manager had treated her as if he suspected she'd just come out of prison. She wished now she hadn't put herself through such an embarrassing ordeal.

She wondered what had possessed her to return to a part of London which evoked so many painful memories. She'd taken the room because it was cheap and accepted a job as a cook in a World's End café, purely because Peggy and Arthur, her employers, weren't concerned about insurance cards, tax codes, or even what she'd done before. But now she regretted both decisions.

At first she'd been glad to work from eight in the morning until six in the busy café since by the time she got home in the evening she was too exhausted to dwell on all she had lost. But now the ever present stink of fried food, the mountains of washing up, and the lack of appreciation from her employers were wearing her down.

On the bus ride home from Kensington, she'd

been close to tears – not just because she hadn't got the job, or that she'd have to stick Peggy's café a little longer, but because she still missed Oaklands so much. If she was back in her old room she'd see a green haze on the trees, lambs in the fields and a golden sea of daffodils out on the lawn. In London the seasons weren't as clearly defined as they were in the countryside. There was the odd window box bright with spring flowers, and suits in pastel colours in every shop window, but there wasn't anything like the thrill of seeing green shoots thrusting out of the soil, or finding clumps of primroses in the hedgerows. Every day now she found herself hating the drab grey streets more. She longed to feel the wind in her hair, to hear birdsong instead of traffic, to stand on a hill and gaze at a beautiful view, to feel she was part of a bigger scheme of things, to have some purpose in life other than mere survival.

Aside from her own troubles the whole country seemed to be in a state of depression. Edward Heath had ordered the farcical three-day week back in December, when the miners went on strike, and although Heath had now resigned and Harold Wilson had taken over, things still looked bleak.

Mrs Smethwick, Mel's landlady, was cleaning the brass on the front door as she turned into Stevendale Road. From a distance she looked like Andy Capp's wife: a cross-over pinny in pinks and reds, nylon scarf tied over her curlers, cigarette dangling from her lips, and a large protruding bottom.

Mrs Smethwick cleaned the brass daily, more for an excuse to spy on her neighbours and goggle at the new young executives who were moving in than out of any desire to make number forty-seven attractive.

Many of the Victorian terraced houses in the

road now sported coach lamps and paved front gardens with evergreen bushes in tubs. Estate agents were fond of describing these as 'town houses of character' or even 'artisans cottages'. But even they would be hard pressed to find something inspiring to say about Mrs Smethwick's house. The area between pavement and house held a collection of open dustbins, and an ancient armchair left to rot all winter. The window frames sagged, the paint was chipped and a broken downpipe had left a green slimy streak from roof to street level.

As Mel drew nearer, her landlady grinned at her, revealing an absence of upper teeth. 'Did yer get the job, ducks? Yer don't 'alf look smart.'

'It wasn't quite what I wanted,' Mel replied, smiling politely even though she loathed the woman. 'How did you know I was going for an interview?'

'I put two and two together,' Mrs Smethwick said, small bright eyes glinting with pride at her powers of deduction. 'I seen yer newspapers with rings round. And then you went out all done up.'

Mel felt she might just write something nasty about the woman one day and put it in her bin – but not yet. She needed the cheap room a little longer.

Trudging up to her room on the first floor, she covered her nose with her hand. The house always smelt dreadful: a mixture of boiled cabbage, cats, nappies and the unspeakable emissions from her neighbours' bowels.

Mel's room had been advertised as a 'serviced flatlet for business person'. In fact it was a poky ten-by-eight room with a diseased mattress on the bed and an electric hotplate and sink in a cupboard. The servicing meant that Mrs Smethwick emptied the wastepaper bin, put a fresh sheet on the bed once a fortnight and pushed the hoover round the bits that showed. As far as Mel could see she was the only one of the six tenants who had a job and sometimes the noise in the house was on a level with living at London airport.

Back at Christmas she had stayed in bed all day reading, pretending to herself it was just another Sunday. When her mind switched back to the Christmas tree in the drawing room at Oaklands or the dining room laid up with silver, starched white napkins and crystal wine glasses, she had pulled the covers over her head and sobbed.

Mel put a coin in the meter, then switched on the kettle and fire. Someone was cooking curry upstairs and by evening the smell would be trapped everywhere in the house. If it hadn't been so cold she would have gone for a walk after the interview to delay returning here.

There were no comforts – not a radio, television or even a bedside lamp. Everything in the room belonged to Mrs Smethwick, from the unmatched thick china to the picture of swans hiding a nasty stain on the wall. Mel knew she was almost at the end of her tether.

How many more plates of pie and chips could she dish out before screaming aloud? How many more nights could she come home exhausted and cry herself to sleep before she cracked up?

Nick's face haunted her. He was on her mind from the moment she opened her eyes in the morning until she fell asleep at night. Daily she blamed herself for the events of that last morning at Oaklands and cursed her stupidity for not having left six months earlier. As for Magnus, that hurt even more because as well as missing him desperately she didn't know what sort of state he was in. Could he walk yet? Was his speech distorted like many stroke victims? She knew he was back at

Oaklands before Christmas because she'd telephoned but the girl on reception had said he was confined to a wheelchair. Whenever she'd phoned since, Mrs Downes or Sally had answered, and she'd had to put the receiver down without speaking.

She pined for her pretty room, the beauty of her surroundings and the other staff who had been her friends. She was so lonely that sometimes death seemed preferable to the constant pain inside her.

'You're just tired,' she whispered, looking at herself in the mirror as she took off her navy-blue suit and hung it on a hanger. Her hair and eyes were dull, even her skin had a yellowish tinge. She had lost weight too, and her shoulders looked gaunt. Even her bra was too big now.

Back in the autumn she had intended to write to Magnus, to tell him exactly why she left in such a hurry and why she could never come back. But she had no idea if he was able to read a letter himself, and if it fell into the wrong hands it would be awkward for him. Now she knew she could never write: she must stay away for good, for his family's sake.

It was tempting to pack her bags, go to the airport and get a flight somewhere, yet she knew now that running wasn't the answer. She had to start living again. What she needed was a job she could be proud of, and a permanent home for herself.

The rattling sound of a milkfloat woke her and the grey early morning light indicated she had slept right round the clock from four in the afternoon until almost six the next morning.

Shivering she got out of bed and switched on the fire and kettle, getting back under the covers until the kettle boiled and the room warmed a little.

By the time she'd had a second cup of tea, she realised she felt calmer, much better than she had for weeks. Maybe this was a sign she was getting over Nick at last?

Peggy's café was in the shabby World's End part of King's Road, where the big houses were divided into bedsitters and occupied by itinerant artists, musicians and a great many refugees from the sixties who clung to the area along with their philosophies of astrology, brown rice and free love. There were still a few hippie shops, with the inevitable handmade candles, incense, Indian clothes and packets of Tarot cards. Peggy's café was tucked between a smart lighting shop and a large junk shop called Bizarre, the only one left in the area that offered cheap home-cooked meals from six in the morning till well past nine at night.

Mel winced as she crossed King's Road. She could see Peggy through the steamed-up window, a cigarette hanging from the corner of her mouth. She'd managed to break Arthur of the habit of sticking his fingers in the cups, and got them both to agree sauce bottles looked more attractive with the tops wiped, but she still couldn't find a way of preventing them from smoking behind the counter!

'Hullo, love,' Peggy called out cheerfully. 'You're early!'

Peggy was well past forty but she had the body of a twenty-year-old and bouffant, bleached blonde hair. Despite her messy habits she took great pride in her appearance. Today she was wearing tight pink trousers and a matching spotted short top which showed up her rounded bottom and narrow hips to advantage. It was a shame her face didn't match up to her body: she had deep lines round her eyes, and the pink foundation she plastered on emphasised them even more. Mel had often seen lorry drivers pinch or slap her youthful bottom only to be startled when she rounded on them and they saw her face.

'I woke up full of beans today,' Mel grinned, nipping behind the counter and going through to hang up her coat and find an apron to tie over her jeans.

It had been a matter of pride never to let on to Peggy and Arthur just how dejected or alone she was. Because of her confident air, her manner of speaking and her knowledge of gourmet foods, she'd inadvertently given them the impression that she came from an illustrious background. It suited her to play along with this myth. Peggy was an inverted snob, sneering at anyone she believed came from a higher branch of the social tree, and therefore she asked no direct questions. If she chose to imagine Mel was slumming it out of some misguided rebellion, that was fine. Barbed sarcastic comments were easier to live with than sympathy or curiosity.

'What's the special?' Mel asked as she came back behind the counter.

'How about that goulash?' Peggy suggested, pouring out a cup of tea for her. The radio was on as always and Slade's 'Cum on Feel the Noize' blared out.

'That needs slow cooking,' Mel said thoughtfully. 'I could do that for tomorrow. What about lasagne?'

'I don't know what the customers did before you came,' Peggy sniggered. 'Cor you ain't 'alf changed our image, love.'

Mel smiled. Peggy would be very disappointed if she was to discover that she hadn't picked up her cooking skills by eating in fancy restaurants or going to a posh finishing school, but by standing at Antoine's elbow and studying recipe books. Six months ago Peggy and Arthur had sniffed disapprovingly at the herbs, spices and garlic she used, but time and the customers' enthusiasm for the hearty casseroles and special pasta dishes she created had mellowed their attitude.

'How did the curry go down yesterday?' Mel sat down at one of the tables. There were only two customers so far, both sitting with giant bacon sandwiches and half-pint mugs of tea, their noses deep in the *Daily Mirror*.

'One complaint it was too hot, but the rest liked it.' Peggy wiped a greasy cloth over the glass cake display cabinet. 'Art had the last bit for 'is supper.'

Mel saw the glass coming up more smeared than it had been at the start, she forgot herself and suggested Peggy got a clean cloth.

'Getting a bit above ourselves aren't we?' her employer snapped.

There were countless things here which Mel frowned upon: the way uncooked chops were left out in the hot kitchen, cooked and raw meat shoved in the refrigerator together and crumbs left on the floor all night, encouraging mice. But she had to be diplomatic about it, for jolly and fun-loving as Peggy was most of the time, she could round on Mel quicker than a snake, spitting out venom with such ferocity it left her shaking.

There were a great deal of inconsistencies in Peggy and Arthur. They spent an inordinate amount of money on clothes, and their flat above the café had every last luxury, yet they wouldn't buy a new fridge or lay new flooring which would be easier to clean. They liked the way Mel's cooking packed the place at lunchtime, yet they wouldn't give her more money. The more she took on, the less they both did. Even the improved menu was something to snigger about rather than praise.

On several occasions she'd heard Peggy ask customers, 'D'you want the fancy muck or a fry up?'

The café filled up quickly, with a mixture of labourers, lorry drivers and students coming in for a mountainous breakfast.

'Glad to see you back today,' Tony one of the regulars called to her through the hatch to the kitchen. 'My breakfast was swimming in fat yesterday!'

It wasn't until after the lunch hour that Mel sat down for the first time. She sipped her coffee and picked at the left-over lasagne, idly looking through the situations vacant. One job caught her eye.

'Chief, cook and bottlewasher wanted for new Supper Rooms in Fulham. Must be smart, hardworking and adaptable. Accommodation available if required. Good wages and bonus to right person.'

Mel jotted down the number and stuck it in her pocket. It was worth a try. She might be able to get round her lack of references by suggesting they called to sample her cooking.

It was quiet late in the afternoon. There would be another rush before six, but under the pretence of buying tights, she slipped off to a public phone.

'Could you call round tonight?' a man said after she explained where she worked. 'I know Peggy's café, I've been in there several times and I was impressed with the specials. Are you the dark-haired girl?'

The man introduced himself as Conrad Deeley. He gave her a good feeling: his deep resonant voice reminded her just a little of Magnus although he had a trace of an Irish accent. If his place was only half decent and he wanted her as cook, she'd take it. Nothing could be as bad as Peggy's.

'Yes, that's me,' she said. 'Camellia Norton, though they know me as Mel.' She didn't know why she'd suddenly reverted back to her real name after so long. Perhaps it was just instinctive: she'd had enough of pretence. 'I could come straight from here,' she said quickly, afraid someone else might beat her to it. 'But I have to warn you I'm not dressed for an interview and I'll stink of chips!'

'You'll stink of garlic here,' he replied and laughed unaffectedly. 'Just ring the bell on the side door. I'm not ready to open yet.'

On the bus to Fulham Broadway, Mel pictured Conrad Deeley as around sixty, big and balding. She had the idea that his restaurant would be in a basement. But she was wrong on both counts.

The windows and door of the narrow building were covered in something white which prevented her looking in, but the outside frames and fascia board had been painted a glossy dark green. It was sandwiched between a greengrocers and a chemists, and she guessed that like its neighbours inside it was just one long room with a kitchen right at the back. There were two more floors above, the top one attic rooms with tiny windows. She quite liked the idea of living here: Fulham Broadway was a bustling place with a street market during the day and it had an interesting mix of residents ranging from working-class families and immigrants to young executive types who had bought houses here in the property boom of 1972.

When the side door was answered by a young, thin weed of a man with wire-rimmed spectacles and a Fair Isle cardigan, her heart sank.

'I have an appointment with Mr Deeley,' she said. 'Is he here?'

'I am Deeley, and you must be Camellia. Do come in.' His voice confirmed he was the man she had spoken to, but the deep tone was at odds with his puny appearance. He winced at the cold wind and quickly shut the door behind her. 'Well that wind must have blown the chip smell away, you smell like frosty clean washing.'

Mel was disappointed. Everything about Deeley was untidy, from his lank mousy hair to his paint-splattered shoes. He didn't look capable of running a restaurant. If it hadn't been for his warm voice and his welcoming manner, she might have turned and left immediately.

'Everything's in chaos,' he said with a friendly boyish grin. 'I'll just hope you have a good enough imagination to get an idea of how it will be when it's finished. I'll quickly show you the kitchen for now, then after we've had a cup of tea and a chat, I'll show you round properly.'

There was a strong smell of fresh paint and new plaster in the narrow passage. He led her past an uncarpeted staircase, down another two steps. As they reached the kitchen Mel's spirits lifted instantly.

Setting aside a mucky floor littered with tools, odd bits of timber and a couple of sacks of plaster, it was superb: attractive pale-green fitted units, plenty of working surfaces and a huge cooker. Even at a glance Mel could see Conrad knew what he was doing. It had clearly been designed with heavy duty use in mind. The lighting was excellent, the positioning of the double sink, cooker and refrigerator was practical, the walls were tiled from floor to ceiling for easy cleaning, and he was in the process of unpacking a vast array of professional copper-bottomed saucepans.

Although it was dark outside, the big window and a glazed door leading out onto a backyard gave the impression that by day it would be a light, cheerful place to work, a far cry from the gloomy, cramped and awkward kitchen she'd endured at Peggy's café.

'I'm looking for someone who will work with me, not just for me,' he said pointedly. 'It's my intention to make Conrad's Supper Rooms "the" place to eat in South West London. The best meat and fish, fresh vegetables, simple food but beautifully cooked and presented. Until I can see how it's going to go, I can't afford to take on a lot of staff. In the beginning it will be a case of doing anything and everything between us.'

She liked the way he said 'us'. As he opened cupboards for her inspection and exuberantly spoke of other equipment he had ordered, she found herself forgetting his appearance. She was charmed by his enthusiasm and astounded by his business-like knowledge of food preparation.

As he led her upstairs into a room at the back piled high with green-stained tables and chairs, he began to rattle out a potted history of himself: how he'd once been a teacher in a boys' school but left because he wanted to be a writer and taken a job in a restaurant to keep the wolf from the door. 'I hardly knew how to peel a spud when I started,' he laughed. 'I worked my way up from washing up, and waiting at tables to cooking, and I found I was born to it.'

Whilst speaking at a hundred miles an hour, about this restaurant down in Hampshire, his family back in Ireland and what a hopeless teacher he had proved to be, he made a pot of tea. Then he pulled a chair down for Mel to sit on by the fire, and asked her a few questions. His face was pale, with a small mouth and a sharp chin, but behind his thick glasses large brown eyes danced with unsuppressed merriment and intelligence.

Conrad, or Con as he preferred, came from a large family back in Limerick. 'If I'd been a puppy or kitten,' he said cheerfully, 'I'm the one in the litter they would have drowned,' and without the slightest pause proceeded to tell her why.

'I didn't fit in you see, I was always sickly and gormless. So when I was nine they sent me off to live with my Great-aunt Bridget in Galway. Luckily, she and I got on like a house on fire. She was a bit odd you see, like me. If I didn't want to go to school she'd let me stay home reading books or we'd go walking along the beach. I was thirteen when she died. I went home for a bit, but couldn't settle in the school where my other brothers had been, so they shipped me off to my grandfather, Great-aunt Bridget's brother, in England. I liked him as much as I'd liked Aunt Bridget. He was a bit of an old reprobate, made all his money in the construction business. He was over seventy and a great one for the ladies and he could've been captain of the Irish drinking team! But he sent me to a small school in Weybridge and I caught up with all the schooling I'd missed. We had a wonderfully close relationship and when he died while I was at University he left me all his money.'

'Sounds like you led an enchanted life,' Mel giggled, a little embarrassed.

'It was enchanted once I was sent away from my own family,' he agreed. 'I thank God daily for his intervention. I couldn't begin to tell you what a mean-spirited, bigoted and sanctimonious bunch they are. Fortunately they were so angry at me inheriting they've cut me right off now.'

He went on to explain the money was held in trust till he was thirty, which his grandfather had referred to as 'the age of reason'. After describing his five years working in a public school, which he'd loathed, he returned to the part he'd already told her about – the writing and the restaurant.

'I wrote all day, was a skivvy by night,' he

laughed. 'I got a few short stories published and I embarked on the book, thinking I was going to be another James Joyce. But it got rejected by every major publishing house, so I decided to put it on a back burner and take cooking a little more seriously.'

Mel smiled as he told her how his dreams were all coming together now he had his inheritance. He was now thirty-two, and he seemed far more astute than his appearance or his confidences had suggested.

'I've bought this place outright,' he said, blushing slightly. 'The way I see it, if it doesn't make a great deal of profit I've still got Grandfather's money held in bricks and mortar. I've got a home, I can have the kind of cosy restaurant I want, and I can sit up here and write during the day.'

Five or six months earlier Mel might have been suspicious of a complete stranger prepared to spill out so much personal information at a first meeting. In her days back at the Don Juan she would probably have put him down as a fool. But now, with heightened sensitivity, she recognised that this frank outpouring stemmed from loneliness.

His enthusiasm was infectious. Already she was looking around her and imagining this rather grubby room emptied of the chairs and tables, the boxes of coffee and sugar and turned into a comfortable sitting room. There was a desk under the window, with a typewriter and a small mountain of paper.

'Is that the book?' she asked.

He nodded. 'I'm rewriting it again. I know in my heart it's good, it just needs reshaping. Besides writing gnaws at me. I'm obsessed by it.'

'Would you let me read it?'

He blushed again and hung his head. 'I'd love it

if you would. No one else has ever shown any real interest.'

Mel sensed he really meant 'no one has any interest in me at all'. She knew how that felt. 'Well I'm interested in everything about you,' she blurted out, suddenly aware she really did want to work for him. 'Now are you going to show me around?'

'You'll have to use your imagination,' he warned her again. 'And I'd be glad of any suggestions about how to make it more homely.'

The flat was entirely self-contained. Con said the previous owners of the building had let it out separately from the shop. Down two steps from the main room, at the back, was a tiny kitchen. To the front were two more smaller rooms, one intended as a study-cum-office and the other his bedroom. Everywhere was uncarpeted and full of boxes.

'This is no way to impress you.' He glumly indicated the piled-up stock and furniture. 'But believe me I will get it shipshape.' He leapt up, opening yet another door leading to a narrow staircase. 'There's two more rooms up there, and the bathroom. That's where you'll live!'

Mel liked the rooms upstairs immediately, even though they were empty. They were small with sloping ceilings, and both had recently been painted white.

'I don't want a snotty, smart place,' he shouted through the door from the kitchen, as he made a second pot of tea. 'I want my supper rooms to be noted for jollity and warmth, like the places in Dublin. Do you know what I mean?'

Mel had never been to Dublin, but she did know. Although Conrad had been away from Ireland for many years his personality was unmistakably Irish. It reminded her a little of Aiden, all that gaiety and irreverent humour. But Conrad wasn't a ladies man: it was impossible to imagine he had a wife and police record tucked away. She could imagine him jigging around at a ceilidh, even playing the fiddle himself, but not making passes at her.

Maybe she'd end up doing the lion's share of the work, worrying herself silly about the place, but she felt her steps had been guided to him and his restaurant.

He barely asked her what she'd done before Peggy's café – just whisked through a menu he'd drawn up and asked if she was familiar with the dishes.

'I can manage all that,' she assured him, secretly thinking his desserts were unimaginative, and that she'd say so too before long. 'I'd really like the job.'

'I haven't even shown you the restaurant yet,' he said in some surprise. 'Or talked about wages.'

As far as she was concerned in the hour or two she'd been talking to him, he'd revealed enough of his character and his taste for her to know exactly what the end result would be. She approved of the stained-green chairs and tables stacked up to the ceiling, and the kitchen was first class. But it was Conrad himself she was sold on. As long as he was prepared to match what she earned at Peggy's, she was prepared to take a gamble on him.

Just the way he laughed about his family told her that accepting they neither loved nor needed him had been a long and painful process. He had an asexual quality which she knew would be easy to live with. Under the skin they were brother and sister already.

'Con, it just feels right to me,' she said. There was a bubbling feeling of joy growing inside her, much like the one she had felt when Magnus offered her a new start. 'I expect you've got other people to see, but I hope you'll choose me.'

'Then the job's taken as of now,' he grinned. 'Will

twenty pounds all found be enough money? To be reviewed and a bonus sorted out when we open?'

That was what she'd earned at Peggy's, but she'd had to pay rent on top. 'Wonderful,' she said with a big smile.

'Well, hand in your notice tomorrow and phone me to say when you can start and move in,' he said, his eyes dancing with pleasure. 'I knew as soon as you phoned that you were the one.'

Three weeks later Mel was on her knees washing the kitchen floor. Conrad was sitting on a stool just inside the restaurant compiling a shopping list.

'And we'll need some oven cleaner,' she called out.

'Give us a chance to get it dirty,' Conrad laughed, moving closer to the doorway to watch Mel. Her hair had broken loose from its rubber-band, falling on her flushed face and she had a grey tidemark halfway up her arms. There was paint splattered on her jeans, grease on her tee shirt and her big toe was protruding through old plimsolls. But she looked happy. She'd entirely lost the haunted look she had on the night of her interview.

Mel sat back on her haunches, holding the wet cloth in sore-looking hands. 'We have to think ahead,' she explained. 'If we wait till the cooker's dirty, we'll soon be in queer street. And you must get some tile cleaner too. They'll have to be washed over daily.'

'What a fountain of wisdom you are!' he mocked her. 'A spell in Ireland would do you the world of good. Kitchens with chickens scuttling around them, too much gossiping to clean the grate let alone the cooker. This place is going to be fun remember!'

'Health inspectors don't have a sense of humour,' she threw back at him. 'You, my

497

unworldly little leprechaun, are in for a few sharp shocks!'

'Did you bully Peggy too? Incidentally, I did buy some rubber gloves for jobs like that. Your hands look like my mother's!'

'We'll have slaves to do the dirty work soon,' she shouted back at him as he went towards the restaurant door. 'Don't forget the oven cleaner!'

Outside a man was painting 'Conrad's Supper Rooms' in gold lettering on the dark green façade. Tomorrow, Friday 15 April, was opening night.

Mel had thought it was hard working at Peggy's, but in the last three weeks she'd worked even harder, unpacking glasses, china and cutlery, cleaning up after workmen, shifting furniture and cooking in advance for the freezer. Now they were almost there.

She finished the floor, working backwards towards the restaurant. Then leaving it to dry, she perched for a moment on a stool by the bar and surveyed their joint handiwork with delight.

Con was a genius. He had taken one long narrow room without character and had stamped his own on it. The white roughly plastered walls, with green tables, chairs and carpet, gave a feeling of light and space, and a large mirror on the back room wall reflected even more. Brass wall lamps with green gingham shades added a country kitchen effect, while modern art prints in primary colours prevented it from looking clinical. The bar just inside the door was very small, but that added to the cosy, intimate ambience of the place. It was time now to hang the white lace curtains on the brass rails. Tomorrow there would be flowers and candles on each table.

Peggy and Arthur had been furious when Mel gave them her notice the morning after her interview. They had ranted on and on, saying she was letting them down and that she was ungrateful. After listening to an unending vicious tirade all morning she had walked out after the lunch hour, forgoing the wages she was owed.

Peggy's attitude hurt her badly. Mrs Smethwick was just as cutting, when she heard her best tenant was leaving, but Mel didn't care about her.

But Conrad's delight that she could move in immediately made up for everything. By the next afternoon he'd had a carpet laid in her room, and bought her a second-hand wardrobe and chest of drawers. It was a far cry from her beautiful room at Oaklands, but she intended to buy a few things to make it more homely.

'Don't you trouble your head about Peggy,' he said sympathetically. 'This is your home now, Mel, and I will appreciate you. It's going to be a wonderful adventure.'

Con was right – it did feel like an adventure. It also felt as if everything she'd ever learned had been a preparation for this job. While Con concentrated on getting men to finish the work down in the restaurant, and seeing to the publicity for opening night, she was free to turn the flat upstairs into a home, to work at her own pace sorting out store cupboards, preparing the kitchen and buying equipment Con had overlooked. Together they planned ahead, working in tandem until late at night as they stocked up the freezer with desserts and casseroles.

Now that the back-breaking work was done, Mel knew it would never be so hard and thankless here as it had been at Peggy's. On summer afternoons she could sit outside in the little backyard, where she planned to plant some flowers. There would be time to read, to look after her appearance as she had at Oaklands. With Con she could linger over cooking, creating rather than rushing against time for people who didn't know the difference between a processed pea and a fresh one.

But best of all she could be herself again. There was no need to pretend she had a busy social life, and Con wouldn't sneer as Peggy did at her efforts to improve the culinary standard, or take offence when she concerned herself with hygiene.

There was only one cloud in Mel's mind: the more distant past.

She had already told him all about Magnus, Nick and Oaklands. On her second night she had sat down with him and revealed the whole story. He was so very open about himself, and she wanted to be equally honest. Con had been very sympathetic. A great storyteller himself, he was fascinated by the mystery of her mother and the men in her life, and she felt the disclosures had strengthened their friendship.

Yet Mel hadn't been able to admit yet about her days in Chelsea. Tomorrow the restaurant would be open, and it was just possible someone might come in who knew her in those days. Peggy's had been closer to Chelsea, but the likelihood of anyone she knew coming in there was small. She must tell Conrad soon, however much she hated the idea. It would be terrible if he heard it from someone else.

Mel's curiosity got the better of her around eleven on opening night. She had heard laughter all evening, even above the music, but now Con had changed the tape to an Irish jig, and the polite, warm laughter had turned to wild hilarity.

Everyone in the supper rooms was here by invitation. Mel had been a little concerned that these people might accept the free evening and never come back as paying customers, but Con said it was 'casting bread on the waters'. Judging by the jollity he had cast enough.

In the main they were media people, who lived locally. The landlord of the local pub and his wife were also there, as well as two men who owned an upmarket interior design business in Chelsea and two women who had an exclusive dress shop. Con might look like a little bookworm, but he was surprisingly astute about people. He'd hand picked those present, not only because they were influential, but because everyone of them had an outgoing personality. If they had a ball themselves, they'd be bound to broadcast to everyone what a good place it was.

Because it was a party night, they'd only put on a limited menu: a choice between garlic prawns or homemade pâté as a starter, Boeuf Bourgignon or chicken and mushroom casserole as the main course. Judging by the empty plates and the requests for seconds, everyone loved the food.

When Mel peeped round the door, she was staggered and amused to see Con doing an Irish jig on a piece of board. She had never seen anything like it and by the rapt faces of the guests, they were just as amazed as she was. His torso and arms were absolutely still, but from the knee down, his legs and feet had a life of their own, intricate steps performed fast and precisely, while his toes and heels drummed out the beat.

Earlier that evening when Con had appeared in his new dark-green jacket, bow tie, and smart haircut she'd been charmed to discover he could metamorphose into an elegant gentleman. Now dancing, without his glasses, he looked for the world like a leprechaun, brown eyes twinkling as fast as his feet.

'Conrad, you are a gem.' A buxom redhead in a green satin cocktail dress got up from her seat as the music finished and planted a kiss on his flushed cheek. 'You, my darling, and your restaurant are made!'

Applause and shouting followed, suggesting everyone in the room was in agreement with the redhead. Mel went back to prepare the Irish coffees and smiled to herself. She had a feeling that woman was Marcia Helms, from the local paper. Con had invited her because she frequently gave restaurants write-ups and though she was often very scathing, when she did like a place she went overboard.

It was almost one in the morning before Con finally locked the door after the last of the guests. He came through to the kitchen with his face aglow.

'It's going to work, Mel,' he said, hugging her tightly. 'Marcia promised she'd write us up, and the chap from Brown's Advertising booked a table for six for next Saturday. I know it's a bit early to say people will rush in off the street, but I just know they're going to.'

'I didn't know you could do Irish dancing,' Mel wiped away a lipstick stain from his cheek. 'You're a dark horse.'

'I used to be a bit of a star turn when I was a kid,' he admitted rather shamefacedly. 'Aunt Bridget sent me to classes in Galway. I can't believe I did it tonight though, I must have had one too many whiskies.'

Conrad was supremely happy that night as he fell into his bed. His dreams had become reality. But even as he hugged himself in delight that his restaurant had turned out exactly as he planned, that tonight had been a real success, he recognised that much of his happiness was due to Mel.

From that first night she came for the interview he knew he'd found a friend. After she'd gone he'd been ashamed at himself for gabbling on at her. It was a failing of his: he'd never managed to learn to keep a still tongue and he'd found to his cost that people took advantage of him because of it. But in the three weeks Mel had been here he'd found she wasn't like other people. To her confidences were a disclosure of a person's inner self and as such she treated them as a gift. They worked so well together. He didn't think he'd ever spent so much time laughing in his whole life as he had these last three weeks.

'Bless you Mel,' he whispered in the dark.

On Sunday afternoon Mel decided she must talk seriously to Con. Saturday night had been steady, with people coming in off the street to eat, and they'd had several telephone inquiries with five firm bookings for the next week. Today they'd been closed, but Con had been up at the crack of dawn, darting about, full of wild excitement.

'Can we talk?' she asked, handing him a mug of tea. Since moving all the tables and chairs downstairs they had worked together to make the sitting room a bit more homely. With a second-hand suite from a nearby junk shop, Con's books on shelves on the walls and a carpet, it looked better, but it really needed redecorating. The walls were papered in a hideous salmon pink.

'Don't tell me! It's going to be a "don't count your chickens" pep talk,' he said as she sat down in an armchair opposite him. 'I can't help it, Mel. I'm naturally excitable. It's the Irish blood.'

'No, it's nothing like that,' she said. 'It's about something which happened to me over three years ago. I'm afraid someone might recognise me and tell you. I want you to know the true story just in case.'

Con put his paper down and sat back on the settee. He was back in jeans and his worn Fair Isle cardigan again today, with a dark growth of stubble on his chin. He looked more like a teenager than a man of thirty-two. She hoped her story wasn't going to upset him. He'd led a much more sheltered life than she had.

It was so hard to force herself back in time, to explain who she was then, and why she'd behaved as she had. Looking back at those days in Oakley Street, it all seemed even grubbier than it had at the time. But talking about it was cathartic, like opening a window in a fetid room and airing it.

'Is that all of it?' he said raising one eyebrow when she'd finished. He hadn't interrupted once; she wondered if it had really sunk in.

'Yes.' She hung her head. 'That's what took me off to Ibiza and you know what happened from then on.'

'Mel, don't look so troubled,' he leaned forward and reached out to her hand, covering it with his own. 'We've all done things we wish we hadn't. If I admitted to you some of the things I got into when I was younger, you'd be afraid to be up here with me.'

Somehow she doubted his misdeeds amounted to more than stealing a few sweets from Woolworths, but his chivalry touched her. There was nothing hidden in Con. When he was angry he roared it out, when he was happy he laughed. She knew whatever he had to say on the subject today would be his last word on it. 'Tell me what you really think?' she asked.

He looked at her for a moment, his small face very boyish and innocent. 'I think how lucky I am to have you here working for me and being my friend,' he said at length. 'I think you've worn a hair shirt for too long and that you care far too much about others' opinions. There are people out there who do terrible really wicked things. You

504

were just young, vulnerable and perhaps foolish, that's all.'

'What do I do if someone does recognise me?' she asked. 'Should I be Amelia Corbett? Camellia stands out in people's minds.'

He smiled at her affectionately. 'To me you are just Mel, and that's all anyone needs to know here. But I think you should revert to your real name officially for your own peace of mind. Hiding away behind a false one only brought you more trouble. What is most important though is that you stop worrying about the past. It's over and done with. Just laugh if someone recognises you – there's no need to even think of explaining or admitting anything.'

'What about Magnus and Nick,' she said, tears springing to her eyes. 'I've tried to tell myself I've moved on, that I don't care anymore about them, but that's not true, Con. It still hurts and I feel it isn't ever going to go away.'

Con lapsed into thought. He and Mel were both scarred by bad childhood memories. Even as young as four or five he knew his mother didn't like him the way she did his other brothers and sisters. Being loved by Great-aunt Bridget and his grandfather had made up for it to some extent, especially when his grandfather had made him his heir. Yet deep down he knew that he would rather have heard his mother say she loved him than have any amount of money.

'You have to have faith,' he said eventually, sighing deeply. 'In God, fate or whatever. I personally believe everything is preordained and that we have as little control over our fate as we do over the weather. If you can believe that too and allow yourself to flow with the tide, one day it will turn and you'll find decisions are no longer necessary. Maybe that will mean that you see Magnus and

Nick again and resolve everything; maybe you'll just wake up one day and find you really don't care anymore.' He smiled at her. 'Of course that's the easy, lazy Irish way, letting fate take you where it will, but it works for me.'

'How did you get to be so wise?' she asked.

'The same way as you,' Con grinned. 'Too much time spent alone as a child observing others, thinking I was out of step with the rest of the world. I like women very much, but I don't really fancy them. My Aunt Bridget said I should be a priest and perhaps she was right.'

Mel took his hand and squeezed it. She didn't think he meant he was homosexual and she wasn't going to ask. His aunt had hit the nail right on the head: he would make a very good priest.

'I've never had a male friend like you before,' she said very quietly. 'I think you are right too, about fate or whatever it is. That's what brought me here and I'm gladder about that than anything else.'

Chapter Twenty-One

'This is beginning to sound as improbable as one of those old Edgar Wallace mystery films,' Magnus said, leaning on his garden fork and smiling wryly at his son.

It was June, six months since Nick went on his crusade to Littlehampton, Rye and London. Although for most of his time he had been working in London the mysteries surrounding Camellia's birth were still his major preoccupation. Today as he worked alongside his father in the garden he had been airing his theories about Sir Miles and his growing conviction that he'd had Bonny killed to shut her up.

Nick dug his spade deep into the ground, then turned over the clump of soil, bending to pick out a clump of weeds. 'Don't humour me,' he said heatedly. 'Maybe I am getting carried away but we're stuck. You can't have a blood test without a sample of Mel's blood to test alongside it. And even if we hired a private detective to find her, I don't think she'd come back here unless we had some real evidence to show her.'

'I think I'd better have a rest now,' Magnus said, taking off a battered old Panama hat and wiping his forehead with a handkerchief. 'My goodness it's hot.'

All through May it had been cold and wet, but the sun had come out at the beginning of June and for the last three days it had grown steadily warmer. Today the temperature was up in the high seventies, and the view across the valley was serene and beautiful in the sunshine.

Nick looked sharply at his father, checking for any signs that might indicate he'd been overdoing it. On the face of it he had made a full recovery from his stroke – he was walking again, albeit with a slight limp and he had regained full use of his left arm – but Nick was still anxious.

It had been a great relief to him when Magnus took on a manageress back in January. Jayne Sullivan, a widow in her early forties, had vast experience in the hotel business. She was efficient, with an outgoing personality, all the staff liked her and she was happy to come to help out at Oaklands for a year or so until she'd decided where she wanted to settle permanently. Nick felt she was heaven sent. Her presence made it easier for Magnus to accept his semi-retirement. Since spring arrived he had spent most of his time pottering in the garden, and the fresh air and light exercise had brought back his old rugged appearance. Few guests realised the big broad-shouldered man with thick white hair, and skin the colour of mellow pine striding around the gardens, was in fact the owner of Oaklands.

Magnus walked over to a garden seat in the shade, picked up a bottle of water he'd left there, took a long drink, then sat down.

Nick continued to dig for a few minutes alone, thinking about his father. The garden had always been very dear to Magnus. But planting flowers and a little weeding was one thing; building a rockery, complete with waterfall was quite another. Nick sensed this sudden desire for a large gardening project was really an attempt to block out the anxiety his father felt for Camellia. Nick knew he couldn't deter him – Magnus was the most stubborn person in the world once he'd decided on something. All Nick could do was to make sure he didn't overtire himself.

It pleased Nick to look at his father. He was entirely at one with his surroundings: his worn checked shirt and faded khaki shorts suited his character better than bow ties and dinner jackets. Each deep line on his face, the broad nose, the wide mobile mouth, suggested a life well spent. Age might eventually thin that unruly mop of white hair, his firm straight body might succumb again to stiffness and frailty, but somehow he knew his father's mind would stay active till the last breath left him.

Camellia's disappearance had brought them both anxiety and sorrow, yet it had also brought them far closer. Nick was certain that the reason Magnus had managed to walk again was tied up in his conviction that she would come back before long.

'Let's try another advertisement,' Magnus called out. 'Not everyone reads the personal column in the *Telegraph*.' They had placed two advertisements pleading for her to get in touch, but there had been no response.

Nick dug his spade firmly into the soil and walked over to his father, flopping down on the grass in front of him. 'I don't think she's in England,' he said, picking up the bottle of water. He was stripped down to just a pair of shorts, tanned even darker than his father, his hair bleached white-gold from the sun. He opened the bottle and drank from it. 'I bet she's gone back to Ibiza.'

'She *is* in England,' Magnus replied with conviction. 'I know that person you all call "The Phantom" is her. She's just checking.'

'You think it's Mel?'

'Of course it is.' Magnus wiped his eyes almost angrily. 'Why else does she keep ringing until I answer it? I kept a log for a while and it proves my point. After she's heard my voice it doesn't start again for at least two weeks. She just likes to check I'm okay.'

For a moment Nick just stared at his feet, idly picking some mud off his plimsolls. He trusted his father's intuition. If he was right at least it showed Camellia still thought about them.

'Well if you didn't pick up the phone at all,' he said thoughtfully, 'she might get so anxious she'd come here.'

'I don't want you to use emotional blackmail,' Magnus said sternly. 'That's wrong under any circumstances. And you, my son, are becoming obsessive!'

Nick knew his father was right. Reason told him that it wasn't normal for a man who hadn't had any sort of real relationship with a woman to be so intense about her. Magnus was concerned about her safety, and grieving because he missed her, but Nick was allowing it to dominate his whole life. He knew all those letters by heart now: he had spent hours and hours poring over them, looking for something new he might have overlooked. He had written copious notes on everything he had been told, then questioned each and every known incident.

He was certain that Helena Forester was the person with the answers.

Back in February Nick had joined a repertory company in Bromley in Kent and found himself a tiny flat in Hither Green in South London. It was a great deal easier in London, especially while working in a theatre, to get information about Helena Forester. Posing as an admiring fan and would-be biographer he had collected up scores of press-cuttings, reviews, articles and pictures of her. He knew her favourite perfume, which actors and actresses she admired; he even had pictures of her Spanish-style home in Hollywood. But she was a very private person, almost reclusively so. She rarely gave interviews, she didn't mix with the super rich jet set and she hadn't been back to England for at least twelve years. Considering what a big star she'd been during the fifties and early sixties, she had almost faded from the public eye now. Her last film, in 1967, had been a box office flop. The more he discovered about her the less approachable she seemed.

In one rare in-depth interview way back in 1958, she had talked about her childhood in Stepney before she was evacuated to Suffolk. Her descriptions of the narrow dark streets, the two small rooms she shared with her widowed mother, the colourful neighbours and the appalling poverty were all so vivid, Nick could see, smell and hear the East End. But however bleak her mother's struggle to survive on the meagre wages she got as a theatre dresser sounded – picking up bruised fruit and vegetables in Covent Garden market on her way home, unpicking cast-off clothes to remake them into dresses for her daughter – Helena had clearly been a happy, dearly loved child. She spoke almost nostalgically of day trips to Southend and Epping Forest with her mother and her aunt, of street parties, picnics in the park and the closeness of the slum community.

Nick had trawled through theatre archives until he managed to find some old faded photographs and programmes of the revue at the Phoenix theatre in which she had appeared as the war ended. He found one picture of a very young Helena dressed in a maid's costume, doing a comic sketch with her friend Edward Manning. There was also an article and photograph of Ambrose Dingle, the producer who had almost ruined Magnus's night at the Savoy, along with a picture of 'The Dingle Belles' his dancing troupe. One of these leggy showgirls was Bonny.

Helena's career seemed to have taken a step backwards after this point. He wondered why Helena, Edward and Bonny had left the West End stage together to tour provincial towns. Magnus remembered Bonny claiming that Ambrose Dingle had sacked her when she got food poisoning and that the other two had walked out in sympathy. Yet Nick felt there must have been more to it than that.

The stage version of *Oklahoma* which Helena joined in 1949 was well documented. The critics proclaimed her performance as 'Brilliant, feisty, and unforgettable' – yet she only stayed in it for a few months, leaving in October of 1949. The filming began for *Soho* in February 1950. It was interesting to discover that Sir Miles Hamilton's company had been involved in the backing of both productions.

A lucky find of old Hollywood magazines from the fifties in Portobello Road market, turned up a reference to Helena as aloof, mysterious and shy – in direct contrast to what Magnus had said about her. Much of the gossip about her in these magazines revolved around Edward Manning, who had joined her in Hollywood. Both Edward and Helena strenuously denied being lovers.

There were a great many articles and photographs devoted to Edward, far more than to Helena. He was startlingly handsome, with the kind of blond, bronzed and blue-eyed charm which ought to have made him a matinee idol overnight. But as far as Nick could ascertain the man never got more than the odd walk-on role in a couple of obscure films. He was photographed posing on a diving board in skimpy swimming trunks, in dark glasses and open-necked shirt behind the wheel of his Cadillac, and resplendent in a white tuxedo with a glass of champagne in his hands.

It struck Nick as odd that Helena never once referred to Bonny when she described the early years back in England. Surely even when they'd fallen out there would have been times when it was natural to mention an old dancing partner, even if only in vague terms.

But the strangest thing of all about Helena, was her apparent reluctance to behave like a star. From that first film *Soho*, through all the Hollywood musicals, there were countless studio pictures taken in costume on the set, and many of her caught unawares by press photographers, but there were none of her at glittering parties, premieres or holidaying in exotic places.

As Nick studied the old photographs, he was staggered by her beauty: those huge dark eyes full of fire and passion, that sensual wide mouth and delicate bone structure. Her nose and chin were small but well-defined, as though created to draw attention back to her glorious eyes. With each passing year she appeared to gain rather than lose beauty. Even in the latest one he'd managed to find, in which she'd passed forty, Helena was perfection.

It was frustrating to know she held the key to all those secrets, and yet be unable to reach her. Even if he was to go out to Hollywood, it was extremely unlikely that she'd agree to talk to him. Letters to a studio would end up in sacks of fan mail, his phone calls would be ignored. And if Bonny had hurt her too, it was unlikely that she would want to hear anything about Mel.

*

'Look, son,' Magnus laid one big hand on Nick's bare leg. 'I'm not suggesting we forget Mel, but I am going to insist you pull yourself together. You are an actor, or so you've been telling me for years. Put all your energy into this new role.'

Nick knew this was an order. When his father insisted on something, he felt he had to obey him. But there was also a sense of relief in being taken in hand. He knew he couldn't go on dwelling on this mystery for ever.

He had left the Bromley repertory company two weeks ago and was waiting to start filming *Delinquents* in the Lake District in a few days' time. He had high hopes for this screenplay: it was the kind of role he'd dreamed of for years. He was to play the part of an Outward Bound instructor, teaching young offenders. Daniel McKinley, a much talked about young actor, was cast in the lead role of the brutish tearaway in his charge, and doubtless he would get all the acclaim. But Nick was impressed by the script. It had a fast-moving plot and realistic hard-hitting dialogue, funny, yet inspiring. He felt this might well be a breakthrough in his career.

Looking at his father, Nick felt a surge of love for this man who had stood by him through thick and thin.

'Could you try and contact Helena?' he pleaded.

Magnus gave a wry grin. 'Okay, I'll try. But don't start building up your hopes Nick, she must get a ton of fan mail every day and she might not appreciate hearing from me anyway. Now let's get back to work. I want the rocks in place before the day's out.'

A month later Nick was standing on the shore of Lake Windermere, watching the film crew stow their equipment into a launch. The sky was a menacing black, and a brisk wind was making the lake choppy. In a few moments he would have to dispense with his warm sweater and dive from a rowing boat into the icy water to rescue Dan. Behind him the rest of the cast clustered around the warmth of the mobile canteen, drinking coffee and smoking. He could hear their laughter and guessed the jokes today were based on bets as to how many takes would be necessary for this particular scene. He fervently hoped he could do it right first time: it was too cold to face plunging in more than once today. Yet despite his nervousness, he was happy. His role in *Delinquents* was the most satisfying part he'd ever played.

Dan, who played Gary, the seventeen-year-old Glaswegian lout he was to rescue, reminded Nick of himself a few years earlier – an arrogant kid, who when he wasn't bragging about his acting talent, was either rolling up a joint or chatting up some young girl who was watching the action. Yet perhaps because of Nick's understanding of Dan's character, a bond had already formed between the pair of them.

In the script Gary has only one ambition in life: to be a bigger, tougher villain than any he'd encountered in several years of approved schools. Nick, as Alan, the committed sportsman-cum-social worker, puts Gary and a group of other equally troubled teenagers, all serving Borstal sentences, through a series of exhausting activities, with the intention of showing them how to use their toughness and courage to a more useful end.

'Ready?' Tim Hargreaves, the director, asked in a gruff voice, touching Nick's elbow. Normally he expected the cast to be ready the moment he bellowed at them, but there was a hint of concern on his big face today.

'As ready as I'll ever be,' Nick grinned. 'I hope Dan's a better swimmer than I am a life-saver!'

'Just make it look good.' Tim pulled up the hood of his anorak and adjusted the life jacket round his wide girth more securely, then stepped into the motorboat with the camera men. 'Rather you than me!'

Dan was already sitting in his rowing boat, wearing only shorts and a sleeveless singlet, bare arms rippling with muscle, the only person in the company not shivering. 'Do I really have to look such a prat?' he said sourly to Nick as he gingerly climbed into another small boat alongside him. 'I bloody well rowed for my school.'

'It's harder to look a prat than to do it properly,' Nick smiled as he picked up his oars. Dan couldn't be described as handsome – his features were too rough hewn – but it was a face full of character. 'Just watch me, I'm an expert on looking a prat!'

For all his arrogance Dan was a fine young actor. The moment he'd got his boat in the right position for the take some thirty yards from the shore, he began to flay his oars around in just the way a novice would.

Nick had the reverse problem: he had to look as if he'd been born in a boat, skimming across the lake effortlessly while shouting instructions to Dan.

Dan stood up in the bows, waving his arms in feigned anger, right on cue. As the boat rocked, he staggered and fell into the water backwards.

Dan's portrayal of a non-swimmer was so realistic even Nick thought for a moment he was in difficulty. Anxiety made him row harder, and he forgot about the biting wind. When Dan sank beneath the water, Nick was up in his boat, diving in without a moment's hesitation.

He had underestimated the weight of his tracksuit and plimsolls as he reached out for Dan and pulled him to the surface. The water was so cold he felt paralysed, but still he had to gasp out his lines while hauling a twelve-stone lad pretending to be semiconscious back to the boat and heave him into it, unaided.

'Cut!' Nick heard the magic command from the motorboat and sank down into the bottom of the boat beside Dan.

'Bloody hell, Nick,' Dan burst out as he lay panting like a netted fish. 'I didn't think you had it in you.'

Nick had known the part of outdoor pursuits instructor was perfect for him when he read the script, but he hadn't anticipated that his feelings for young Dan would echo the storyline or that Dan in turn would come to admire him. Nick's first reaction to the lad had been horror: he strutted around the set like a rooster, boasted about himself, put others down, and generally behaved like the spoiled pampered brat he was. But as filming started, so did a kind of chemistry between them, which, as the days passed, grew stronger. Nick had some real experience with rock climbing and he shared it with Dan. In return the lad helped him out in other directions. One evening about ten days into filming, instead of rushing off into Windermere to get drunk and pick up a girl Dan hung around waiting for Nick. He claimed to want to discuss the next day's shooting, but in fact he was curious about Nick. To Nick's surprise Dan had seen all six episodes of *Hunnicroft Estate* and couldn't understand why Nick wasn't famous.

'Because I was a conceited prat,' Nick said lightly. He went on to chart his rapid decline from star to nobody. 'Watch out you don't fall into the same trap,' he said finally as Dan sat hanging on his every word. 'You're a bumptious young bugger just like I was and you need friends in this business. If you do make the big-time from this one small film, don't think it's down to your talent. It's just luck.'

After that evening Dan sought Nick out every time they had a break in between scenes. He stopped boasting and name dropping and from behind the brash bold exterior stepped a child, desperate for some affection and attention.

The story built to a dramatic climax when Alan, instructing the boys in rock climbing, falls into a crevice because his line hadn't been properly secured. All the boys see this as an opportunity to escape from the gruelling course and make a break back to Glasgow.

They flee, but by the time they have reached the road at the bottom of the mountain, Gary finds he has a conscience after all. Dan played the scene superbly, torn between freedom and his fear for the safety of the man he has come to admire.

The other boys take his change of heart as betrayal, but Gary eventually sways them, revealing the qualities of leadership and reason Alan had brought out in him during the course.

Sending some of the boys for help, Gary climbs back up to Alan. The final scene, as he inches his way towards the injured instructor, is achingly emotional as Alan realises that the lad really does have all the finer qualities he'd hoped for.

'Perfect,' Tim called out jubilantly at the final take. 'If that doesn't win a few awards then I'll retire.'

Nick felt strange as he drove back to London. He felt he ought to be excited – everyone was predicting both he and Dan would soon be inundated with film offers – or at least a little sad at saying goodbye to all the new friends he'd made. But he felt nothing. It was almost as if his emotions had shut down.

When he got to his small flat in Hither Green that afternoon and saw the mess he'd left behind him a month ago, his numbness left him. The bed was unmade, thick gritty dust on every surface. The kitchen was even worse, the sink full of unwashed dishes, a couple of rotting black bananas surrounded by flies, and ants marching in a thick orderly line up the wall and into the cupboard. Suddenly he switched back to reality.

'Yuk!' he exclaimed, opening a window to let out the hot, smell-laden air. His flat overlooked the railway lines by Hither Green station and the noise from the trains usually made him keep it closed, but noise was preferable to a stink. 'So this is how the star really lives! Don't even think of going out tonight. This has to be tackled.'

He was halfway through washing the kitchen floor when the phone rang.

'Thank goodness you're back,' his father's deep voice rang out.

'I got home a couple of hours ago,' Nick said. 'Why? Is there something wrong?'

'Something right at last,' Magnus chuckled. 'Guess who's coming to Oaklands?'

'Mel?' Her name just popped out.

'No, son.' Magnus's voice dropped a little. 'But we're halfway there. It's Helena. She's coming here in two weeks' time.'

'What? You're having me on!'

'Of course I'm not,' Magnus said.

'But how? Why?' Nick had to sit down.

'I'd better come clean,' Magnus explained. 'You see some time ago I read a tiny article in the local newspaper about a film company looking for locations in the West Country. Amongst other things they were looking for a suitable country

519

house. I thought it might give Oaklands a bit of a boost, so I sent off some photographs. Anyway, I had a letter back thanking me for my interest but saying Oaklands wasn't suitable, they were looking for something more sinister. They enclosed the bit of blurb about the film *Broken Bridges* they were intending to make, presumably just as a public relations gesture, and low and behold, I saw Helena Forester was to be the star.'

'And you didn't tell me?' Nick felt a flush of anger.

'Would you have concentrated on your acting if I had?' Magnus retorted. 'No you wouldn't, you'd have been up at the film company's offices making a nuisance of yourself.'

Nick's anger left as quickly as it had come. His father was right of course. 'Well, come on, out with the rest of it!'

'When you were last here I'd just written to her. I didn't expect a reply – I thought the letter to MGM studios wouldn't even reach her. But I wrote anyway and invited her to stay here while she's in England.'

'She accepted? You mean it's definite?'

'Yes, first I got a letter from her secretary thanking me for the offer, the usual stuff: Miss Forester would be in touch etc. But yesterday I got her personal letter. Shall I read it to you?'

Nick could hardly contain himself. 'Go on,' he said, perching on the arm of a chair.

'Dearest Magnus,' his father read. 'What a delightful surprise to hear from you after all these years. I've often thought about you and wondered where you ended up, just as I have wondered about so many people I knew back in those post-war years.

'I was so sorry to hear about your wife's death, but heartened to hear your children have all done so well for themselves. That must be a consolation to you.

'I'd be more than happy to take you up on your invitation, at least for a night or two while I get adjusted to being back in England and find a suitable house. Your hotel sounds and looks idyllic from the brochure you enclosed, and I know I can count on you to be discreet. It will be so good to talk over old times. I don't often get excited these days, but I am thrilled at the thought of seeing you and England again after so many years away. My secretary will be in touch to make the arrangements.

'Until then, yours affectionately Helena.'

Nick gave a long low whistle. 'That's great Dad. Are you sure she wasn't an old flame too?'

'Quite sure,' Magnus laughed softly. 'You do understand we have to keep this under our hats?'

'Of course,' Nick replied. 'Will you let me know when she's coming so I can get down there?'

Magnus hesitated. 'I think it would be better for me to see her alone first,' he said slowly, as if he'd been churning things over in his mind. 'For one thing we don't want to intimidate her, and for another we don't want her thinking I want a leg up for my actor son.'

Nick was disappointed at not meeting the famous actress, but he kept it to himself. 'How's the rockery looking?' he asked instead.

'Finished.' He could almost see his father smiling. 'I got the pump sorted out. The waterfall works perfectly now and the plants are plumping up beautifully. It changes that whole part of the garden. But what about you, Nick, how did the film go?'

'I thought you were never going to ask. Absolutely marvellous. I think things might work out for me at last, but right now I'm cleaning up my flat. Let me know when Helena's coming won't you?'

'I'll let you get back to your chores,' Magnus's voice grew a little husky. 'I'm proud of you, son.'

The night before Helena's arrival, Magnus began to get nervous. Everything was in readiness: the menus planned, the staff informed who the important guest was. They had always prided themselves on giving their guests privacy, but in this case Magnus had to be sure no leak came from his end. Only two other couples were staying. The London barrister and his wife were too well-connected themselves to be unduly excited if they discovered the 'old family friend' was an actress, and the two Australian botanists had spent so much time in remote parts of the world they probably wouldn't know the Queen if she walked in.

Magnus downed a large whisky in the bar, said goodnight to the staff and made his way upstairs.

He was putting Helena in the Blue Room and on an impulse he went in to check everything. It was in fact a suite, the one he always gave to special guests. Until Ruth died, it had been his and Ruth's private rooms.

As he stood on the pale blue carpet a shiver ran down his spine – not an unpleasant sensation, just a gentle reminder of Ruth, for she'd loved this room so much. He could see her now, small and plump with wavy brown hair, sitting sewing on the window seat, constantly looking out at the view she never tired of.

Despite redecoration and new furniture, Magnus had kept the essence of Ruth's original scheme. She had chosen blue as the dominant colour because it faced south. In winter the two small settees in smudgy pink and blue sateen flanked the gracious Adam fireplace, and the matching curtains were replaced with heavy dusky pink velvet. But now the settees sat by the windows, the fireplace was filled with a huge jug of fresh flowers, the cooler, lighter curtains in place. Ruth's dainty Edwardian writing bureau was still here, no longer overflowing with menus, diaries and odd bits of mending, but filled instead with a selection of writing paper, booklets about the West Country and a telephone.

Once a Welsh dresser had stood on his right, laden with bits of bric-a-brac. In those days the blue walls were a mere backdrop for pictures and photographs, a room cluttered with mementos of the past. All the clutter was long since cleared, taken away by Sophie and Stephen in silent disapproval that Magnus no longer wanted it. How could he explain to them that he felt Ruth's presence even more strongly after her death than he had during her life? Those items she arranged so carefully were nothing more than milestones in their life together and unnecessary now. He could look back over their years together in one glorious long sweep, like the view from the window. He didn't need reminders of anything; it was engraved on his heart and mind for all time.

The room was perfection now, from the hand-printed silk paper on the walls, to white bone-china doves sitting on the mantelpiece. He knew Ruth would approve.

Magnus opened the window wide and leaned out. The night air felt like a lover's warm kiss on his cheeks. He could hear an owl somewhere in the distance and closer the splashing of the fountain round the side of the house. Earlier tonight people had been sitting out on the terrace. Many of them had stayed there until it was dark, lingering over their drinks, enjoying one of those rare almost Mediterranean summer nights. He had seen couples strolling arm in arm down across the lawns, and he was glad to see there were still romantics who liked to look at starry skies, to feel damp grass beneath bare feet and kiss in the seclusion of a beautiful garden.

He had found Mel looking out this window one evening in her first summer here. The room was free at the time and for some reason he had imagined it was a burglar. He had crept in silently, without turning on the light.

She was leaning out the window, just as he was doing now. He stood for a moment before speaking, but then he realised she was crying. She didn't hear him walk across the thick carpet, and she jumped in surprise when he put his hand on her shoulder.

'What is it, Mel?' he asked. 'Why are you crying in here?'

He couldn't see her face clearly, but there was enough light to reflect on the tears on her cheeks. 'Because it's so beautiful,' she said.

'So why cry?' He put one finger under her chin and lifted her face up. Her eyes were mere slits in a white face.

'It's just that I don't think I belong anywhere as beautiful as this,' she said. 'Every day I wake up feeling brand new, like everything that went before was a bad dream. But late at night like this I get to thinking *this* is the dream and that tomorrow I'll find it gone.'

He put his arms round her and let her cry on his shoulder. With hindsight he felt he should have done more.

Why hadn't he questioned her that night, and dug until he got at the whole truth?

He already trusted her to take cash to the bank, he had begun to involve her more and more in the running of the hotel, he valued her assistance out in the grounds in the afternoons, and she helped him there even though it was her free time. Looking back he couldn't understand why he hadn't been suspicious of such a perfect employee. She watched Antoine cooking and read books on food and wine. She studied the bar, the flower arrangements, everything and anything, all the time asking questions. When she went out it was just to walk. She was friendly and helpful to his guests, but never overly familiar.

He got into the habit of confiding in her, about guests, plans for the hotel, even things about Ruth and his children. She was so interested in him; she filled a part of his life that had been empty for too long. Then when she first met Nick and he sensed the current between them, he was overjoyed. If only he'd stopped to consider then why Mel held Nick at arm's length, instead of lapsing into daydreams about a big white wedding, and grandchildren playing in the grounds.

What a blind and stupid fool he was!

Magnus closed the window, then went over to the bedroom. Mel had chosen the material for the cover on the four-poster bed, deep-sea blues and greens. He remembered how fussy she was about this suite and the bed: the cover had to be just so, smoothed to perfection, just touching the carpet on both sides, the pillows folded into it with precision.

'Oh Ruth,' he murmured, picking up a small pressed flower picture from the dressing table that she had made. 'Where do I go from here?'

'Magnus,' Jayne Sullivan called him from the bottom of the stairs, her voice as crisp as the starched white shirts she always wore. 'The car's just pulling in, it's her!'

It was four o'clock, yet it seemed to Magnus as he hurried down the stairs that it ought to be nearer ten at night. He'd been unable to sleep the previous night and had got up soon after six, working in the garden all morning to take his mind off Helena and the images of Bonny she was bringing back.

As he stepped out the front door to greet her, the chauffeur opened the back door of the grey Daimler. A glimpse of dark glossy hair, one slim leg stretched out and the years slipped away.

'Ellie!' he called out and strode across the gravel drive, arms outstretched. 'It's so good to see you!'

She looked every inch a star, and far younger than the forty-seven he knew her to be: big dark eyes, skin as taut as a young girl's and black waves rippling down onto the shoulders of a white suit.

'Magnus, you old devil.' She ran to meet him. 'You look so bloody marvellous!'

Later as he had tea with her in her room he saw she hadn't quite halted the years. Her movements were a little slower, and on closer inspection there were tiny lines around her eyes. There was just the faintest suggestion of a double chin, and she didn't laugh quite so readily as he remembered.

The first time he'd seen her in that theatre in Oxford, he remembered likening her face to a pansy, yet those huge dark eyes had been full of fire then. Now they spoke of sadness. Even when he told her humorous stories about starting the hotel, he felt she was holding back, or worse had forgotten how to laugh from the belly the way she once did. She even reprimanded him for calling her Ellie, saying she'd left that name behind a great many years ago.

'Are we going to skirt round all the delicate areas?' she said suddenly. 'We can't talk about the old days without mentioning her name!'

Magnus blushed. They had been speaking for almost an hour, about his hotel, her films, his wife and children, yet he hadn't been able to bring himself to go further. She didn't invite confidences now, the way she had years ago. Her voice still had that same, deep husky quality, but there were overtones of an American accent and a different, much more brusque manner about her. 'I didn't like to,' he said. 'You know of course that she died?'

The colour drained from her face so fast Magnus thought she was going to faint.

'I'm so sorry,' Magnus got up from his seat and went to sit beside her on her settee, taking her hand in his and squeezing it. 'How tactless of me. I thought you must know.'

'I didn't,' she said weakly. 'It's such a shock. When did this happen?'

'In 1965.'

'But Camellia! She would only be fifteen then. Oh Magnus, how terrible. How did John take it? He must have been torn apart – he loved Bonny so much.'

Magnus's heart began to beat alarmingly fast. 'John died years before,' he said. 'I thought you'd know that.'

'Oh no.' Her hands flew up to her face. 'When, how? Oh Magnus, tell me?'

Magnus explained, and to his surprise Helena began to cry. 'I can't bear it,' she sobbed, her tears making her mascara run. 'Why didn't Bonny write and tell me about John? And that poor little love on her own. Why didn't you write and tell me?'

'I didn't know myself until last year,' Magnus said.

From the shock and distress on her face it was clear that Helena hadn't hardened her heart to Bonny. He passed on the information about both John's and Bonny's deaths almost as if he'd read of them in a newspaper. He couldn't possibly explain *now*, how he had learned of them, or tell her any of the more recent events.

'Can you leave me?' she said shakily when he'd finished. 'It's been an awful shock. I need time to rest.'

Magnus needed to rest himself, he felt drained. It would give him time to consider how he was going to broach the rest of his news and questions. 'Would you like dinner downstairs?' he asked. 'Or would you like to dine with me in my room.'

'With you, please,' she replied, her eyes still full of tears. 'I don't think I'm up to meeting your other guests.'

She was very pale and Magnus was worried about her. 'Would you like some brandy?' he asked.

She shook her head. 'I don't drink any more, Magnus.'

'Don't be afraid to ring down to reception if you need anything,' Magnus said as he left the room. 'I'll see you at dinner.'

As Magnus went along to his room, he wondered about that 'I don't drink any more'. It sounded almost as if she'd had a problem with drinking. Could that be the reason she'd faded from the public eye in the last ten years?

He couldn't imagine the Ellie he knew becoming an alcoholic, she was too strong willed, and she had left England with the world at her feet. Was it possible that fame and fortune hadn't brought her happiness after all?

It was half past seven when Helena knocked at his door. Her nap seemed to have restored her and she looked breathtakingly beautiful in a loose-fitting long purple gown, cut low at the front to reveal voluptuous cleavage. The purple enhanced her sultry colouring and gave her a regal appearance.

528

'The years have been very kind to you.' Magnus kissed both her smooth cheeks. 'Go on, disillusion me. You've had a face lift!'

She laughed, making her eyes sparkle. 'No I haven't, you cheeky devil. I was just lucky having a dark skin to start with. We wear better than blondes.'

Joan Downes had put his small supper table by the window and laid it beautifully with candles and flowers. Helena was thrilled by the panoramic view of the valley, and she lapsed back into the old easy manner Magnus remembered.

She was excited to be back in England and about her role in this new film, and admitted that she was now something of a has-been.

'When they do these coach trips round Hollywood showing the tourists the famous people's houses, I'm told they say: "Do any of you remembere Helena Forester? She was a big star in the fifties. This is where she moved to when she retired." I suppose it's better to have people think you're retired than just plain washed up. But it makes me sound so old.'

'Tell me about *Broken Bridges*?' Magnus asked. He was glad she'd retained her honesty.

'Oh, it's just perfect for me to make a comeback. It's about a middle-aged lady who falls in love with a young man and turns to murder when he jilts her,' she chuckled and her eyes twinkled wickedly. 'Rupert Henderson, who I understand is something of a heart-throb here, is my co-star and it's being directed by Stanley Cubright. I don't know if you're familiar with his work but he's renowned for his stars getting Oscars. I must admit I'd love to get one, before I hang up my hat for good.'

As she told Magnus about the script and the rest of the cast, the years seemed to slip away. She was just the old Ellie he knew. Funny, irreverent and self-effacing.

'Don't tell me you're dieting?' Magnus said later, when he noticed how little she'd eaten.

'No. Though I ought to be.' She smiled, that delightfully sensual lower lip curling, and patted her stomach. 'I guess it's jet lag. The chicken is wonderful and the sauce is divine but I can't manage any more.'

Magnus poured himself a glass of water, wishing it would turn into wine miraculously. Normally he didn't hold with people who fortified themselves with drink, but this time he needed it. He was going to have to ask her about Bonny soon.

'You didn't tell me how you found out about Bonny dying?' she said suddenly as if picking up his thoughts. 'Was the reason you invited me here something to do with it?'

Magnus had forgotten until now that one of the main reasons he'd liked Ellie had been for her intelligence and her directness. Clearly she hadn't lost either quality.

He fiddled with his napkin for a moment, not exactly certain which question he should answer first. 'I would have invited you here even if Bonny had been alive,' he said carefully. 'For old times' sake. But you're right, there was something I wanted to talk over with you. After giving you such a shock earlier, I'm a bit loath to go into it now.'

'Oh Magnus,' she laughed lightly and patted his hand flirtatiously. 'You're talking to me, someone who cut her teeth on trouble and bad news. Come on, out with it.'

'Bonny claimed that Camellia was my child,' Magnus said quickly before he lost his nerve. 'This was back in 1954.'

Helena's eyes opened wide in shock. 'That's

530

ridiculous,' she exclaimed. 'You aren't going to tell me you believed her?'

'Yes, I did,' he said with an embarrassed smirk. 'In fact I gave her money for several years. It was only when Camellia came to me here –'

'Camellia came here?' She cut him short, her voice sharp. 'So you've seen her? How is she? Where is she?'

Magnus stood up. 'Come on over to a more comfortable chair and I'll tell you everything.'

Once they were settled in armchairs he began with how Camellia arrived at Oaklands under an assumed name, and how and why he discovered her true identity. Although he spoke of the letters Mel had found from him, he didn't mention those from Jack and Sir Miles Hamilton.

To his utmost surprise Helena began to cry again as he described how Mel had run away after his stroke.

'Damn Bonny,' she exclaimed angrily. 'I thought she might have grown out of lying, but obviously she hadn't! Of course you aren't Camellia's father, Magnus.'

'Can you be absolutely certain?'

'Oh yes. I went with her to a doctor's in Harley Street for a pregnancy test.'

Helena's expression was so open and full of dismay that Magnus felt he could believe her implicitly. 'When exactly was that? Do you remember?'

'The beginning of May in 1949. She was six weeks pregnant then.'

'You're absolutely sure?' Magnus asked, running his hand over his chin. If Helena was right about the date, he couldn't possibly be the father.

'Yes. You see I'd only just started rehearsals for *Oklahoma*. Bonny came to the theatre to ask me to go with her for the test and it was confirmed that day. That's why she got married in such a hurry. How on earth could she blame you?'

'I saw her before her wedding. It wasn't planned. I just ran into her in London,' Magnus admitted shamefacedly.

'Oh Magnus, that was June.' Helena shook her head, but there was an understanding look in her eyes.

'I didn't see her after that day until September 1954,' Magnus went on. 'It was at a party in Sussex and both Ruth and John were there too. She told me then that I was Camellia's father and that she was born two months premature.'

'Magnus, what a sucker you are,' she exclaimed. 'I can't believe you fell for that! I was there with Bonny when Camellia was born. She was tiny, only five pounds but she was a full-term baby.'

'You were there, at her birth?' Magnus hadn't expected that.

'I was the first person to hold Camellia, I even named her.'

Her eyes were soft now, just the way Ruth's looked when she spoke of babies. 'John was abroad and I stayed for a month till he got back from America.'

'What was she like as a new mother?'

Helena didn't answer immediately. She put her head back on the cushions of the chair and closed her eyes. 'Like a little girl with a dolly,' she said softly. 'She was surprisingly maternal. She loved all the bathing, dressing and feeding. I kept expecting her to get bored with it, but she didn't. You'd have been very surprised, Magnus. She was made to be a mother.'

The words were hardly out of her mouth when she suddenly jerked upright in her seat.

'Did she continue to be a good mother? I mean

later after John died? You see when I last saw her Camellia was only four.'

Magnus was somewhat taken aback by the depth of passion in her voice. He would have expected the Hollywood years to have blunted the compassion and sensitivity he remembered so well in the young Ellie.

He had no choice but to tell her what he'd learned of Camellia's childhood and adolescence. He wanted to stir up her sympathy so she would help both Nick and himself. But as he told her how things had been back in Rye and her eyes filled with tears again, he wondered if he'd gone too far.

'Camellia's a sunny, kind, caring and gentle person,' he added, trying to put into words things which had come to him during his spell in hospital and since. 'I can't see how she'd turn out like that without a strong groundwork of love and affection. Whatever Bonny put Mel through, at the end of the day Mel loved her mother, and she still does despite everything.'

Helena dried her eyes. Her face was white and he could almost see the tension rising within her. 'There's more, isn't there?' she said. 'Tell me everything, Magnus. Don't hold it back.'

'Tell me first what split you two up?' Magnus asked.

'Jealousy,' Helena spat out the word, her mouth in a tight straight line. 'She hated seeing my name on billboards, reading about me in newspapers. She said some cruel, evil things that last day we met and in the end she told me to push off and never come back.'

'Surely she didn't mean it?'

'Oh she did, Magnus. She was like ice.' Helena turned her face away from his. 'I phoned her so many times but she wouldn't speak to me and she returned all the presents I sent for Camellia. I expect that's why she didn't let me know about John dying too.'

Magnus felt it was time to reveal the parts he'd kept hidden, about Jack Easton and Sir Miles Hamilton.

Helena scarcely reacted to the mentions of Jack. But she did look agitated about Sir Miles Hamilton and turned away slightly so Magnus couldn't see her face.

Magnus put one hand on her shoulder and drew her back to face him. 'What did she have on him, Helena? Was he a lover to both of you?'

Her eyes were wide. This time it wasn't surprise but fear.

'Tell me, Helena? It won't go any further than this room.'

'You've got it all wrong,' she said, but although she tried to compose herself her voice was shaking. 'He wasn't a lover to either of us. He was far too old.'

'Bonny had no aversion to older men, as I remember.' Magnus decided the time had come to stop pussy-footing around the issue. 'My son believes Sir Miles is Camellia's father. He also suspects Bonny didn't commit suicide, but was killed to shut her up. Sir Miles has the best motive. What do you say to that?'

For a moment she stared at him in horror. 'No, Magnus.' She shook her head vigorously. 'You are way off beam. Sir Miles isn't Camellia's father and neither is he the kind of man to bump anyone off.'

Magnus knew with utter certainty that Helena was concealing something. She couldn't look into his eyes. He felt he had to shake her up.

'I understand your loyalty to Sir Miles when he's helped your career so much. But Camellia is out there somewhere, bewildered and alone, and I know you've got at least some of the answers that might help her. What made you an alcoholic, Helena? Was it the burden of too many secrets?'

She was off the settee so fast and backing away towards the door that Magnus hardly had time to catch his breath.

'How dare you,' she asked, eyes flashing with anger. 'I am not an alcoholic and I came here as your guest, Magnus, not to be cross-examined. Despite the fact you were a married man when you had your affair with Bonny, I always thought of you as truly honourable. I wanted to see you again because I admired you. Now I find you only invited me to pry and poke around, just like everyone else.'

She gathered up the skirt of her long dress and opened the door. 'I'll be leaving in the morning,' she flung back at him. 'I've told you all you need to know. Your son is free to marry Camellia. She is not your child.'

She left the door wide open and raced along the landing towards the Blue Room. Magnus stood at the door for a moment, a feeling of nausea rising inside him.

He went back into his room and poured himself a stiff drink. 'Well, you really cocked that up!' he said to himself. 'You bumbling fool!'

It was after three in the morning when Magnus finally got weary of trying to sleep. His head was buzzing with conflicting emotions. Delight that he could tell Nick he wasn't Mel's father, shame that he'd laid into Helena so brutally, and frustration that the whole truth was so close, yet unreachable. He put on a plaid dressing gown over his pyjamas and went into his sitting room.

Julie had come to collect the dinner things about ten thirty, and he'd nearly bitten the poor girl's head off for asking how the evening had gone.

What would the staff think when Helena left suddenly in the morning?

What could he do now? It was unlikely Helena would have second thoughts. She'd always been determined about everything. And he'd insulted her by suggesting she was an alcoholic.

Dejectedly Magnus opened his door. He might as well go down to the kitchen and make himself some hot milk. That was what Ruth had always prescribed for anxiety.

As he passed the Blue Room he heard a faint sound. He stopped, pressing his ear to the door. For a moment he thought he was hearing the ghost of Ruth, for she had cried that way when she was in the final painful stages of her life. But it was no ghost, it was a flesh and blood woman sobbing her heart out. He gingerly tried the door, expecting to find it locked, but to his surprise it turned in his hand. Opening it just a crack, he looked in.

The way the bedside light in the adjoining bedroom cast its weak golden beam onto the sitting room carpet was all so familiar. How many times had he crept in as he was doing now. Ruth would brush the tears away when she saw him and try to smile, making out she had no pain.

Helena's face was turned away as he silently walked into the room. Black wavy hair was spread out on the pillow, her shoulders and arms golden-brown against the white sheets, shuddering as she sobbed. She wore a cream lace nightdress with narrow shoulder straps, the matching negligee tossed onto the floor.

'I'm so sorry, Helena,' he whispered, going over to the bed and sitting down beside her. 'I didn't mean to hurt you. To be honest I was like a big schoolboy at the thought of you coming here. The prying was only because I wanted to get you to help me find Camellia.'

She didn't reply, but he didn't sense any further anger, only sorrow.

Lying down beside her and taking her into his arms was the only way he knew of helping, as it had been with Ruth.

She was silent for some time, but the fact she didn't recoil suggested she needed him.

'Oh, Magnus, I want to make things right,' she whispered eventually against his chest. 'But you don't know how hard it is.'

'Not now,' he whispered back. 'I'm just a friend now, not an inquisitor. Whatever it is that's troubling you can wait. Go to sleep now.'

He didn't fall asleep until a long time after she did. It was so long since he'd held a woman in his arms he could only savour the sweetness of it. The softness of her breasts against his chest, her hair on his face and the delicate flowery scent of her. He thought perhaps he'd finally learned all the aspects of love now. The innocent longing for his sweetheart, the warmth of marriage. Passion for a mistress and the tender sweetness of fatherhood. In those last months with Ruth there had been more, a distillation of every kind of emotion mixed into a bewildering potpourri. Love, anger, tenderness and bitterness, rage and quiet calm. Gentle Ruth had known and seen everything. She faced death with the same courageous spirit that had carried her through knowing he loved another woman. At the end she found the words to absolve him from guilt.

'Don't grieve for me,' Ruth had said. She had become so thin she looked like a child in the big bed. 'We had so much happiness together, that's all I remember. If I could turn back the clock and be eighteen again, I'd still pick you. Maybe I'd try harder to understand you needed a bigger world than me and be at your side as you conquered it, but I wouldn't change one thing about you.'

The sun woke Magnus, as it played around the edge of the curtains. Helena was sleeping peacefully now, lying on her stomach, her face buried in one curved arm. Silently Magnus inched his way to the edge of the bed, taking care not to wake her.

It wouldn't do to be here when she woke. Silent comfort in the night was one thing, by daylight it could be mistaken for something else. Whatever secrets Helena knew, she must make the decision to deal with them herself. He would have to learn patience.

Chapter Twenty-Two

Magnus was on his knees weeding a rose bed. He'd come out in the garden at eight to do some watering while it was still cool. Now it was nearly eleven and very hot, but he was still pottering. He felt he ought to be happier: Jayne had informed him earlier that they were booked solidly through till October, and Nick had sent him a preview of the publicity planned for his film *Delinquents*. But his thoughts were all centred on the events of last night, wondering if Helena had forgiven him and whether she'd open up more before leaving Oaklands.

'There's nothing quite as lovely as an English garden, is there?'

Magnus was startled to hear her husky voice so close, especially as she'd been on his mind. He jerked his head around. She was wearing a lilac sleeveless dress, her hair swept back into a chignon and her sly grin suggested she'd crept up behind him deliberately.

'There's you, which is equally lovely,' he said gallantly. 'But creeping up on an old man and making him jump could prove fatal.'

Her laugh was as attractive as her face, low and musical. 'Old age hasn't diluted your charm,' she said, and she put one hand under his elbow to help him up to his feet.

'Did you sleep well?' Magnus asked.

'You know I did,' she reproved him with a soft

little laugh. 'I just hope discretion was the reason for leaving rather than shock at seeing me minus the war paint?'

Magnus felt soothed by her openness. 'Definitely discretion. I'm just sorry that your first night in my home was so upsetting. I handled things very badly.'

Last night he'd wondered if her eyelashes were false, but she wore only the minimum of make-up now and they were certainly real.

'Old friends can be that penetrating and be forgiven.' She bent over to smell a rose and sighed deeply with pleasure.

'Are you all dressed up like that to leave?' he asked hesitantly. 'Can't I persuade you to change your mind?'

'There's no persuasion needed,' she smiled. 'I'd like to stay – well for another night or two maybe. If I looked dressed up, it's just because I've got to go and see a cottage later. But I hoped you might come with me.'

'I'd like that,' Magnus smiled with relief that she bore no hard feelings. It looked like being a good day after all. 'Where is it?'

'In a village called Kelston,' she said. 'Someone from the film company called just now about it. Do you know it?'

'Yes, it's not far away and very pretty,' Magnus said. 'In fact Nick and I often go to the Crown there, for a bit of olde England. But aside from the pub, it's a bit isolated. Wouldn't you be better off in Bath?'

Helena looked at him, her eyes twinkling. 'Magnus,' she said. 'You've just said my favourite word – not pub but isolation. It sounds just perfect. The owners are going abroad and though they only want to let it for now, they may want to sell it later. Have you got time to sit down and have a chat, or have I got to get down on my knees and join you at the weeding?'

Magnus had moved the swinging garden settee down by the rockery just a couple of days earlier because it was the most secluded part of the garden and an ideal place to sit in peace, well away from any noise from the terrace bar or the swimming pool. He led Helena over there, then rinsed his dirty hands under the waterfall.

Her reaction to the swinging seat pleased him. She gave a squeal of pleasure, rushing to it like a child and sitting down, swung it hard with her feet.

'I just love any kind of swing,' she said gleefully. 'I've always wanted an ordinary rope and plank one, hung under a tree, but if you had one in Hollywood, without a child in the house they'd think you'd lost your marbles.'

'Am I clean enough to sit beside you now?' he asked, standing in front of her and showing her his clean hands like a Boy Scout at inspection.

'Of course you are.' She reached out, took his hands in both of hers and drew him down beside her. 'Your hands say a deal about you,' she said thoughtfully, running one perfectly manicured fingertip round the end of his short square nails. 'Strong, capable, but adventurous too.' She turned his palm up and looked at it. 'A long life-line. One big romance and two smaller ones.' She pinched his fleshy mound of Venus. 'That's a good healthy sign. Lots of passion and warmth. Ruth was a lucky lady.'

'She deserved a great deal better than me,' Magnus sighed. 'Why did I get involved with Bonny? Can you see that in my palm too?'

'Perhaps we ought to look and see if we have an identical line,' she smiled wryly, her lower lip curling. 'Because I've asked myself that question hundreds of times. She gave me more headaches than anyone I've ever met. Yet, I loved her and so did you. If she'd been born a few centuries earlier she would have been the King's mistress at least. But let's not talk about her just yet. I want to hear more about Camellia.'

It felt good to sit back on the soft cushions and talk about Mel. The waterfall in the rockery gurgled and splashed, and they didn't even hear the club members beginning to arrive for lunch. Because Helena understood how he had once felt about Bonny Magnus could speak openly. With Nick he had felt obliged to tone down both his memories and feelings.

'I didn't realise just how much Mel meant to me until I was ill with pneumonia,' he explained. 'I was aware I was very fond of her, and that I'd never felt that way about any other member of my staff. I depended on her too and felt we were close friends, but then you don't analyse your feelings about people do you? At least not until something makes you realise they might just walk out of your life.'

'You never connected her with Bonny then?' Helena asked. 'Not even a suspicion?'

Magnus sighed deeply. 'It was always in my mind that one day a girl might turn up and announce herself as Camellia Norton. With someone as devious and unpredictable as Bonny there was a strong chance she would renege on the promises she'd made years before. On the night Mel arrived here, sick and wet through, I did get a sharp jolt. Not only was the name Amelia similar to Camellia, but she was the right age. I said some pretty tough things to her that night. Looking back I suppose I felt threatened.'

'Did you question her about her background?' Helena asked. 'I mean when she was better and before you offered her a job?'

542

'A little, but my housekeeper did most of the digging while Mel was still ill. She said she'd been brought up in London, that both her parents were dead and she'd been travelling and working around the continent. There wasn't anything to be suspicious about – so many young people at that time just bummed around as she had. But you've got to bear in mind that I'd always had a picture of a girl who looked like Bonny in my mind. I expected her daughter to have inherited her character too.'

Helena smirked knowingly. 'You expected a Marilyn Monroe look-alike to come wiggling in singing "My Heart Belongs to Daddy"?'

Magnus chuckled. 'I suppose so. The only photograph I ever saw of Camellia was shown to me by John, just a couple of hours before Bonny claimed she was my child. Now had I been shown it *afterwards*, I would have studied it. But we all know how precious little notice we take of other people's snapshots.'

'Magnus, I really can't believe you would just accept what Bonny told you on trust,' she said, shaking her head in disbelief. 'You knew what a storyteller she was. If I'd been in your shoes I would have insisted on documentary evidence.'

'Even if you were afraid that by doing so your wife might find out about it?' Magnus raised one eyebrow questioningly. 'Besides Bonny didn't ever ask for money, she just wanted me to share her guilt. The money side came much later after John died, and I offered it. Perhaps part of me wanted to believe Camellia was my child. Bonny had engraved a place for herself in my heart remember – those feelings don't ever quite leave one. You know what they say: "There's no fool like an old one"?'

Helena fell silent for a moment or two, mulling

everything over in her mind. 'But Camellia was here for two years, Magnus, surely during that time some odd things about her must have come to light. Childhood memories, places, things like that. I avoid telling anyone about my early days, but every now and then I slip up and something comes out.'

'All she revealed was her character – honest, brave, kind-hearted and extremely hard-working,' Magnus replied. 'She told me just before her first Christmas here that her mother had committed suicide, and she also told me she'd been very fat as a teenager. Now both of those rang true, but neither of them were pointers to Bonny. Any initial suspicion I'd had about her just wafted away. When Nick fell for her I became puzzled again. They were so right for each other.'

'Tell me about Nick?' she asked. 'You said he was an actor. Is he like you?'

'He's turned out to be a fine young man,' Magnus said with some pride. 'Better looking than I was at his age. He's got none of my practical nature or his mother's patience, but in the last year or so he's matured considerably. He works hard, takes his acting very seriously and he's fun to have around. He's looking forward to meeting you – he's been a life-long fan of yours.'

Helena blushed prettily. 'What did you suppose was Mel's reason for holding him at arm's length?' she asked, swinging the seat gently.

Magnus shrugged. 'At first that she was playing hard to get or that she was afraid of getting involved with the boss's son. Mel wasn't one for talking about herself and I didn't think it was my place to question her about Nick. Besides he wasn't actually living here. It was only when I got pneumonia that I began to think more deeply about what the real impediment between them could be. I came up with two possibilities: that she had a child somewhere or that she'd run from a violent husband. But you know how it turned out, I told you all that last night.'

Magnus looked round to see that Helena was mopping at her eyes.

'For a girl who was tough enough to get to Hollywood,' he said with a grin, 'you are very sentimental.'

'I just feel so bad about all this,' she sniffed. 'If only I'd known John died, I'd have come back to see Bonny, even at the risk of her turning on me again and sending me away with a flea in my ear. I wonder now if she tried to contact me then, and the letters just never reached me.'

Magnus's speckled eyes wrinkled up with amusement. 'Helena, you know as well as I do that if Bonny had wanted to contact you, she'd have found a way.'

He expected her to laugh, but instead Helena began to cry harder. 'Do you have a picture of Camellia?' she sobbed.

'Only if you stop crying,' he said. 'If anyone walks past they'll think we're having a lovers' tiff or something.'

She smiled wanly and wiped her eyes. 'I'm sorry, Magnus, whatever must you think of me.'

'I think you are a softie,' he said, reaching into his back pocket and pulling out a picture. 'I've got lots of others in my office,' he smiled as he handed it over. 'But this one's my favourite and for some perverse reason I've taken to carrying it around with me.'

It was the one he'd taken as she was dressing the tree that first Christmas. This one was the first of the series, before she toppled from the stepladder and landed on her back on the floor. She was leaning forward to place the fairy at the top of the tree, her tongue peeping out from her lips, an intent expression on her face. She was wearing jeans and a red sweater, her hair caught up in two bunches.

Helena stared at it for a moment. 'She's not at all what I expected!' she said eventually.

'Nothing like her mother!' Magnus agreed. 'But she's lovely, isn't she? A bit taller than Bonny, about five foot seven or eight I'd say, a womanly shape with proper hips even though she's slim. Mind you after I knew who she was I found similarities to my daughter, Sophie.'

They were interrupted by Julie coming to ask if they wanted some lunch. Magnus hastily put the picture back in his wallet.

'What would you like to do?' He turned to Helena. 'Go inside or have something out here?'

'Let's stay here,' she said and smiled at the small blonde waitress. 'It's Julie, isn't it?' she asked.

Julie blushed nervously.

'Yes, Miss Forester,' she squeaked.

'Mrs Downes told me it was you who pressed some of my clothes for me while I was having dinner last night?' she said. 'Thank you so much, it was very thoughtful of you.'

'I liked doing it, Miss Forester,' Julie said, twitching with excitement. 'My mother used to take me to see your films. I just loved them. I hope you have a lovely stay in England. We can't wait to see your new film.'

'It will be awhile yet,' Helena said. 'But you and your mother must come to the film set one day and see it being made. I'll arrange it all with Mr Osbourne and have a car sent for you.'

Magnus thought Julie might very well curtsey before long. She was the colour of a beetroot now, her eyes like saucers.

'Thank you so much,' Julie squeaked again. 'What shall I bring you for lunch then, Mr Osbourne?'

'A surprise picnic,' Magnus said, wondering if little Julie would be able to work for the rest of the lunch-hour now. 'Just ask Antoine to put something in a basket.'

Once Julie had scuttled off, he turned back to Helena.

'That was nice of you,' he said.

'My fans are very precious to me,' she replied softly. 'There have been times in my life when without their affection and support I might have cracked up.'

'Ruth was one of your fans,' Magnus said, smiling at the memory. 'I think she saw *Soho* about four times. She recognised you from the night at the Savoy and she was thrilled you made it. Sometimes I wonder if it was your influence which started Nick on the idea of becoming an actor. He and Ruth used to cut out your pictures and stick them in a scrapbook. I always wished I could admit I'd once known you pretty well.'

'Did Ruth ever find out about Bonny?' Helena asked.

A cloud passed over Magnus's face. 'Not who she was, but she knew there was someone,' he said sadly. 'She didn't tell me right until the end. But that was the way Ruth was. Her family's happiness and mine were always more important to her than her own feelings. I miss her so much, Helena.'

Helena squeezed his hand in silent sympathy.

'Tell me about you,' Magnus said in a gruff voice. 'Why didn't you ever marry? Didn't a big enough love come along?'

'A huge one, over before I even met you,' she said glumly. 'The first, the greatest and the only real one. His name was Charley King, the fireman who dug my Aunt Marleen out of the bombed block of flats. I had lost my home, and Marleen was

547

blinded and had her back broken. He took me home to his mother's house in King's Cross.'

'So what went wrong?'

She let out a big sigh. 'I wanted fame and fortune, he wanted marriage and children. Maybe I was too young, too selfish and headstrong, I don't know exactly now. But I do know that if I could start all over again, I'd marry him, have half a dozen kids and settle for sweet ordinariness.'

'What happened to him?'

'He went to Australia. I kept in touch with his mother for some time, but not after she joined him and his wife and family out there. I often wonder if he's seen my films, and whether he ever forgave me. I hope he's happy, he deserved to be.'

The way she said that took Magnus right back to 1947 when he so often took both Bonny and Helena out to supper after their show. In those days she was just Ellie, the quieter one of the double act. He had been impressed then by her compassionate nature, and it pleased him to think she hadn't lost that quality on the road to becoming famous. But she had been such a joyous young girl, full of fun and laughter. She so richly deserved her success, but it saddened him to see that she hadn't been happier.

'What went wrong in your life?' Magnus asked. 'Can't you tell an old friend about it?'

She hesitated for a moment and he half expected her to clam up as she had the previous night. 'I should never have allowed myself to be talked into going to Hollywood,' she blurted out. 'I should have stayed in England and made more films like *Soho*. But I let myself be manipulated because I'd lost sight of my real goals. By the time I woke up to what was happening, it was too late. I let them trap me into a contract I couldn't get out of and I made one after another of those banal musicals.' She paused and he saw her eyes were full of bitterness.

'Go on,' he prompted.

'The moguls over there don't care about talent or art,' she spat out. 'When they find a formula that brings in money, they squeeze it to the last drop. They wouldn't let me grow as an actress, they stunted me. When the last film was a flop they blamed me, not themselves, and I was forced into retirement because they said I was too temperamental.'

'When you've finished this film will you stay in England or go back?'

'I thought I had no choice in the matter until this morning,' she said thoughtfully, her smooth brow crinkled by a frown. 'I thought I was too deeply rooted in America to transplant myself back here.'

'But now?'

'What I thought were roots look more like mere possessions today,' she grimaced. 'And I have no real friends – only a psychiatrist who I have to pay to talk to.'

'You have a psychiatrist? What on earth for?'

She looked at Magnus, with a trace of suspicion.

'You're in England now,' he reminded her. 'There's no journalist hiding behind the trees with microphones, and I don't pass on privileged information.'

'As the Yanks like to say, "I'm pretty screwed up", Magnus. I've been hiding behind costumes and pills for years. When you said I was an alcoholic you were wrong, drink hasn't been my problem. I was put off that by my Aunt Marleen. But I have suffered from chronic depression. When I was offered this part, I was feeling very low. I'd lost my confidence, even the sense of *who* I was. But I managed to recognise it as a possible liferaft. When your letter came, that, my old friend, was like finding a dry blanket in the raft and a gallon of fresh water.'

'And I almost overturned the raft?'

She tucked her arm through his and smiled. 'My psychiatrist said I would be tested when I came back here. Maybe if you hadn't come in last night when you did, I might have slipped back. It's rather ironic isn't it? I've paid fortunes to doctors and shrinks over the years, dredged through old painful memories with strangers, all to no avail. But a few probing questions from an old pal, followed by a hug, achieved a great deal more than all that expensive therapy.'

'Are you serious that you have no one back in America?' It seemed incredible that a woman as lovely as Helena should be so alone. 'Not even a man friend.'

'Well, there's Edward,' she said. 'I don't know if you remember but he was a friend right back from 1945.'

Magnus nodded.

'He's coming over soon to join me.'

Magnus felt himself stiffen, to his surprise he realised he was a little jealous. 'He's in the film too?' he asked.

Perhaps Helena heard the starch in his voice. She smiled. 'No, he isn't, and we aren't lovers, Magnus.'

'It's none of my business if you are,' he retorted quickly. 'I just hope you'll have room for me as a friend too.'

Julie came back at that point loaded down with a large wicker basket and a folded picnic table and their conversation was halted temporarily.

'That, as Edward would say, was "topping",' Helena said half an hour later as she slumped back in the swing seat holding her stomach and grinning broadly. 'I've never had a picnic like that one before.'

To Magnus it was nothing outstanding. Just crusty bread, chicken, ham, cheeses and salad. 'You must have had better than that,' he said disbelievingly.

'Americans aren't picnic people,' she said. 'They go for lavish barbecues and stuff, but they somehow miss the point of picnics, which should be taking quite ordinary food somewhere extraordinary to eat it. My mother and I used to go to Victoria Park in Bethnal Green for picnics. We'd have bread and dripping in waxed paper, an apple each and a bottle of ginger beer, and that was a real feast.'

Magnus knew exactly what she meant. He could remember sharing equally basic food in the woods around Craigmore with some of the other children who lived on the family estate. The fancy picnics he remembered going on with his parents and their friends were never as much fun.

'So does Edward like bread and dripping picnics too?' he asked.

'Actually he doesn't,' she said. 'In fact he finds it very irritating that I have such love for "common" things, particularly British common things.'

'He sounds a bit of a snob.'

She sighed. 'Oh Magnus, he is. I love him like a brother, we've been through so much together, and I've got everything to thank him for, but there are times when I wish I could walk away from him for good.'

'Then why is he coming here to join you?'

'Because he controls me, Magnus,' she said in a small voice. 'I feel guilty about telling you this. It makes me sound so disloyal when I've already said what a good friend he is. But I'm afraid it's true, and I'm too spineless to put a stop to it.'

'You were never spineless,' Magnus said stoutly. 'From what Bonny had to say about this man, years ago, he wasn't great shakes as an actor and he was only a passable pianist. But then she was a bit jealous. So how come he got in a position to control you?'

'I met Edward even before I met Bonny,' she said. 'We were partnered together in a comic sketch for the revue at the Phoenix. Bonny was one of the Dingle Belles. He was a few years older than me, a very correct, starchy young man and as it turned out, a very lonely one too. My friendship with Bonny began on VE Day when we got into some mischief together with a couple of GIs, but Edward and I were already firm friends.' She paused for a moment as if thinking how to explain.

'Bonny and I were a case of opposites attracting, but Edward and I were more like twin souls in many ways. Like me he had no family, aside from a very old grandmother. We were both unsure of ourselves and we both loved the theatre passionately. Bonny provided all the excitement of a fun fair, Edward was the soothing voice of calm and reason. I loved them both.

'Over the years I spent performing with Bonny, my friendship with her tended to dominate, just because of the way she was, but Edward was always there. Even when he was miles away in another town, I still kept in touch. I knew Bonny inside out, but I knew Edward too, and often he was the one I ran to when Bonny let me down. After Bonny got married and I made *Soho*, Edward and I became even closer. When I finally found myself in Hollywood in 1951, everything was so alien. People fawned round me, I couldn't make out who were good people and who were just using me. I needed someone I could trust implicitly and so I asked Edward to join me there.'

Magnus nodded. He could quite understand the old Ellie giving an old friend a leg-up, but he still found it hard to imagine her being under anyone's control.

'Well, once Edward arrived, I felt so much better. He soon became the buffer between me, the studio and the press. He was so good at organisation, and he helped me get a house, staff who could be trusted and how to handle my money. I introduced him to everyone as my manager, because that's exactly what he did, he managed me.'

'Did you pay him?' Magnus asked.

She didn't speak for a moment, but tucked her hand into his arm companionably. 'Maybe that was the first mistake. I should've had it on a proper business footing right from the start and drawn up lines of conduct. But that's hard to do with a good friend, isn't it? Edward had a private income you see, from his grandmother, so he didn't actually need a job as such. Of course I reimbursed him for all expenses and he had his own apartment in my house. He also had small parts in films sometimes, usually when they wanted an archetype English gentleman. As I've said, he handled my money for me, he paid the bills and acted as secretary and everything else. If that included a car for him or a new suit, that was all part of my expenses.'

Magnus shook his head slowly. 'That sounds like a recipe for disaster.'

'Not in the way you mean,' she corrected him. 'Edward accounted for every penny, spent by him and by me. Without him looking after my money for me I would probably have spent everything as fast as I earned it. He invested it for me and very wisely too. But what I didn't see coming was the danger of allowing myself to become so dependent on him. You see I had no decisions to make. I got up in the morning and my clothes for the day were laid out by the maid, instructed by him. The car arrived to take me to the studio, at the end of the day's shooting it took me home. Edward would decide which engagement to accept for me that night, he'd even advise the maid again what I should wear. More often than not Edward escorted me to these parties or functions. Hairdressing, manicures, massages, Edward arranged all that. His taste was impeccable. Before long he even shopped for clothes with me, or for me.'

'That sounds monstrous,' Magnus exclaimed.

'It does telling you now, while I'm sitting here as free as a bird and looking back on it,' she said with a funny little smirk. 'But at the time I was very glad of it. Each day's shooting was exhausting, and I was frightened by all the high-powered people around me. Edward made it possible for me to give my best each day without any worries. I didn't know then what I should wear to these dinner and cocktail parties, I was just glad he did.'

'Didn't he have any lady friends?'

She didn't answer immediately and Magnus repeated the question, remembering that Bonny had always claimed he was homosexual.

'Yes, but never what you'd call romances,' she said warily. 'I mean he went out to meet women from time to time, but he never brought them home. He had always been a bit odd about women, Magnus. I think I'm the only one he ever really liked.'

Magnus nodded. It sounded to him as if Bonny had been right. He didn't like the sound of him one bit.

'So at what stage did you become depressed, and why?' Magnus thought it better to change the subject, even if it was still painful.

She looked thoughtful.

'I used to have panic attacks right back while I

was making *Soho*,' she said. 'But I was on home ground then, surrounded by people who had my best interests at heart. But when I got to Hollywood they got far worse. I felt cut off, frightened; kind of intimidated by everything. I saw a doctor who gave me some tranquillisers, but though they helped me calm down, I sometimes felt I was losing touch with reality.'

Magnus was beginning to get the picture: a beautiful talented young woman thrown into an artificial world peopled by hyenas and sharks who preyed on her vulnerability. 'But if Edward cared about you, didn't he try to get you sorted out?'

She nodded. 'Oh yes, he tried. He took me to classes to learn relaxation exercises. He gradually weaned me off the pills and even encouraged me to have a drink rather than rely on tranquillisers. For a time I was much better, I was eating and sleeping well, but the downside was that I started to put on weight and the studio didn't like it. Finally, in 1961, I found a doctor to prescribe me some dieting pills and they worked. I drank only orange juice, I lost the weight, I felt on top of the .world again for awhile, but they were addictive, Magnus. Soon one a day wasn't enough, it was three, four, six or even ten and I was so hyped up I couldn't sleep at night. Before long I was taking barbiturates to sleep, and something else to wake me up the next day. Edward would have stopped me had he realised what I was doing, but he didn't until it was too late.'

Magnus listened in horror as she described the spiral she was trapped in. Loss of memory, the spurts of wild elation followed by black depression, and her ever increasing reliance on Edward to hold things together for her.

'When the work dried up in the mid-sixties, he was still there for me,' she said in a low voice.

'Thanks to him, I was financially secure and I could afford to see the best psychiatrist in town.'

Magnus didn't believe in psychiatrists. He couldn't see how the level-headed girl he'd once known could ever need that kind of 'quackery'.

'Did this "shrink" help?' he asked.

'In some ways, yes. He made me look deeply at myself. But as he was so very fond of telling me, I alone had to make the decisions to deal with what I'd learned and for a long, long time I did nothing about it. Those years were my "hermit" period. I rarely left my house and I saw no one. I read books, I swam in my pool, exercised a little, but I was almost suicidal and quite often I got drunk just to black it all out. If it hadn't been for Edward's continuing care and support I would probably have ended it all during one of these benders. Then one day when I'd finally given up hope of ever getting offered another part, Stanley Cubright came to see me with the script for *Broken Bridges*.'

'And that pulled you together?'

'It did. As I read it I knew the part was made for me. I had all the excitement I felt when I read *Soho*. Nothing had affected me like that for years. Edward was against it oddly enough. He said returning to England would make me feel more isolated, but for once I didn't listen. I just knew I must come home and make this film. So I accepted the part. And that's where you came in.' She paused, looking hard at Magnus.

'Now could I have possibly said I didn't need or want Edward here with me after all he'd been through with me?'

Magnus hardly knew what to say. On the face of it Edward Manning had been a saint and true friend, yet for all that he knew he wasn't going to like the man anymore than Bonny had done. 'I think you have to take control of your life again,' he said carefully. 'And if Edward is the friend he seems to be, he'll be happy to see you do that.'

'Help me with him, Magnus,' she pleaded suddenly, clutching at his arm so hard her fingernails dug into his flesh.

'You're frightened of him?' he said. 'Why Helena?'

She loosened her grip instantly. 'I'm sorry,' she said blushing and dropping her eyes from his. 'Heavens above, Magnus, you're going to think I'm absolutely cuckoo now, or worse still that I'm going to add to your worries.'

'I don't think either of those things,' he said firmly. 'But I'll offer you a deal.'

'A deal?' she frowned.

'Yes, you help Nick and myself find Mel so you can tell her yourself everything you know about her birth, and I'll help you keep yourself together until you can manage it all by yourself. If necessary I'll even elbow Edward out.'

She hesitated.

'Come on now,' he said more firmly. 'Surely you can do that?'

'There's so much more than I've told you, Magnus.' Her voice dropped to almost a whisper.

Magnus assumed she was talking about herself and Edward. 'You can tell me when you feel up to it,' he said. 'But we can put the business of finding Mel in hand straight away.'

'You don't understand,' she said, her eyes filling with tears. 'I mean about Camellia. You see I can't see her until I'm ready to tell her the whole truth and I don't know if I have the courage for that.'

Magnus turned right round on the seat until he was facing her squarely. He could see panic in those dark eyes, and her lower lip was trembling.

'Is the truth that bad?' he asked, lifting her chin up, forcing her eyes to meet his.

'Yes,' she whispered.

'Will it be worse for Camellia than her hiding out in some strange town believing she's the cause of everyone's unhappiness?' he asked. 'Is it bad enough to deprive her of a man who loves her, a home where everyone cares for her?'

'No,' she whispered. 'I want her to have all that. None of it is her fault.'

'Then you have to find your courage, Helena,' he said. 'Otherwise you and I have no deal.'

She was silent for some time, sitting absolutely motionless. Magnus wondered what could possibly be so bad that she needed so much time to think about it.

'Okay,' she said at length. 'But what I have to tell her is for her ears only. I don't want you questioning me any more. If she chooses to keep what I tell her a secret then you must accept that decision.'

'Fair enough,' Magnus stood up and held out his hand to her. 'Now shall we go and look at that cottage?'

Helena took his hand and stood up. She smiled and suddenly the years fell away. She looked just the way she had as a young girl, the last time he'd seen her, in the dressing room of the Hippodrome in Catford in 1947. She had been repairing her stage costume, sitting in the corner wearing a shabby sweater and a tweed skirt. He was taking Bonny out for a late supper, planning to tell her it was the end of the line for them because Ruth was expecting Nick. That night he'd wished he had had the nerve to advise Ellie to get away from Bonny and pursue a solo career, yet he knew she was so loyal to her friend that she'd hang onto the bitter end.

'You haven't changed much, Ellie,' he said softly, leaning forward to kiss her cheek, just as he had that last night.

'Nor you, you handsome devil,' she laughed, her dark eyes dancing. 'But before we go gallivanting off to this cottage, I've got a couple of phone calls to make.'

'Dare I go as far as to ask who to?' he said as they walked back across the lawn towards the house arm in arm.

'To a couple of newspapers,' she said, looking round at him with an impish grin. 'One of them must want an exclusive on the faded Hollywood star who wants to find her old dancing partner's daughter.'

'Make sure they go for it and I'll take you out to dinner,' he said. 'If they don't I'll throw you in the swimming pool fully dressed.'

Magnus was still wide awake at two thirty in the morning, his mind churning over everything that had happened during the day. Helena was going up to London the next day for an interview with the *News of the World*. She'd taken the cottage in Kelston for an initial six months' rental with a view to buying it at a later date.

The two-hundred-year-old thatched cottage was delightful, big enough for her to employ a live-in housekeeper if she wanted one, yet not too large that she couldn't live alone in it if she chose. The garden was exquisite with views over open countryside. The furniture, carpets and curtains the owners had left behind when they moved abroad were all entirely in keeping with character of the cottage, yet there were all the modern appliances Helena had grown used to in America.

He was excited by the idea of finding Mel too. It was a far better plan to give Mel a chance to contact Helena without him being involved. That way she wouldn't feel she was being hunted down.

But it was the questions he couldn't ask which were keeping him awake. Helena was frightened of Edward. It didn't make sense if he'd looked after her for all those years as protectively as she said. And even then, it didn't seem quite healthy for a man to bind himself to a woman with such devotion when the relationship was merely platonic: what had there been in it for Edward? And what was it that she knew about Bonny's past? It had to be pretty shocking to have made Helena so distressed. He hoped it wasn't going to make things any worse for Mel.

On top of this Magnus felt a stirring inside himself towards Helena. He could argue with himself that he was an old fool and that she couldn't possibly be attracted to him, but yet when they were in the cottage together, exploring and examining everything, he'd felt absolutely certain her mind was in tune with his.

They'd been standing in the kitchen, listening to the agent explaining how the Aga worked, when she'd suddenly giggled.

'What's so funny about Agas?' Magnus asked her when the agent walked out of earshot.

'Absolutely nothing,' she said. 'I just thought what a perfect excuse it would be to call up and ask you to come round and relight it.'

'You don't need any excuse to get me to call,' he'd said. 'In fact you'd better start inventing them to keep me at bay.'

'Magnus,' she said, tipping her head on one side and giving him that adorable wide smile, 'fate seems to have thrown us together again for some good reason. Maybe this is a chance for us both to grab some happiness.'

Chapter Twenty-Three

'Mel! Wake up!'

She opened her eyes at Conrad's command, saw him standing beside her bed, and closed them again. 'It's Sunday,' she said sleepily. 'I don't get up early on Sundays, especially wet ones in September.'

'You do for something like this,' he retorted and flicked back her curtains. 'Besides it's going to be warm and dry today.'

The excitement in his voice rather than the bright sunshine forced her to respond. She lifted her head from the pillow, groaned when she saw it was only eight o'clock and slumped back, looking quizzically at Conrad. He was dressed in jeans and a checked shirt, flushed and panting as if he'd just run up the stairs.

'It had better be good,' she said warningly, rubbing her eyes.

'It's not just good, it's thrilling,' he replied, thrusting a newspaper into her hands. 'Read it!'

'Something about Nick again?' She was suddenly wide awake and sat up eagerly, buttoning up her pyjama jacket. A couple of months ago she had read an article in a magazine about the making of a film for television called *Delinquents* in which Nick was co-starring with Daniel McKinley, a young actor who seemed to get his photograph in the papers almost daily. She hoped this was going to be Nick's big chance to prove himself.

'No it's not Nick,' Conrad smiled ruefully. 'But I think it might be even better than that.'

Conrad's Supper Rooms had been open now for six months and although they hadn't become a Mecca for the arty Chelsea set as Conrad had originally hoped, they were very popular with the young middle-class people who had moved into Fulham in the 1972 property boom. Conrad found these materialistic people stultifyingly boring. They seemed unable to talk about anything but investments and he sniggered at their clone-like tendency to turn their homes into identical Laura Ashley showrooms with waxed floors and stripped pine furniture. Yet however dull these people were, they appreciated good food and wine, tipped well and kept coming back.

It was hard for Conrad to accept his customers weren't ever going to be exciting and that every night couldn't be the party he had once envisaged, but he consoled himself that at least he was making a good living. He could afford to employ a daily cleaning lady, a student to wash up at weekends and a waiter. And besides he had Mel, and she was worth a crock of gold.

Hardly a day passed without Conrad thinking how lucky he'd been to find such a gem. She remained cool and calm no matter how busy they were, with an ability to plan and think ahead which astounded him. They could work together as a team without any battle for supremacy, understanding each other's strengths and weaknesses. While Conrad was the ideal host, using his charm and warmth to make sure even the most sober of diners had a memorable evening and ate and drank far more than they intended, he wasn't always so good at serving people quickly or totting up their bills correctly. Mel responded intuitively at such times, slipping into the restaurant to lend a hand,

and while he continued to charm and entertain, she would have a table cleared, the desserts ordered or a bill prepared without undermining him in any way.

Yet it was Mel's companionship he valued above all else. Although he was a gregarious man, liked by almost everyone who met him, he had never formed such a close relationship with anyone, man or woman, before. He could be himself with Mel. She alone knew his inadequacies, his failures with women and the sad parts of his life he had tucked away, just as he knew all her secrets too. In many ways they were alike: they'd both had a troubled childhood and painful adolescence, both quietly hungered for love and affection and though outwardly they seemed outgoing and sociable, they shared the same deep need to be alone at times.

As the months passed they had slipped into a comfortable oneness. In the mornings while Mel prepared the dishes for the evening, Conrad stocked up the bar and did any necessary shopping and accounts. They kept the afternoons free for Conrad to work on his book while Mel transformed the little backyard with flowers, or lay reading and sunbathing.

Sundays, by mutual unspoken agreement, had become their special day. If it was warm they would take off in Conrad's Mini for a walk in the countryside, or a trip to Brighton. Sometimes they visited friends they'd made in the restaurant. On dull days it was a museum or art gallery or just a boozy lunch in one of the riverside pubs, then home to snooze in front of the television.

Conrad had woken before seven this morning, and seeing bright sunshine after several days of September rain, had decided they should make the most of it. It might be the last chance this year to spend a day outside in the country.

He had got up and dressed, then gone out to buy a newspaper. His plan was to come back, prepare a picnic, then wake Mel with a cup of tea and discuss where they should go.

But while queuing for his *Observer* in the busy newsagents, he saw Helena Forester's picture on the front of the *News of the World*, and a wave of nostalgia made him buy that too.

Helena Forester's face had evoked afternoons spent in the cinema as a student, and later on when he was a young schoolmaster. Musicals were Conrad's secret vice. Some of his more macho student friends and the other masters at Marshfield might have ridiculed him for wallowing in such frivolous nonsense, but he just loved those beautiful costumes, extravagant sets and dance routines. It was a harmless vice and far more enjoyable than solitary walks, or lying cloistered in his room reading. But most of all it was Helena Forester's face and wonderful contralto voice that had thrilled him. Sometimes he even wondered if it was her luscious full lips and dark flashing eyes that had spoiled other women for him. After her, real women paled in comparison.

Conrad walked slowly back home, reading as he went. He had a pang of guilt as he read how long it was since she last made a film. A once ardent fan, he had barely noticed her absence from the screen. But now she was staging a comeback as a serious actress in *Broken Bridges*, a British film to be made in the West Country.

It was good to read she was happy to be back in England after so many years' absence, that she'd missed fish and chips, street markets and even the English rain. She sounded as lovely as she looked.

He was almost at his front door when a paragraph halted him in his tracks: 'So much has changed while I've been away. Little theatres I once

564

played in are now Bingo halls, the small shops have become supermarkets and there's rarely a queue these days for the cinema because people stay in and watch TV. But the saddest thing of all was to discover my old dancing partner had died several years ago and her daughter, Camellia, orphaned. I hope she'll read this and get in touch. There is so much I would like to share with her.'

'Why did you think I'd be excited by this?' Mel stared at the newspaper in astonishment.

'Not the skinhead bit. Down there.' Con impatiently stabbed at the picture of a glamorous dark-haired woman in the right-hand column. 'You do know who she is?'

The face looked vaguely familiar. 'Should I? She's very beautiful. What is she? A film star or singer.'

'Oh Mel, it's Helena Forester. She was as big in the fifties as Doris Day,' he said in exasperation. 'Surely you've seen her films?'

The name did ring a distant bell, but she was still bewildered. 'I don't think I ever saw one, but then I hardly went to the pictures when I was a kid. What's all this about?'

'Read it through,' he insisted. 'Most of it's on page three, especially the thrilling part. I'll go and make some tea.'

Mel had just finished the article when Conrad came back into her room with two mugs of tea. She was frowning, as if unable to fully comprehend what she'd just read. She looked up at him, dark eyes begging to be reassured. 'It can't be me! Can it?'

'How many other Camellias have you met?' he said archly, putting the tea in her hand.

She shrugged. 'None, but there must be others.'

'With a mother who was a dancer and also happens to be dead?'

'Dancers are more likely to give their kids daft names,' she said flippantly, but as she sipped her tea she read the interview yet again.

'H,' she whispered, colour draining from her face. 'There was a letter in that file I found from someone who signed herself "H". And there was a photo taken with Mum and Magnus. Is this her?'

'Where's the photo?' Conrad moved over to her chest of drawers as if about to turn out the contents.

'It's not here, Con. I left it down in Bath,' Mel said.

Conrad slumped down onto her bed in disappointment. 'It has to be the same person. The more you read that article the more you notice the importance of those few lines. It's almost as if she agreed to the interview just to find you. She says she's staying in Bath – she might even be at Oaklands!'

Mel closed her eyes for a moment. She could see that photo as clearly as if she was holding it in her hand. Two pretty girls with youthful, taut faces, wide smiles, in feathered headdresses and sequinned costumes, Magnus standing between them with his arms around both their shoulders. She couldn't tell whether this forty-year-old voluptuous dark-haired actress was the second girl.

Had Magnus instigated this? Had he found the file hidden in her old room and followed it up?

Her heart began to thump alarmingly. She wanted to believe the message was for her, that Magnus, Nick and this old friend of her mother's were trying to find her, but she couldn't quite believe in that kind of good fortune.

'But why is she so vague? I mean why doesn't she come out with her friend's name?'

'Fear of impostors turning up on her doorstep?'

Conrad suggested. He was disappointed in Mel's reaction. He had expected her to bound out of bed and shriek with delight. 'Maybe when she discovered how your mother died she became afraid the press might make something more of it. Who knows. Ring up the paper now! Tell them who you are and ask them to contact Helena.'

'Not yet,' Mel lay back down again. 'I need to think about it first.'

'Think about it!' Conrad leapt to his feet, infuriated. 'What is there to think about? You've turned yourself inside out agonising over who your father was, yet now someone's turned up who might know the truth, and you back down. Jesus, Mary, Mother of God!'

She half smiled at this so very Irish outburst.

'You are very bossy, to be sure,' she replied mimicking his accent. 'Would you be so kind as to take yourself off downstairs while I get my head together?'

Conrad glowered at her. 'And they say us Irish are thick!' He flounced off towards the door. 'I'll give you an hour, that's all,' he threw over his shoulder as he went down the stairs.

Mel lay in her bed, listening to Conrad banging saucepans in the kitchen. Half of her longed to get up and rush to the phone, as he would, but the other half was urging caution. These last six months of working and sharing a home with Conrad had been happy and secure. She had a life of her own again, peace and contentment, she'd learned to laugh again, made friends with a couple of girls who worked in Fulham Broadway along with several couples she visited with Conrad. Even her rather monastic white painted room had become dear to her, she had stopped looking over her shoulder at the past. Was it wise to take a gamble on something which could possibly involve more pain and humiliation?

An hour later when Conrad knocked tentatively at her door, she was up and dressed. Curiosity had overridden her caution.

'I brought a cup of tea,' he called out. 'If you don't want to see me I'll leave it outside.'

'Don't be daft,' she laughed, opening the door and grinning at him. 'You'll be pleased to know I have decided to contact Helena, but not by phone. I don't want the press knowing my business. I've written to her.'

Conrad's smile almost split his face in two.

'What did you say?' He came right into the room and sat on her bed. Mel picked up the sealed letter and waved it at him.

'Just the bare facts. My date and place of birth. About Dad and Mum's deaths. I said I found a letter from someone who signed herself "H" in Mum's things and asked if it was from her. Finally I just said I'd love to meet her and I gave her the address and telephone number here. Now I'm going to post it off to the *News of the World*.'

'I don't suppose she'll get it until next Saturday or so, if it's got to be sorted and posted on by the newspaper.' Conrad looked a little dejected at this. 'Let's go up to Hyde Park today and take a boat out on the Serpentine. At least it will take our minds off it.'

The week seemed endless, made worse by a sudden change in the weather making it too wet and cold to go out in the garden. On Thursday afternoon Mel made a trip to Kensington High Street to buy a new dress just in case, but there was a distinct nip in the air which reminded her that autumn was well on its way – the time of year when shattering things seemed to happen to her.

When by Saturday there was still no word, she decided it must all have been a coincidence. After all, if Bonny had such a famous friend she would have shouted it from the rooftops.

That evening they were rushed off their feet. A party of ten was extremely demanding and noisy, and every other table was full too. Although Mel had more than enough to do in the kitchen, every now and then she had to dart into the restaurant to help out as John the new waiter and Conrad didn't seem to be able to keep on top of it.

It was during one of these table clearing sorties, around ten, that she saw a man peering through the window above the lace café curtains. It was raining hard and the man was drenched. He looked German: his face was very angular and bony, with close-cropped white-blond hair and vivid blue eyes.

She smiled at him and he came in, wiping raindrops from his tanned face.

'Is it too late for dinner,' he asked, shutting the door behind him.

He didn't have a German accent, but a cultured English one. He was older close up than he'd seemed at first glance – perhaps in his forties – and very tall and straight-backed.

She would not normally have been keen to serve another person this late in the evening, but she didn't have the heart to send him out into the rain again.

He looked for the world like a Nazi officer: the white-blond crop, the piercing blue eyes and thick blond brows. His tan and his slim athletic build suggested an outdoor occupation, yet at the same time he looked very correct in his expensive pale-grey suit and stiff-collared shirt. Something prevented him from being truly handsome, despite his perfect bone structure and dazzling white teeth. His lips were a little thin, and his eyes cold. But just the same he was unusually attractive.

Camellia looked around the restaurant. Most of the diners were still on their main courses, talking and laughing as if they had all night. This man would probably be in and out before they'd even got to dessert.

'No, it's not too late, not if you don't mind waiting while I just clear this table,' she said with a welcoming smile. 'Take a stool at the bar for a moment.'

She poured him a glass of wine.

'On the house,' she said as he felt for his wallet. 'You'll have to take pot luck I'm afraid – I think we're down now to steaks or our special chicken casserole.'

'Nice place,' he said as she passed by him with a loaded tray. 'Is it yours?'

'Oh no,' she smiled with amusement, pausing with the tray balanced on her hip. 'I'm just the cook. It belongs to Conrad Deeley. He's in the kitchen at the moment, but he'll be out to see to you in a jiffy.'

'Mel?' Conrad shouted from the kitchen. 'Have we finished all the chocolate mousse?'

'It's in the fridge,' she called back, then looking at the stranger she shrugged. 'He has many talents, but finding things for himself isn't one of them. I'd better go.'

'What's Mel short for? Melanie?' he asked.

'No, Camellia.' She had long since given up hiding her name. Con had been right: people didn't have long memories and no one she knew from her days in Oakley Street had ever come in to eat.

'Very pretty,' he replied, looking her up and down. 'It suits you.'

She disappeared out to the kitchen, found the mousse for Conrad and tucked a clean tablecloth under his arm for the table she'd just cleared. 'I told the Nazi at the bar we've only got chicken casserole or steak left,' she whispered. 'So don't you go tempting him with anything else, it's too late to ponce around now.'

Conrad grinned, clicked his heels together and attempted a mock salute before disappearing back into the restaurant.

He came back into the kitchen a few minutes later to pick up two desserts. 'I reckon the Nazi fancies you,' he said in a stage whisper. 'He asked me if you were my wife. But I spoiled it for you – I said you merely live with me.'

Mel smiled. She knew he'd said no such thing – he was too much of a gentleman. 'Has he ordered yet?' she asked.

'I haven't got around to him yet. Table four are ready to leave and I'll have to do their bill. He's all right though, he doesn't seem to be in a hurry.'

A rush of further orders for desserts prevented Mel from going back into the restaurant again. Some twenty minutes later she popped her head round the door and was surprised to find that the blond man had vanished.

'I suppose he got fed up with waiting,' she said to Conrad who was sweating profusely as he cleared table four. 'Last time I'll give anyone a free glass of wine.'

'I wasn't pretty enough for him,' Conrad grinned. 'And speaking of wine, let's both have a glass, I need a pick-up.'

Another week passed and there was still no word from Helena Forester. Conrad had been convinced she would turn up at the door in a limousine. When she didn't his excitement turned sour.

'She could have acknowledged your letter anyway,' he said several times. 'She's clearly not the sensitive, caring sort of woman I took her for, but just another self-centred phoney.'

It had rained all week, and as Mel wanted something to distract her from the thoughts of Magnus and Nick which kept popping into her head, she had spent the afternoons painting their living room. Its new look with apple-green walls and white doors and skirting board lifted her spirits a little, and Conrad encouraged her further by buying some very expensive curtains from Heals in Tottenham Court Road. It cheered them both to have a bright and pretty room to relax in, especially now the wet, cold weather prevented them from going out quite so much.

The phone rang on Sunday afternoon. Mel was lying on the settee reading, and Conrad answered it downstairs in the restaurant kitchen.

She knew by the way he came thundering up the stairs that he was excited. She looked up at his glowing face as he came into the room and smiled.

'It was your Mum? She's decided to forgive you and come over here for a holiday?'

Conrad laughed. He looked so boyish. It wasn't just his skinny frame, his small elf face and spiky hair, but a childlike quality which shone through even when he attempted to be adult and sophisticated. He had bought new glasses recently with heavier tortoiseshell frames which he was convinced made him look more business-like, and had his hair styled regularly. But his brown eyes still flashed with irreverent humour, and his hair stayed unruly. The small boy in him would still be there when he was sixty.

'Much more interesting than my Mum doing an

about-face,' he said. 'It was a chap called Michael Dunwoody who owns a restaurant in Brighton. He wanted to put a proposition to me.'

Mel groaned. People were always putting propositions to Conrad. He could be very gullible. 'What about?'

'Buying him out. His place is in a prime site but he's in financial difficulties. He wondered if I'd be interested in buying it, with him managing it for me, creating the same kind of set up as here.'

The proposition was at least original, but it bothered Mel that Conrad was so easily lured into wild ideas. 'If he couldn't make his own place pay, he's hardly likely to make much effort just managing it,' she said, stretching out more comfortably and loosening the waist of her jeans. She couldn't understand how Conrad could even consider owning another restaurant; he had his hands quite full enough with this one.

'Maybe, but it's worth looking at.' Conrad pushed her legs over and sat down beside her. 'It's all set up and equipped and he's prepared to let me have it far cheaper than I'd get it on the open market. It would be a good investment.'

It sounded the perfect way to lose his money, but Camellia had discovered early on that opposing his scatterbrained ideas only made him keener on them.

'So when are you going to meet him?'

'No time like the present,' he grinned. 'At least in this rain there won't be any traffic on the road.'

'Just promise me you won't make any decision immediately,' she said gently. She knew she couldn't deter him from going, but it was worth trying to slow him down. 'Just look and talk today. The restaurant is doing well, Con, but that's because you're here all the time, giving it the personal touch. And you wouldn't have time for your writing if you had another business.'

He didn't reply, but got up and went over to the window, looking down at the small garden.

Mel had read his book, and she thought he was a brilliant storyteller. His characters were vivid and funny, and the plot was fast moving. She wished he would concentrate on it whole heartedly. She was a little worried their more materialistic customers were beginning to influence him, however much he laughed at them. Conrad was an artist, not a businessman.

'I'm sorry I got you all fired up about Helena Forester,' he said unexpectedly. He turned back to her and his brown eyes looked huge and troubled behind his thick glasses. 'Perhaps it was wishful thinking on my part. I wanted something really nice to happen for you – you deserve it.'

Mel was touched by his concern for her. Conrad could be fiery, impulsive and hare-brained at times, but beneath that was a sensitive, deeply caring man. 'Something nice happened when I met you,' she said. 'I'm very happy here, Con. I shouldn't want anything more.'

'But you still think of Nick a great deal, don't you?' he said, moving over to the settee and running his hand over her hair almost paternally. 'Sometimes I get the idea that you're running on only one valve, and there's another one rusting away through lack of use.'

'Yes, I do think about Nick a great deal,' she admitted. 'And sometimes I think how much I'd like to meet another man, fall in love, get married and have babies. But I'm not pining for that. I'm content for now with my peace of mind and your friendship.'

Mel didn't think about her needs very often and never voiced them. But as she spoke she realised she was living in a kind of waiting room, letting life flow comfortably past her. At least Conrad reached out for what he wanted and allowed himself to be receptive to new ideas and experiences. Perhaps she should take a leaf out of his book.

'You give too much of yourself, Mel,' he said, wiggling a finger at her like a schoolmaster. 'Without you I'd never have got this place off the ground. I dread the day coming when you'll want to move on because heaven knows how I'll manage without you. But all the same, a big part of me wants to see you truly happy and fulfilled. I want to see that other valve start moving, to see a glimmer in your eyes for something other than a new supper dish or making this flat look pretty.'

'There's a glimmer in my eyes for that frayed collar.' She got up from the settee and caught hold of his shirt collar, wiggling it. 'So take it off and put something smart on. You can't let this Dunwoody chap think you might be in financial difficulties too.'

Conrad left twenty minutes later, wearing a baggy tweed suit which made him look like an Irish farmer on a Sunday. She didn't have the heart to tell him he looked better in his jeans. She heard the garden gate slam shut and the roar of his Mini as he sped out of the small lane at the back.

Sighing she picked her book up again. She hoped he wouldn't like this man Dunwoody; it all sounded a little fishy to her.

The front doorbell woke her. She glanced at her watch and saw that it was after five. She must have dropped off soon after Conrad left. Pushing her feet into her slippers she went downstairs to answer it.

To her surprise it was the tall blond man who'd left the restaurant the previous Saturday night. She was embarrassed to be caught in worn jeans and a grubby tee shirt, by someone so attractive.

'Remember me?' he asked. 'I called to apologise for running out last Saturday night. You must have thought me frightfully rude. But I suddenly found I'd left my wallet in my other suit. Thank goodness I discovered that before I started to eat or I might have spent the night washing up for you.'

Mel was startled but pleased that he'd even considered making an apology. Such good manners were rare these days. He was less formally dressed than at their first meeting, in a casual light-brown suede jacket, open-necked checked shirt and beige slacks, but even so he still looked as if he'd stepped straight out of a tailor's window.

'Did you find anywhere to eat later or did you have to go to bed hungry?'

'I found one of those late night hamburger places.' He leaned on the doorpost nonchalantly, and gazed at her.

Mel blushed. If this was only an apology, a phone call would have sufficed. Could it be he was going to ask her out? She wasn't sure how she felt about that; he wasn't quite her type. 'Next time you'd better book a table,' she said. 'It was nice of you to apologise. I actually thought you'd grown tired of waiting to be served. We were very busy that night.'

'I guess I'd better come clean,' he smiled. 'Helena Forester sent me! I'm her manager – my name is Edward Manning.'

Shock made her jaw drop open.

Delight, disbelief and embarrassment precluded any intelligent questions. His expensive clothes, the suntan and a hint of an American accent all fitted in with someone in the movie business. But she was a little uneasy that he'd found it necessary to make an incognito visit first.

'You'd better come in,' Mel's voice trembled. 'I just wish I looked a little tidier!'

'Did Helena get many letters,' she asked as she gave him tea. 'I mean from Camellias?'

'Thirty-four in all, and no more than four were even named Camellia,' he said with a wry smile. 'Most of them were stage-struck teenagers, their letters full of all the films they'd seen of her, and how they knew all along there was some link between them.'

'How did you know I was the right one?' Mel asked.

'Quite simple. You had the correct date of birth, the right surname.'

'So why did you check me out last week?'

He looked penetratingly at her, his blue eyes suddenly very cold. 'We had to be absolutely certain. Helena is very vulnerable. I didn't want her to become involved with anyone who might be slightly off centre.'

This explanation was slightly offensive, but Mel decided that it was at least an honest one. He wasn't the easiest man to talk to – he seemed humourless and reserved, and she had a feeling he didn't actually approve of this mission. But then as Helena's manager it was his job to protect her interests. Mel felt she would need to charm him into being less guarded.

'Tell me about Helena,' she asked. 'You see I'm entirely in the dark, my mother never spoke of her. I'm afraid I haven't even seen one of her films, though Conrad who is a great fan has filled me in with some of her background. Have I ever met her? I mean when I was small.'

When he didn't answer immediately Mel thought perhaps she'd said the wrong thing.

'Helena Forester isn't an easy person to describe,'

he said at length, as if choosing his words very carefully. 'Her public image as one of the greatest musical comedy stars of our time is rather at odds with her private one. She is an intensely private person, Camellia, extraordinarily beautiful with a warm and loving nature.'

Mel wondered if Edward was something more than Helena's manager. He sounded as if he'd lifted that description from a press release, but at the same time there was passion in his eyes which said he adored her.

'Bonny Norton hurt her very badly many years ago,' he went on, looking at her hard, as if he held her accountable. 'They fell out and perhaps that is why she never told you about Helena. As I understand it, you were about three or four at the time of their last meeting, too young I suspect to remember it. But Helena is a very compassionate and forgiving woman. When she discovered on her return to England that both your parents had died, her first concern was for you.'

'How did she find out? Did Magnus tell her?' Mel felt a rush of wild excitement. 'Is she staying at Oaklands with him?'

'Magnus? Oaklands?' He looked baffled. 'I'm afraid neither of those names mean anything to me.'

'Magnus Osbourne was a friend of my mother's. I thought perhaps he knew Helena too.' Mel felt a little foolish, and disappointed. But if Edward didn't know about Magnus and Bonny, she wasn't going to volunteer the information. 'It was just an association of ideas. You see I used to work at his hotel in Bath, and I thought she might just be staying at Oaklands.'

'She has taken a house quite near to Bath,' he said stiffly. 'But that is because the film is being made nearby. As far as I know she has no acquaintances in the town. I believe she got the news about your parents from an old friend in London. But you can ask her about that yourself.'

'When can I meet her?' she asked bluntly. She didn't think she could stand being kept on tenterhooks for another couple of weeks.

'My plan was to take you to her now,' he said. 'If that is all right with you of course.'

'Now?' Mel stared stupidly at him.

'The restaurant isn't open on Sundays is it?' he said. 'It's only a couple of hours drive. You can stay with her tonight and I'll bring you back in the morning or pop you on the train.'

There was no sensible reason she could think of as to why she shouldn't go immediately. But all the same it did seem a bit sudden.

As if sensing that she needed further reassurance, he took an envelope out of his inside jacket pocket. 'Take a look at these,' he said more gently, pulling a batch of snapshots from it. 'Helena has kept them close to her all these years.'

They were all pictures of Mel, from tiny baby to the age of about four. In one she was looking at a birthday cake with two candles, in another she was naked in a paddling pool. The most recent one was of her sitting on the steps outside their Mermaid Street house, a plump, serious-faced four-year-old, nursing a dolly.

'Does that tell you how she feels about you?' Edward asked pointedly.

Mel felt a prickle in her eyes.

'Don't make her wait any longer to see you.' His tone was suddenly warm and persuasive. 'She has so much to talk to you about, so many years to make up for. Come with me now – there's nothing keeping you here is there?'

Mel glanced about her. She had her book to finish, and Conrad would want to tell her about the place in Brighton when he got back. But that wasn't as important or as exciting as discovering a little more about her mother.

'Well, no,' Mel said, aware that if he left without her she'd be kicking herself within half an hour of his departure. 'It's just that I look a mess. I wanted to look my best when I met her.'

He smiled then, as if he'd finally decided he approved of her. 'You look lovely to me,' he said. 'But there's nothing stopping you changing first if it will make you feel more comfortable.'

She left him sitting on the settee looking at the Sunday paper while she ran upstairs to change. Her new navy and white striped dress had seemed perfect when she bought it last week, but now as she put it on she wasn't so sure. The rather demure white sailor collar, and the long bias-cut skirt now looked a little old-fashioned and far too summery. But it was too late to find anything else, so she dug out tights and a white cardigan, brushed her hair, tied it back at the neck and slipped her feet into her navy-blue platform shoes.

Edward looked up and smiled as she came back down to the living room with a small overnight bag, make-up on and her raincoat over her arm.

'I wish all ladies could transform themselves so quickly,' he said. 'You look very pretty. I think Helena will be startled to find the chubby little girl she remembered has turned into such an elegant young lady.'

'I could have done even better with a little more time,' she laughed, and picked up an old envelope and pen to write Conrad a brief message.

'Helena's manager, Edward Manning, turned up to take me to Bath,' she wrote. 'I'll be back tomorrow sometime. Love Mel.'

'Are you always a girl of so few words?' he

asked, raising one blond eyebrow sardonically as he glanced at the propped-up note on the table.

'Not usually,' she grinned. 'But whatever I put won't be enough for Con, and we haven't got time for me to write a full report have we?'

Edward's car was a new dark-blue Jaguar, and Mel sank into the soft leather seat, sighing with appreciation. She had never ridden in such a splendid car before and it seemed like an omen for a whole new chapter in her life.

'How long have you known Helena?' she asked as they reached the start of the M4. Edward had barely spoken since they left Fulham and it was making her just a little tense.

'Since 1945,' he said. 'We were in a show together in London. I was an actor then, but I've been her manager now for almost twenty years.'

He went on to tell her about other shows they'd been in together, saying that sometimes he played the piano. It grew more and more obvious he adored Helena. Mel found it touching how they'd kept in touch by letter when they couldn't work together and how Edward had taken pianist's jobs in towns where she was performing, just to be near her.

'Did you know my mother?' she asked.

'Yes, I did,' he said. 'She was one of the dancers in that same first show.'

Mel waited, expecting him to go on reminiscing, but he added nothing more. 'You didn't like her, did you?'

'No,' he admitted, glancing round at her. 'I'm sorry if that's hurtful to you, Camellia, but I'm afraid we never really got on.'

'I'd rather people were honest,' she said, hoping this might make him open up a bit more. 'But most men seem to have been fascinated by her.'

When he didn't answer immediately, Mel looked round at him. He was gripping the steering wheel so tightly, his knuckles were white.

'Tell me why you didn't like her,' she said, a little unnerved by such a display of tension.

'She was . . .' He hesitated as if unsure whether to voice his opinion. 'Well, poisonous is the only word that fits. I'm very relieved to find you aren't like her in looks or character.'

'So what did she do to upset you?' She felt indignant. Bonny didn't warrant quite such a vicious description, especially to her daughter.

'To me personally, very little,' he replied with a shrug. 'But she played havoc with other people's lives and minds. But you'd know this anyway, my dear. I'm quite sure she didn't change once she'd married your father.'

Mel felt Edward's animosity towards her mother must have been based on jealousy. She didn't feel she could ask any more questions about the two women's friendship, or tell him about the letters she'd found. Instead she moved on to speak about more general things – the restaurant, London, films she'd seen – but in lulls in the conversation she pondered on his relationship with Helena.

She was pretty certain they weren't lovers, but for such a close platonic friendship to have lasted nearly thirty years seemed a little odd, especially as neither of them had married other people. Mel liked Conrad very much, but she couldn't possibly imagine either of them being content to stay together forever without love, romance or sex.

'Are you always so quiet?' Mel asked once they had passed through Reading. It was dark now and she was bored with watching the windscreen wipers swish away the rain. She had tried to get a clearer picture of Helena by asking him questions about her old films and their life in Hollywood, but though she had discovered Helena had a Spanish-style house in the Hollywood hills, a swimming pool and a red Cadillac, and that Edward played a pianist in *Dreamers*, one of her earlier films, she hadn't gleaned anything personal. Edward was so guarded and unresponsive. He could describe a dress Helena wore or the interior of her house in detail, yet he didn't offer any insight to how she felt, her interests or other friends. Stranger still was his reluctance to talk about himself.

'I guess I'm one of life's listeners,' Edward smiled, but barely took his eyes off the road ahead. 'Forgive me for not being better company for you. But Helena will more than make up for it when you meet her. She's a talker too.'

He turned on the radio and Mel lapsed into thought. When she'd first read about Helena she had spent a great deal of time daydreaming about what their meeting could mean to her. Helena might know for certain who her father was. Supposing it wasn't Magnus after all – there was nothing to prevent her going back to visit him at Oaklands. She had even imagined Nick greeting her with open arms, all past grievances forgotten.

As Edward's arrival at Fulham had been unexpected, and their departure so hurried, it was only now as they sped towards the West Country that her mind turned back to those daydreams. She could see Oaklands so clearly in her mind: the trees in the drive turning gold, yellow and russet, the view of the valley shrouded in wispy autumn mist. Magnus would have the fire lit again in the drawing room and there would be those hearty spicy soups on the menu.

She was absolutely certain Magnus would hold no hard feelings against her for running off, but she wondered if he had someone else now in her place, and what he'd done with all the things of hers she'd left behind. There was her bank book. She'd hardly considered it all this time, but perhaps she could get it back, draw out her savings and buy a car.

Yet it was the vision of Nick which made her tingle from head to toe. The memory of him hadn't faded: he was still there in her heart, head and in her blood. If she closed her eyes she could see his chiselled cheek bones, his wide mouth and blue eyes so clearly that she could almost reach out and touch him. She had long since forgiven him for all the cruel things he'd said – perhaps he too had since come to realise that she had no choice but to behave as she did. She offered up a silent prayer that Helena would scotch all ideas of them being related.

Mel was jolted out of her reverie as Edward turned off the motorway and halted at a round-about.

'Where are we?' she asked.

'Near Chippenham,' he said almost curtly.

Mel knew that the Chippenham road led to Bath and she looked out eagerly for familiar sights. But the rain was so heavy she could barely see a few feet ahead of the headlights.

'Do we go right into Bath?' she asked. They had just flashed past a signpost but she couldn't read it.

'No, we turn off before there,' he said, glancing round at her. 'It's a shame it's so dark and wet. It's very pretty around here, but of course you must know it.'

'Only Bath itself and around Oaklands,' she said. 'You should go to Oaklands yourself one day. It's set on a hill overlooking a wonderful valley with the river running through it. I loved it there.'

Edward made no comment, not even to ask why she left if she liked it so much. But then he hadn't asked her anything about herself.

'Did I tell you that Helena's house is on the river,' he said some minutes later. 'I'm staying there for the time being until I can find her a good housekeeper. It's a rather isolated spot, especially in this sort of weather, and the house is in need of modernisation. But you'll see for yourself soon, we're nearly there.'

With that he turned off the main road and into a narrow lane, overhung with trees. There were a few groups of cottages here and there, but mostly the lane seemed to be winding through farm land, up and down, twisting and turning like a switch-back. At one point they met another car and Edward had to reverse back into a wider part to let it through. They went on for another five minutes or so, the road going steeply downward before finally turning off into a bumpy, rutted track.

Mel felt uneasy. She could see no lights any-where. The wind was howling, rain was battering down and the lane was pitch dark, overhung with bushes.

'Only a few yards of this,' Edward said cheer-fully and almost immediately turned onto a gravel drive. 'Well, here we are at last.'

'It looks a bit spooky,' Mel blurted out, then giggled at how childish she had sounded. From what she could see of the house with only one dim light hanging in the stone porch, it actually looked very pretty, with pointed eaves and lattice win-dows. It just wasn't what she expected.

'You wait till you see it in daylight,' Edward said with far more enthusiasm than he'd shown for anything else so far. 'It's a beautiful old house and an idyllic spot. The garden is a bit neglected but we've got plans in hand for that.'

As she opened the car door, the wind snatched at her. She grabbed her overnight bag and raincoat from the back seat and ran to the porch for shelter.

'Where's Helena's car?' she asked as Edward scurried through the rain towards her.

'She hasn't got around to getting one yet,' he said, putting a key in the lock. 'She gets ferried to and from the film set every day. She's got her eyes on a Mercedes though.'

The fusty smell that wafted out as Edward opened the heavy, old oak door, set Mel's nerves jangling again.

'Oh dear, don't say she's been delayed,' Edward exclaimed at the dark hall in front of them. 'She said she'd be back well before seven.'

He switched on a light. The hall was entirely in keeping with the quaintness of the outside of the house but it was very shabby. The floor was uneven flag stones, with just one badly worn rug to soften it. The staircase was solid oak, with an ornate carved newel post, but again the runners on the stairs were almost threadbare and the brass stair rods were tarnished as if they hadn't been polished for years. A large grandfather clock in the hall had stopped at quarter past three. Even the small oil paintings of horses in heavy gold frames looked slightly menacing.

But it was predominantly the smell that worried her. Mel recognised it as lack of use. The smell of windows kept firmly shut, unaired beds, old people. 'It's very cold,' she said, pulling her raincoat round her shoulders.

'I'm so sorry about this,' Edward tutted and switched on an electric radiator. 'Not very welcoming for you, is it? But don't worry, she's bound to be back at any minute.' He went on ahead down the passage and opened a door.

Mel followed him, pulling her coat more firmly round her shoulders.

The room was in darkness. As Edward moved

across to switch on a table lamp she had an irrational urge to turn and run for the front door.

Even when light flooded the room and she saw a copy of *Vogue* and a used teacup on a low table, a small voice inside her head told her that no one had been in this room for days. In one sense the room was entirely perfect. Deep comfortable settees either side of a huge fireplace, antique highly polished small tables and a thick traditional red patterned carpet. From the dark wooden beams to the brass poker and coal scuttle, the glass-fronted china cabinet full of figurines and the roll-top desk everything was just so, without a speck of dust. Yet it seemed all wrong.

'I don't like it,' Mel said impulsively. French windows led out to the back garden and the blackness out there was scary. 'I don't want to stay here.'

Edward looked round at her in surprise. 'Oh Camellia, I'm so sorry you're frightened.' He took a step towards her and put his hand gently on her shoulder. 'This is too bad of Helena, she should've been here to greet you. But don't worry. I'll light the fire and make us a drink. She'll be bursting in here any moment full of apologies.'

The fire was already laid. Edward lit a gas poker and shoved it in under the wood and almost immediately bright flames shot up. Mel perched on the edge of the settee nearest to it.

'That's better,' he said, and drew the thick tapestry curtains over the French windows. 'It will be cosy in no time at all. If Helena does go through with buying this house we'll have to make sure she gets central heating put in. I know we English are supposed to be a tough breed, but after living in a warm climate you notice the cold and the dampness.'

Edward's solicitous remarks and the efforts he

put into making everything more welcoming should have reassured her, but Mel still felt uncomfortable. The rain and wind outside were so loud. Where exactly was she? How close was the nearest house or shop?

'Oh good, she's left a note,' Edward said jubilantly, picking up a sheet of bright blue paper from the desk in the alcove by the fireplace.

'Dearest Edward,' he read aloud. 'Sorry but I think the meeting's going to take longer than I expected. Have a drink and just hang on. I'll be back as soon as I can. Whatever must you think of me! Love, H.'

He handed it to Mel, with a glum smile. 'There must have been a change of plan after I left this morning. This sort of thing is always happening. The director gets a new idea, one of the producers changes his mind about a location. It's very annoying.'

Mel felt less edgy then. Nick had often complained about the time he wasted in theatres and studios for very similar reasons and she felt soothed by seeing the letter. The handwriting and single initial was most definitely identical to that in her mother's letter.

'I suppose it can't be helped,' Mel said, holding her hands out to the blaze.

Edward looked at her, his expression one of resignation. 'I can't count the times Helena and I have arranged to do something and had to cancel at the last moment. Now about that drink? A gin and tonic perhaps, or we've got Scotch, wine, and I think rum.'

'I'd rather have some tea.' She smiled at Edward. It wasn't his fault things had gone wrong. He was probably as bored at being stuck with her as she was with him and he was trying to be charming.

'I'm sorry if I was a bit hysterical just now. I suppose I'm just nervous.'

'That's quite understandable,' he said and bent over to move the gas poker to another part of the fire. 'If I'd known Helena would be late I'd have taken you to a pub for a while. But have a real drink, it's been a long drive and it will help you relax.'

Mel fancied a gin and tonic, but she thought it better to wait until Helena arrived. 'Not just now,' she said. 'I really would like tea.'

'Okay,' he said getting up from the fire. 'It will take a minute or two, the kitchen is a little antiquated. I could rustle up a sandwich too if you'd like one?'

'That would be nice,' Mel smiled. 'Shall I help?'

'No, you stay here,' he said. 'It's cold in the kitchen.'

Mel looked at her watch after Edward left the room. It was five past nine. She picked up the magazine from the table and flicked through it, but lost interest in a couple of seconds when she realised it was last month's which she'd already read.

It was getting warmer and she stood up to take off her raincoat, at the same time looking more closely at everything. The owners of the house must be very old. There was a collection of Victorian porcelain figurines in the china cabinet, some grim, dark oil paintings of stags and Highland cattle on the walls and dated parchment lampshades on the table lamps. If she were Helena she'd have packed them all away and replaced them with something jollier and more up-to-date. Flowers and pot plants would make the room more inviting too.

Almost the second that thought popped into her head she realised why the room didn't seem quite right. There wasn't one item that wasn't in keeping with its style and period. Surely Helena would have brought a few of her own things in here, a couple of framed photographs, some cherished mementoes?

But the lack of flowers was perhaps most remarkable. An actress used to receiving them would surely see them as essential. And wouldn't they be doubly important if a guest was expected?

The unease she'd felt as they came up the rutted lane came back twice as strongly. What kind of woman would send a total stranger to collect a young girl, and expect her to travel a hundred miles to an isolated cold house, then not be there to greet her?

Edward came back in five minutes later with a tray in his hands. There was a plate of sandwiches, a fruit cake, a white bone china teapot with cups, saucers, milk and sugar.

'That was quick,' Mel said.

'Helena must have guessed you'd be hungry, she'd cut some sandwiches in readiness,' he said, looking faintly embarrassed. 'I hope you like ham.'

They sat down, Edward in an armchair, Mel on the settee, the tray of tea between them on a coffee table.

'Milk and sugar?' Edward asked as he poured the tea into the cups.

'Just milk, no sugar,' she said and sat back a little more comfortably.

The tea was too hot to do more than sip it. But it tasted a little peculiar.

'Um, that's hot,' she said, putting it down on the coffee table. Edward picked up the milk jug.

'Perhaps I didn't put enough in,' he said. 'I don't take milk myself, so I never know how much to put in.'

Under ordinary circumstances Mel would have

found nothing odd about that remark. But she'd given him tea back in Fulham and he'd drunk it with milk. She was puzzled and glanced at Edward. He looked tense, a tightening around the mouth and the eyes and his hand shook as he put more milk in her cup.

Mel tried the tea again, only another sip, but the odd taste was stronger still. Could he have put something in the milk?

She thought her imagination was playing tricks on her. What would he gain by drugging her?

'May I use the phone?' she asked. 'Con's bound to be a little worried. I ought to tell him where I am exactly.'

Edward frowned. 'The phone's dead I'm afraid.' He didn't meet her eyes and got out of his chair to bend over to take the gas poker out of the fire. 'The lines round here are very old and it seems they went down in last night's high winds. The engineer will be here first thing in the morning.'

Taken as one isolated incident, a phone being out of order wasn't important. But added to everything else she felt was strange here, alarm bells began to jangle. Would a sophisticated actress, used to living in some splendour, really choose to stay in such a damp cold house? Now she came to think about it, surely a woman in her position would be far more likely to arrange to meet someone for the first time on neutral territory, in a hotel or restaurant.

Mel looked suspiciously at Edward and all the curious little things she'd observed about him during the evening, all came together. He was too smooth, too cagey, and, aside from Helena, he didn't like women. His long silences, the guarded, often curt way of speaking, his cold eyes, were all so creepy.

'Edward, please don't take offence at this, but I'd like you to take me to a hotel,' she said, trying very hard not to show her panic. 'I'm not a bit happy being here, especially without a telephone. I'm sure Helena will be tired too when she gets back. We can meet up tomorrow when we're both fresh.'

'Now that's ridiculous,' he replied and his eyes flashed with irritation. 'Helena will be upset if you aren't here when she gets back. Now just drink your tea and relax. It's tipping down out there too. You don't want to be rushing off somewhere else at this time of night.'

She wanted to insist, but a sixth sense told her that she must keep calm and think this through before putting herself in an even more vulnerable position.

'Just another half an hour then,' she said as compromise. 'But if she isn't back here then, I'll go.'

'Oh, she'll be back within that time.'

Mel felt there was a note of relief in his voice. It could of course mean that he was merely relieved she wasn't about to make a scene. On the other hand it could mean that half an hour was all the time he needed. She looked at the cup of tea in front of her, saw a couple of white flecks floating on the surface and she thought perhaps it might contain some kind of sleeping draught. She certainly wasn't going to risk drinking it.

'I expect it's just the quiet here giving me the jitters,' she said with a tight little laugh. 'Con always recommends tea for calming you down.' She picked up the cup and pretended to drink some, then put it down and took a bite of her sandwich. 'Do you think I could have some salt on this?' she asked. 'I know salt isn't good for you, but I can't eat anything without it.'

Edward frowned, but he got up and went out to the kitchen. Camellia looked around her quickly. There was a tall brass vase standing in the corner by the French doors, the moment he was out of earshot, she leapt up, rushed to it and tipped the tea in.

As Edward came back with a salt cellar she was back on the settee apparently drinking the last dregs of her tea. He smiled at her. 'Would you like another cup? There's plenty more in the pot.'

'Not just now,' she said, hoping her face wasn't as flushed as it felt. She took the sandwich apart and sprinkled it with salt.

Edward began to tell her something about Rupert, Helena's co-star, but Mel was only listening with half an ear as she tried to reason things out. Why would he want to drug her? So he could take her somewhere she wouldn't normally go willingly? To keep her quiet for some other purpose?

All at once she guessed the truth. He intended to kill her.

Her first instinct was to run for the door, but she resisted it. For one thing he would catch her before she even got to the hall. It would also alert him that she had guessed his plan. He was far bigger and stronger than her and even if she managed to get beyond the door he'd be able to out run her. If she calmly played along with him, giving him every reason to think his plan was working, then she could outwit him.

'Are you warm enough?' Edward's solicitous question startled her. She hadn't heard a word he'd been saying before that.

She thought fast. 'A bit too warm now I think,' she said, faking a yawn. 'I'm getting sleepy.'

He smiled at her. Mel thought it was smug, as if that were what he hoped to hear. She slipped off her shoes and moved to a more relaxed position on the settee, curling her legs up on it.

'Tell me the story line in the film?' she asked. 'Is it a love story?'

She leaned one elbow on the arm of the settee,

looking right at him as he began to describe Helena falling in love with a man half her age. Edward was an outstandingly handsome man. She wondered what his background was and why he hadn't ever got decent parts in films and become famous himself. Could it be that he lived in Helena's shadow?

By Mel's reckoning a strong sedative would make most people start to feel sleepy within fifteen minutes, faster still if they were already tired. As she looked at him she allowed her eyes to droop, then blinked and opened them again.

Above the crackling fire and the wind outside, she could hear another sound, she listened carefully until she identified it. Then she remembered Edward had said the house was by a river.

Suddenly everything fell into place.

None of this was chance. It had been planned meticulously. Helena hadn't wanted to find her because she cared about her old dancing partner's daughter. She was afraid that Bonny had passed some information to Mel.

Edward was waiting for her to fall asleep then take her out there and drown her. He knew it would work because he'd done it before: to Bonny. The only difference was that Bonny was probably very drunk long before he slipped her the sedative.

Mel thought back to those days prior to her mother's death. The late night phone calls, her excitement and even the mention of getting them both passports. Edward must have been that man she was in contact with. He was the one she went to London to meet.

There wasn't time now to concern herself with what secrets Bonny knew that were serious enough to warrant murder. Mel had to escape before she met the same end. But how on earth was she going to do it?

She let her eyes droop again, jerking her head up every now and then in exactly the same way she'd seen other people dropping off. Edward stopped speaking, almost in mid sentence. She sensed he was studying her.

She took his silence as the final proof of his intentions. Any normal person would speak, offer her a cup of coffee or even suggest she went upstairs to bed.

Where was Helena? Was she sitting in a hotel room somewhere close by waiting for the news that loyal, obedient Edward had finally severed the last link with her past? Or could he be acting on his own initiative out of some misguided desire to protect her?

Some ten minutes later Mel had allowed herself to sink right down onto the settee, faking deep sleep. Edward had been silent all this time. She felt he was watching her, biding his time. She'd had time now to work out a plan of sorts. She didn't think he would attempt drowning her in his smart clothes. If she faked sleep well enough she thought he might leave her alone in the room to go and change. Then she could either slip out into the hall and out the front door, or if he was still downstairs, unlock the French windows and escape that way. She hoped it could be the front door, she didn't relish the thought of negotiating a river in the dark.

Minutes seemed like hours as she lay there. It wasn't easy to feign sleep while being watched, and she was so frightened she was afraid he could hear her heart thumping. The wind was growing even stronger. She could hear the trees outside creaking with the force of it.

She heard him move, just a faint shuffle, then his hand touched her cheek. How she managed to give a soft sigh instead of a flinch, she didn't know, but perhaps knowing your life depended on it made one a better actress.

At last he moved away and the door creaked as he opened it. She waited, sensing he was looking back at her and kept her eyes shut.

To her disappointment she heard a key turn in the lock after he'd shut the door behind him. Again she waited. She knew he was still outside, listening.

Finally he moved away and she heard the sound of his feet on the stairs.

She was onto her feet immediately and over to the French window. Holding her breath she parted the curtains, silently drew the top bolt back, then the bottom one, then pushed at the doors.

They wouldn't open. The doors were locked by a key in the centre and it wasn't in the lock.

Frantically she looked on the mantelpiece, ran her fingers along the ledge above the window, even quietly opened the desk drawers to look for it. But the key wasn't there.

She felt paralysed with terror now, looking this way and that, her mind unable to function. Then she heard him coming back down the stairs.

When the door opened and Edward came in, Mel was back on the settee, concealed beneath her was the only weapon she'd been able to find in such a short time. A brass candlestick. It was only about eight inches long, but heavy. She hoped it was enough.

A smell of rubber and a distinctive rustle suggested he had put on a waterproof coat. His step was different too, she thought he might be wearing wellingtons. He stopped, she felt he was watching her again, then after a few seconds she heard him draw the curtains back.

Like that night when the police raided Dougie's flat, she could feel her bowels loosening. She felt sick too and every hair on her body was standing on end. But as she heard him slide back the bolts and turn a key in the lock, she peeped.

He was wearing a mackintosh and long rubber fisherman's waders. As he pushed the doors open and a cold blast of rain-laden wind came in, she leapt to her feet, candlestick in hand.

Charging at him with her head down was pure instinct. She caught him in the chest, just as he turned and he staggered back, out into the garden.

'You bastard,' she screamed involuntarily. 'You aren't drowning me.' Lifting the candlestick she whacked it down on his shoulder with all the force she could muster. He reeled back in shocked surprise and Mel was off like the wind down the garden in her bare feet.

Above the wind, rain and the sound of the river she couldn't hear if he was following her. It was too dark to see anything clearly, but there appeared to be high stone walls on both sides of the garden and the river was presumably just beyond the dark shape of trees in front of her. But as she skirted round a walled raised flowerbed in the centre of the lawn, Edward surprised her by appearing again in front of her.

'You aren't going anywhere,' he yelled at her and, grabbing one of her arms, swung her round.

Mel had dropped the candlestick as she fled. All she had as weapons were her hands and nails. With her one free hand she clawed at his face, bringing up her knee hard in his groin as he hauled her nearer to him.

He yelped as her nails tore into his face, letting go of her arm. She tried to run again, but he leapt after her catching her in a flying tackle, bringing her down onto the ground and pinning her down with his own body.

Mel was winded, but terror gave her strength. Somehow she managed to buck enough beneath him so they rolled together, and this time she used both hands to claw his face.

Edward swung his fist at her. It caught her by the right eye and crashed her head back against the bricks of the raised flowerbed, but as he got to his knees ready to haul her up, Mel drew her two feet up to her chest, then shot them out at him.

The force with which she kicked him was sufficient to send Edward staggering back and give her enough time to get up. She was off again, running for her life through the garden towards the river. She no longer cared how deep and cold it was, she knew it was her only chance of survival.

He was right behind her, so close she could hear his laboured breath. She barged through a bush and saw a narrow wooden jetty, with a small white motor boat moored there. The river was as black as tar, swirling past in a torrent. But any hesitation she might have had vanished as she heard Edward thundering through the bushes behind her and she leapt in without a second thought.

The water was icy, almost paralysing her, the strong current tried to suck her down, but she struck out in a fast crawl, going with the flow.

Mel had always been a strong swimmer. Bonny's fear of water hadn't affected her and in fact she had been the fastest swimmer in the class at senior school. But swimming in a pool or even in the sea on a summer's day, was quite different to being in a rain-swollen river in the dark, with a current that threatened to pull her under at every stroke.

She hoped for another garden backing onto the river, but she could see nothing but shrub-covered banks which appeared to be growing steeper the further she swam. To her further horror she heard the sound of the boat's engine being started up behind her, and she knew he would catch up with her in minutes.

There was no alternative but to strike out for the bank on the opposite side from Edward's house, to conceal herself until he'd passed by, then somehow climb out and make a run for it. The river wasn't very wide, but the current made it difficult to make much headway. She had her hand on a branch when she saw Edward coming, the white bows of the boat and his blond hair showing clearly in the darkness.

She hauled herself under a low-lying bush, trying hard to grip her dress which was floating up to the surface like a parachute between her legs. He was going very slowly, looking intently at both sides of the river as he went. She held her breath and let herself sink right under the water, offering up a silent prayer that he wouldn't catch a glimpse of her striped dress.

There were thick weeds and roots under her feet, but she stayed down until her lungs were bursting. As she re-emerged gasping for air, she was just in time to see him going round a slight bend. It was obvious he'd come back, he would know she couldn't have swum much farther in that time; she just hoped that by then she had managed to get out of the river.

It was the most difficult thing she'd ever done. The heavy rain had turned the bank into thick slimy mud and as fast as she got one foothold, so the other would slide back. Reaching out for a bush she nearly toppled back into the river when she felt sharp thorns, but she gripped it regardless of the pain. Hauling onto another branch she finally managed to reach the top.

More thorn bushes tore at her face, cardigan and legs, and she could hear the boat returning. With rasping breath she forced her way through another bush and hid behind a tree trunk just as Edward got back to the spot where she'd climbed out.

He cut the engine. Mel held her breath. He was just beneath her. Could he see marks where she'd scrambled up the bank?

She was even more terrified now than she'd been earlier. Setting aside the discomfort of being soaked, freezing cold and her feet bare, she knew Edward wasn't going to give up easily, there was too much at stake. She had no idea where she was, or which direction to go in to find help. Her watch said five past ten, but it must have stopped when she jumped in the river.

The boat engine started up again and moved away back in the direction of his house. She took off her sodden cardigan, tried to squeeze out some of the water, then rolled it up and put it under her arm. She hurried through the last of the trees and bushes, but once she was up to the top of the bank she found herself in an open field with no cover to conceal her.

Stopping for a moment she scanned all around. Across the field was a hedge. There could well be a country lane behind, but if there was, Edward almost certainly knew of it. She had no way of knowing where the nearest bridge across the river was either, but it might be quite close and if he got in his car he could quickly catch up with her on a road.

She decided to go to the right, keeping close to the bushes. She could see nothing ahead of her, not even a distant light, but at least it was away from Edward's house, and if he was following her on foot, at least she had a head start. It was only now that she felt the pain of her injuries. Her jaw and cheek throbbed, there was a bump on her head as big as a walnut and dozens of sore places from thorns on her legs, hands and face.

The rain lashed down and she was so cold it was painful. She broke into a run to try and get warmer, but almost immediately she caught her foot on a stone in the grass, so she had to slow down and try to look where she was stepping. She reached a thorny hedge. It was too high to see over, so she followed it along looking for a hole to crawl through. Another rock caught her foot, and this time she knew it was cut open by the pain. Hobbling on she came to a small hole in the hedge and attempted to crawl through it.

There was barbed wire. It caught her back, and as she struggled to free herself she heard her dress rip. A noise startled her, making her draw back under the hedge in fright. But when she looked again she saw that what had appeared to be a bush was, in fact, a cow.

She had never been nervous of cows, not in daylight, but making her way through a field full of them in darkness was quite different. Each time one moved, she jumped, and when she stepped in a still warm cowpat she recoiled in horror. Then she heard a car.

The glow of headlights proved she was correct in thinking a lane ran behind the far hedge to her left. But the slow speed at which it was being driven proved without any doubt it was Edward. Dropping down onto her stomach, she crawled back towards the hedge she'd just come through. The car stopped. She heard the door open and close behind him.

Shaking with fear and cold, she lay under the hedge, imagining him peering into the field. A gleam of a torch frightened her still more as it slowly scanned around, its beam reaching almost to where she lay. Not daring to lift her face to look, her heart palpitating, she waited and waited, tense with the expectation that any minute he would grab her.

Just when she could stand the suspense no

longer, she heard the click of the car door again. She lay still until the engine started again and he moved off.

Her foot was hurting so badly now that she could no longer bear her weight on it. When she came to a thicket of dense bushes, she crawled underneath them, unable to go any further.

It was the safety of those bushes which made her stay. Even though she was wet and freezing, and she hurt everywhere, common sense told her it would be foolhardy to try and walk any further until it was light. Again and again in those long hours as she lay curled up in a ball, she saw Edward's headlights pass by less than a hundred yards from her.

She relived so many scenes from her past, purposefully only selecting good ones, and trying to steer her mind away from the image of Edward suddenly hauling her out from the bushes. Eating hot buttered crumpets in Norah's tea rooms with her mother. Cheering her father when he came striding out of the pavilion in his cricket whites to bat. A day out with both her parents, sitting in the back of the car singing 'The Animals Went in Two by Two' and Bonny making up sillier and sillier new verses.

Planting spring bulbs in the garden with Bonny, hanging the decorations on the Christmas tree. Suddenly these happy memories seemed to far outweigh the sad ones, warming her inside as if she was back in front of the fire at Mermaid Street, drinking cocoa before going up to bed.

She had to survive until morning. There was still so much she had to do. Helena and Edward had robbed her of her mother, and she had to see not only that they were punished, but that all those dark secrets which had caused her death, were brought out into the open.

When the first weak grey light crept into the sky, Mel ripped off a strip from the hem of her dress and wound it round her foot for a bandage, then crawled out of the bush.

Anger alone kept her moving through those wet, cold fields. Ears strained for the sound of Edward's car, her feet, legs and arms throbbing and jangling with pain. She thought of Magnus and Nick, wondering how many miles she was from them. There was so much she wanted to say to them.

And Conrad. Was that phone call from Brighton part of the plot? Had Edward snatched that note she'd left him while her back was turned? Was he lying in bed right now, worrying, imagining that she'd run out on him?

There was more barbed wire on the next hedge, thorns and still more cowpats and stones to stumble over. But the sky was getting lighter and lighter by the minute.

Then at last she saw a house in the distance, just as she was ready to drop with exhaustion. A farm house, built of old grey stone. A barn and some outhouses clustered round it, and faint grey smoke curling out of the chimney. It was some distance away, in a dip, and another two hedges to negotiate before she'd reach it.

Those last two fields seemed endless, stumbling along with no shelter if Edward should come back. Sliding on mud, her feet getting torn by stones, wind battering her and crying aloud with pain which now seemed to be in every part of her body.

A dog bounded up to her as she crawled the last twenty or thirty yards. A big black and white farm dog, obviously put off his guard by her position.

'Good boy,' she said weakly, reaching out to pat him. 'Bark please, get help.'

The dog seemed to think it was a game, he lay

down in front of her, wagging his bushy tail, red tongue lolling almost as if he was laughing at her.

'I know I look funny,' she whispered. 'Just be a good guard dog and make a noise!'

'Kim!' A loud bellow came from the farm house. 'Kim! Come here!'

'Go and get him.' Mel struggled to her knees as the dog looked back in the direction of his master's voice. It was only when she got to her feet unsteadily that the dog barked, running round her, then stopping crouched down, just as if he was rounding up a sheep.

'What's all that noise for?' The man's exasperated voice came closer.

'Help me,' Mel shouted, yet even to her it came out more like a yelp. 'Help me!'

No man had ever looked more beautiful than the big man striding towards her. He was huge, powerful great shoulders in a red checked shirt, cord trousers tucked into Wellington boots, black hair tousled as if he'd just got out of bed.

'What on earth!' he exclaimed, running the last few yards to her.

'Help me,' she croaked out. 'There's a man out there trying to murder me.'

Chapter Twenty-Four

Conrad peeped hesitantly round Mel's open bedroom door at seven on Monday morning.

Instead of finding her still asleep as he expected, he saw that her bed hadn't been slept in. The jeans and tee shirt that had been lying on it last night were still in exactly the same place. She hadn't come home.

'Not another bloody mystery,' he exclaimed. He had a thumping headache and his mouth tasted like a sewer after the bottle of whisky he'd drunk the previous night. He didn't even feel up to making himself breakfast, and he'd been hoping Mel would go and buy the bread and vegetables for him.

He'd arrived at the Four Seasons bistro in Brighton just after six the day before to find it didn't open until seven. He stood in the rain and hammered on the door for some minutes, until a dim-witted girl who said she worked in the kitchens, opened it and told him that Mr Michael Dunwoody never came in until seven and that he hadn't told her he had an appointment with anyone.

Nothing but a Wimpy Bar was open and after stewing in there for an hour, drinking three cups of muddy coffee, Conrad had lost his usual good humour. He got back to the Four Seasons just in time to see a portly man in his fifties wearing an expensive suit get out of a brand new Mercedes and open the door with a key.

He ought to have twigged right away that something was wrong, especially since Dunwoody had looked completely blank when he introduced himself. But instead of checking first that he had got the right man and the right restaurant, Conrad launched into a volley of questions about the man's turnover. Ten minutes later he found himself back in the street, smarting with embarrassment. Dunwoody wasn't a reasonable man at all. At the words 'financial difficulties' he laid into Conrad with a fierce verbal onslaught declaring in no uncertain terms that his bistro was the most successful and well-known on the whole south coast and he wouldn't sell it to anyone.

Conrad tried to apologise and explain that it must have been a malicious hoax, but Dunwoody treated him like a lunatic and forced him to leave.

All the way home in driving rain, Conrad turned the incident over and over in his mind. He couldn't see why anyone would go to the trouble of setting him up like that, unless they wanted him out of his own place for a few hours.

It didn't help when he stopped halfway home to telephone Mel and got no reply. In his imagination his restaurant was already ransacked, with her tied up in a broom cupboard and the hoax caller sprinkling petrol on the carpet.

He was relieved to find his home and business intact when he eventually got back to Fulham. If Mel had been there he might have seen the funny side of the lurid pictures he'd had in his mind on the drive back from Brighton. But she'd gone out and hadn't even left a note, so he sat drinking whisky, morosely dwelling on who might have wanted to test his gullibility.

He didn't remember going to bed. When he

woke he found he was still fully dressed, including his shoes. His head felt as if someone had taken a sledgehammer to it.

Now with Mel missing he felt uneasy again. She had never stayed away for a night before; in fact she had never gone out on a Sunday night without him. Why hadn't she left a note or telephoned?

He went down to the restaurant kitchen, made a pot of strong coffee and took a couple of aspirin for his headache. He toyed with the idea of crawling back into bed, but the shopping had to be done, and the cleaning lady would be in at any minute. She always made enough noise to wake the dead.

The phone rang just as he was in the middle of shaving. Dabbing at his face with a towel he went down the stairs. Somehow he knew this was going to be the kind of day when everything went wrong.

'Conrad's Supper Rooms,' he said, hoping it was Mel.

'Am I speaking to Conrad Deeley?' The caller had a deep voice with a rural accent he couldn't place.

'Speaking. How can I help you?'

'My name is Brian Parker. I've been asked to ring you with a message.'

Conrad felt a surge of irrational anger. He was sure this was going to be another wind-up. 'Oh really, where do you want me to rush off to this time?' he said sarcastically.

'I beg your pardon,' the man retorted. 'Camellia Norton gave me your number because she thought you'd be anxious about her. You certainly should be – I found her in a terrible state.'

Conrad's stomach lurched. 'I'm sorry,' he said quickly. 'You caught me off guard. What do you mean, a terrible state? Where is she?'

'On her way to Royal United Hospital,' the man said. 'I'm a farmer, Mr Deeley. I found her in one of my fields about an hour ago. It seems she had been brought to a house somewhere near here and then attacked.'

'Attacked?' Conrad began to shake. 'Who by? Why?' He fumbled for a chair and slumped down on it to listen. He heard how the farmer had gone out to start his milking and found Mel in his field on the point of collapse.

'She's in good hands now,' the man said more gently, perhaps realising how shocked Conrad was. 'I don't think her injuries are serious, but she's in deep shock, suffering from exposure and exhaustion. She had escaped from the man by jumping into the river and then made her way over the fields barefoot. I called the police of course.'

'Who did this?' Conrad was beside himself now, suddenly aware that this might be why he'd been lured away.

'I'm afraid I can't tell you anything more,' the man said. 'She wasn't very coherent as I'm sure you can imagine. All she managed to do was tell me your number.'

'I'll come down there right away,' Conrad said. 'Bath General you say?'

'Will you let me know later how she is?' the man asked. 'Both my wife and I are very concerned.'

'Of course, and thank you for helping her.' Conrad recovered his good manners. 'I'm sorry I was a bit short with you at first. I'll explain why later. Now if you'll just give me your address and phone number?'

Mel was trapped in a thick, cold fog, turning first one way, then another to escape, but her legs wouldn't move and hideous contorted faces kept leering at her through the gloom, with long thin arms reaching out to clutch at her.

She was aware that one of these faces was

Edward, his blue eyes the only colour amongst the greyness, but though she felt the others were known to her she didn't recognise them or the voices that were calling to her. She felt something grab her round the neck, like a tentacle from an octopus and as she grappled with it, a wraith-type figure with black holes where eyes should be floated past her cackling with fiendish laughter.

'You should have stayed away,' it called in an eerie wheezing voice.

Somehow she knew this was her mother. She tried to run from her, covering her eyes and ears, but the tentacle held her tightly, slowly squeezing her throat.

'No,' she shouted, lashing out with her hands. 'I don't know anything. It's nothing to do with me.'

'What's nothing to do with you?' A crisp, human voice spoke and suddenly the fog, the tentacle and the wraith vanished. 'Was it a nasty dream?'

Mel opened her eyes and saw a nurse looking down at her. She remembered then that she was in hospital. 'They were all there, trying to get me,' she whispered, her voice a mere croak.

The nurse was barely older than herself, with a sweet face and a pink and white complexion. She put one cool hand on Mel's forehead and smiled soothingly. 'No one's going to get you,' she said firmly. 'You're quite safe here in hospital. I'm Grace Powell, one of the night nurses. Now how about a nice cup of tea and then if you feel up to it perhaps I can let your friend in to see you? He's been waiting so patiently for you to wake up.'

'What friend?' Mel stiffened.

'Mr Deeley,' the nurse replied. 'Don't you want to see him?'

Mel sighed with relief. 'Conrad's here? When did he come? What time is it?'

The nurse laughed softly. 'So many questions. It's nearly eight. By all accounts Mr Deeley's been here since midday. Now let's get you sat up first and see how you feel when you've had some tea.'

Mel's hands were shaking too much to hold a cup, so the nurse gave her one with a spout and held it to her lips for her.

'That's better,' she said approvingly when it was finished. 'Now how do you feel?'

Mel had to get her bearings first. She was in a single room, with a light over her bed and more coming through a glass porthole in the door. She could hear the murmur of voices coming from somewhere else. She guessed her room was just off the main ward and it was visiting time.

'I'm stiff and sore,' she said eventually. 'Every bit of me aches.' She looked down at her arms, covered in deep vivid scratches. Her foot was bandaged and it throbbed. Gingerly she lifted her left hand to her cheek.

'That looks and probably feels worse than it is,' the nurse said in sympathy. 'You've got a nasty black eye and a bump on your head, but your right foot's the only serious injury. You had to have quite a few stitches there. Do you remember being brought in?'

'Vaguely,' Mel said. The big farm kitchen was very clear in her mind. It was warm and a woman with short dark hair had sat her in a chair by an Aga and wrapped her in blankets before feeding her hot, sweet tea. There were pots of geraniums on the windowsill and a smell of frying bacon, and a fat tabby cat had tried to get up on her lap. It had felt like waking with a start from a terrible nightmare, remembering the terror, but being unable to recall actual events. She couldn't do anything but cry and ask them to phone Conrad.

The police and ambulance arrived simultaneously. Mel tried to get a grip on herself, but although she could tell them her attacker's name and that his house was on the river, she had lost all sense of which direction it was in. Later on at the hospital, when another policeman came into her cubicle in the casualty department to question her further she thought she did a little better, but she was so exhausted she kept dropping off.

'From what I hear you had a terrible time with that man.' The nurse sat on the edge of the bed. 'But you mustn't worry anymore. The police are out searching for him, and you are quite safe now. Can Mr Deeley come in? He's been pacing up and down that corridor wearing it out while you were asleep, and Sister insists all visitors leave the ward by eight thirty.'

'Yes, please,' Mel said weakly. She knew the police would be back soon to question her further, but she needed to talk it all over first with someone she could trust.

'Oh Con.' She held up her arms weakly as he came hesitantly through the door. 'You can't know how good it is to see you.'

His appearance brought it home to her that she wasn't the only one who'd been through an ordeal. He looked terrible: unshaven, his eyes bloodshot and his jacket thrown on over a tee shirt. But he embraced her with all his customary warmth, murmuring little endearments with a choked voice.

'You look ghastly,' she said, once he'd lowered her back onto the pillows.

'I've seen you looking better too,' he retorted and his lips quivered. 'My excuse is that the farmer called just as I was about to start shaving. I never thought to finish and get dressed properly before rushing out. Heaven only knows what people here are thinking of me.'

'Just how bad do I look?' she asked. Her jaw ached intolerably, her foot throbbed and her hair smelt and felt like something retrieved from the bottom of a pond.

Conrad wished he could find a jokey reply, but he was too shocked by her injuries for humour. Her left eye was almost closed, in a deep purple mass which spread right down her cheek, and her face was very badly scratched.

He picked up her hand and held it gently. 'You're alive, that's what counts,' he said softly. 'I just hope that when they catch that man someone roughs him up too.'

'It was the one who came into the restaurant and left without eating. The one I said was a Nazi.'

'Was it?' he said in surprise, pulling up a chair. He had spoken to a police officer earlier while Mel was still asleep and got the gist of what had happened to her, but the police hadn't been able to ascertain why she had left London with a stranger, or what he had to do with her mother. They were even more puzzled by the way she kept repeating Helena Forester's name.

Con listened as she explained how it all came about. 'Well, that at least explains why I had to be lured away,' he sighed. 'The man obviously did a lot of homework.'

'He killed my mother too, Con,' he said.

'The police are a bit puzzled about that, Mel,' he said anxiously. 'I hope you don't mind but I had to fill them in with a bit of your background. They went off to interview both Helena and Magnus.'

'You didn't tell them I thought Magnus was my father?' she gasped.

'No, I didn't,' he reassured her. 'It isn't really relevant to this. I just said you used to work for him and that he was an old friend of your mother's. It seems Helena *was* staying at Oaklands, though she's got a cottage somewhere nearby now. Apparently Magnus has been escorting her around quite a bit.'

Mel's stomach lurched. 'Then he must be in this too?'

Conrad looked puzzled, brown eyes blinking hard behind his glasses. 'What on earth makes you say that?'

She began to cry. All the thoughts she'd collated together in the last twenty-four hours had led her to believe Edward had been alone in disposing of Bonny, although perhaps ordered to do so by Helena. But Magnus had good reason at that time to want Bonny silenced too, whatever he'd said to the contrary. Wasn't it just possible that he took an active part in the conspiracy?

'I don't know why I didn't see it before. They're all in it together,' she sobbed. 'It's a horrible tangled web and I can't trust anyone anymore. Now I understand why Magnus had that stroke. He thought it was all going to come to light. Once he found the letters after I left Oaklands he must have thought I'd discovered more than I told him. He got in touch with Helena and they cooked up the appeal to find me just to get rid of me once and for all.'

All Conrad knew of Magnus were stories from Mel, and he'd often cynically considered that he couldn't be quite the paragon of virtue she described, not if he had an affair with another woman while claiming to love his wife. He knew nothing about Sir Miles and all he knew of Helena was from film magazines. But he couldn't possibly imagine all three such well-known people conspiring to kill Bonny or Mel.

He expressed this view to Mel.

'I agree there's something very fishy about it all,' he added. 'But I don't agree Helena and Magnus are responsible for Edward coming after you.'

'Magnus might not be, but she is,' she insisted.

Conrad felt she was temporarily unhinged and that aside from offering her affection and concern, he could do and say nothing that would make her feel less threatened at the present.

'I think you should sleep on this,' he said. 'I'll drive home to London now and return tomorrow after I've put a note on the door saying we're closed for a few days. I'll bring down some washing things and a nightdress for you, and we'll talk about it again then.'

She just continued to sob.

'Go back to sleep, Mel,' he said, bending over to kiss her goodbye. 'You are safe in here. I promise you it will all look different in the morning.'

Grace Powell came in the next morning with some breakfast on a tray. Last night after Conrad had left Mel had been very weepy and Grace had sat with her for some time to comfort her. But she had been pleased to see a big improvement today; earlier Mel had drunk a cup of tea unaided and asked to be allowed to get up to use the toilet.

'I'm going off duty soon,' Grace said. 'But I intend to see you eat all this before I go. I've got porridge and scrambled eggs for you with soft bread and butter, so don't make the excuse you can't eat it.'

'I'm actually hungry,' Mel said in some surprise. 'In fact I feel much better.'

'Then you'll be even more pleased to hear we've had three inquiries about you in the last half hour.' Grace put the tray on the bed trolley, then helped Mel to sit up. 'The famous Helena Forester no less, someone called Osbourne with a sexy deep voice and last, but I don't think least, Nick.'

'Nick?' Mel almost leapt out of bed.

'I had a feeling that name would get some response,' Grace laughed. 'He sounded a real dish. Said to give you his love and he was driving down from London today. He said he has a million things to tell you.'

After a long and deep sleep Mel felt able to look at things a little more dispassionately. 'What did Osbourne of the sexy voice say?' she asked. 'That's Nick's father,' she added with a smile.

'His concern for you came down the line like hot syrup,' Grace said with a smile. 'He asked me lots of things about your injuries but his message was "Tell her I want to come and bring her home".'

Mel's eyes prickled and a lump came up in her throat.

'Don't you dare start crying again,' Grace said severely. 'I felt sorry for you last night – I didn't think you had anyone in the world but Mr Deeley. Now I know you've got so many chums I won't waste any more sympathy.'

Mel wanted to laugh, but her face hurt too much to do anything more than chuckle.

'Well don't you want to hear what Miss Helena Forester, star of stage and screen, had to say?'

'Not really,' Mel shrugged. This morning she might be prepared to give Magnus the benefit of the doubt, but she'd hardened her heart to Helena.

'Well, I'm going to tell you anyway. She said, "Tell Camellia that I'm devastated by what has happened and that my thoughts and prayers are all for her." She also asked if she could pay for you to have a private room.'

Mel made no reply but went on to eat her breakfast.

'I told her you were in a room on your own.'

Grace sat down on the end of the bed. 'I wish you'd tell me the whole story. I know there's a lot more to it than you've said.'

Mel looked up from her porridge. She could see the nurse was bursting with curiosity. 'Yes, there is, Grace, but some of it still baffles me, so I can't really explain to anyone. But in the meantime I don't want any visitors aside from Conrad, not even Nick. And I don't want anyone shifting their guilt by trying to pay for my treatment.'

Grace's blue eyes opened wide in astonishment. She had already seen the papers this morning and Edward Manning's picture was on the front of it, with an appeal for anyone who might see him to contact the police. Mel wasn't named as his victim, but they'd made a big thing of Manning's role as Helena Forester's manager. One of the other nurses had passed on the news that the actress had been staying at Oaklands, and Grace already knew that Osbourne owned the hotel.

But now Mel was saying she didn't want to see anyone aside from the skinny little chap who looked like a librarian. She just couldn't make head nor tail of what was going on.

'The police rang to ask how you were, but Sister spoke to them,' she went on. 'They are coming in soon to see you. Do you want me to tell the Day Staff to send them packing too?'

Mel looked up and smiled. 'You can't send police packing,' she said. 'But I mean it about the other visitors. I don't want to see them. However much fuss they make.'

'Just tell me why?' Grace pleaded.

'Because, my nosy little nurse, I'm confused and I need time to come to terms with everything.'

The nurse waited until Mel had eaten everything, then took away the tray. 'I'll see you this evening,' she said as she left the room. 'Don't try walking on that foot either.'

The police came just after nine, in plain clothes. Williams, a frosty-faced WPC, was about thirty-five with bad skin and red hair. Her male companion who looked about fifty, introduced himself as Price, not mentioning his rank. He was humourless, a thin, rather seedy-looking man in a beige trench-coat, with bleak pale-blue eyes and thinning hair. Mel had to assume the policewoman had been brought along as a witness. She didn't speak throughout the interview.

Mel had felt quite calm and collected until Price began questioning her in depth, but within minutes he made her feel tense and frightened again. He took her right back to the first time she saw Edward Manning in the restaurant, then every step of the way until she finally reached the farm where the police were called the next morning.

He pulled her up on every last thing. What Manning was wearing, the car he drove. What he spoke about on the journey to the West Country, his manner towards her and why she should suddenly feel threatened when they got to the house by the river.

When she reached the point when she suspected Edward had put a sedative in her tea, Price looked disbelieving. He kept stopping her, questioning why she didn't panic if she thought she was in such danger. The way he raised one eyebrow when she explained how she decided to fake sleep gave her the distinct impression Price thought she had an overactive imagination.

'I just *knew* he intended to kill me,' she said stubbornly. 'I was terrified, of course, but playing along with him was my only option. If he'd known I'd tumbled what he was doing he might have knocked me out. Anyway as it turned out I was right about him and his plan to get rid of me. Why else did he come back into the room wearing a mackintosh and waders?'

When Price didn't reply immediately Mel grew angry.

'I suppose you think I've made the whole thing up. That I'm some sort of loony that races barefoot around the country in a storm for attention? Why don't you look for the house and check it all out.'

Price smiled as if she was a simple-minded child. 'We have found the house. We checked it out yesterday afternoon. Manning's grandmother lived there until her death some fifteen years ago. But we didn't find any evidence that anyone but Manning had been there. Not your shoes, overnight bag or raincoat. We could find no sedatives there either. Of course it's possible he returned to the house after you escaped him and cleared all these things away, but that seems unlikely if he was quite as deranged as you say, especially as you have claimed he came after you in his car later.'

'He was going to kill me, just like he killed my mother,' she insisted. 'I suppose Helena Forester has convinced you that I'm the crazy one, that I freaked out for no reason and jumped in the river to make my story look good. But then she would, she's up to her ears in this.'

Price cocked his head to one side, for the first time in the interview he looked surprised.

'Now why would you think that? We inter-viewed Miss Forester yesterday after your friend, Mr Deeley, informed us about your connection with her. She has shown nothing but the utmost concern for you. She told us that Manning collected a bunch of letters from the *News of the World* offices for her, and that was confirmed by Mr Osbourne, in fact they went through them together. By all accounts they were both disappointed to find there wasn't one from you amongst them. The only thing that struck me as odd about Miss Forester was that she had enlisted Mr Osbourne's help in trying to find you. I believe you left his employ in rather a hurry. Why was that Miss Norton?'

'Ask them,' she snapped. 'They're the ones with all the answers.'

Conrad arrived back at the hospital just before twelve, with a bag containing Mel's washing things, nightdress, dressing gown and slippers, along with flowers and a box of chocolates. He felt rested and calm again after a good night's sleep, he'd even put on his best grey suit. His wide smile vanished though as he walked into the room and found her lying hunched up on her side, crying into the pillow.

'What on earth's happened?' he asked, dumping his bags on the floor and rushing over to her bed. He'd phoned the hospital around eight in the morning before he left London and had been told by the Ward Sister that she was very much better, and quite cheerful.

Mel sobbed as she told him about her interview with the police. It wasn't a twenty-four-year-old woman in shock he heard, but the anguish of a very young girl. It was as if she had slipped back mentally to the time when her mother's body was discovered. She had withheld evidence then out of shame and anger, but now nine years later the combination of painful memories, fear, guilt and an insensitive policeman had pushed her over the edge.

'Oh baby,' Con put his arms round her and held her tight. He couldn't bear to see her locked into such misery. 'I'll go down to the police station myself and put them straight.'

'You don't understand,' she sobbed. 'Those letters have blighted my life. Because of them I'm up to my neck in trouble again. Anything you or I say to the police will bring more trouble down on me. They'll check me out, dredge up all the old dirt before they even so much as ask Helena Forester her birthday. I wish Edward had killed me, Con, that way I'd be free of all this. I can't take any more.'

Conrad left the hospital with a heavy heart. The Ward Sister had curtly told him that Mel needed rest and peace to get better, as if he was responsible for upsetting her again. She'd also pointed out that the official visiting hours which were between two thirty and four in the afternoons and seven to eight thirty in the evenings. Mel had told him not to go to the police, so he had a couple of hours to kill until two thirty. As he'd never been to Bath before, he drove on into the city to look round.

The sun had come out again. He parked his car in Victoria Park and decided to walk from there. Although Mel was in the forefront of his mind, he soon found himself becoming enchanted by all he saw around him. The park was glorious: huge trees turning gold and orange, flowerbeds ablaze with colour, lush lawns stretching right up to the terraces of imposing Regency houses.

The enchantment grew stronger still as he walked through the town, past the elegant big stores in the wide main street, and through the narrow lanes leading off. There seemed to be flowers everywhere – hanging baskets, riotous window boxes, tubs outside the dozens of restaurants and coffee shops. He bought a couple of rolls and guided by a helpful assistant made his way down to the famous Poultney Bridge to eat them.

Conrad had always considered Dublin to be

unsurpassable for its beauty and atmosphere, but as he stood looking over the wall at the fast-flowing river tumbling over the weir, he felt Bath was comparable, with its old buildings built in a serene golden stone, willow trees drooping down to the water and brightly painted canal boats. When he looked up he saw how the city was almost like a huge amphitheatre, the graceful houses rising in tiers up towards the green hills beyond. As Mel had so often told him, there were tourists everywhere, cameras strapped around their necks, clutching guidebooks, and gasping at everything in awe. But this town was more than a living museum dating back to the Romans; it was a place dearly loved by its residents. Little old ladies hobbling by on sticks, young mothers with prams, burly workmen shinning up scaffolding – they all looked happy to be here. The pretty park by the river wasn't crowded with holiday-makers, but working people snatching their lunch hour in a place of peace and tranquillity. Conrad understood now why Mel had fallen in love with this city.

He shivered as he gazed down into the river. But for Mel's quick thinking and courage, she might very well have ended up being fished out of it. As it was she might never fully recover from the ordeal.

There was only one way to heal his friend: to peel back that cloak of secrecy and reveal the whole truth to her. It was time someone stepped in on her behalf, someone who had no vested interest.

Conrad turned away from his view of the weir and walked purposefully to a telephone box.

At nine o'clock that same evening Conrad turned into the wooded drive towards Oaklands. He had spent the afternoon with Mel, then returned to the small guesthouse in Weston village to freshen up and change his shirt. By seven thirty he was back at the hospital, where he'd found Mel just as withdrawn as she'd been earlier. She had seen an evening newspaper and the news that Edward still hadn't been apprehended hadn't helped. Conrad couldn't cheer her much. He was so nervous about going to Oaklands behind her back that he'd had difficulty in stringing more than a couple of sentences together.

The front door opened even before he'd parked his rusting little Mini between a big grey Daimler and a black Bentley by the stable block.

He guessed the man silhouetted in the porch light was Magnus, though his height, upright stance and broad shoulders hardly fitted the image of a seventy-year-old stroke victim. As Conrad got out of his car the man moved forward to greet him, and he noticed then that one leg dragged slightly.

'You must be Conrad? Welcome to Oaklands. I'm Magnus Osbourne. Come on in.'

Mel had spoken of this house so often that Conrad felt he'd been there before. But even so, the hall was grander than he'd imagined: no sagging settees or worn rugs like the country house hotels in Ireland. He took in the twinkling chandelier, the handprinted wallpaper and the glossy white paint and felt uncomfortably aware of his unprepossessing appearance and his cheap suit.

Through a half-open door he caught a glimpse of an elegant candle-lit dining room and heard the low rumble of voices and the clink of glasses. The bar was busy too, full of businessmen in lounge suits. Classical music played softly in the background.

'I thought it better to meet in my private sitting room,' Magnus said, leading Conrad towards a wide staircase before he could see anything more. 'The drawing room is a little public and some of my guests might wander in. Sir Miles has managed to get here, even at such short notice – he arrived about an hour ago.'

As Magnus ushered him into his masculine sitting room and the assembled company stood up to greet him, Conrad's nerve left him.

He thought he had prepared himself, but now he felt dwarfed and intimidated by such an impressive group. He wondered how he had the temerity to think he could break them down.

Helena, in a regal blue dress, dark hair waving over her shoulders, was even more devastating in the flesh than on screen, taller and more majestic than he'd expected. Mel's loving descriptions of Nick Osbourne hadn't quite prepared him for such physical perfection either. Just one glance at his height, sun-kissed blond hair and athletic body and he was back at school, gazing at the golden boys who had it all.

Then Sir Miles Hamilton: old and fat, but still so distinguished. He wore a formal dark suit, but beneath it a maroon silk waistcoat with a small gold motif. Baggy jowls, bright dark eyes embedded in flesh, balding head glistening under the light from a table lamp, but though he had to reach for a silver-topped cane to help himself out of the chair, his step toward Conrad was sprightly.

Magnus made the introductions and Conrad shook hands with all three of them. Then as Helena and Sir Miles returned to their seats and Nick went to a trolley to pour drinks, Magnus began to speak.

'Conrad has asked us to meet tonight because he has something to put to us. I know you are all as curious as I am, but first I'm quite sure you'd like to know how Mel is.' He looked back at Conrad. 'We have of course rung the hospital, but their reports have been disappointingly guarded.'

Conrad felt he ought to stand, but his legs were

turning to jelly, so he took one of the two smaller armchairs.

'Physically she's recovering well,' he said, leaning forward in his chair, one hand on either knee. 'She has a very bad cut on her foot which has several stitches, but the rest of her injuries are superficial. Mentally, however, she is in a very low state. That's what prompted me to ask if I could speak to you all.'

Magnus took the last spare chair, while Nick passed around the drinks. He then joined Helena on the settee and looked to Conrad to continue.

'I feel a little awkward.' Conrad blushed with nerves, his heart thumping. 'I've known Mel such a short time and it may seem impertinent to you that I'm sticking my nose in her business.'

'The police said one of the first things she did when she was found was to ask the farmer to ring you,' Nick said. 'As far as I'm concerned that gives you the right to act on her behalf.'

Conrad was grateful for Nick's support; the man must be wondering if he was more than just her employer and friend.

'I told Magnus on the telephone today that Mel has confided in me totally,' he said, looking to the older man for reassurance. Magnus smiled encouragement. 'And Magnus in return gave me a frank report on the lengths he and Nick have gone to to try and find her in the last year. I was very tempted to tell Mel this tonight, but I resisted because it's my belief that until the entire truth can be handed to her, such news would only offer a strand of comfort, not a cure.'

He paused and looked at each one in turn, just as he once had with a class of boys.

Helena was nervously pleating her skirt with her fingers. Sir Miles looked uncomfortable, but this might have been due to old age and tiredness. Nick was leaning forward, his whole stance impatient for a revelation. Magnus alone sat back entirely relaxed.

'I'm not going to beat about the bush,' Conrad went on, hoping he could keep his nerve. 'Mel believes Edward killed her mother because of something Bonny knew and maybe threatened to disclose. Clearly Edward had reason to believe Bonny had passed on this information to Mel, which was why he attempted to kill her too. As it was Helena's newspaper interview which revealed where Mel was, she quite understandably believes Helena must be involved too.'

'That's the biggest load of tosh I've heard in years,' Sir Miles roared out before Conrad could even catch his breath. 'The girl's a fool if she believes that Helena had anything to do with it.'

'Mel is no fool,' Conrad said indignantly. 'She is distraught right now, but then it would be strange if she wasn't after narrowly escaping death. As I see it, at the centre of all this is the file of letters Mel found on Bonny's death. Each one of you has been drawn into this business because of them, and someone in this room knows the secret at the core of them which prompted Edward to kill Bonny. Until they are prepared to tell Mel, she would be foolish to trust any of you.'

'She can trust me,' Nick blurted out. 'I've done everything I can to find out. How does she feel about me?'

'Tortured,' Conrad said simply. If he'd met Nick under any other circumstances he would have doubted whether he was capable of loving anyone but himself. But he had felt Nick's love for Mel as Magnus had spoken earlier of all he had done. There was absolute sincerity in those blue eyes, and so far he'd hung on every word Conrad had said as if that made him feel closer to her. 'From the moment she realised you were Magnus's son she lost her peace of mind. Unless she is given hard evidence that she isn't related to you, I don't think she can cope with seeing you again. If you care so much for her you must bring pressure on the other people in this room to reveal what they know.'

No one spoke for what seemed like minutes. Nick looked around challengingly. Magnus was watching Helena as if willing her to speak. Sir Miles was staring at his lap intently, his chin disappearing into folds of loose skin.

'I have that hard evidence.'

Everyone started as Helena's husky voice broke the silence. Nick turned to her eagerly on the settee. Magnus leaned forward in his chair and Sir Miles opened his eyes very wide, looking at her with some consternation.

Conrad looked closely at Helena, suspecting theatricals. Yet her gaze was steady and unwavering, her dark eyes glinting with strange lights. Her full lower lip quivered with emotion.

'I wish I could tell you it all now and be done with this mystery,' she said in a low voice, and her eyes began to fill with tears. 'But what I have to say is for Camellia's ears only. Conrad, you must convince her that my sole reason for that interview was to meet her and tell her my story. She has nothing to fear from anyone in this room.'

Conrad felt elated. He had been intending to threaten them next by saying he was going to take the entire story to the police. He was greatly relieved that this might not be necessary. 'I will pass that on, providing you can tell us now why Manning should want to kill Mel.'

She hesitated for only a second. 'He knew once I'd met up with her that his place in my life would be usurped.'

Conrad was confounded by this reply, but it

sounded like the truth. Magnus half rose in his chair as if compelled to reach her. Nick looked as baffled as Conrad felt. Sir Miles looked distinctly alarmed.

Until now Sir Miles had seemed less involved than the others. He had sat in his chair, hands folded across his large stomach as impassive as a judge. But now he was truly participating. There were beads of perspiration on his forehead, he licked his lips nervously and his eyes were firmly on Helena.

Conrad took a deep breath and jumped in before he lost his nerve. 'Well sir! Are you prepared to tell me what part you've played in all this?'

'The fool,' Sir Miles snapped back. 'A stupid old fool who should have faced up to his indiscretions years ago, and taken note of things he was told instead of dismissing them out of hand.'

Conrad was just going to ask him what he meant when he saw exactly what Nick had seen.

The old man's eyes had been almost buried in loose flesh, but as he spoke they opened wider and the truth was there to see. They were almond-shaped like Mel's. The resemblance was uncanny.

'Now Helena has stated her intention, I too must do my part to put things right.' His voice boomed out across the room, clear and unwavering. He looked at the actress as if for approval. 'Like Helena, what I have to say is for Camellia's ears only. But I can tell you now Conrad, that none of us here tonight was involved in any way with Bonny's death, and neither did we know that Manning had intercepted Camellia's letter to Helena. To my shame I have to admit I alone suspected Manning was irrational and unstable and I hold myself accountable for not acting on that gut feeling. But in my own defence I would say that I couldn't conceive of the man planning something like this.'

Silence fell, but the tension remained in the air. Conrad sensed he would achieve nothing by pressing anyone further tonight.

'I'm very grateful to you all for your honesty,' he said. 'Tomorrow I shall tell Mel everything which has been said tonight and I'll let you know her response.'

'Will you ask her if she'll allow me to bring her back here to recuperate?' Magnus asked, his deeply lined face full of concern.

Conrad remembered how Mel had once described this man as a lion. Now he understood why. It wasn't just the broad nose, the mane of hair or the straight-backed way he sat, but something within him, proud, indefatigable.

'You must ask her that yourself,' Conrad said. 'There is a danger that if Manning isn't caught soon he might come here.'

The police had no leads yet on Manning's whereabouts. Helena had believed him to be in Manchester. The police had asked for the public's assistance in spotting his dark blue Jaguar, but so far none of the reported sightings had been substantiated. Helena hadn't even known he still owned his grandmother's old house. She thought he had sold it several years earlier.

'I doubt that he'll attempt to come here. But I can make Oaklands like Fort Knox if necessary,' Magnus said with the kind of authority that suggested he would kill Manning himself if he as much as stepped over the threshold.

'We'll have to see what Mel says,' Conrad rose to his feet. Such considerations were hardly important at the moment, she would be in hospital for a while yet. 'I would ask though that none of you make any move towards her until she's ready.'

Nick's lip curled petulantly. 'Me too?'

'Especially you.' Conrad got a certain kick out of

saying this. He wasn't in the habit of having the upper hand with people of Nick's class and type. 'She's very confused still, Nick. Give her time to hear what Helena and Sir Miles have to say. Give her a bit of space.'

'Conrad's right.' Helena turned to Nick and put her hand over his, squeezing it in sympathy. 'I know if I were in her shoes the last thing I'd need is a young man pressing for a romantic entanglement.'

'I suppose you're right,' Nick shrugged. 'I do have to go back to London tomorrow anyway. I guess I was jumping the gun a bit thinking I could just charge into the hospital and whisk her off somewhere.'

'Just a bit,' Conrad smiled. On one hand he admired the man for being prepared to admit the depths of his feeling so openly. But on the other he was remembering how badly Nick had hurt Mel when he threw her out of Oaklands. Nick needed to put that right before thinking he could whisk her away anywhere.

Magnus stood up. 'Well, son,' he took a step towards Conrad, 'I can see Sir Miles at least is wilting and I'm quite certain you've had enough for one day too. Have we covered everything you intended?'

Conrad felt so small and insignificant next to this man but he wasn't quite finished.

'Almost everything,' he said to Magnus, then looked towards the other three. 'There is one last, very important thing I need to stress. In the six months Mel has worked for me we have become very close. Life has struck her more body blows than most of us could take, but yet she has remained a fine, good person without a trace of bitterness. Right now she is quivering on the edge of a mental breakdown. I want you to bear that in mind, because if one of you should push her over that edge you'll be accountable to me.'

Sir Miles gave a little snort, which could have been confirmation he agreed or irritation that such a little weed was giving orders. Nick looked taken aback. But Helena's fearful expression was the one which floored him. It confirmed at least part of his suspicions.

Chapter Twenty-Five

As the car turned into the drive of Oaklands Mel leant forward in the passenger seat, looking eagerly around her. Touched by her obvious delight to be back Magnus slowed right down so she could see everything.

'There's a badger set over there.' He pointed into the woods to the right of the drive. 'I saw a mother and her babies early one morning back in the summer.'

Mel smiled happily. It was all just as she remembered seeing it for the first time, three years earlier: the leaves changing to gold, orange and deep russet, a smell of damp earth and the soothing sound of wind rustling the tree tops. Even Magnus was much the same – a few more lines on his face perhaps, and his stroke had left him with a slight limp, but he was as rugged as ever. Even his old tweed jacket had that same woody, country smell she remembered from the day he offered her a job at Oaklands.

'Sometimes I doubted I'd ever see you, or all this again,' she said with a deep sigh.

It was the second of October, eight days since Edward took her away from Fulham. She had been kept in hospital when the deep wound in her foot became infected. But she'd been glad to stay there. It gave her body a chance to heal, and time to think things through.

When Conrad had told her about the meeting at

Oaklands, just before he returned to London, she had been stunned by his audacity, but the knowledge she had one true friend on her side soothed some of the pain within her. As Conrad went on to tell her how Nick had traced her life back to try and find her, she was shaken to the core. She had imagined he was still harbouring bitter thoughts about her. The next morning a long and loving letter arrived from him, giving her all the details of his search. He spoke of his deep sorrow about the cruel things he'd said when he made her leave Oaklands and of his hopes that they could start afresh when she was better.

Mel was now intensely curious about what Helena and Sir Miles had to tell her, but during her stay in hospital it had been enough to have Magnus coming to see her every day. Their reunion had been an emotional one. While she was thrilled to see Magnus had made such a good recovery from his stroke, he was horrified by her scarred face and felt himself to be partially responsible. But with each successive visiting time, the sad parts of the last year were wiped out. Each day she felt both the external and internal scars fading. The mysteries of the past, and what might happen in the future, could wait.

'Well, here we are.' Magnus halted the car just before the house so she could see the view of the valley. 'I think the weathermen must've known you were coming home today and arranged the sunshine specially.'

Mel's eyes prickled, not just because everything was even lovelier than she'd remembered, but because he called it home. The sun was a fiery orange ball, about to slip down behind the green lush hills. Wispy pink cotton wool clouds scudded across a still bright blue sky. Here and there, between trees, she caught glimpses of the river,

632

sparkling in the sunshine, and fronting all this was the autumnal magnificence of the gardens. Heavy rain hadn't spoilt the display of huge chrysanthemums and Michaelmas daisies, and there were still a few roses lingering. The Virginia creeper was fiery red on the walls of the house, the pyracantha was studded with scarlet berries and each tree seemed to have selected a different shade of yellow, orange or gold to outdo its neighbour.

'Oh, Magnus,' she whispered. 'It's heaven.'

'It's a chilly heaven,' he laughed. 'And Joan and Antoine will be champing at the bit to see you.'

Magnus had never found it easy to talk about his feelings. Ruth had teased him about this many times, often jokingly claiming he didn't have any. While Mel had been in hospital Magnus had talked her through all the recent events, but he had found it impossible to describe the emotional switchback he'd found himself on in the past few weeks.

Helena's arrival had been the start of it. Dining with her, helping her settle into her cottage, visiting her film set to watch her work and above all sharing the anticipation of finding Mel had drawn them closer. He couldn't begin to explain the excitement they had both felt as they opened the package of letters from the *News of the World*. There were dozens, nearly all from stage-struck teenagers. Sadder still were the ones from ex-dancers, women Helena had never met, claiming they had been in shows with her. But the excitement turned to acute disappointment when they realised there was nothing from Mel.

As the days passed after the article and they realised Mel had either not read the paper, or worse still didn't want to get in touch, the sorrow grew even deeper. Helena was all for hiring a private detective and bombarding the newspapers

with messages in the personal columns. Her determination kept Magnus's spirits up, but meanwhile
he was developing an intense dislike for Edward,
which at times bordered on hatred.

With hindsight he could see he had picked up on
the man's true character, but at the time he had
seen himself merely falling prey to jealousy. He
hadn't liked the bumptious way Edward arrived at
Helena's cottage, assuming not only that he could
take up residence there for the duration of the
filming, but making it quite clear Magnus wouldn't
be a welcome visitor. The man's good looks,
impeccable clothes and starchy manner all irritated,
but it was his possessiveness towards Helena that
most riled Magnus.

It was around one in the afternoon, some hours
after Mel had been found by the farmer, that the
police called at Oaklands to question Magnus. To
have the news thrust at him that Mel was injured,
lying in hospital in Bath was bad enough, but when
he was told Edward was responsible he felt
murderous. Then to be told the next day that Mel
had refused all visitors plunged him into despair.

Now he thanked God for Conrad's intervention.
He obviously cared deeply for Mel, and he had true
guts to insist on that meeting.

After the roller-coaster ride of sorrow, anger,
hatred and suspicion, came joy. Few things had
moved Magnus as much as the moment when he
walked into the hospital room, and saw Mel.
Bruised and battered as she was, she opened up
her arms to him in welcome. He knew then without
any doubt, that daughter or not, she was part of his
family.

But as Conrad had said, she was trembling on
the edge of a breakdown, however hard she tried to
pretend otherwise. He just hoped that whatever

Helena and Miles had to say to her wasn't going to nudge her closer to that edge.

'Welcome home, Mel!' Joan Downes's voice rang out even before Mel hobbled into the hall on Magnus's arm. The housekeeper rushed forward, her plump face alight with pleasure, eyes bright behind her thick glasses. 'You don't know how much we've all missed you. My goodness I'm glad to see you back.'

Mel was enveloped in a warm, enthusiastic hug, then Antoine stepped forward, his long thin face as lugubrious as ever, but his dark eyes dancing.

'*Ma chérie,*' he said, kissing her on both cheeks, then holding her two elbows studied her face. 'As beautiful as ever.'

Mel giggled. He had always been one for extravagant compliments, even when flattery was inappropriate. 'You old charmer,' she said. 'I look a fright and you know it. Have you got any old sacks down in the kitchen I can wear over my head till I look more presentable?'

Although the swelling had gone down on her eye and cheek, it was still yellow and purple, crisscrossed with small vivid scars. But while her face looked awful it didn't hurt any longer. Her foot was the only part of her which did: even hobbling along on her heel was painful, and she'd been warned to keep off it.

'I've got a tray of tea ready in Magnus's office,' Joan said. 'We wanted to have it down in the kitchen, but we didn't think you could manage the stairs. We're so pleased to have you back, Mel, it hasn't been the same place without you.'

An hour or so later Magnus collected Mel from his office to help her up the stairs to her old room. It was dusk now. Although it had been good to catch up on all the news, and hear stories about guests and the other staff, Mel was drained and anxious. She had felt almost crushed by the pressure of their unasked questions. As old friends they were entitled to more of an explanation than they'd been given, but she couldn't bring herself to tell them anything. She didn't know if she'd ever be able to.

'That was a bit too much for you, wasn't it?' Magnus said as he opened her old bedroom door. 'I thought it might be, but Joan and Antoine are hard to put off. In a day or so we'll talk together and decide if we can tell them the whole truth. Their loyalty and affection for you is without question. I think, too, you might find it easier once the air has been cleared.'

She couldn't reply for a moment. The sight of her old room brought a lump to her throat. The curtains were drawn, the bedside light left on welcomingly and someone, perhaps the new girl she'd heard about called Julie, had unpacked the clothes Conrad had brought down from Fulham, and laid her nightdress and dressing gown on the bed.

'Just as you left it?' Magnus raised one bushy white eyebrow.

'Even better,' she sighed happily and sat on the bed. She noted the vase of flowers on the small table by the window, a teddy bear sitting on the chair and a bowl of fruit by her bed. She knew that someone called Jayne Sullivan had been using this room in her absence, but she'd left now and Mel's books were back on the shelf as if they'd never been taken away. She knew somehow that all the other things she'd left behind would be in the drawers and wardrobe. 'I dreamed of this room all the time I was gone, especially when I was living in a horrible bedsitter before going to work for Con.'

But she hadn't remembered quite how the lamp

cast a rosy glow on the sloping ceiling, the softness of the carpet or the delicacy of the pink and white decor. She felt now almost as she had the first time she saw it.

'The teddy bear is from Nick,' Magnus said, picking it up and putting it in her arms. 'He thought it would keep an eye on you for him.'

She held the bear to her cheek in delight. His fur was the same golden colour as Nick's hair and he wore a red spotted bow tie. No one, apart from her mother had ever bought her a soft toy and it had a special kind of poignancy. 'I can't wait to see him,' she said. 'But I'm a bit scared.'

'You'll find he's changed.' Magnus sat down on the chair by the window, looking tired and very thoughtful. 'He said recently that looking into your past helped him come to terms with his own. I don't fully understand what he meant by that, but I've a feeling you will.'

Mel nodded.

'He's become more mature,' Magnus went on. 'Gentler, more sympathetic. His mother used to describe him as a bullock. Looking back she was absolutely right – he was stubborn, hot-headed and very arrogant.'

'You must both have been very shocked by the things he found out about me,' she said in a small voice.

'Not shocked as in disgusted, if that's what you're thinking.' He smiled in reassurance. 'It was more enlightening. For someone to go through what you have and end up so capable and kind-hearted, without any kind of chip on your shoulder shows great strength of character. Anyway both of us have our share of skeletons in cupboards too.'

Mel gave a tight little laugh. 'I can't spare any kind thoughts for Edward,' she said. 'And to be honest I still don't trust Helena even after all you've told me about her. If she's so wise and caring, why did she cart a weirdo like Edward around with her for so many years?'

'There's a time in everyone's life when they need someone to lean on,' Magnus said, moving to sit beside her on the bed. He wanted to voice his own feelings about Edward, but not now. 'But I'm sure Helena intends to tell you all about that herself.'

'I still don't see how he had that letter in his house from her if she had nothing to do with all this,' Mel said stubbornly.

'It was a very old note,' Magnus said. 'Helena said she gave up using the bright blue paper and signing herself "H" years ago – it was a phase she went through at the time she stopped calling herself Ellie. According to the police, Edward had a whole stack of memorabilia stored away in that house. Like a magpie, he'd kept everything she ever gave him. Helena had been to that house only once in her life and that was donkey's years ago when his grandmother was still alive. She thought he'd sold it several years back. I can't help wondering what reason lay behind that smoke screen. Any normal person, knowing that Helena was coming to work in the area and intending to rent a place would have offered it to her. In fact when he came down to Bath with the letters from the newspaper, he stayed at Helena's cottage, yet his own house was only a few miles away.'

'The whole set up stinks to me,' Mel said. 'And he's in love with her!'

Magnus smiled at her stubborn refusal to consider that Helena too was a victim. He wished he could admit to Mel how much he cared for Helena. It was the first time since Ruth died that he'd felt desire for any woman, and he had begun to hope that their futures lay together. But until Helena had spoken to Mel and life got back onto an even keel again, he had to keep that to himself.

'I'd describe Edward's feelings for her more as psychotic obsession than love,' he said gently. 'But you of all people should be able to understand how someone can be trapped by old friendships, and how they look away rather than face that something is very wrong?'

Both Dougie and Bee flashed into Mel's mind. She did know exactly how people became trapped in relationships.

'I still find everything about her weird,' she shrugged. 'You said yourself she is overly emotional. Edward had a stack of photos of me that she'd been hoarding. I think she sounds completely neurotic.'

'And I think you'll find that statement funny once you've met her,' he retorted. 'Now when can I arrange for her to come? I don't think my curiosity or my nerves can hold out much longer.'

On top of his concern for Mel, Nick and Helena, and his anxiety that Edward was still at large, Magnus was worried about his own health. He knew he was a prime candidate for another stroke: his blood pressure was too high, he wasn't sleeping. It was imperative that he found some way to relax, but he couldn't while so much was still unsettled.

'I don't want to talk about Helena.' Mel tossed her head. 'Tell me more about Nick and this film – he didn't say much about it in his letter.'

Magnus laughed heartily. 'You always were one for avoiding confrontation by changing the subject.'

'Nick's more interesting than Helena,' she said stubbornly.

'He's what they call a hot property now,' Magnus said proudly. '*Delinquents*, an appropriate name if I ever heard one, is going to have its TV premiere on Friday week. So everyone wants to interview him.'

'It's that good is it?' she asked, a flash of her old vitality coming back into her face.

'If it's half as good as everyone is saying, Nick will never have to do another dog food advert again,' Magnus said.

He saw a troubled look flit across Mel's face and guessed what she was thinking.

'It won't make any difference to Nick or me what muck gets raked up when Edward is caught and tried,' he assured her. 'Our only concern is for you – because we both love you, Mel. But now it's time I went downstairs and began cracking the whip. Why don't you relax and watch some television and I'll bring some supper up later for you?'

'Okay,' she agreed. She was tired and she couldn't face any more questions downstairs. 'Can you ask Helena to come tomorrow?'

Magnus pulled a surprised face, his eyes glinting mischievously. 'You really are contradictory. A few minutes ago you didn't even want to talk about her. Now you want to see her!'

She blushed. 'A girl can change her mind, can't she?'

'As often as she likes,' he said, getting up from the bed. 'But don't go prancing around on that foot. If you want anything press that bell and someone will come running.'

When Magnus had gone downstairs Mel looked at the bell push. She knew exactly why he'd installed it, and it wasn't for her to ring and ask for tea.

'As if Edward could get in here!' she said aloud, but the comfort and security of the room didn't entirely banish her nervousness. Everyone had avoided mentioning the fact that Edward was still at large to her. They seemed to have forgotten she was just as likely to read the papers as anyone else.

Conrad had been a little jumpy the day before. He said he was only thinking about the restaurant and wondering if the woman he'd hired from an agency to do the cooking would be any good, but she knew he was lying. He was nervous about her safety.

The police had scoffed at her suggestion that Edward might come here: his car had been found abandoned near Newhaven and they were certain he'd left England as a foot passenger on the ferry to France. But she felt she knew better. Edward had nothing more to lose now he'd lost the affection of the woman he loved. Nor would there be much difference in his mind between being sentenced to prison for one, two, or half a dozen murders. And a man as obsessive as he was would almost certainly want to strike back at the person he held respons-ible for his plight: Camellia Norton.

The next morning Mel sat at her dressing table brushing her hair, despondently. She had vaguely imagined that when she woke up today her scars and bruising would have faded more, yet they looked even worse. Putting a little foundation over them didn't help one bit, nor did arranging her hair so it swung forward on her face. She looked and felt ugly.

She had been in bed by nine o'clock last night, but even though she was tired and her old bed felt so much more comfortable than the hospital one, she hadn't been able to sleep. She could hear an owl hooting, the wind in the trees, even snoring coming from one of the guest's rooms along the landing. Nevertheless her room seemed very dark and still after the lights and continual noise of the hospital.

The thought of Nick kept her awake for a long time. She'd believed herself to be in love with him for so long, but now the barriers had been removed, she felt apprehensive. What if the feelings they thought they had for one another were just fantasy? And how could they step tentatively into a romance with everyone around them watching like hawks?

Sleep came eventually, but with it nightmares. This time instead of seeing Edward's face, it was Nick chasing and cornering her. Drenched in sweat she woke with a start, relieved to find it was morning. Then Magnus came in with a cup of tea and told her that Helena would arrive at ten, and suddenly she was terrified all over again.

It took some time to select the right clothes. Jeans were too casual, a pretty Laura Ashley dress with a frill round the hem was too milkmaidish, a suit much too formal. Finally she plumped for black flared trousers which would hide her scarred legs and a black wool tunic top with just a string of red beads round her neck to make it look less severe. She left her long hair loose as it seemed to be the only part of her undamaged, and added a pair of dangly red earrings to detract the eye from her face.

A tap on her door at exactly ten made her jump. She hadn't heard a car on the gravel outside or any voices coming up the stairs.

'Come in.' She sat back on her bed; there was no time now to check her face again.

The door opened but Helena faltered in the doorway.

Mel could only stare, her mouth dropping open. Even after Conrad's and Magnus's descriptions, the reality of Helena's beauty was awesome.

Black hair in soft waves framed an ageless face,

her skin the colour of clear honey. Her eyes were huge and dark, her wide soft mouth trembling as if she were a young girl on her way to punishment.

It was her timidity which surprised Mel most. The perfectly manicured long nails, the understated elegance of the plain navy dress and matching shoes were predictable. But she had expected a boldness and confidence which were completely missing from Helena as she hovered at the door.

'How are you, Camellia?' Her voice was a soft contralto, almost a caress.

'Not so bad,' Mel said glibly. 'I look worse than I feel. Come in and sit down.'

Helena shut the door and moved inside, but then just stood there, looking round her. 'When Magnus showed me this room I could imagine you here,' she said. 'It's a bit like seeing a painting back in the frame.'

She took the small buttoned-back chair by the window. 'I don't know where to start, Mel,' she said, attempting a smile.

'Well, Magnus said you were going to tell me what the secret was that made Edward try and bump me off. Start with that,' Mel said impatiently. If Helena thought she was going to treat her like a star, she was mistaken.

'I want to, but I can't just launch into it,' she said, her voice shaking. 'You see when the police contacted me and told me what Edward had done, I felt destroyed, absolutely devastated.'

'You don't need to go over all that.' Mel forced herself to smile. She was beginning to find Helena's nervousness infectious. She ran her finger over the bell and pushed on the side of her bed experiment- ally. 'Everything there is to say has already been said. I don't hold you responsible.'

'But I am accountable,' she said, leaning forward in her chair as if to stress the point. 'I inadvertently

643

provided the fuel for his rage. He's been like a brother to me for half my life, and I knew how jealous he can be. I should have known better than to trust him to pick up those letters from the newspaper.'

'But I wasn't close to you,' Mel said evenly. 'Unless you suspected he'd killed Bonny, why should you think he'd want to harm me?'

Helena was silent for some time, her eyes distant and troubled.

'When Magnus told me about Bonny drowning and the possibility that it wasn't an accident, I never for one moment thought Edward might be responsible. But with hindsight, now other facts have come to light, I feel I ought to have.' She paused and took a deep breath.

'Did Edward tell how he, Bonny and I all met up back in 1945?'

Mel nodded. 'He was very dismissive of my mother,' she said crisply. 'In fact he described her as poisonous.'

'He didn't think that of her in the beginning,' Helena said firmly. 'But let me explain how it was back then when we began rehearsing. It was the mood of the country, the hardships we'd all endured during the war, the hope for the future which set the tone of what was to come.

'Just picture me, Mel! I was eighteen, I'd lost my mother in an air raid, and cleaned offices and waited at tables since before I was fourteen. I had absolutely nothing, not even a decent dress, then suddenly I go from singing a few songs in a seedy nightclub to getting my big chance on a West End stage. Bonny was just sixteen then – she'd been touring in a dance troupe for the past year. Edward had done a few bit parts in plays and revues, and he and I became friends immediately. He was very gentlemanly, very calming and we had a great deal in common. I didn't actually get to know Bonny until quite a bit later – the day we heard Hitler was dead and victory was imminent.

'Bonny and I spent VE day together. We wore silly sailor caps, waved streamers, blew hooters and kissed servicemen, just like everyone else that day. That night we ended up at a party thrown by some American airmen. The events of that night and the things which followed in the next few weeks forged an indestructible bond between us. We were hungry for everything then – for nice clothes, for glamour, success, money and fame. And at that time we thought it was all just around the corner, ours for the taking.'

'And Edward, where did he come into this?'

'He thought he and I were going to become permanent stage partners,' she said with a faint smile. 'We were good in the comic sketch we did together – it always brought the house down. But fate conspired against all three of us. It's a long story which I'll tell you one day, but the end of it was that the three of us had to leave the show and find other work.

'We landed up touring provincial theatres and seaside towns, and doing pantomimes. Bonny and I devised a singing and dancing double act, and Edward played the piano. It was only then that a certain friction between Edward and Bonny became apparent.

'They were always sniping at one another. Edward thought Bonny was a bad influence on me, and she resented not having my exclusive friendship. I loved them both, for entirely different reasons, and as they rubbed each other up the wrong way, eventually I learned to keep the pair of them in separate compartments of my life.'

'But you were mainly with Bonny?'

'Oh yes. We were a real force together. She was a

brilliant dancer, while I was only passable, but I could sing and together we were red hot. But what I want you to understand isn't our stage act, but the strength of our friendship. We were chums, sisters and at times mother and daughter. Few people are blessed with that kind of closeness. Whatever happened later, I'll always treasure those memories.'

Mel thought of Bee and herself. She knew just what Helena meant. 'I wish Mum had told me about you,' she said. 'Why didn't she?'

'I'll come to that later,' Helena said. 'It's tough enough trying to explain why and where, without all the filling-in bits. Anyway, I continued to keep in touch with Bonny even after I went off to America, but later when Edward joined me I suppose I allowed him to think she'd dropped out of my life.'

'But she did anyway. So why should he kill her?'

Helena hesitated. 'There are some things I still don't know the answer to,' she said eventually. 'You see the last time I came back here was when you were four. Bonny and I had a bitter fight, and quite honestly after that there was nothing left for me in England. But Edward came back every six months or so. My business associates back in Hollywood, prompted by the police inquiries here, have been checking through old diaries and papers to see whether one of his visits coincided with Bonny's death. So far they haven't turned anything up, but they did find an address in Rye – the one you were living at when she died. That leads me to suppose that Edward intercepted a letter from Bonny to me and took matters into his own hands.'

'Do you think it was a blackmail letter?'

Helena shrugged. 'It could have been, or it might just have been a plea for help – but my guess is that she merely spoke of our secret.'

'What is this secret?' Mel could contain herself no longer. 'For God's sake tell me who my father is and be done with it.'

Helena shook visibly, and her eyes welled up with tears. 'He's not one of the men you've contacted. His name is Raymond Kennedy. He was the producer at the Little Theatre in Hampstead.'

Mel was so staggered at hearing a name unknown to her that she barely noticed Helena get up and move over to the window.

'A producer,' she said thoughtfully. 'The plot thickens. Did he promise to get her to Hollywood too? Or was that what your row was about? He pushed you and not Bonny?'

When there was no reply Mel looked round. Helena was leaning her face against the window and her shoulders were heaving.

'I'm sorry,' Mel said awkwardly. 'That was a bit callous wasn't it. But you see I'm so tired of half-truths and intrigue.'

Helena turned round to face her, tears streaming down her face.

'Why cry?' Mel looked at the older woman in bewilderment. 'I'm nothing to you, just a girl with a fixation about her roots. There's no need to get emotional about it.'

'I can't be anything but emotional about you,' Helena replied, dropping down to her knees by Mel. 'You see, I'm your *mother*.'

There was absolute silence for a moment. Even the birds twittering outside in the garden seemed to hush.

Mel sat like a statue, too stunned to speak. Helena's tears were making her mascara run and her wide mouth was slack and quivering.

'You're mad,' Mel gasped. She felt she was in the middle of a weird Greek tragedy. 'How can you be my mother?'

'I am,' Helena insisted. 'I planned to tell you so very gently, but I guess seeing you again after all these long years made me too hasty and blunt.'

'Don't you think I've been through enough?' Mel leapt to her feet, forgetting her injured foot in the moment. A sharp pain caught her and made her scream out in agony.

'You mustn't walk on it,' Helena exclaimed, catching hold of her and pushing her back onto the bed.

Mel recoiled from her touch.

'Get out you bitch. You're as crazy as Edward.'

'I will go when I've made you understand.' Helena knelt down by Mel who continued to stare at the older woman in horror. 'Look at me, Mel, really look. My eyes are a different shape, but they are the same colour as yours. Our faces are both oval, the same cheek bones and skin-colouring. But it's our lips that give the game away. I can't understand why no one else has seen it.'

Mel wriggled further up the bed away from Helena, but shocked and scared as she was, she didn't ring the panic button. There was no madness in Helena's dark eyes, only pain. She looked hard at her lips and saw for herself the irrefutable truth. So many men had remarked on the sensuality of her protruding lower lip. Now, as she looked at Helena's, she saw what they all meant.

'You were my baby, but I never told a soul!' Helena whispered. 'I've carried the ache inside me all these years. Success and money couldn't banish it,' Helena's voice crackled. 'I made a pact with Bonny. For my silence, she would love and protect you. But if I had known that John died, and that Bonny ceased to be a loving mother, I would have been back a long time ago to reclaim you, no matter what happened to my career.'

'I can't believe it.' Mel began to cry.

648

'Then look at these!' Helena ordered, snatching up her handbag from the floor and pulling out some photographs. She glanced at them briefly, then thrust two of them into Mel's hands.

Mel swallowed hard as she looked at them. One was of her when she was about four sitting in her father's big armchair, a plump, serious-faced little girl with long straight dark hair, in a smocked dress, white socks and patent leather bar shoes.

The second picture was much older, creased and faded, but it looked like the same child. It was taken in an old-fashioned studio and the little girl stood before a fake flower-covered archway. She turned it over and saw a faded name and address on the back, it was 'Abraham's, Mile End Road, East London', dated December 1932.

'This is you?' Mel asked, even though she could see for herself it was Helena.

'Yes. I thought all pictures of me as a child were lost during the war,' Helena said. 'But fame has one advantage and that is that people send you things. Apparently my mother paid to have this picture taken by making the photographer two shirts. He sent me a copy when I made my first film. He knew my mother was killed in an air raid and I suppose he guessed all records of my childhood were gone.'

She took out another picture and handed it to Mel. This time Helena was around nine or ten, much fatter and plainer than in the earlier picture, with a small slender woman with wavy hair and a sweet pretty face. 'He sent me this one too. That's my mother, Mel, Polly Forester. You see how fat I am? I've heard you were plump at that age too.'

Mel felt as if the years had been stripped away. Helena looked exactly as she had at the same age, a roll of fat around her middle, chunky legs and the high cheek bones concealed beneath surplus flesh.

'Bonny adopted me?'

'No. There was nothing legal about what we did. I dare say it's actually criminal. It was certainly a crime in the moral sense. But in our foolish and reckless way we believed we were helping one another.'

'I don't understand.'

'I'll have to backtrack again. Bear with me, honey, if it seems part of this is irrelevant, because I have to let you see the full picture. It starts with Bonny falling in love with Magnus in 1946. If it hadn't been for that we might have ended up in Hollywood together, but when she met him her ambition flew out of the window. All she wanted was marriage, a home and children.'

'So she really did love him?'

'Oh yes. Bonny played with many men, as I'm sure you know, but she truly loved Magnus. But he was married and I know you've heard his side of all that already.'

Mel nodded.

'Then you know too how she came to get involved with John Norton?'

Again Mel nodded. 'Did she love him too?' She hated to think that the kind loving man she remembered had been used.

Helena must have picked up her feelings because she took Mel's hand in hers and squeezed it. 'I can't say truthfully that she loved him at the outset, and she did trick him into marrying her. But I promise you as God is my judge, on the day they took their vows in church, Bonny had fallen deeply in love with him. But I'm getting ahead of myself because I haven't yet told you why this marriage took place, and what was happening to me.'

Helena paused for a moment to go and get herself a drink of water from the bathroom. She came back again and sat down on the bed beside Mel.

'When Magnus parted from Bonny she took it very hard and went home to her parents in Dagenham for a while. I joined a pantomime in Hampstead, which is where I met Raymond Kennedy, your father. Ray and I had an affair, for a few months, a light-hearted jolly one, which as it turned out, should have ended finally when I went back to touring provincial towns with Bonny. Anyway, the upshot of it was that Bonny had been seeing John occasionally during these months we had apart, and she'd decided that come hell or high water, she was going to marry him. Towards the end of our tour together we had a long weekend in London. Bonny went off to meet John. I went to Hampstead to see Ray again. That weekend was a turning point for both of us. Bonny became engaged to John and I got a lead part in the stage version of *Oklahoma*. A few weeks later I discovered that I was pregnant.'

'Was Bonny pregnant too?' Mel felt so confused.

'No she wasn't, but perhaps because of my predicament, and the fact we couldn't perform together again, she told John she was. To this day I don't really understand why she made up such a stupid lie. She said it was because John wanted to wait a couple of years before marrying her and Bonny could never wait patiently for anything. So there we were. I'm really pregnant and desperate not to be. Bonny wishing she was. John wouldn't go ahead with wedding plans without proof of her pregnancy. Somehow Bonny talked me into posing as her for a test in Harley Street. She said she'd pretend to have a miscarriage right after her wedding.'

Mel stared open-mouthed. It was too bizarre. Yet she remembered only too well how adept Bonny was at getting what she wanted, at any cost.

'The wedding went ahead and I was their

bridesmaid,' Helena added. 'They moved to John's house, The Chestnuts in Somerset.'

'But what about you?' Mel asked. 'I mean what were you doing meanwhile?'

Helena sighed deeply. 'I was in *Oklahoma*. I tried to have an abortion, but I couldn't go through with it. I carried on with the show, wearing a tight corset, hoping for a miracle.'

'But what about Ray?'

'I didn't want to tell him, for various long-winded reasons which I can tell you another time. In the meantime Bonny was my lifeline. She was the only person I could share my predicament with. In those days to be having a baby outside marriage was still considered terrible and shameful. I wrote to her every few days, and she wrote back long sympathetic letters always saying she would help me when the time came. I decided I would stay in the show until October, then I planned to move to somewhere nearer her, like Bristol, get a cheap room and then get help with having you adopted.'

'But Bonny took me?'

'Well, it wasn't quite as straightforward as that, honey. You see when I got down to Bonny's house in October, John was away in America and she admitted he still believed she was pregnant. She had always been hare-brained, but this time she'd dug a deep grave for herself. I tried to persuade her to sit down and write and tell him the truth, but there was a good reason why she felt she couldn't do that.'

'Why?' Mel asked.

Helena sighed. 'I didn't intend to tell you this just now, but I guess I'll have to. You see Bonny had a backstreet abortion back in 1945. She got a bad infection afterwards, and she'd had problems ever since. After she married John she went to see a specialist. He told her she couldn't ever have children.'

Mel nodded, she could imagine how devastated any woman would be to hear such a thing and also why Bonny would be reluctant to admit it to John.

'And then she came up with this plan,' Helena went on. 'At first I was appalled, but slowly she got me round to her way of thinking. She needed a baby to present John with on his return. I needed a home for mine. I had no money or family. She had everything. A loving husband, a beautiful home and security. We were to swop identities, I would pass myself off as Mrs Norton at the nursing home, then give the baby to her. No one would ever know that Bonny hadn't given birth, not even John.'

Mel was flabbergasted. 'You agreed to that?'

Helena nodded, her eyes filling with tears again. 'The alternatives were much worse,' she whispered. 'Either we'd be in a dingy cheap room somewhere, struggling to make ends meet, or I'd have to get you fostered while I went out to work. I knew first-hand just how difficult things were for a single mother. I was brought up that way myself. Polly was the best mother anyone could have, she'd given up her stage career willingly and happily for me, but we had some very hard times. Then there were terrible rumous that babies put up for adoption were being left in overcrowded orphanages or even being shipped off to Australia. At least I knew Bonny and John would love and take care of you.'

Mel could understand that back in 1949 life would have been awful for a lone mother and child. 'But I don't see how you got away with it? Surely someone must have suspected?'

'It was a great deal easier than anyone would believe. You see no one asks you to prove your identity when you have a baby. In those first years after the war with the health service being set up there were few proper records. The house in Somerset was miles from anywhere. No one around there knew Bonny and for the last three months we just swopped roles when necessary. We made padding for Bonny to wear under a maternity dress. I bleached my hair blonde and posed as her to visit the doctors for check-ups. She bought a black wig for times when she was pretending to be the visiting friend and for accompanying me to the nursing home when I was in labour.'

Mel gasped. The reference to hair dye made sense at last. How many times she'd read and reread that line wondering what significance it had. 'But how could you plan such a massive fraud. Didn't you feel guilty about it?'

'Not then.' Helena looked up, pain etched across her lovely face. 'All that anguish was to come later. We were like little girls playing house, both excited that we'd found a solution. The last three months of my pregnancy were so happy – we shared everything, trimming your crib, making your clothes and doing up your little nursery. Bonny became your mother mentally long before you were born.'

Mel was torn with conflicting emotions. Half of her knew this story was true, and was trying to accept it. The other half was clinging to sweet, tender moments in her childhood, unable to believe Bonny wasn't her natural mother.

'Whatever else I have to reproach myself with, at least I didn't hand my baby over to a cold stranger,' Helena said in a croaky voice. 'Bonny was with me throughout my labour; she took you into her arms just seconds after you were born. She loved you from that first moment. When we took you home to The Chestnuts, she took over looking after you entirely. It was as if she was the rightful mother.'

'And John? Did he know?'

'He didn't come back from America until early

January and he was so thrilled to see his daughter, he never questioned anything. No man I've ever known was such a natural father as John. He delighted in everything about you.'

Mel knew this was true. She could remember him bathing her, washing her hair, always attentive, never too tired to bother with her. 'But didn't you have qualms about it?'

Helena broke down then, put her hands over her face and sobbed. Mel felt she ought to take her in her arms and comfort her, but she couldn't.

'So many,' Helena sobbed. 'But John and Bonny could give you everything I couldn't. There were times when I wanted to pick you up and run away with you, but by then I was in too deep. You were registered as John and Bonny's child, and Bonny's parents, and all John's friends and relatives were standing by waiting to be invited down to see you. Cards and presents came with every post. I had nowhere to take you.'

Mel fell silent thinking about it all. The one thing she didn't need to question was the bond between Bonny and Helena; it was remarkably like the one between Bee and herself. If she and Bee were to be taken back twenty years earlier and put in the same circumstances as Bonny and Helena, she felt they might very well have chosen the same path.

'But if you'd come through all that together, why did you fall out?' she asked at last.

Helena dabbed her face with a lace-edged handkerchief. 'We'd made a deal. I was to be Auntie Ellie, friend of the family, and in return for my silence, Bonny would write each month and send me pictures and full progress reports about you. I told Bonny then that I was afraid jealousy would creep in at sometime. I was right, it did.'

'Conrad told me about how you became a big

star after your first film *Soho*. I suppose Bonny didn't like that?'

Helena's eyes opened wide in horror. 'Oh no, it wasn't that. No one was prouder of my success than Bonny. She collected every review of mine, sat through my films umpteen times. She was so happy I'd made it. No, it was me who was jealous.'

Mel had been expecting Helena to blame Bonny for everything. When she so frankly admitted she held herself responsible, and remained unflaggingly loyal to her old friend, it put her character into a whole new perspective. She hadn't tried to whitewash anything. Mel suddenly knew that she could trust her.

'You know how life was for you in your first four years,' Helena said by way of explanation. 'Even though you were too young to actually remember it, you hold all that love John and Bonny showered on you inside you. You were the pivot their lives turned on. I was in America for much of that time, but even when I came back to England I had to limit myself to just a couple of days with them, because it was too painful for me seeing their delight in you. I sent presents, wrote and telephoned frequently, but I always had to remind myself that you were their baby, not mine.'

'So what happened?'

'I came to visit you in June 1954, when you were four and a half. I should've made it a flying visit like the previous times, but John was away on business. I'd always been nervous about giving myself away when he was there, and I weakened when I saw you, Mel. It was as if I was seeing myself again as a child. You were a plump, serious little girl with big soft eyes and a knack of slipping your hand into mine which made me feel as if someone was turning a knife in my heart. I had a splendid home in Hollywood, a big car, money, expensive clothes and millions of adoring fans. But for two days as we romped together on the beach, went to the fair in Hastings, ate cotton candy and ice creams, I knew I would gladly trade everything for you. Bonny hinted that I should go back to London on the second night, but I ignored her. I thought only of myself, and I was greedy for more time with you.'

She heard Bonny sigh and glanced round. Bonny had picked up a magazine, but she didn't seem to be reading it. Yesterday on the beach, Bonny had been just like she was at eighteen or nineteen, all dizziness, golden limbs and flying hair. She'd chattered about friends and neighbours, giggled at nothing in particular, and when Camellia wasn't in earshot she'd made saucy comments about the bodies of the men on the beach, just as she had in the old days. But today her manner was changed, more guarded. Helena knew she should ask her what was the matter, but she didn't. She didn't want to hear it.

Camellia put the last jigsaw piece in. 'That's it,' she crowed, clapping her hands together. 'Come and look, Mummy. It's all finished.'

'I'm busy,' Bonny said in a sullen voice. 'I'll look at it in a minute.'

Camellia didn't appear to notice anything odd about her mother's tone. She got down from the table, skipped across the room to the window overlooking the street and stood up on a stool to look out.

'Come and look, Auntie,' she called out. 'There's a waterfall.'

Helena joined the child at the window. The overloaded drains could no longer carry away the heavy rain and it was cascading down over the cobbles in a fast-flowing river, lapping against the steps up to the old houses.

She missed so many English things. Quaint old streets like this one, fish and chips wrapped in newspaper, the jollity of the pubs and summer rain. Rain never seemed so fresh, soft or clean anywhere else in the world compared with England and it had a smell all of its own.

'My goodness!' she laughed. 'It's a good job there are steps up to the house, otherwise we'd be paddling in here.'

'If we had a little boat we could sail it down the street,' Camellia said wistfully, pressing her little nose up against one of the small leaded panes.

Helena looked sideways at the child and felt that old familiar pang of longing. The last two days had shown her how very empty her life was.

Helena looked down at her green silk dress and matching shoes. 'If we put on coats and wellies we could race paper boats,' she suggested.

Camellia looked up at her, dark eyes suddenly alight with excitement. 'You mean out there, now?'

'Yes, why not,' Helena laughed. 'Let me undo your frock and you go and put something old on. You don't mind, Bonny, do you?'

Bonny looked up from her magazine. 'If you're daft enough to sail boats in the gutter that's your funeral,' she snapped.

Helena might have changed her mind if Camellia hadn't already shot off out the door to change. But it wasn't fair to spoil a child's fun just because an adult wanted to be disagreeable.

It was the best fun that Helena had had in years. Dressed in an old mac and boots of John's, with Camellia in a yellow sou'wester, coat and boots, they made their way up past the Mermaid Inn to the top of the street, then dropped the paper boats Helena had made in the water.

The boats weaved, dipped and turned and, as one overtook the other, Camellia ran after them screaming with laughter.

'My one's winning. No, your one is now,' she called out and Helena ran after her, cheering and shouting just as loudly.

Helena was aware of net curtains moving as the older residents checked to see who was making all the noise, but she didn't care. The first two boats sank after becoming water-logged, but they hastily made more.

They forgot about the time, or how wet they were, and it wasn't until the rain turned to drizzle and the cascade of water turned to a mere trickle that they went back indoors.

Helena took off her coat and boots in the small hall and then turned to Camellia. She had fallen over a couple of times and she was wet right up to her waist.

'Skin a bunny,' Helena said, pulling the child's dress over her head taking her vest with it. 'And off with those knickers and socks.'

It was the sight of the plump little stomach and bare bottom that made her grab Camellia, lifting her up to nibble and tickle. She didn't hear Bonny move across the room towards them in the hall above the sound of Camellia's laughter.

'What on earth are you doing?' Bonny's harsh tone made her put the child down hastily.

'Just playing,' she blushed as if caught red-handed at something shameful.

'It was super, Mummy.' Camellia was rosy cheeked and excited. 'You should have come out too.'

'I could see when I wasn't wanted.' Bonny turned on her heel and flounced back into the lounge.

'Go on up and get changed.' Helena tapped

Camellia's small naked bottom. 'Stay and play with your dollies for awhile. I want to talk to Mummy.'

As Helena went back into the lounge she saw Bonny pouring the last of a bottle of gin into her glass. 'Don't be a kill-joy, Bonny,' she said. 'I don't get to see her very often.'

Bonny looked coldly at Helena. 'Just as well. Fancy taking Camellia out in the rain. She might have caught pneumonia!'

'Don't be ridiculous.' Helena laughed nervously, but she shut the door so Camellia wouldn't hear. 'It's the middle of summer. Besides a bit of fresh air is better for her than sitting in here watching you sulk and drink.'

She regretted that remark the moment she said it. Bonny's eyes turned dark with anger.

'You think you're so bloody clever, don't you?' Bonny leapt up and knocked over her bottle and glass. 'You sweep in here with new clothes and toys for Camellia, turn her head with all that attention, then have the cheek to tell me how to behave. She's my kid, not yours. I don't want you coming here anymore.'

All at once Helena saw this wasn't a tiff which could be smoothed over and laughed about later. Bonny's whole body was bristling with resentment, she'd clearly been working up to this for some time.

'You don't really mean that do you? What about the promises we made one another and our friendship?' Helena asked quietly, fear clutching at her insides. 'Doesn't that count for anything?'

'I've kept my side of it. I've loved Camellia, cared for her. She's my whole life,' Bonny spat at her. 'But you aren't satisfied with your side of it, are you? You've got the whole world falling at your feet. Now you want Camellia too.'

'Of course I'd like Camellia too,' Helena retorted.

'Every time I see her I regret what we did. Just becoming successful doesn't make natural feelings go away. But I know you and John love her, you are her mother and father. I wouldn't jeopardise her happiness.'

'Don't get smarmy with me,' Bonny yelled and struck Helena hard across the face.

Helena put her hand up to her cheek, it stung a little but she was more stunned by the viciousness in Bonny's voice than the blow.

'I wasn't being smarmy. I was sincere and I only want what's best for Camellia.'

'Well, get out of my life once and for all. I don't need you swanning in here reminding me that Camellia isn't really mine. You make me feel worthless.'

'That's silly, Bonny,' Helena lowered her voice, afraid Camellia would come in. 'You're such a good mother. You wanted marriage and a home and you've made a real success of it. You've got dozens of friends, people admire you. I might be famous, but it's empty, Bonny. You can't know how empty.'

'Too damned bad,' Bonny snarled. 'Just because your life turned out to be empty doesn't mean you can come down here and tamper with ours. Clear off and don't ever come back.'

'Surely you can't mean that, Bonny?' Helena began to cry, frightened by the sound of finality in Bonny's voice.

'Oh yes I do. And if you do come back I'll destroy you. I'll go to the newspapers and give them so much dirt on you and your precious, perverted Edward that all those Hollywood producers will turn their backs on you too.'

'Bonny, listen to yourself.' Helena caught hold of her friend's wrists and held them. 'Anything you might say about me will only incriminate you. All I can lose is money. You might lose a husband and child. I told you jealousy would turn up one day. I'll get out of your life if that is what you want, but don't threaten me.'

'It's not jealousy,' Bonny said stubbornly. 'I just want my daughter all to myself. I want peace of mind. I can't have it when every month I have to write to you, never knowing when you'll turn up. It's bad enough looking into Camellia's face and seeing you staring back at me. I don't want you here too.'

Helena slumped down in a chair and covered her face with her hands. She wanted to tell Bonny that Camellia was her life-line, that without contact with her she was afraid she might shrivel up and die. But she guessed this had all been coming for some time. Perhaps it even proved just how much Bonny loved Camellia.

'Okay, you win,' she said eventually. 'I'll get out of your life. Not for you, but for Camellia and John's sake, because they are innocent and I don't want them hurt. I won't come back unless you write and ask me to.'

'I don't want you sending presents either,' Bonny said, putting her hands on her hips. 'We don't need you.'

Those last words hurt the most. Helena just looked at Bonny, tears streaming down her face. In four little words she'd destroyed everything they once had. All the love, sharing and laughter. Edward was right. She was poison.

'Thank God it was John you married,' she said as she turned toward the door. 'At least I know he'll make sure Camellia grows up with the right values.'

Saying goodbye to Camellia was the hardest thing she'd ever done. When Helena walked into the child's bedroom she jumped into her arms and clung like a limpet. Clearly she'd overheard at least part of what had been said.

'Mummy doesn't mean to be nasty,' she said, her dark eyes glimmering with tears. 'She gets cross with me sometimes, but she always says she's sorry.'

Helena told her that it was nothing serious, that she had to go back to London anyway.

For one brief moment as she silently hugged the child to her shoulder, she imagined herself running off down the stairs with her daughter in her arms. She could afford fancy lawyers to reclaim her child. She could gain public sympathy if she told the whole story.

But she wiped out the idea almost instantly. John didn't deserve that kind of hurt and Camellia's happiness and security would be shattered. It would be as wrong as the pact she'd made initially with Bonny.

Helena shifted in her chair, reaching out to catch Camellia's hand.

'You came hurtling down the stairs just as I was walking out with my case,' she said. ' "One more kiss", that's all you said. It felt like someone had driven a stake through my heart.'

Mel had been crying silently through much of the story as fragments of it came back to her. She could remember chasing those paper boats, the water squelching inside her Wellington boots. A golden memory that had stayed in her mind, though she had lost the image of her companion that day. But Helena had evoked other equally old memories, ones that must have taken place in the ensuing weeks. Memories of Bonny crying, sitting indoors for long periods with a drink in her hand and a mournful expression on her face. And perhaps the most poignant one, of her going through a big scrapbook of papers and photographs, tearing them out and throwing them on the fire, sobbing as she did so.

Mel understood everything now. Why Bonny had never told her about her famous friend, why drinking became a habit, and why she'd tried to get Jack and Magnus's attention that summer. This time she didn't push away Helena's hand, but silently held it in hers.

'I did write, even though I said I wouldn't, but the letters were always sent back marked "Not known at this address", in her writing,' Helena said eventually, wiping her mascara-streaked face with her hanky. 'I wanted to know about how you were, what you looked like and things so badly, but there wasn't anyone I could get information from, not without making people suspicious. I just wish now I'd gone back to England and Rye sometimes. But I thought by staying away I was doing the right thing for all of us.'

'What was Bonny going to expose about you?' Mel asked tentatively. That seemed to be the last remaining secret.

'That Sir Miles Hamilton is my father,' Helena said.

Mel's mouth fell open. 'He's not! He can't be!'

'You aren't the only one with muddled parentage.' Helena half smiled. 'Until I was eighteen, I thought my father was Tom Forester, a docker who'd been killed at work just before I was born. My Aunt Marleen told me the truth when she was ill in hospital, long after Mum was killed. Secrets seem to run in our family, don't they?'

'That's incredible. But why didn't your mother tell you?'

'Polly was a dancer too. She fell in love with a married man who also happened to be titled. When she found she was pregnant she ran off and hid to save him from scandal, and brought me up alone pretending she was a widow. But Miles wants to tell you his side of this himself. At the time when Bonny threatened to expose this, Miles had no idea that I was his daughter. I was just his protégée. He learned it pretty soon afterwards, Bonny wrote and told him.'

'So that explains his letter,' Mel gasped. 'Good God. He's my grandfather! Magnus said that Nick had seen a resemblance, he was convinced he was my father.'

'I know,' Helena smiled ruefully. 'The day I came here to see Magnus, all my chickens came home to roost. I was always so sure I'd done the right thing by keeping quiet about you and Miles, but in fact all the time I thought I was protecting you both, I was putting you in danger.'

'It's all so muddled,' Camellia sighed. 'I can't get my head round it. I still don't see exactly why Edward had to kill Bonny.'

'Until Edward's caught and he makes a confession, we won't know it all for sure,' Helena said. 'But there is one thing more I must tell you, because Edward's reasons for doing what he did almost certainly rest with it. I got myself into a terrible mess after I returned to America after seeing you and Bonny that last time. I suffered from depression right from the time I left you with Bonny and John. In those first four years I could cope with the bad days because I was hearing about you from Bonny each month and I could phone whenever I wanted reassurance. But once I lost that life-line I got really screwed up. Edward kept me going then – he was the truest friend anyone could ever have. But I guess when he discovered about your birth, he thought it was fear of being exposed which made me that way. Of course if he'd admitted he knew about it, I would have told him that my mental problems were caused by grief, not fear. The story might have had a different ending then.'

'And Bonny told Jack and Magnus they were my father just for attention?'

Helena's expression held both surprise and warmth as if she was touched by Mel's perceptiveness.

'Yes, I think so, honey. You see, I was the one she'd always turned to before when she had a problem or just needed reassurance she was loved. It's sad to think she felt compelled to turn to her old men friends, and make up something so damaging for all of them, just for a measure of comfort, especially when she had a husband who worshipped her. Bonny was Bonny – impulsive, flighty, ridiculous, and a dramatist sometimes. Yet I think I understand why she did it. I hope you do too?'

Mel could only nod. A lump was growing in her throat. Helena was everything Magnus had said – a woman with a big heart, loyal to a fault and generous too. That last statement about Bonny said so much: the kindest, truest epitaph.

'Can we be friends now?' Helena asked in a small voice. She was looking at Camellia as if her life depended on the answer.

'I'm not sure what we can be,' Mel said truthfully. 'Reason tells me I ought to be overjoyed. I've got a new mother and a grandfather and there's nothing to stand in the way of Nick and I becoming lovers either. But I just feel stunned, and a bit bruised.'

'I'm sure you do. Finding you have a new family doesn't take away the hurt of knowing why Bonny was killed – and it can never replace her.'

Mel nodded. 'I suppose that's it. I loved her. She wasn't a good mother, not after Dad died. But we had times together that were so sweet, and good.'

'So did I,' Helena said softly, and her hand reached out to caress Camellia's scarred cheek. 'I loved her too. You and I both saw the other Bonny behind all that greed and scheming. She was like a sparkler – too hot for comfort, but bright and beautiful. Both of us have suffered deeply, because we cared for her, but perhaps that common ground will help us now.'

'She wouldn't have liked to grow old and wrinkled,' Mel sighed. 'And if she'd lived she would have destroyed us all, one way or another.'

'Wherever she is now I bet she's laughing about this,' Helena smiled. 'Maybe if we can think on that we'll get over it too.'

A silence fell between them. Mel remembered that night in Fishmarket Street when she was fifteen and she'd cried because she was so fat and plain. Bonny had comforted her by saying she'd once had a friend who'd been fat too and that she turned into a beautiful woman. Now she knew Bonny hadn't hardened her heart towards her old friend. Edward must have convinced her he would reunite them.

'I want to hug you, but I can't,' Mel said bluntly. She turned her head slightly so she didn't have to see those big sad eyes.

'The world wasn't made in one day. I carried you for nine months, and held you in my heart and mind for another twenty-four years,' Helena said in a tremulous voice. She stood up and stepped away from where Camellia sat on the bed. 'We've got the rest of our lives. But there's something you need more than a new mother right now.'

'What's that?' Mel looked up. Helena was smiling again.

'A love affair,' she said, and her eyes glinted with wickedness. 'My Auntie Marleen, who was a character and a half, always advocated that remedy

667

for everything from falling hair to sore feet. Perhaps it's not what a mother should say to her daughter, but then I haven't earned the right to that title yet.'

Chapter Twenty-Six

Sir Miles sat in a high-backed chair by the fire in the ground floor drawing room, Mel on the settee a few feet from him, her bandaged foot up on a padded stool, covered by a thick sock. It had turned very cold and a high wind sent flurries of autumn leaves past the windows, so even at the risk of appearing rather casual about meeting her grandfather for the first time, Mel had chosen to wear jeans and a red sweater.

The Westminster clock on the mantelpiece had just chimed eleven o'clock and though the old man had talked almost continually since arriving at ten thirty, it was clear from his brusque manner that he found confessions difficult.

'There's no need for you to feel awkward or embarrassed Sir Miles,' Mel said gently. 'I do understand.'

She was finding it hard to digest the idea that he was her grandfather. He looked and sounded so much like Winston Churchill – the same kind of round face, fleshy jowls and lack of neck, not to mention a manner of speaking that commanded attention. But his rather flamboyant green tweed jacket and his green and gold cravat pleased her, and she felt that at heart he was a nonconformist.

'You don't have to use my title,' he said stiffly. 'Miles is perfectly acceptable to me. Helena privately calls me "Smiley", but as we haven't found a great deal to smile about yet, that doesn't seem particularly appropriate.'

Mel took heart at this, since it implied he too wished for an easier rapport with her. She felt deeply for him. He had stayed at Helena's cottage the night before and it was only then that the suspicions which had started when Nick called on him earlier in the year were finally confirmed, and his daughter told him the whole story. From the pride in his face when he spoke of Helena, Mel could tell that it had been a source of joy for him to discover he was a father late in life, but she didn't think he'd yet accepted the idea that he was also a grandfather.

Miles's age and background made it very hard for him to speak of his illicit love affair with Helena's mother. He had told the story in a crisp, unemotional way, but Mel could see some parallels to the affair between Bonny and Magnus. Miles had met Polly, a chirpy little Cockney chorus girl, when she was in a show at the Catford Hippodrome in 1925, and fallen deeply in love with her despite his marriage and social position. When she disappeared without trace some eighteen months later, he said he had been devastated but had to assume she'd met another man who was free to marry her.

When he moved on to relate the sequel to Polly's story, told to him by Helena, his voice shook. Clearly some forty odd years later he was still troubled by the knowledge that the mistress he loved had chosen to turn her back on the stage and bring up his daughter in poverty, rather than subject him to any scandal or disgrace.

'Well, let's find something to smile about,' Mel said brightly. She was feeling sparkly today. She and Nick had spoken for nearly an hour on the telephone the day before and he was coming down from London this evening. Although she'd only been at Oaklands for two days, her foot was less painful now and being able to talk over with Magnus everything Helena had told her, had put it all into perspective. She saw Miles's past as rather romantic; it didn't disturb or shock her in the way Helena's revelations had.

Now she wanted to clear up all the debris from the past and start afresh. Early this morning she'd written a long letter to Conrad about it all, though now she thought she'd better open it again and add the part about Miles. It was the kind of juicy story he loved and she knew he wouldn't pass it on to anyone else.

'Helena's new film sounds so exciting, and I'm dying to see her thatched cottage too. Magnus said it's very pretty.'

He did smile then at the sudden switch to lighter topics. Helena had been so sure last night that Camellia would never accept her as even a friend, let alone a mother.

'You are a sweet girl,' he said generously. 'Just as Magnus and Helena said you were. I hope in my clumsy way that I've managed to explain how things were for me back in those days. I would hate you to think I knowingly abandoned a woman who was carrying my child. I couldn't have married Polly, but I would have supported her and Helena. It was a great sadness to me that Mary and I never were blessed with children.'

'They aren't always a blessing,' Mel said wryly. 'But tell me about my early days. I know you were a guest at Bonny and John's wedding, and I imagine you and your wife must have come to our house before John died?'

'Many times in the first two or three years of your life. We came to the house in Somerset too,' he said and at last there was a real smile on his lips. 'It was in spring of 1950, you were just a few months old and Mary never stopped cooing over you. She insisted on us taking you out for a walk in your pram. The hills were so steep I was forced to push you myself. It was the first and last time I ever pushed a pram.'

Mel liked this image, even though she could no more imagine him behind a pram than dancing in a tutu. 'Was I a nice baby?'

'Wet and squawky as far as I remember,' he said gruffly. 'But Mary thought you were an angel. Of course, had I known you were my granddaughter then, I certainly would have taken a much closer interest. But that weekend was a very jolly one. John and Bonny were excellent hosts. I remember we had pheasant for dinner and I was astounded that someone as giddy as Bonny could cook so well. She loved her garden too. It was a mass of spring flowers, quite lovely.'

'So you liked her then?'

He gave Mel a sharp look. 'Yes, I did like her, then,' he agreed, if somewhat reluctantly. 'She was such a child – excited, happy, full of bounce and vitality. I had my reservations when John married her; she had something of a reputation you see and I thought she was after John's money. But that weekend I saw exactly why John adored her. She was delightful.'

'And your opinion changed when she wrote to you about Helena?'

'Yes, I was profoundly shocked – not only by the revelations which knocked me sideways, but by the viciousness of the letter. Of course now I know the background I realise it was written in a moment of spite, out of grief that she'd lost her dearest friend, but that is no excuse. My feelings as I read it must have been similar to yours when you discovered John Norton wasn't your real father. All those years I had imagined Polly left me for another man. Now

I hear that the young actress whose career I've been pushing is in fact my daughter.'

He paused for a moment, as if to gather himself, and wiped his perspiring brow with a handkerchief. He shot an odd sort of look at Mel, as if unsure how far he should go in his confessions. He cleared his throat and went on.

'Bonny didn't demand any money. Her motive appeared to be purely to cause maximum distress. She threatened to take the story to the newspapers.'

'Then she didn't tell you I was Helena's child?'

'No, not that. I do wish now that she had. She hinted at knowing something even more damaging, but I assumed this was that Helena had been involved in something illegal or criminal. My fears at the time were all for my wife. Mary was a very kind, caring woman, who'd supported me loyally my entire married life. It wasn't fair that someone should destroy her peace and happiness out of sheer malice.'

'You were very brave calling Bonny's bluff,' Mel said. 'What would you have done if she'd gone ahead and exposed everything publicly?'

'I don't know,' he admitted, again wiping his brow. Mel hoped she wasn't submitting him to too much stress: he was after all over eighty. 'I spent a few sleepless nights thinking on that of course. I wasn't entirely convinced it was true at that point. Polly Forester might not have been "my" Polly. Even if she was, Helena might have been another man's child. So I went over to America to see Helena.'

'Why hadn't she told you before?'

'Helena said it was because she hadn't absolutely believed the story her Aunt Marleen had told her. But in my opinion, she is just very like her mother – unable to make waves which might hurt others. We checked on everything together; we even had blood tests. But even before it was confirmed, we both knew that Marleen was right. Helena has the Hamilton colouring, the mouth and nose. You have inherited those too, along with my eyes, which come from my mother's family.

'Anyway, I felt less anxious after talking to Helena. She convinced me Bonny wouldn't make good her threats, that her intention was just to cause friction between the two of us, nothing more. As it turned out she was right, and I bitterly regret that I took Manning into my confidence about it. But at the time I thought it best that we should be prepared for a scandal, and as Manning was Helena's manager I believed he had a right to be forewarned.'

Another piece of the puzzle dropped into place for Mel. She could see now how faced with strong evidence of her maliciousness Edward's antagonism towards Bonny had accelerated into hate. It was even understandable, given that he didn't know the whole story, that he held Bonny responsible for Helena's unhappiness and depression.

'When do you think Edward discovered the truth about me?' she asked.

Sir Miles sighed deeply. 'Helena believes it was well before he killed Bonny, but I don't think that's right. In the light of what we know now, he most certainly would have found a way of disposing of you too if that had been the case. I have to admit that I inadvertently fuelled his rage by feeding him information over the years. I've been a doddering, interfering old fool.'

Mel smiled: he couldn't often have admitted such things. 'Tell me?'

'As you know it was two years before John's death that I received that dreadful letter from Bonny, and as you can well imagine I didn't pay any further social calls to Rye. But I met John alone twice for lunch in London in those two years, and I allowed him to think I was getting too old to go visiting. When John died, Mary and I were on holiday in Kenya. That was fortunate for me as it meant I had the perfect excuse not to attend his funeral and come face to face with Bonny. We did of course send flowers and a message of sympathy.

'Manning called on me in London some four or five months later. I showed him John's obituary in *The Times* and we discussed whether or not Helena should be told. We decided, bearing in mind that she had just begun a new film, that it would be in her best interests to say nothing.'

'That was very wrong of you,' Mel said.

'With hindsight, it was,' he agreed, rubbing his hand thoughtfully around his several chins. 'But believe me, Camellia, I was, like Edward, only attempting to shield Helena from any distress. We guessed she would want to go and see Bonny, and bearing in mind how acrimoniously her last visit had ended, we felt she was better off in ignorance.

'My wife died two years later. I notified Bonny because Mary had been fond of her. Mary, of course, knew nothing of my change of heart towards Bonny and had continued to send you cards and presents for birthdays and Christmas, right up till her death.

'But Bonny ignored my letter; she neither came to the funeral nor sent a letter of condolence. I felt perfectly justified then in severing all links with her. I certainly didn't want Helena to become involved with the woman again.'

Mel could remember getting many cards and presents from her parents' old friends when she was little. Then like the visitors they'd once had, they all gradually stopped coming. She wondered if Bonny managed to upset all those people, or whether she had in fact distanced herself purposely.

'I saw Manning many times in the subsequent years,' Miles went on. 'Twice or three times in London, but mainly over in Hollywood when I went to see Helena. She was in a bad way at that time and both of us were desperately worried about her. It was during one of these visits about three years ago when I asked Manning if he and Helena had heard about Bonny's death. I had only learned about it myself from the newspaper reports about you and that friend of yours who died from a drug overdose in Chelsea, and I'd taken the cuttings with me to show him.'

'You knew about that and showed him?' she exclaimed.

Miles blushed furiously and dropped his eyes to his lap. 'I'm sorry. I know now from both Nick and Magnus that you didn't deserve all the sensationalism that followed that incident. I don't wish to hurt you now by bringing it up. But the name Camellia Norton was emblazoned in the papers and of course I recognised it, as anyone would who had once dangled that child on his knee.'

'How did Edward react?' she asked. 'I mean to Bonny's death?'

'He seemed as surprised as I was when he read it,' Miles said with a grimace. 'He was pretty unpleasant about the news, but there was absolutely nothing about his manner to make me think he'd had any prior knowledge of her death. He insisted that we keep it from Helena as it would upset her.'

Mel frowned at him.

'I know, I had no right to act as a censor,' Miles said with a shrug. 'But put yourself in my shoes for a moment. My only child, one I can't even openly acknowledge is chronically depressed, a golden career on the stage all but finished. Over the years I have been led to believe that much of Helena's deep unhappiness is attributable to Bonny Norton. Would you under those circumstances give her more distressing news?'

'Maybe not. But go on. Do you think Edward guessed the truth when he saw my picture?'

'Perhaps. He kept the cuttings saying he might broach the subject with Helena when she was feeling better. Maybe when he'd had time to study the pictures more closely he saw the similarities I can see for myself now. You have to remember he knew Helena better than anyone, right from when she was eighteen. Anyway, when I returned home to England, I heard from my manservant that you'd called at my home. The next time I spoke to Manning on the telephone I reported this to him and he did seem a little rattled. Asked me all kinds of damn fool questions. But as you left no address I couldn't pass anything more on.'

Miles cleared his throat. 'As Magnus may have told you, Helena accepted the role in *Broken Bridges* without telling Edward. One has to assume he was thrown into a state of panic when he found out. Not only was it the first time in years that she'd made a major decision for herself, but the film was to be made here in England. On top of that Helena didn't tell him, or myself, that Magnus had contacted her. We both thought that Oaklands was just a country house hotel that the production secretary had selected for her.

'Edward came to see me first when he arrived in England, and telephoned Helena from my house, though I didn't hear what they talked about. Helena has said since he was a little churlish about her meeting up with Magnus, and renting a cottage without his approval, just as she expected, but he seemed pleased at the publicity she'd got from the

News of the World, and indeed offered to call at their offices to pick up any letters. One has to presume that he devised his plan for abducting you at that point.'

Mel thought Edward was probably a far better actor than anyone had ever given him credit for. 'What did you think of him? I mean before all this happened?' she asked.

'I trusted him implicitly, as anyone would who had seen him caring for Helena with such devotion,' Miles said firmly. 'But I didn't ever like him. I thought he was queer. In all senses.'

Mel half smiled at the old man's bluntness. She had a feeling he knew a great deal more about Edward Manning, but he was old fashioned and would never discuss such things. 'Let's hope they catch him soon,' she said. 'Then maybe we can put all this behind us.'

Miles put his head to one side and looked quizzically at her. 'You sounded just like your father then,' he said.

'I didn't know you knew him?'

'It was me who suggested Helena for the part of Prince Charming at the Hampstead theatre,' Miles said with a smile. 'Ray Kennedy was a clever, amusing and astute man. He was a cad to Helena, but I liked him.'

'What went wrong between them?' Mel had intended to ask Helena about this the next time she saw her, but it wouldn't hurt to have Miles's opinion too.

'Stupidity on Ray's part,' he said. 'He made the mistake of trying to run two women at the same time. He was an excellent producer, but he never really achieved his full potential. I heard he was killed in a car accident a few years ago.'

The crackle of car tyres on gravel made Mel start. It

was just before four in the afternoon and she'd come down to the kitchen about an hour ago out of boredom. Ever since Miles had left before lunch she'd been unable to settle to read, although she had written more to Conrad. As the kitchen was the hub of the house, and Joan and Antoine were only too pleased to have a further opportunity to chat, it seemed a good place to while away the time until Nick arrived.

Joan stood on tiptoe to peer out the small window on the level of the drive. 'Yes, it's him,' she said and waved a finger at Mel. 'And don't go rushing on that foot.'

She might as well have saved her breath. Mel jumped up, grabbed the pair of crutches Magnus had given her and hopped off at speed down the passage on one foot.

At the top of the stairs, a couple of guests stared at her in surprise, as she bounced along to the front door. Nick was just getting out of his MG as she stepped into the porch. She stopped short, leaning on her crutches and panting, overwhelmed by the rush of emotion fizzing up inside her.

In the year since she'd last seen him he'd changed from looking like a struggling artist to a man of means. He was wearing a tweed jacket, his blond hair was short and well styled and he was a few pounds heavier. As he slammed the car door shut, and turned, Mel knew instantly that she had neither imagined nor exaggerated the feelings between them.

She heard him gasp her name, and saw the joy in his eyes as he opened his arms and ran to her.

One moment she was standing, the next she was in the air, as he lifted her and twirled her round. Her crutches fell clattering onto the flagstone floor.

'You are supposed to keep off your feet!' he said accusingly, sliding one arm under her bottom and carrying her back into the hall. 'You haven't even had the stitches out yet.'

'I couldn't stay waiting in a chair like Queen Victoria,' she laughed. 'You don't know how long today has been.'

She had been longing for this moment ever since Conrad told her how Nick had searched for her. She had anticipated nervousness and fright, even a sense of anti-climax when she saw him. She hadn't expected suddenly to feel strangely shy.

He was even more beautiful than she remembered. Was it really possible for a man to have eyes so brilliantly blue, hair quite that shade of ripe corn? Or did love make everyone look special?

'I want to kiss you,' he whispered, glancing round and seeing two guests staring with interest at them. 'I can't really whisk you upstairs can I?'

'We could go in Magnus's office,' she suggested, clinging to his neck, the smell of his warm skin sending shivers of delight down her spine. 'But put me down. We're making an exhibition of ourselves.'

Magnus's fire was lit, his brown leather Chesterfield pulled up beside it. Nick put her down on the seat, then joined her cupping her face in his hands.

'My poor darling,' he whispered, running his thumbs down her scarred cheeks, and looking right into her eyes. 'I could kill that man myself for doing this to you.'

Mel felt his breath warm on her cheek. As he pulled her into his arms every nerve-ending leapt in response.

Two years of wanting exploded into passion the moment their lips touched. They devoured one another, tongues, lips, fingers touching, arms pulling each other closer still, every muscle straining for all that had been denied them.

They forgot that the curtains were open, that any

second a member of staff or Magnus might walk in. Time and place ceased to have any meaning in the joy of holding each other at last.

'We must stop,' Mel gasped eventually.

Sighing deeply, Nick pulled back. His face was flushed, his lips swollen with desire. 'This is crazy.' He turned slightly to cradle her head against his shoulder, lips buried in her hair. 'I've thought of nothing else but kissing you all the way from London, but I never thought it would be quite as wild as that!'

'Me neither,' she admitted. 'What are we going to do now?'

'I don't know,' he said glumly. 'I imagined it all being quite chaste. Chatting and holding hands over a candle-lit dinner table until we got to know one another again. I intended to be a perfect gentleman until you were all healed up and we could go off somewhere romantic for a weekend.'

'Maybe it's better like this,' she smiled, pleased that his plan had echoed her own hopes. 'I've been frightened for days that I was deluding myself all this time. I was scared when it actually came to it, I might feel nothing.'

He lifted her face, looking down at her with such tenderness that all her anxiety slipped away. 'You do feel the same as me, don't you?' He kissed her eyes and caressed her cheek. 'For me it's like a gnawing pain inside – the need to hold you, to reach inside you.'

The last time Mel had been with a man was back in Ibiza, over three years ago. She had hardly thought of sex all that long time; it was as if her mind had shut away the memory. But now Nick's words were turning the key and unlocking that part of her.

'I want you too,' she whispered, taking his hand

and kissing the tips of his fingers. 'Body, mind and soul. But not here, it wouldn't seem right.'

He laughed softly and cuddled her to him. 'Funny isn't it? People come and stay here all the time to put the sparkle back in their marriages, for honeymoons and illicit weekends. But us two who belong here can't do it.'

'My stitches come out tomorrow,' she said, kissing his nose, eyes and lips. 'Couldn't we go back to London and stay in your flat?'

'You wouldn't like that much.' He nibbled at her lower lip. 'It's very seedy and the other tenants are noisy. Let's slip away tomorrow night to another hotel for a few days.'

Mel didn't reply for a moment. Magnus was arranging a surprise party for next Friday to coincide with the first showing of *Delinquents*. There was an official launch party being held in London for it, but because of the circumstances here, Nick had declined his invitation. Magnus felt that such an important event should be celebrated, and he'd invited Sophie, Stephen and their respective husbands and wives, along with some of Nick's old friends to Oaklands.

Miles had put forward a suggestion that Mel and Nick could come and stay in London with him for a few days before, while all the preparations were being made, with Helena joining them if she could get some time off from filming, to arrive back here at exactly seven thirty when all the guests would be waiting. Mel had promised Magnus faithfully that she wouldn't give the game away, but now she had a feeling Nick's idea might mess up the whole plan.

'If we're going to go away we'd better make it a whole week,' she said. 'Because I think Miles was planning to invite us up to London next week.'

Nick made a horrified face. 'I don't fancy that, he's a bit crusty.'

He had been absolutely stunned when Mel had told him all about Helena and Miles – delighted, but a little overwhelmed too. He doubted Mel had even considered what having such an illustrious grandfather and famous mother could mean for her, but he had.

'He is my grandfather and he grows on you,' she laughed. Until half an hour ago Mel had thought it was a wonderful idea, and a golden opportunity to get to know both Miles and Helena better. But Nick's arrival had changed everything. 'But I must admit I'd sooner be alone romping with you than minding my "p"s and "q"s in London.'

'I'll speak to Dad,' Nick said, nuzzling into her neck. 'He must know we need to make up for all this lost time, without any distractions or prying eyes.'

Mel was sure Magnus would understand. But she also knew he was becoming increasingly anxious that Edward hadn't been caught. She was worried enough herself, though she was putting on a good act of being unconcerned. She hoped he would feel able to let them out of his sight.

Nick kissed Mel's nose as he helped her out of his car outside Helena's cottage. It was two days since he'd arrived back at Oaklands and Mel had been invited over to Helena's cottage for the evening.

'I'll just say hullo and then shoot off,' Nick said. 'I'll come back for you about ten.'

It was too dark to see the cottage in any detail, but the bright light in the porch showed up enough of the lattice windows and the shrub-filled garden to sense it was the kind of cottage seen on chocolate boxes.

The door opened before they reached it and Helena came rushing out to greet them. 'I've been in such a tizzy,' she said excitedly. 'I didn't get home from the set until six and I've been rushing around straightening everything up. Do come in. It's a bit chilly tonight.'

'This is such a lovely room,' Mel said, looking around her. Nick had gone back to Oaklands and she and Helena were sitting by the fire with a bottle of wine. This cottage really did look as if it belonged to a famous actress, all the things missing from Edward's house were here. Flowers, a basket of fruit, framed photographs, so many of them of herself as a small child, and heaps of glossy magazines. Helena had obviously added many of the homely touches to an already beautifully furnished room. There were big, bright cushions on the deep comfortable settees, a couple of large china cats on the mantelpiece and a huge parlour palm on a low table by the windows.

'I just love it,' Helena said with a wide smile. 'It's the sort of home I always wanted. I hope I might be able to persuade the owners to sell it to me. You should see the garden, it's got a view to die for. I relish the thought of the changing seasons. I missed that in Hollywood.'

The evening had none of the tension of their first meeting. Over the wine Helena told Mel many vivid and funny anecdotes about her touring days with Bonny back in the forties. Mel told Helena a little about her time in London, about Bee and how she came to Oaklands and found Magnus.

It was as Helena showed her the other rooms in the cottage that Mel saw the real similarities in their characters. Both were at heart homemakers, even though neither of them had had much opportunity to settle into a real one. Helena had a girlish enthusiasm to learn about cooking, gardening and interior design which Mel related to.

'Will you help me do up this room?' Helena

asked, showing her the biggest of the bedrooms. It was a pleasant enough room, with low lattice windows and black beams, but it was decorated in a dull blue and it seemed chilly. 'I'd like it as my room, because it's bigger than the one I'm in now. But I don't really know where to start.'

They sat on the bed and discussed colour schemes and how one wall could be fitted out with wardrobes. Mel suggested a deep rose-pink wallpaper. 'Not something pretty-pretty,' she said. 'One of those dramatic Victorian designs, perhaps just one wall and then the rest plain. You could have a splendid four-poster bed, the room's big enough, with cream lace drapes, and a thick, thick, cream carpet.'

When Helena opened her vast wardrobe, Mel felt as if she was fourteen again and back in her mother's bedroom. Helena had even more clothes than Bonny, and dozens of exquisite evening and cocktail dresses.

Helena seemed to sense Mel wanted to look at them all, and drew one after another out, telling her about parties she'd worn some of them to.

Mel sighed over an emerald-green chiffon one, holding it up to herself the way she always did with Bonny's dresses.

'Try it on,' Helena urged her. 'I've put on a few pounds recently and it's too tight for me now. I bet it will fit you perfectly.'

It fitted as if it had been made for Mel. As she swirled in front of a long mirror, with Helena looking on smiling, she had a feeling of having come round in a big circle, back to home.

'You must keep it,' Helena said. 'I doubt I'll ever lose those pounds, not the way I've been eating lately.'

'I love it, but you can't give it to me,' Mel said. 'Besides I never go anywhere grand enough for it.'

'You will soon,' Helena said. 'With Nick about to be a big star, and Miles and I dying to take you out with us and show you off, you'll need lots of glamorous clothes. Besides it feels good to see you in it, a bit like old times. Bonny and I used to wear each other's clothes.'

'How did it go?' Nick asked as they drove home later, Mel holding the dress across her lap.

'The time just flew by,' Mel said. 'I thought it would be kind of sticky in places, but it wasn't. I like her so much. It was almost as if she'd always been part of my life.'

'All ready?' Magnus asked as he came up the stairs to help Mel down and carry her case. Nick had driven down to a garage to get some fuel. It was Saturday morning now. The stitches in her foot had been taken out on Friday as arranged, but it was too sore that day to leave immediately.

'Just about,' she said, leaning on a walking stick. 'I feel a bit guilty at leaving you to do everything for the party.'

'You would only be in the way,' he said with a wide grin. 'Just make sure you get him back for Friday night.'

She nodded and blushed.

'It's okay,' he smiled and tweaked her hair. 'I may be getting old but I have my memories. Love is very precious, Mel, and you two have waited a very long time. Just be careful with that foot. No long walks or running through the dew barefoot.'

'It's a bit cold for that,' she laughed. There had been a light frost when she looked out this morning and though the sun had come out now, it was still cold enough for gloves and a thick coat. 'But I'll promise anyway if it makes you happy. Just you promise me you won't tire yourself out getting this party organised?'

'Nick!' Magnus called from the doorway just as he was preparing to drive away.

'What the hell does he want now!' Nick frowned with irritation and turned off the ignition as his father beckoned.

'He probably wants to tell you the facts of life,' Mel joked. 'Listen to him, he may have a few handy hints.'

Nick got out of the car and went back into the porch. 'What now?' he frowned. 'Yes, I've got enough money and I've checked the oil in my car.'

'I wouldn't call you back for anything so trivial.' Magnus drew him into the hall. 'I've just had a call from the police. A man flagged a woman down on a road in Wales late last night, then turned her out of the car and drove off with it. The woman described him as dark-haired with a moustache and glasses, but they are sure it's Manning.'

'She'll be quite safe with me,' Nick said flippantly, but as he turned to walk away Magnus grabbed his shoulder.

'There's more,' Magnus said. 'The FBI in the States have passed on some information about two young women who were found drowned in the last three years, again believed to be suicide cases, just like Bonny. It seems they both had a connection with Manning.'

Nick gulped. 'But he's blown it with Mel. Surely he wouldn't dare to come back and have another pop at her?'

'Maybe not, but he's got a gun,' Magnus admitted, licking his lips nervously. 'That's why the woman handed over her car without protest. He was heading in the direction of the Severn Bridge.

Now doesn't that suggest he's making his way back here?'

Nick's earlier irritation was now replaced with concern for his father. Deep frown lines furrowed his forehead and his eyes were muddy with anxiety. Earlier this morning he'd looked on top of the world. Now suddenly Nick was reminded of that stroke. 'Perhaps I ought to take Mel somewhere safe and come back here to stay with you?' he said.

'No, son, Mel needs you far more than I do and the police will be patrolling around here. Just try to prevent her from seeing any newspapers and phone me each evening for reports on what's happening.'

'I'd better go.' Nick looked round anxiously as he heard the sound of the car radio being switched on. Mel was bent forward tuning into a station. 'I'll find some way to disconnect that too. Don't worry, Dad. No harm will come to her with me.'

'With luck he'll have been caught long before you get back,' Magnus said, patting his son's shoulder. 'Just do your best to keep this from Mel, she's been through quite enough.'

'What did he want?' Mel asked as Nick slid into the driving seat.

'Nothing much,' Nick leaned towards her. 'Just that if we were going anywhere near Brixham could we bring back some crabs and lobster.'

'Are we going near there?' She was excited now they were finally pulling out of the drive.

'You'll have to wait and see!'

'So Brixham was a red herring. It's Lyme Regis!' Mel exclaimed as they drove down the steep hill into the town late in the afternoon. She was immediately enchanted by the cobbled streets, the tiny cottages and shops with bow windows.

'Mum always claimed it was a romantic place,' Nick turned to smile at her. 'We used to come here a lot in the summer when I was little. Dad and I used to go out mackerel fishing, Mum used to sit on the beach or wander about the town. I think she'd approve of me bringing you here.'

'I hope you aren't intending to take me mackerel fishing,' she laughed. 'I don't find the smell of dead fish one of life's aphrodisiacs.'

The Bay Hotel was situated right on the seafront with only a walkway before it, so they left their car in a back street and walked down some steep steps to reach it. Nick went on ahead carrying their cases; Mel was much slower, holding onto the rail and stepping very gingerly. The wind was strong, coming straight off the sea, but the salty tang, the smell of seaweed and the pounding of waves on the shore were invigorating after being cloistered indoors for so long.

'I'd forgotten I couldn't drive right up to it,' Nick admitted ruefully, as he dumped the cases at the bottom of the steps and ran back up to help her. 'Is your foot hurting? Maybe I should've picked a flat place?'

'My foot doesn't hurt,' she reassured him. 'I'm only limping out of habit. By the end of the week I'll be running up these steps.'

The Bay Hotel was a little less grand than Nick remembered, but Mel was delighted by its pink-washed façade, the slightly drunken-looking ancient windows and its close proximity to the sea. The cobbled walkway along the front was deserted, not a café, amusement arcade or shop in sight to spoil its old-world charm, just a gentle curve of quaint old cottages and houses that had remained intact for centuries despite the bombardment of sea spray.

'You must be Mr and Mrs Poitier.' A man with a polished, ruddy face leapt to help them as they came through the door. He introduced himself as James Grant the proprietor and beamingly welcomed them to his hotel. 'Now would you like some tea first or shall I take you up to your room? It's all ready for you.'

Nick had been in here often for afternoon tea with his parents and he was pleased to find it even cosier than he'd remembered. A huge log fire was blazing in the bar and comfortable armchairs and a strong smell of lavender polish reassured him he hadn't made a mistake in choosing this place to stay. Two middle-aged ladies were sitting reading magazines, and they looked round with interest at the new guests.

'I think we'll see our room first.' Nick struggled to keep his composure as Mel grinned like a Cheshire cat. 'My wife is a little tired; as I said on the telephone she was in a car accident recently and we've come away for her to recuperate.'

'Why Poitier?' Mel whispered as Mr Grant took their cases and led them up an old winding staircase.

'I thought it was more exotic than Smith,' Nick whispered back behind his hand. 'Besides I hoped someone might think I'm Sydney.'

'You aren't quite the right colour for that,' she giggled, as she struggled upstairs.

James Grant smilingly put down their cases, pointed out the minibar, the sea view and wished them a happy stay.

'Versailles revisited,' Nick said once the door had closed, running his hand over the gilded headboard on the double bed and smirking at the ivory satin bedspread. 'A real bridal suite.'

'I think it's wonderful – don't be such a snob,'

Mel tapped his cheek playfully. 'It has a perfect, almost decadent atmosphere.'

Mr Grant, or perhaps his wife had at least been consistent in indulging their taste for gold. The wall lights were gold cherubs, all the furniture was cream with gold mouldings, the full-length mirror had a heavy gilt frame and the dark red pelmet above the window had gold tassels. It wasn't exactly in keeping with a two-hundred-year-old inn, but to Mel it looked romantic.

She limped across the room to look in the bathroom. She expected more gold, but there everything was white except for the dark mahogany around the bath and washbasin and the wall of mirrored tiles. If she hadn't been used to the splendour of Oaklands she would have considered it very grand.

'Come here,' Nick said from the bedroom. Mel looked round the door and saw him standing by the window. 'Hurry up, the sun's about to set.'

It looked like a huge blood orange, sinking down fast towards the sea, cutting a wide pink swathe through the water almost to the shore. The cob jutted out almost like a black serpent and alongside they could see lights on fishing boats, twinkling and moving as the boats bobbed up and down on the swell.

Nick stood behind Mel, his arms round her waist, his chin resting on her shoulder as the sun slipped slowly into the sea. The sky was dark grey, but pink around the sun. Slowly it turned to purple as the sun dipped further and further into the sea. For a brief moment there was a fiery crescent, then all at once it was gone, sunk into the blackness.

Mel nuzzled her cheek against Nick's. 'I've never actually seen it disappear before,' she said thoughtfully. 'I always lost patience.'

He turned her in his arms, holding her face between his hands and lifting it up to his.

A light on the hotel sign flickered on, catching his blond hair and highlighting the curve of his lips. Down in the bar music was switched on and the sound of The Stylistics' 'You Make Me Feel Brand New', played above the sound of the sea. 'They're even playing our song,' he whispered, smiling.

There had never been a sweeter moment in her life: all hesitation gone, a feeling she was about to step into eternal bliss. Even before their lips touched the electricity flowed between them.

Passion was tempered now with the knowledge it was to be consummated. Their lips and tongues teased and played, their breath hot and sweet, their fingers searching out soft places. Slowly Nick unzipped her dress, sliding his hand in and gasping at the silkiness of her skin. She pulled out his shirt and ran her fingers up his spine, feeling goose bumps of pleasure rising under her touch.

He ran his hands down her neck onto her shoulders so delicately Mel found she was holding her breath, dropping her arms to her sides. Her dress dropped to the floor, quickly followed by her bra and Nick stared in awe.

Mel took his hands and held them to her breasts.

He sighed with pleasure, bending to kiss her erect nipples and she trembled with emotion, running her fingers through his soft hair. His rapt expression brought a lump to her throat.

'They are so beautiful,' he whispered, holding each nipple between his fingers as he moved back to kiss her again. 'I never felt this way before.'

All at once they were overtaken by a fierce thirst. Clothes were ripped off, tossed away heedlessly, two bodies straining to be as one. As they kissed, Nick sunk onto a straight-backed chair by the window and pulled her down with him to sit astride him.

The window was less than a foot away. Anyone passing along the sea walkway could have looked up and seen them, illuminated by the hotel sign, but they needed release too much to move away to the bed or even to close the curtains.

Mel's hunger matched Nick's. Other men had held her like this in the past, but not once had she experienced such savage joy or such oneness.

Tenderness washed over her as she held him to her shoulder. He was quivering, panting against her, sweat turning cold with the draught from the window.

'I love you,' she whispered, lifting his face so she could look into his eyes. 'Stay with me forever?'

The hotel sign lit up his face, golden and glowing, softer than she'd ever seen it before. 'Could I leave you now?' he whispered back, his eyes glistening with tears. 'We were meant for one another.'

He lifted her up, carried her over to the bed and laid her down on the satin covers. Then he switched on the bedside light before returning to the window to draw the curtains.

The feel of the silky material against her bare skin made her writhe sensuously. As Nick turned from the window she held out her arms for him.

He paused, just looking at her. He had imagined her naked so often, but even in his dreams she had never looked so beautiful. Her skin was honey-coloured, her dark hair shiny and tousled against the cream satin. The soft light hid her remaining scars and emphasised her long slender limbs, full firm breasts and small waist.

But the rush of tenderness he felt made him suddenly shy of his own nakedness. He took a hand towel from the radiator and put it over his arm like a waiter. 'Will madam be requiring anything else?'

Mel smiled. She knew why he felt he had to clown, and loved him for such absurd, unexpected shyness. 'A great deal more,' she said, and wriggling up the bed she held out her arms again. 'Come here and I'll show you.'

Time and place ceased to have any meaning as they held one another in that big warm bed. Mel felt as if she was coming back to life. As they explored each other's bodies, long suppressed desire and emotion welled up and overflowed.

She sensed Nick was intent only on pleasing her now, his own needs put aside. She watched him as he caressed and kissed her breasts, delighting in the sensuality of his touch, but moved more by his desire to thrill her. He made her feel as if her skin were virgin, as if each sensitive spot he discovered was new to her too.

Slowly he kissed and licked his way down her body, his fingers probing deep within her. Again and again she felt she was on the point of orgasm, writhing against him, trying to draw him inside her, but still he continued to play with her.

'Tell me what you like best?' he whispered. But she couldn't answer. Everything he did, everywhere he touched was magical. She wanted to thrill him too, yet she couldn't move, only moan and hold him, wanting release, yet not wanting the bliss to end.

When he finally moved right down her body, Mel held her breath, her whole being wanting to scream at him to lick her there, and yet an exquisite shyness preventing her.

But he knew that was what she wanted; each touch and tentative lick was mere teasing. He was waiting for her to demand it.

'Please kiss me there,' she called out at last, unable to contain herself any longer. 'Please Nick, please!'

She heard him make a little chuckling sound and at last he obeyed her. He parted the lips of her sex and began to feast on her lasciviously.

Wild, heady sensation, white hot in its intensity engulfed her. She clawed at his hair and shoulders, all thought of modesty gone. 'More,' she shouted, widening her thighs and holding him trapped against her. 'I'm coming!'

She was still trembling from her orgasm when he entered her. His hot deep kisses, the taste of her on his lips and the urgency of his need for her made her cry with love and ecstasy.

There were more tears as they lay entwined, damp and sticky with perspiration. There was so much she wanted to say, yet her heart was too full to express it.

All those other men she'd been with, all the cheap, squalid, humiliating things she'd done were washed away. She knew somehow that this was the beginning. Here in this hotel room, past mistakes and misfortunes were wiped out for good.

'I knew you were meant for me the first night I saw you,' he murmured, lips in her hair. 'Like my whole life up till then had been waiting for you.'

Her silent tears broke into a sob at such tender, beautiful words.

'Oh Nick,' she whispered, lifting his face so she could see him better. His eyes were soft and adoring. No man had ever looked that way at her before. 'I wish I could tell you how you make me feel. Just saying "I love you" isn't enough.'

He leaned up over her, just smiling. His lips were swollen with kissing, the glow of the bedside lamp highlighting his cheek bones.

'Do you remember those miracle stories they told

us at school, ones from the Bible where lame men walked and stuff?' she asked.

'You're not going to tell me I've made your foot better?' he laughed softly.

'You might very well have done, I haven't checked it yet,' she smiled. 'No, I mean like baptism washing away sins. I tried meditation, celibacy, even prayer to wash away the past. I never thought love could do it, but it has.'

Nick didn't reply, just snuggled down on the pillow beside her. He was quiet for so long she thought he'd fallen asleep. Then he sighed, and reached up to trace round her lips with one finger.

'I thought you'd dropped off,' she whispered.

'It isn't gentlemanly to fall asleep before your lady does,' he said. 'I was just wondering how I'm going to go downstairs for dinner tonight pretending I'm Mr Poitier with his convalescing wife, when really I want to go down there and buy a magnum of champagne and tell anyone who'll listen that I'm the luckiest man in the world.'

'Dinner,' she said thoughtfully. 'Now you're talking. I'm starving!'

Nick sat up in bed, snatched the pillow from under her head and held it over her face. 'You unromantic pig,' he said in a mock severe voice. 'There I am pouring out my innermost thoughts and all you can think of is food.'

'Let me go.' She struggled against him. 'I promise I can be twice as romantic, and twice as sexy with a full tummy. I won't even giggle when Mr Grant calls you Mr Poitier.'

They drove out of Lyme Regis late on Friday afternoon. Mel had never had a real holiday before and now she understood why people set such store by them. It had been such a blissful lazy time:

hours of lovemaking, breakfast in bed, long wallowing baths, lunches in quaint old pubs, gentle walks around the town followed by delicious dinners in the evenings. It was the first time she'd ever slept close to the sea. Lying in Nick's arms listening to the waves pounding the shore, it seemed the most blissful, soothing sound she'd ever heard.

They hadn't fooled anyone in the hotel that they were Mr and Mrs Poitier. Mr Grant admitted he recognised Nick's face from the papers and the curious and often affectionate looks they got from the older guests suggested that most of them recognised young love.

The scratches and bruises were gone now, the faint pink lines here and there easily concealed with a little make-up. Rest and fresh air had brought colour back to Mel's cheeks. Even her foot had healed completely. That morning she'd had her hair washed and trimmed in a hairdressers, in readiness for the evening's party. Nick still hadn't guessed there was a surprise in store for him when they got back.

'We'll get away again soon.' He reached out for her hand as he drove, instinctively sharing her sadness that the holiday was over. 'Why don't we tell Dad tonight that we're getting married?'

'Is that a proposal?' Mel wriggled nearer to him. 'Or just an excuse for another holiday.'

'Do you want me to attempt to kneel while I'm driving?'

'No, that can wait,' she joked. 'But what are your prospects young man?'

'If the critics are kind after tonight, excellent,' he grinned. 'I've got a month's filming in Rome lined up for early next year. Who knows after that.'

'Rome!' she exclaimed. 'You haven't mentioned that before.'

'I've been saving it for a surprise.' He patted her knee affectionately. 'If we got married at Christmas you could come with me and it could double as a honeymoon.'

'Are you serious?' Mel's eyes grew wide with delight.

'Never more so.' Nick turned into a petrol station and pulled up by the pumps. 'I don't ever want us to be apart again. But you've got as long as it takes me to get some petrol to make up your mind.' He dropped a kiss on her nose. 'This is a limited offer.'

As Nick filled the car he blew kisses to her through the window and Mel felt tears prickling her eyes.

He liked to tease and clown, and he made jokes about things to hide the true depths of his feelings, but she knew he was entirely serious about marriage. She knew too that she wanted it more than anything else.

She took a lipstick from her bag, found an old envelope stuffed into the glove compartment and wrote 'Yes Please' in large letters. The moment he had disappeared into the garage shop, she propped it up on the windscreen so he'd see it as he came out.

Nick picked up a couple of bars of chocolate and while he waited to be served he glanced at the display of daily papers.

The headline 'Armed and Dangerous' on the front of one of the tabloids attracted his attention, so he picked it up. As the folded paper dropped open, he gasped in horror at the photograph of Edward Manning.

A cold chill ran down his spine. He looked over his shoulder to make sure Mel was still in the car, then read through the story as fast as he could, his heart thumping.

'Can I help you, sir?' the woman behind the

counter called out, but he ignored her and continued to read on.

All week he had prevented Mel from seeing the news on television and even buying a paper, by pretending he wanted to cut them off from reality. As his daily phone calls to Magnus had revealed there had been no more sightings of Manning since that night in Wales before they left, he had been lulled into a false sense of security.

The previous afternoon a widow in her early sixties had been shot in the shoulder at an isolated house some ten miles from Bristol. She was discovered by the evening paperboy, lying outside by an old shed. She regained consciousness when the ambulance arrived and was able to tell the police that a man had come to her door demanding that she give him the keys to her car. She had handed them over, guessing that this was the man she'd read about in the papers, but he took all the money in her handbag, ripped out her telephone and shot her anyway. She was trying to get help when she collapsed outside. If it hadn't been for the paperboy she would have bled to death by morning.

Nick's head spun. He didn't know what to do for the best. If he insisted on taking Mel back to Lyme Regis she would be instantly suspicious. Yet how could he risk taking her back to Oaklands?

He paid for his petrol and the chocolate. As he came out of the shop and saw Mel's note on the windscreen, and her grinning face behind it, he was stumped. She was so happy. How could he dash it all by telling her about Manning?

Taking a few deep breaths to calm himself he walked back to the car. 'So you'll marry me?' he said, forcing himself to smile and look normal. 'Well, that's worthy of another celebration. Let's turn round and go back to Lyme Regis?'

'Don't be so ridiculous,' she laughed gleefully,

ruffling his hair. 'Your film's on TV tonight. Magnus would be savage if he couldn't watch it with us.'

Nick went cold all over, immediately guessing why she'd insisted on having her hair done that morning, and why she'd bought a new dress earlier in the week. Magnus had arranged a surprise party.

Nick had a straight choice: either tell the truth and see the anxiety and fear come back in her eyes, not to mention disappointing all the guests, or say nothing and go home and just hope the police would be extra vigilant tonight.

'If you insist on going back for tonight, will you at least promise you'll come to London with me tomorrow morning,' he asked. 'I want to buy you a lovely ring.'

'That sounds like a pretty good deal,' she grinned. 'We can have champagne tonight at Oaklands and I can buy some new clothes in London too.'

Mel dropped off to sleep soon after leaving the garage. Nick was glad: it freed him from being forced to make bright conversation. He slowed down, trying to think of some plan. Could he pretend to break down? But he knew that wouldn't work. If she'd promised Magnus they would be back this evening, she'd insist they got there somehow.

Manning was bound to know *Delinquents* was on TV tonight. He might also guess there would be some sort of celebration at Oaklands, and that Mel might be there. But surely no man on the run would risk turning up in a place that the police would be certain to be watching? Perhaps it was really the safest place for her to be.

It was pitch dark when Mel woke up, dark hedges

lining the road. 'Where are we?' she asked. Looking at her watch she saw it was half past six.

When he didn't answer she glanced sideways at Nick. He looked a bit strained.

'Are you all right? Shall I drive for a bit?' she asked. 'Or are you having second thoughts about marrying me?'

'Of course not,' he scoffed. 'I was just wondering if Dad would let me share your bed tonight.'

'You aren't going to ask him?' she giggled. 'I'd die with embarrassment.'

'Well, he knows we haven't been just holding hands all week,' Nick retorted.

As they drove through Bath just after seven it seemed to Nick that there was an unusually heavy police presence. He spotted four Panda cars in the space of five minutes, and he had a feeling they were doing more than just watching out for drunken hooligans on a Friday night.

As they approached the driveway into Oaklands, Nick saw two more Panda cars parked up on opposite sides of the road, some thirty yards apart. Two uniformed men were standing by the gates, clearly on guard.

'What's going on?' Mel asked, leaning forward in her seat.

Nick thought quickly. 'I expect Magnus has invited Helena tonight and asked them to make sure no fans get in. Unless of course it's got around what a sensation I am,' he added, hoping that would distract her.

As he slowed right down to turn into the drive, the two men stepped out in front of the car flashing torches.

Nick opened the window and stuck his head out. 'I'm Nicholas Osbourne,' he called out. 'With Camellia Norton. Do we have to advance and be recognised?' He offered up a silent frantic prayer that the police wouldn't say anything to alarm Mel.

'You're okay sir.' The policemen backed away, signalling him on. 'We were briefed you were coming. Drive on in.'

'That's a bit heavy,' Mel said suspiciously, turning in her seat to look at Nick as he drove up the drive. 'Are you sure you aren't keeping something back from me?'

Nick was very glad it was so dark, not only because she couldn't see his face, but because by turning to him she'd missed the two policemen on foot with a dog in the woods to her right.

'I suspect it's you keeping things back,' he said glibly. 'Who else is coming tonight aside from Helena? And why did you get your hair done today?'

'I didn't know Helena was coming tonight until you told me. And I got my hair done for your benefit,' she said sweetly.

Nick thought she was almost as good a liar as himself.

The floodlighting around the house was on. Nick hoped Mel had forgotten that Magnus normally only used the front lights during the autumn and winter. 'Good God! It's busy tonight,' he exclaimed, feigning astonishment at the number of parked cars. 'I just hope Dad doesn't rope us two into serving behind the bar?'

Magnus must have been looking out for them, as he opened the front door the moment they got out the car. In the light from the porch he could well have been mistaken for a film star himself. He was wearing a dinner jacket and bow tie and his white hair was slicked back.

'You're looking very dapper, Dad,' Nick called out, taking Mel's arm and moving her swiftly towards the safety of the house. 'I would have thought with all these cars out here you could afford a doorman!'

'I heard you driving in,' Magnus said, coming forward and clamping his arm round Mel's shoulder protectively. Nick saw him glance nervously back into the shadows. 'It's cold out here, let's get you inside.'

Nick noticed how quickly Magnus shut the door and his distracted manner, but Mel was equally distracted, looking towards the sound of voices coming from behind the closed bar door.

'Welcome home.' Magnus kissed Mel's cheek and slapped his son on the shoulder. 'I'm afraid I've got a few pressing things to do before I can relax with you and hear about your holiday. Why don't you nip upstairs and change? By the time you've done that I'll be free and we can have a drink together before the film starts.'

Mel began to walk towards the stairs, but she looked back over her shoulder and grinned at Nick. 'You see!' she said. 'I knew he wouldn't approve of your jeans.'

Magnus waited a second until she'd turned onto the stairs, and caught hold of his son's arm. 'For the first time in my life I hoped you'd be feckless and not turn up tonight,' he said in a low voice. 'Manning shot a woman not fifteen miles from here yesterday.'

'I know, Dad,' Nick whispered. 'We were on the way back when I saw it in a paper. Without telling Mel the truth there was no alternative but to come here. I'll take her to London first thing in the morning.'

'I suppose too you've guessed about the party?'

Nick nodded. 'Yes, it dawned on me when she was so anxious to get back. But Mel doesn't know I've twigged, so I'll fake surprise, for her benefit.'

He looked towards the closed bar door. 'I take it they are all in there waiting?'

'There wasn't time to stop them coming,' Magnus sighed deeply, putting one hand up to his head as if the weight of so much responsibility was too much for him. 'But I've done everything possible to make it secure. I cancelled all bookings, closed the club until further notice, and the police are patrolling the grounds. I've even put a double bed in Mel's room so she's got you for protection during the night. As long as everyone stays inside and keeps the windows and doors closed, she will be safe. I don't really believe he'd risk coming here tonight, but I can't help wondering if we should warn her though.'

'No, Dad,' Nick put his arm across his father's shoulders. 'She's so happy and secure right now, we can't shatter that for her. We'll make sure someone's with her at all times. The police are outside. Tell everyone else to be vigilant, but not to say anything to her. Let's make this the happy carefree party she's expecting, for her sake.'

He picked up their cases and raced up the stairs to find Mel standing in her room looking in astonishment at the double divan which had replaced her old single one.

'Dad just told me,' Nick said. 'He said he needed all the other rooms tonight, but I suspect he just didn't want us creeping along passages.'

'Shame we can't christen it immediately,' she giggled, flinging off her clothes. 'But the film starts in just over half an hour and I'm dying for a drink. But bless Magnus – I didn't fancy sleeping alone again.'

Ten minutes later they came back down the stairs – Mel in her slinky long cream dress, Nick in a navy-blue suit and striped tie.

As Nick opened the door to the bar, a barrage of

party poppers erupted, smothering him in paper streamers.

Mel stood back shaking with laughter. Nick was transfixed, eyes wide with shock, mouth hanging open.

'What the Dickens is going on,' he gasped, seeing at least thirty of his family and friends dressed up and grinning at him. 'I don't believe this!'

If Magnus had once doubted his son's ability to be a convincing actor, Nick's display of feigned amazement put him straight. Everyone, including Mel, was taken in.

Again and again this week Magnus had been tempted to abandon the idea of the party and not just because of Edward Manning. Everyone, family, friends and staff were intensely curious about Mel – why she'd left Oaklands, why Manning had tried to kill her, what her connection with Helena was. On top of that Magnus knew they were also all wondering where he came into the story – how he knew Sir Miles Hamilton and Helena and why the police had questioned them all. A few moments ago when he'd warned everyone to say nothing to Mel about Manning or the police presence outside, it created even greater confusion.

Magnus was at heart an honest man, and he would have found it more comfortable to tell the truth than lie or evade the issue. But he was only one of the supporting cast in this drama, and unless Helena and Miles were prepared publicly to reveal their relationship to Mel, he couldn't offer a plausible explanation about any of it, to anyone.

Sophie and Stephen were both bristling with indignation, convinced they were the only people being kept in the dark. Joan and Antoine were a little hurt he couldn't take them into his confidence and he knew the rest of his staff were whispering about this mystery together.

Glancing about him Magnus saw it in all their faces. Sophie had made a great effort with her appearance tonight: she'd had her dark hair put up in a French pleat at the hairdressers, with make-up and her black cocktail dress she was, if not glamorous, at least sophisticated. But though she was smiling and chatting to everyone, every now and again she'd glance balefully in Magnus's direction. Stephen was very smart in a dark lounge suit, a full glass in his hand, June, his wife by his side, but he appeared to be studying Miles and Helena as if trying to work it all out. Even Joan and Antoine, although clearly touched that they'd been included tonight, looked slightly strained.

But Magnus knew he had to put all this out of his mind. The party was for Nick, and what counted tonight was his youngest son's happiness.

'I'm as proud as punch of you.' He took a step closer to Nick putting one hand on his shoulder, his voice gruff with emotion. 'This is my way of showing it.'

'Oh Dad, you silly sod,' Nick hugged his father tightly. 'Am I really going to be put through watching it with all of you?'

'You just wait till you see the size of the television I hired for the night,' Magnus said. 'Now how about some large drinks before we go into the private cinema in the dining room?'

Mel was so busy watching Nick's face, she didn't notice Helena come through from the back of the crowd to stand by her side.

'You look wonderful, Camellia. I hope you feel as happy and well as you look.'

Mel turned her head in surprise at the now familiar husky voice.

Helena looked like a film star tonight, in a floor-length blue and green chiffon low-cut gown, with wide, almost mediaeval sleeves. Diamonds

706

sparkled at her throat, wrist and ears, and her dark curls cascaded onto her shoulders. The glamour threw Mel, bringing back an unexpected twinge of resentment.

'I'm fine now, thank you,' she said.

A fleeting look of hurt in the woman's velvety dark eyes immediately shamed her for giving such a stilted, cold reply.

'I'm sorry, that came out all wrong,' she added quickly. 'I think I meant past hurts don't matter any more. Tonight and all the tomorrows are what count.'

'A commendable sentiment,' Miles's deep gravelly voice came from her right. He pushed his way past a couple of Nick's actor friends. 'And my dear, you look ravishing.'

'And so do you, Smiley,' she said, reaching out to touch his waistcoat. It was red silk, embroidered with gold thread and she had the oddest feeling he'd put it on for her benefit. 'This is absolutely spectacular.'

She knew in that instant she'd made amends to both of them by using Helena's pet name for him. Delighted smiles passed between them.

'It has been said, that a man of my age should wear more discreet clothes,' Miles said with a rumble of laughter in his voice. 'But I have always maintained that if everyone was to dress as they feel, we'd all understand one another a great deal more quickly.'

'Then I should be wearing red,' Mel admitted. 'That's my favourite colour. What would that say about me?'

'Ah, ha!' he exclaimed. 'Red signifies a huntress. But as you chose cream tonight that suggests to me that you have found what you were looking for. Am I right?'

Mel looked from Miles to Helena. She sensed that

they were both still uneasy. This was all new for them too.

It was a strange moment. The room was filled with Nick's family and friends. To them, aside from Nick and Magnus, she was merely an ex-employee turned girlfriend – a curiosity perhaps, because of the recent events, but nothing more.

Mel was aware her idea of family life was distorted. She'd only really ever observed it as an interested outsider – sometimes with yearning, but more often with cynicism. She had the choice now either to claim these two strangers as her family and be prepared for the difficulties which would come with it, or to back away politely and keep the independence she valued. It wasn't easy. She wasn't sure she could ever be what they wanted, and once she'd committed herself she would have to stick by her decision.

'Yes. I have found what I was looking for,' she said carefully. 'Me.'

Miles looked a little perplexed, but Helena's eyes showed true understanding. She lifted one hand and caressed Mel's cheek, her tender gesture showing that she knew Mel had placed a foundation stone on which all three of them could build.

Magnus elbowed his way through the crowd with a tray of drinks. 'Nick told me you'd like gin and tonic,' he said, handing a glass to Mel. 'Brandy for Miles, lemonade for Helena and whisky for me. I need it too. If I ever get the idea of throwing another surprise party, lock me up until the madness has passed.'

'It was worth it though, wasn't it?' Mel said. 'I've never seen Nick look so surprised. I thought he'd guessed when he saw the police on the gate. Are they really necessary? I mean do you get followed by fans much, Helena?'

Helena had to think quickly. People did turn up

on the film set every day, but the real draw was Rupert Henderson, her young co-star. 'It isn't me people are likely to chase after, but Nick,' she said with a wide smile. 'There was a great deal in the local papers about him while you were away, and Magnus has had his hands full for the last two days with people wandering into the grounds hoping to see him. After tonight it will probably be worse.'

Magnus shot her a look of gratitude. 'Speaking of Nick's film, it's about time we all went in and took our seats,' he said. He put his arm around Mel. 'And I haven't even had time to tell you how gorgeous you look tonight, or ask about your foot.'

'The foot's all better, and I'm glad I look human again. But you haven't told me what's happened about Edward? And where's Con? He said he was going to come.'

'Con couldn't find anyone to stand in for him tonight,' Magnus replied, glad that as usual she'd strung all her questions together. 'But he said he'd come down – if not this coming Sunday, the next. I think he's finding it a bit of a struggle without you. Now let's get Nick and get in the dining room. We can do all the chatting after the film.'

The dining room had been turned into a cinema, with the biggest television Mel had ever seen put up on a table. Magnus had replaced the dining tables and chairs with the more comfortable wicker armchairs and settees from the orangery. Nick, Mel, Helena and Magnus took the biggest settee right in the front, with Miles in a chair next to them. The rest of the party gathered to both sides and behind them.

'I'll bring round the ices,' Nick joked, a little embarrassed to find himself the focal point of the whole evening. But he was glad to discover that he had at least drawn all the guests' attention away from what was going on outside. He'd peeped out through the curtains just before coming in here and he'd seen the police patrolling the grounds with torches.

Magnus had half expected some of the guests, particularly the actor friends, to interrupt the flow of the film by making ribald comments, but the story was so powerful that they quickly became immersed in it. In fact Magnus found himself forgetting that the tough instructor who bullied, cajoled and reached the hearts and minds of those young offenders, or shinnied up rock faces seemingly effortlessly, was his son. But every now and then, mostly when the camera caught Nick in a close-up, and he saw the lad's clear blue eyes, and his angular cheek bones, he felt a pang of sorrow that Ruth wasn't here beside him.

Mel, sitting between Magnus and Nick, was so enthralled that when they got to the part where Nick fell into the crevice, she cried out in fear.

In the final poignant scene where the young tearaway changes his mind about running away to the city and climbs back to help Nick, both Helena and Mel were sobbing. Magnus glanced round over his shoulder and saw that Sophie was too. He hadn't seen her react emotionally to anything since she was a young teenager.

As the credits rolled and Nick Osbourne's name flashed onto the screen, Magnus leapt to his feet.

'That's my boy,' he yelled, his eyes as damp as Mel's.

'Oh Dad.' Nick embraced his father fiercely, too choked up to say anything coherent. A babble of laughter and chatter broke out, hands reached out to pat his back, but his father's pride and delight meant more than anything.

'You were absolutely wonderful.' Mel hugged Nick, still sniffing and dabbing at her eyes.

'Dan was better,' Nick said. 'He made the film. Did you see that expression on his face when he was fighting? He really looked like a hard nut.'

'Which one was Dan?' she joked. 'I only saw one face throughout the whole film.'

They all moved back into the bar, the two waitresses coming in to move back the chairs for dancing later and to set up a table for the buffet. The barman was opening bottles of champagne and everyone was talking at once, trying to get Nick's attention. But Nick stayed firmly by Mel's side, introducing her to his friends, smiling happily at their extravagant praise.

'Look who's coming!' Nick whispered to Mel a bit later as Sophie elbowed her way towards them, dragging her husband Michael by the hand.

Mel thought she looked very attractive tonight. It was good to see her in a smart dress, instead of baggy tweeds and twin-sets. She hadn't any idea that Sophie had such a good figure or such nice legs.

'You were very good, Nick,' she said in the same kind of snooty voice she used to speak to Oaklands staff. 'I'm very proud of you.' She stopped suddenly, as if aware her tone was all wrong. 'I mean it, Nick,' her voice softened. 'You made me cry.'

Mel glanced at Nick, hoping he wouldn't come back at Sophie with sarcasm. To her delight he reached forward and gave his sister a warm hug. 'That's a nice thing to say, Soph. My family's opinion is more important to me than tomorrow's papers. I'm really glad you came – it's a long way from Yorkshire.'

Sophie smiled – really smiled from the heart – and for the first time ever Mel saw Magnus in her face. She shared none of his strong features, but just this once she had her father's joyful expression.

'Hullo, Mel.' She turned to Mel almost timidly.

'I'm so sorry to hear about what happened to you. It must have been terrible. But you look well now. Are you feeling better?'

It was enough that Sophie hadn't been waspish with Nick; the last thing Mel had expected from his sister was that she'd be nice to her. 'I'm absolutely fine now,' she said in a rush, wishing she knew how much Magnus had told his daughter. 'It's nice to see you again, and Michael.' She smiled at the whey-faced man with thick glasses standing just behind his wife. 'Isn't this a lovely party?'

Mel expected Sophie to move on then – she had never been any good at sustaining a conversation beyond two or three sentences – but to her further surprise Sophie blushed and dropped her eyes.

'I'm sorry if I was sharp with you in the past,' she blurted out.

'Were you? I didn't notice,' Mel lied.

'I was. I suppose I was a bit jealous because Dad was always talking about you.'

There was nothing Mel could say to that so she just smiled. She wondered if Sophie realised they would soon be sisters-in-law.

'Dad seems very chummy with her now,' Sophie nodded her head towards Helena who was talking animatedly to one of Nick's actor friends. 'I don't know that I like it. I hear she's an alcoholic.'

'Sophie!' Nick exclaimed. 'She isn't and anyway do you have to judge people so harshly?'

'I'm sorry,' she retorted, but her old acid tone was back, probably to stay. 'I can't helping worrying about our father, it's in my nature.'

As Sophie flounced off with Michael following meekly behind, Nick grinned. 'Now there's another person who must've been swopped at birth. She hasn't got an ounce of Mum or Dad in her. Somewhere out on the Yorkshire moors there's a couple of ogres who she really belongs to. Poor old

Michael! I wonder what he did wrong in his previous life.'

As the champagne flowed, so the noise level in the bar rose. Nick had taken Mel around the room introducing her to friends. She'd seen some of them before at Oaklands – a young doctor and his wife, a jeweller and his fiancée – but most were actors.

The ringing of the bar bell made them all turn. Magnus was standing behind the bar with a smile which lit up the room.

'I just want to say a few words,' he said, once everyone was hushed. 'To thank you all for coming tonight and sharing my pride in my son. It came as quite a surprise to me to find he has some talent. There was a time when I worried because he couldn't get the hang of anything useful like bricklaying.' A ripple of laughter broke out at this. 'Now if you'd like to raise your glasses with me I'd like to propose a toast. Not just to Nick, or to the success of *Delinquents* but to all actors and actresses, for their skill at entertaining us and for enriching our lives.' He lifted his champagne glass. 'To Nick, *Delinquents* and the world of entertainment.'

His toast was repeated by everyone, amongst cheering and clapping. More party poppers were fired into the air and Joan Downes was clicking away with her camera.

'Your turn now, Nick,' someone yelled from the back of the bar and the cry of 'Speech' was taken up by everyone.

Nick moved over towards the doors which led onto the garden, took a swig of his drink and grinned broadly. 'I'm not much good at impromptu speeches,' he began. 'I'm used to getting my lines written for me. But I would like to say thank you to all of you for not sleeping during the film or walking out to get a drink. I'd also like to thank my father, not just for this party, but for being such a brilliant dad all these years and for not insisting I became a bricklayer, or even a plumber. Maybe the reviews tomorrow will be so bad that I'll have to ask him for a job as a waiter or groundsman, but I think I should warn him now I drop plates and I can't do stripes in lawns.

'Finally, before you all start yawning, I've got something further to share with you all. Today I asked Mel to marry me. Unless she's changed her mind since seeing me on the screen, she accepted, and we want to get married as soon as possible.'

A barrage of cheering and clapping started and Mel was pushed forward for Nick to kiss her.

But as Nick released her and they turned back to face the cheering group in front of them, Mel knew she'd found far more than a fiancé. She had a real family at last. All the apprehension she'd felt earlier about what that meant vanished at seeing their reaction to Nick's announcement.

Magnus had tears of joy running down his cheeks; he wasn't even attempting to hide them. Miles was perched on a bar stool, smiling so broadly he looked almost ridiculous. Helena's mouth was quivering, her eyes like two dark woodland pools. Even Sophie and Stephen were cheering and clapping with everyone else. As for Joan, she had her face embedded in Antoine's chest, her shoulders heaving.

In the ensuing barrage of congratulations and kisses, no one noticed Magnus slip from the room. Stephen organised more champagne to be opened, Joan tearfully came forward to hug them both, and even the kisses from Sophie and Stephen were warm and sincere.

Then just as Magnus was missed, the door opened wide and he came back in, grinning like a new father. Everyone turned to look at him expectantly.

'An engagement isn't truly possible without a ring,' he said. 'I know Nick probably intended to choose something with Mel tomorrow, but it's my belief this is the one Mel should wear, tonight and forever.'

He held out a single diamond ring.

'This was Ruth's,' he said, his voice trembling and his eyes damp again. 'Both Sophie and Stephen were married before Ruth died and I know she would have liked one of her children to wear it into marriage. I couldn't find a more fitting hand to put it on than Mel's. To me she has always felt like another daughter.'

For a second there was complete silence, as an almost visible current flowed between Magnus, Nick and Mel.

'Are you sure, Dad?' Nick said in a quavering voice.

'Just put it on her finger,' he said huskily.

Nick took the ring and Mel's left hand and slipped it on.

A champagne cork popped like gunshot and wild cheering broke out.

'I love you,' Nick whispered to Mel as he leaned closer to kiss her.

An hour or so later Mel slipped away from the party, into the drawing room. She was a little drunk, the cigarette smoke in the bar was making her eyes sting, and she wanted a few minutes alone.

The party was in full swing, Lena Zavaroni's 'Ma he's Making Eyes at Me' was belting out from the dining room, and all the younger guests were in there dancing, joining in with exaggerated raucous voices. There had never been quite such a noisy party at Oaklands before.

As she left the bar, Nick was deep in conversation with his brother Stephen, Magnus had his head together with Sophie, Helena was talking to a couple of actors and Miles had fallen asleep in an armchair with his head lolling forward onto his chest.

It had been such a perfect evening, all her dreams and hopes coming together, yet for some inexplicable reason she had suddenly felt sad.

To her surprise the fire in the drawing room was still blazing away. Magnus must have built it up expecting people to come in here. It was peaceful and fresh after the noise and smoke in the bar, but she'd expected it to be cool too.

Perhaps it was partly because Ruth's ring was twinkling on her finger, but she felt very much aware of Nick's mother's character as she stood looking around. The calming blues and greens of the decor reflected her love of the countryside, the comfort of the room showed her desire to cosset and protect, even those vast handsewn curtains showed the woman's patience.

Ruth, or so Mrs Downes had told her, never minded guests' children jumping on the furniture and lovingly touched up scratches on the beautiful walnut coffee table without saying a word in complaint. Would she be saddened to find that children seldom come to stay here now? That Oaklands had gone beyond being a family hotel?

There was still a box of toys and jigsaws in the walnut sideboard. Once Mel had taken them out and marvelled at the woman who'd found time to make a complete layette for the baby doll instead of thrusting it away in a tattered old dress as most hotel owners would do. She wished she had known

Ruth. Everything she'd ever heard about her told her they would have been friends.

It was so hot Mel opened the curtains a little and unlocked the French windows to let in some cool air. She looked out for a moment. The small courtyard was lit up outside, but beyond the low ornamental wall that surrounded it, she could see nothing, almost as if a black curtain were hung there. But she could hear the sighing of the wind in the trees and the distant hoot of an owl.

The courtyard was at its best in summer – urns overflowing with flowers, a small fountain playing in the little pool. She could remember dodging the pale mauve tassels of wisteria as she took drinks out to the guests lounging in the sun. But the pool was still and black now, a carpet of fallen leaves covering the ground. It looked as sad as she felt and chilly, so she pulled the door to and moved back across the room to sit by the fire.

Helena came in just seconds later.

'Oh, there you are,' she said, a slightly anxious look clouding her eyes. 'You had me worried for a moment.'

'Just gathering myself,' Mel admitted. 'I love parties, but I got a bit tired of being the centre of attention, and all the questions.'

'I know exactly what you mean,' Helena smiled and perched on the end of the settee across the fire to Mel. 'It's been difficult for all of us tonight – I mean the questions – but much more so for you. You aren't used to having a spotlight turned on you.'

'A shrink would probably say I'm insecure,' Mel grinned sheepishly. 'I go looking for black clouds, even when the sky is blue.'

'Me too,' Helena laughed, tossing her head, her eyes dancing. 'I used to cry buckets when I got one bad review against nine excellent ones. Eventually one has to accept that absolute perfection is extremely rare, perhaps even nonexistent. But what black clouds have you found tonight?'

'None,' Mel admitted. 'I just suddenly felt a bit sad. I don't know why.'

'I do.' Helena gave a rueful smile. 'At the times in our life when we are happiest, our mind often flits back to wishing we could share the moment with someone who for one reason or another can't be there. On the opening night at the Phoenix back in 1945, I can remember feeling absolute joy at the curtain calls, yet deep sorrow that my mother wasn't in the audience. Magnus wished Ruth were here tonight, I'm quite sure Nick did too. Miles said earlier how much Mary would have enjoyed the party.'

'I haven't been wishing anyone else was here, aside from Conrad,' Mel said, not quite understanding what Helena was getting at.

'No?' Helena raised one perfect arched eyebrow. 'What about Bonny?'

'She never even crossed my mind, except to think but for her I wouldn't be having to be so evasive about everything.'

'So she did cross your mind?' Helena looked at Mel, her lips quivering with a smile. 'Maybe you didn't consciously miss her, but it amounts to the same thing. I know I thought how much she would've relished tonight. She would be overjoyed to find you'd become engaged to Nick.'

Mel was deeply touched. It hadn't occurred to her that Helena would continue to cast Bonny in the role of mother, or stop to consider her views on Mel's engagement. 'You think so?'

'I know so,' Helena said and getting up off the arm of the settee she came over to Mel's chair, crouched down in front of her and took Mel's hand between both hers. She looked like an exotic orchid in her flowing green and blue chiffon. 'Just because someone is dead doesn't mean you should shut them out. Of course if Bonny had been here tonight, a few sparks would have flown. But then you know what I mean by that!'

They both laughed in complete understanding. Mel's sadness flew away.

'She would have stolen the show,' she admitted. 'Dressed to kill in something revealing, flirting with every man in sight. She'd probably have rolled back the carpet and given us a tap dance too.'

'I might have joined her.' Helena smiled with affection. 'We had some wonderful times together, Mel, one of these days we must sit down together and I'll tell you them all. I never had as much fun with anyone as I did with Bonny.'

The warmth in Helena's voice moved Mel. 'Why aren't you bitter?'

'Now what have I got to be bitter about?' Helena's eyes widened at the question. 'I regret agreeing to give you to her and John, but if I hadn't, you and I might have had a very hard time. I'm sad too because we couldn't work something out between ourselves so that I shared in your growing-up. I have been angry that Bonny neglected you later on. But I don't feel bitter.'

'But why not? I would if I was in your shoes.'

Helena shrugged. 'I know Bonny loved you. Just the way you are proves that. If you had been a burden to her she would have got in touch with me when John died. I believe her silence then proves that you were the most valuable part of her life.'

'She had a strange way of showing it!'

'Maybe.' Helena reached out and tilted up Mel's chin to look at her. 'But would I have done better? I was in a bad way too remember! Look at you, Mel – you're warm, intelligent and I know from Magnus how resourceful and hard-working you can be.

Can you honestly say none of that was down to Bonny's influence.'

It was Helena's loyalty to her old friend which tugged at some string inside her. Everyone who knew Bonny had maligned her – even Magnus – leaving Mel almost nothing to cling onto. Helena, who had more than enough reasons to hate her, was honest and compassionate enough not only to forgive, but to treasure her memory.

'I ought to get back to the party,' she said a little reluctantly. 'But we must spend some time together soon. I want to hear all your stories, but right now I should be with Nick.'

They both stood up but Helena cupped her two hands around Mel's face, looking right into her eyes. 'We've got the rest of our lives to get to know one another,' she said softly. 'I'm so happy I've found you again, and so delighted at the way you've turned out. That's enough for the moment.'

Something stirred inside Mel, a sensation of warmth melting an icy place inside her. She put her hand tentatively on Helena's cheek and caressed it tenderly. 'Are you going to tell the world I'm your daughter?' It was a bit juvenile to ask such a thing, especially when she wasn't even sure she wanted it herself, and she felt a little embarrassed.

But Helena's wide exuberant smile proved she was more than ready to nail her colours to the mast. 'Oh darling! I want to scream it from the rooftops. I'll call a press conference tomorrow if you'll let me. But the decision about that must rest with you. Your emotions might be too raw still for such a thing.'

Mel's inner reserve broke down at this forthright statement. The icy lump inside her dissolved completely and when Helena drew her into her arms, this time there was no resistance. The spontaneous sweetness of the embrace broke through the barricades as no mere words could. Two bodies and minds fused together out of mutual need as they cried on each other's shoulders.

'Very touching!'

Mel's eyes shot open at the sound of a male voice just feet away from them.

It could have been a workman, entering the door from the courtyard by mistake, a greasy brown flat cap on his head, a dark donkey jacket and mud-splattered trousers. But he was pointing a squat, black gun right at them.

'Edward!' Helena gasped and stiffened, but instead of moving she held Mel even tighter to her.

Mel's legs turned to water. But for Helena holding her she might have collapsed with terror.

'You didn't think I'd give up did you?' He took a step closer to them and waved the gun. 'Move away from her, Helena. Now.'

Mel was incapable of moving, and Helena clutched her tighter, manoeuvring her round so that even though Mel was facing Edward over Helena's shoulder, her body was shielded.

'Put that gun down, Edward!' Helena's voice roared out like a sergeant major. 'You're in enough trouble without this.'

Mel felt as if she was taking part in a weird version of musical statues. 'Baby Love' by Diana Ross and the Supremes was blaring out from the dining room, she could hear laughter out in the hall, but she was motionless, staring into Edward's cold blue eyes, while held captive by Helena who had her back to him. A quick terrified glance at the older woman's face showed that she was actually watching Edward in the mirror over the mantelpiece and was calmly playing for time.

All at once Mel realised why the police had been

at the gate tonight. If she hadn't drawn the curtains back and opened that door onto the garden, Edward would never have been able to pinpoint where she was in the house, much less gain entry.

'Let go of her, Helena, and move away,' his voice rasped, eyes chilling Mel to the bone as he stepped closer still. 'Now, or I'll blow your brains out too.'

'No, Edward,' Helena's voice boomed out. Clearly she hoped she might be overheard. 'Mel's done nothing to you. Shoot me if you must, but I won't let you hurt her.'

Helena's courageous words were all very well, but Mel was terrified that at any moment the door might open and Nick or Magnus walk in. She looked over to the open door onto the courtyard, hoping against hope that a police officer might suddenly appear. But the wind was merely blowing leaves in, and beyond the floodlit strip was inky darkness.

'Edward.' Helena sounded like a reproving old aunt. 'Think about what you are doing! Now why don't you sit down and give me that gun. Then we can talk.'

Mel buried her head in Helena's shoulder, peeping out at Edward in horror. He looked nothing like the impeccably groomed man who'd come to the restaurant. He had dyed his hair and eyebrows dark and he had a small thin moustache which had to be fake. He looked insane now: his face was contorted and twitching, his glassy blue eyes red-rimmed, his nostrils flared. The veins on his neck stood out like ropes and his Adam's apple was leaping up and down in his throat. He had gone far beyond talking to anyone.

'You betrayed me,' he cried out. 'I nursed you, I made excuses for you. I was your friend when you had no one. But you never trusted me enough to tell me about her!' He waved the gun accusingly.

'You let me believe we were coming back to England for a new start, together. But all the time it was just because you wanted to find the kid you gave away to that bitch Bonny.'

Mel felt Helena quivering, but she still held her tightly, inching imperceptibly towards the door. 'I didn't ever tell you about Camellia because it hurt too much. And when I decided to come to England it was to make a new start. You know I've always cared deeply for you. Even now, after all you've done, I still care enough to help you. Put the gun down, Edward, please stop this, for my sake.'

'I've done everything for your sake. I've given my whole life to you. Bonny would have destroyed you if I hadn't silenced her. Look at you now. You won't even turn to face me. You care far more about *her* than me! What have I got to lose by shooting both of you, and whoever comes through that door?'

'Oh, Edward,' Helena cried out. 'Please, please, don't fire that gun!'

'Turn round damn you,' Edward screamed. 'That girl in your arms is just a piece of garbage. She was a cheap hooker and she's only interested in you now because you're famous. She'll never care for you like I did.'

Helena caught hold of Mel's hand, pressing it to her breasts in a silent message to hold on. She took a deep breath. 'How did you get in, Edward?' she asked. Her voice was lighter, almost as if he were just a visitor. Yet at the same time her body seemed to expand sideways to shield Mel still more. 'You must have been very clever to get by the police?'

'They're damn fools every one of them,' he replied with a growl, but for a moment he sounded less tense. 'It was easy enough to come up through the fields and across the garden. I've been round the house dozens of times tonight. They were so busy having a chat and a cigarette, a whole army could have got in.'

Helena pushed against Mel with her knees, edging backwards, closer still to the door. 'Edward, darling – ' she put a little pressure on Mel's right shoulder – 'I'm going to turn round to face you. I want you to think carefully about what you are doing and where it will end.'

Mel knew what Helena wanted, yet her limbs were shaking so much she didn't know if she could do it.

Helena began to turn slowly, pushing Mel round with her so she would face the door. 'Edward I beg you,' she said. 'We've been friends for so many years. I don't want the police to catch you. Please! Go now!'

The door was only three feet away from Mel and the order from Helena was unmistakable.

'Get out the way,' Edward yelled.

'I won't,' Helena's voice rose an octave. 'Go, Edward, if you care anything for me.'

Mel sprang forward, grabbed the knob and tried to turn it.

The loud report from the gun, a smell of cordite and a blow to her head came simultaneously. One moment Mel's fingers were scrabbling with the door knob, the next she was on the floor.

She heard the sound of breaking glass, male voices shouting, but she was more aware that she couldn't move. There was a pain in her head, and she could see nothing. She opened her mouth to scream and it was only when her lips encountered a mass of hair that she realised Helena was lying on top of her, pinning her to the floor.

Stunned and afraid to attempt to move she heard noise coming from all directions – shouting from the hall, loud male voices outside, a woman screaming, the sound of feet running along the terrace, and another loud report from a gun – but over and above all this she heard gasping breath.

'Oh my God! He's shot them both,' she heard Nick shout out from the direction of the French windows, and the floor beneath her seemed to vibrate as he ran to them.

'Gently.' A male voice she didn't recognise spoke. 'Lift her gently.'

As Nick and the uniformed officer slowly lifted Helena from her and light flooded onto Mel's face, the scream of pain and terror that had been stifled earlier came out. Involuntarily her hands moved, one to the pain in her head, the other to the warm, sticky patch on her chest.

She lifted her fingers and saw blood and screamed again.

The whole room seemed to be full of smoke, and through it faces loomed at her.

'Mel, it's me,' Nick's voice cleared the mist a little. 'You're safe now, it's okay. Where are you hurt?'

'I don't know,' she croaked, trying to get him into focus. 'My head.' She lifted it from the floor slightly and saw the huge red blood stain all over her cream dress.

Her heart was beating. Aside from her throbbing head there was no pain. Her legs and arms could move and all at once she realised. It wasn't her blood, but Helena's!

'Don't move,' Nick said, pushing her down, but he was too late. One glance towards Helena lying just a couple of feet away confirmed what had happened. One of the policemen was holding a handkerchief to her chest, thick, deep-red blood seeping out from beneath it, staining the blue and green chiffon. Her face was chalky, her eyelashes and brows standing out in dark relief.

Mel was onto her knees and leaning over Helena

before anyone could prevent it. 'No, Mummy,' she cried out involuntarily. 'No, Mummy, no!'

One of the policemen tried to draw her back, but she saw Helena's lips move and fought him off.

'Are you hurt, darling?' Helena's voice was so faint Mel had to lean right over her to hear what she was saying.

'No, no,' Mel shook her head, her hand smoothing back the dark hair from her mother's face. 'I'm all right, just a bump on the head.'

'What did you call me just now?'

For a moment she didn't understand. All she could see was the policeman vainly trying to staunch the flow of Helena's blood and the dimness of her dark eyes.

Helena's lips moved and Mel remembered. 'Mummy,' she repeated, taking Helena's hand in hers and kissing the fingertips frantically. 'Mummy.'

'That's all I wanted to hear.' Helena's lips moved to smile, her voice just a faint croak. 'I wanted – ' she paused, struggling for breath – 'to tell you so much. I guess Magnus will have to fill in the gaps.' A bubbling rasping sound came from her throat, and blood trickled out of the corner of her mouth. 'I'm so very proud of you.'

Mel saw the light fading in Helena's eyes. Tears gushed from her eyes, falling onto her mother's beautiful, serene face.

'Don't leave me,' she begged. 'I love you. Please don't go!'

'It's my cue.' Helena's lips barely moved. 'I love you, my darling!'

Mel heard her own scream but it seemed to be coming from some far distant place. She was aware of arms lifting her, of both Nick and Magnus's voice trying to calm her, but then a thick black

blanket seemed gradually to enfold her until at last
she was silenced.

Chapter Twenty-Seven

'I can't go, Nick. Please don't force me to,' Mel sobbed. Nick was standing beside the bed looking down at her, ready for Helena's funeral in a dark suit and tie.

She had woken that morning believing she was prepared mentally for it. She'd washed her hair and put on a black wool maxi dress, but as the clock hands moved closer and closer towards the afternoon, panic overtook her.

'You have to go, darling,' Nick said gently, taking her hands and drawing her off the bed. She was very pale and she'd lost weight alarmingly. The black dress accentuated the gauntness of her face and the dark shadows around her eyes. Even her hair hung like a limp dull curtain. 'I know you feel that you just can't take any more, but you have to be there today.'

Mel had been carried up here by Nick, just after the shooting, ten days ago. She hadn't left the room since. Aside from Doctor Searle who had come that night to check her over and give her a sedative, she had refused to see anyone other than the police, Nick and Magnus. Alternating between moments of terror and black depression, she wouldn't even allow anyone to open the curtains. It was a gloomy sanctuary, but it felt safe.

'You don't understand,' she sobbed, struggling with him. 'It's my fault she died. If I hadn't left that door open Edward couldn't have got in. I was so scared I didn't even try and protect her. Could you live with knowing that you were such a coward?'

Ten days ago to the hour, she and Nick had been sitting in the Royal Standard pub by the Cob in Lyme Regis, eating fish and chips for their lunch. She had thought then that she'd stepped into a world where there would be no more heartache. But less than twelve hours later, everything was smashed to pieces. Helena's body was on its way to the mortuary.

Sedatives had brought her long hours of welcome oblivion, but as they wore off, cold reality came back and she relived every moment of those last minutes with Helena, over and over again.

She would be happy to have visions of Edward's death. She'd asked the police to recount exactly how he ran across the lawn to the rockery, chased by one of their dogs, then turned his gun on himself. Nick had said he'd had to drain the pool and waterfall, because it ran bright red with Edward's blood. She wished she'd seen it herself – it would be a far better image to have trapped in her mind than seeing the blood oozing out from Helena's chest and the light slowly leaving her eyes.

Mel was bitter that she'd had so little time with her mother. There were so many questions that would now remain unanswered, so much left unsaid. But the rage inside her was greater still than the bitterness. Helena's early life had been so tough; hardship and tragedy dogged her footsteps. Even when she achieved fame and fortune, it was overshadowed not only by the past, but by packs of jackals feeding on her success.

Mel couldn't understand why when at last the tide seemed to have turned for both of them, and true happiness seemed within their grasp, a huge destructive wave should have come again and dashed them both. She truly wished she'd died beside her mother.

'You aren't a coward – that's a ridiculous thing to say,' Nick retorted. 'Even if you'd calmly let Manning shoot you, do you really think that would have been the end of it?'

'He didn't want to kill Helena,' she sobbed. 'Only me.'

'He'd already shot another woman, just for the keys of her car and she's still seriously ill in hospital,' Nick said evenly. 'There's evidence he killed two other girls in America, just the way he drowned your mother. He had gone totally insane, Mel! The chances are he would have shot you, then Helena, quickly followed by whoever came through the drawing room door next. Now put this jacket on and pull yourself together. You've agonised over all this enough.' He held out the black jacket for her.

'Nick, you don't understand,' she implored him. 'I'm some kind of awful jinx, wherever I go, whoever I get involved with, there's trouble.'

Nick sighed with impatience. He felt deeply for her but it had been the longest, most fraught week in his life. Press had been clamouring at the door, and the telephone hadn't stopped ringing. There were a million and one things to do and he'd had to put his own feelings on hold while he attended to everyone else.

Yet Nick had his own mountain of guilt to live with. He should have anticipated that Magnus would want to throw a surprise party for him, to make up for missing the official launch in London, and with a madman on the loose he should have stopped it. But then he'd compounded his stupidity by bringing Mel back to Oaklands without warning her about Edward.

That night he'd believed he was saving her

unnecessary anxiety, but now it looked rather more like pure selfishness on his part. He'd wanted Mel to shine beside him as he basked in everyone's admiration. At the point when Helena was shot he was pouring himself another large drink, gleefully imagining all the film offers about to come his way. He hadn't even noticed that Mel was no longer in the bar, not until the shot rang out.

More disgraceful still to Nick's mind was that he had rushed down the stairs early the next morning to look at the reviews in the daily papers. What sort of man would care what the critics had to say about his performance in *Delinquents* in the aftermath of such a tragedy? It was painfully ironic that one of the reviewers had complimented him on his 'exquisitely sensitive' performance!

Helena's murder was on the news by lunch-time. The *Bath Chronicle* devoted the first two pages to it in their second edition that day. On Sunday every newspaper in the country had it splashed across their front pages.

When the news first broke that Manning had abducted a girl and attempted to murder her, all the media focus had been on him. Mel wasn't even named. He was intriguing to the press only because of his position as manager to a famous actress. Since going on the run, turning a woman out of her car at gunpoint and subsequently shooting the widow near Bristol, he'd become even hotter news. But once he'd returned to one of Bath's most prestigious hotels, to kill that first victim, but instead murdered Helena, then killed himself, every sharp-nosed journalist in the country sensed there was another story tucked away. It didn't take long for the name Camellia Norton to be leaked.

The newspapers had struck a rich seam of gold. By Monday morning Mel's name was in the headlines, as papers recounted her mother's death in 1965 and revealed the probability that she too had been murdered by Manning. They dug up the story of the events in Chelsea in 1970 for good measure. They had discovered that Bonny and Helena were old dancing partners, and that Sir Miles Hamilton had been instrumental in helping Helena's film career. Not even Magnus escaped their scrutiny. Along with hints that he was Helena's lover, they slanted his background with the implication that he had been a devious and unscrupulous post-war speculator.

Nick, Magnus and Miles met on the Monday evening to discuss what to do. They knew the press would continue with this barrage of half-truths and innuendoes unless they could offer something to defuse them.

Nick was astounded by Miles's courage when he said he intended to prepare a statement for *The Times*. He was stricken with grief at losing Helena, but he took the view that by acknowledging her as his love child, and Camellia as his granddaughter, he could in some way protect Camellia and by association, Nick and Magnus from further scandal.

On Wednesday morning *The Times* printed Miles's statement. Entirely factual, it stated exactly why, how and when everything took place. The only fact omitted was that John Norton had believed Mel to be his child. Copies of it were sent by his secretary to all the other papers with a clear warning that any deviation from the truth would result in libel action.

They were astounded in the days that followed by how each paper treated the same story. The *Mirror* gave it a hearts and flowers touch, the *Sketch* played up the 'tragedy caused by secrecy' angle. When Sunday came round again the *News of the World*'s version made Miles sound like a villainous stage-door Johnny who had deflowered a young dancer and left her and his child to perish in the slums of Stepney.

But Helena's courage in protecting Mel prevented too much being made of her handing over her baby to a friend. She was a tragic heroine, and there was no mileage in laying blame at her door.

Nick read every word written on the subject. He was convinced Miles had done the right thing. But however glad he was that there was no further need for secrecy or lies, either within Oaklands or without, and that Camellia and Miles could now take their rightful places as chief mourners at the funeral, he was still troubled by a shameful inner bitterness that his personal triumphs had been eclipsed. All he could do to purge himself of guilt was to be what everyone needed – comforter, organiser, the rock everyone else could lean on.

But his endurance was at breaking point now. Mel hadn't once asked how he felt or considered he might need comfort too. She had refused to see Miles, and she didn't seem to realise that Magnus was locked into deep grief too. Unless Nick shocked her back into reality she might just wallow in dangerous self-pity forever.

'I won't hear any more of this.' His eyes flashed as he grabbed Mel's arm and stuffed it into the sleeve of her jacket. 'Stop behaving like a child and get a grip on yourself. I don't think you've grasped yet what Helena really did, and it's time you thought about it.'

Mel stopped crying, shocked by his anger.

'She *gave her life* to save you,' he hissed through clenched teeth. 'I dare say she thought Edward wouldn't shoot her, but whatever she thought, she acted purely out of instinct. Don't demean that act by saying you can't cope with her funeral. Miles and my father are grief-stricken too. You aren't the only one. Now pull yourself together.'

His angry words sank in, the first thing to have made any real impression on Mel in the long days since Helena's death. She put her other arm into the jacket without protest.

'That's better,' he said approvingly. 'Now brush your hair.'

She did as she was told, and put on a little lipstick, then the black wide-brimmed hat Nick had been out and bought for her. But even as she went through the motions of obedience, inside a small insidious voice was speaking to her: 'Go along with this today, say goodbye to Helena, but you don't have to live with this guilt. They'll soon get tired of watching you. Tomorrow or the next day you can die too if you want to.'

'And you must speak to Miles today,' Nick added, pleased to see Mel was at last co-operating. 'I don't think you've any idea what he's been through in the last few days. Not just losing Helena, but making that statement to the press.'

Mel stared at Nick.

'Think about it, Mel? He had first to admit to his younger brothers and their families who all adored his wife about his affair with a dancer and the resulting child. Then he had to do it publicly,' Nick said curtly. 'That isn't easy for a man of over eighty, especially one in such a state of shock. But he did it for you, so he could acknowledge you openly and protect you from any further harm.'

Mel's lips quivered. Nick had tried to make her read the newspapers all week, but she'd refused, just as she'd refused to go downstairs, or eat more than a couple of mouthfuls and even open the curtains. She felt ashamed now. Nick was right, she had been behaving like a child.

The bright daylight out on the landing made her

blink. She paused at the top of the stairs, somewhat taken aback to see that everything was just as it had always been. Somehow she'd expected it to look different. Yet it was extremely quiet. Usually there were voices from somewhere, the low buzz of machines in the kitchen, a typewriter tapping or just music in the background.

Nick took her hesitation as further panic. Grasping her arm firmly he led her down the stairs. 'Just take today in stages,' he suggested gently. 'Don't try to look too far ahead.'

Mel was irritated by his patronising tone, coming so soon after his curt words in the bedroom. She shot a sideways look at him, but her sharp retort died on her lips. He looked deeply troubled and tired.

All at once she realised she hadn't kissed him or held him once since the night of the party. She had allowed him to hold her, to tell her he loved her and she had expected him to look after her, but she hadn't considered that he might want reassurance.

'I'm sorry, Nick,' she whispered, taking his hand in hers and turning on the stairs to kiss him. 'I've been forgetting about you, haven't I?'

'I'll remind you in a week or two.' He half smiled wearily. 'Let's just get through today somehow.'

An overpowering, cloying smell of flowers caught them as they turned on the last flight of stairs. Mel looked over the banister and saw wreaths, bouquets and arrangements lined up all along the hall.

'At the last count there were thirty-five,' Nick said. 'There's four times as many at the church. Helena said her fans had forgotten her, but she was wrong.'

Tears started up in Mel's eyes again, but as Magnus came out of the drawing room, she gulped them back.

'Good girl,' he said with a smile, but his eyes were as dead as her heart felt. A black suit and tie looked strange on him, as if he was wearing someone else's clothes. Even his hair was cut short and slicked down. 'Will you go and speak to Miles? He's in there.' He indicated the drawing room.

Mel blanched. She didn't want to go in there ever again.

'Don't be frightened, Mel.' Magnus took a step closer to her, putting both hands on her shoulders. 'You have to see the room again sometime and as for Miles, well he's a brave old man who's lost the dearest person in his life, and he's your grandfather.'

Mel looked into his eyes, and drew just a little strength from the compassion in them. As always Magnus had struck right at the heart of the matter. Miles needed comfort more than anyone. She didn't know why she hadn't realised that before.

Miles was sitting in the same winged chair he'd taken at their first meeting, but as she hesitated in the doorway, he hauled himself up with the aid of his silver-topped cane.

The carpet had been cleaned by professionals, not even a slight discoloration left as a reminder. But the dramatic change in Miles's appearance made her forget that she was walking across the spot where Helena died. It was as if all the padding under his flesh had disappeared, leaving nothing but folds of yellowing skin hanging over his shirt collar.

'Camellia!' he said, his voice tremulous and weak, and he tottered as he took a few steps towards her. 'How are you, my dear?'

'I'm – ' she stopped short. She took off her hat and put it down on the coffee table.

'You've been better?' He tried to smile, but his eyes were bloodshot and weary, and his mouth

736

couldn't manage more than a twitch. 'It was a silly question wasn't it? At my age I should know the right things to say at times like these, but if I ever knew them, I've forgotten.'

Suddenly everything Nick had said upstairs struck home. 'I'm so sorry.' She took the last few steps to him quickly and impulsively put her arms around him. 'I should have talked to you.'

'Oh, Melly, I understand,' he growled in her ear. 'I was afraid to see you too.'

She was just a little surprised by him calling her Melly. But she held onto him tightly; it didn't matter what he chose to call her.

'John and Bonny called you Melly when you were a baby,' he said and his old veined hand smoothed her hair tenderly. 'I found it very confusing then because of Ellie, but now it seems the appropriate name for you.'

A distant memory came sharply into focus. She must have been four or five and she was down at the quay in Rye with her father. He held her tightly by the shoulders as they looked down into a fishing boat. The hold was full of silver fish, many of them still wriggling. 'They are herrings,' he said. 'Some of them will be sold just like that, but the rest they take over to the smoke houses and hang them up till they turn all brown and salty. Then they are called kippers.'

'Why do they give them a different name if they are still the same fish?' she asked.

He swung her up into his arms and kissed her, his moustache tickling her cheeks. 'Well, your name is Camellia, but that's a bit grand sometimes, so I call you Melly.'

'Mummy doesn't like it,' she said. 'She says it sounds common.'

'Mummy thinks kippers are common too,' he laughed. 'But I like Melly and kippers. They are

737

just special names. I eat kippers when I'm away from home, and when I'm out with you on our own, I call you Melly.'

She knew now why Bonny had taken a sudden dislike to that pet name. It had nothing to do with it sounding common – it was just too similar to Ellie for comfort. But things had come a full circle now. This old man was her only living relative and she had to try to fill the place in his life that Helena had vacated.

'I'd like to have a special name for you too,' Mel murmured against Miles's chest. His black suit smelled of mothballs – she wondered if it was the same one he'd worn for his wife's funeral. 'I can't call you Smiley, it doesn't seem right anymore.'

He didn't reply for a moment, just rubbed his cheek against her hair and held her.

'There's always Grandpa,' he said.

Mel sat in the middle of the seat in the funeral car, Miles to her right and Nick on the left and she held each of their hands tightly. Magnus was in the car behind with Joan, Antoine and Julie, the chambermaid. There were nine or ten private cars following behind, some people from Helena's film set, others club members who had met Helena here at Oaklands. All the other mourners would be going straight to the church in Kelston. The sun reflected off the highly polished hearse in front of them making dazzling prisms of light. It seemed wrong that it should be shining so brightly. Mel couldn't see the coffin for flowers.

Slowly they moved off, up the slight slope past the covered swimming pool, and on through the woods to the gates. There were few leaves left on the trees now and those that fluttered down as they passed felt like a final tribute to Helena.

As the car drove slowly down Widcombe Hill,

the spectacular view of Bath reminded Mel of the first time she saw it. She had gasped then with astonishment at the beauty before her, a city built of dull, golden stone, rising in tiers around the Abbey, as splendid as it must have been in the days when the rich came to take the waters.

She felt that morning that this was where she belonged. Even now, after all that had happened, she still felt it.

'Lovely isn't it,' Miles said gruffly. 'Helena said she felt she'd come home when she got here.'

Mel squeezed his hand. He was crying silently, big tears rolling down his cheeks. 'She had come home,' she whispered. 'And now she can stay forever.'

People stood and gawped as the cortège made its way slowly through the town, but the driver took the route through the quieter streets up past Victoria Park and out through Weston village.

Mel felt a lump rising in her throat as they drove along the winding road to Kelston. It was a route of sensational views at every turn: steep green hills to her right, and on her left, way below, the river meandering through green fields. She knew Helena had wanted to make a permanent home here, if not in the thatched cottage at Kelston then somewhere nearby. Magnus had said she'd joked that as this was a place where time appeared to stand still, maybe she wouldn't grow old and doddery – that she could learn all those things she'd never had time for, like baking cakes and making jam and finding out which were weeds and which were flowers.

They had to stop for a herd of cows meandering along the road. The farmer looked round in alarm as the church bell began to toll, hastily shooing the cows into the field, then took off his hat and stood with bowed head as the cortège passed.

On any other day in Kelston, one would be surprised to see more than two or three people. But today a phenomenal crowd had congregated: mourners in dark clothes, local people hoping to see some famous faces, banks of reporters and police trying to control the crowd and direct where cars were parked.

'Jackals,' Miles snarled as a reporter lunged in front of their car to take a photograph. 'Have they no respect?'

Every pew in St Nicholas's Church was full, scores more people standing reverently at the back. Banks of flowers detracted from the cold grey stone, their perfume filling the air and their beauty matching Helena's.

As Nick led Mel and Miles into the front pew, she saw Conrad in the one behind. The doleful eyes behind his thick spectacles, the severe haircut and dark suit poignantly reminded her that he had adored Helena long before Mel even knew she existed. Somehow it helped to know that everyone in this church was linked by a mutual loss.

The men from the film crew carried in the coffin on their shoulders, placed it on the trestles before the altar and filed into their seats. Mel glanced behind her, stunned by the sheer number of people, all unknown to her. In uniform dark clothes it wasn't possible to separate fans from directors, actors and actresses, or even those who'd flown over from Hollywood from those who'd known Helena as a young girl here in England.

Mel joined in the hymns, the twenty-third Psalm and the prayers dry-eyed, and locked in grief, unable to see anything more than the coffin just a few yards from her. But as the vicar took his place in the pulpit Miles took her hand in his.

She had noticed nothing more than the vicar's voice until now – melodious, and deep with just a trace of a West Country burr. Now she saw he was elderly, small and plump with a shock of white hair and pale-blue gentle eyes.

'Compared with most of you here today, I had only known Helena a short time,' he began, resting his hands on the balustrade of the pulpit. 'I met her here in this church and called on her twice at her home. In the light of this brief acquaintance, it might seem presumptuous that I ask you to put aside your grief and see today's service as a celebration of Helena's life, but I believe that is what she would have wanted.' He paused, looking down at the upturned faces below him.

'Helena Forester was a great actress and singer, who gave pleasure to millions of people throughout the world through her many films. But today I want to take you away from the glitter of Hollywood and speak of the woman, not the big star.'

Mel felt a slight shift in the congregation, almost as if they'd settled back into the pews to hear a story. They were so quiet and still she could hear the many candles spluttering.

'Helena was born in London's East End, brought up in the dressing rooms of a theatre where her mother was a dresser. During the war she faced more hardship than many of us can possibly imagine. Her mother was killed in the Blitz and at the age of thirteen Helena was scrubbing out offices to pay for her keep with her aunt. When this aunt was blinded and her back broken in a doodlebug raid, Helena had to fend for herself.

'I have received a great many telephone calls and letters in the past week from people who knew Helena back in the forties. Many of them were from fellow entertainers – comedians, magicians, singers and dancers – mostly too old, sick or too far away to attend today. But they all felt compelled to share with me their memories of this talented young girl who had performed with them. Helena paid her dues in the entertainment world first by singing in a Soho nightclub, then singing and dancing in revues, variety shows and pantomimes all over the country, before she reached the West End theatres. Throughout all these often humorous heart-warming stories set in a background of hardship and appalling living and working conditions, one thing shone out above everything else – Helena's character.

'She had a big heart. Always the comforter, the shoulder people cried on. A funny girl with a golden voice, who took joy and sadness in her stride, never complaining, steadfast in her fierce ambitions. She was a loyal friend. Many of you here today have told me how she never broke a promise or breached a confidence. But above all else, Helena was courageous.'

The vicar's voice filled each corner of the ancient church. A shaft of sunshine danced down through a stained-glass window and came to rest on a marble statue of the Virgin Mary.

'That courage was put to the ultimate test last week, and proved beyond all doubt when she risked her own life to protect her daughter, Camellia. It is a terrible tragedy that Helena died, and she will be missed by all of us, yet the nobility of her purpose must lift us beyond grief and fill our hearts with love and admiration for her.'

Mel's eyes filled with tears. Both Magnus and Nick had made similar statements, but here in this little church, hearing them from a stranger, they struck through to her heart.

'Banish any feelings of guilt you may have.' The

vicar looked directly at Sir Miles and Mel. 'To feel guilt is to demean the sacrifice Helena made so willingly.

'I ask that you join me now in a prayer to celebrate Helena's life. To remember her with love and pride, with gratitude that you were privileged to have known her and above all to honour her courage.'

It was over. The coffin was lowered into the grave, prayers were said and slowly the crowd began to disperse. So many damp eyes, so many hands held out to Mel and Sir Miles in silent understanding and from others emotional words of heartfelt condolence.

The press had been kept at bay by police outside the small churchyard and they'd gone now.

Miles looked exhausted – not an impressive peer of the realm now, but a tired old man swaying on his feet. He had wept openly throughout the burial, but afterwards he'd bravely dried his eyes and spoken to the many people who came up to him. Nick and Mel took his arms and led him back to the waiting car.

Just as she was about to get in beside her grandfather, she glanced back across the churchyard. Magnus was standing by the grave alone, his head bent to his chest, his shoulders heaving.

'You go with Miles, Nick,' she said, putting one hand on his arm. 'Take Mrs Downes in this car. I'll stay for a minute with Magnus and come back in the other car.'

Nick looked back at his father and his heart swelled up with pain for him. He remembered seeing Magnus like that when his mother died, not knowing what to do or say to comfort him. He had a feeling that Mel would know.

She joined Magnus silently at the grave. He was

holding the cards from the flowers in his hands. Always the one person who thought ahead, he'd collected them up for Mel, afraid rain might wash away the messages. Tears rolled unheeded down his cheeks, a terrible forlorn cry of anguish coming from deep in his chest.

The sun was sinking now behind a big yew tree, casting a pink light on the hundreds of flowers and wreaths which concealed the mound of earth ready to cover Helena. A man was standing back by the church, a shovel in his hand, discreetly looking the other way. In the distance she could hear the sounds of cars being started, but here there was absolute quiet aside from Magnus's sobs.

She knew then that he had fallen in love with Helena, and that he'd allowed himself to dream of them sharing a life together. He held himself responsible for Helena's death, just as she and Nick had. But now in a moment of clarity and shared pain, Mel knew that none of them were to blame.

'Come away now,' she said gently as his sobs subsided, slipping her arms round his waist and holding his head against her shoulder.

'Oh, Mel,' he sighed. 'What is there now?'

The wind was cold, whipping round her legs and fluttering the skirt of her black dress. She could remember asking herself that same question when Bee died. She knew now that time did heal all wounds.

'There's you, me, Nick,' she whispered. 'And Sophie and Stephen. Maybe soon you'll have grandchildren. We'll hold Helena in our hearts forever. She isn't gone.'

He straightened up then, wiping his sleeve across his eyes. 'It was picking up these cards that started me off,' he said, holding them out to her. 'So many loving messages. Yet I never said to her what was growing in my heart.'

'Some things don't have to be said,' she said simply. 'Some of the sweetest memories are just a special look, a brush of the hand. She'll know what lies behind our tears and our silences.'

He half smiled. 'I just wish –'

'No.' Mel stopped his words with one finger on his lips. 'No wishes or if onlys. Helena wouldn't want that. As the vicar said, we have to celebrate her life and honour it, thank her too for bringing us back together. Maybe in a week or two we can think of some way to do that properly.'

'You're right, of course,' he sniffed and then put his arm round her shoulder. 'You know even if Helena hadn't finally told us she was your mother, I would have guessed eventually. You are becoming more like her every minute. But we must get back to Oaklands – everyone else will be there by now.'

After the cold wind in the churchyard it was good to be back in the warm. Mrs Downes had called in several local women to get things ready while they were all at the church, and they'd built up the fire in the drawing room and laid out a buffet in the bar.

Mel felt a wave of panic as she walked in with Magnus and Antoine. Except for Conrad, almost everyone there was a stranger to her. She didn't think she could speak to anyone.

'It's okay.' Nick saw her stricken face and came forward with a glass of brandy for her. He took her jacket and hat from her. 'They are just people who cared for your mother. They all understand you aren't up to talking much.'

Conrad came forward first, silently holding out his arms, his mournful face showing just how much he felt for her.

'You poor darling,' he said hoarsely as he

hugged her. 'If I'd known this was going to happen I'd have torn my heart out before showing you that newspaper.'

For a moment she hugged him back wordlessly. She wanted to apologise for not returning his many calls in the last week, for not acknowledging the beautiful letter he'd written, and yet she knew he understood about that dark world she'd fallen into. 'Please don't regret anything, Con,' she whispered against his shoulder. 'You taught me to accept fate, and that's what this is. I'm so very glad I met Helena, even if our time together was so short. And so very glad that I have you as a friend.'

They talked for a little while, about the restaurant, her engagement to Nick, and his role in *Delinquents*, then Mel felt compelled to go and speak to other people. 'I'll come back to you later,' she said, pressing his hand in hers. 'You mingle too, there are plenty of people here who loved Helena's films as much as you, especially Miles – he'll be pleased to talk to you again.'

It wasn't the ordeal she'd expected. Nick was right, they were just people who cared, and by circulating and having a few words here and there, gradually she found she was building up a picture of who everyone was and what Helena meant to them.

The statuesque redhead, hands laden with rings, was Suzanna Ashleigh from Louisiana, an ex-dancer who had worked with Helena in Hollywood. She greeted Mel with unexpected warmth.

'Helena was a real pal to me when I first arrived in Hollywood,' she confided, in her languorous Southern drawl. 'I was one of those dumb broads they used to call starlets. No talent, just a good body and a pretty face. She always said I reminded her of her Aunt Marleen, and she used to tell me these stories about Marleen's fancy men. She called them Spivs. There was a hidden warning in those tales, a sort of, "listen to me girl or you'll end up washed up in some trailer park". Gee, without her around I would've got in deep trouble too! She was one of the biggest stars at MGM then, but she never showed off. Ya know she lent me one of her evening dresses once. It was gorgeous, white chiffon, made by Myna Lowe, the dame who made a lotta Ginger Rogers's clothes. I was going to a big party and I wanted to look a sensation. Well I looked a sensation all right, but I had one too many martinis and somehow ended up in the pool with it on. The dress was ruined and I thought she'd kill me. But guess what she said when I finally got around to owning up?'

Mel smiled. She liked the woman's frankness. 'Last time I lend you a new dress?'

Suzanna laughed. 'The hell she did! No, she said "Well did you have a good time?" I said I did, but I was real sorry about her dress. She said, "Well, that's all that counts. If I had as many good times as I have dresses, maybe I wouldn't need a shrink." ' Suzanna stopped short and looked a little embarrassed. 'I guess I shouldn't have said that, honey.'

'Yes, you should,' Mel retorted. 'She told me about that, she didn't make a secret of it.'

'Well, all I can say it was a damned shame she kept you a secret,' Suzanna said. 'But I guess that was why she always seemed so sad.'

Rupert Henderson, Helena's young co-star in *Broken Bridges* had no humorous stories to tell. As he spoke of acting with Helena he was struggling not to cry. His angelic choirboy face, soulful brown eyes and storm of blond ringlets were enough to make a woman of any age want to mother him.

'She was such a great actress.' He bit his lip and tried hard to smile. 'But she was a lovely woman too, so generous with her praise, so patient and kind.'

Nick had told Mel a great deal about him. They had crossed paths many times at auditions, and Nick said Rupert was as conceited as he used to be. But he didn't come across as at all conceited to her. He was truly distressed.

'She made it all so easy,' he said wistfully. 'She explained to me all the emotions a woman of forty would feel falling for a lad half her age. The terrible fear of being out of control and of being hurt, the anxiety that her body is past its best and the jealousy when her lover looks at girls his own age.'

Mel guessed he had been a little in love with Helena. She wondered if he had anyone he could shared his grief with. 'What will happen to the film now?' she asked.

He shrugged. 'I don't know, nothing's been decided. All our big scenes together are in the can already, but there's still the whole bit to do when she finds her lover has another younger girlfriend, and her revenge. There was some talk about altering the storyline – something like her being disfigured in an accident, so we can get a stand-in, but I don't like the idea of that.' He broke off, blushing, realising how tactless he'd been.

'I don't think Helena would mind that,' Mel soothed him. 'I think she'd even see the black humour in it.'

'You are very like her.' He ran his eyes over Mel appraisingly. 'Not in looks so much, more your direct manner. I'm glad I met you. Perhaps we could meet for a drink sometime and talk about her.'

Mel guessed Nick wouldn't like that, although she knew Rupert wasn't asking for a date. 'Maybe,' she said. 'I don't know whether I'm going back to

London or staying here. I expect it's the same for you.'

As the day slipped into early evening, Mel found she was moving out of the hopelessness she'd felt for the past week, just by speaking to all these people. Many of them had worked closely with Helena. Some like Suzanna had reason to feel indebted to her, others told her funny stories which gave a different insight into her mother's character from the things Miles or Magnus had told her previously.

A relaxed atmosphere had crept into the room, perhaps aided by the drinks Magnus plied them with and the warm fire. The women had taken off their hats. One sat on a settee beside Miles with her legs tucked beside her as she chatted to him. Conrad was squatting on a stool in front of an elderly woman who'd apparently been a magician's assistant, and toured with Helena and Bonny right back in the 1940s.

Miles and Nick were perfect hosts, getting drinks, urging people to eat, circulating and making sure no one was left alone. Although they often came to check that Mel wasn't overtiring herself, mostly they kept their distance, perhaps realising she needed to hear all these stories alone.

Helena was tough and single-minded. She could do a scene in one take where other actresses took nine or ten to get it right. She was a faultless mimic and often had the whole cast in stitches with her imitations of everyone from breathless starlet to director. She always had time for her fans, never refusing to give an autograph and there were many actors and actresses, who but for her support and kindness might have given up the profession for good.

But again and again Mel heard how Edward manipulated her.

'I never liked the man,' Stanley Cubright, the director of *Broken Bridges*, stated emphatically. 'I wasn't a director back in those days when Helena first came to Hollywood, just a camera man, and I guess I was annoyed that she got some dude over from England who knew nothing about filming to be her manager. But right from the start he dominated her, made her think she couldn't trust anyone.'

'But she had other friends didn't she?' Mel had heard at least a dozen friends mentioned today.

'She had plenty on the set,' Stanley said with some bitterness. 'She liked to mix with the crew and the dancers, she felt easy with them, but Edward soon put a stop to her meeting them socially. We had no "class" you see. He organised her private life and unless he felt that a dinner or cocktail party would further her career in some way, he declined invitations for her. But you gotta understand honey that in those days, guys like me didn't dare speak out for fear of losing our jobs. He was ruthless. Know what I mean?'

Mel nodded. No doubt in Hollywood Edward's essential English gentleman act, coupled with a little covert homosexual activity had opened many doors for him. He began to enjoy having power.

'I suppose he thought unless he kept her on a tight lead he might be dumped, and then he'd be no one again,' she sighed. 'But everything I know about Helena suggests that she'd have remained loyal to him anyway. Why couldn't he have settled for just having a good time by her side?'

'He didn't know what a good time was,' Stanley chuckled. 'Not in the sense you or I understand it. We used to call him "the Butler".'

Mel smiled. 'I thought he looked like a Nazi! I

still don't really understand why Helena allowed him to get so close in the first place.'

'I read somewhere that our friend is our need answered,' Stanley said. 'Helena needed a family, and Edward became it. Brother, sister, ma and pa. He was a good-looking dude, and to be fair to him, he stood by her when she had her problems. But he always worried me, honey. Word got out he used to cruise the downtown bars. We used to hear whispers of stuff you don't like to think about. You know what I mean?'

Mel nodded. She knew exactly.

'Don't dwell on it.' Stanley patted her on the shoulder comfortingly. 'That priest said it all this afternoon – let's celebrate Helena's talent, charm and her courage, and put the rest aside. In a month or two I'll call you up to see the film we've got in the can. It will make you cry, but they'll be tears of pride. I promise you.'

Chapter Twenty-Eight

On the twelfth of December, just weeks after the harrowing events of October, St Nicholas's Church at Kelston was once again full of people. But this time there were no mournful faces or dark clothes. Hamiltons to one side, Osbournes to the other, brightly coloured frivolous hats, beaming smiles and whispers of joyful anticipation.

Nick and Conrad in grey morning suits stood side by side at the altar rail waiting nervously. The church was ablaze with candles, garlands of holly and ivy festooned the end of each pew, and banks of vivid poinsettia, scarlet carnations and the heady smell of pine brought Christmas and the awaited wedding together.

'Ready?' Conrad whispered as the first notes of the wedding march wheezed out from the organ.

'As I'll ever be,' Nick grinned. 'Have you got the rings?'

Reverend Matthews, the vicar of Kelston, had encouraged Nick and Mel to go ahead with their original plan of getting married before Christmas. He had visited Mel at Oaklands a few days after the funeral and since then they had met often to talk. He felt that it was by no means always right to delay wedding plans out of respect for the dead. He pointed out that Sir Miles was growing increasingly frail, and that a happy occasion might very well help him through his grief, giving him something else to focus on.

Nick was overjoyed when Mel finally agreed to go ahead. In the first week or two after the funeral she had been unpredictable. Sometimes she disappeared for hours, without telling anyone where she was going; other times she seemed too jovial. On several nights she'd woken screaming from a terrible nightmare, going over and over all that had happened, but the next day had been so withdrawn he couldn't reach her. She went up to help Conrad in Fulham for a few days and when she returned she was calmer, much more like her old self. It was then she agreed to the wedding.

But it was sharing with Magnus in making the wedding arrangements which brought happiness back into Oaklands. Once laughter had been heard coming from Magnus's office as the two of them compiled a guest list, everyone of the staff perked up. Antoine baked the cake, a huge three-tier one. Joan Downes organised a spring clean and suddenly there was excitement in the air, driving out the gloom and despondency.

Mel had so much to do, her panic attacks all but disappeared. Magnus had some purpose again, striding around with lists, barking out orders in his old manner. Miles became a regular visitor, staying for days on end and allowing all the staff to pander to his every little whim.

Nick had asked Conrad to be his best man. Although they hadn't known each other long, there was already a strong bond between them. Now he was here in the church, awaiting the moment when Mel would sweep up the aisle on Miles's arm, and he felt as excited and happy as a child at Christmas.

It was so good to see family on both sides of the aisle. The Hamiltons had turned out in force in a show of solidarity for Miles: his two younger brothers, with their wives, children and grandchildren. On the Osbourne side were Sophie and

Michael, Stephen and June, and half a dozen cousins Nick hardly knew.

Further back were a handful of friends: some actors, some old members of staff and a few old friends of Helena's they'd got to know at the funeral. But more important to Mel was the sight of Jack Easton's stocky figure and flame-red hair and Bert Simmonds's kindly face and broad shoulders. Both men had written warm, compassionate letters soon after Helena's death, offering Mel their support and affection. Their presence here today meant so much to her. They stood for links with Bonny and John, and for her they completed the family circle.

A gasp from behind him made Nick turn, and his eyes prickled at the first sighting of Mel in her wedding dress, framed in the church door, holding her grandfather's arm. Conrad looked first at Mel then back to Nick, his eyes glinting behind his glasses. 'She didn't change her mind then,' he whispered.

As Mel stepped forward to Nick's side at the altar rail, he trembled. She had never looked so beautiful, the simple white velvet dress enhancing her olive skin, dark eyes shining through the delicate veil, her hair pinned up with a garland of rose buds and gypsophila, her lower lip quivering with emotion.

The bell that had tolled so mournfully that day in October, now rang out in joy as Nick took Mel's arm and led her outside to be bombarded with confetti.

It was a cold crisp day, the churchyard trees gaunt without their foliage, but the sun shone weakly and the happy faces and bright wedding finery made the small churchyard as colourful as high summer.

'Happy, Mrs Osbourne?' Nick asked, his dark blue eyes gleaming with delight.

'Extremely, Mr Osbourne,' she replied, lowering her eyes like a Victorian bride. 'I would go as far as to say this might turn out to be the happiest day of my life.'

Mel slipped upstairs at seven that evening to take off her wedding dress. All the guests had left now, aside from Miles and Conrad who were staying the night. They had arrived back at Oaklands from the church just before twelve and the reception had gone on until five when the Osbournes' coach arrived to take them back to Yorkshire. The Hamiltons had drifted off soon after, back to Hampshire, followed later still by the other guests.

Tomorrow she and Nick would be flying off to New York for a brief honeymoon. Their real honeymoon would be in Rome in the New Year.

Sitting down at the dressing table she took off her veil and headdress, glad of a few moments alone. Her wedding had been all she hoped for and more. It really had been the most wonderful day in her life, despite the attack of nerves she'd had earlier.

She smiled at herself. It had all been so silly really, but at the time it had seemed like a warning to abandon the wedding. A dream had started it, and as Nick was sleeping at a friend's flat for propriety's sake, she'd had no one to turn to.

She had dreamed of the figures of a bride and groom on a wedding cake, and a huge knife coming down between them. In the early hours, before it was even light, she'd sat up at the window and cried, afraid that all the trials she and Nick had been through had created an illusion of love. She cried too for all the people she'd cared about in the past and lost. Later she picked up the photograph of herself and Bee and that brought on new tears.

But now twelve hours later all sadness and anxiety had left her. She had a huge family: dear kind people who had welcomed her with all their hearts. Tomorrow she would be setting off to New York, her passport bearing her new name, a suitcase full of new clothes and a whole new adventure about to begin as Mrs Osbourne.

She stood up and slipped off her wedding dress, fleetingly wondering if one day her daughter might choose to wear it too. She smiled at herself in the long mirror. She looked naughty in the white lacy basque and stockings and not a bit virginal, but tonight she would play the part for Nick.

As she stepped into the long flowing red crushed-velvet dress she'd bought for tonight, the colour and fabric reminded her fleetingly of the tunic and shorts she'd worn that first night in the Middle Earth club. She'd changed so much since those days, yet she had few real regrets now. She had experienced so much more than most girls her age – a lot of heartache, but a great deal of fun too. It was better to go into marriage knowing what she did. One day she'd tell her children all about it. 'Well, maybe an edited version,' she giggled to herself.

It was so good to have seen Bert Simmonds today and to find that the images locked in her mind of that kind, caring man were all real. One day she'd go back to Rye, stay in the Mermaid Inn with Nick and walk down the High Street on his arm holding her head high.

'We do a pretty good wedding here at Oaklands,' Magnus said an hour later as he stretched out luxuriantly in an armchair. 'Even if I have to say it myself! There's usually someone who upsets a few people, but they were all remarkably well behaved. A better class of guest you see.'

Nick and Mel both laughed. It was good to see Magnus relaxed again and making jokes. They were on the settee together, Mel lying with her head on Nick's lap. Miles was sitting opposite Magnus by the fire, Conrad in another chair beside them.

'That chap Easton looked a little uneasy I thought,' Miles said. 'Your Aunt Gertrude asked him what connection he had to Camellia and he didn't know what to say.'

'Well, childhood-sweetheart-of-the-bride's-other-mother is a little hard to say,' Nick laughed. He knew Miles found it a little odd that Mel had invited Jack, but then Miles was an old man and his prejudices ran deep. He seemed to have forgotten that Magnus was an old love of Bonny's too. 'Especially to someone as deaf as Aunt Gertrude. I was very glad he came, he's a good man. Did you see the canteen of cutlery he gave us?'

'It's so wonderful,' Mel enthused. 'I never thought I'd ever own proper silver cutlery. But even better was the letter he gave me that he'd been holding onto from Lydia Wynter. Imagine her leaving me six thousand pounds?'

It wasn't the size of the legacy which thrilled her, so much as Lydia's warm words, and the knowledge that she had cared so deeply about Bonny and her child.

'For richer and richer,' Nick smiled down at her, stroking her forehead. They had heard from Helena's lawyers in Los Angeles. Once everything had been sorted out Mel would be inheriting everything from her too. 'Just think – last night I thought I was marrying a girl with a few bob in a post office book. Now I discover she's an heiress.'

'That must have been quite a shock to you, my

dear,' Miles said gently. 'Though the nicest kind. I met Lydia you know at Bonny and John's wedding. She was a gracious, fine-looking woman and one I thought had a strong moral code. I'm pleased to discover I was correct. How very sensible she was to entrust Easton to hold onto your legacy until you were of a sensible age.'

'You know nothing much about the past bothers me now,' Mel said thoughtfully. 'It was wonderful to see Bert Simmonds too. It rounded everything off just perfectly.'

She looked across at Conrad, expecting that remark to spark off questions. He had such a fascination for family intrigues and all the time she and Bert were talking earlier, he'd been watching her intently. But to her surprise Conrad didn't even appear to be listening. He looked as if he was off on another planet.

'What's up, Con?' she asked. 'I thought you'd want to know what the gossips are saying in Rye?'

He blushed, right down to his neck, his eyes blinking furiously behind his specs.

'Come on, out with it,' she said, suddenly realising that he had been uncharacteristically quiet for the last couple of hours. 'Is there something wrong back at the restaurant?'

'No, it's dull and boring, but doing okay,' he said reluctantly. 'I'm sorry if I was miles away, but you see I've had something else on my mind.'

'Well, tell us,' Mel said.

'I can't, not now. I want to ask you something, but it's too impudent.'

Mel laughed and sat up straight. 'Impudent! You and me are old chums, you can ask whatever you like, within reason.'

'Yes, come on,' Nick encouraged him. 'As Dad used to say when I was a nipper, don't be afraid of the gold braid.'

Conrad smiled, but he still looked very unsure of himself. 'It's about Helena. Ever since Miles broke the news about you all, I've heard people saying they'd like to know the whole story. As you can imagine it's been hard for me not to reveal I know the complete, unedited version and I've spent a great deal of time thinking about every aspect of it.' He paused, looking nervously at Mel.

'Go on,' she urged him. 'You aren't going to ask if you can sell it to the *News of the World*?'

He looked indignant. 'Jesus, Mel! You know I wouldn't dream of doing that. But the more I've thought about it, the more aware I've become of just how dramatic it is.'

'You want to write it?' Mel grinned. 'You do! Don't you?'

'Not a newspaper story,' he shook his head and wrinkled his nose in disgust. 'No, I meant more of a biography.'

Magnus snorted, it was hard to say whether in disgust or approval, and Conrad blushed again.

'I know it's impertinent when there's hundreds of well-known biographers out there who'll come asking. But at least you can trust me to write it truthfully with some sensitivity.'

Miles sat bolt upright in his chair, looking straight into Conrad's eyes.

Magnus smiled and took a sip of his drink. He knew Miles had good reason to be wary of journalists, and he probably felt much the same way about biographers.

Nick put his arm around Mel's waist and held her, almost as if he expected her to spring out of her chair in indignation.

There was absolute silence for a moment, while everyone's eyes turned to Mel.

'I can't actually think of anyone more suitable to write it,' she said at length. 'You've seen every film.

You know so much detail about her Hollywood days. But I think Miles is the one to decide, not me. Grandpa, what do you think?'

Miles turned to smile at Mel, as he did every time she called him Grandpa. 'Someone will write it one day, with or without my consent,' he said with a shrug. 'Better this lad who adored Helena, and cares about you, Melly. I'll probably be pushing up the daisies before it's finished anyway.'

'Don't say that, Grandpa. I'm counting on a few years of your company,' she replied. 'And if Con is to do it, he'll want help from you about Polly. What do you think, Nick?'

'Helena thought Con was a good sort,' Nick said, drawing Mel back closer to him until her head was resting on his chest. 'I think she'd approve. But we have to consider everyone else. I assume Con will give Dad and me a mention?'

'I wouldn't have to write about Magnus and Bonny,' Conrad said hastily. 'I could just say you were a friend of John Norton.'

'How do you feel about it, Magnus?' Mel asked.

'I'm a great believer in nepotism.' His eyes twinkled. 'For my part I'd rather have Con do it than some ferret with an eye for sensationalism. But she was your mother, Mel. Ultimately the decision has to lie with you.'

Mel thought for a moment or two. An image of herself and Bonny came to her – they were running along Camber Sands hand-in-hand, laughing and singing as they jumped over tiny waves. She had put her wedding bouquet on Helena's grave before they left the churchyard this morning and it had reminded her there was nowhere to place any flowers for Bonny. But Bonny would much rather be immortalised in a book than have a few flowers wilting somewhere for her.

Con could spin word-pictures so clear they

jumped off the page. He'd make the funny things sing, the sad parts really moving. With his sharp understanding of human nature he'd bring every character to life. It would be a wonderful thing to pass on to her children and grandchildren.

'Yes, Con. You can go ahead, but with one proviso.'

'Whatever you say.'

'Bonny is to be treated with the same sensitivity as Helena.'

Nick was surprised by this request. He moved round on the seat so he could see Mel's face. It was as serene as it had been in church today.

'She loved me,' she said simply. 'All the trickery and lies were separate. Helena made me see that before Edward surprised us. I learned to love Helena in those last few minutes with her, but I loved Bonny from birth.'

Magnus frowned. He looked to Mel, then Nick, then back to Mel. 'You sound as if you've found one of your missing pieces.'

'Do you remember likening Bonny to a beautifully wrapped parcel?' she asked Magnus.

He smiled. 'I never got to the bottom of the wrapping,' he said wryly.

'I think I have,' she said softly. 'I think the file of letters was intended to be the final piece.'

Everyone looked puzzled.

'I could never understand why she kept those letters,' Mel said, looking at them each in turn. 'But the reason came to me when Grandpa found a few letters from Bonny to Helena up in the cottage. In the same way Helena couldn't bring herself to destroy all evidence of giving me to Bonny, Bonny hung on to those letters from Magnus, Miles, Jack and Helena. She wanted me to see them one day. I'm sure of that now. Not then, not without her

761

explaining the rest of the story, but she kept them for me.'

She leaned back against Nick. 'Bonny didn't expect to die young. She sailed through life intending to put everything right, one day.'

'Who of us is ever quite prepared for death?' Magnus smirked. 'I go to bed nightly intending to put my affairs in order, but I haven't done it.'

'Exactly. That night when Edward was chasing after me, I kept thinking how much I still had to say to Nick, to Magnus, and to you, Con.'

Magnus nodded. 'I take your point. The Bonny I knew couldn't have imagined getting ill or dying.'

Mel sighed. 'Bonny had a great many flaws, but I've read those loving letters she sent to Helena before they fell out. There's such detail about me, each tooth, each word, what I weighed and ate. There was one which explained why they moved from Somerset to Rye: she felt guilt pressing in, always afraid she might meet someone from the nursing home where I was born. Yet she had so much compassion for Helena too. The woman who later drank herself stupid, who spent all the money and forgot even to buy food was as unhappy and lonely as Helena was herself.

'I'm sure she did write to Helena when I was older to try and make things up, and that Edward intercepted the letter. I suspect that he conned Bonny, just as he conned me. Maybe he promised that he'd take the two of us to America. Maybe that was why she seemed so happy and excited in those last few weeks, because she believed she was putting everything right at last.'

'And she trusted the wrong person,' Nick said thoughtfully.

'I had an argument with her not long after I'd turned fifteen. Amongst other things I asked her why she gave me a ridiculous name like Camellia.

You see other kids always called me Camel or Cami-knickers. That afternoon when I got home from school, she insisted that I was to go out with her. She didn't take me very far, just to a road a few hundred yards away. There in a garden was this beautiful bush smothered with white flowers.'

'A camellia?' Magnus smirked.

'Yes. She said she'd named me that because it was the most beautiful thing she could think of, and so was I as a baby. She promised me that one day people would say it suited me.'

'She was quite right,' Nick said. 'It does, perfectly.'

Mel shrugged. 'I know now that it was Helena's choice, not Bonny's, but that doesn't matter. What does matter is the way they shared me in those early days, the strong bond of love between them. That's what the name represents to me now.'

The five of them fell silent. Magnus had that proud lion look again, resolute and dignified. Miles's eyes were damp. Mel's face had a golden glow as if lit from within.

Nick and Conrad looked at one another and smiled. 'Write it, Con,' Nick said.

'What do you think of *Legacy of Love*, for a title?' Conrad's eyes had a spark of fire in them. 'I think that's what both women left behind.'

Buy *Lesley Pearse*

Order further *Lesley Pearse* titles from your local bookshop, or have them delivered direct to your door by Bookpost